Thirty-Nine Steps from Baker Street

J. R. Trtek

By the same author: *The Hapsburg Falcon*

ISBN: 151715300X
ISBN 13: 9781517153007
Library of Congress Control Number: 2015919017
CreateSpace Independent Publishing Platform: North Charleston, SC

Cover Image: *Statue of Eros, Picadilly Circus, London c. 1914-18.*
(Courtesy Kodak Collection / Science & Society Picture Library)

But there can be no grave for Sherlock Holmes and Doctor Watson... Will they not always live in Baker Street? Are they not there this moment, as one writes? Outside, the hansoms rattle through the rain, and Moriarty plans his latest devilry. Within, the sea-coal flames upon the hearth and Holmes and Watson take their well-won case... So they still live for all that love them well; in a romantic chamber of the heart, in a nostalgic country of the mind, where it is always 1895.

—Vincent Starrett

Editor's Note:

Those who uncompromisingly take to heart the sentiment expressed on the previous page may perhaps do well to read no further. Several events contained in the following narrative have been told or alluded to elsewhere—and sometimes quite differently—in the novels *The Thirty-Nine Steps, Greenmantle,* and *Mr. Standfast* by John Buchan, as well as the Sherlock Holmes short story "His Last Bow." The tale fully revealed in this book, rather than gleaned piecemeal through those episodes just mentioned, most definitely does not transpire in 1895. Its way stations do not encompass the sitting room of 221B Baker Street, and while horses' hooves are heard on occasion, those claps are but muted echoes from a landscape where Queen Victoria is a fading memory.

Thirty-Nine Steps from Baker Street is not a typical Sherlock Holmes story. Taking place before, during, and after the First World War, it is not so much a mystery tale as it is a saga of espionage. Holmes and John H. Watson, real people rather than the timeless literary creations some believe them to be, are seen at a point in their lives much later than portrayed in almost the entire accepted Sherlockian canon, during years when their everyday partnership had become a thing of the past and the personal relationship between the two men accordingly altered.

Those wishing to understand the provenance of the following text before starting it may read Appendix A without fear of learning too much too soon. The other addenda that close this book contain detailed references to events in the narrative, however, and the reader is advised to peruse them only after completing the story itself. Comments on the aforementioned novels and short story will also be found in many of the attached and probably far too numerous footnotes, which are also intended to clarify some terms and references for the modern American reader and those not familiar with Holmesian lore.

And to address in advance the likely discontents of those self-styled and often self-important keepers of the flame who may recoil at what follows, please remember that you have been warned.

Book One: Cerberus

CHAPTER ONE: BOOTS FOR A CORPSE

In the period immediately following Sherlock Holmes's retirement to the South Downs, I continued to enjoy his company with regular, if decreasing, frequency. By the turn of a new decade, however, my habitual pilgrimages to the former detective's cottage in Sussex had dwindled to but yearly events, as had his own excursions into greater London. And though our correspondence enjoyed a more respectable pace through the spring of 1912, thereafter I found myself waiting an increasingly longer time to receive his replies to my letters before they stopped altogether toward the end of the following year. In the meanwhile, though Holmes was rumoured to often hike the seaside cliffs of his district, he did not seek close contact with any of his neighbours, nor did he invite old acquaintances to share the comforts of his modest home.

It was a situation I began to find altogether unsettling.

Had these misanthropic habits expressed themselves a quarter century earlier, I should have felt but minor concern, surmising that the detective was engaged in some urgent investigation requiring he remain incommunicado. My attentions would then have gravitated back to the demands of medical practice or to the joys of recounting Holmes's previous adventures to the reading public while I waited for him to re-enter the commonplace world. As it was, throughout that last peaceful winter and early spring preceding the Great War, I used composition to divert my thoughts from concern for Holmes's reclusive behaviour, an anxiety that at times dulled my concentration when occupied as an occasional physician.

I had recently ended my own practice in Queen Anne Street but continued to reside there, remaining active as an occasional alternate for Dr. Henry Blanding, the son of an old associate who had followed his father into the profession. The young man's offices were also in Marylebone,[1] not far from Portland Place, and for several days in the early summer of 1914, I found myself serving as replacement for Blanding *fils*, seeing to regular clients and treating those new patients who entered his consulting room in need.

These supplicants impressed me as a diverse and rather interesting set—among their number were an Italian opera singer bothered by inflamed tonsils, a young American plagued with migraines, and a society matron whose ailments, I suspected, were actually those of her Pekinese, which she sought to comfort with benefit of more than veterinary advice. Then, during the penultimate morning of my duty, I received perhaps the most curious visitor of the lot.

He was a tall, gaunt fellow about my age, clothed in a long dark coat topped by a shovel hat. His angular chin sported a small goatee beard, and spectacles tinted faint blue sat astride the man's hawkish nose. One might have thought him to be in some religious order but for the aroma of stale cigars that clung to his thin figure and the expression his eyes cast through those thick lenses, a look such that I initially thought him to be in the throes of an alcoholic stupor.

"I must apologise for interrupting your afternoon," he said with an obvious American accent, a characteristic of speech that caused me to

---

[1] Marylebone is a district of London, formally within the City of Westminster, encompassing not only Watson's Queen Anne Street residence but also the famed house at 221 Baker Street where he and Holmes shared quarters for years.

perceive in him a certain resemblance to the iconic figure of that nation's mythology, Uncle Sam. Yet something else about the voice struck a different chord within me, and as we both took to chairs facing one another, my heart skipped as I silently realised that the stranger before me was none other than Sherlock Holmes himself, in disguise.

I leaned back, at first averting my gaze from him, pleased at having seen through the impersonation, yet curious as to why he should approach me in this furtive manner at all.

"In truth," I remarked with a nonchalant air, "it is not yet midday."

"Oh," said he, putting a hand to his mouth—and I could now clearly discern my friend through the affectation he presented—"I've no timepiece. Earlier than I believe, you say?"

I motioned upward. The man cocked his head, apparently at last heard ticking from above, and beheld the clock upon Blanding's consulting room wall.

"Ah, indeed!" he said, squinting at the numbered face. "It's still morning—unless it's the evening, in which case I've gone without my dinner, you know. But my stomach doesn't feel empty, and I remember the sun has not yet set. Oh, forgive my confusion. I'm so harried, and I am so troubled."

"No matter. You are not a regular patient here, I understand."

"That's correct, sir. Stricken as I am and passing by these offices, I thought to seek help, no matter who might provide the physic."

Still wondering why my friend insisted on this farce after so many months of silence, I continued to assume the role of one deceived, even as my mind sought to formulate a hypothesis. "And would you describe your symptoms, please?"

"They're all here!" the man said, eyes widening behind the spectacles as he sprang forward and pointed to his right temple. "In here. The mee-graines." He leaned back in his chair, drew himself up as if he were a scrawny cat defending its prey, and nodded. "They're fierce, I tell you."

"Migraines, yes."

"Have you treated such before?"

"Of course," I replied, feeling the first twinges of annoyance at my friend's continued ruse.

"Recently?" he asked. "Have you kept apace of the newest developments and research? What's your opinion on the use of ergot?"

"Once you have recounted your experiences in more detail," I said calmly, "I may perhaps prescribe a treatment. Is the pain accompanied by—?"

"Have you read the works of Thornberg or Powers?" the disguised Holmes asked. "Possibly Osland's many papers?"

"Please," I insisted, "if you will simply tell me—"

"You're not one for trepanning, are you?" he enquired warily.

"Certainly not!"

"Have you treated anyone else for them recently?"

I paused and took a deep breath, finding it increasingly difficult to continue this absurd charade.

"Tell me," he persisted, "have you lately received a sufferer with complaints similar to mine?"

With patience now at an end, I suddenly reached out with devilish purpose, intending to burst my friend's bubble and rip the false goatee from his face.

“Ouch!” came a pitiful shout in Holmes’s familiar voice. “For God’s sake, man, let it go!”

I released my hold on what I now recognised as a natural growth of beard and lurched back in my chair, embarrassed and contrite.

“Holmes, I apologise most sincerely!” I stammered. “I could not help myself in exposing your disguise. I say, you are you, are you not, Holmes?”

“That is a supposition you have proved true in a most forceful manner, Watson,” he replied while caressing his chin. “Though, if I may say, it would have been preferred that your excellent perception had extended to the goatee as well.”

“I believed it merely glued to your chin, an adjunct to the impersonation. I could not imagine—”

“Nor could I some months ago, but the business at hand requires all this to be genuine, other than my change in hair colour.”

“Yes, I was going to remark that it does not become you, either.” I looked sheepishly at my friend. “That is, if you do not take offense at the comment.”

“If anything, Watson, I endorse your sentiment.”

Holmes removed his spectacles and smiled once more. “It was a complete surprise to find you here, and without a bit of putty about the face and perhaps false brows, I thought it quite likely that you would see through this disguise in which I am cloaked, but my own imp of the perverse compelled me to proceed nonetheless.”

He sighed. "I confess that, a tender chin aside, I am rather glad that it all transpired as it did—fortunately, without you swooning over me this time[2]—and I congratulate you on a still-discerning eye."

I shrugged. "No doubt, it still cannot compete with yours."

"Well, I admit it is evident that you have now become a frequent passenger in motorcars, an invention that you have traditionally despised. The faint differentiation of skin around your eyes, where goggles would be fitted while riding through the country, testifies to that."

"Yes, I have—"

"Then, too, you remain clean-shaven, other than your moustache, but both sides of your face have now been scraped with equal precision, suggesting that you are no longer the one applying the razor. You always had difficulty in achieving perfection with regard to the left cheek, you know."

"I recall previous comments to that effect, but as for the issue of motors—"

"That someone else shaves you suggests your personal accounts are much healthier than they were before I set up camp in Sussex."

"Yes, that is why I was able to—"

"It cannot be due to your practice, from which you have presumably retired," Holmes said, glancing about the room, "though you obviously step in for Dr. Blanding for days at a time—these are his offices, yet you have made them somewhat your own, with that tobacco jar and various other

[2] This is likely a reference to the occasion, two decades earlier, of Holmes's reappearance after being presumed dead following his duel with Professor Moriarty at the Reichenbach Falls. As chronicled in "The Adventure of the Empty House," a disguised Holmes accosted Watson and only later revealed his true identity, prompting the doctor to faint—for the first and only time in his life.

personal possessions I recall from our Baker Street days. No, I believe you and your literary agent have recently extracted money from one more sad, unsuspecting publisher in return for the right to print yet another of your fantasies based upon our past work together."

"The Birlstone affair," I replied cautiously.

Holmes sighed. "I shudder to think what misconceptions the public will draw from *that* account." He smiled sardonically as he raised a brow. "Do you include mention of Professor Moriarty?"

"Yes, of course I do."

"You should reconsider that, old fellow—it will only serve to baffle your readers.[3] But, such matters aside, you remain active, and that is to be admired. Your retirement is certainly not complete, is it?"

I studied my friend. "Evidently, the same may be said of you."

Holmes regarded me with an expression of whimsy. "Indeed, Watson. I have cast aside all the trappings of leisure."

"You term it *leisure* now? In the old days, I believe you employed words such as *inactivity, boredom,* and *ennui* in its stead."

"Yes, so I did. Well, no matter what turns my vocabulary may have taken since, when the nation's premier comes to my sitting room and insists that I answer his call to play the game of espionage, who am I to contradict him?"

I sat up abruptly. "What—"

---

[3] The Birlstone affair is recounted in *The Valley of Fear*, published later in 1914. Holmes's comment refers to the fact that Professor Moriarty was initially introduced to readers in an earlier story, "The Final Problem," where Watson supposedly learns of the detective's nemesis for the first time. However, in *The Valley of Fear*—which takes place before "The Final Problem"—Watson appears to already be familiar with Moriarty.

"I will provide explanation in time," Holmes said thoughtfully, leaning back in his chair. "You know, when I realised you were here rather than Dr. Blanding, it was all I could do to restrain my excitement—as well as my embarrassment. I must apologise for the very long period of silence, Watson."

"It does not signify. You have been pursuing an investigation at the behest of the premier, you say. But you indicated you came here to talk to Blanding."

"I did. I wish to discover what additional insight may be gained concerning one of his patients: Franklin P. Scudder."

"Scudder? Oh yes, the American with migraines. I treated him just a week ago, I believe."

"I was attempting to elicit more about him when you initiated that vicious assault upon my facial hair. Some shreds of information about Scudder have already been passed on to me, most of them apparently originating with his valet. It was he who discovered the body, you see."

"What?" I cried. "The man is murdered?"

"That is not certain," said Holmes, raising his hand. "What I have been told is that Scudder lies dead in his flat. Perhaps if someone else had given you that news," he added with mild amusement, "your thoughts would not have turned so rapidly to those of homicide."

"And what is your own assessment of that possibility? Of homicide, that is."

Holmes shrugged. "You know my methods, Watson, as well as their limitations. I have not yet had opportunity to examine either the body or its resting place, and so speculation would be meaningless at this time.

Even so, I have no intellectual stake in the manner of death as such, other than how it may serve my particular purpose."

"What is that purpose?" I asked. "And how did the Yard contact you? I and all your friends have found that an impossible task of late."

The detective smiled. "It was not Scotland Yard that summoned me in this instance, Watson, though their Inspector Magillivray is expecting me shortly at Scudder's flat. No, this particular investigation is a corollary, shall we say, of my enterprise on behalf of the government."

"Ah."

"And now that we speak to one another as our true selves, I do hope you may be forthcoming about Scudder."

"Of course. Ask me what you like, with the understanding that he is—was not a regular patient of young Dr. Blanding. I saw him but once, when he came in from the street complaining of headaches, as you did moments ago. You desire his medical details?"

"Those are not now of primary concern, though they may become relevant in future," replied my friend. "Rather, I wish to know all you can relate about the character of the man himself."

"Gladly," I said, rising to fetch the slim file on Mr. Scudder that, during the previous week, I had deposited in a cabinet on the far side of the consulting room.

"Of course, you may not be able to reveal more than has already been conveyed to me," Holmes said as I searched the cabinet drawer. "Still, prematurely ending the pursuit of evidence can—"

"'Have the effect of negating what has already been gained.' I believe that is how you often put it," I said as I took hold of Scudder's file. Turning round, I saw Holmes's smile suggest no small satisfaction with my quoting him.

"It appears you were far more attentive than I supposed," my friend said, eyes sparkling. "In fact," he went on, "I have recently added a statement to such effect in *The Whole Art of Detection.*"

"And how is that book coming these days?" I asked. "I keep wondering when your magnum opus will finally be completed."

"Composition has slowed these past two years, Watson," he said. "First, by the enterprise that requires this disguise, and second, by work on a very different volume, which is forthcoming."

"Truly? And what is this other piece of which you speak?"

"I wish to surprise in my own time," said Holmes mischievously. "If my desire does not offend."

"I believe I have demonstrated extreme patience in the past, my recent lapse notwithstanding."

"Yes," replied the detective, once more caressing his goatee.

"I have but one hope in regard to your two literary efforts," I said while regaining my chair.

"Oh? And what is that?"

I stared at the papers on my lap and then added in an even tone, "That either volume will be more interesting than *The Martyrdom of Man.*"[4]

"Tush, Watson!" my friend said with a chuckle. "On with the details of Mr. Franklin Scudder, if you please."

"Very well."

---

[4] *The Martyrdom of Man* by Winwood Reade was a book viewed by Holmes as "one of the most remarkable ever penned." Watson's opinion of the work appears to have been somewhat different.

I leaned back, looking down at the notes that sat before me. "As previously mentioned, I treated the fellow for migraines. Yours have subsided, I assume?" I asked puckishly.

Holmes silently gestured for me to proceed.

"And so," I said, now in a serious tone, "Franklin P. Scudder is—was an American, age thirty-two. From his dress, I gathered that he enjoyed a healthy income. Born in the state of Kentucky, he attended university and apparently had seen much of the world in his relatively short life, for he was a correspondent for some newspaper in Chicago—he did not indicate which. Scudder had reported on the late Balkan hostilities and most recently travelled through the Continent by way of Hamburg, Norway, and Paris before arriving in London."

I halted and looked at my friend. His look became expectant.

"And what about the man?" Holmes asked. "What did you perceive to be his outstanding traits of personality, especially methods of dealing with adversity? Have you insight regarding topics such as those?"

"Well, it seemed he was a master of several languages," I said hesitantly before setting the folder aside to give my friend an apologetic look. "I recall him sprinkling his conversation with various epigrams in the original German, French, or Italian. He had a keen interest in the past, citing books he had recently read concerning his own nation's civil war, as well as the history of Greece."

My voice trailed off, and I spent a moment gathering my thoughts. "I am afraid that is all I can say. I have no words to illuminate his person, I fear, other than to remark that he was a rather pleasant chap—certainly, I can make no pronouncement with respect to the qualities you mention.

Sadly, I was viewing him as a physician, intent on alleviating his migraines."

My friend nodded again. "Yes, of course." He smiled with a kindly expression. "Perhaps I should not grasp at straws until I first observe Scudder's flat."

Holmes paused, looking at me as if intending to continue, but then he bowed his head and remained silent.

"And so something is once more afoot, after all these years," I remarked in a deliberately offhand manner as I rose from my chair to put away Scudder's file.

"Indeed it is, old fellow."

Again the detective seemed about to ask something of me but appeared hesitant to do so. Then, as I strode to the cabinet, he spoke.

"I suppose it would an imposition to ask you to share my current paucity of leisure," Holmes remarked. "However, Watson, would you consider accompanying me to Scudder's flat today?"

"Today and any day, as the opportunity arises," I said with genuine delight.

I deposited my file of papers and shut the cabinet drawer. "And it is far less an imposition than having one's chin whiskers pulled." I looked at my friend with eyes that threatened to brim over. "It would be a joy to accept your offer, Holmes."

"Can you close this early?"

"Time be damned," I replied, walking back across the consulting room. "In more ways than one, I suppose. There are no appointments scheduled for the afternoon, and on the morrow but two, which I will simply drop."

"You need not go so far as that."

"I choose to do so. One never knows what each day may bring," I declared. "If I am to be of use to you, I must first be available."

"I take it," he said with a faint smile, "that you have not wed again in my absence."

"Indeed," I said with mock severity. "I have not."

"I realise it must be a shock to have me reappear so abruptly after these many months, let alone ask for your assistance in the field."

"Old soldiers never completely stand down," I told Holmes, and I thought I saw a watery glint in his own eye before he once more donned the tinted spectacles. "I will close up once I fetch my coat and hat," I said, "and then we may depart."

"In truth, I should wish to meet you inside Scudder's building rather than journey there in your company," Holmes declared as he stood.

I gave a start, surprised by my friend's statement.

"You will have your full explanation in time, recall."

"Of course," I replied, stepping toward a closet door. "I know better than to question your instructions. And so, we are to meet at Scudder's flat, you say?"

"Yes. It is in a new building a few blocks away, near Portland Place."

"I am familiar with it, having watched the structure go up last year."

"Good, then directions will be unnecessary. When you pass through the front entrance, that Inspector Magillivray I referred to earlier will greet you in the lobby. He is a rather prim-looking man with a clean-shaven lawyer's face and a prominent dimple upon his chin. I take him to be an amateur woodworker, an avocation he pursues in the early morning, before reporting to the Yard, for though his waistcoat betrays a light sprinkling of sawdust, his jacket and shoes are—"

"Do you wish me to bring anything?" I asked abruptly.

"Yes, Watson," Holmes replied in an abstracted tone. "Your medical bag is hereabouts?"

"It is."

"Good. Please have it with you."

I promised to do so as I withdrew my coat and hat from the closet. Putting one arm into the former, my back to the detective, I added, "I must say, I feel myself limbering up already, Holmes. I can once again feel the thrill of the hunt, though you have not yet disclosed the nature of the quarry. It is all very much like strolling through a familiar forest of old—"

I stopped suddenly, for having turned round, I realised that my friend had already left the room.

After closing Blanding's office and sending his assistant home for the day with instructions to call off Friday's appointments, I stepped onto the pavement and made my way to New Cavendish Street and thence into Harley Street, passing near Queen's College on the way toward Scudder's flat.

Traversing this burgeoning local community of physicians and surgeons, sprinkled with clerks and shop-girls, as well as an occasional policeman, I found myself feeling as if I inhabited a metropolis that had become suddenly fresh, one into which Holmes's returning presence had breathed new life. The avenues were filled with traffic, though motors now claimed majority status, scooting past horse-drawn vehicles whose numbers had sharply declined in the past decade. My stride became more confident as I basked in the glow of sentimental reflection, and I marched briskly in late morning light toward the new building near Portland Place.

Entering that block of flats, I immediately espied a man standing at the lobby entrance who fit Holmes's brief description of the Scotland Yard inspector perfectly, down to the sober look in his eyes and a dimple set at the midpoint of his chin.

"Dr. Watson?" he enquired. "I am Inspector Magillivray. I have already let in Mr. Holmes through a rear entrance as arranged, and he awaits us above."

While the building's porter looked on from across the lobby, the inspector and I shook hands before he directed me away from the lift.

"The flat in question is on the top floor, but Mr. Holmes instructed that we are to employ the common staircase. Follow me, please."

As we ascended, the inspector cast a smile in my direction, billycock hat in hand. Trailing behind, I thought I could detect the aroma of wood glue wafting from him.

"I am very pleased to make your acquaintance at last," Magillivray said. "You were a mite before my time at the Yard, but Inspector Hopkins spoke often of you before he retired, and I have read all your stories about Mr. Holmes. Most instructive, they are."

I nodded appreciatively as we trod the risers upward.

"Are there to be any more?"

"What?"

Stories, I mean." The inspector slowed somewhat to accommodate my measured pace toward the top. "They seem to have become a bit sparse of late."

"I have been writing a new piece," I informed him. "It will be coming out later this year."[5]

"Oh, that will grand," he declared as we reached the upmost storey. Magillivray smiled and gestured in the direction of the corridor that lay before us. At its far end stood Sherlock Holmes.

"Halloa again, Inspector," called out Holmes. As we approached, my friend nodded to me with an apologetic expression. "And, Watson, do forgive me for slipping away unannounced."

"I considered it a spur to keep me alert and in practice," I assured him.

"Shall we go inside, then?" Holmes impatiently asked Magillivray, motioning to the door nearest us. "From the condition of the knobs and locks, I have assumed No. 15 to be Scudder's flat."

"It is indeed, sir," replied the inspector, stepping to the door and fitting a key into the lock. "I suppose I did fail to tell you the number, did I not?"

"And where is Scudder's man?" Holmes enquired.

"The one who valets him?" Magillivray said, pausing with the key still in its lock, unturned. "The boys are bringing him back here, for he has been held at the local station since he came to us with his report of Scudder's death. Fortunately, I was on hand when he told his story and, recognising the American's name from Mr. Bullivant's list, took charge of the matter at once."

---

[5] During the years 1912 and 1913, only one new Holmes story appeared: "The Adventure of the Dying Detective." In September 1914, however, *The Strand Magazine* would begin serializing *The Valley of Fear,* mentioned in footnote 3. When, earlier in this chapter, Watson speaks of writing as a means of coping with Holmes's unexplained silence, it is likely that he is referring to the composition of that novel.

I made note of this Mr. Bullivant, whose name was completely new to me.

"That was fortunate indeed," remarked Holmes. "And so, will I have an opportunity to speak here with the valet?"

"Oh yes," said the inspector.

"Good. Now then," my friend said, smiling expectantly, "may we enter the flat?"

Magillivray quickly unlocked the door, opened it, and then backed away, allowing Holmes to pass before him. I followed.

"It is the only set of rooms occupied on this floor at present, as I suppose you deduced," said the man from Scotland Yard upon entering the flat. "The body is in the bedroom, Mr. Holmes. It appears to be a case of suicide."

The remark did not cause me to break stride as we crossed a cluttered sitting room, where two empty bottles of spirits sat prominently beside one another upon a table. Holmes approached the windows and within seconds had shut every curtain and blind. Then, after snapping the switch for additional light, he turned round and round slowly, giving the area a quick visual examination.

"If you wish me to leave, Mr. Holmes, I will do so," Magillivray said. "Mr. Bullivant indicated you might wish privacy."

I glanced at Holmes after this second mention of that mysterious name, but my friend showed no inclination to enlighten me. Instead, he waved his hand. "Pray remain, Inspector. You may be able to assist us with the body. It is in the adjoining room, you say?"

He stepped to a large trunk that lay upon the carpet, lifted its lid, and then quickly closed it before passing through an open doorway.

Magillivray and I followed him into another room, there finding, upon a bed, the corpse of a man in pyjamas. Its jaw was horribly mutilated by what I took to have been a gunshot, for a revolver lay beside the body.

Stepping with care so as not to disturb the mess that had resulted, Holmes pulled shut the curtains, motioned for me to turn the switch, and then planted himself at the foot of the bed to take stock.

"Behold the remains, Watson, the face now past recognition," he said. "Do you nonetheless discern the obvious?"

I stared intently at the figure on the bed, sensing Magillivray step up behind me as I pondered the scene for several seconds.

"Are you referring to the fact that this was not suicide by gunshot?" I replied after a moment.

"I am."

"What?" said the inspector. "You mean he didn't kill himself?"

"That the man took his own life is not yet a logical impossibility," remarked Holmes, "though I would hesitate to lay a wager on it. Still, there is a glass of what may be more than mere sleeping-draught there upon that bedside table. I suggest you take it to the Yard for analysis, for I suppose it could contain poison."

"I believe the valet said he did mix such a draught for Scudder, but I will do as you recommend," Magillivray said. "And so then, Mr. Holmes, you believe someone else shot him while he slept?"

"To be sure, someone else fired the gun as he lay sleeping," the detective remarked. "However, it was already the eternal sleep."

Magillivray looked at me with a questioning expression.

"There is far less blood than would be expected had the revolver been fired into the jaw of a living man," I explained. "He was already dead when the bullet struck."

"But if he wasn't killed with the revolver, how did he die? And if Mr. Scudder was no longer alive and therefore unable to fire the shot, who discharged the gun?"

"Dr. Watson may, perhaps, be able to respond to your first query after examining the body more closely," Holmes replied. "In the meanwhile, I will attempt to enlighten us with regard to the second issue. Of course, the third question already has an answer."

"But I asked no third question," said Magillivray.

"I have answered it, nonetheless."

"And what is that question?"

"*Why* the shot was even fired," said Sherlock Holmes.

"And you say you have a reason for that?" replied the inspector. "What would it be? To disguise how the man actually died?"

"With the rest of the body seemingly undisturbed, quite ready to disclose the real cause of death to any thorough examiner? Hardly," my friend declared.

Magillivray made a pleading gesture. "Mr. Holmes, will you perhaps explain—"

"Patience, Inspector," said the detective with a soothing tone. "I will elaborate shortly. Watson," he went on, looking me in the eye, "is my proposed division of labour acceptable?"

"It is eminently fair." I turned and re-entered the sitting room to doff my coat. Both it and my hat found a place upon a chair, and then I removed my jacket as well. With cuffs loosened and rolled up past my elbows, I smiled at Magillivray as I returned to the bedroom and stood beside a small table, upon which I had left my bag.

"Will you assist me, Inspector?" I asked. Then, as Sherlock Holmes busied himself about the rooms of the flat, Magillivray and I separated the corpse from its pyjamas before I myself performed a more careful examination of the remains.

It was slightly more than a quarter hour later when I stepped into the sitting room, where Holmes reposed in an armchair, deep in thought.

I discreetly cleared my throat, and he glanced up, his eyes luminous.

"I cannot with absolute confidence declare cause of death without a complete autopsy," I said. "However, after feeling the region of the man's liver, I believe excessive drink may have played a role. There are other signs not inconsistent with that theory, and of course it is supported by the presence of those bottles there."

Holmes did not look toward the direction in which I pointed but merely nodded.

"It is certainly true that the man did not die from any physical attack upon his person," I added.

"Yes. Thank you, Watson."

"And have you reached any conclusions of your own, Mr. Holmes?" Magillivray asked from the open bedroom doorway.

"I have compiled a speculation or two," said my friend, speaking in abstracted tones. "But I have also formulated one additional question of importance."

"And what is that?" asked the inspector.

Holmes stroked his goatee twice and then rose from the chair to walk past me and Magillivray and into the bedroom.

"I wish to know," he said, "whether the man's shoes fit his feet."

The inspector looked dumbfounded, but I gestured for him to follow, and we stepped through the doorway after Holmes. Approaching my friend, I watched as he knelt at an open wardrobe door and rummaged about.

"Here, Watson, can you help me rise?"

I assisted the detective to his feet. He held in his hands a pair of well-polished short boots.

"Thank you. Now then," Holmes said, "which of us will put these on the body?"

Magillivray cocked his head and awkwardly scratched the nape of his neck. "Well, sir, since you seem the most enthusiastic about it..."

"Then I will shoe the corpse," replied my friend, who stepped to the bed and attempted to insert the dead man's left foot into its corresponding boot.

"It is a mite too small," I commented. "The boot, that is."

"So it is. Let us see about the other."

The inspector gave a start. "But why–"

"It is not uncommon for a person's feet to be of unequal size, and it is not unheard of for some individuals to wear shoes of a size more appropriate for the smaller of the two. Ah, but observe! The right boot is not large enough to fit its matching foot, either."

"But what does that mean, sir?" asked Magillivray.

"I told you earlier that the corpse's jaw was not shot off to disguise the cause of death," replied Holmes. "It was, instead, meant to disguise the identity of the victim. That Scudder's boots do not fit these feet confirms that. This body does not belong here."

“The body does not belong here?” said Magillivray. “Do you mean to suggest that these are not the remains of Franklin Scudder?”

“I thought I had asserted it most emphatically,” replied the detective.

“Well,” the man from Scotland Yard said, crossing his arms. “I don’t know what Mr. Bullivant will make of that.”

Holmes set the boots aside, and again I found myself yearning for some introduction to this person repeatedly referred to by both men, but about whom I knew nothing.

My friend gave a deep sigh. “Well,” he said, “there is nothing here that will lead us to Mr. Scudder, wherever he now may be. I have found these rooms to be quite sterile, insofar as meaningful clues are concerned.”

“But how was this body transported here?” the inspector asked.

“I suspect that it arrived in the now-empty trunk which lies upon the sitting room carpet,” replied Holmes. “It could easily have held this corpse. Have any of the porters yet been questioned at length?”

“No,” said Magillivray.

“I suggest you talk to the one currently on duty. He or one of his fellows may have assisted in moving the trunk up here.”

“And what of Scudder? He will not return?” the inspector asked.

Holmes motioned toward the dressing table as I closed my medical bag. “I take those to be the man’s keys there upon that chain. I believe this is one bridge Mr. Scudder has most definitely burned.”

“Aye,” said the inspector, picking up a key and comparing it to the one with which he had opened the rooms. “The two match, sir.” He turned toward my friend. “But there is no evidence you have found which suggests where Scudder went, assuming that our body here is someone else’s? And nothing concerning who fired that shot into the dead man’s jaw?”

"Not a single datum," answered Holmes. "No evidence whatsoever. And, more often than not, the complete absence of evidence is itself evidence of purpose. In this instance, it is evidence of one purpose in particular."

Before Magillivray could beg further explanation, a knock came from outside.

We stepped into the sitting room, and the inspector opened the door to the flat, revealing a mousey young man whose dour face was framed by two policemen.

"Why must I needs be brought back here?" the man whined. "Looking at that body the first time was more than enough for me."

"You were valet to the unfortunate Mr. Scudder?" asked Holmes immediately, before anyone else could respond.

"I was, yes," replied the man, who gave his name. "I saw to him now and then, but he wouldn't take my advice and go to the doctor yesterday. He looked a fright, and I told him he needed the leeches. I'd already put him on to visiting a physician about his headaches—he saw some Dr. Blanding the other week, as I have already told you coppers, but this was far different."

The man's gaze then fell upon me, and he noticed the medical bag in my hand.

"You?" he asked. "Are you Dr. Blanding, perhaps?"

"He is Dr. Blanding's associate," said Holmes before I could reply, and I discreetly declined to add any elaboration. "If you will merely remain here in the sitting room—there is no need for you to return to the bedroom, I assure you—I will have a few words with you."

Before stepping back into the hall, the two policemen nudged the valet past the door, which Magillivray quickly shut, and for perhaps ten minutes Holmes gently barraged the man with questions about Franklin Scudder, under the pretence that both he and Magillivray were from Scotland Yard. I could discern my friend's disappointment all through the examination, and after the conversation had ended, the man was sent out to once more be retained in custody by the policemen.

Holmes looked down at the carpet and pursed his lips.

"A benevolent if pitiful sort," he declared. "If I'd had half a crown, I might as well have given it him and sent the man on his way, for he produced nothing of additional value. Holmes glanced about the sitting room. "There is no more use in my staying here, either, I fear," he declared.

"Do you wish me to convey anything to Mr. Bullivant, sir?" asked the man from Scotland Yard. "Or will you be reporting to him yourself?"

"The latter," was my friend's crisp reply. "Indeed, I am to meet with him within the hour." He turned toward me, a subtle smile upon his face. "You will attend as well, old fellow?"

"Of course," I said, somewhat stiffly. "If for no other reason than to once again see my dear friend Bullivant."

Holmes quickly turned away, and I suspected his movement toward the window was meant to disguise mild, involuntary chuckling.

"As before, Watson," he said in a light voice as he parted one set of curtains ever so slightly to glance outside, "we must not be seen together. I will employ the same rear door I used to enter this building. You, meanwhile, will descend the stair. In perhaps a quarter hour, a taxicab will pull up before the main entrance. Approach and make certain I am its passenger before stepping into the vehicle."

"I will."

"Now then," Holmes said, addressing the inspector. "To all others, assert that the body in the bedroom is that of Mr. Scudder. Make your report to that effect, adding whatever valid details you wish to use in order to embellish the assertion, overlooking the observations made by myself and the doctor—indeed, omitting the very fact of our presence here. And recall the need to analyse that glass of liquid, though I expect it will yield nothing extraordinary."

"Of course. I believe the inquest is to take place tomorrow, sir."

"Everything presented there must support what I have just told you, Inspector Magillivray," said my friend as he stepped toward the door. "And I will see you soon, Watson."

Immediately after Holmes had departed, Magillivray and I left the flat to stand near the stair in the company of one of the policemen who had escorted Scudder's man.

"The valet has been taken to one of the empty flats down the hall," the inspector informed me. "We will walk him about these rooms later, despite any objections he may have to it. Of course, that will be after the wagon arrives to take the body away—which should occur within the next few minutes."

Magillivray then leaned close to me. "I will put up the show of a thorough investigation here, on into afternoon, just for the sake of appearances, as Mr. Holmes wishes. Oh, and if you have the opportunity, Dr. Watson, you might put in a good for me with Mr. Bullivant, whom you apparently know well."

I nodded in a self-conscious manner and then, having judged that enough time had elapsed, left the inspector and made my descent. As I came to the first floor, I saw a man approach the staircase. He was well dressed and athletic, with a drooping moustache set on a tanned face that appeared about forty years of age. We smiled briefly at one another, and I slowed, allowing him to gain the stair before I reached the landing.

"Thank you much," he said in a resonant voice before rapidly skipping down the steps to the ground floor, where I saw him stride hurriedly out the main entrance.

"You have seen Afghanistan," I whispered in jest to myself, for the man's weathered face had reminded me of those words: Sherlock Holmes's first comment to me, spoken that auspicious day in the laboratory at St. Bart's, a third of a century ago.[6]

He who had preceded me down the staircase might well have seen Afghanistan recently, I reflected—or India or perhaps South Africa. I thought no more of the incident, however, as I reached the ground floor and stepped outside to gain the pavement, where I waited for a taxi bearing Holmes to appear.

Five minutes later, it pulled up before me.

"Go," said Holmes to the chauffeur as I sat down beside my friend and closed the door. The vehicle shot off along the street, initially heading south, and Holmes leaned forward and lowered the hand that had been obscuring his face.

"Well, Watson, are you now ready for my explanation of all this rigmarole?"

---

[6] Holmes's first words to Watson, as reported in *A Study in Scarlet*, were actually, "How are you? You have been in Afghanistan, I perceive."

"I am," I replied cautiously. "But do you think it wise to talk of such matters here?" I added in a whisper, nodding toward the front of the motorcar. "Should we not find a more discreet place?"

"I think this is perhaps the most discreet venue we have at the moment. Do you not agree, Jack?" Holmes asked the chauffeur in a loud voice.

The person at the wheel, a blond-haired youth barely twenty years of age, twisted round for an instant.

"I reckon it'll at least do, sir." He smiled and then quickly returned his attention to the street ahead before making a sharp turn toward the west.

I glanced at Holmes, who said, "Did you not observe that the vehicle's taximeter is idle?"

"Yes." I took a moment to think. "And so our chauffeur is one of your agents."

"He is. Jack, this is Dr. Watson."

"*The* Dr. Watson," said the youth, briefly looking back in our direction once more. "Pleasure to meet you, sir."

I smiled as he turned back round to watch the traffic.

"An American," I whispered.

"Very good," Holmes said. "Yes, his name is Jack James. I signed him on in Chicago."

"My," I remarked, "you've been quite far afield these past several months, have you not?"

Chapter Two: Heads of Cerberus

"Some time ago," said Sherlock Holmes as our taxi turned into Wimpole Street, "I was approached by my brother, Mycroft, on behalf of the British government—"

"A government which, at times, he is," I interjected, remembering the pronouncement Holmes had once uttered about his massive sibling.

"Well, Mycroft's bureaucratic horizons, if not his girth, have contracted ever so slightly in recent years," the detective advised me. "They now encompass only a portion of the government rather than its entire expanse—in particular, that aspect associated with the gathering of intelligence.

"He came to me more than two years ago with a request that I undertake important business for his superiors. Engrossed, as I was, with my continuing study of bees and comprehensive work on *The Whole Art of Detection*, I politely declined.

"Two weeks later I refused him once more, with an emphasis that was not altogether congenial to the notion of family. A few days after that, I was visited a third time. The entreaty in that instance, however, was brought by the premier himself. His manner was less insistent than Mycroft's, but of course the weight of his station was far greater. As I told you earlier today, I could not refuse him."

Holmes smiled thoughtfully.

"And so I entrusted my bees to a worthy assistant, grew this goatee, and changed the colour of my hair, as well as my wardrobe," he said, raising his arms as if to display them.

"And altered your personal habits in no small degree, to judge from the stench of cheap cigars that never leaves you."

"Yes," said Holmes wistfully. "I fear my briar and cherrywood will never be the same."

"I am certain your pipes will forgive you in time."

"Let us hope so. But then, Watson, if you now are accepting rides in motors, I can be granted my own excursions away from past practice."

"Yes, but perhaps I should make clear that—"

"In any case," Holmes went on, "the endeavour upon which the premier set me is no less than that of neutralising a German espionage ring that resides here on our own island. The government's hope was that I might turn this nest of spies to our country's advantage."

My eyes widened at the revelation.

"The group is headed by one Heinrich Von Bork.[7] He is the nephew of Count Von und Zu Grafenstein, whom you may recall."

I searched my memory, at first to no avail. Then, abruptly, I remembered.

"Klopman, the nihilist, would have assassinated the count had you not intervened by extinguishing gas lights in the hotel lobby."

"And I would not have done so had you not detected that trace of cinnamon in the papal emissary's drawing room, Watson. Your olfactory abilities always surpassed mine. Tell me, have you yet set your pen against that particular case as well?"

"I have not, though I thank you for suggesting it."

---

[7] Von Bork is Holmes's antagonist in "His Last Bow," a story that does not reveal the German's given name. In that same tale, there is mention of a cousin of Von Bork named Heinrich, but that does not preclude the possibility that both men had the same first name, or that the author of the short story confused Von Bork with his cousin.

"Hum. The reading public will have me to blame, should your inevitably distorted version of events ever see the light of day. But on with my own tale. Von Bork is an extremely clever man, truly in a class by himself, and capable of great mischief. You see, things had been going wrong for our nation's government in recent years. They were not events that the public would have noticed or even have inkling of, but to men such as Mycroft and Bullivant, they were setbacks that appeared most ominous."

"That brings up a point in need of clarification—"

"Many of our agents in other lands found themselves under suspicion. Some were being caught without apparent effort, and no one could understand why all this was happening. There was evidence, however, of a strong and secret central force."

"Holmes, might you please—"

"And then pressure was brought to bear upon me to look into the matter."

"Can you not—"

"Bullivant—more properly, Sir Walter Bullivant—is a spymaster," my friend said abruptly. "He is among the foremost players of the game, a chief of the Secret Service, reporting directly to Mycroft. He is my immediate superior, in fact." Holmes smiled. "Forgive me for leaving you twisting in the wind, so to speak. I could, of course, not fail to observe your most curious expressions at the several mentions of his name back in Scudder's flat."

"Well," I said with exaggerated disdain, "that simple introduction just uttered would have sufficed at the time."

"I was well aware of that," said my friend coyly. "However, I thought it necessary that you suffer for the injustice levied upon my goatee."

"Consider me to have been suitably punished. And is Magillivray one of Bullivant's men as well?"

"The answer is both yes and no. Magillivray is a go-between of sorts. He is Sir Walter's clandestine man in Scotland Yard, yes, feeding Bullivant information and doing his bidding, but he is not privy to any of the Secret Service's, well, secrets. He follows orders without knowing their purpose, but I believe that more should be confided in the man. He lacks a certain imaginative quality, but the inspector is both clever and tenacious. As a fully informed participant, Magillivray would be a much greater boon to Bullivant than he is at present."

"Before I left Scudder's building, he indicated he would put up the pretence of a thorough investigation."

"Yes," said Holmes. "I had already passed on to him that directive from Bullivant, and Magillivray will comply wonderfully, I am sure. Sir Walter, you see, does not wish the public to view that anonymous corpse as anything but a case of suicide, which no doubt is what Scudder himself intended."

"You believe the man is still alive and at large?"

"Of course."

"And who was—is Scudder? A spy, I gather."

"You are correct," replied Holmes. "He is a rather accomplished American agent whose information of late has been shared with Whitehall.[8] There are indications he has uncovered something of great

[8] Whitehall is a road in central London lined with administrative buildings, so that the name is often used as a synonym for the British government itself. Meanwhile, in *The*

importance but not yet correlated all his evidence in order to bring a full report to his government, a representative of which is supposed to be present when I—we meet with Sir Walter presently."

"And now that I am somewhat acquainted with Sir Walter Bullivant, I suggest you continue with your own narrative, Holmes. I fear my question diverted you. You were speaking of Von Bork and his spy apparatus."

"Yes. Having been persuaded to look into the apparent disruption of our own intelligence gathering machine, I discovered the cause to be Von Bork's previously unknown organisation, which operates out of a wonderfully gabled house overlooking the Essex shore—a residence that is, ironically, not that far from my own abode on the South Downs.

"Some time ago, as part of a grand ruse, I travelled to Chicago in the United States and there posed as an American of Irish descent, one Altamount—it was as Altamount that I came to you complaining of migraines. Well, in time, I managed to wend my way back across the Atlantic and get myself recruited for Von Bork's far-flung organisation, bringing with me Jack here."

The young man did not turn round but merely raised one hand briefly as he negotiated the taxi around a stalled horse-driven wagon before turning into Crawford Street.

"Together," Holmes said, "we conscientiously began assembling intelligence for Von Bork, most of it spun from our imaginations. And in the meanwhile, having gained Von Bork's trust, I also recruited two others

---

Thirty-Nine Steps, Scudder is portrayed as a freelance agent. Watson's narrative makes clear that he was actually operating under the command of Washington, which apparently had directed him to cooperate with British Intelligence.

for his organisation here in Britain whom you should find familiar: a Mr. Hollins and a Mr. Steiner."

"Hollins and Steiner? Two of your former agents from the Baker Street days?"

"The same. I should very much have wished to enlist instead Frank Farrar and Shinwell Johnson for this particular mission, but they, of course, have become somewhat too well known here in London to pose as potential German spies."

"Their fame hardly exceeds yours," I noted.

"Yes, but their skills at disguise also pale accordingly," said my friend.

"I should never have thought that unmatched pair would, together, make a successful detection agency."

"Nor I, but their enterprise has flourished this past decade, has it not?"

"Indeed, it has," I remarked. "So you have taken over Von Bork's spy machine, in effect?"

"Well, in part. The four of us supply him with much of his information, most of it false, and he periodically forwards it on to Berlin. The Germans believe they know everything, when they in fact know little or nothing. The troubles that the Secret Service had been experiencing have nearly vanished. It is a neat and tidy arrangement, though how long I am to maintain my pose as Altamount I do not know. I hope it will not be of indefinite duration, however. Ah, we are getting close. Please maintain speed, Jack," Holmes said primly to the young American.

The detective had glanced outside at two young women smiling at our chauffeur, who in his turn had slowed the motorcar in order to better appraise the pair.

"There will be time for frolic when there is time," Holmes said good-naturedly. "Not before."

"As you say, Mr. Holmes," Jack sighed with disappointment as the vehicle increased speed, leaving the damsels behind.

"I should have expected our destination to be somewhere in Westminster,[9] if we are to meet a government spymaster," I said. "But we have been travelling in the opposite direction."

"We will still be encountering a bit of Westminster away from Westminster," said Holmes lightly. "Pull over now, Jack."

The taxicab suddenly veered toward the kerb and came to rest.

"Increasingly these days," my friend said, "matters of espionage are directed from locales away from the formal halls of government. It is a bit of a far cry from that quaint era, now past, when the two of us dabbled in such foreign intrigue now and then."

"You mean cases such as the Bruce-Partington business,[10] for instance?"

"Yes, whether one is speaking of the investigation that actually occurred some years ago or the highly embroidered version you later foisted upon the reading public, the notion is still the same. We will be meeting Bullivant in that house," Holmes revealed, pointing several doors down.

---

[9] An area of central London and the location of the aforementioned Whitehall Road, Westminster has been the home of the British government for centuries.

[10] Almost twenty years earlier, in 1895, Holmes and Watson had been involved in a case involving the theft of military secrets.

"I will exit first and wander around and in through the back, as I did at Portland Place, for I have a key. Jack here will run you on a ways and then let you out. Please walk back along a winding path, and when you ring the bell, do so twice and wait a moment before ringing once more."

"Two then wait then one," I repeated. I glanced again from the taxicab at my eventual destination: a dun-coloured house lodged among others of its type. "A rather unassuming place," I observed.

"Unassuming and therefore, it is hoped, easily overlooked. Mycroft has dubbed it Safety House.[11] There you will meet Sir Walter Bullivant, for whom I have danced these past two years."

Holmes then made a show of slipping some coins into Jack James's hand and stepped from the taxicab.

"When the house door is opened, be certain to ask for Mr. Sherrinford," he directed.

Shovel hat pulled down over his forehead, Holmes then closed the door and strode quickly away. James drove me on for three more blocks before veering to the kerb and stopping, this time quite abruptly—throwing me forward, almost off my seat.

Quickly, the young man turned round, his nose pinching at the malodour his improper braking had produced.

"Sorry, sir. Sometimes I have the devil of a time getting the hang of this contraption."

"Use the lever and not the emergency brake," I reminded him gently, speaking from my own experience. "Do heed that advice, for otherwise, you

---

[11] It is possible that Mycroft Holmes's coinage may be the source of the term "safe house," which did not come into general use within the espionage community until later in the century.

may someday ignite the linings, and most certainly damage your transmission in the meanwhile."

"I'll keep that in mind," the young man said, extending his hand toward me. "Make as if you're giving me fare also, if you will, Dr. Watson," he requested with a twinkle in his eye.

Without hesitation and with raised brows, I cooperated in the ruse.

"Thank you, sir. Mr. Holmes would want us to be careful. Again, it's nice to meet you. Perhaps the next time you can give me some advice about cresting hills in this flivver."

I smiled in an avuncular manner. "Slipping the clutch can be a brutal business, that is the truth, but I will be happy at some point to impart to you what small insight I have gained concerning the practice. In the meanwhile, it has been a pleasure to meet you, Mr. James."

"Jack, if you will, Dr. Watson."

"Very well—Jack. We will meet again to discuss those hills."

"I'm sure we will. And we'll be meeting again and again for other purposes as well, I reckon, before all this business with Mr. Holmes is done with. Take care of yourself, sir."

I left the taxicab, medical bag in hand, and strolled along the pavement before rounding a corner to begin a circuitous journey that brought me to Safety House.

Reaching its door, I rang in accordance with the instructed pattern, and after a few seconds, the door was opened by none other than my friend's brother, Mycroft.

The elder Holmes sibling had lost not a fraction of his massive figure during the many years since I had last seen him, and he retained an expression as cunning as ever there was—his eyes quickly casting a critical glance over me, silent testament to the continued sharpness of that analytical mind whose powers exceeded even those of his more famous brother.

"Well," said he, extending a fleshy hand, "this has been a day of surprises, at least one of them now pleasant. Dr. Watson, I confess you are perhaps the fifth least likely person I should have expected to call at this door. I assume you are seeking Mr. Sherrinford," he remarked coyly as our handshake ended, before I could utter the password phrase I had been given. "In with you then, and let us be quick about it."

I stepped over the threshold, and Mycroft Holmes rapidly closed and bolted the door, which, I noticed, was equipped with a peephole as well as letterbox. Looking round, I found myself standing in a plain-looking entry devoid of any decoration. A dull, musty smell hung in the air, though I also detected the faint, incongruent aroma of fine tobacco.

"One distinct disadvantage of this place is the absence of service," my host said, extending his arms as if to prompt me to remove hat and coat. "We dare not employ regular help because of concerns about security, and to require Foreign Office clerks to serve as footmen, let alone as maids, would be too much to demand, even of those poor fellows. Permit me, please," he said as he took my coat. "Yes, thank you," he added as I gave him my hat as well.

"You don't actually reside here, do you?" I asked as Mycroft turned to place my articles in a wardrobe.

"Oh heavens, no," he replied. "That would be a vile purgatory, indeed, would it not?" He turned round to face me once again and then glanced at my bag, which I had set upon the carpet. "Shall I place that with your other items?"

"Allow me to do so," I insisted, uncertain as to either the man's ability to bend sufficiently far to reach the handle or my capacity to gracefully transfer the valise to his pudgy fingers. And so, instead, I merely lifted the bag from the floor and set it beneath my coat, already hanging in the wardrobe, before stepping back to await Mycroft Holmes's direction.

"Off to your left, there," he indicated. "The main sitting room is beyond that doorway."

I proceeded along a short hallway, stepping past a small alcove of shelves, upon which lay open boxes with names emblazoned upon their sides, and then into the next room, where I immediately caught sight of a large man with a fat, sallow, clean-shaven face, sitting in a basket chair beside a small table. His sleepy eyes regarded me calmly, like those of a contemplative steer, as he put down a cup from which he had been drinking. So this, I thought, was the mysterious Mr. Bullivant.

"Doctor," said Mycroft Holmes, stepping to my side, "may I present John S. Blenkiron, from America. John, this is Dr. John H. Watson."

"John H. and John S.," said the man in a bluff, friendly voice as he rose. "Let us promise to never reveal what lies behind our respective middle initials."

"Dr. Watson is my brother's former associate," added Mycroft.

"Of course he is," said the man as he shook my hand.

I realised, as he stood before me, that though Blenkiron's face was broad, he possessed a figure that was far from plump, and as the American's hand grasped mine, I sensed great strength in it.

"You are still associated with that famous detective in a literary sense, aren't you?" he said. "I know you continue to churn out the magazine tales of his adventures."

"I fear he does, all too frequently," declared Sherlock Holmes from the open doorway. "The doctor has proved most impossible to house-train in that way."

My friend stepped into the sitting room, an expectant look upon his face.

"Sherlock," said his brother, "this is Mr. John Blenkiron, of whom I have spoken."

"Ah," said my friend, suddenly reassuming the voice of his alter ego, Altamount. "Always good to meet a fellow Yankee."

"Indeed, indeed," said Blenkiron, good-naturedly taking the detective's hand. "And I deduce that you are Sherlock Holmes," he added with a chuckle.

"That declaration reassures me." Doffing the shovel hat and removing his spectacles, Holmes glanced down into Blenkiron's cup before sitting in a chair and then stared at his brother. "As I remarked to Watson only a short while ago, I do hope this masquerade is nearing its finale."

"Only time will tell, my boy," Mycroft replied enigmatically, seating himself upon one portion of a large sofa.

Blenkiron resumed his position in the basket chair. "One never knows when any inning of the big game will end," he said in response.

Suddenly finding myself the only one standing, I at once took to an armchair beside the American.

"And so, Sherlock," the elder Holmes said, "it appears you have now brought the good doctor into our enterprise—without prior consultation, of course, which will not please Sir Walter, but the move has my strong approval." Mycroft smiled at me and then looked back at his brother. "I do hope you intend him to do more than simply replace that young man from Chicago as your chauffeur."

"I had not considered that possibility," said the detective, "but I suppose Watson could take over for Jack now and then. Until recently, Watson has rarely deigned to approach a motor, you see, let alone been desirous of taking control of one. Sadly for my old friend, the horse-drawn trade is approaching extinction, leaving him a stranger in a strange land."

"On the contrary," Mycroft chided his sibling. "He appears quite familiar with the landscape, especially that of motors."

"Well, perhaps somewhat," admitted Sherlock Holmes. "He did ride with me here in a taxi, and it is evident that he has made several excursions about the country of late, as passenger in another's vehicle."

"Tut-tut," replied Mycroft. "Why, it is obvious that the doctor has been the frequent operator of a motorcar for at least several months. Indeed, he is the owner of one, and an enthusiastic owner at that. Are you not?" he asked of me.

"Well," I said, eyeing the younger Holmes with caution, "the truth is, yes, I own an automobile."

"Clamp him in irons!" cried the detective with mock distress. "This cannot be the real Watson but rather an impersonator. And to think I failed to see through your disguise, sir."

"You are most amusing," I said calmly. "As always."

"Mr. Holmes, you've not kept up with your good friend's interests, it seems," Blenkiron gently interjected, reaching for his cup.

The detective shrugged. "Yes, involvement in Brother Mycroft's conspiracies has certainly caused me to lose touch with those I thought I knew well." He stared at me with an expression of disbelief I took to be at least half genuine. "Is it be true, Watson, that you, of all people, have capitulated and now possess and operate an automobile?"

"It is housed in a motor stable, if you would ever care to examine it."

"And what make is it?" Blenkiron asked with apparent interest.

"A Carleton-Herriott," I answered.[12]

The American whistled before sipping from his cup.

"And you did not know of this acquisition?" Mycroft asked of Sherlock Holmes, as if to taunt. "When the signs are all in plain view?"

"I fear I must have missed them," the younger brother replied with an astringent tone. "I did take note of that well-defined area around the good doctor's eyes in which the flesh is less lined and tanned, suggesting the frequent wearing of protective goggles."

Mycroft sniffed. "Yes, I expect that would have caught the attention of any schoolboy, even a nearsighted one."

"I, meanwhile, am apparently becoming all too careless in my dotage," declared Sherlock Holmes. "Perhaps you may further enlighten me, dear brother."

"When I shook the doctor's hand, I detected calluses on these portions of the fingers and palm," Mycroft began, illustrating with his own. "They are consistent with the use of only two or three different types of machine tool, including a screw-cutting lathe. I take it that even a Carleton-Herriott's handmade fasteners wear out in time, and that replacements must be cut by hand?"

---

[12] This is a fictional name, for no such automobile appears to have existed.

"Yes," I replied. "In the long run, the lathe has proved a good investment, as the vehicle's screws are, of course, not uniform. And, I must admit, I find the cutting tool a minor joy to work by myself."

"Of course, the calluses in themselves are not conclusive evidence of a motoring enthusiast," Mycroft said. "However, those same fingers also display mild staining, and not from materials I associate with the practice of medicine—a practice from which our good doctor appears to have retired, though only in part," Mycroft declared as his brother opened his mouth to speak. "I take it you act as an occasional substitute for one or more of your colleagues?" he asked me.

"He does," said Sherlock Holmes glumly, before I could respond. "There is no need for further elaboration on that point, I think."

Mycroft smiled at me without glancing toward his brother and then leaned back in the sofa to continue. "The man I employ to tend my motor has cautioned me about the need to frequently dress the leather cone covering the vehicle's clutch with neetsfoot oil. The stains on his fingers from that substance are about the same hue as those you sport on your hands, Doctor."

"Yes, of course," I commented.

"And the left portion of your left shoe is similarly stained. If a clutch cone dosed with neetsfoot oil is the cause, that places you in the chauffeur's seat, does it not? I conclude that your stained and callused hands are testament to your enjoyment of tending the vehicle by your own effort, and thus evidence of enthusiastic ownership. An admirable attitude," asserted Mycroft Holmes. "It is, however, one I find myself unable to share—I require a mechanic to keep my automobile in fine condition."

"As if you have any need of a fleet motor," whispered Sherlock Holmes.

"Did you say something, brother?"

"What? Oh, I remarked on the absence of street odour. A consequence of the reduced horse population, think you not?" said the younger Holmes.

Mycroft frowned.

"I've had my man employ collan oil instead of neetsfoot for my car's clutch cone," said Blenkiron with amusement. He then related his own past experiences with automobiles, much to the interest of Mycroft and me. Sherlock Holmes, meanwhile, silently chafed as the conversation became dominated by the topic of motoring and its tribulations.

"Perhaps you should purchase a Fox Type-V, made in my country," suggested Blenkiron after a while.[13] "I saw one here in London but yesterday for only one hundred seventy-five pounds. The parts are standard, fashioned uniformly," he added. "You wouldn't need that lathe to cut screws of individual size."

The house bell suddenly rang twice and then, after a pause, once more.

"That should be our final guest," declared Mycroft Holmes. "I will fetch him."

As his brother rose and then ambled from the room, Sherlock Holmes looked at me, his lips forming a single, silent name: Bullivant.

I nodded, noticing that Blenkiron's face still held a subtle expression of amusement as he once more sipped from his cup.

---

[13] Watson again uses a fictitious manufacturer's name, for Blenkiron is undoubtedly referring to the Ford Model-T.

"I trust, Mr. Blenkiron, that your dyspepsia is not proving too much a hindrance during this meeting?" asked Sherlock Holmes.

"Why no, sir," replied the American, who then gave a mild start.

"Drinking warmed milk could merely be personal preference," Holmes said. "But I chose to assume it is a reflection of digestive troubles."

Blenkiron nodded.

"Well played, sir," he declared, lifting his cup at my friend. "Let me admit to suffering from such problems. The milk calms me down below."

At that moment, the elder Holmes brother returned in the company of a large-framed man with a florid face. As we all rose from our chairs, the newcomer's shrewd eyes immediately fixed upon me through tortoiseshell spectacles.

"Who is this person?" he demanded before there had been any introductions. "Why is he here?"

There was an awkward moment of silence before Mycroft Holmes stepped forward.

"This is Dr. John Watson, Sir Walter," he said. "You may have heard of him as my brother's former consulting associate."

"I don't give a damn if he's Jesus's current batman," exclaimed Bullivant. "Get him out."[14]

I looked at both Mycroft and Sherlock Holmes with some embarrassment and made as if to go, but from the corner of my eye I sensed a discreet gesture from Blenkiron suggesting I remain.

"I have placed my life in Dr. Watson's hands on more than one occasion, Sir Walter," declared Sherlock Holmes. "I have no hesitation in

[14] A batman is the personal servant of a British military officer.

trusting him with the destiny of our nation, and I request that he be allowed to remain."

"The hesitation is mine, not yours, Mr. Holmes." Bullivant transfixed me with his stare. "What purpose does he serve here?" he asked, looking once more at Mycroft.

The older Holmes did not respond, but rather deferred again to his brother, who said, "I have recruited him for my enterprise, as I have recruited the others."

"Yes," replied Bullivant, "but Messrs. James and Hollins and Steiner do not sit here in the innermost circle, do they? It was a breach of security to inform him of this house's existence, let alone allow him to enter it. I am your immediate superior, Mr. Holmes, as I have constant need to remind you. You should have asked permission for this rash act, permission that would not have been granted in any event."

"Sir Walter, I can more than vouch for the doctor," asserted Mycroft Holmes. "And, if I do not appear too pre-emptory, please do recall that I in turn am *your* immediate superior. I confess it was I who granted Dr. Watson entry, and I also should very much prefer that he remain."

Bullivant exhaled with force and then reluctantly nodded.

"Very well," he said in a tired voice, motioning for us to sit down as he took to the remaining empty chair. "Mycroft, on your recommendation, we will let the matter drop. Let us get on with the business, then. So, Mr. Blenkiron," he said, now ignoring me altogether, "What had you heard from your man Scudder before he disappeared?"

"I have only one small item that he passed on to my government a few days ago," the American admitted. "That item, however, would appear to have great significance."

"Yes," said Bullivant. "Mycroft indicated you had something of importance. What the devil is it?"

"It is, Sir Walter, just a pair of phrases: 'Black Stone—part of Cerberus.'"

Mycroft Holmes appeared intrigued, while Bullivant awkwardly cleared his throat. Sherlock Holmes merely sat and watched, his face impassive.

"And what are those phrases supposed to mean?" asked Sir Walter.

"Aside from the mythological reference, I do not know," admitted Blenkiron.[15] "The only other thing I can tell you is that, whatever their meaning, they must have a heap of import for the Germans."

Bullivant again cleared his throat and then spoke. "Have you any thoughts, Mr. Holmes?"

The detective leaned back and made a steeple with his fingers.

"It appears the two phrases must be taken together," he said, "and thus we must pay equal attention to the nonmythological one: Black Stone. Mr. Blenkiron, you say the American government came by this through Franklin Scudder?"

"It was all he was able to write upon a small scrap of paper which he left for one of our agents to retrieve at a designated site," the American replied cautiously.

In the corner of my eye, I saw Mycroft Holmes and Bullivant both shift in their chairs.

"Was it Traill's, John?" asked the elder Holmes brother.

---

[15] In Greek and Roman legend, Cerberus was a multi-headed hellhound that guarded the gates of Hades, preventing its inhabitants from escaping.

"Yes," admitted Blenkiron after a moment. "So you know of the bookstore, Mycroft?"

Bullivant sniffed loudly.

"Of course we do," said the older Holmes brother, smiling.

"Traill's Bookshop in Haymarket Street," Blenkiron said to Sherlock Holmes and me almost immediately. "I myself own it as a pastime, for I love books and enjoy dealing in them, but in addition, it has served my country's intelligence service as a way station, in somewhat the same manner as this house serves you."

"Yes," said Mycroft. "That is what we have been given to understand. You have owned it for the past two years, have you not, John?"

"Yes, and it was my intention to eventually share with you knowledge of the place and its role, Mycroft."

"Which you have just done," replied the elder Holmes brother with another gracious smile. "As we shared with your government information about my brother's mission to your country—from the beginning."

"I get your point," said the American.

"If we may return to the issue at hand," Sherlock Holmes interjected, "it should be noted that while Cerberus, whatever it is, incorporates the Black Stone—whatever, in turn, that happens to be—it by implication has other parts as well. The mythological Cerberus had three heads *in toto*, did it not?"

"Three was the most common number mentioned," said Blenkiron, "if I'm remembering my classics correctly."

"Well, at the moment, only the Germans—and, perhaps, Franklin Scudder—know the exact count," said Mycroft Holmes. "I refer to Mr.

Scudder in the present tense, for I expect he is still alive. Did your examination of his flat near Portland Place support that belief, Sherlock?"

"It did," replied the detective. "The body in Scudder's flat is most definitely not that of Scudder. Dr. Watson and I have established that."

Blenkiron cocked his head slightly, and Mycroft Holmes nodded.

"I thought such might be the case," the latter said. "I had been informed that the body was found in pyjamas, and from what little I do know of Scudder, it seemed unlikely that he of all people would be caught sleeping, as it were."

"Where may he be, then?" asked Bullivant. "And why has he not reported? Why could he not simply go to the American embassy?"

"Or more pointedly," noted Mycroft Holmes, "why has he not fled to your bookshop in the Haymarket, John?" He drew himself up and gave Bullivant a look of mild reproach. "Of course, were Safety House available to the agents of our allies, as I have frequently urged, its address might have previously been given to Scudder as an additional haven from his pursuers."

Bullivant clasped his hands together. "I grant that you are correct in that hindsight, Mycroft, but hindsight provides precious little solace in our present situation, does it?"

"The reason Scudder has not attempted to find refuge on Haymarket Street is because he was directed not to," said Blenkiron, apparently desiring to steer the discussion away from further discord. "The shop's real purpose is not known to anyone else—other than you British now, I hope. Scudder had left his note there earlier with complete discretion, but he had also been directed to not approach the bookstore if he ever felt he were being closely watched or pursued. We don't want the identity of the shop compromised—even at the risk of an agent's safety, I must confess."

The elder Holmes shrugged. "In our present situation, I trust the experience and judgment of my brother. Well, Sherlock, what can we do to find Scudder?"

"By which question," the younger Holmes replied, "you mean what can *I* do to find him."

Mycroft smiled. "You know I never enjoy stating the self-evident to you."

"And I am equally aware that you savour even less having the obvious laid out for *you*," said Sherlock Holmes. "However, for the record—if this secret gathering even has a record—I think it obvious that Scudder knew he was being watched and that his life was in danger. He no doubt made arrangements to make it appear that he had committed suicide—apparently by obtaining a body from some latter-day Burke and Hare[16] and then setting up the scene in his flat before somehow escaping the building, hoping that his pursuers would believe he had taken his own life."

Intent on justifying my presence at this council, especially to Bullivant, I steeled myself, leaned forward and said, "If he did escape the building."

All eyes turned toward me, and I meekly added, "Could he not, perhaps, still be within that same block of flats?"

My friend ignored the scowl that appeared on Sir Walter's face.

---

[16] William Burke and William Hare killed a number of people in Edinburgh during 1828, selling the corpses as subjects for dissection in anatomy classes, at a time when cadavers for medical research and training were difficult to come by.

"I admit that was a thought I pondered there in Scudder's sitting room as I waited for you to finish your examination of the body," he said. "It would be a bold move on the man's part, but the likelihood of it hinges upon his personality and character. Do you have any understanding of that character and nature, Mr. Blenkiron?"

The American leaned back and imitated Holmes's previous gesture of making a steeple with his fingers. "I may have some small insight into him, I suppose, but, to be honest, Franklin Scudder has remained a cipher to many of us, even though he's one of the best players of the game I've ever seen—but then, because he is one of the best, perhaps he should be expected to remain an unknown.

"The man is honest, certainly, but he is also half crank, half genius. He's brilliant at working a crowd. I've seen him pose as a Harvard professor lecturing on Ibsen—Ibsen, for God's sake—and fooling everyone within earshot, myself included, and I knew it was a ruse at the time! However, his one fault is a decided preference for playing a lone hand."

"Ah," said Holmes. "Cooperation is not in his blood."

"Exactly," said Blenkiron.

"And if he is loath to bring in partners of his own trade," the detective went on, "he would be even less likely to seek assistance from a stranger."

"That's a fair bet, Mr. Holmes," replied Blenkiron. "For Scudder to, say, barge into another man's rooms and take up residence there would be most unusual for him."

"But this is an unusual situation," I observed.

"In fact, Doctor," said Bullivant dismissively, "it is a situation not at all unusual for the game, is it, Mycroft?"

The elder Holmes brother sighed. "Well, it is certainly not uncommon. I will grant you that, Sir Walter. Sherlock?"

"I have been wrong before." The detective glanced at me and smiled. "Indeed, I have been wrong far more often than the public suspect; however, if I must choose in this instance, I opt to believe that Scudder is not in hiding at Portland Place. All of London may be a dangerous place for him, but it still gives him a wider pitch in which to find solitary concealment than does the enclosed block of flats where he began. Even if the building were being watched, as I am certain it was and may still be, I believe an agent of Scudder's calibre would have found means to leave unnoticed."

"Perhaps by posing as a tradesman," suggested Mycroft. "A milkman, say."

"Precisely, my astute brother."

"In any event," said Bullivant, "I understand the inquest concerning the body found in the flat is to be tomorrow."

"Yes," replied Sherlock Holmes. "That is what Magillivray conveyed to me."

"The inspector will orchestrate the proceedings nicely," noted the spymaster.

"He is a good man," observed Mycroft. "I believe the time is coming when he should be granted admittance to this circle."

Sherlock Holmes discreetly looked at me and smiled.

"Perhaps," admitted Bullivant, who also cast a glance in my direction, albeit a darker one. "Particularly since the circle seems to be expanding with every passing day."

"I suggest that Dr. Watson be present at the inquest," said Holmes abruptly. "It is natural that he should be asked to testify," my friend said, as all eyes fell on him. "He treated Scudder for headaches only last week."

"And what relevance do headaches have to this situation?" asked Bullivant sourly. "Other than as metaphor. Magillivray will be at the inquest, after all."

"The inspector will be intent on making his case to the jury," Sherlock Holmes explained. "The doctor's testimony could help influence that panel to make the very judgment you desire, Sir Walter, and he would also be able to observe the proceedings at greater leisure when not being questioned, all in the bargain."

"You believe there may be German agents present?" asked the American.

Holmes shrugged. "For all I know, Mr. Blenkiron," he said with a wry smile, "some of your own agents may be there as well. Another pair of eyes would simply be helpful, and I must travel to Sussex early tomorrow to meet with my other master," the detective declared, "the estimable Heinrich Von Bork."

"My brother's suggestion is reasonable, Sir Walter," said Mycroft. "As a physician who treated Scudder recently, Dr. Watson's presence would create no suspicion, and his testimony—properly given—may be very helpful," he added glibly.

Bullivant thought for a moment and then waved his hand in an exasperated manner. "Of course," he grumbled. "Do as you wish. However," he said, leaning forward in Blenkiron's direction, "We still have these cryptic references to Black Stone and Cerberus to sort out."

Blenkiron nodded. “I have put my people onto it as, no doubt, you will yours, Sir Walter, all the while hoping that Scudder eventually turns up with an explanation.”

There followed several minutes of discussion among Bullivant, Blenkiron, and Mycroft Holmes on matters of which I had no understanding, and so, as the conversation ground on, I glanced about the room while Sherlock Holmes merely stared at the ceiling.

Eventually, Bullivant slapped the armrests of his chair and got to his feet. “All right, then. Everything seems in order, I suppose. Unless there is more you want from me, Mycroft, I will go.”

“I believe we have covered all items in the agenda,” said the elder Holmes brother, smiling gently. He and the rest of us also rose. “Thank you for attending, Sir Walter. I will convey more as needed.”

And with that, after acknowledging everyone but me, the spymaster left the room in the company of Mycroft Holmes.

“Well, Dr. Watson,” said Blenkiron, settling back in his chair and once more reaching for his cup of milk as the house door closed, “you have had your christening with Sir Walter Bullivant.”

I could only smile awkwardly as Mycroft Holmes reappeared.

“And that ceremony completed,” said his brother, “it becomes necessary to instruct the doctor in what to say at tomorrow’s inquest.”

“And how to say it,” added Mycroft.

“That is, how to say it in such a way that people will believe you,” amended Blenkiron.

“Once that is accomplished,” declared Sherlock Holmes, “I will extract you from this coven of deceit, old fellow, and make certain to get you back to the safety of Queen Anne Street for the night.”

§ § §

On the following day, as both witness and secret observer, I attended the inquest into Franklin Scudder's presumed death. My testimony included a description of having treated him for migraines, but following the instructions of Blenkiron and both Holmes brothers, I also declared—quite untruthfully—that I could see the troubling suggestion of suicidal tendencies in the American after the fact.

A man I later supposed to be one of Sir Walter Bullivant's agents appeared in the guise of a partner in some publishing firm and identified Scudder as the agent of a paper firm from across the Atlantic, explaining that the deceased had brought him propositions concerning wood-pulp. The American's valet, that sad little man who had discovered the body, said nothing that was new to me, and the glass of sleeping-draught turned out to have been quite harmless.

It was late afternoon when the jury finally declared that Scudder had taken his own life while being of unsound mind, the self-execution accomplished by means of a gunshot to the head. The man's effects were authorised for transfer to his nation's consul, and the hearing disbanded.

As I joined the small, slowly departing crowd, I saw from the corner of my eye one of the other onlookers gracefully step in front of another man, who had paused to allow him to join the exiting queue.

"Thank you much," came a resonant voice, and I looked up at once to see that same weathered face with drooping moustache that I had encountered on the stair at Portland Place the day before.

Stirred into sudden alertness by my second encounter with this individual, I looked back into the room for Magillivray, who had presented Scotland Yard's case, but I failed to espy the inspector, who had evidently left the room through another door. Torn between the choice of either following the anonymous man or alerting Magillivray, I decided to pursue the former.

Discreetly and at a distance, I trailed my quarry from the government building and then along a crowded pavement. My immediate fear was that the stranger might seek a taxicab or lonely hansom at any moment, but he kept striding along so briskly that soon I instead became anxious about matching his pace on foot—it was clear that he was a devotee of long, strenuous hikes.

The man had gained some distance on me when, fortunately, he stopped to enter a milliner's, where he spent the better part of a quarter hour. I bided my time somewhat awkwardly in front of a bakery and then once more took up pursuit when he left the hat shop, no longer as far ahead of me as before.

In much the same matter, I followed him with stops and starts across the expanse of the City,[17] finally approaching that block of flats in which Franklin Scudder had resided, and where I had first encountered the man I now surreptitiously pursued.

While I stood some distance from the building, I observed the man pass a loafer near the main door, and as I watched, the loafer suddenly looked up and across the street. I turned my head quickly in the same direction and saw, framed by a first-floor window in the house opposite, the head of another man, his face obscured by a curtain. There was a nod from the person at the window, and the loafer gave a hand signal in reply as my moustached quarry entered the block of flats.

---

[17] "The City" here refers to the historic heart of London, encompassing only that part inhabited through the Middle Ages and not the greater metropolis as a whole.

I now fully understood that I had stepped into very deep waters. That Scudder's building was being watched there could be no doubt, but by whom? The loafer and his partner could well be Magillivray's men from Scotland Yard, or perhaps members of Bullivant's Secret Service. John Blenkiron had admitted that American agents were present in London, and these might be two of his countrymen instead. Alternatively, I knew, they could be men in the pay of some other foreign power.

In addition, I could not be certain what the apparent signals between the two individuals had signified. Perhaps the man had meant nothing to the pair, or possibly he was one they earnestly sought. When, after some time, the object of my pursuit did not emerge from the building, I concluded that he must reside there. And, since I had seen him the previous day coming from the first floor, I concluded that his flat was in that portion of the block.

Accosting him alone in his rooms would expose my interest in him, I feared, and so I turned away, having decided that I should seek out assistance before proceeding.

Sherlock Holmes, I recalled, had departed for Sussex that morning to rendezvous with the German spy leader Von Bork. John Blenkiron had seemed most friendly, but he was an American, and I knew not if he were still in London and—if he had remained in the metropolis—where he was quartered. I could attempt to contact him at Traill's Bookshop, but I suspected I would be rebuffed without knowledge of some special password. That left Sir Walter Bullivant and Mycroft Holmes as my only sources of help. Given my previous experiences with both men, I knew which one to seek first.

I hurried south toward Pall Mall, intent on determining if Mycroft Holmes might be biding his time at the Diogenes Club, the distinctive institution that he himself had helped found. A haven for the misanthropic, the club was established to benefit those having no wish for the company of their fellows, yet who could still appreciate the comfort of plush chairs and the latest in reading material.

The Diogenes Club, in short, was famed for containing the most unsociable men in town.

I passed the more venerable Carlton Club and quickly strode on to that plain door before which I had stood more than once in years past. After steadying my nerves, I rang. An attendant responded, and after presenting my card, I was led along the club's unusual entrance corridor.

We almost at once encountered the unique glass panelling that comprised the left-hand side of the hall, allowing me to see into the club's large main room, where no member is permitted to take the least notice of any other one. The panelling, which separated the entry hall from the main room, served a dual purpose, however: while allowing a newcomer to view the inhabitants of the main room, it also gave members sitting there forewarning of incoming visitors.

As I stared through the panes, searching for the rotund frame of Mycroft Holmes, I saw instead, sitting in an armchair reading a periodical, Sir Walter Bullivant. It seemed odd that the spymaster should, by coincidence, be a member of the Diogenes Club, but I thought not to question my good fortune. The attendant guided me to the right and into the Stranger's Room, graced with but a single bow window looking out onto Pall Mall and the only room within the club where talking was permitted.

The attendant asked whom I sought.

"I came looking for Mycroft Holmes," I told him quickly. "But I just espied Sir Walter Bullivant in the main room. May I please have a word with him?"

The servant nodded and left me standing by the window. I fingered the brim of my hat and glanced outside as I waited for Bullivant, finding the interval was extending far longer than I should have expected.

At length, the attendant returned.

"Neither Mr. Holmes nor Sir Walter is present, sir," he informed me.

"But I saw the latter as I entered," I once more asserted. "He was in a chair, reading."

"I'm afraid I did not come across him, sir," was the man's reply. "Perhaps we should both observe again from the hallway—silently, if you please?"

I followed him from the Stranger's Room into the corridor. Looking once more through the glass, I saw that the armchair which had held Bullivant was now empty.

"But he was there," I said, indicating where Sir Walter had been.

"Pointing is no more allowed than speaking, sir," whispered the attendant.

Contritely, I dropped my arm and hid the forefinger and then led the attendant back to the Stranger's Room.

"But he was there," I said softly but urgently, once we had returned. "Sir Walter was in the main room, in an armchair, calmly reading."

"I believe we both observed, sir, that he is not occupying any chair at present. Indeed, I surveyed the entire main room and found that he is not present at all."

I nodded reluctant agreement. "And Mycroft Holmes is not about, either?" I asked.

"As you had mentioned Mr. Holmes initially, I did keep an eye for him also, but to no avail."

"May I leave a note for either gentleman?"

"I am afraid that is not allowed anymore, sir. Indeed," the attendant added, "many of our members come here to evade such intrusions."

"Well then," I muttered, turning toward the entrance corridor, "I may as well depart."

We both marched back down the hallway, and the attendant opened the door so that I might leave the building. Standing for a moment on the pavement, gazing at the bow window from which I had but minutes before stared toward my present location, I considered going on to various government offices in Westminster in search of Mycroft Holmes. By now, however, the afternoon had begun to advance toward evening, and I decided those offices would be closing to the public.

It was then that I thought to undertake a pilgrimage to the Safety House, believing that whomever I might find there would be able to direct me to one of the men I sought. And so, flagging down a taxicab—this time, one not operated by Jack James—I proceeded in that direction.

Employing caution, as I was certain Sherlock Holmes would have advised, I instructed the chauffeur to take me a slight distance away from the house itself and then walked in a roundabout manner to the front door I had confronted the day before. I stared at the letterbox and then squarely at the small peephole, which I should never have noticed had I not already been aware of its existence. Then, after a deep breath, I rang in the pattern I had been told previously.

There was no response. Again I rang, once more to no effect.

It was quite possible that the house was empty at this time, but I began to fear that, perhaps instead, the appropriate pattern of ringing was changed each day, so that my signal would naturally be ignored.

Stepping back from the entrance, I began to slowly walk away, pondering what further action I might take. Eventually, having trod several blocks at random, I found I had no answer to my question, and so in a disheartened state, I found a second taxicab to deliver me home, where I spent a restless and anxious night.

CHAPTER THREE: THE MAN WHO FLED

While rising the next day, I realised I had overlooked the possibility of seeking Inspector Magillivray's assistance. However, as I sat upon the edge of my bed in early morning light and contemplated a visit to Scotland Yard, arguments against that choice rapidly came to mind.

Sherlock Holmes had indicated that the inspector was Bullivant's man, to be sure, but he had also explained that Magillivray was not privy to all portions of the spymaster's plans and intentions. Indeed, though I had been granted at least a momentary seat at the inner circle in Safety House, the inspector was not yet deemed worthy of such inclusion, and I found it difficult to conceive how I might impress upon Magillivray the possible importance of the moustached man without revealing too much of what I knew of Scudder's mission, knowledge which Bullivant might not desire the inspector to have.

It also occurred to me that, once I had engaged Magillivray at length, it would be all too obvious to him that I knew even less of Bullivant and his operations than did he, and that such ignorance might, in turn, cause the inspector to become suspicious of my own position, intentions and loyalties, since I had earlier claimed familiarity with the spymaster.

Thus, as I prepared to make my toilet,[18] I had already weighed all arguments and decided that it was best to exclude the inspector from my current problem. I resolved instead to return to Portland Place and there conduct my own investigation as best I might. At the very least, it seemed,

[18] This is a now old-fashioned way of referring to the act of washing and dressing for the day.

I might learn the identity of the man whom I had twice encountered and thus attach a name to the tanned face and drooping moustache.

So it was that, almost forty-eight hours after first entering that block of flats where Scudder had roomed, I approached the building a third time. Recalling my last experience, I sought out the loafer I had seen the day before, but he was nowhere in view. In like manner, the window across the street, to which he had signalled, was vacant—indeed, it was now completely curtained shut.

Feeling somewhat more assured by this apparent absence of observers, I entered the building and strode casually across the lobby toward the porter, who was not the same individual I had earlier seen serving in that capacity. This man sat reading the previous day's *Evening Standard*, but he put it down upon noticing me.

"How may I help you, sir?" the porter asked, getting to his feet.

I paused, suddenly unsure of myself, for though I had practised my opening remarks many times on the way to Portland Place, I was now gripped by fear that the other man might become suspicious if I appeared to be seeking my quarry too earnestly. The expectant look in the eyes of the porter only heightened that anxiety, and finding myself years out of practice in the arts of such ruses, I found myself immediately frozen and speechless.

I cleared my throat, creating an interlude which allowed me to do the same for my mind, and then said idly, "There is a gentleman residing here I wish to see. He has recently arrived, I believe, from India."

This last remark I added with trepidation, for I had no assurance that the subcontinent had been the man's previous residence—I thought Afghanistan an unlikely choice, but South Africa or, I supposed, the Levant could not be excluded. I silently hoped I had made the correct choice as I waited for the porter to respond.

"Ah, I suppose you must mean that Captain Digby who's taken to lodging with Mr. Hannay up on the first floor," he said after a moment.

"Indeed," I said with a sigh of relief. "It is Captain Digby, though I must confess," I added with a nervous smile, "that I am but a casual acquaintance and can never recall the man's given name."

"It is Theophilus, I've been told," replied the man with a curious tone. "Don't quite see how a man could forget that name, though I reckon the captain himself may wish he could, eh?" he added with a chuckle.

I was at once alarmed by my apparent faux pas, but fortunately, the porter mistook my expression of concern for one of offense instead.

"Oh, not that I was making light of a fine soldier such as he must be," the man said anxiously, stepping closer. "No, please forgive me if I seemed disrespectful, for I would never intend that.

"I've observed the man but once, and that was enough to make clear that I was in the presence of a professional fighting man, all right. He possesses a superb military bearing, even out of uniform. And that voice! So commanding, it is. And he's obviously quite disciplined in the personal sense, too, you understand: very well groomed, with hair parted precisely in the middle and his face shaved perfectly clean. Even sports a monocle, to finish the portrait."

My heart sank at the porter's extended description of Captain Digby, for it made obvious to me that he was not the man I sought. Yet, I believed, there was still a chance that success might be salvaged, and I reached for it.

"You said he is residing with someone here?" I ventured.

"With Mr. Hannay—Richard Hannay, the South African chap," the porter replied, and upon hearing those last three words, I felt hope return in sudden fullness.

"Ah, yes," I said boldly. "Mr. Hannay, with the drooping moustache and tanned face."

"That's right, sir. You plainly know him."

"Indeed, I do. It is through him that I made my acquaintance with Captain Digby, you see."

"Well, you've accomplished more than any of us here have, I can tell you. The captain's been here just a very short time, but he seems to keep to himself in Mr. Hannay's flat pretty much round the clock, day and night. I've seen the man but once, as I just told you. Bit of a reclusive, he is—that's the medical term for it, I believe."

"I see."

"Mr. Hannay, on the other hand, is about as friendly as possible, as you must know, being of his acquaintance. Has he ever done any of his little Scottish pantomimes for you?"

"No."

"Oh, you must ask him to perform one for you some time. Just last week, he was regaling me and the lift operator with his impersonation of a sheep herder whose dog was going—"

"Do you know if Mr. Hannay is in?" I asked abruptly.

"In fact," said the porter, taking no offense at my interruption, "he's out most of the time, including the present—I saw him leave less than an hour ago."

"Oh."

"But then, it is Captain Digby you've come to visit, I believe you said, and he never goes out. Shall I step up to the first floor and see if he's accepting callers? I would just be doing my job. Here, let me—"

"No, thank you," I replied, fumbling for an explanation. "The fact is, Mr. Hannay's presence will be required also," I added on impulse and then, with sudden inspiration, patted the chest of my coat as if the pocket held a document.

"There are some personal legal issues involving the captain that require settling," I said. "Papers to be signed, and Mr. Hannay had agreed to act as witness. Nothing can proceed unless he is present as well."

"Oh," said the porter in a very deferential tone. "Yes, indeed, I see. Very personal legal business it is, then."

"I will return later, I think."

"And should I mention your enquiry to Captain Digby or Mr. Hannay?"

"No," I replied as I turned to go. "I would, in fact, very much appreciate it if you would not. Extreme discretion must attend this matter, I am afraid."

"Oh well, then mum shall be my word," the porter told me, winking. "Discreet business and mum it shall be, yes."

I nodded and then strode back across the lobby, confident that I had identified my moustached man. Then, a few feet from the door, I paused and turned, having half-consciously contemplated the fact of Theophilus Digby's presence in the meanwhile.

"Excuse me," I called to the porter. "I realise that you told me earlier, but when did the captain take up residence here?"

“Two days ago,” the man replied. He scratched his head, tilting his cap slightly. “Yes, it must have been Thursday, for Paddock—that’s Mr. Hannay’s valet—he first made mention of the captain that very morning. You see, it was the same day as they found poor Mr. Scudder’s body up on the top floor.”

“Oh? A body?” I said, feigning lack of knowledge concerning the tragedy. I stepped closer to the porter, who, *Evening Standard* once more in hand, approached to meet me halfway.

“Yes, nasty business that was,” he told me as if confiding in a very close friend. “Have you not heard of it?” He began to leaf through his newspaper. “I should think there must be details in this edition. Well, in any case,” he said, lowering the paper from his face, “the gent was an American, you see. Shot himself clean through the jaw while in his nightclothes—terrible, most terrible it was. And I had helped the poor soul get his trunk up top but the day before.”

“I am so sorry to hear of the tragedy,” I remarked. “Tell me, was the trunk very heavy?”

“Oh, it were not a light load,” the man said with a smile. “And not well packed inside, you know, for whatever it was in there kept jiggling this way and that. The awful thing was that it wouldn’t quite fit within the lift, you see. Otherwise, we’d have just taken her up that way. But no, it was to the stairs with her, and all the effort that accompanied it. I tell you, I’d have preferred hauling a body up them steps instead of that trunk, if I’d had my choice.”

“I sympathise.”

“But at least I did not have to endure all that business with the police on Thursday,” the man declared. “Instead, Stephens was on duty. Spared me a heap of trouble, I can tell you, him being here when they found the corpse."

He then regaled me with a most detailed description of that day's events, obtained from his fellow porter. I listened patiently to the lengthy story, and then, as I contemplated my next step, an idea occurred to me.

"I wish to make a request," I said, interrupting the man's third version of the police removing the body from No. 15. "Have you paper and pen? I need to compose a short note."

"Writing implements?" said the man. "Why, of course. You wait here—I'm afraid I never got your name, did I, sir?"

"Mr. Price," I said upon a whim. "And you said you had paper and pen?"

"We do, indeed. Just a moment."

While the man strode off to fetch the items I had requested, I made my way to a bench at the far end of the building lobby. Moments later, as I sat there, the porter returned.

"This will do, I hope," he said. "I found several sheets of writing paper, but only a pencil."

"Yes, this will suffice," I replied, taking the items from him.

He then offered me a small box to place upon my lap as an impromptu writing desk, and I hastily composed a note on one sheet of the paper, which I then folded and addressed to "Sherlock or Mycroft Holmes, or Sir Walter Bullivant" before handing back the pencil and unused paper to the generous porter. I placed the note in my coat pocket, bade him farewell, and left the building.

Regaining the pavement outside, I glanced at the house across the street and saw that the window where I had noticed an observer the day before was still curtained. In addition, the loafer had not reappeared, but nonetheless I walked in an unassuming manner for several blocks before hailing a taxicab.

Several minutes later, I found myself yet again ringing the bell of Safety House to no result. I had recalled while at Portland Place, however, that the door of the house was fitted with a letterbox, a memory which had prompted my composing the note on borrowed paper. As no one came to open the door for me, I withdrew the folded page from my coat pocket, slipped it past the horizontal flap of the letterbox, and then left with the intention of visiting various government offices in Westminster, where I still held out some hope of locating either Mycroft Holmes or Sir Walter Bullivant.

That task, however, proved far more daunting that I had expected, for later, as I stood before the first official entrance I encountered, I realised that, despite my personal familiarity with Mycroft Holmes, I had never in all the years of our acquaintance learnt either his formal title or the specific ministry in which he was employed. Thus, I knew not where to search for him—and, indeed, my several attempts proved fruitless: No one to whom I spoke knew of the elder Holmes brother, and when one of my long chains of enquiry brought me back to the office at which I had started, I abandoned hope of quickly finding my friend's sibling.

Meanwhile, I recalled Sherlock Holmes mentioning that Bullivant held a place of importance within the Secret Service, but when I asked for directions to that organisation's offices, I was met with suspicion and obfuscation.[19] As late afternoon began to wane, I found myself no closer

---

[19] At the time, the bureau later known popularly as MI-6 was headquartered in Whitehall Court, constructed in the 1880s.

to finding assistance than I had been upon arising from my bed some hours earlier.

I attempted to convince myself that I had done my best under the circumstances as I returned to Queen Anne Street, where it dawned on me that I had had no meal since breakfast. I ravenously devoured my supper and then waited anxiously for some reply to my note. The evening passed, however, without the ringing of either my house bell or my telephone, and for a second night I suffered lack of sleep.

The following morning, I rose later than my usual hour and was preparing to sit down to Sunday breakfast when I heard my housekeeper greet a caller at the house door.

It was Jack James, and his appearance gave me sudden relief.

"Mr. Holmes has read the note you left, sir, and says you have performed magnificently," the young man declared before I could utter a single word. "But he doesn't wish to delay in taking advantage of your achievement. Can you leave here immediately, Dr. Watson?"

"Sixty seconds will suffice," was my reply, and, after apologetically suggesting to my housekeeper that she enjoy the fruits of the cook's labour instead of me, I finished donning my jacket only as I reached the kerb, where Jack James sat at the ready, behind the wheel of that same taxicab he had driven three days before. Holmes occupied half of the passenger compartment, head bowed so as to obscure his face.

"Off we go again, gentlemen," said the young American as I stepped into the vehicle and closed the door.

"Portland Place is within walking distance, of course, but every minute may count in this instance," said Holmes as we roared off. Lifting his face toward mine, he added, “Stop at least a block short, Jack, if you will.”

“Right,” said our chauffeur.

“We returned from Von Bork’s headquarters in Essex less than an hour ago,” my friend told me. “Fortunately, I decided to stop at Safety House rather than return to the flat that I maintain as Altamount south of the river. Your note, which I took to have been put through the letterbox slot, had been left by someone in Mycroft’s mailbox within Safety House, apparently unread, but I routinely scour my brother’s letters, as he no doubt peruses mine. At least it stays within the family,” he remarked with a wan smile. “You have uncovered items of a most interesting nature, Watson, and I expect they will prove vital to our cause. And so you believe Scudder has been sharing the flat of this fellow Hannay the past few days?”

“Yes, under the assumed identity of Captain Theophilus Digby.”

“Hum. By your brief written report, Hannay was at the inquest, resides at Portland Place, and obtained a fellow lodger at the very time that Scudder disappeared from his own flat.” Holmes smiled. “It is a confluence that is quite suggestive, I admit, and Mycroft and Sir Walter will be most appreciative.”

As the remark left his mouth, I felt a satisfying if somewhat grim sense of accomplishment. “My conclusion may be false, however,” I said modestly.

“Rather, I suspect it is my own opinion concerning Scudder’s movements that will prove incorrect. The man, in this instance, appears to have gone against his usual habit and sought assistance—and from an apparent stranger, at that." Holmes shrugged. "*Mais nous verons.*"[20]

I gave him a more complete description of my questioning of the porter at Hannay's building, mentioning my pose as Mr. Price and the invention of legal documents to be witnessed. Then, two blocks from the block of flats where I believed Scudder still resided, Jack James stopped our taxicab.

Holmes jumped from the vehicle.

"I will this time exercise my skills with locks at the rear of the building and meet you inside on the ground floor," the detective said. Then, pausing for a moment, he added to Jack James, "Once the doctor has left the cab, scurry to Scotland Yard and try to get in touch with Inspector Magillivray. Have him come to Portland Place at once. Tell him it is most urgent."

"Yes, sir," said James as Holmes closed the door of the taxicab.

"Tell him it concerns Scudder," the detective added as he departed, "but be most discreet about it."

"I will, Mr. Holmes."

"Onward, Jack," I said, and we sped off for another three blocks before stopping once more. I left the cab, wished the young man good luck on his search for Inspector Magillivray, and strode briskly back toward Portland Place, taking a side street along a bit of vacant ground, where I passed a hoarding,[21] behind which I casually noticed discarded milk cans and an overall.

---

[20] "But we will see."
[21] A hoarding is what Americans usually call a billboard.

I then rounded one more corner and caught sight of the block of flats itself, and as a church clock struck eight, I entered the building to find Holmes being confronted by the same porter with whom I had spoken before. As the lift operator watched, cowering from within his cage, the porter turned toward me upon hearing the door close, as if pleading for assistance.

"Ah, it's you again, sir!" the man cried. "Not a moment too soon! Please help me with this intruder!" He once again faced Holmes. "You're in with the murderer, aren't you?"

"Murderer?" said the detective cautiously.

"Help me, Mr. Price!" the porter bellowed again.

"This man is in my employ," I said sharply, approaching the pair.

"What?" The porter looked momentarily confused. "He's with you? But he came in from the back, sir. Broke the lock, he did."

"I never break locks," Holmes asserted with annoyance. "Go, examine it for yourself, man. I have left the mechanism intact."

Then, in a different voice, a gruff tone that was neither his own nor that of his creation Altamount, he continued. "It's what he told me to do," Holmes said, pointing at me. "I'm his investigator, like he said." With a jaundiced eye, he added, "I'm an investigator for Mr. Price here."

The porter appeared to stand down and cast a wary look in my direction, still appearing quite confused.

"Is that correct, sir?" he asked.

"Yes," I replied hurriedly, my eyes meeting those of Holmes before turning toward the other man. "I asked him to meet me here, but discreetly. Evidently," I said, giving Holmes an amused smile, "my man took the request a bit too literally and gained unlawful entry through the rear of the building. I apologise for the trespass."

"I'll accept that, I suppose," the porter said nervously. "Trespass is the least of my worries at the moment."

"Yes," said Holmes. "You mentioned murder."

The porter looked at Holmes with continued suspicion before addressing me instead.

"It's your Captain Digby, sir. He's in the flat above, on his back, a knife though his chest."

"Great God!" I exclaimed.

Holmes drew himself up and was about to speak when there was noise from above. Turning round, I saw three people watching from the staircase.

"There is nothing going on about here," called the porter to the newcomers. "Get away! It is a trifle. One of the boarders and two man-servants," he said to me. "I suppose they heard the ruckus I was having with your fellow here."

"May we see the body?" asked Holmes as the trio of observers slowly ascended the stair and out of view.

"But the police will be here presently, I expect," the porter replied. "Paddock caught the killer red-handed, sitting right in the flat itself. Claimed to be the milkman, he did, but where's his cans, eh? And I had seen the real milkman leave but a while earlier. Even had to tell him to stop his whistling in the building, he was so loud."

"Who is Paddock?" asked Holmes.

"He's Mr. Hannay's valet. Always arrives at seven thirty, but he was a tad early today. Opens the door of Mr. Hannay's flat with his latchkey and finds a strange gent in the sitting room, biding his time. The man gave some wild tale about being coaxed to part with his overall and milk cans—because he claimed to be the milkman, as I just told you. Said he gave them to some other fellow in the flat to use in a jest of his—or so the murderer said."

I gave a start, remembering that I had seen those very items on my way to the building.

"Paddock went on into another room and there found Captain Digby, covered with a sheet," the porter said. "Stabbed right through the heart, he was. Paddock took custody of the man and led him out in search of a policeman."

"And this presumed murderer did not take flight or struggle?" asked Holmes, who was slowly walking toward the staircase.

"No," said the porter, who instinctively followed my friend across the lobby. "A very docile killer, I suppose, but a killer nonetheless, eh?"

"The police will, no doubt, be returning in force," Holmes said.

My friend glanced at the porter, whose eyes were fixed on him, and then said to me with an obsequious tone, "Perhaps, Mr. Price, you should enter the flat to look for those other legal documents you mentioned, seeing as how Captain Digby is now deceased."

"Yes, I suppose you are correct," I stammered in reply. Then, quickly regaining my confidence, I asked the porter, "Will you please take us to Mr. Hannay's flat?"

"I'm not certain that I should," the man replied.

After energetic coaxing on my part, however, he relented and hesitantly led us up the common staircase to the flat in question. The porter tried the door, finding it unlocked.

"I'd best stand guard, should I not?" he suggested.

"Indeed," I said, stepping in front of him to be nearer the door, which was now ajar. "That is an excellent suggestion."

Looking at Holmes discreetly for assurance, I continued. "Let me propose instead, however, that you stand outside at the building entrance. Watch for the police to arrive, and warn—or, rather, notify us of that at once."

"But should I not be in the rooms with you, as you do whatever it is you are going to do?" the porter asked nervously. "And what, if I may ask, will that be?"

"I am glad you agree," I said, taking the man by the shoulders and leading him toward the staircase. "Go down and watch for the police, please. We will be but a few minutes."

Holmes swept past me and into the flat, while the porter stepped to the railing and haltingly began his descent.

"Oh, it is all out of Conan Doyle, isn't it?" he moaned.

"What do you mean by that?" I asked sharply.

"Well," the porter said, pausing on the staircase, "there is this murder, with a body on the floor and a knife in it, as well as mysterious milkmen."

"Yes, but why did you mention the name of—"

"Mr. Price!" called Holmes from within the flat. "I believe you'd best look at this, sir!"

I stared at the porter as he gazed up at me.

"Later," I said brusquely before he continued on to the ground floor. I turned and entered the flat, closing the door behind me.

The abode of Richard Hannay was far more elegant than the simple digs that Franklin Scudder had occupied above. The sitting room was large and well-furnished, but I noticed at once that it was in profound disarray. Drawers had been pulled from chests, their contents rummaged, and books lay in confusion, many lying open upon chairs, shelves, and the carpet.

Holmes leading, we proceeded to what I took to be a smoking room. It, too, had been left in chaos, and in its centre, partially covered by a tablecloth, lay the body of a man in evening dress. Pulling back on the cloth, Holmes exposed the face.

Though he had shaved, altered his hair and brows, and applied stain to his skin to simulate weathering, the dead man was immediately recognizable to me. He bore a remarkably calm expression, despite the fact that a very long knife was embedded in his chest, as the porter had warned us.

"I take it that the deceased this time is actually Scudder?" said Holmes as he pulled the cloth back farther and began to search the pockets of the man's jacket and trousers.

"Oh yes, it is Scudder."

"There is nothing of significance on his person," Holmes remarked. "Loose coins, a cigar holder. This pen knife and a bit of silver in the trousers. Ah, here's something in the side pocket of the jacket..."

I bent down with anticipation.

"Hum," said my friend in disappointment. "It is just an old crocodile-skin cigar case, and an empty one at that."

"Holmes," I said as he put back the items, "what do you make of the fact that the rooms have been—"

"Ransacked? Yes, one could not miss that, could one? Let us determine the thoroughness of the search."

A quick exploration revealed that, in addition to the disruption of the sitting and smoking rooms, cupboards and chests and boxes had been violently disturbed in every other reach of the flat. Even the pockets of clothing still hanging in wardrobes had been turned out.

"Not one small area has been left untouched," observed Holmes as we stood in the bedroom. "And each time, the same rude, rapacious techniques have been employed. Whatever the intruders were seeking, the odds are that they did not find it."

"Can you be certain?" I asked. "After all, the last place one looks is always where the quarry is found."

"True enough, old fellow, but in this instance the entire flat was turned topsy-turvy. The probability is that, had the searchers found what they sought, it would have occurred with some part of these rooms still left to be searched, an area which would then remain intact. Yet no portion has escaped the rampage, do you not agree?"

I shrugged. "And what of the fellow whose flat this is? Mr. Richard Hannay, whom I followed after the inquest?"

Holmes cocked his head, swept his eyes around the room, and then gave a small smile. "Well, he does apparently hail from the African continent, judging by various mementos that lie scattered amid this rubble. I also fancy him to have had some military experience, given those regimental collar badges that have been mounted and framed there upon the wall. Do you recognise the device on them: crossed flags mounted on lances?"

"The image is unfamiliar to me. The Fighting Fifth[22] wore St. George killing the dragon," I mused.

"I expect these badges are from a South African unit—perhaps he fought against the Boers. In any event, he appears to have had a career as an engineer—most likely a mining engineer, given the titles of many of these books that have been strewn about the place. The most relevant fact about Mr. Hannay at present, however, is that he must be in flight for his life."

The detective then appeared to fall deep into thought. "The question is, where does he seek refuge?"

"But could it not have been Hannay who put the knife to Scudder?"

"That is unlikely. I believe Hannay must have come across the body last night, pondered his possible courses of action, and then escaped the building earlier this morning, after deciding that he was in danger as well. This block of flats was being watched now and then from the street side, you say?"

"Yes. But how can you be certain Hannay merely found the corpse, rather than rendered Scudder into one?"

"It is not a certainty, only a probability. But come along," said Holmes, leading me back to the smoking room. "See the ash there upon the carpet, near this entrance? From the shape and nature of the scattered remnants, I would say that a cigar was dropped there, near the door, but hours ago. Why? A strong possibility is that Hannay switched on the light upon entering, saw the body and, in shock, dropped his cigar. Notice, in

---

[22] Watson is referring to the regiment in which he originally served: the 5th (Northumberland Fusiliers) Regiment of Foot. He was later attached to the 66th (Berkshire) Regiment of Foot during the Second Afghan War.

fact, that an unfinished cigar lies there in a tray upon that table—it is likely the very one that Hannay let go in his surprise. It is the same brand as will be found in the humidor upon that far table.

"Then, of course, there is the matter of the cloth covering the body. Why would a corpse be so treated? Murderers generally do not shroud their victims, other than to hide them, and this one is all too evident—lying, as it does, in the middle of the room. No, that was a gesture of respect for the deceased. Showing such sentiment after the fact, why would Hannay have murdered the man in the first place? Again, it is not impossible but rather improbable."

"And you say that Hannay spent some time weighing his options?" I said.

"Certainly, he appears to have stayed the night. His bed has been slept in, and I cannot imagine that the evening passed without Hannay contemplating what course he might follow."

Holmes gave a quick turn of the head. "Then also, allow me to show you points of interest in the bath," he said.

We strode together to the bath entrance, where Holmes gestured toward the tub. "Someone recently bathed here," he said. "I doubt it was Scudder who took that dip, for he has been dead for hours, judging from the state of the body. And look you here, Watson, in and about the sink."

I paused, staring steadily at the porcelain for a moment, noticing nothing. Then I comprehended what I beheld and declared, "There are a few cut hairs visible. What—"

"You said that Hannay had a drooping moustache," my friend reminded me. "I suggest he trimmed it here—either removing it entirely or making it shorter."

"As disguise?"

Holmes smiled. "Mycroft was correct, indeed."

"What?"

"The milkman," he said. "The man whom the valet apprehended claimed to be the milkman. Let us take him at his word. If so, then I expect it was Hannay who talked him out of his accoutrements and left the building in that guise. Recall that my prescient brother had suggested just that strategy for the late Mr. Scudder during our meeting with Bullivant."

"Holmes, on my way here, I observed a set of milk cans and overall stashed behind a hoarding."

Holmes laughed with enthusiasm.

"Now I must, at all costs, find Hannay," he said.

"What?"

"Oh, we must certainly rescue him for our nation's well-being, Watson, but we are also obliged to recover Mr. Hannay because a man of such wit and invention must be saved—for the sake of the world!"

"But in what part of London do we search?" I asked, as Holmes's laughter faded and we left the bath for the smoking room.

"None, for I doubt he remains in town. We should, however, still cast our glances toward the railway stations. St. Pancras is the closest, and I expect that by now he has already departed it aboard a train."

My friend turned to me, saw my expression, and then pointed across the room.

"There is a Bradshaw[23] upon that chair, where it has been neatly stacked atop an atlas, rather than casually tossed about as have all the

---

[23] George Bradshaw published the most popular railroad timetables during the Victorian era. By the late nineteenth century, his name was applied to any such set of schedules.

other volumes present. No doubt, Hannay left both there after having thoughtfully consulted them this morning. He is from Africa, remember, and I suppose he may find it easier to hide in remote, wild country. Perhaps he is a master of veldcraft[24] in his own land, for all that we know. Indeed," the detective said, becoming contemplative, "let us concentrate on that phrase, his own land.'"

I frowned.

"The atlas is of Britain, and Hannay is a Scot surname, is it not?" Holmes asked.

"There is a Clan Hannay, I believe, yes."

"Hum," said Holmes. "Our man may be a distant relation. Nonetheless, if he has Scottish roots..."

"The porter outside told me the other day that Hannay is skilled in mimicking Scottish characters."

"He may have acquired that skill in childhood," said Holmes. "Perhaps he was born and spent his early years in Scotland, and if he has retained some familiarity with his presumed ancestral homeland, then perhaps he may have taken a fancy to escaping northward, to the Scottish moors. Given his background, he may find it easier to remain hidden there than here in London. However," the detective said, "there is one item we must try to locate before we begin the search for Hannay. And we must do it before the police arrive, Watson."

"What item is that?"

"We must find whatever it was that the intruders were seeking, for recall that I do not believe they uncovered it." Holmes stood in the centre

---

[24] Veldcraft is another word for fieldcraft: the methods of living, travelling, and making observations in the field, especially without being seen.

of the room and slowly turned round. After rotating three-quarters of a circle, he stopped.

"Halloa, *there* is an anomaly."

Holmes stepped to a table that sat by the fireplace and looked down at a tobacco jar whose lid lay beside it.

I came to his side and stared at the open jar, noticing that the contents had been slightly disturbed. I watched as Holmes reached down and poked his fingers into the tobacco. His hand, however, came away empty.

"Alas," I said in disappointment. "There is nothing in the jar, Holmes."

"Oh, you are quite mistaken, old fellow."

"Truly?" I replied. "What is inside the container, then?"

"Tobacco."

"But it is a *tobacco* jar."

"Yet not an empty one! If the intruders had searched this jar in the same style by which they rummaged through the rest of this flat, they would have simply spilt the contents onto the table.

"That did not occur," declared Holmes. "Yet the lid is off the jar, and tobacco remains within, though disturbed even before I touched it. Fingers have dipped into the container, as mine just did. I expect they were not those of an intruder, but rather Hannay's fingers, perhaps innocently seeking to fill a pipe, and I believe he must have found something buried within the jar, for otherwise he would not have been so distracted as to not put back the lid."

"If he did discover anything," I observed, "it would have been rather small."

"Yes," answered my friend. "It was small, in order to fit inside the jar. And, of course, you have noticed that books were the principal items scattered about during the search."

"Are you suggesting they were looking for a small book?" I said. "You mean, perhaps, a small notebook?"

"Yes. I believe that is what the intruders were seeking: Scudder's notebook. They did not find it, however. And, in overlooking the tobacco jar, they allowed Hannay to recover it instead."

We then heard, from without, the door to the flat being opened.

"Mr. Price? Sirs?" called the porter's voice. "I think the police are coming now. What will we—?"

"Thank you!" shouted Sherlock Holmes as he stepped toward the sitting room. I followed quickly behind, past the chair where Hannay's atlas still sat.

The porter stood at the open door. "I said I think—"

"On behalf of Mr. Price, I thank you," repeated Holmes. "We have recovered the documents and will now depart."

"But—"

Holmes strode past the porter and into the hallway. I followed right behind. The porter closed the flat door and turned to explain further as he walked quickly after us.

"I did as you asked, sirs," he said. "I went down and stood on the pavement to watch from there, Mr. Price. I have seen the police approaching from up the street just now. Do you not think that—?"

"My man has already thanked you," I said, glancing back as we rapidly trod the staircase between the first and ground floors. "And I thank you, sir. You have been of inestimable assistance."

With the porter descending behind us, Holmes and I reached the bottom of the staircase and rushed across the lobby. My friend turned left and headed toward the rear of the building. I still followed immediately upon his heels.

"But, sir," called the porter, who had now also stepped from the staircase and continued to dog us in earnest. "Should we not—"

"Excellent work," I told the man as Holmes reached the rear door and opened it. "However," I said, pausing, "your previous reference to Doyle was entirely irrelevant."

As the porter opened his mouth, I stepped outside and closed the door sharply behind me.

"This way, Watson," said my friend, and I followed him out to the side street and then on along its quiet pavement, rapidly taking one corner after the other until we both had reached a location just off a farther portion of Portland Place.

"Should I not separate from you?" I asked. "You have not wished that—"

"Yes, Watson. We must gather our forces and meet again at Safety House. Go back to your residence and wait there for me to ring you up, or for Jack James to fetch you. By that time, I hope to have roused Sir Walter and Mycroft. Where did you say you found the milk cans and overall?"

I gave Holmes directions to the site, which was but a short distance away.

"Good," said my friend. "I doubt that examining them will yield anything of value, but one never knows."

And with that, my friend rushed on alone.

I stood for a moment on the deserted pavement, before a chemist's shop, and then began to walk briskly back to Queen Anne Street. I stoked my courage with every step, hoping to find the nerve to ask my housekeeper to convince the cook to prepare a second breakfast.

CHAPTER FOUR: COUNCILS OF WAR

"I regret that I was travelling these past two days and therefore away from London," declared Mycroft Holmes from the sofa in the sitting room at Safety House late that same afternoon.

"An act that is rather out of character," murmured Sherlock Holmes from his armchair. He glanced at me and added, with a faint smile, "But such appears to be the prevailing style with many in this room."

"Blenkiron had expressed a wish that I show him Scapa Flow[25] before he left for Paris," replied the elder Holmes brother. "Unfortunately, I did not return until late last evening. It was a journey I was loath to take, as my dear sibling has noted, but Blenkiron is somewhat my counterpart in the American government,[26] and I could not refuse his request. Moreover, over the past few years of corresponding with him, I must admit that I've taken a bit of a liking to the man."

"Yes," said Sherlock Holmes. "He is one after your own mind."

"And yours as well, in fairness," replied the elder brother. "Still, I wish I had been at the Diogenes Club when you called, Dr. Watson, or stopped here to find your note. Had that been the case, Mr. Scudder might still be alive, and we would have in our hands his secrets—whatever they turn out to be."

---

[25] A large natural harbor in the Orkney Islands of Scotland, Scapa Flow served as chief base for the British Navy during the First and Second World Wars, before being closed in 1956.

[26] In novels written by John Buchan, Blenkiron is portrayed as a highly competent American agent. This comment in Watson's narrative suggests that he was that and much more.

"I believe they are contained in a missing notebook," said Sherlock Holmes. "That notebook, at present, is most likely in the hands of Richard Hannay."

"And Hannay, you suggest, is on his way to Scotland." Mycroft shrugged and then smiled wistfully. "Perhaps I should have remained at Scapa Flow a bit longer and thus met him on the way down."

Just then, we heard the back door open.

"Ah," said Mycroft, "that should be our fourth: Sir Walter."[27]

It was not only a fourth but a fifth as well, for seconds later, Bullivant entered in the company of Inspector Magillivray.

"After some thought," Sir Walter said immediately, before anyone else could speak, "I have decided to take your advice, Mycroft. Inspector Magillivray," he told his companion, "this is where many of our councils of war, so to speak, are conducted. You are now admitted to that circle. I believe you have personally met everyone here, except Mycroft Holmes."

"Well, of course I know of you through Sir Walter," Magillivray said to the elder Holmes sibling, as the latter rose with us to shake the inspector's hand. "Never before made your acquaintance in the flesh, however, as I have your brother and Dr. Watson." He turned to Bullivant. "I'm flattered, Sir Walter, to be part of this august group."

"Yes, well, just go ahead and sit back down, all of you," said the spymaster with a slight bit of embarrassment. "I defer to you, Mycroft," he added in a humble voice. "You are senior here, after all."

---

[27] In this instance, Bullivant apparently has a key to Safety House and can let himself in. However, when meeting earlier with Watson, Blenkiron, and the Holmes brothers, he must ring to be admitted. There is no explanation in the text for this seeming inconsistency.

"Are you certain, Sir Walter?" asked the detective's brother. "I did not mean to pull rank on you the other day, you know. Nominally, you are under my supervision, but of course, I consider myself more properly just an observer and go-between for Squiddy.[28] Please assume the lead, as has been our tradition. I insist."

Bullivant shrugged.

"Very well," he agreed, becoming the last of us to take to chair or sofa. "At the outset, I apologise for being here later than you requested, Holmes," he told the detective. "I thought it best to be tardy but with all the information I could gather on our man, rather than arrive promptly and empty-handed."

"I understand," replied Sherlock Holmes.

"It was, of course, Dr. Watson who first identified Richard Hannay as an individual of interest to us," Bullivant said, with a tone that suggested some odd, newfound respect for me. "I think we must surmise at this point that the American agent Scudder, having created the false impression of his suicide, took up residence in Hannay's flat, only to be murdered by persons unknown, but persons whom we suspect to be in the employ of, shall we say, a certain Teutonic power."

"Shall we say Berlin?" interjected Mycroft Holmes.

"We shall say Berlin," agreed Sir Walter. "In any event, I—with some valuable assistance from Inspector Magillivray—have been able to collect several pieces of data on Mr. Hannay.

[28] It cannot be known for certain, but this is likely a reference to the prime minister, H. H. Asquith, one of whose nicknames was Squiffy, a nod to his fondness for drink. "Squiddy" appears to represent Watson's fictionalization of the sobriquet.

"He is a native Scot, age thirty-seven. His father was a man of business whose affairs led him to reside in the Cape Colony some time ago. Hannay accompanied him there as a child and subsequently spent much of his adult life in Rhodesia. Though he has visited Britain before, his current stay has been for only the past three months."

"Scotland would be the place of his earliest memories," said Holmes. "There is a suggestion that he retains a strong sense of that background."

Bullivant glanced toward Magillivray, who smiled nervously.

"Oh yes, I believe he does," the inspector said. "A prime source of information on Mr. Hannay came to me quite by chance: a barrister whom I will not name, a man who has become acquainted with Hannay through business connections."

Sherlock Holmes made as if to speak, but Magillivray continued without pause.

"I had worked with this individual a while ago, on a rather curious missing person case," he informed us, "and after Sir Walter rang me up a few hours ago to speak of Mr. Hannay, I thought I might contact the barrister and see if he were acquainted with our Scottish South African. And, low and behold, he had indeed crossed paths with the man. Quite a fortunate coincidence."[29]

"Inspector," Mycroft Holmes said gently, "I believe we were considering whether Hannay has any conscious sense of his Scottish heritage."

---

[29] It is likely that Magillivray is referring to his role in events that are portrayed in the partly fictionalized novel *The Power-House* by John Buchan. If so, then the barrister mentioned is almost certainly Edward Leithen, who was the protagonist of that and other Buchan novels.

"Oh yes, of course," Magillivray said. "Well, according to this barrister, Hannay often entertains acquaintances with wonderful impersonations of Scots characters. The man recalled in particular a marvellous pantomime of a harried gamekeeper from Dunbar who—"

Sherlock Holmes cleared his throat and then said, "Dr. Watson also heard testimony to that effect at the Portland Place flat."

"Yes, I see," said Magillivray. "Well, I am happy to corroborate it. He can certainly mimic his fellow native Scots, and that suggests a familiarity with the culture, does it not?"

Bullivant gently raised his hand and resumed. "Hannay became a mining engineer and, among other activities, prospected for copper in Damaraland."

"That is a part of South-West Africa," explained Mycroft Holmes for my benefit.

"Which is German territory," supplied Sir Walter with a thoughtful look. "Indeed," he added warily, "Hannay is reputed to speak German rather fluently."

"Well, I was told that many of his father's business associates were German, you see," Inspector Magillivray declared.

"You believe Hannay may have connections with Berlin?" Sherlock Holmes asked Sir Walter. "That he is perhaps a German agent?"

"One must admit that there are tantalising coincidences, such as his fluency in the German language."

"I grant that it was by chance that the inspector's barrister friend knew Hannay," said Holmes, "but that Scudder, an accomplished agent, should fortuitously elect to room with a spy for the Kaiser strains the concept of luck a bit too much, I think."

"Perhaps," admitted Bullivant.

"I have the impression that Hannay has done quite well by himself," Holmes said.

"He possesses a small fortune, yes," Magillivray declared. "Prospecting and engineering work have both paid off handsomely for him."

"Does his CV[30] have any other facets?" enquired Mycroft Holmes.

"Hannay's military record reveals that he fought in the Matabele Wars,"[31] Bullivant replied. "He was a member of the Imperial Light Horse, and he also served with our military intelligence during the Boer War, stationed at Delagoa Bay."

Mycroft Holmes raised his brows.

"And that is the sum total of our knowledge of Mr. Hannay, at least insofar as appears relevant to the situation," declared Bullivant.

"Relevant to our perception of the situation," amended Sherlock Holmes.

"The question is, how should we act upon it?" his brother asked.

"We must follow Hannay to Scotland, obviously," said Sherlock Holmes, pulling a Bradshaw from his coat pocket. He held it up to view. "This I took from the fellow's flat. There are no markings within, but St. Pancras is the station nearest his Portland Place residence." My friend began to leaf through the timetables. "We know that Hannay left his building—"

---

[30] "Curriculum vitae," or résumé.

[31] The Matabele Wars pitted the British South Africa Company against the Ndebele people, whom the British called the Matabele. These conflicts raged between 1893 and 1897 in the region once known as Rhodesia and which is now the country of Zimbabwe. Since Hannay was thirty-seven years old in 1914, he must have been a combatant while still in his teens.

“Posing as a milkman, I’m told,” said Mycroft Holmes with delight.

“Yes,” Sherlock Holmes said, not looking up from the Bradshaw. “Disguised as a milkman, he left his building no later than six thirty, given the porter’s story, and there was a train leaving St. Pancras at seven ten, which would put him in, say, Galloway by late afternoon today.”[32]

“In other words, about now,” murmured Magillivray.

“Well, we have no one up there at present,” said Bullivant. “And the local authorities cannot be told of Scudder’s notebook; that information is far too sensitive to share with them, in my opinion.”

“They’ll already be looking for Hannay in any case,” said Magillivray. “I was not present when the Yard got wind of Mr. Scudder’s murder and the accusations by Hannay’s valet against the milkman.”

The inspector cleared his throat and then continued, somewhat hesitantly.

“I am told that the porter in Mr. Hannay’s building complained of a pair of men who invaded the scene of the crime: a Mr. Price and his anonymous agent,” Magillivray said. He glanced knowingly at Holmes.

“Are these two being sought by the police?” asked the detective with an innocent smile.

“Yes,” said the inspector. “Indeed, I volunteered to take charge of that portion of the investigation myself.”

“Good man,” volunteered Bullivant with a mischievous smile.

“However, my colleagues have since declared the milkman innocent and fixed upon Hannay as the likely murderer,” Magillivray went on. “They have also surmised, as have we here, that he is headed for Scotland.

---

[32] Galloway is a region of southwest Scotland.

Authorities as far north as Edinburgh have been directed to apprehend the man."

"Recovery of the notebook is essential," said Bullivant. "I suppose one or more of us must board a train and follow him."

"Yes," admitted Sherlock Holmes, glancing upward and then toward his brother with a coy expression. "However..."

"An aeroplane would be faster," completed Mycroft Holmes.

"An aeroplane?" exclaimed Sir Walter.

"Can you conceive a more rapid method of travel?" asked the elder Holmes brother. He leaned back in the sofa and placed the tips of his opposing fingers together. "I fancy I could easily requisition a Royal Flying Corps pilot from Hulton[33] to take one of us north in a two-seater. Well," added Mycroft, "I should rather say, one of you."

"Would the craft need to be fed more petrol during the journey to Galloway?" asked Sherlock Holmes.

"Yes, but that may be arranged without difficulty," Mycroft replied. "A route can be mapped out, one that includes refuelling. Are you proposing to go, Sherlock?"

"In truth, I was going to suggest the doctor."

I turned my head in disbelief toward my friend.

"Well," said the detective with a defensive air, "an aeroplane really cannot be that many steps removed from an automobile, can it? And you are on quite good terms with motorcars, so you say. I'm not demanding that you pilot the contraption, Watson."

---

[33] In his memoir, Watson probably meant Halton, a village in Buckinghamshire, northeast of London, where the Royal Flying Corps' No. 3 Squadron was deployed at the time. Halton is now the site of one of the largest Royal Air Force stations in Britain.

I could think of nothing in response.

"Will you not go to Scotland instead?" asked Bullivant of Sherlock Holmes.

"Oh, I am going to Scotland, Sir Walter," replied the detective. "However, I propose to follow Hannay's route there by train, as you initially suggested. If everyone is correct in assuming he is off to Scotland, the man's departure from St. Pancras is a near certainty, but we cannot yet be sure of his exact movements from that point onward.

"I believe the Scottish moors are his eventual destination, but circumstances may force a change in that plan. I will follow his supposed initial route and pick up any information about his subsequent path that I can, however difficult or improbable that task might seem.

"At the same time, we do need a man in Galloway as quickly as possible. That must occur by means of an aeroplane. Do you propose to go, Sir Walter—or you, Inspector Magillivray?"

"Magillivray is needed here, to help shepherd the police investigation of Scudder's murder," said Bullivant. "It has already gotten somewhat out of hand, and for our purposes, it must not become more so."

"And I shall require you to remain in London for at least the next day," said Mycroft Holmes to Sir Walter, "There are matters with Section 5 that require a degree of finesse, and I believe only you can supply that touch."[34]

---

[34] Section 5 refers to that British intelligence group devoted to domestic counter-espionage and known in the public imagination as MI-5. Oddly, that is the very group which seemingly should have been in command of the search for Hannay in the first place. That Bullivant and company were involved in the hunt instead, that no other agents were available, and that matters needed some "finesse" suggests that bureaucratic and legal boundaries were overstepped in this affair, for it would appear that Bullivant was actually in Section 6, whose charge was espionage abroad. Watson's memoir offers no further explanation.

Sherlock Holmes frowned at this reference, and Magillivray looked steadily at the sitting room carpet, while Bullivant appeared to ignore the comment.

"There is that special agent in the south," Sir Walter said cryptically to Mycroft, who shook his head as his brother raised his brows. "Not enough time for him to get here?" asked Bullivant.

"There is that obstacle, yes," agreed Sherlock Holmes, "but the obvious disadvantage is that removing that man from his present duties leaves no one else to perform them."

"Granted," said Bullivant, glancing discreetly at Mycroft Holmes, who nodded.

I looked to my friend for explanation of these last comments, but none was forthcoming.[35] Instead, the detective said, "The doctor, after all, is rather familiar with Galloway, having angled there for the elusive trout on more than one occasion."

"So you're a fly-fisherman, are you?" asked Bullivant with seeming interest.

"Yes," I told him. "Since my youth."

He emitted a pleasant grunt and then said, "Well then, Doctor, are you willing to play the game with us? Will you fly to Scotland to fish for Hannay?"

I looked the spymaster squarely in the eye.

"Are you certain, Sir Walter, that you would wish to entrust me with that task?"

---

35 The meaning of this exchange is revealed later in Watson's narrative.

The man sat and thought for a moment, his eyes glazing over as he contemplated some unspoken thought. Then, after briefly bowing his head, Bullivant said, "I'm afraid I hadn't got your limits earlier, Dr. Watson. Perhaps I'm not the first to admit to that, and such confessions from others are not uncommon."

From the corner of my eye, I saw Sherlock Holmes gently nod.

"That failure of judgment aside," Bullivant went on, "for my past failings are irrelevant at the moment, I agree with Holmes that you should be the one to fly north. You among us are the only one who has set eyes upon Richard Hannay, after all, and I now appreciate the dogged skill that you can bring to this endeavour. Will you accept the charge, sir?"

"There is no one else?" I asked. "Young James? Hollins or Steiner?"

Bullivant and Mycroft Holmes looked uncomfortably at one another, while Magillivray glanced innocently about the room.

I saw the hint of a smile on the lips of Sherlock Holmes as he said, "They are true and faithful underlings, but as capable as they are in their way, they nonetheless do not possess the particular resources that reside in you, Watson. It took me a while longer," he added, speaking to Sir Walter, "but at last, I too got Watson's limits, and rather vast those limits are."

"There is the matter of my age," I offered as a final objection.[36]

"And who was it recently declared that time be damned?" asked Sherlock Holmes, leaning back in his chair. "Watson, the die was cast when you first accepted my offer to visit Portland Place."

---

36 Perhaps a couple years older than Sherlock Holmes, Watson was in his early sixties at the time.

I gave a great sigh, nodded philosophically at my friend, and then said to all present, "If it is the consensus that I should, then yes—of course, I will go."

"Well done," murmured Mycroft Holmes.

"For King and Empire," was Magillivray's homely pronouncement.

Bullivant paused for a moment and then asked Mycroft Holmes, "He'll be despatched from Hulton, you say? Where would he be deposited?"

Sir Walter's clinical phrasing led me to cautiously eye my friend's older brother.

"Hum," grunted Mycroft. "Well, we want him to begin in Galloway, I suppose. Dumfries might be a good choice. I believe there's a plain near the town that the flying corps boys fancy. And Dumfries is on the rail line."

"It is one of the stops of the train I believe Hannay has boarded," noted Sherlock Holmes.

"You know, I have a godson in that region," said Bullivant. "Sir Harry Christey. He's an ambitious young politician, though a bit of a black sheep in that regard: a Free Trader, I must confess.[37] He might be available to render you some assistance, Doctor—provided, of course, that you don't disclose the true nature of your mission. I can write a brief letter of introduction—he is not aware of my actual post and believes I'm Secretary to the Foreign Office or some such. If nothing else, he may be able provide a motor for your use."

"And I will have one of my agents, Hollins or Steiner, send word to Herr Von Bork that I am off to Scapa Flow to scout its defences," said

---

[37] In general, British Conservatives at the time supported the use of tariffs to shore up the nation's industries and imperialist policies, while Liberals supported free trade without tariffs. Bullivant's comment suggests that he was a member of the former group.

Sherlock Holmes. "I cite your recent sojourn there with Blenkiron as inspiration for the ruse, Mycroft. In the eyes of the Germans, it should serve as a handy pretext for my train journey north."

"And the two of you will employ the usual methods to communicate with Sir Walter by telegram?" asked the elder Holmes brother.

I looked warily at Sherlock Holmes, who smiled reassuringly as he said, "With your permission, Sir Walter, I shall take the doctor to Mr. Macandrew to review code and cipher protocols."

"There should be no difficulty with that," Bullivant replied. "I will ring up Macandrew and make arrangements. I take it you wish to see him presently?"

"If possible," said Holmes. "I believe Dr. Watson will prove a quick study."

"Yes," said Sir Walter, once more eyeing me with an expression of confidence. "Yes, I am certain he will be. Well then," he said, slapping one knee of his trousers, "we all have our assignments, it would seem."

"I will arrange the doctor's transport by air to Galloway," Mycroft Holmes declared. "Brother Sherlock will pack for his great rail expedition after taking Dr. Watson to visit your Mr. Macandrew, and I will manage the bureaucratic matters here in London, with your assistance. And you, Inspector Magillivray, will attempt to restrain your colleagues in the Metropolitan Police."

"As best I can, sir," the man from Scotland Yard replied. "As I said earlier, others took command of the Scudder murder case before I could become involved, but I believe I have convinced them to not yet publicly declare Hannay the prime suspect, though they continue to view him as the guilty party. Regardless, both they and the police up north will be pursuing him vigorously."

"As will the Germans," said Sherlock Holmes.

"But *which* Germans?" asked Mycroft. "I refer to the phrase *The Black Stone*, Sherlock."

"I understand your allusion, dear brother."

"But we do not know what Scudder meant by that," said Bullivant.

"Taken in the context of all that has happened, Sir Walter," said Mycroft, "I and my younger brother think we have evidence of another circle of German operatives at work on our island, a spy ring distinct from and perhaps independent of Von Bork's."

"It would fit the imagery of Scudder's cryptic note," added Sherlock Holmes.

"Cerberus," I murmured. Then, after a pause, I added, "But there were at least three heads on that beast, and therefore, should we not have, in turn, Von Bork's spy ring, this Black Stone group, and..."

"And one more after that," said Mycroft Holmes, nodding glumly. "Aye, there's the additional rub, indeed."

Within another quarter hour, I left Safety House through the house door, while Sherlock Holmes departed by way of the back. After walking a roundabout path of a few blocks, I waited at a specified intersection, where Jack James pulled up in his taxicab. Hopping aboard the vehicle, I found Holmes leaning back in his seat, his brows furrowed.

"I might ask if you were deep in thought," I said lightly. "But then, when are you not in deep thought?"

"These days, more often than I care to admit," my friend replied with a wan smile. "To Lime Street, Jack."

"Ah," said the American. "Mr. Macandrew's office."

The motorcar turned a corner and headed south. We had travelled in that direction but a short time before something caught Holmes's attention most dramatically.

"Halloa!" he exclaimed. "Jack, fall back if you will, but keep that car ahead in view!"

"The light brown one with black trim?"

"That is the one, yes!"

"Oh, of course, sir," said the American after a moment. "We've seen that one before, haven't we?"

"Many times," said Holmes, leaning back. "Not along this route, however. I fancy trailing him, Jack, as long as it does not take us out of our way."

"As good as done, sir."

I looked expectantly at my friend.

"That is the automobile of Baron Von Herling, chief secretary of the German legation," he said. "He is the man who oversees Von Bork's espionage activities. Indeed, one can observe him through the rear window of the vehicle."

I leaned forward and saw the backside of a man's head, topped with a homburg, through the somewhat dingy pane.

"And you find his presence in this district unusual? It appears to me that he is being driven toward the City, which I should think would be a common destination for a diplomat in this metropolis."

“Oh yes, I have followed him there many times, Watson. While claiming to be collecting secrets for Berlin, I have often instead been clandestinely observed my Teutonic bosses, in order to better grasp the workings of their apparatus. Von Herling is a not infrequent visitor to the heart of London, but his usual route there is not this one, suggesting that he is coming from a location different from his usual haunts.”

“And that suggests he is engaged in business of a nondiplomatic nature?” I suggested.

“Just so. Be careful, Jack!” Holmes suddenly admonished. “You approach too close to Von Herling’s motor. Leave the recommended minimum distance, if you will, and vary the distance between ourselves and the other automobile on occasion.”

“Sorry, sir,” replied the young man, allowing the other vehicle to gain ground on us.

“You have rules for this game of follow-the-leader?” I asked with a bemused air.

“Very much so, Watson, for I have written a short monograph on preferred methods of automotive pursuit,” said Holmes in a distracted tone.

“And so you have some acquaintance with motors yourself,” I observed.

“It is a professional interest only,” Holmes replied primly. “Of course, my piece exists at present as a classified Secret Service document, unavailable to the public. Perhaps after the war, I will have Blenkiron publish a limited edition. In addition to his bookstore, the man possesses a small press, you know.”

I watched our quarry ahead.

"Do you think Von Herling may be on business related to Scudder?" I asked.

"Who can say?" Holmes replied. "If the baron manages Von Bork's apparatus, it is not inconceivable that he has his hands in the affairs of the Black Stone as well."

At length, we entered the City by way of the Whitechapel Road, following Von Herling's vehicle past Finsbury Circus and on to Meerston Street, where the motorcar we had so doggedly followed finally pulled to the kerb.[38]

"Drive past, Jack," Holmes ordered. The detective leaned back. "Sadly, we have not the time to determine who or what Von Herling is pursing here. I will note the address, however."

We rambled on southward, veering somewhat east, and in time arrived in Lime Street, a short distance from Leadenhall Market. Holmes and I separately left the motor and in our individual ways trod a neighbourhood with narrow houses on which were emblazoned lists of names, mostly attorneys and notaries public. Some distance ahead of me, my friend entered a building where the last name displayed was a J. N. Macandrew, identified as an average-adjuster.[39] After a moment, I followed.

Once inside, I was briskly led by Holmes up steps to the door of a small, dingy office on the first floor. There we were received by a pale boy who nodded to my friend and then escorted us up a maze of wooden stairs

---

[38] Finsbury Circus is an elliptically shaped park in the City of London, while Meerston Street appears to be a fictional name.

[39] An average-adjuster is an expert in marine insurance and law, who may be hired by an insurance firm to apportion loss in a maritime claim.

and dark passages that ended in a cluttered, grim waiting room lit by one dingy window.

"I'll fetch him for you, sir," said the boy, who vanished through the door.

"Pray, Watson, have a seat," said Holmes, motioning toward a worn table around which sat three chairs.

Out of deference to my yet unmet host, I declined the armchair and took one of the other two, which were spare and somewhat rickety. I looked down at the table, upon which sat two Law Lists, a directory of London and a tall pile of shipping journals.[40] A large calendar hung on the wall, whose paper was dark with grime. The calendar was flanked by an old photograph of the court of a livery company[41] and a bad print of some dignitary.

"It is the 1st Earl Stackpile," said Holmes, looking at the portrait.

"The one who was Lord Chancellor so long ago?"

"Yes, Watson." My friend touched his finger to the picture frame. "You may recall my trifling and unsuccessful investigation for his son, who later succeeded to the earldom." Holmes smiled.

"I do not remember the matter."

"It was a breach-of-promise case, and one in which I failed quite miserably," declared Holmes. "Ah, the trials of my inexperienced youth."[42]

I suddenly became conscious of a musty aroma and looked at the empty grate, where a pile of spent cigarettes lay.

---

[40] A Law List is a publication compiling the names and addresses of those engaged in the practice of law and information of interest to the law profession.

[41] Livery companies are descendants of the medieval trade guilds and are now largely social and charitable organizations.

[42] From the information Holmes gives, it would appear that the portrait was of Hugh Cairns, 1st Earl Cairns (1819–85). Cairns was Lord Chancellor until 1880, and his eldest surviving son was successfully sued for breach of promise in 1884.

"How long will we be in this rabbit-warren, do you think?" I asked.

"It depends on how good a student you turn out to be," came a high-pitched voice from behind, and I turned round to behold a short man bending under the weight of the thick books he carried. "However, as rabbit-warrens go, this one does offer a few amenities."

Embarrassed, I rose awkwardly, but the stranger smiled and motioned for me to sit back down.

"You'll need pencil and paper, which I have in abundance. Good day, Mr. Holmes," he said amiably to my friend.

"My associate Dr. Watson," said Holmes, who nodded and sat in the chair opposite me. "And Watson, this is the encyclopaedic Mr. Macandrew."

The man ceremoniously bowed and then dumped his books upon the table and reached into a drawer, extracting a ream of foolscap[43] and several pencils.

Holmes took a deep breath and stared at me with amusement.

"Well, gentlemen," said Mr. Macandrew, "we shall now review the basic principles of codes and ciphers..."

"Those last rules were rather simple and clear, of course," I recalled to Sherlock Holmes that evening in his spare Camberwell[44] flat, where he dwelt as Altamount when in London. "Use of the words *hot* or *cold* negates the sentence immediately following, whereas either *calm* or *quiet* means it

---

[43] Pronounced "full-scap" or "full-scape," foolscap is a size of writing paper, traditionally 13.5" x 17". A standard paper size since the fifteenth century, its name derives from the watermark once used to identify it: a jester's hat, or fool's cap. It was the most widely used paper size throughout Britain and Europe until the introduction of international standard paper sizes in the 1970s.

[44] Camberwell is a district of Greater London south of the Thames.

is the preceding sentence that should be taken opposite its original meaning. That completes Mr. Macandrew's list, does it not?"

"It does indeed," said my friend. He glanced to either side as the other three men smiled at me.

"Time hasn't blunted your edge, Doctor," remarked Steiner.

"No, indeed," agreed Hollins. "That's what I told the three of you, isn't it? Dr. Watson will catch on immediately, I said. Just like in the old Baker Street days. Quite different from our time with old Macandrew, eh?" he said to Steiner.

"It took us nearly a week to get it all straight, didn't it?" said his compatriot.

"Good job, sir," interjected Jack James, who stood beside me, arms crossed. "You're ready to send in code with the best of them, I figure."

"I do not dispute that evaluation," said Holmes. "And, Watson, you have memorised the addresses to be used in contacting Sir Walter?"

"Of course."

I leaned back in my chair, one of four placed round a small table in the dimly lit room, and rubbed my eyes. "Much of the work you do in your new avocation of espionage seems more in the fashion of a bank clerk's routine."

"So it often appears to me as well," replied Holmes. "But, as with detection, routine is the commonplace that breathes vitality into the enterprise."

"Another line worthy of inclusion in your book?"

"Hum," said my friend. "It has possibilities, has it not?"

Holmes pushed his chair slightly away from the table.

"And so," he said to Steiner and Hollins, "you two will journey to Von Bork and inform him of my supposed visit to Scapa Flow."

"That we will, sir," replied Hollins.

"Sooner rather than later, if you can," Holmes directed.

"We'll leave for the Essex coast at first light tomorrow," declared Hollins.

"You don't want us to just send him a telegram in German code, if we can remember how to do so?" asked Steiner. "That would reach him sooner."

"I desire soon but not too soon," said Holmes. "I wish to be well on my way before Von Bork knows I am leaving. Though he appears to trust us, I do believe he occasionally has us watched, at the insistence of his superiors."

"The Baron Von Herling whom we saw earlier today, you mean?" I asked.

"Yes. The baron often visits Von Bork at that gabled seaside house, and I suspect he has ordered all of us—myself, James, Hollins, and Steiner—to be quietly observed from time to time. That has been one reason why Altamount has not desired to be seen too often in your presence, Doctor."

"And you got nothing from following Von Herling earlier today, sir?" Hollins asked.

"Nothing of substance, other than an address in the City," replied Holmes. "Quite possibly I will have you and Steiner look around those premises in a few days. It was more important, of course, to get the doctor to Mr. Macandrew for his instruction."

"But you were explaining, Mr. Holmes, why you did not wish us to telegram Von Bork that you were leaving for Scotland," said Steiner.

"Yes," declared Holmes. "I do not wish to have a German agent observe me board a train bound for Galloway when Scapa Flow was the supposed destination. By the time word gets to Von Bork of my trip, there will be no opportunity for him to trace my movements; I will already have left, and once on my way, most difficult to track."

"As difficult to track as Hannay?" I posed.

Holmes sighed.

"Hannay may prove a true challenge," he admitted. "We can only hope that our abilities will exceed his skills—and those of the Germans."

There was a moment of silence, and then Holmes said the Steiner and Hollins, "I suppose you two may go now. See them out, if you will, Jack."

James led the pair of agents from the flat, which was located just off Coldharbour Lane. As we heard the young American close the door, Holmes leaned back in his chair, the look in his eye one of appraisal as he considered me.

"You do feel up to this, old fellow?" he asked. "Beyond the façade of bravado, that is."

"Well, it is more than a decade since I have been on the scent," I remarked. "I have not had the two years of recent practice that you have enjoyed in getting back into harness."

"I should not refer to the experience entirely in terms of pleasure. As you have remarked, this spying business has some of the elements of detection, but only some."

"I understand. Nonetheless, I believe this is something I can do. Certainly, I know it is something that I want to do. Indeed, something that I must do."

"I understand the impulse."

I studied my friend as he gathered up the papers on which he had written examples of code work for my benefit.

"Do you miss Baker Street?" I enquired as I looked about the sparsely furnished flat.

"I think of it now and then."

"You have not returned to our former digs?"

"Not recently," Holmes replied quietly. "But then," he said, "our final visits to 221 were not happy ones, were they?"

"You do not still blame yourself for—"

"But I have had my bees," the detective asserted. "They have allowed my mind to focus—until that focus had need to turn toward my duel with Von Bork."

"That is a somewhat one-sided combat, though, is it not?" I said, understanding my friend's unspoken desire to change the subject of our conversation. "And the man is not even aware that he is engaged in a struggle with you."

Holmes shrugged. "Perhaps it is not a fair fight," he admitted.

"It can hardly be fair if you are one of those contesting it."

My friend gave a wan smile. "As always," he said, "you overestimate my capabilities and achievements."

"Someone must," I replied. "You, after all, underestimate them more often than not."

"I believe my assessments to be objective. That is how you have always portrayed me, is it not: objective, rational. And detached."

We looked at one another for a moment, and then I glumly nodded.

"Holmes, if I have ever slighted your—"

"In truth, I am rather glad that you have on occasion misrepresented me, Watson," he said softly, with a smile I recognised as disingenuous. "Those who have read your little entertainments have obtained from them a somewhat incorrect notion of my character, making my foes more prone to misjudge me."

"And so you grant that my stories have some redeeming value," I declared puckishly.

"To the extent that they confer a subtle advantage upon me vis-à-vis my enemies, my answer is yes. And then, too," he added as his expression became one of earnest sincerity, "you have allowed me to see myself as others no doubt see me. An ounce of self-realisation is precious indeed."

"Well, they're off," said Jack James, returning to the sitting room.

The young man made as if to continue speaking and then stopped as he noticed Holmes's expression. The detective looked up at the American, his visage suddenly changed, and James resumed.

"I take it I'm to ferry the doctor to his plane tomorrow morning?" he asked cautiously.

"If by 'morning' you mean that period of time commencing at midnight, then yes, you are correct, Jack," said Sherlock Holmes. "Dr. Watson must be at Hulton before dawn."

James whistled. "How far is that, Mr. Holmes?"

"Something like thirty miles, I believe, as the crow flies."

"Well, we won't be flying to get there," said the American. "And I'll have to watch it in the dark, for we'll be leaving in the middle of the night."

"Yes," said Holmes. "You will. Oh, and Jack?"

"Yes, sir?"

"By the time you return to London, not only the doctor but also Steiner, Hollis, and myself will have departed town. As the only one left here in London, and unchaperoned as you will be, please do not—"

"Get involved in another brawl over a girl," said Jack James. "Yes," he declared. "I'll be good this time. I promise." The young man smiled at me and motioned toward his right cheek, which I now noticed carried the mark of a bruise nearly healed.

"Just see that you keep that promise this time," insisted Holmes with a wan smile. He turned toward me. "Well, Watson, you must return to Queen Anne Street in order to gain at least a few hours of sleep. And you, Jack, need to be turning in as well."

Holmes then informed young James as to the time he should come round to fetch me for the trip to Hulton, and he also gave me final instructions concerning what items I should pack for my journey. The detective then rose from the table, prompting me to do the same.

"May you encounter few impediments," Holmes wished as we slowly walked toward the door of his flat. "However, some will undoubtedly arise."

"The first will be my housekeeper, and then the cook," I said cheerfully. "I am certain the former has been puzzled by my suddenly irregular hours, and the other recently inconvenienced, no doubt. This journey will throw both into a state of complete disarray, I fear."

"One is advised to have servants who can roll with the punches, as we once said in the boxing ring."

"Yes, as it was true of landladies," I said, immediately regretting the words. "It is always best if they can bear the inconvenience without complaint," I added quickly.

"Indeed," Holmes said somewhat mournfully. "Indeed it is."

With some awkwardness, we spoke no more during the final few steps toward the door. I nodded, as if to silently mark an end to my visit, and extended my hand to a friend of more than three decades.

"We will next meet in Scotland, then?" I said.

"That is my hope," Holmes replied, taking my hand as we bade one another farewell for the moment. "What is vital, however, is that one or the other of us meet Hannay—alive—in Scotland or elsewhere."

I followed Jack James along the corridor and out the door at the rear of the building. Moments later, on another street, we boarded the now familiar taxicab.

"Would you mind just a bit of a detour before dropping me in Queen Anne Street, Jack?" I asked.

"Anything you want, Doctor, as long as I can get you home at a decent hour. I think Mr. Holmes wants you well rested for tomorrow."

"I shall be fine. Go north if you will, and cross the Vauxhall Bridge."

"That's the way we'd be going in any case, sir, to get you home."

"Yes, but keep going until you find Oxford Street and there turn east, if you will."

"As you command, Doctor."

In the deepening night, we proceeded across the river, reaching Grosvenor Place before skirting the east end of Hyde Park and then turning into Oxford Street.

"Baker Street will come up presently," I said. "Turn left into it, please, Jack."

The young American did as requested, and suddenly I found myself once more on the familiar ground where Holmes and I had shared lodging for so many years. I had no doubt that time had altered the neighbourhood slightly, though perhaps many changes were likely swallowed up by the night, so that I did not notice them at this hour.

"Slow the motor now, please."

The vehicle crawled along Baker Street, and in the gloomy distance I saw the object of my fancy.

"Pull over, if you will," I directed.

The young man gently veered into the kerb, and we stopped just short of a house whose fanlight I recognised at once. The number was less easily perceived, but I knew what it read: 221.

Jack James sat patiently behind the wheel as I slowly emerged from the taxicab and set foot on the old pavement for the first time in several years. A small group of boys, all of them no doubt born after I had left this place, ran past and on into the darkness—one of them laughed and called me his old uncle. A young couple beneath a street light smiled at the comment, and I grinned as well to indicate I had taken no offense at the remark.

Then I walked slowly up to the door whose threshold I had crossed countless times in what now seemed some other life. I paused before it, thinking I might witness Holmes and myself suddenly bursting forth from the house and out into the evening to unravel some mysterious enigma, uncover a hidden identity, or expose another nefarious cabal.

Idly, I began to wonder who inhabited this place now, all the while wishing that the house walls might still harbour the faint spiritual remnant of those they had sheltered for so long. A faint noise came from within, puncturing my reverie, and I slowly stepped away from the house, turned round, and strode back to the taxi.

"You don't want to stay longer, Doctor?" asked Jack. "I'm happy to just wait here."

"No," I said hoarsely as I slammed the taxi door shut. "I take it you can navigate to Queen Anne Street from this address?"

"I can," said the young man. "I can, even in the dark, for I've driven here many times before, sir."

"Oh?"

"Yes," Jack replied. "Mr. Holmes regularly has me bring him here, you see. Just to sit and look at the place, much as you did."

"Ah," I whispered, with bittersweet thoughts in my mind.

As our vehicle pulled away from the kerb, I did not turn to look at 221 as it passed. Instead, I forced my thoughts in the direction of the morrow, when I should take to the sky for the first time in my life and be off in pursuit of Richard Hannay. Sitting in the darkness of a rumbling taxicab, I willed myself to embrace this new chapter, ending what I now realised had been an unconscious and unintended purgatory, years in duration.

CHAPTER FIVE: THE AIRMAN AND THE CONSTABLE

It was perhaps a half hour before dawn when Jack James and I finally entered Hulton. We had taken a wrong turn that set us back a good twenty minutes, but fortune smiled thereafter, and after retracing our path and choosing correctly a second time, we passed through the village and found, beyond its far outskirts, the estate whose owner had allowed the Royal Flying Corps to house aeroplanes on its grounds and conduct manoeuvres from its fields.

As we approached along a winding drive running some distance from the manor house, I saw in our vehicle's lights a lone figure standing by the path ahead. Dressed in military uniform, the man waited until James stopped the taxicab and then drew near.

"You are the gentleman sent at the direction of Mr. Mycroft Holmes?" he asked as I opened the taxi door.

"Yes," I replied. "I am, uh, Mr. Price."

"Mr. Price, yes," said the officer. He looked me over in the predawn light. "I must admit, sir, that you're not quite what I expected."

"I hope I do not disappoint," I replied in good humour.

Determined to not be offended by the man's comment, I stepped onto a moist gravel path, leaving the taxi door ajar.

"Well, I'm Major Reardon," he said, placing his left hand on his cap brim while extending the opposite arm. "I meant no disrespect by the remark, sir," he explained as we shook hands. "I simply worry that we may not have made adequate provision for your age and physical condition."

As he looked at me with concern, I contemplated the fact that this officer had likely been an infant or small child when the *Orontes* brought me home from Afghanistan.

"Your craft is in the final stages of preparation," Reardon said, pointing toward the horizon, where in the distance I perceived an amorphous outline contrasting with the dawn mist. "One of our wing captains has been designated to fly you north."

"Thank you, Major," I said, reaching into the taxi to grasp my valise, in which I had personal items and a change of clothing.

"Can I stay and watch her go up?" asked Jack James from behind the wheel of his vehicle.

"Of course," I said with a smile. I closed the taxicab door and turned round. "Unless you have objection, Major."

"None whatsoever. Simply make certain that you not go beyond the gravel," Reardon told young James before turning back toward me. "Come along with me, please, Mr. Price."

I followed the officer across the adjoining field toward what I now saw to be an aeroplane tended by two mechanics. "I'll have one of the men put your bag into the craft, though you'll find your feet will be somewhat cramped as a result," he said. "Then we'll put flight clothes on you."

"Do they merely cover my current dress?" I asked. "The flying clothes, that is. Are they akin to motoring garments?"

"Yes," said Reardon. "You could liken them to such." He looked me up and down again in the emerging morning light as we walked. "The additional clothing should not incommode you. Here, you two!" he called to the pair of workmen as we approached the aeroplane.

One of the mechanics stepped over to meet us, taking the valise from my hand.

"Stow it under the observer's seat," the captain ordered. "Is everything checking out?"

"Oh, yes sir," the workman replied. "She's all fuelled and ready to go."

"Fine. Come with me then, Mr. Price."

I followed him across another portion of the field, in a different direction than before, toward what at first I thought was barren expanse, until I saw a shape emerge from the fog. It was a small hut, with a tall figure leaning against the entrance, arms crossed. As we approached, the man snapped to attention, and I saw he was dressed in a midthigh-length leather jacket buttoned down one side. A leather cap clung snugly to his head, and goggles were perched above his forehead. In one hand, he held a pair of furry gloves.

"Mr. Price, this is our Captain Harper, one of the wing leaders and your pilot for today's excursion. Harper—"

"Sir?"

"Here's your passenger: Mr. Price. A messenger of sorts for the Foreign Office, or some such. Do you know whom you represent?" Major Reardon asked me with a hint of sarcasm.

I chose not to respond.

"Special envoy to Dumfries, aren't you, sir?" Captain Harper asked with gentle amusement, breaking the awkward silence. "That's where I understand I'm to convey you. Halloa, Mr. Price," the captain said to me with an honest smile.

He extended his hand, and we greeted one another.

“Will it be good flying weather, Captain?” I asked, pointedly ignoring the major, who stepped into the hut. “It’s rather foggy at present.”

“I reckon we’ll be fine, sir,” Harper answered. “The mist isn’t very high, and I’ve gone up when it was much thicker than this. We’ll get on top of it within seconds, and I understand we are likely to have clear skies all the way to the border. We’ll be stopping twice to take on petrol, though in a pinch, only one refuelling would be needed. Of course, the extra landing will give us more opportunity to drop some personal ballast,” he added with a boyish smirk.

“Ah,” I said. “One doesn’t seek relief in the air?”

“I’ve always thought a pot’s a mite too tricky to handle up there,” Harper replied, his smile broadening. “And I wouldn’t suggest standing to lean over the edge of your cockpit.”

“I will take your advice to heart, Captain.”

“That’s prudent of you, sir. The stops shouldn’t add much time to the trip. I’ll get you to Scotland well before noon.”

“By the high road rather than the low, apparently.”

“Couldn’t get much higher, I think.”

“We need to get the gentleman into flight clothes,” Major Reardon interjected impatiently as he emerged from the hut. “I’ll leave you to it,” he added as he strode across the clearing toward the aircraft.

“Yes, sir,” said Harper respectfully. “You don’t want to be riding at five thousand feet dressed for lunch at Simpson’s, do you, Mr. Price? Here, let’s step inside and get you decked out proper.”

Minutes later, I emerged from the hut clad for the air: I wore a coat similar to Captain Harper’s, though it was somewhat small for my frame, and my head was covered by a wool balaclava topped with a leather cap. In my hands were goggles and leather gloves.

"We don't really have what you might call a standard kit," Harper told me as we walked toward our aircraft. "Your shoes will do in place of boots—we had no idea of the size of your feet, and so we did not attempt to scrape up a pair for you. Just make certain you wear those goggles," he said. "The slipstream can be brutal."

"Pardon? Slipstream?"

"Oh, nothing supernatural," the captain said light-heartedly. "It's a fancy new term for the air that will rush past you in flight. There'll be dust in it at times, and the engine will be spitting oil constantly. One must protect the eyes, sir," he insisted as we reached the aeroplane, where Major Reardon was conversing with the two mechanics.

"Ah, Mr. Price," said Reardon in a more friendly tone than before. "You look ready to join the squadron, what?"

"Appearances can be deceiving, I fear" was my reply.

"I think you'll do fine, sir," said Captain Harper. "In any event," he said, glancing at his superior officer, "we'll lift up as gently as we can."

"However you do it, Harper," said the major, "make certain you reach Dumfries by midday."

"Oh, yes sir, I've already assured Mr. Price that we shall."

"I'll send one of the men to wire your Mr. Mycroft Holmes that the craft is in the air, once that has become fact," Reardon told me. "We have arranged for Harper here to remain with the aeroplane in Dumfries should you require it. If at any time that becomes unnecessary, however, do advise the captain to that effect."

"I will."

"Good luck, Mr. Price," Reardon said, extending his hand. "I don't know what this is all about, but it must be important, and I wish you all the success in the world."

"Thank you, Major."

Captain Harper and one of the mechanics then assisted me into the observer's cockpit, which was positioned forward of that which the pilot would occupy.

"You've got your own set of controls in there," the captain told me. "Just make certain you don't touch them," he advised with a grin.

In the growing light of dawn, I could see those levers and gauges clearly, and I leaned back to put the greatest possible distance between them and myself.

"I'm sorry if all this inconveniences you, Captain," I said as Harper climbed into his own seat behind mine.

"No inconvenience at all, sir," the officer replied. "This is why I went to Bristol in the first place.[45] Flying is a pleasure, and we'll be flying some distance."

"Three hundred miles," I said, turning round to face the captain, an objective I found not fully possible to achieve in my flying gear.

"Yes," replied the pilot. "Well, if any of our planes can make it, sir, it's this one. New model. Not overly fast, but terribly stable in the air."[46]

I heard him laugh.

---

[45] This is probably a reference to Bristol Flying School at Larkhill on Salisbury Plain. It was founded by the British and Colonial Aeroplane Company, later known as the Bristol Aeroplane Company, and at the time was recognised as one of the finest flying schools in the world.

[46] From Watson's sketchy description later in the narrative, the aircraft appears to have been an early version of the Avro 504, which was first delivered to the Royal Flying Corps in 1913. Produced in greater numbers than any other plane of the First World War, it quickly became obsolete but saw continued use for many years as a training aircraft.

"You won't be falling out. However, Mr. Price, you also won't be able to hear me once the engine is going. If I need to signal to you, I'll give you a pat on the back."

"I understand. I will just try to appreciate the view."

"You won't need to try, sir. There's really nothing like it, to be sure. Oh, and goggles down, remember? And gloves on, if you will."

I adjusted the goggles to fit with reasonable comfort over my eyes and pulled on the leather gloves to await the aeroplane's launching.

Harper and the two mechanics began final preparations for departure, and Major Reardon stepped a short distance away. Beyond, on the gravel path, Jack James stood and watched. I saw the young man wave, and I waved back.

"Is that your chauffeur?" asked the captain.

"Yes."

"Well," Harper said, "here is where I take over from him."

I leaned back and stared into the foggy distance.

"Major Reardon?" Harper suddenly called to his superior. "Do you think we could get Mr. Price's man over here to help you hold the tailskid?"

"Oh, if you like," said the major. "I believe I can handle it alone, but let me fetch the lad."

Presently, Jack James came running toward us. Breathing deeply, he asked, "I get to help in this? Is that right?"

"Yes," said Major Reardon. "If you will join me in grasping the tailskid, it would be most appreciated."

"Be glad to," replied Jack. "Just show me what the tailskid is."

"Come along," sighed the major.

"Chocks in position?" Harper asked the mechanics.

"Both are set," replied one of the men.

"Turn on the oil supply," Harper said to the workmen as Reardon and the young American took hold of the craft's rear support. "She uses castor oil, Mr. Price," the pilot said. "The petrol won't dilute it, but when it burns, we'll get a bit of a stink."

"I have been breathing London air for over three decades, Captain. I am certain I can withstand it."

A syringe was used to inject a small amount of fuel into each cylinder of the engine. Then, as one mechanic stood at the ready, his gloved hands grasping the wooden propeller, the other workman stood behind and took secure hold of his belt.

"Ignition is on," called out Harper to the mechanics. "Contact."

Swinging the propeller blade did not appear an easy proposition, and positioning oneself to do so was made somewhat awkward by the presence of a single long ski sled that protruded from beneath the rectangular fuselage, between the main wheels. It required three strong pulls on the blade to bring the aeroplane's engine into life.

As the second mechanic yanked the first one away from the suddenly spinning rotor, there was a loud cough from beneath the cowling, a sharp kick, and then acrid smoke wafted past my face, a cloud immediately dispersed by the sudden, fierce blast of wind from the rotating blade. I felt my face flatten against the manmade gale, even behind the windscreen, and was thankful for the presence of my goggles.

After a moment, Harper signalled to the workmen to pull the chocks from the wheels and for Reardon and Jack James to let go the tailskid. Feeling powerless, I realised the craft was now beginning to move. As we rolled across the field, our path began to swing to the left, causing me concern, and I found myself gripping the edge of the cockpit with gloved hands as we hit the first of several bumps in the field.

My heart raced as we picked up even more speed, and an old childhood memory suddenly sprang from the past into my consciousness. I recalled running down a steep hillside at breakneck speed, my velocity increasing to such a degree that my legs, seemingly, could not keep pace, and I feared I would fall at any moment. Much the same sensation welled up in me now, except that instead of the dreaded tumble, I abruptly felt the bumping cease and grasped that we had risen into the air.

Then my heart skipped again as I heard the engine cough and sputter, as if it were going to stop at any moment. The intermittent bursts continued as we passed up through the morning mist and swiftly through to its top, as Captain Harper had promised. Then the engine regained vigour, and we found ourselves suddenly lit by the rays of dawn.

Now gasping, I felt the craft tilt somewhat to the right and watched the fogbound landscape swivel beneath me until the sun lay at our backs. The wings then came back level, and we flew on a straight angle up, higher into the sky. At a distance well above the trees—indeed, higher than any landform I could imagine we might approach—our ascent slowed, and we assumed a constant altitude, at which point the pilot turned the craft again, placing the morning's glow to our right.

I felt a tap upon my shoulder and turned round as best I could. From the corner of my eye, I saw Captain Harper's right hand extended outward, the thumb pointing upward. I gave him a smile he could not see and nodded my head vigorously while duplicating his gesture, whereupon which he patted me on the back again and then settled into the business of keeping us aloft.

In time I became acclimated to my high station, and as the sun climbed into the sky and the fog evaporated, I grew ever more enthralled by the sight of what lay below us, confirming Captain Harper's expectation.

The fields were a quilt of contrasting greens and browns, sometimes stitched together by stone walls and country paths, and the trees and forests were shimmering balls of verdant fluff. We passed over what I took to be Aylesbury and then flew on, eventually approaching Oxford. There we made a slow turn round the town, and I caught sight of the Radcliffe Camera, where Sherlock Holmes had first confronted Professor Moriarty face to face.[47] I thought fleetingly of the handful of other cases that had taken the detective to Oxford and then turned round to have one last look at the dreaming spires in morning light.

"'She needs not June for beauty's heightening,'" I intoned, contemplating the literal truth of those words on this gorgeous morning, though I could not hear my own utterance through the roar of the engine.[48]

We flew on, eventually reaching the Midlands. Birmingham hove into sight, and once more I felt a tap upon my back. Turning round in my seat, I saw, at the edge of my vision, Captain Harper gesturing downward. I nodded, turned forward again, and felt our craft tilt slightly toward ground. We descended gracefully, but as landing became imminent, I instinctively

---

[47] Radcliffe Camera is a building which initially served as Oxford University's library, eventually specializing in science. Well before 1914, its book collection was moved elsewhere, and it became a reading room for the Bodleian Library. That it was the place where the paths of Holmes and Moriarty first crossed is a rather significant revelation, if the narrative can be trusted, and it leads to more than one question—e.g., was that initial meeting at Oxford as teacher and student? If not, when and under what circumstances did it occur? Sadly, there are no more references to the event in Watson's account.

[48] This quotation, as well as the reference to "dreaming spires," is from the poem *Thyrsis* by Matthew Arnold. Its citation may give some hints about Watson's taste in literature, but it might also be relevant to the matter of assigning dates to the events in this text.

clasped my hands to the edge of the cockpit once more, suddenly feeling alarm as I heard the engine sputter as it had during our original ascent.

Captain Harper shouted, but I could not understand his words. To my relief, however, the aeroplane came down safely in a field east of Birmingham, and as we touched soil, there was a firm jarring, followed by a series of jolts, and then I felt only gentle shaking as we eventually rolled to a stop.

For the first time, I noticed three individuals in the field, running from a small copse of trees that bordered the open space. With our engine stopped and the propeller rotation slowing to a halt, Captain Harper again patted me on the back.

"Did you enjoy it, sir?" he called out.

"Very much so!" I exclaimed.

"Ha! Perhaps we'll see you take your ticket before long."

"Beg pardon?"

"'Take your ticket,' Mr. Price: learn to fly and obtain your pilot's certificate."

"Ah, I understand," I replied. "I must ponder that option for a while, I suppose. However, I cannot wait for the second leg, though I have concerns about the engine."

"The start-and-stop? Don't fret," the pilot said. "That's the way we have to run her at the beginning and end. Did you not notice the same when we took off from Hulton?"

"I most certainly did," I replied. "And I thank you for your explanation."

"You're more than welcome," the officer told me as he stood up, clambered over the edge of his cockpit, swung round, and hopped onto the ground. “She’s a fine craft, she is: light and responsive, a joy to fly.” He looked up at me. “I take it you’d like to stretch your legs also while they refuel us?”

“Yes, if you do not mind.”

“Not at all,” he replied as the three men approached our craft at a jog: They were, as had been the case in Hulton, two workmen and an officer, and they reached our craft before Captain Harper could assist me down to the ground.

“Halloa,” said my companion, extending his hand to the officer. “Cecil Harper.”

“Edward Ashley Tate. And halloa to you, sir,” he added, glancing up at me. From his uniform, I took him to be a captain in the regular army, equal in rank to Harper, but not of the Royal Flying Corps.[49]

“Shall we refuel her, sir?” one the workmen said, wiping a hand on his overall.

“Yes, Cooper,” replied Ashley Tate. “You and Seldon go bring the motor and fill her up.” He turned round to face the aeroplane, once more taking notice of me. “Need a hand down, sir?”

I accepted the offer, and both captains assisted me from the craft. I found my legs somewhat unsteady after having been folded within the cockpit for some time, and I spent a moment limbering up while the two officers conversed. Then, from the distance, I heard a loud report and, turning round, saw the two mechanics reappear in a small motor-lorry. They drove it to within a few feet of the aeroplane and stopped.

---

[49] The Royal Flying Corps was an arm of the British Army, while the Royal Naval Air Service was the corresponding air service of the Royal Navy. The two organizations were merged to create the independent Royal Air Force in April 1918.

"The army doesn't possess that many motors," said Captain Ashley Tate, "but we have one of them here, I'm proud to say."

"They'll be refuelling her," Harper said to me. And then, in a lowered voice, he added, "Do you need to relieve yourself, Mr. Price?"

I smiled gently. "To be honest, Captain, that would do me a heap of good."

"Understood, sir. I'll likely be taking a turn myself before we lift off again. I'm afraid that, out here in the fields as we are, your only choice is there within those trees." He pointed in the direction of the copse, and I gave a resigned nod.

"Can you handle the garments adequately on your own, sir?"

"I believe I can manage, Captain Harper."

"Is there a need for paper, sir?"

"No," I replied. "None required. I will see you back here presently."

I trod across the field as the workmen began to refill the aeroplane's petrol tank. Feeling myself far from Queen Anne Street, I let my thoughts carry me back to Afghanistan. Any inconvenience I was about to suffer, I realised, would be minor compared to those I had experienced during the retreat from Maiwand decades ago. I overcame what obstacles I encountered among the trees and, within a few minutes, in finer fettle than before, returned to the company of the two captains and the mechanics, who were finishing their task.[50]

---

[50] That Watson would include in his account a detail as intimate as this walk into the woods, no matter how obscurely related, seems somewhat out of character and casts some doubt on the authenticity of this narrative. The First World War changed mores, however, and this story, if genuine, would probably have been composed sometime in the 1920s. Perhaps by then the doctor had acclimated to Jazz Age attitudes, and his sense of circumspection accordingly loosened at bit.

The officers, who stood smoking some distance from the aeroplane, looked up at me as I approached. “Feeling better, sir?” shouted Harper.

“Yes,” I said, putting on my gloves again. I stood in the morning air and stared at our craft. “All is well with the machine?”

“She checks out fine,” replied my pilot. “The captain’s men aren’t flight mechanics, but they know how to load petrol well enough. I gave her a quick going over, and I think we’re still in business.” He dropped his cigarette and stamped it out in the moist grass. “Well, I think I will step over and have a go myself. By the time I return, I believe we may be able proceed with our journey. And oh,” he said to the other officer, “I just remembered—it was Teddy Morrison who was stationed at Farnborough.”

“Yes, of course,” replied Ashley Tate. “Damn, I just could not recall his name.”

“Well,” said Harper as he strode toward the copse, “Teddy himself is rather forgettable, isn’t he?”

Ashley Tate raised his cigarette in agreement and then turned toward me. “Good flight up here, sir?”

“Yes, very enjoyable.”

The officer watched Harper retreat into the woods. “Never been up in one of these aeroplanes yet,” he said. “Maybe that will change someday.” He tossed his cigarette away and began to walk back toward the craft. “I don’t know what mission you’re on for the higher-ups, Mr. Price,” he said as I followed him, “and I’m not angling to find out, but I’ll tell you this: I received orders early this morning, in no uncertain terms, to expedite your journey without fail. I hope we’ve accommodated your needs.” He pulled out a watch. “As Captain Harper mentioned, our men are not flight mechanics, but they do the best they can.”

"I'm sure the captain will have no complaint," I told him.

Ashley Tate smiled. "And in the meanwhile, we—those two workmen and I—are to wait here every day for you to return," he said. "Up to a fortnight, at least."

"I must apologise for the inconvenience," I said.

The officer chuckled. "All in the line of duty, sir. From near dawn to dusk, whenever you choose to return, we will be here with more fuel. Are you experienced at this flying business, if I may ask?"

"I must confess that I'm no expert on aeroplanes. This is my first flight."

Ashley Tate clasped his hands behind his back and nodded. "Not your first journey through the Midlands, though, perhaps?"

"Oh no, I am quite familiar with the area. Birmingham in particular," I added, looking off toward the direction in which the city itself lay. Idly, I began to silently recall, among others, the affair involving Hall Pycroft,[51] until one of the mechanics called to his captain and disturbed my reverie.

"She's full up, sir!" the man declared.

"That's good, Seldon," replied Ashley Tate, who then turned round toward the copse to catch a glimpse of his fellow officer. Harper was still shrouded within the trees, however, and so all four of us stood quietly for a moment, waiting for the pilot to return. Presently, he emerged from the foliage and rapidly approached us.

"All set, then?" Captain Harper asked.

---

[51] Hall Pycroft was Holmes's client in "The Adventure of the Stockbroker's Clerk," which took place in Birmingham in the late 1880s.

The mechanics both nodded, and the other officer said, "I believe you're ready to take to the skies again." He extended his arm. "Good luck to you both."

"Thanks much," said my pilot, shaking other officer's hand. With a smile, he added, "Stick around for a bit, if you will. We'll give you a jolly farewell from above, eh?"

Ashley Tate smiled and nodded before offering me a handshake as well, a gesture I readily accepted, and then Harper instructed the mechanics on how the aeroplane's engine should be prepared using a syringe we carried with us. He also carefully explained the procedure for starting the motor, making clear that one man should be ready to pull the other away from the propeller once the motor was engaged.

Captain Ashley Tate and his crew had brought with them large wooden blocks which were set as chocks once the craft was turned and positioned for launch. I was assisted into my seat once more, and Harper advised me to hold on tightly this time as he assumed his position as well.

With Ashley Tate grasping the rear of the aeroplane as instructed, the engine was finally coaxed into action and, cheered by the three who would remain on earth, we rolled across the Midlands field and once more lifted skyward, finding our way above the treetops, over which we made a grand circle while gaining much altitude.

Then, from that airy mount, Captain Harper turned the aeroplane nose down, and we sped toward the ground, faster and faster. The framework began to vibrate wildly, and I could hear the craft scream, when suddenly the horizon vanished and all was sky. My mind filled with sensation only, crowding out the ability of words to express fear, and then the ground appeared again, only now above my head. As earth rotated before my eyes upon that unnatural axis, I suddenly understood we were in a vertical loop, and as my stomach once more settled into its proper place, I saw terra firma also restored to its customary position.

Now on an even keel, we circled lower, and I saw three small figures waving and jumping in the midst of the field we had just departed, and I along with Harper waved in reply. Our wings tipped slightly and then came back level, and after feeling a pat on my back and replying with a vigorous upward display of my thumb, I felt us turn once more to continue our wending path toward Scotland.

We traced a route parallel to the major roads heading north, passing over what I took to be Stafford and Stoke-on-Trent. At first it appeared as if we would split the difference between Liverpool and Manchester, but gradually we veered more in the direction of the latter, and at length, Harper set us down in a field that was near a town he indicated was Stockport.

"Did you fancy the loop?" he asked as he once more assisted me from the aeroplane.

"I fancied it and then some," I assured him. "It was most thrilling!"

"It's not difficult to do," the young man informed me. "One simply needs to make certain to start out with a speed of over a hundred. If you don't have enough in the beginning, you'll not have enough to make it over and wind up hanging there, upside down, and end it all by chasing your tail."

"'Chasing your tail'?"

"Getting into a spin," Harper explained. "Aside from catching fire while in the air, it's perhaps the worst experience one can have up there," he said as we saw a horse-drawn lorry approach. "Spins tend to be fatal."

“Have you ever experienced either?”

“Fire or spin?” The officer smiled at me. “Not yet,” he replied, stepping over to the wooden propeller to rap it with the knuckles of one hand.

The lorry stopped several feet from our craft, and three men debarked. They identified themselves as a Mr. Jenkins and his sons Alfred and Thomas. With hardly any other words exchanged, the three fuelled our aeroplane with petrol carried in their vehicle, giving demonstration that they had performed such duties many times before. They then moved our craft into position for take off without any instruction, setting their own pair of chocks in front of the wheels.

Captain Harper took the taciturn manner of the strangers in stride, and I for my part did not openly display any curiosity about the trio. I saw that, whoever these men were, they were well versed in starting up the aeroplane’s engine and equipped to do so—complete with their own syringe and container of oil. With an absence of ceremony, our reascent into the air was accomplished most efficiently.

By now I had become somewhat accustomed to treading the sky, and removed from Captain Harper by the noise of the engine, as well as our seating arrangement, I found myself once more alone with my thoughts. My recollection near Birmingham of the case involving Hall Pycroft had brought to mind, in turn, other adventures experienced in the company of Sherlock Holmes—who, I suddenly comprehended, had largely been far from my mind since leaving Hulton.

Conveyed by Captain Harper, finding myself in the midst of an uncertain trip north in search of Richard Hannay, I realised that I had been thinking of myself more as Sir Walter Bullivant’s instrument than the venerable assistant of a famous detective. Indeed, many of the cases I had shared with my friend now seemed to pale in comparison with our current exploit, a mission upon which the British nation's own safety might depend.

As Captain Harper guided the aeroplane over the Lake District, I espied the area of Fell Foot and thought to myself how quaint even the gruesome business Holmes and I had faced there now appeared in contrast.[52]

As we caught sight of the Solway Firth,[53] I began to grow more anxious, for I realised that my air journey was drawing to a close, to be followed by the start of the real challenge facing me: finding Richard Hannay.

Captain Harper brought our aeroplane down lower, and we crossed the few miles of open water. Scotland's coastline was ahead, I knew, and from my past visits to the area for the purposes of fly fishing, I recognised before us the mouth of the River Nith.

Harper, no doubt, was also aware of the local geography, for he flew upstream along the course of the waters, which would lead to Dumfries, our destination. After several miles, it was apparent that the pilot was aiming for an open field just off what I recalled was the Abbey Road, south of town.

Our landing was much smoother, by comparison, than those we had experienced near Birmingham and Manchester. By now I had become

---

[52] The Lake District is a mountainous area in the northwest portion of England notable for, as might be expected, its lakes, but also for forests and mountains, the latter known as fells. There is no known narrative by Watson of the case obliquely referred to in this passage.

[53] The Solway Firth is an inlet that forms part of the border between England and Scotland.

accustomed to the engine's intermittent functioning while taking off and landing, and Harper skilfully guided the craft to a halt within a short distance of the road.

"Welcome to Scotland, Mr. Price," he said as the propeller stopped circling and he pulled up his goggles. "That was a bit more than a bonny wee jog, wasn't it?"

"A bit more indeed, Captain."

The two of us debarked from the craft. Feeling far more confident in myself, I left the aeroplane unassisted in this instance, after handing Harper my valise. Climbing down, I began to strip off my flight garments to once more reveal my tweeds, and from the bag I retrieved the cloth cap I had stashed within.

"You're the picture of a country gentleman now, sir," the captain remarked as he gathered my flying clothes and placed them in the cockpit where I had sat. He looked round. "Is anyone coming to meet you?"

"No," I said circumspectly and then, thinking of the great service this young man had done without full knowledge of its circumstances, I stepped toward him, my hand outstretched, and declared, "Words cannot express my gratitude, Captain."

He smiled, and we shook hands most heartily.

"I confess I feel so remiss," I added. "I have quite forgotten your given name."

"Cecil," he said with a modest smile. "Cecil Wallace Harper. And you are more than welcome for the service, Mr. Price. That is, Mister...?"

"James Price," I responded without hesitation—and not without guilt at the deception. Nonetheless, I was more than honest when I said, "I shall not forget you, Captain Harper."

"Nor I you, sir. For a first-time passenger—of your age, if I may say—you withstood the hardships magnificently. I shall be proud to share the clouds with you any time, Mr. Price."

"And I will never refuse your company, Captain, up there or here on the ground. But I have not asked what happens to you now? Your Major Reardon told me to inform you when you and your craft would no longer be needed, but until that time, what will you do, stranded as you are?"

"It'll be the camping life for me, Mr. Price. Simply put, I'll stay pat. I've done it many times before, sir, so don't waste a moment in worry. I will be fine."

"But you will need to eat."

"I have an allowance of coin and can venture into the town for food."

"But who is to protect your aeroplane?"

Harper shrugged. "I reckon I'll attract a small band of local boys at the least. I'm sure they'll not resist the offer of serving as guards for her, particularly if I give them some of that coin I mentioned. There's no need to fret about either me or the plane, I assure you."

"Very well."

I was ready to bid the pilot farewell, but as I looked at him cheerfully setting up camp beside his craft, I could not help but try to purge myself of the aura of dishonesty I felt I had attached to myself.

"Captain Harper," I began, "you are showing great fortitude in doing me the service you do, and perhaps I should explain why—"

"You needn't," he told me. "If I were meant to know your business here, Major Reardon would have informed me of it. What you call fortitude," he added gently, "is merely discipline. There is no reason to apologise to me, nor any obligation to explain yourself. I have my duty, and you have yours. No more elaboration is needed, sir."

I nodded, accepting the wisdom of the young man's words.

"Except to bid you farewell, Captain," I said. "For now."

"Yes, sir," he agreed, giving me a friendly, offhand salute. "Godspeed to you, Mr. Price."

Smiling in my civilian garb, I offered him the same military gesture, only with the snap I had shown during the Afghan War.

"My," said the captain, evidently impressed. "You must be true army, then."

"Assistant surgeon, 5th Northumberland Fusiliers," I replied briskly. "Subsequently seconded to the Berkshire Regiment of Foot."

Cecil Harper gave me one more salute, this time as sharp as mine and then some.

"Carry on then, Doctor," he said with a chuckle.

I nodded and then turned to make my way up the road toward Dumfries with a bittersweet feeling, realising that this earnest young man, who knew me as Mr. Price, had at last, unknowingly, addressed me correctly.

It was a walk of about three miles into town following the Abbey Road, which paralleled the river. The day was clear, and I thought I heard curlews and plovers crying, though it was only later on my hike that I saw some few of the latter in flight. I passed several people going the other way, all in carts or on bicycle, and was overtaken more than once by riders heading for Dumfries. At one point, I encountered two men on foot like myself, a pair who hailed me in friendly fashion from the other side of the road as they approached. They studied me with interest, and I was certain that, like others who had seen me, they found it odd for a gentleman in fresh tweeds and carrying a valise to be tramping into town from this direction.

I was not unacquainted with Dumfries and its surroundings, having visited the area two or three times before the turn of the century in pursuit of trout, and as I caught sight of the old bridge crossing the Nith, I could almost imagine myself twenty years younger, coming back to my inn after a brisk walk down the road and back. Almost at once, however, I felt the weight of my valise, perhaps also the weight of years, and I crossed the river intent on finding Bullivant's godson as soon as possible before beginning my improbable search for Richard Hannay.

Halfway across the water, I heard a train whistle in the distance and was reminded of Sherlock Holmes, who would not arrive in Dumfries, if he were to arrive there at all, until later that day.

I entered the town proper and shared its streets with shepherds traipsing about in the company of their dogs, as well as assorted old men in ragged tweeds, women with weathered faces, and gaggles of children who glanced at me with youthful curiosity. From memory, I located an inn where I had lodged during one of my past visits. Its interior was heavy with the accumulated odour of clay pipes and whisky, and upon entering I saw that it held only two grizzled men, who sat in a corner.

After a moment, a third fellow, whom I took to be the innkeeper, came through an open doorway as I closed the front entrance behind me. He was tall and thin, middle-aged, with a freckled face and bright blue eyes, and he warily stroked his clean-shaven chin as he noticed my valise.

“Greetings,” the man said with a curious nod. “You'll be wanting a room, perhaps?”

“Well, I may require lodgings,” I replied, stepping to a counter and putting down my luggage. “However, I am most urgently attempting to locate the residence of an acquaintance.”

I took from my jacket a paper upon which Bullivant had written the name of his godson and directions to his grounds.

“I am seeking this man,” I declared, showing Sir Walter's scrawl to the innkeeper. “Do you know him?”

“Sir Harry Christey?” the innkeeper said, raising his brows as he read. He frowned slightly and cocked his head. “Well, sir, I have heard of him, to be sure. His estate—called Dunfeardon, as it is written on this paper—is rather a bit off to the northeast. You must take the Lockerbie Road in the beginning and then after you—”

“How far is it?” I asked with slight impatience. “Do you know anyone who might be willing to take me there, by motor or cart?”

“It's hine awa!” shouted one of the men in the corner.

“There might be one person I could ask,” said the innkeeper, ignoring the interruption. He gave me an oddly cautious look and then added, “Allow me a moment. I'll find someone to fetch the individual I am thinking of.”

“Thank you,” I replied. “You are most kind.”

The man smiled and then stepped out the front door. I leaned against the counter, my gaze falling upon the pair in the corner. One of them, he who had shouted about Bullivant's godson's home being far away, raised his pipe to me, and I nodded with a smile.

“Ye be daundering?” he asked.

"Well, I suppose I am doing more than just strolling," I replied, pointing to my valise.

"Be needing a gillie?" asked the second man.[54]

"No, I'm not here for sport, in truth."

Both men smiled amiably and then slowly returned to their own conversation. I allowed myself to turn away from them, and my eyes caught sight of a newspaper sitting upon the counter: a copy of *The Scotsman*, whose pages had been folded so as to present a short posting about the murder in Hannay's flat.

Glancing furtively at the two men as they mumbled to each other and enjoyed their pipes, I picked up the newspaper and quickly read its notice of the killing, which included a description of Hannay's man Paddock seizing the poor milkman, who subsequently had been released. The paper indicated that the suspected murderer, whose identity was not revealed, was said to have escaped from London by rail and headed north. Hannay was mentioned only parenthetically, as the owner of the flat in which the murder had occurred, and no details of the murder itself were provided.

I put down the newspaper, wondering how extensive the manhunt had become, and hoping that Magillivray had managed to steer suspicion away from Hannay.

The front door opened, and the innkeeper stepped back inside.

"All is arranged," he said with an air of anxiety as he closed the entrance behind him. "I've asked one of the lads to fetch someone to take you."

---

[54] A gillie is an assistant to a fisherman or hunter.

"To Sir Harry Christey's estate? That is excellent," I replied, eyeing at the man studiously. "You know, I have stayed here before."

"Oh? Here in Dumfries?"

"Yes, but I also meant here, in this inn."

"Truly?" he said, his manner suggesting that he did not believe me. "Your face is not familiar."

"Well, that was a good fifteen years ago or more."

"Ah, I see. That was before my time here, to be sure."

The innkeeper stepped behind the counter. He glanced at the copy of *The Scotsman* and frowned, and it occurred to me that he realised I had looked at it before replacing the paper upon the counter in a different position than before.

"I was just reading about that very gruesome murder," I remarked.

"*An uisge beatha seo*," intoned one of the grizzled men from across the room, holding up a glass of whisky.[55]

"Aye," replied the other, and the pair of them clinked their glasses together before emptying them, their chuckles only just subsiding when the front door opened again and a young man in police uniform stepped inside. Behind the constable, who appeared to be barely twenty years of age, a small boy watched, wide-eyed.

"Halloa, sir," said the policeman gently. "May I ask you for your name and place of origin?"

"Why, I am from London," I said.

"And your name, sir?"

---

[55] "Behold the waters of life."

I paused for a moment, finding myself uncertain of a proper response. I had taken the alias of James Price on impulse, fearing that if German agents discovered that John H. Watson were involved in the search for Richard Hannay, they might suppose that Sherlock Holmes was on the case as well. I realised at once, however, that I carried no proof that I was Mr. James Price. On the other hand, I could present my letter of introduction to Sir Harry Christey from Sir Walter Bullivant, but that document referred to me by my real name.

"Who are you?" the policeman repeated.

I noticed the innkeeper's rapt expression and saw that the two men in the corner had stopped mumbling to one another to listen as well.

"I am John—that is, James Price," said.

"John or James Price?" asked the young constable.

"I told you: I am James Price."

"Can you prove it, sir?"

"What need have I to prove my identity, officer?" I asked forcefully, trying to wrest of control of the conversation from him.

"You have my need, sir," the constable replied calmly. "Once more, I ask you to prove you are who you claim to be."

I thought again of the letter of introduction written by Bullivant, but now—having presented myself as Price—was of the opinion that changing my story would only compound the problem. Then I hit upon an obvious solution.

"I carry no identification," I said primly, "for I am on a secret mission for the government. I was conveyed here in an aeroplane piloted by an officer of the Royal Flying Corps. He and his craft await me south of town, along the Abbey Road. I suggest you ask him to verify my identity."

"Aye," shouted one of the men from the corner. "There be a tale and half. He come falling oot of the sky to save us all."

He and his friend began to laugh again.

"Well," said the policeman, "I still must take you into custody for the time being, sir, while we confirm this tale of yours. May I ask what your exact business is in Dumfries? And—once more—where do you hail from?"

"I told you my mission is a secret one, and I have already informed you that I arrived from London. I do not see why—"

"London be where that murder happened," the innkeeper interjected. I turned round to face him, and he cringed from behind his counter as he asked, "You wouldna happen to know anything about that, eh?"

"I know only what I read in your newspaper there," I said with a casual air.

"He called it gruesome just a mite earlier," the innkeeper told the policeman.

"Yes," I said in a fit of irritation. "How else would you describe the act of plunging a long knife through the chest of a man?"

The innkeeper's freckled face contorted into a wicked smile, and he abruptly gained the confidence to step closer to me, though still from behind the counter.

"Oh, so that's how it were done, eh?" he said, giving the constable a look of triumph. "I wouldna ken, having read only the newspaper here, which dinna give any details about the manner in which the murder was committed."

I felt suddenly numb at realising my error.

"So how did you come to know that detail, Mr. Price?" said the constable, laying heavy emphasis upon his last two words. "Perhaps, sir, there is now even more reason why you should come along with me."

I silently weighed the courses open to me and decided it was best to comply for the moment. I picked up my valise and turned to accompany the young policeman out the door.

"Just like Conan Doyle," exclaimed the innkeeper as I stepped over the threshold. "Me and Sherlock Holmes, a pair of deductive twins we are."

I stopped and turned again, only to witness the men in the corner salute the innkeeper with their empty glasses. Feeling the constable's light hand upon my shoulder, I merely sighed, determined that silence was the better part of irony, and swept round yet again to leave the inn in the company of the policeman.

"I'm taking you a place where we may keep you for a while, sir," he said, removing his hand from my shoulder. "I'll trust you'll make no attempt to escape and in return will make no spectacle of this."

"I thank you for that small consideration," I said coldly as we strode down a major street, the boy walking behind us while many passersby gave us second and third looks.

"You are welcome, sir, and I appreciate your cooperation and understanding. You see, we've been alerted to watch for the fugitive from that Portland Place murder—"

"I am someone else."

"I'm sure we will both be quite happy when that is proved, sir. Until then, I hope you are able to sympathise with my situation, for I feel I must keep you in custody."

"How far are we to go?"

"Well, sir," said the young policeman, "the fact is I have no place to hold you other than the prison itself, and so it is there that we are headed. It is about half a mile distant."

Silently, I followed alongside the constable, marching back across the bridge spanning the Nith, and then to the right along the second street we encountered. Lugging my valise, I finally caught sight of the prison: a stone and brick fortress resembling in its way a latter-day castle, with turrets and steeples.

"I won't put you in a cell, sir," said the constable, finally shooing away the curious boy as we approached the building. "You will, however, remain under supervision."

"Let me say again that, if you take the Abbey Road south, you will come upon a military aircraft tended by its pilot, a Captain Cecil Harper. He will identify me."

"I reckon we will do just that, sir," the constable said as he held the door open for me. "But all in due time. To your left once we're inside, if you please."

I was settled into a room whose furnishings consisted of a desk and three chairs, with a window that looked out onto a spacious lawn. I set my valise upon the tile floor and then selected what I judged to be the most comfortable chair in sight.

"I'll return presently," said the policeman before he closed the door. I heard a key being applied to the lock and then receding footsteps.

After a few minutes spent imagining how I might have avoided finding myself suddenly incarcerated, I got to my feet and slowly walked to the window. I spent a while staring through the pane, admiring flocks of birds that occasionally flew past.

It was during such a moment that I espied an aeroplane against the clouds. The sight gave me a turn, for I instantly feared that perhaps Captain Harper had seen fit to abandon me. Soon, however, those worries faded, for as the craft drew somewhat closer, I saw that it was a monoplane, rather than the biplane in which I had made my journey northward.

I observed the craft make slow, lazy circles whose centres gradually drifted toward the northeast. It seemed a suspicious pattern of flight to my untrained mind, and in time I attached an odd malevolence to the aeroplane. Whoever was piloting it, I decided with no rational justification, that person must have some purpose not altogether wholesome.

Just then, I heard the lock turn, and the door opened to reveal my young warden.

"You are still doing well, sir?" he asked.

"As well as might be expected," I replied somewhat brusquely. "Has anyone interviewed the pilot I mentioned?"

"Not just yet," the policeman said in a tone that suggested he did not take seriously the story I had told. "We will get onto that in a bit. In any event, sir, I came to ask if you would care for me to arrange an afternoon meal for you."

"Yes," I said, turning toward the window again. "If I am going nowhere, I suppose I might as well eat."

"Very well," the young man said awkwardly. "Oh, and I'm afraid I haven't introduced myself to you, Mr. Price. Constable Charles Taylor, it is."

I made no response, maintaining my vigil at the window.

"Well, I'll be by to check on you later, sir," Taylor informed me before closing and locking the door.

I sighed and stared upward through the glass pane. The monoplane was still visible, now circling nearer the horizon.

The late afternoon sun was lowering ever more as I neared the end of a book I had been lent by one of the other local policemen. As I once again imagined being rescued from my imprisonment by Sherlock Holmes, Charles Taylor opened the door, accompanied by another of his colleagues.

"Mr. Price?" he said timidly.

"Have you come to clear my table?" I asked with sarcasm, nodding toward the plate, utensils and cup that still sat next to me.

"Ah yes, I suppose I did neglect that, did I not?" said Taylor, stepping into the room while his companion remained at the open doorway. "In truth, Mr. Price," he said as he gathered up the remains of my meal, "I've come to inform you that we have spoken to the army pilot who brought you here."

"Indeed," I said smugly. I thought to pull out my watch to underscore my irritation, but refrained from that excess. "Are you saying you now believe who I am?"

"We tend in that direction, yes." Taylor held the plate and other items as he spoke. "There's no doubt that the officer is genuine, and his vouching for you is good enough for us."

"And so may I now go?" I asked calmly.

"Well, it's not quite as simple as all that."

"No," I replied, setting the book down in the space just occupied by my plate. "It never is, is it?"

The young man was visibly cowed by my expression. “But you see, sir, we had already contacted Edinburgh, and they are sending some men here to talk with you.”

“Why? You just told me that Captain Harper’s identification of me is good enough for you.”

“For me—” the young man looked back at his companion—“For us, it’s good enough, yes, but it’s not good enough for Edinburgh. They insist on having their people speak to you as well, and we have been directed to retain you in custody until their representatives arrive.”

“But Edinburgh is a hundred miles away.”

“Actually, sir, I believe it’s just under eighty as the crow flies.”

“In any case, will these men from Edinburgh be arriving shortly?”

“That’s just the point, Mr. Price. They won’t be here until tomorrow.”

“Tomorrow?”

“Yes. You see, they have received other notifications of similar apprehensions or sightings, and Edinburgh has many investigators traveling about, looking into those reports. The ones who are to interview you hope by tomorrow morning to be in Moffat, and that’s just over twenty miles away.”

“Tomorrow?” I repeated.

“Yes, tomorrow,” replied Charles Taylor, cringing. “I canna help it, sir. We’ll have to keep you through the night, I’m afraid.”

“Here,” I muttered. “In Dumfries Prison.”

“In truth, Mr. Price,” said the young man hesitantly, “I should like to take it upon myself to offer you a bed for the night in my home. My wife and I have a spare room you can have, along with my sincere apologies.

Dinner and breakfast are part of the bargain, of course. It's the least I can do to make amends for the trouble caused you."

I sat back and looked at my valise, which had sat untouched throughout the afternoon, and wished I had taken the precaution of packing more in the way of naïve hope.

The next morning, I woke in my small cottage bed at once determined to make up for loss of the previous day. Rising without hesitation, I dressed and prepared with alacrity for the hours ahead. Opening the door of my room, I entered the sitting room to find the constable's young wife smiling over a full breakfast at the ready: eggs, link sausage and bacon, buttered bread, fried mushrooms, tattie scones, and black pudding, in addition to coffee, which I consumed in abundance.

"Once more, Mrs. Taylor," I said as I lifted my cup, "you have prepared another exquisite meal."

"You are more than welcome, Mr. Price," said the woman.

I smiled at her, recalling the previous night's dinner of Scotch broth, roast grouse, potatoes and pudding, with clootie dumplings for dessert. Her resentment at my arrival that evening had appeared to match my own sour attitude at being detained in Dumfries, but as the night wore on, we had found ourselves softening toward one another. With the excellent food and her husband's conciliatory words both lightening the mood, we were all on quite genial terms by the time I retired to the spare bedroom.

The shortness of the bed, which required me to wear a spare set of stockings to keep my protruding feet warm, had been an inconvenience I overcame with stoicism, and while I had been preoccupied with my own failure to obtain the objective of meeting Sir Harry Christey, I had nonetheless enjoyed a sound and refreshing night's sleep, my first in several days.

As I finished a last round of coffee, Constable Charlie Taylor entered the room and smiled gently as I caught sight of him.

His manner remained apologetic. "Did you sleep well, Mr. Price?" he asked timidly. "Is the breakfast there enough for you this morning?"

"More than enough, thank you," I replied, nodding appreciatively at Mrs. Taylor. "I am very much grateful to you both for your hospitality."

"We're happy to have provided you some comfort," said the young woman, who looked at her husband sternly. "It's to be regretted that mistakes were made."

"Well," I said before Charles Taylor could respond. "Such things happen." After a good night's sleep, I had become more philosophical regarding my recent setbacks. "I can only hope your colleagues from Edinburgh arrive relatively soon," I told the constable.

"That is my wish also," he said. "If I am not too bold, may I suggest that we make our way to the prison in short order?"

And so it was that, within the half hour, I found myself back in the same room at Dumfries Prison where I had been detained the day before. The space was now altered somewhat: a cloth lay upon the table, decorated with a small bouquet of flowers in a vase. More books had been left as well. As I had the day before, I set my valise down in a corner of the room and took to the most comfortable chair.

"You needn't remain here, Mr. Price," said Charles Taylor. "But as we don't know when the inspectors from Edinburgh will arrive, I think that it best you stay put until they appear. That will allow you to leave us sooner rather than later, which I suppose to be your preference."

The policeman departed, this time leaving the door ajar. Once more alone, I strode casually to the window to enjoy the view of early summer, and there, against the billowing clouds, I again saw the suspicious monoplane making its curious loops in the sky.

Frowning, I wondered what had become of Sherlock Holmes.

It was not until late afternoon—and two books later—that my captivity ended.

I heard a motor in the distance, though from my vantage point I could not see the vehicle approach. Then there were muffled voices from without, the closing of doors, and footsteps approaching down the hallway. Turning from the latest volume which I had taken up, I stared toward the open doorway and saw two men wearing ulsters and billycock hats enter in the company of young Charles Taylor.

The strangers halted once they glimpsed me. Each looked at one another and then at the local policeman.

"He can't be the man," one of the newcomers said.

"Too old," said the other. "Begging your pardon, sir," he added.

"But then," said the first stranger, as his partner cast a jaundiced eye at Taylor, "we are now told you have a person who will vouch for you. A military pilot, eh?"

"Yes," I said, closing the book and getting to my feet. "He can—"

"We are from Edinburgh," the second man interjected, addressing me. "I am Inspector Wilson, and this is Inspector Thomson. You've given your name, I believe, as Mr. James Price?"

"That is correct."

The inspector glanced across the room at my valise. "And your business here in Dumfries might be what, sir? Our understanding is that you claim to be on some sort of government mission."

I paused for a moment. Then, calmly, I responded by saying, "I am here to consider sites for a proposed aerodrome in the area."

"Truly?" said Charles Taylor with astonishment. Then, with embarrassment, he bowed to the two inspectors. "My apologies, sirs."

"And why did you not declare so at the beginning?" asked the first man, the one identified as Inspector Thomson.

"The existence of the proposal is not supposed to be generally known," I said.

"We understand," said Inspector Wilson. "Well then," he added, glancing at his companion as he spoke, "I suppose we should go see this pilot, then—in the spirit of *pro forma*?"

Thomson nodded. "The orders were to be quite thorough," he said, "even though he's obviously not—"

"All right," muttered Wilson. "Let's be off, then."

Charles Taylor rode with me in the back of the motorcar driven by Inspector Wilson, beside whom sat Inspector Thomson. The vehicle was a Fox Type-V, the very model that Blenkiron had recommended to me days earlier in Safety House, and so I leaned forward as we rumbled down the Abbey Road and shouted to Inspector Thomson, "Have you found satisfaction with this motor?"

"What?"

"I said, do you like this vehicle, Inspector?"

"Oh, the motorcar. Yes!" he replied loudly. "She runs quite well, I think. Wilson does most of the driving. Bill?" he shouted to his companion. "You like this motor, do you not?"

"Yes, I do," the other inspector affirmed. "And the mechanics back in Edinburgh are fond of her as well. A gem to maintain, they tell me."

"Reliable?" I asked.

"Very much so!" shouted Wilson. "Haven't had a problem all the while we've been gadding about in search of that London murderer. All the way from Edinburgh to West Linton, on through Biggar and Moffat, and then here into Dumfries. We need to make Gretna by nightfall before making the loop back home through Langholm and Galashiels."

"And we're not the only ones out looking," added Inspector Thomson.

"Has the murderer been identified?" I asked.

The men from Edinburgh paused and looked at one another.

Then Inspector Thomson said, "He's said to be one Richard Hannay, a Colonial."

My heart sank a bit with the realisation that Magillivray in London had apparently failed to turn his colleague's from the belief that the South African was guilty of killing Scudder.

"He may have altered his appearance somewhat," Inspector Wilson said, "but for what it's worth, Hannay is in his late thirties, speaks fluent German, is tanned with a long moustache, and is likely to be travelling light, perhaps with no baggage at all."

"And you are searching along the roads?"

"Along the roads, across the moors, in every glen and atop every hill," Thomson said. "And we'll find him, Mr. Price. You can rest assured that we'll find him."

I leaned back beside Charlie Taylor, feeling somewhat disconsolate, realising that I had already lost more than a day in police custody and was completely ignorant of Sherlock Holmes's whereabouts, let alone his success at finding Hannay. Moreover, as I comprehended the resources of the authorities set against my own, I now appreciated the foolhardy nature of my own enterprise.

Then, as we caught sight of Captain Harper's aircraft in the distance, I yet again espied the monoplane against the clouds, still making its ominous circles overhead.

"Are you searching for this Hannay from the sky as well?" I asked Thomson. "Using aeroplanes in your search?"

"Not to my knowledge, no," said Thomson. "However," he added, glancing at his partner, "that is rather a thought, isn't it?"

We pulled up to the aircraft and stopped. Captain Harper was there, holding court with a small group of children and a handful of men and women. A girl of perhaps ten knelt on the central ski sled that lay beneath the fuselage. The captain, who sat eating an assortment of meats and bread from a cloth spread over the ground, looked at me as I left the motorcar and smiled. He got up and walked over to us as his small entourage watched.

"Halloa, Captain," I said, shaking the officer's hand. "You have acquired a bit of a following, apparently."

"Yes. It's not unusual for that to happen when we land in the countryside." He held up the chunk of bread he still held in his left hand. "As you can see, I'm not wanting for anything."

"As you had predicted. Captain," I said, "Might you affirm to these two gentlemen that we are acquainted, and inform them whence we have come?"

"Of course. I so gave the same information yesterday to this constable," he said, indicating Charles Taylor.

"May I present Captain Cecil Harper of the Royal Flying Corps," I declared to the Edinburgh inspectors, before introducing each one to the pilot, who shook their hands in turn.

"Well, sirs," said the captain, "I've been acquainted with Mr. Price here since about dawn yesterday, when we departed Hulton in Buckinghamshire. My commanding officer there is Major Reardon, and I have—"

"That's quite all right, Captain," said Inspector Wilson, raising a hand. "We need no further explanation. There was a brief confusion about Mr. Price's identity," he said, glaring at Constable Taylor, who had remained silent during our motor trip. "That uncertainty has already been removed. We thought merely to convey Mr. Price to you before leaving Dumfries to fulfil our own duties."

"And I thank you for that," I told the two inspectors before pulling Harper aside for a short talk in private. "And so you have prospered, despite my absence?" I asked the captain.

"As you can see, Mr. Price, I've been leading a life of luxury, though I'm forced to become my own rigger and fitter."[56]

---

[56] At the time, two mechanics were assigned to each plane in a Royal Flying Corps squadron. One, called a rigger, was responsible for trueing up the aircraft's wings and fuselage, which were made of wood and braced with wire and turnbuckles. The fitter, meanwhile, looked after the engine.

"I have been detained by the local police since yesterday," I informed him. "They thought me to be another man, a fugitive, and were initially unwilling to believe my story about you flying me here."

"Yes. As I said a moment earlier, they came to me, and I vouched for you. For me, it's been a whirlwind since midday yesterday. I had several invites to stay the night, which I've declined, preferring to camp here with the plane. Some local men have agreed to take turns guarding the craft, however, should I take brief leave of her."

"I believe we will have no problem in getting the local constabulary to assist in that endeavour."

"The more the merrier. And what of you, sir, now that you appear to be a free man again?"

"I still need to speak with someone in the district, hopefully by this evening. I trust I will find you here for the next two or three days?"

"You will indeed," replied the officer. He glanced back at his craft, where a boy was shouting to the girl on the ski skid to move over and make room for him. "I think I'll need to tend to matters here right now, sir. Perhaps I will stay the night at one of the cottages about—and I'll leave word with those who will guard the aeroplane as to where I'll be. However, I shall be at the ready should you need me. Me personally, that is," he added, "for the plane herself is somewhat low on fuel, of course. My understanding is that more petrol is to arrive later today, according to what Major Reardon told me before we departed Hulton."

With that, I returned to the company of the local constable and two inspectors, informing them of my need to go to the home of Bullivant's godson, Sir Harry Christey. Charlie Taylor told them where the residence was, and Inspector Wilson gently refused my request.

“As I mentioned earlier, Mr. Price, Inspector Thomson and I must be in Gretna by late afternoon, which it’s nigh getting onto as we speak,” he said. “Sir Harry’s estate is apparently up toward Moffat, whence we came. There’s simply no time for us to convey you there and then make our destination by the deadline. Then, too,” he added, looking sideways at the constable, “it’s really the fault of the locals that you’ve been detained for so long, and so they should be the ones to accommodate you. I am afraid the best we can do is take you back into Dumfries.”

It was an offer I accepted, but there now seemed small likelihood of my finding any vehicle to convey me by a decent hour to the residence of Bullivant’s godson, which lay some distance to the northeast. It would be dark ong before I should arrive there on foot, and with no guide I was likely to become lost in the meanwhile, were I to set out on my own. There apparently being no one immediately prepared with cart or horse or motor to convey me to my desired destination, I resigned myself to staying another night in Dumfries when Charles Taylor turned to me in the motorcar as we sped back to town.

“I’ve just recalled something regarding your Sir Harry Christey,” he said. “He’s in politics, isn’t he?”

“Yes,” I said. “I believe his godfather mentioned that fact to me.”

“Ah, well then,” the constable replied, a weary but hopeful smile on his face. “I believe I can manage to get you to him by this evening, Mr. Price.”

CHAPTER SIX: THE SPEAKER & THE INNKEEPER

"We're not very political, the missus and I," the constable said quietly as the automobile re-entered Dumfries. "On the other hand, Murray the tobacconist is a rather fierce Liberal and has been trying to get me to attend a rally this evening up in Brattleburn, and I just recalled that he said Sir Harry's going to be one the speakers, along with some Colonial personage—an old Australian premier, I think."

"And where is Brattleburn?"

"It's a bit of a ways to the northeast, but still closer to Dumfries than Sir Harry's residence. And the journey is not a long one if you've got a motorcar, which is true of one of Murray's friends. The two of them are attending the rally tonight. You could simply ride along."

"Yes, but I had hopes of reaching Sir Harry sooner than this evening."

"Ah, I see. Well, alternatively, I believe I can instead arrange for a cart to take you to Sir Harry's residence, departing earlier. May I see those instructions again, sir?"

I produced the directions to the Christey estate that Sir Walter had written down for me, and upon reading them, Taylor declared getting me there by cart would pose no problem at all.

"Most likely, though," he advised, "I canna get it arranged until a bit afore supper, and then the trip itself would be a long one, for the fellow I have in mind to take you would be making many stops along a circuitous route. Nonetheless, he would get you to this address shortly after nightfall."

"But Sir Harry will no doubt have left for that rally by then," I said.

"Aye," said Charlie Taylor in dismay. "That would pose a problem, would it not?"

"And simply hiking to Sir Harry's would not take me there any sooner?" I asked. "Even if I started out presently?"

"No, I would reckon," replied Taylor. "The distance is too far."

"Well," I said with disappointment, "I suppose I will wait for that ride to the rally. In the meanwhile, perhaps a walk around Dumfries and vicinity will clear my mind."

"Very well," said Taylor. He gave me an inquisitive look as our moton stopped before the prison. "Are you perhaps thinking as well of the need to scout out the location for that aeroplane field?"

"Yes," I answered, untruthfully. "That is my purpose here, after all. It is not supposed to be known," I added in a conspiratorial tone.

"I quite understand," replied Taylor.

And so, after bidding farewell to the two inspectors from Edinburgh, I asked the young constable to see if Murray and his friend would convey me to the evening political rally, where I hoped to finally introduce myself to Sir Harry Christey. In the meanwhile, I set out about Dumfries in hopes of finding some suggestion that Richard Hannay had recently passed through the village. It also occurred to me that I might perhaps stumble upon evidence of Sherlock Holmes as well.

I strode toward the centre of town and was twice accosted by local folk who asked me if I were associated with the flyer who was camped along the Abbey Road. I freely admitted to the relationship and did not give a negative response to my greeters when they asked if an aerodrome was planned for Dumfries—evidently, word had quickly spread of my supposed intent.

In time, I found myself nearing the town's small train station and decided to pause there to see what idle enquiry might turn up. I was not long in finding success far beyond my modest hopes.

An old man and his dog sat front of the station office. Of the two, I was noticed first by the canine, a glaring brute whose expression gave me second thoughts about approaching, but I steeled myself and did not turn back.

"Halloa," I cheerfully called out.

The dog snorted, while its owner lifted his face, revealing bloodshot eyes that stared vacantly from below a moth-eaten tweed cap. Squinting, he punctuated the animal's incipient, low growl with a repetitious, "Aye, aye, aye?"

"I see we are both enjoying the summer weather," I declared. The dog stopped growling, but then it discreetly bared its teeth in my direction. "That is to say, all three of us," I added.

"Dunno about enjoying, necessarily," the man said plaintively. "Experiencing, aye, but that goes without saying."

"Quiet about, is it?"

The dog suddenly stood and began viciously barking at me. I reared back, before the old man turned in his chair and kicked at the animal, which shied away and began whimpering before settling itself upon the ground several feet away.

"Quiet enough now," said the old man, who suddenly tilted in his chair and became flatulent for the better portion of a minute. "I misspoke, it seems," he added as he leaned back.[57]

It was now obvious to me that he was inebriated.

"Have you encountered strangers in the past day or two?" I asked cautiously. "Perhaps a suspicious-looking man?"

"Aye, I have, as a matter of fact."

"Truly?" I said with sudden interest. "When and where?"

"Now and here," he said, once more pulling his cap down over his eyes.

"Yes, that is right amusing."

"If ye think so."

I smiled, but only the dog seemed to be paying me any attention now, and the glint in its eyes silently suggested the interest was nothing if not a malevolent one. Thus, seeking to put more distance between myself and the pair, I turned to make my way farther into town, but not wishing to leave even this noxious stranger in any mood other than a pleasant one, I asked in the spirit of good fellowship, "Can you suggest an establishment where I might find some good whisky?"

"No, but I can point ye away from some bad brandy."

I nodded and then turned again to go.

"I'm a strong teetotaller, ye know," the old man bellowed. "I took the pledge last Martinmas, and I havena touched a drop of whisky sinsyne. I

---

[57] This is another detail that, one thinks, Watson would be very unlikely to include in his memoir. Some may, with justification, find it yet another piece of evidence that this narrative was not penned by him.

was sair temptit at Hogmanay, ye know, but I dinna touch a drop then, either. That's what I told the fellow what ran away from the train."

I stopped and turned round.

"He wouldna listen to me, though," the man went on. "Just wanted to get off the carriage. Dunno where he thought he was going."

The dog had curled up, facing away from us, and I stepped back to the station porch.

"What man was that?" I asked.

"The man on the train. The slow train, do ye ken? Day before yesterday it was."

"What did he look like?"

"Mature, fit type of a man," my companion drawled, between hiccups. "A collared shirt he wore, good flannel as near as I could make out, but not as fine as his tweeds. Aye, but the best about him were the boots. Good and strong—and nailed. I thought—"

"Was he tanned and did he have a moustache?" I enquired.

"Who is there about who doesn't have a touch of sun, eh? Except perhaps you. And as for moustaches, who can remember? You have one. Is not that enough?"

I paused, uncertain what to ask next, but the man took the opportunity to say more. "I canna remember today any more than I could yesterday, when the parson kept asking me about it," he proclaimed.

"Parson?"

"Aye, the parson which come in on the train from the south. Curious fellow, asking about much like you."

"Did he have a goatee?"

"They dunna allow those on the train," said the man. "At least, not the proper ones. A dog, yes," he added wistfully, glancing at his own animal. "But never—"

"Chin whiskers!" I said. "Did he have chin whiskers and eyeglasses? Was he tall and did he—"

"Aye, aye," insisted the man, holding up his hands. "All those things and more, I suppose. He just kept asking and asking, like you. Asking about all manner of meaningless stuff."

"And where is this parson now?"

The old man shrugged. "Where are any of us, if ye ken what I mean?"

"Please," I said. "Can you tell me where this parson might be?"

He looked up and tilted his cap back, revealing a leathery forehead. Rubbing his dirty, pink nose, the man replied, "Reckon I guessed he was going off to find the man who left the slow train."

"And where was that?"

"Aye, up farther north. Up the way, along the tracks."

He thought for a moment. "What did I tell the parson? It wasn't as far as the one station—the one by the tarn. No, two stations down from that. Actually, not at the station at all. We were stopped, you see, waiting for a train going west to let us pass. There were police on the west-going carriages, and they was coming down the line, to board us."

"But where was this?"

"It was by the river."

"Which one?"

"The one we were stopped aside of! We were not moving, just waiting for the policemen to get on board. I remember seeing a culvert. And the dog here was barking. Lay his teeth into the man's trouser leg he did, but the fellow got loose and made off. Had the mutt tied to me waist with a rope. It's best that way, when you be on the train."

"Yes, go on."

"Well," said the man, impatiently, "the dog tries going after the man, but it's tied to me waist. So when the dog jumps out, it pulls me with him. Just tumbled out, you know," he added, looking down at his knees. "See the stain there. A pity."

I saw a myriad of stains, all of them old, upon the man's worn trousers. "And then what happened?" I asked.

"And what would you think?" replied the man indignantly. "I got back onto the carriage, of course, pulling the dog up with me. The train ran on to Dumfries here, and then you come along."

"And the man who left the train?"

"What about him? He left the train along the track up north, by a culvert. Have ye not been listening? Havena seen him since. Dunna need to. Do you?"

"And the parson," I said. "What did you say became of him?"

"I told ye: the parson took the slow train up north too. Yesterday. Saw him buy the ticket."

"Thank you."

The man coughed and then leaned back, planting his palms on his knees. "Funny man, that parson," he remarked.

"Oh?" I said. "How so?"

"Only man the dog here ever has took a liking to. Most funny."

"I am certain it was," I replied, glancing at the animal, who immediately bared its teeth again. "Good day, sir."

"May that it be," he called after me as I strode away from the station. "May that it be."

I now felt some small glimmer of hope, for despite my own stalled pursuit, there was no doubt in my mind that the parson had been Sherlock Holmes, who perhaps had succeeded in tracking Hannay's movements into the Scottish hinterlands.

This belief was but minor consolation, however, as I spent the remainder of the afternoon desperately roaming about Dumfries in search of more information that might pertain to the fugitive from Portland Place. In various inns, taverns and shops, however, my enquiries came back dry as a bone.

Later, as I hiked the outskirts of town, I encountered Constable Charlie Taylor.

"Halloa, Mr. Price," he called to me from across the way, hand waving and eyes flashing. "I have word from Murray, sir!"

I crossed the pathway and greeted him. He accepted my hand bashfully, perhaps still smarting from the error of his overzealousness.

"The tobacconist and his friend will take you to the rally tonight, Mr. Price, in the motor."

I expressed my gratitude to the young man and commented on my affection for the area, leading me to remind him of my past visits for trout fishing.

"Perhaps you will return for that sport exclusively," he said. "Have you decided yet upon a possible site for the airfield?"

"Perhaps," I replied, lying yet again. "There are, however, several factors that will weigh upon the final choice."

"I see," said Taylor. "Do you wish a bit to eat before leaving for the political rally, Mr. Price?"

"Well, I had not considered that."

"My wife would be happy to provide, if you like."

"I do not wish to impose—"

"There's no imposition at all," the young policeman said. "We'd be honoured to have you accept."

"I confess I have enjoyed myself immensely at your table."

Taylor smiled. "Then you will accept?"

And with a nod, I fell into step with him, the two of us ambling on back toward the centre of Dumfries. Along the way, I espied Captain Harper, who caught sight of me as well and approached. He gave Charlie Taylor a cautious eye.

"And how are your efforts coming, Mr. Price?" asked the airman.

"He's picking a spot for your aerodrome," the constable interjected. "Do you know when it's going to be built?"

Harper's face assumed a wry grin, and he looked at me with a sparkle in his eye. "Oh well, I wouldn't know that," the captain said. "Mr. Price is the man who would have the answer."

"As to the timing of construction, I am not privy to the government's intentions in that regard," I stammered, wishing to change the subject of our conversation.

"My wife and I are providing Mr. Price with a meal, Captain," said Taylor, unknowingly fulfilling my desire. "Perhaps you might join us?"

"I should not wish to impose," Harper replied.

"I earlier used that argument without effect," I declared jovially. "Come along with us, Captain. In return for the treasured memories from above that you have given me, I wish to facilitate the tickling of your palate."

The pilot nodded acquiescence with a bemused grin.

"If the two of you do not mind," said Charlie Taylor, "I'll run ahead and along home to have Averil prepare another two plates. You remember the way, Mr. Price?"

"Of course."

"Very well. We'll expect you both shortly," the policeman said before setting off in the direction of his cottage.

"You have made a lasting peace with the local constabulary, it appears," Captain Harper observed.

"Yes, and then some."

"And how is your survey for our new field coming, sir?" the young man said puckishly.

"Quite well," I replied, with raised brow.

The airman clasped hands behind his back and strolled along with me. "Well, sir, whatever your business here really is, I hope it *is* going well."

"I confess I have no idea," I told him. "And thank you for your discretion."

"Duty, sir."

"Yes, duty."

"And I suppose I should eat rather quickly," the pilot added. "The petrol for the aeroplane may arrive this evening."

Captain Harper and I were treated to a meal of fish soup and steak pie, and the two young men exchanged pleasantries concerning their respective positions and duties while Mrs. Taylor and I listened.

Eventually, after a dessert of pudding, I saw the pilot off along the Abbey Road to reunite with his aeroplane and there await the arrival of more fuel.

Constable Taylor stood with me outside the cottage for a short while thereafter, until a gleaming motor pulled up in the fading light of early evening.

"You be Mr. Price?" shouted the man sitting next to the chauffeur as both I and Charlie Taylor approached the vehicle.

"Yes," I answered, looking at the tall, thin, grey-haired individual. "You are Mr. Murray?"

"That I am, sir: Gavin Murray. Well, Charlie," the tobacconist said playfully to the constable, "I guess ye don't need to make your introductions now, do ye?"

"I suppose not, Mr. Murray," Taylor replied, eyeing the chauffeur, "except for—"

"And this one at the wheel is my friend and political compatriot, Mr. Boyd Watson," added the tobacconist quickly.

"Did you say Watson?" I enquired, stepping up to the second man to extend my hand. "I know a Watson."

The stout, clean-shaven man took my hand. "And I know several Prices," he replied, eyes flashing. "So you're to join us at the rally tonight? Jump in, then."

"Aye," said Murray. "It's a glad welcome we extend to our fellow Liberal kith and kin from England, eh?"

I looked across to Charlie Taylor, who appeared discreetly embarrassed, and I gathered that he had gently lied about my reasons for wishing to attend. I smiled at him, however, silently grateful for the innocent deceit, and then looked at the two men in the automobile.

"Yes," I said, "and it is heart-warming to be so greeted." I got in the tonneau of the motor and sat back.

"I will keep your luggage safe in the meanwhile, Mr. Price," said Taylor.

"Thank you," I replied, having decided the valise would be an impediment. I did not know what would be the result of my meeting with Bullivant's godson, but if I were granted the use of his motor, I could easily return to Dumfries for my belongings.

"Ready, Mr. Price?" asked Murray.

"Quite ready, sir."

And with that, we were off. The better part of an hour was spent on winding roads that led eventually to the town of Brattleburn.[58] We drew up along the side of a central street and were immediately accosted by several people, most of them older men, one of whom wore a rosette. As we left the motor, I noticed that Murray was now sporting a similar badge as well.

"Shall we go into the hall then?" the tobacconist asked of me and my fellow Watson. "Sir Harry and the guest speaker have not yet arrived, but they are expected shortly."

I nodded assent, and in the company of my two travelling partners and those who had greeted us, I walked down the street and then through a door that opened onto a spacious hall already filled with perhaps half a thousand people. To my mild surprise, the majority were women, with most of the remainder being men near my age, though a few younger ones were scattered among them. All the chairs I saw were occupied, and so as

---

[58] No such town exists. It should be noted, however, that Watson uses the same fictitious name that is found in Buchan's *The Thirty-Nine Steps*.

Murray joined his beribboned colleagues on the dais, Boyd Watson and I made our way to the side of the hall and there stood together amid a crush of fellow attendees.

"I hear the Australian is a good speaker," Watson shouted in my ear amid the growing din. "I reckon he will give the Tories a good drubbing tonight."

"Indeed," was all I offered in response while admiring the draped banners and numerous bouquets that adorned either side of the stage. A lectern had been placed in its centre, and there I watched Murray in heated consultation with other presumed organisers of the event. At length, I began to feel rather warm in the crowded hall and wished for some form of refreshment, but as I looked round the expanse I saw no relief for my thirst, though I did espy two policemen standing by the door.

More people entered the hall, pushing both myself and Boyd Watson ever farther to the side. I detected some slight commotion at the open doorway, and then the house lights darkened. As the great space dimmed, an anxious rustle of anticipation passed through the crowd.

Though several individuals were standing in front of me, limiting my view, I did witness a small entourage stride across the hall from the direction of the open door as Murray, standing on stage near the lectern, raised his hands and began to clap earnestly. A wave of applause spread throughout the large room, and I fell in with my fellow attendees, slapping palms together fervently for what reason I knew not.

Several male voices shouted encouragement, which caused me to once again recall that most of those within the space were female. One heavy-set woman rose ponderously from her chair to clap with enthusiasm and then whistle in such a shrill manner that my ears were discomforted.

Beside me, Boyd Watson took some liberty in lightly jabbing me with his elbow.

"Even our women can beat the Tory men, eh?" he shouted, and I nodded briskly, hoping my rapid agreement would cause him to stop poking me.

At length, the crowd settled, and those who had just entered the hall mounted the dais to take seats on the far side of the lectern, out of my line of vision. It was then that a devious-looking minister, whom Boyd Watson told me was the chairman, brought the meeting to order. Even at such a great distance, his bright red nose was a sight to behold, and I stood there, my attention fixed upon on that great glowing proboscis rather than the man's words, until my companion broke that concentration with another nudge to the ribs.

"Aw, the luck," Boyd Watson said disconsolately. "Crumpleton's not going to be speaking."

"Who's Crumpleton?" I asked, causing a man in front of me to turn round and silently frown with disdain.

"Crumpleton's the old Australian premier," Boyd Watson whispered. "He was to be the featured speaker tonight, aside from Sir Harry. They've got another bloke here in his stead. He'll be speaking second."

Someone near told us to be still, and I began to pay closer attention to the minister, who suddenly said, "And I present Sir Harry Christey!"

The hall erupted with loud applause, in which I joined, and I craned my neck to get a better look at the man I had sought these past two days. He was tall and relatively young, with light hair and sparkling dark eyes. I confess I found his cocky smile most infectious, and unconsciously I began clapping more earnestly as, dressed in a tweed suit and sweater vest, he grasped the podium with both hands. My fellow attendees had apparently the same reaction, so that after a moment Sir Harry was forced to raise his palms to quiet the multitude.

"Let's make the Tories feel it!" he said in a somewhat high and nervous voice, which spurred another roar from the crowd. "They can already hear it!" the young politician said with a laugh. "And let's make sure they appreciate it when the time comes!" He motioned downward, gesturing for the noise to abate, and after perhaps a minute, it finally did.

Sir Harry laughed again and then pulled from his jacket copious notes, which he attempted to arrange upon the lectern surface. His speech began awkwardly, with the man grasping his papers and reading from them and then stuttering a bit when he looked up to confront the crowd. But, as if remembering what he had written, the speaker ploughed ahead at full steam, declaiming like Alexander or Tree, until he once again could not recall his next point.[59]

In content, Sir Harry talked both of both peace and reform. "The so-called German menace is little more than a Tory invention," he asserted. "It is a ploy intended to cheat the poor of their rights and dam up the great upwelling for social reform." There were hoots of agreement. "But organised labour knows the Tory way with tricks," the speaker went on, "and we'll teach them a few ourselves!"

The crowd erupted with cheers and laughter, entranced by Sir Harry's words if not his delivery. He continued with an exhortation about the need to reduce the size of the navy as a show of good faith to Berlin, before demanding that Germany do the same. Fellow workers in both

---

[59] These are likely references to Sir George Alexander and Sir Herbert Beerbohm Tree, both of whom had been prominent actors in the Victorian era.

nations would unite in peace if it weren't for the Tories, he asserted. Indeed, he claimed, the entire world might be one if the opposing party could be wiped from the face of the planet, a statement that brought down the house.

I had, in the meanwhile, managed to slowly insinuate myself next to the wall, so that I might find some small relief by leaning against it. Thus, my view of the podium had become completely blocked. As Sir Harry ended his remarks, loud applause erupted, and with a sense of propriety—and a desire for personal safety—I joined in. I then heard but did not see the red-nosed chairman introduce a second speaker, described as an Australian Free Trader named Twisdon. My loud sigh was lost in the second round of clapping for this new presenter. Crossing my arms and lowering chin to my chest, I wondered how long this next oration would last.

"I suppose you already have heard much of my land of Australia," Mr. Twisdon began, and by his sixth word I had lifted my head, stepped away from the wall, and begun to gently nudge myself forward through the crowd. One fellow gave me a mild push back, but I cared not that I might have given him offense, for my mind was completely taken with the speaker's voice—which, despite the introduction, I recognised as that of Richard Hannay.

"Ours is a land without Tories," said the man supposedly named Twisdon. "In Australia, there are only Liberals and Labour." That statement brought another loud cheer from the crowd, forcing me back once more toward the wall, and I fought again to move ahead, so as to gain a glimpse of the speaker. As the latest round of applause subsided, I attained my goal and beheld Hannay, one hand raised as he continued his strenuous invective.

"In the long haul," he was saying, "we can all work together. We can all do the right things. We can make the Empire a decent place in which all may live." Hannay bowed as he concluded, and in the glare of the lights, I recognised the tanned face, though I noticed that his moustache had been greatly trimmed.

The hall erupted yet again, and amid the cheering and clapping, I found I could not advance through those still crowded before me. I could only watch and listen as the chairman urged Sir Harry Christey to rise again to stand beside him, with Hannay on the other side. The three men joined hands and raised their arms into the air, prompting more cheering from the audience. At length, the chairman proposed a vote of thanks to Sir Harry, ignoring Hannay altogether, and the hall approved the notion with a loud, "Aye!"

The rally itself now appeared to be at an end, and I saw an opportunity to advance toward the podium and latch onto Hannay. But as the meeting dissolved, everyone in chairs now suddenly rose to their feet, and those immediately before me milled about in conversation. The great mass of humanity within the hall began to assume the nature of a vast liquid cauldron, with currents that impeded my progress, or in some instances even drove me farther from my objective.

As I stood, occasionally on tiptoe, I saw Hannay and Sir Harry converse with the minister, Murray and others, but every time I glimpsed them anew, I saw that they had advanced closer to the door. I tried to force my way through the crowd with greater imperative, but those efforts only earned the scorn and anger of my fellow attendees.

"Here, sir!" said one. "There's no need to be so rough!"

"You've disturbed my wife with that shove, ye impudent sod," snarled another.

"Wait your turn," I was told by yet another, who then added, "Are you a Tory spy?"

This question, spoken as an accusation rather than in mere jest, suddenly inflamed those within earshot, and I was threatened with being dragged outside and beaten, until Boyd Watson approached and vouched for my good intent. By then, however, I could no longer see either Sir Harry or Richard Hannay in the great hall. With the other Watson in tow, however, I at last was able to cross the floor and step outside into darkness, where I found Murray conversing with the red-nosed minister.

"Ah, Mr. Price," said the tobacconist. "A very stirring rally, do ye not think?"

"Where is Sir Harry and the other speaker?" I asked breathlessly.

"Sir Harry and that fellow Twisdon? Why, they're off to Dunfeardon, Sir Harry's estate, I believe."

"You mean they have left?"

"They left some five minutes ago, I'm afraid. Had you something to say to them?"

"It was Sir Harry I wished to meet!" I said. "And Twisdon as well," I added disconsolately. "Is it possible to follow them to Sir Harry's residence?"

"Tonight?" Murray glanced at Boyd Watson curiously. "I do not see how you might accomplish that. Watson and I must return to Dumfries this evening. Of course," he added in a hesitant voice, "you may always enquire as to whether any other of our fellow rallygoers might be headed in that direction. Shall I ask around for you, Mr. Price?"

“Yes,” I replied on impulse. “It would be most appreciated.”

Twenty minutes later, I found myself in the tonneau of a different motor, crammed between two masons from Lockerbie.

“How far is it to Dunfeardon?” I asked.

“What say ye?” shouted the chauffeur, a fellow from Eaglesfield, whose wife sat beside him.

“I said, how far to Dunfeardon?”

“Oh, I reckon ye’ll have about five mile, once we set you off on the trail.”

“What?” I exclaimed, leaning forward, which caused the two masons to fall toward one another into the space I had vacated. “I thought we were going to Dunfeardon!”

“It’s no on our route,” the chauffeur calmly told me. “That fellow Murray said you wanted help in getting there.”

“Well, yes, but—”

“And it is help we’re providing ye. Ye’d likely no wish to start your walk from Brattleburn now, would ye?”

“But it’s well into evening,” I said. “And five miles—”

“Is five mile,” interjected one of the masons.

“Are we dropping him at the wood?” asked the other mason. “There be the inn just beyond it, on the path.” The man bent forward in the seat to look me in the eye. “Ye can stay the night there and start out at dawn, if ye’ve no fancy for walking in the dark, there.”

“Aye,” said the man from Eaglesfield. “There is your solution, sir.”

“The wood is coming up ahead,” his wife quietly noted.

"So it is," said the chauffeur, who pulled his motorcar to the side of the road and brought it to a halt. He turned round and smiled at me in the darkness. "Here ye be, then. The inn is along that path, not far," he indicated by pointing. "Ye can even see its lights from here, I think."

I saw nothing as I stepped from the automobile, but I felt that I had no other choice if I were to have any hope of seeing Sir Harry Christey—and now, Richard Hannay—before dawn, and so I bade farewell to my brief companions, whose names I never learnt, and stepped off the road and onto a winding path that led through a small copse into abruptly hilly terrain, with a pass between the low peaks.

All was darkness save for the light of the moon, and after the better part of an hour, I ran into a road where, in the distance, I did at last see dim light ahead. It took me a short while to reach its vicinity, where I encountered a small stone bridge spanning a stream. On the other side was a cottage.

The chimney calmly smoked in the moonlight, and flickering candlelight was visible through dingy windows. I walked toward the house, half-seen twigs snapping and gravel crunching beneath my soles, and stepped onto the porch. Hearing nothing from within, I knocked softly.

I stood for what seemed many seconds, breathing the aroma of peat smoke, before the door was finally opened by a young man with a ruddy, boyish face who held a long clay pipe in his right hand.

"Good evening," he said. "It's a mite late to be on the road. You are in need of a place to rest?"

"This is the inn?" I asked.

He smiled gently and raised the pipe to his lips for an instant then exhaled. “It is an inn,” the young man replied. “For these parts, though, I suppose it is *the* inn. I am its landlord, and at your service.”

He moved to the side, as if inviting me to enter, and I took that presumption, stepping over the threshold. Near the hearth was a sturdy chair and table, upon which lay an open book.

“You have no lodgers at present?” I asked.

“None,” he said. “My grandmother is upstairs. Margit, our housekeeper, is still in the back, I believe. She can prepare a small repast if you are—”

“I am not hungry, no,” I said briskly. “I am, however, in great need of transport to a place called Dunfeardon.”

“Dunfeardon?” the young man said, stepping to the table before motioning for me to sit in a chair.

I politely shook my head at the offer.

“Ah yes, Dunfeardon,” he said. “The Christey manor, isn’t it? I know its general location, and it’s really not that far—as long as you’re not on foot.”

“But I am.”

“Oh, I see.”

He again sucked on his pipe and considered me with a thoughtful expression.

“May I ask a question, sir?” the young man said at last, his face momentarily obscured by a smoky exhalation. “Why do you lack transport other than your legs? You do not seem quite dressed for hiking, and this is hardly the hour—”

"I urgently need to see Sir Harry Christey, and I was travelling with acquaintances whom I thought would deposit me at Dunfeardon. My assumption was incorrect, and this is where I find myself. They recommended your establishment as a place where I might seek assistance."

"Ah, I see. Well, what kind of assistance do you seek? A place for the night or transport to Dunfeardon?"

"The latter," I said. "If it is at all possible at this hour."

The young man shrugged. "It is...possible."

"You have a motor, then?"

"I have a motor bicycle."

"Can it accommodate me?"

"There is a sidecar. Have you any baggage outside, Mister...?"

"Watson," I said, at last foregoing my seemingly useless alias. "John Watson. I carry nothing at the moment."

"Good. I am Ewan Clark," he said, taking the pipe in his left hand and offering me the other. I accepted it warmly, and then the young innkeeper reached for his book on the table and with thumb and forefinger bent a page to mark his place. "You've spoken of urgency, and so I assume you wish to set off immediately, despite the hour."

"I do, yes."

He nodded and stepped to the hearth to knock out his pipe. "Then I will make preparations to take you to Dunfeardon."

"That is all rather kind of you," I said with genuine emotion.

Ewan Clark looked at me and smiled shyly.

"I love adventure," he declared. "I inherited this place from my father, and it provides little in the way of that. I must do my adventuring in the mind," he added, gesturing toward his book. "Milton, for the present. However," he went on, "lately I've had a touch of real excitement, and this will merely add to it. Excuse me for a moment."

And with that, he left the room.

I heard low talking in the back of the house and then the tread of footsteps upon stairs somewhere beyond the wall in which the hearth was set. I stepped to the fire to warm myself and turned over the book to observe that it was indeed *Paradise Lost.*

Once more, I heard footsteps—now descending—and returned the volume to its original position upon the table. As I looked up, Clark reappeared from the back of the house.

"I've told my gran and Margit that I'm taking you to Dunfeardon," he said.

"I do have some money that I can—"

"The thrill will be more than enough pay for me, sir," he insisted, motioning toward the book. "Beside this and the events of the past two days, even Satan there can't hold a candle. Just a few moments more while I change clothes, please."

The innkeeper disappeared yet again, and I slowly cast my eye about the room, taking in its homespun quality and cosy air. After a moment, I noticed that an old woman had materialised from the back of the inn. Almost at once, the young man stepped around her and into the room. He was dressed in boots and a long coat, goggles upon his forehead.

"My grandmother is already in bed, and Margit here will tend to things while I am gone," he said, indicating the woman, who did not smile as she was introduced to me. "Shall we go, then?"

"Yes, of course. This is awfully kind of you," I said again as the young man strode to the door. He held it open for me to pass on ahead and out into the night.

"I've done rather a lot these past two days," he said cheerfully. "After two weeks with no visitors, I'm suddenly in the midst of one adventure after another." He closed the door behind him and, in the moonlight, directed me to a shed in the distance.

"And what adventures have those been?" I asked idly.

As we approached the shed, the innkeeper said, "For one, I've helped a man from South Africa, a mining magnate from Kimberley.[60] He had been pursued by a gang of illegal diamond buyers across the Kalahari into German Africa, assaulted and nearly killed on board the ship bringing him to Britain—and an associate of his was murdered in London to boot. I read a bit about that killing myself in the newspaper," he proclaimed while opening the door of the shed to reveal the dim outline of a motor bicycle within.

"A nasty business it was," he declared. "As I told him myself, all pure Rider Haggard and Conan Doyle."

"Well, the parts about the Kalahari and Africa sound like pure Rider Haggard, to be sure," I said primly, my interest in the young man's story suddenly deepening.

By this time, the innkeeper had pulled the vehicle out of the shed. It appeared a sturdy contraption, with a sidecar as promised.

"And what became of this South African?" I said earnestly, for I knew who that South African man must have been. "When did you last see him?"

[60] Kimberley was a focal point of the diamond business in South Africa.

The man paused in his preparation of the motor bicycle and turned to face me in the moonlight. For the first time, his expression seemed one of suspicion.

"Why would you be asking about that?" he said in a voice that confirmed my perception of his changed mood. "Coming here as you have, on foot and at this hour, I thought you an honest man and not one who might be connected with the two that were chasing my mining magnate earlier today."

"What two men?"

"My, curiouser and curiouser you become." He stepped toward me, arms at his side, and I thought I saw his hands formed into fists.

"Yes, I am pursuing your South African friend as well," I said abruptly, deciding now to brook no dishonesty on my part. "I pursue him, but as a friend and ally."

The innkeeper halted in his advance upon me, and he lifted his chin, his eyes narrowing. "And how is that?"

"This is not about diamonds," I told the young man. I reached into my jacket pocket, a gesture that appeared to give my companion alarm, and so I moved my hands back to my side. "May I show you a paper?" I asked calmly. "It is a letter of introduction to Sir Harry Christie, on official stationery, from a high government official."

"Truly?" The man's voice was neither sceptical nor credulous.

"I speak the truth," I said. "Shall I give you the paper, so that you may see for yourself?"

"Perhaps." He stepped closer to me. "Yes," Clark said after a moment. "Yes, show me this letter of yours, then."

I slowly pulled the paper from my jacket pocket and handed it him. Eyes straining in the moonlight, the young man read the letter. He gave it back to me and then spent a moment in thought.

"Well," Ewan Clark said at length, "will we get you into the sidecar, then?"

The innkeeper had a spare set of goggles, which I donned after reversing my tweed cap. Then, astride the vehicle, the young man started up his motor bicycle, producing a rough din far in excess of that emitted by my own automobile, of which I thought briefly, safe and sound back in London.

"Here we go, sir!" cried my companion, and with that we set off into the night, out to the road and then in a northerly direction, toward Dunfeardon and Sir Harry Christey.

CHAPTER SEVEN: FISHING IN BERKSHIRE

The innkeeper's motor bicycle pulled up at the door of Sir Harry Christey's residence just before the hour of three in the morning, after a tortuous journey during which we twice lost our way and each time angered local residents by waking them to ask for directions. At length, however, I had the satisfaction of arriving at my desired destination, albeit much later than I had originally intended. Still, I held high hopes that my true quarry, Richard Hannay, was within reach. I knocked on the door loudly and without reservation, for Ewan Clark's motor bicycle was still running, and I was certain that it alone had caught the attention of Sir Harry's household.

"You are certain you wish to remain?" I called to my companion, who sat astride his vehicle. "I doubt my reception will be a warm one at first."

"I will stay until you are received one way or the other," he said. "If a hasty retreat is called for, you need only hop back into the sidecar, and we'll scoot from here as quickly as we can."

I smiled wanly in the dark at the innkeeper and then was enveloped in light as the door opened behind me. Turning round, I beheld none other than Sir Harry Christey, whose speech I had endured but hours earlier. He had changed clothes since the rally, but the fact that he was attired at all in the middle of the night caught me up short.

"Yes?" he said in a quiet but assertive voice, glancing at the motor bicycle before once more fixing his eyes upon me. "What do you do, coming here in this manner? It is not yet dawn, sir."

"I seek the man named Richard Hannay," I said at once. "Is he here, Sir Harry?"

"I am acquainted with no Richard Hannay," he replied in a tone that made me believe him instantly. "And I do not believe I know you, either. How do you come to be so familiar with me?"

I then realised that I had gotten my greeting completely backward, and fumbled in my jacket pocket for the letter of introduction. After a moment, I held it before him.

"I am here on instructions from your godfather, Sir Walter Bullivant," I said. "I believe this will present me properly."

Sir Harry took the folded paper with reservation and bent toward the light from within while opening it. He read it with deliberation and, when finished, turned back to face me.

"Well, I am pleased to meet you, Dr. Watson," he announced. "Is, perchance, that fellow on the motor bicycle Sherlock Holmes?"

"*Doctor* Watson? Great Hannah!" shrieked the innkeeper behind me. "You are *that* Watson?"

"I am," I said, not turning round.

"The one that Conan Doyle writes about?"

I stood there in the warm entrance to Sir Harry's residence and sighed. "That is one way of putting it" was all I chose to say, given the state of affairs at the moment.

"I'm afraid I lied to you, Doctor, just a moment ago," declared Sir Harry. "Hannay has been with me since late this afternoon. We attended a political rally—"

"I know," I said hurriedly. "I was also there. I attempted to approach the two of you, but the crowd was such that I could not reach you before you had departed."

"And you've come here—" he glanced at Clark, who had shut down his vehicle's motor and come up to stand beside me—"by somewhat unconventional means in the middle of the night, all for the sake of Hannay?"

"Indeed, I have. Is he inside?" I enquired anxiously.

"I am afraid he left less than an hour ago."

"To where?" I asked. "It is imperative that I find him!"

Sir Harry seemed oddly unmoved by my urgency. "I rather doubt you would be able to do that, Dr. Watson. Come in. You too, if you like," he told the innkeeper as he stepped back to allow us to enter.

My companion apologised for the state of his dress, but Sir Harry waved him off. I introduced the two, and then our host led us through the house and on into a large, cheerful smoking room, whose dying fire still crackled intermittently. We sat down beneath deer's heads and old prints that lined the walls. Sir Harry brought the fire back to life and then invited us to sit in armchairs.

"You know all about Hannay, then?" he said straightaway. "Scudder, the milkman, the notebook, all of it?"

"I know of Scudder and the milkman," I answered. "The notebook has been speculation up to this point."

"I should take it, then, that you are not aware of the assassination plans."

I looked Sir Harry squarely in the eye. "No. Did Hannay glean something from Scudder's notebook?"

"Yes. Agents of a foreign power intend to murder Karolides, the Greek premier. It is to happen a few days from now, when the fellow visits London."

"Good God," I declared. "Thankfully, there is ample time to forestall the crime. You said Hannay left but an hour ago. Where is he headed?"

Sir Harry gestured to a curtained window.

"Out there," he said. "Somewhere among the hills. I sent him forth upon an old bicycle—not motorised like yours," he added to Ewan Clark, whose eyes by this time had increased twofold in diameter. "Hannay proposed to hide in the wild for a short while, and then try for London to warn of the plot.

"I have just been writing a letter to my godfather, Sir Walter," he said, indicating several pages and a pen lying upon a table. "I promised Hannay I would do so." He tilted his head and contemplated me. "I suspect I should now give that letter to you, rather than post it. I take it you can convey it to Sir Walter at his cottage near Aldermaston."[61]

"Where, did you say?"

"The town is in Berkshire, on the Kennet. He goes there for midsummer and the week after."[62]

"I doubt he is there now," I said, though I recalled one of Bullivant's contact addresses as being in in Berkshire. "Ironically, I should think the Hannay matter would be keeping him in London."

---

[61] In *The Thirty-Nine Steps*, the town is identified as Artinswell, which appears to be a fictional name.

[62] According to John Buchan's account in *The Thirty-Nine Steps*, Bullivant's godson tells Hannay that Sir Walter goes to his Berkshire cottage for Whitsuntide, the week following Whitsunday, which is another name for the Christian festival of Pentecost. In 1914, Whitsunday fell on May 31, and so Whitsuntide would have been the first week of June. The summer solstice, on the other hand, fell on June 21 in 1914. This discrepancy is relevant to the issue of dating events in Watson's narrative.

“Well,” said Sir Harry, “I suggest you get him to keep to his usual plan, for the cottage in Berkshire is where Hannay intends to go first, to seek out my godfather. To identify himself, he will give Twisdon as his name and be whistling ‘Annie Laurie.’”

I leaned back in my chair, suddenly feeling the weight of my fatigue.

“Sir,” said the innkeeper, bending in my direction, “are you all right?”

“It is just a momentary weariness. Sir Harry,” I said, “you are certain we could not find Hannay out in the countryside?”

“I received the very strong impression that he is skilled at fieldcraft,” said Sir Harry. “And tough as nails, too. Why, the man showed me some African native trick of his: he tossed that hunting knife on display over there and caught the damned thing in his lips, by God.”

Ewan Clark chuckled. “It’s like yet another detail out of Rider Haggard,” he said. “But then, listen to me talk,” the young man went on, “sitting here, as I am, next to someone flesh and blood out of Conan Doyle.”

I was numb to the bone, and so I merely addressed Sir Harry once more. “Can you give me detailed directions to Sir Walter’s Berkshire residence?” I asked.

“Why, of course,” the man replied. “I’ve visited there often enough during my life—even as a boy, I stayed there with my family. It’s a pretty place, with a lawn running down to the stream, and lilacs and—what are they?—oh, yes, guilder-rose lining the path. Quite often—”

“If you can write it all down—the cottage’s appearance, its location, everything—it would assist me greatly,” I interjected.

"Of course," said Sir Harry. "Straightaway. And I will rouse one of the servants to prepare some small meal for you, for you appear rather in, Dr. Watson."

"Thank you," I said, gesturing toward Clark. "I am not certain if also—"

"I trust you will not sup alone," said Sir Harry. "You wish to join him?" he asked, glancing at the innkeeper, who in turn looked my way.

"I believe we should both appreciate some small bit of food," I replied at once, smiling at the young man who had delivered me here.

And so it was that the two of us partook of collops and black bun, washed down with some sugarelly,[63] while Sir Harry looked on, slowly nursing a glass of wine. I freely related to both him and the innkeeper more of my own story, revealing only those parts that corroborated what Sir Harry already knew of the affair. The innkeeper hung on my every word, and our host simply sat back, glass in hand, nodding now and then.

"Well," said Sir Harry at length, "I suppose we must start you off for Berkshire and trust that you will be there to greet Mr. Hannay when he arrives. Are you concerned, Doctor, about your associate, Mr. Holmes?"

"I do not know how to respond," I declared. "Obviously, he has not yet crossed paths with Hannay, and I've received no word from him. Still, I long ago came to trust in the man without reservation, and despite the passage of time, that trust has not diminished. He will reappear, I should think."

"And in glory," added the innkeeper, "as at Dartmoor."

"What?" I said.

---

[63] Collops are slices of meat. Sugarelly, or liquorice water, is a soft drink that was popular in Britain at the time.

"The Baskerville case," explained the young man. "Have you not read it, or recall it from your own experience? Surely Mr. Holmes will turn up here as he did then, and victorious to boot?"

"Ah yes," I replied patiently. "I trust that to happen eventually. Sooner rather than later, however, would be better."

"In any event," said Sir Harry, "how may I assist you in getting to Berkshire?"

"If you can transport me to Dumfries, I will be able to reunite with Captain Harper. He can then fly me down to Aldermaston, assuming that additional fuel has arrived, as he said it would."

"Excellent. When do you wish to start?"

It was already getting on past four in the morning, and though I had had no sleep for close to a day, I knew what my answer must be.

"Shortly," I replied. "I expect if we leave soon, it will be light by the time we arrive in Dumfries."

"Very well, then," said Sir Harry, finishing his wine in one gulp and setting the glass down. He rose to his feet. "I will change and then bring out the motor."

"And may I accompany you?" asked Ewan Clark. "I'd very much enjoy it."

"Two additional men are needed to help start the aeroplane," I said with a gentle smile. "I expect both of you will be invaluable in that regard."

"That's most grand!" Clark declared.

"Indeed it is," agreed Sir Harry.

§ § §

In less than a quarter hour, we found ourselves before the Dunfeardon manor house. My host had supplied me with a spare riding coat, which supplemented the goggles the innkeeper had already given me.

"I know the way to Dumfries, but I will follow you, sir," said the innkeeper.

"Very well. Ready to step aboard, Doctor?" Sir Harry asked.

Wordlessly, I opened the passenger door of the motorcar, prompting Sir Harry to smile as he opened the door on his side, and the two of us got into the automobile.

We rode along winding stretches of road before reaching the main thoroughfare that led back to Dumfries. With the innkeeper on his motor bicycle keeping a distance from our rear, Sir Harry and I engaged in only occasional conversation, all of it pertaining to the local flora and fauna. We encountered no one else upon the road until we were perhaps halfway to our destination, when, in the brilliance of our lights, I saw a lone bicyclist approaching.

Sir Harry immediately slowed the automobile so that, I supposed, we might obtain a revealing look at the oncoming rider. The cyclist, however, proved to be merely a local man, who cursed us most vehemently for the noise and glare of our vehicle.

At length, as the horizon behind us began to glow warmly, we entered the outskirts of Dumfries. I am certain we roused several of the inhabitants while passing through town, though by now several men were out on foot and we encountered two carts while making our way to Constable Taylor's cottage.

Taylor and his wife were already up and about, and it was the young policeman himself who opened the door before Sir Harry and I had even debarked from the automobile. Taylor approached us as the innkeeper pulled up in his motor bicycle.

"I take it you found Sir Harry Christey at last," the constable said to me in a low voice. "The wife and I were a mite worried last night when you dinna return." He looked at Sir Harry and bade him greeting, also giving Ewan Clark a friendly halloa as the innkeeper stepped from his vehicle and pulled off his goggles. "I don't know that we can sit you all together, but I can offer you all a bit of breakfast if—"

"I am safe and all is well," I replied hurriedly. "However, it is imperative that I depart presently. Forgive my abruptness, Constable Taylor, but have you my valise still in your possession?"

"That I do, sir. My wife had taken upon herself to clean your shirt from the other day, and your bag has been repacked, if you don't mind the liberty taken."

"Not at all. Might you fetch it? And thank your wife for—"

I stopped, having noticed Mrs. Taylor, now standing in the still open doorway of the cottage.

"Is all well with you, Mr. Price?" she called out.

Sir Harry and Ewan Clark both glanced at me oddly.

"And who is Mr. Price, Dr. Watson?" asked the former, causing both Charles Taylor and his wife to now give me a look of surprise as well.

"Come," I said after an awkward pause. "Let us all go inside. I will fetch my valise and explain myself, truthfully, once and for all."

Minutes later, I was once more beside Sir Harry Christey, riding south along the Abbey Road. The innkeeper followed us in his motor bicycle, with Charlie Taylor beside him—the constable had declared his desire to accompany us to Captain Harper and the aeroplane, indicating his decided preference for riding in the sidecar.

The sun was just clearing hills to the east when we pulled up beside the open field where Captain Harper's biplane still rested. Smoke rose straight up from a small fire tended by the pilot, who turned and waved to us. As we approached, I saw that the officer was preparing a hearty set of eggs and meat in a large skillet supported over the fire.

"People have been most generous," the pilot said as we approached him on foot. "I've almost been expecting someone to drop off a four-poster."

"Has the aeroplane been refuelled?" I asked immediately.

"Oh yes, it has. Boys from Montrose arrived late yesterday in a horse-drawn army lorry and topped her off."[64]

Quickly, I introduced Sir Harry and Ewan Clark to the airman and revealed to Captain Harper that Richard Hannay had been the object of my journey—and disclosing my own true identity at the same time. I told him of the need to fly to Aldermaston without delay.

The pilot took the revelations in stride, casually tending his skillet as he listened to my confession. Removing the iron from the fire, he set it aside and cast a glance upward.

"So may I have my breakfast before we go aloft, Dr. Watson?" he asked.

"Of course," I said.

"Do you wish to join me?" the officer asked of us. "I have no objection, though there is a shortage of plate and utensils."

---

[64] Located in Forfarshire—now known as Angus—in Scotland, Montrose station was the first operational military aerodrome in the United Kingdom. At the time, it would have been the base for the Royal Flying Corps' No. 2 Squadron. It continued in operation after the creation of the Royal Air Force but was closed in 1952.

"That would render your ration quite intolerably small," said Sir Harry. "You'll need your strength to convey Dr. Watson south."

And so Captain Harper made short work of the eggs and meat, and then quickly disbanded his camp, entrusting Charlie Taylor with the task of returning to their owners the skillet and other few small items that had been loaned him by local residents during my absence.

After donning my flying clothes, I and the other three men joined the pilot in moving the aeroplane into position. Stones were employed as improvised chocks, and Captain Harper instructed my other companions in how to assist in starting the engine.

The cylinders were injected with fuel using the syringe that we had brought from Hulton, and all appeared ready, until a controversy arose concerning who would actually set the wooden propeller into motion. At length, three blades of grass were pulled from the field by Captain Harper, who shortened one of them and then had Constable Taylor, Ewan Clark, and Sir Harry each pick from his fist.

The innkeeper was the winner and cheerfully approached the aeroplane, ready to do his duty. After brief discussion, the constable agreed to grasp the innkeeper's belt from behind while Sir Harry held the tailskid, and so with that arrangement we were ready to depart, now before a small crowd that had slowly gathered in the quiet morning.

With me once more in the forward cockpit and Captain Harper sitting behind in his, the innkeeper gave the propeller a strong heave. Almost at once, he was yanked free of the blade, which made a single rotation and then stopped.

"She's been sitting for quite some time," the pilot called out. "It will take perhaps several tries. Again?"

Once more, Clark stepped forward and pulled at the blade, again to no effect. He was about to take hold of the propeller a third time when Charlie Taylor gently stopped him.

"Here, man," the constable said in a friendly tone. "If it's going to take several heaves, we should all have a chance for a go, eh?"

Light-heartedly, the innkeeper raised his hands. "Why not?" he said. "Tis only fair. We'll take turns then?"

"We'll rotate positions, lads," suggested Sir Harry.

The policeman approached the aeroplane and reached for the blade as Bullivant's godson grasped his belt from behind and the innkeeper now held the tail. A third pull proved to not be the charm, either, though the propeller made almost two rotations before stopping.

"My turn now, chaps," said Sir Harry Christey. "Here, let's trade off again."

Ewan Clark appeared reluctant to take hold of the squire's belt, but Sir Harry coaxed the innkeeper to do so.

"It's all in good fun, lads, eh?" Sir Harry reminded us. "I'd rather you pulled me back than leave me to be sliced up by that blade."

This next attempt also was unsuccessful, leading to three more, with each man succeeding the other in giving the propeller a turn. By now, the trio were approaching the task as a frolic, and laughter erupted after each disappointing try.

"I wish our mechanics had half as much fun as this bunch," said Captain Harper cheerily from behind my back.

The rotation had come round once more to Ewan Clark, who took hold of the blade and began to chuckle again. Then, calming himself, he said with a smile, "This time for St. Andrew," and gave the propeller a mighty pull.

As Charlie Taylor hoisted him away, the engine finally caught hold. Loud coughing and staccato bursts erupted in front of me, and I felt once more the machine-made gale press against my face as I caught the aroma of burning oil. The constable and innkeeper danced for joy, and I waved for them to carefully remove the stones from the front of the wheels as Sir Harry let go the tailskid.

All three of our companions ran quickly back toward the road to join the assembly of onlookers, which had grown to perhaps a dozen other men and women, as well as a quartet of children. Then I felt myself in motion and stared ahead as our aeroplane rolled down the expanse of field, its course initially parallel to the Abbey Road.

Glancing to the side, I saw some of the roadside audience—all of them men and children—running in the same direction. The craft began to veer to the left, as had been its habit each time we had taken to the air previously. Wheels hit ruts and bumps in the grassy field, and then the aeroplane lifted from earth, and once more the captain and I were airborne.

As the engine stuttered, we rose above the trees, circled round and then, while passing over the waving crowd, Cecil Harper dipped our right wing in salute before turning south toward England.

We followed the Nith once more, this time downstream to its mouth, crossed the Solway Firth a second time, and then, as we approached the coastline, I suddenly became conscious of my weariness. I had been awake continuously for more than a day, and now that I was sitting, albeit in the midst of noise and slipstream, I could not shake off drowsiness.

After what seemed like mere seconds, I felt myself being jabbed.

I lifted my head with a jerk and looked down from the cockpit, thinking with disbelief that I espied the profile of Birmingham again. Understanding after another moment that my eyes did not betray me, I realised that I had fallen asleep.[65] I received another poke in my back and, turning round as best I could, saw that Captain Harper was motioning that we were going to land just outside the city, as we had during our journey north.

We touched down in what I thought to be the same field where we had stopped previously, a conjecture that became all the more likely when I saw in the distance the familiar figure of Captain Edward Ashley Tate standing beside a motor-lorry with the same two mechanics as before. I immediately recalled Ashley Tate's pledge that he and his men would be awaiting us every day should we return, and I greeted the three of them heartily, as did Captain Harper. Our craft was refuelled and then, assisted by the mechanics and Captain Ashley Tate, we once more took to the air.

We flew on and on, for the most part following in reverse the path we had taken from Hulton. As we once more passed over Oxford, however, Captain Harper steered us due south rather than to the southeast, so that we were now headed not for our point of origin but rather Aldermaston, which lay some twenty miles beyond. Shortly, we espied what I knew must be the River Kennet, with the village just beyond. An open field lay in the distance, and I pointed in its direction. Captain Harper responded with an upward gesture of his gloved thumb, and we began our descent.

---

[65] The editor has not been able to find any documentation relating to the speculation about to be given, but it is possible that, with his unintended nap, Dr. Watson became the first person to sleep aboard an aircraft in flight.

The landing was far rougher than those we had experienced before, but our plane came to rest undamaged with the pair of us unharmed. As the propeller stopped spinning, I pulled the goggles from my eyes and took a deep breath, three names burning in my mind as I clawed myself out of the cockpit: Hannay and Holmes uppermost, with that of the threatened Greek premier, Karolides, following right behind.

I doffed my flying clothes and prepared to set out along the banks of the Kennet, where I knew Sir Walter Bullivant's cottage to be. From his godson's directions and my estimation of our landing point, I reasoned that my course should be west along the stream.

"I do not wish to be encumbered by my valise," I told Cecil Harper. "I trust you will guard it?"

"Of course," said the pilot. "As I will guard the plane." He looked around. "I reckon that a small band of locals will eventually gather here as at Dumfries, so once more I urge you to not worry yourself on my account. I'll stand here prepared to assist as I am called to, Dr. Watson."

I nodded humbly. "I do hope, Captain Harper, that—"

"Cecil, sir," he insisted. "As you're no longer in the service yourself."

I smiled. "Very well. Cecil it is. And I confess it is more satisfying to have you know me by my true name. But, to get on with the job at hand, I will go in search of Sir Walter's residence. Once I locate his cottage, I shall return and retrieve my baggage, and perhaps you as well, should some of the inhabitants pledge to watch over your plane."

"What will be will be, Doctor."

And so I bade the officer a temporary farewell and set out along the water's edge, proceeding upstream. After perhaps a quarter hour, I found myself approaching a road that, for a short distance at least, paralleled the bank, and so I took to tramping along its gravelly length for my own convenience. Several minutes after gaining the thoroughfare, I heard a motorcar at my back and stepped onto the grass. The automobile passed me, throwing up a whirling cloud of dust, and then stopped about fifty yards beyond where I stood.

As I walked toward the vehicle, I saw the passenger get out. He was clad in standard attire: a long coat, driving cap, gloves, and goggles. The fellow stood by the motor, still manned by a chauffeur, and gazed intently in my direction before waving one hand.

"Halloa, Doctor!" he shouted, and I trod toward the motorcar more briskly than before, recognising the voice and, a moment later, the face of Sir Walter Bullivant.

"And what is your reaction to Holmes's silence?" asked Sir Walter as he lit a cigar in his study.

I began stuffing my pipe with Arcadia mix, waiting for the svelte butler to clear away our coffee cups. My companion understood the reason for my hesitation in answering and smiled gently as I waited for his servant to leave the room.

Then, finally alone with the spymaster, I leaned back, holding my match in abeyance. "My reaction, as I suppose it always has been with him, Sir Walter, is to wait and accept what transpires. I rarely heard from Holmes during the past two years, while he was on assignment for you, and given the nature of our present endeavour, it does not surprise that our friend has failed to appear. I assume him to be intent upon the chase."

I stopped, noticing an odd smile on Bullivant's lips.

"You term him *our* friend," the man said, studying his cigar. "I am not certain that Holmes views me as such."

"He has voiced great respect for you."

"Respect and friendship are not one and the same." He shrugged. "I perhaps have demanded too much of him."

"It is he who demands too much of himself. And yet," I said, "he never fails to disappoint others. He will not disappoint in this instance, either. He will appear—" I said, recalling the words of the young innkeeper. "He will appear in glory."

Just then we heard a knock upon the study door.

"Enter," said Sir Walter.

It was Cecil Harper. "I do hope I'm not disturbing you, sirs."

"Of course not, Captain," said Sir Walter over his shoulder. "The meal was to your satisfaction, I hope?"

"The best I've had in several months," the officer replied, stepping closer. "I appreciate your kindness."

"Nothing's too good for the likes of you, Captain," the spymaster declared. "It was an honour to send my man to fetch you in the motor."

"And it's an honour for me to be your guest, Sir Walter. I'm wondering, however, if I should return to my aircraft and fly her back to Hulton. Enough fuel remains for that jaunt, and I get the impression that Dr. Watson will be under your wing from now on."

Bullivant looked at me, and I returned a questioning expression.

"Yes," said Sir Walter. "In point of fact, the doctor and I will be taking up positions here for the duration, until Mr. Hannay or Mr. Holmes—or both—cross this threshold. You might as well return to your squadron. Shall I call my man to ferry you back to the aeroplane?"

"That would be appreciated, sir, along with another you might spare, so as to assist with starting the engine."

"That can be done," replied Sir Walter, who rose from his chair. I immediately followed his lead. "Excuse me, please, while I fetch my chauffeur."

Cigar in hand, Bullivant strolled from the room, leaving me with my still unlit pipe and Captain Harper, to whom I extended a hand. "I cannot adequately express my gratitude to you, Cecil. Without you, I should have been nowhere."

"All in the line of duty, Doctor," the young pilot said, grasping my hand. "As I've said before, sir, it will be a pleasure to see you once more."

"I'm certain that we will meet again, though perhaps in less pressing circumstances."

Sir Walter returned with his chauffeur, who took Captain Harper from the house and drove him back to the aeroplane in the company of the gardener—each man, I supposed, destined to do his part when the craft was started up for the flight back to Hulton.

Sir Walter and I passed the rest of the afternoon in the study, discussing at first fly fishing before the subject shifted once more to the matter of Richard Hannay and German spy rings.

"The business has certainly grown in depth, breadth, and complexity," Bullivant said. "When Mycroft suggested recruiting his brother two years ago, I could not foresee what would emerge: Von Bork, Scudder, Hannay, and this Black Stone business."

"Not to speak of Cerberus, which may end by encompassing all that you have just mentioned," I added.

"And perhaps even more beyond that," my host replied.

“Yes,” I reflected. “Perhaps we have only plumbed the shallowest end, Sir Walter.”

“Bullivant,” he said.

“What?”

“Call me Bullivant,” the spymaster said genially. “That’s what my friends call me, rather than Sir Walter.”

We spent a moment looking at one another, and then I said, “Yes, as you wish.” Then, after a moment, I added, “And I may be Watson to you, if you should desire.”

He smiled, but then his face assumed a troubled look.

“There is something I must confess to you,” he said.

I watched as he struggled to find the words, or perhaps the courage, to speak his full mind. At last, he began.

“During those first days, after you had discovered that Hannay was mixed up in all this, you attempted to find Mycroft at the Diogenes Club.”

“Yes,” I said, recalling how I had related that fact to those assembled at Safety House. “I sought him in vain.”

“You also asked for me at the club that day,” Sir Walter declared. “You did not mention that fact, however, when we met to plan our response to Hannay’s flight from London.”

“No, I supposed it was not relevant.”

“But you saw me at the club, did you not?”

Once more we stared at one another. Then, nodding, I said quietly, “Yes. You were—”

“In an armchair, reading,” Bullivant said. “Through the glass, from the corner of my eye, I in turn saw you enter the Stranger’s Room. Immediately, I left through another door and stood there, beyond its frame, until the attendant entered. I waved the man over and asked him—by means of a written note, of course—what or whom you were seeking. His reply was that you wished to see either Mycroft or myself."

"And you did not respond," I said evenly, before taking a deep breath. "I knew that I had seen you, however. I could only surmise that you chose not to present yourself because—"

"Because at that time, I had no faith in you. I thought your attention would be an annoyance and nothing more."

"I can understand," I said. "I am but a layman, and perhaps an awkward one at that, in your world of espionage, Sir Walter."

"Again: Bullivant, if you please."

I nodded. "Bullivant."

"There is something more I must tell you, however," the man said. "The next day, you travelled to Safety House to deliver the note that finally alerted us to Hannay's importance."

"Yes," I said. "That is also common knowledge."

"What is not common knowledge is that I happened to be there alone, in the house, at the time," confessed Sir Walter. "While going over several recent despatches, I heard a patterned ring. Going to the door to look through the peephole, I saw you standing there. I could have opened the door, but I chose not to do so. And so you slipped a note through the letterbox."

I put down my now empty glass.

"I picked up your message from the carpet," Bullivant said. "I saw that it was addressed both to me and to Mycroft, and I should have read it then and there, but I did not, for I could not imagine you having written anything of value upon that sheet of paper, John. With incredible stupidity, I dropped it, unopened, into Mycroft's box and left minutes later. Had I only possessed the confidence in you then that I have now, I'd have read that note and—"

"Such errors occur."

"This one should not have happened," he said mournfully. "It was the third time I ignored you, to the detriment of us all, and our country."

"Let us not dwell on that now, Bullivant," I said with forced cheer. "Instead, we should gather as much hope as we can. You have already alerted Mycroft to the assassination plot against Karolides—that threat is forestalled. We now have only to await the safe return of Holmes and Hannay, and Scudder's notebook with them."

"Yes, you are right" he said, casting a thoughtful gaze in my direction. "As I have learnt at great cost, you are a man whose words should be heeded, Watson. We shall wait."

We found the execution of that advice far harder than its suggestion, however.

A day passed, and neither Hannay nor Holmes appeared. There followed a second and a third day, and then I found myself completing a week's stay at Bullivant's cottage with no word from either man.

Long before we reached that anxious milestone, Sir Walter and I had agreed to submerge our concerns in daily trampings to the River Kennet in search of trout. Our success was such that we dined on fish every night, though Bullivant's cook was resourceful, dishing up a different culinary variation on genus Salmo for each successive catch.

We were now, however, within days of entering the month of July, and it was difficult not to believe that the signs pointed to us never seeing

Richard Hannay again, though I could not allow my thoughts to include Sherlock Holmes in that grim augury. My only hope lay, paradoxically, in the continuing absence of my friend, for I could not help but believe that while the detective remained elsewhere, he was exerting himself in a cause not yet lost.

Thus it was that I set out with Sir Walter for yet another fishing excursion, this time on a Sunday evening. The midsummer air was heavy, yet sweet with the aroma of lime and chestnut, and lilacs were bursting with blossoms. We started at a point where the beds of water buttercups were especially dense and then slowly worked our way toward a bridge, nearly reaching it as dusk began to filter into the sky. Breathing deeply, I realised the scented evening was bringing me no joy. It was then that I heard whistling.

"Listen!" said Bullivant at once. He quickly lifted his delicate ten-foot rod and grasped my arm with his free hand. "Do you hear that?"

"'Annie Laurie,' is it not?" I said.

"It is," said Sir Walter, his voice now urgent. "Indeed, it is! Come, Watson!"

Grasping my own split-cane rod, I followed him up the bank toward one end of the bridge, where I now espied the silhouette of the whistler who had attracted our attention.

In his untidy flannels, a canvas bag slung onto his shoulder, Sir Walter began to whistle as well, joining the newcomer in 'Annie Laurie.'

I gripped the wide brim of my hat, twin to Bullivant's, and followed my friend up the last portioni of the slope and onto a pathway leading to the bridge. By the time I had reached the top, I saw that the stranger had paused to watch our ascent from the stream.

Sir Walter nodded to the man. In the gathering darkness, I could not see the stranger's face clearly, but it was evident to me that he was bearded and rather dishevelled, in boots caked with mud and a shirt lacking any collar. The dim figure I saw before me now resembled nothing like the man I had encountered at Portland Place or seen on that platform in Brattleburn.

Bullivant leaned his rod against the bridge. "The water's very clear here, is it not?" he said, addressing the newcomer in an odd tone, almost one of familiarity. "I back our Kennet here any day against the Test."[66]

"Yes," said the stranger, taking a step closer to us. "I've been eager to admire both it and the fish that inhabit it."

I took a sharp intake of breath, for I recognised the voice at once.

Sir Walter turned and looked down at the stream, pointing toward it. "Well then, will you look at that big fellow," he said, indicating a huge trout lurking near the reeds.

"I don't see him," said the newcomer.

"There," declared Bullivant. "Just above that stickle."

"Oh yes," said the newcomer. In the twilight, I thought I saw an odd smile play across his face. "You might swear he was a black stone."

Standing beside Sir Walter, I saw a smile appear on the spymaster's face as well, just before he broke into another bar of "Annie Laurie." Then, still staring at the stream, he stopped his tune and asked of the stranger, "Twisdon's the name, isn't it?"

"No," said the man, taking me aback. Then he abruptly he corrected himself. "I mean yes, of course."

---

66 The River Test is in Hampshire.

“It’s a wise conspirator who knows his own name,” Bullivant jovially observed, grinning broadly while we watched a moorhen emerge from under the bridge. There was suddenly a rumble, and I turned round to see a dogcart approaching.[67]

Sir Walter’s mood changed abruptly. “I call it disgraceful,” he said in a loud voice. “Disgraceful that an able-bodied man like you should dare to beg. You can get a meal from my kitchen, sir, but you’ll get no money from me.”

Hannay stepped off the path to allow the cart to pass. The driver, a young man, raised his whip to Sir Walter, who acknowledged the salute. Then, as the cart reached the far side of the bridge, Bullivant picked up his rod.

“That is my house,” he said to Hannay, pointing back a hundred yards or more toward the white gate of his cottage. “Wait five minutes and then go round to the back door.”

And with that, Sir Walter motioned for me to follow him back up the slope to his residence. We quickly strode through the gate and on into the cottage, where Bullivant instructed a servant to attend to Hannay at the back entrance.

“I’ve told my man to lay out several sets of clothing,” he said as we shed our hats and canvas bags. Sir Walter accepted my pole. “My godson shows up every now and then, of course, and has garments stored here. Indeed, I’m certain that the rather worn and filthy tweeds Hannay was wearing just now came from Harry. I expect it will take our guest a while

[67] Despite its name, a dogcart is a vehicle drawn by a single horse.

to shave, bathe, and make himself presentable. Shall we also change and then meet in the dining room, Watson?"

"I will be ready as quickly as I can, Bullivant. Of course, I should have wished to ask him the most important question at present."

"And what is that?"

"If he had seen Sherlock Holmes."

Bullivant looked at me with compassion and nodded. "Yes, of course. We shall get to that as soon as possible."

Some minutes later, I sat at a round table lit with silver candles, Sir Walter Bullivant beside me. Across from us, bisecting the longer arc between our seats, was an empty chair.

"At long last, we will have Richard Hannay and all that he knows, Watson," the spymaster sighed. "Not just that which pertains to the threat against Karolides."

"Yes," I replied. "But when will Sherlock Holmes be joining us at the table?"

"I believe that can be accomplished presently," said the detective in a cheerful tone, "if only one of you will be so kind as to pull up a chair for me."

I bolted to my feet and turned round to see Holmes standing at the doorway, dressed in a set of brown tweeds a bit too large for his thin frame.

Noticing my expression at the sight of his attire, Holmes smiled and stepped aside.

"I apologise for my appearance," he said, "but I fear the better set of clothes was already spoken for."

From behind my friend stepped Richard Hannay, now clean-shaven, groomed, and clothed in evening dress that fitted him to a tee.

"I'm more obliged to you than I can say," the South African declared to all three of us. "Especially to you, Mr. Holmes, as I've repeated constantly between Galloway and here. I'm bound, moreover, to make things clear and right—with respect to the entire matter. I have so much to tell you, but I won't be surprised if you kick me out," Hannay said to Bullivant.

As the former fugitive spoke, however, my eyes were fixed upon Sherlock Holmes, who gently walked into the room with a slight limp, a sly smile still upon his face.

"So what say you, Sir Walter?" he asked. "Will this man be thrown out?"

"Certainly not!" replied the spymaster with relish. "Moreover, he will be fed, and fed well. Don't let anything interfere with your appetite, man," he told Hannay. "We can talk about everything after dinner. And Holmes, you are most correct in pointing out my lack of manners. It is a joy to behold you, and we must give you a chair at the table without delay."

I, in the meanwhile, had already started across the room to fetch one.

"My journey north from St. Pancras station was quite uneventful, as I should have expected," said Holmes later that evening, while we four all sat in Sir Walter's study, lodged in cluttered comfort amid books, stacks of paper, and trophies.

I sipped my coffee, which came as excellent postscript to a grand meal that had boasted not only champagne but an uncommonly fine port as well. Our earlier conversation at the table had ranged from tiger fish that reputedly catch birds in flight along the Zambesi River to anatomical differences between the manatees of Africa and those of the West Indies. Now, however, our talk was of more serious subjects.

"I believed I had truly little hope of picking up any scent of our fugitive here until I should reach the vicinity of Dumfries," said Holmes, "and indeed, it was at that station that I found his trail. I had adopted the guise of a parson, and in that pose, I idly chatted with several people there. I confess I neither saw you, Watson, nor heard explicit mention of your name."

"That was because I had been rather quickly hauled off to Dumfries Prison after assuming an alias," I replied with mild embarrassment.

"Ha, that is a tale I must hear at some point," my friend genially demanded. "But to continue, I did hear tell of an incident on the slow line north—some episode of an unknown person debarking from a carriage while its train was stopped. Most people's recollections focused upon another man tumbling out because his dog tried to run after the stranger."

"I spoke to that man, the one with the dog," I said.

"As did I," declared Holmes. "The canine was most affectionate."

"Truly?" I said. "I found it rather malevolent."

"Goodness is in the heart of the beholder. In any case, from the testimony of more than one person, I was able to fix upon the spot where the stranger—whom I assumed to be Mr. Hannay—had left the carriage. I took the same line myself that very day and, when the locomotive slowed significantly at a culvert near the area in question, I jumped from the carriage."

"Is that how you acquired the limp?" I asked.

"Very observant, old fellow," Holmes remarked. "And very patient of you to hold that comment in reserve until now. But yes, I confess that I did slightly injure myself when leaving the carriage, though the train was travelling at almost no speed. Still, I was able to hobble at a reasonable clip and wandered off in the direction I had understood Hannay to have taken when leaving the tracks. Very soon, I found evidence of someone's passage through the brush, and I began to follow those marks as far as I could."

"At the time, I was intent on putting as much distance between myself and the train," Hannay interjected. "I wasn't mindful of covering my tracks."

"That was fortunate," Holmes told the man, "for before long, it became clear that you were heading for the mountainous rim off to the northeast."

He leaned back in his armchair and finished his cup of coffee.

"It seemed a logical place for you to go, for it would command a high vantage point from which you might survey the entire moor, all the way back to the rail line as well as south, where the heather gave way to green fields. Bracing myself, I prepared for the long hike ahead of me when, as I paused to watch a golden eagle circle in the sky, I noticed another dark form miming that same motion farther above: a monoplane."

"Yes," said Hannay and I, almost in unison. The South African and I looked at one another and then, as a matched pair, at Holmes.

The detective took a deep breath and nodded. "Since you saw it, Watson, and presumably have already mentioned it to Sir Walter," he said, "perhaps I need not add that, somehow, the sight of that craft making its ominous loops overhead gave me concern. I had left London unaware of any official attempt at aerial reconnaissance to locate Hannay," he said, glancing at Bullivant.

"And none was ordered," the spymaster admitted. "In hindsight, I suppose we could have employed you and your pilot in that manner, Watson. I should have thought of that."

"I was of the opinion that Mr. Hannay would likely be able to elude detection from above," Holmes replied. "Moreover, inspection from the ground is *de rigueur*, and taking a person into custody always requires one to have both feet firmly planted on earth in any case. But we stray from the story. I thought the aeroplane must be piloted by our antagonists, the Germans, and the presence of such a craft there in Scotland in turn required a base of operation.

"I made the assumption that Hannay would also notice the aircraft and, given the relatively barren ground to the north, then decide to head south toward the cover of trees. Thus, I made in that direction as well. In addition, though I knew finding Hannay was an important goal, I also realised that I might accidentally have detected another centre of German espionage operations, which would require investigation. Going south might achieve both objectives, I reasoned."

"And did you locate where the aeroplane was based?" asked Bullivant.

"Not upon that first day. I hiked in its direction, having decided to concern myself directly with Mr. Hannay only if our paths should cross. The aeroplane made its eventual descent too quickly, however, and dropped from view before I was close enough to determine its exact landing area, and so I waited the rest of the day for it to rise again, which it did not.

"Though I could perhaps have camped upon the moor that night, I chose instead to approach a cottage, where a couple and their two sons lived. They were not much for conversation, but their hospitality was more than adequate. I, in return, good-naturedly assisted them in some simple chores. Well fed and having slept soundly that night, I set out the next day with a good pack of supplies from the family and assumed another watch of the sky, which paid off handsomely, for I spotted the monoplane rising within an hour of starting my vigil.

"I did not follow the craft's repeated circling off toward the west, but rather hiked the direction from which I had seen it ascend. It was a land of hills, which broke into ridges separated by dales that were as wide as they were shallow. I found myself in occasional fields of heather, and there was a winding stream I crossed more than once. I came upon a dyke and jumped it, despite a leg that still ached persistently—"

"Perhaps I should examine it presently," I suggested.

"In a while, old fellow. Allow me to continue," insisted Holmes. "I was soon climbing a gentle slope, which I judged part of the highest rise of land in the area. It was there that I came upon a rather well-kept road. I did not follow it but rather hiked alongside a stream, which paralleled the roadway. The bracken was deep there, and the high banks, I felt, would screen me sufficiently from passing motors.

"In time, I came upon a deserted cottage and overgrown garden, beyond which I saw young hay and a stand of wind-blown firs. I infiltrated the trees and walked through them, crossing a small stream, and from the far edge of the woods espied a house, its chimney smoking, some several hundred yards away."

"It looked so innocent and welcoming," said Hannay. "Eventually, I saw it as well," he explained to Bullivant and me.

“I immediately became suspicious when I noticed, in those woods, a wire stretched above the ground,” Holmes said. “I surmised it was part of an alarm system, and that suggested I might indeed have found the German lair. From within, I circumnavigated the stand of firs, again encountering the small stream, and noted that the slope continued upward still more, to a more heavily forested summit. After a moment’s thought, and being most careful of my lines of sight—including that from above—I made my ascent.

“The trees at the top, I found, gave way to an open oval at the very acme of the ridge. It was green turf, I tell you, so well kept that it resembled a huge cricket field. Near the middle was a swivelling wind vane upon a tall pole.”

“An aerodrome,” whispered Bullivant.

“Precisely,” replied Holmes. “I had found the monoplane’s resting place, and in so doing, I felt more confident than ever that I had uncovered the location of yet another haven for German spies.

“I scrambled back down the slope and once more into my protective cover of firs. There I sat and waited for some time, until I heard a roar from above. Peering through the branches, I saw the aeroplane approach from the west and then descend below the treetops at the ridge’s summit to land upon that well-manicured oval lawn.

“I withdrew deeper into the trees and, several minutes later, saw two men emerge from the forest above me, both dressed in flying clothes. They walked down the ridge, passing perhaps fifty yards from my enclave, and so on to the house. I kept watch, but nothing further transpired.

“Late that day, I returned to the cottage where the couple and their sons lived, and there re-established the bonds I had previously forged. I told them I was a naturalist studying the distribution of various species of bee, and they graciously agreed to put me up each night. And, as they provided me with food and a place to sleep, I continued to assist them on their plot each day, before leaving to stand vigil by the house and aerodrome."

"It must have been quite boring for you, Holmes," Bullivant remarked.

"Oh, quite the contrary," Holmes replied. "On the second day, ironically, I chanced to discover a group of swarming *Apis mellifera mellifera.*"

"I beg pardon," intoned Bullivant.

"European honey bees," I said.

"Very good, Watson," said Holmes cheerily. "You were paying even closer attention than I had suspected. Yes, observation of the new colony helped pass the time.

"With each sunrise, I camped within that stand of firs, watching the house and observing the comings and goings of the monoplane and its crew, when not making notes on the activities of my bees. More than once, a motorcar arrived at the house and then left. And so the time passed for me, as I waited for either an opportunity to enter that den of presumed foreign agents or for Mr. Hannay to arrive as a captive, whereupon I was determined to set him loose."

"And I did arrive eventually," the South African said, "except that I did so as a free man, of my own accord."

CHAPTER EIGHT: GANG AFT AGLEY

"After reaching Dumfries on that first day," said Richard Hannay, "I did take the slow Galloway train north, as Mr. Holmes surmised, and got off at a little station along the way. From there, I followed a road that straggled over expanses of brown moor.

"It was a gorgeous evening," he said, and as the South African recounted his trek, commenting on the odd, rooty smell of bogs, comparing the hills to cut amethyst, and relating how he fashioned a walking stick of hazel and whistled as he trod the glen of a brawling stream, I understood how deeply rooted in nature's realm was this man.

"Eventually, I came to a herd's cottage," he told us. "There I asked a woman with a weathered face if I might have a night's lodging, and she offered me a bed in the loft, as well as a hearty meal of ham and eggs, scones, and sweet milk.

"Later, her man came in from the hills. He was a lean giant with a huge stride, and like his wife, he asked no questions. I sensed they thought me a cattle dealer, however, and I played to that supposed impression by speaking a good deal of such animals. The man knew a little of local markets, and I kept in mind all that he related, thinking I might be able to use the information to maintain my false guise."

"That was resourceful of you, Mr. Hannay," said Sir Walter Bullivant. His eyes narrowed behind the tortoiseshell spectacles, and I could see his shrewd mind plotting as he contemplated his guest.

"The couple refused any payment," said Hannay. "They generously fed me breakfast the next morning, and I set off with the intention of returning to the railway line to board a carriage heading back south, for I reckoned that it would be the trains travelling north that would be most closely watched."

"Very clever, indeed," whispered Sir Walter, and I saw Holmes silently nod.

"I got on a southbound train, eventually taking company with an old shepherd and his dog, the two that both of you encountered on your own journeys," he told Holmes and me. "The four-legged one was a wall-eyed brute that I mistrusted from the start."

"Hear, hear," I intoned, and Holmes's eyes sparkled. "The herd related a story about a man leaving a rail carriage outside a station," I said, "and I took that man as having been you."

"It was," said Hannay. "As I suppose he told you, the train came to a standstill at the end of a culvert spanning a river. There was another train waiting for us to pass, we were told, but then I saw that three men had left that train and were headed in our direction. I figured they must be the police, and so I decided then and there to drop from the carriage and slip away. The dog thought I was trying to steal its master's belongings, perhaps, and started to bark. The herd, who was asleep—"

"From drink, no doubt," I interjected.

"Oh, you are quite right there, Doctor," Hannay agreed. "Nonetheless, he woke and began to holler. By this point, I had put several yards between myself and the carriage, but I had been noticed by several onlookers. Fortunately, the dog chose that moment to leap after me, taking his master with him, for the man was tied to the animal by means of a rope. His tumbling off the train stole everyone's fancy, and they dropped any interest in me to laugh at the dog and the herd. I then took that opportunity to dart into cover and start running.

"I had gotten rather far from the train when I first spotted that monoplane rising up from the south. Suddenly, it seemed as if my choice of hiding in the barren countryside had been a poor one, given the likelihood of now being seen from the air, and so I decided to leave the moorland and head for the green country to the south, in search of woods and stone houses in which to hide."

"As Holmes thought you might," said Bullivant.

"Yes," replied Hannay, smiling boyishly at all of us. "Well, later that day, I came to a small plateau where there was a house sitting beyond a bridge, against which a young man leaned, reading Milton."

"Milton?" I said, recalling Ewan Clark. "Did this house serve as an inn? And on the grounds was there a shed in which sat—"

"A motor bicycle?" completed Hannay. "Yes, Dr. Watson, there was. So you passed that way also?"

"I did," I replied, glancing at Bullivant, who knew my own tale already. Holmes stared at me expectantly, but I waved my hand at the South African. "But go on, Mr. Hannay, please. Forgive my interruption."

"Yes, of course," he said. "I made up a story about being a mining magnate from Kimberley, claiming I was being pursued by illegal diamond buyers whose plans I had thwarted. The innkeeper was more than happy to take me in, give me a room, and supply me with meals. The next day, two men came round in a motorcar, and my host, on his own initiative, told them I had stayed the night before and then left."

"An enterprising and inventive lad," said Sherlock Holmes.

"Yes, he was, as well as trusting," said Hannay. "He came up while they were still there to inform me of all this, and I sweetened the pot by penning a false note in German. I then had the innkeeper take it to the men and tell them that I'd inadvertently left it behind, with the request that they return it to me should they find me."

Holmes chuckled and looked at me. "I told you this man must be salvaged, did I not?"

"Indeed, you did. Then what happened, Mr. Hannay?" I asked.

"Well, the two men apparently swore mightily and took off in pursuit. I had the innkeeper go tell the police about the pair and suggest they might have been involved in the Portland Place murder. I expected the men to return later, after they had failed to come across me, you see."

"And they did return?" said Sir Walter.

"Yes," replied Hannay. Looking down into his now empty cup, the man tilted his head slightly. "Thanks to the innkeeper, however, the police had already arrived—two constables and a sergeant—and taken up station within the house, all without knowing I was still holed up inside my bedroom. I saw the two strange men approach in the distance, coming up the hill in their automobile. They stopped the vehicle some two hundred yards away, in the shelter of a patch of wood, and walked the rest of the way up to the inn."

"And had you intended to remain hidden in your room?" I asked.

"At first, yes, but then a better idea occurred to me. I opened a window and dropped to the ground, cushioned by a gooseberry bush. I then proceeded unobserved across the dyke and crawled down the side of a burn to reach the car. I started her, jumped into the chauffeur's seat, and stole away."

Holmes raised his chin and smiled, his brows raised whimsically.

"I immediately left the main roads and took to the byways," said Hannay. "And it was then that I realised what a fool I had been to steal the automobile in the first place, for it was a big green brute that would clearly give me away to anyone who had been told of the theft. I therefore headed for even more lonely roads and made it almost to evening without encountering anyone, but by now I was furiously hungry. Just then, I heard a noise in the sky, and lo and behold, there was that monoplane again, flying near the ground, about a dozen miles to the south of me and approaching rapidly.

"I drove on toward a thick wood I had espied, and once under its cover slackened speed. But then I heard the hoot of another car, and I realised I was almost upon the entrance to a private road from which another motor was emerging. I clapped on my brakes, but the automobile's speed was too great, and I saw that my present course would cause me to ram the other vehicle in the middle. I did the only correct thing and veered to the right, into a hedge, hoping to find something soft beyond."

"And did you?" asked Bullivant.

"No," said Hannay. "My motorcar shot through the hedge as if it were butter and careened toward the edge of a precipice. I stood on the seat and prepared to jump, but the branch of a hawthorn caught me in the chest and lifted me up, holding me there as the vehicle slipped over the edge and pitched down the slope, perhaps fifty feet in all. It landed with a crash in the bed of a stream."

"Well," I said, "your luck was with you."

"The man in the other car was a local politician, as it turned out," Hannay added.

"Yes, Sir Harry Christey," I remarked.

"You met him?"

"I did, within an hour of your having left his residence on bicycle."

"Ah, then you know the rest of the story."

"I witnessed part of it, actually," I said, and proceeded to relate my experience at the political rally, including my unsuccessful attempts to reach Hannay and Sir Harry in the hall, followed by my long nocturnal hike afterward, adding as well the motor bicycle ride with the very innkeeper who had previously sheltered the South African.

"What befell you after you left Sir Harry's, however, I do not yet know," I added expectantly.

"Nor do I," said Bullivant.

"I bicycled that night into the hills," Hannay told us. "However, by seven the next morning, I realised I had made perhaps another fatal choice, for on the summits I once more stood out like a sore thumb. And, sure enough, the ominous beat of the monoplane's engine suddenly sounded from above. Before I could act this time, however, the aircraft had dropped several hundred feet and began circling around my position, and the observer on board caught sight of me through glasses. Then the aeroplane rose and turned eastward, receding until it was only a speck.

"I knew the enemy had located me at last, and that made me do some savage thinking. I wheeled my bicycle a hundred yards from the highway and plunged it into a moss hole, where it sank among water buttercups. Then I climbed to a knoll that gave me a view of the two valleys on either side. The long winding road between them was empty. I could go north or south, but I could not decide which. I felt rather like Buridan's ass.[68]

"And so I pulled a coin from my pocket and tossed it in order to decide. Heads came up, and I turned northward. I had gone perhaps ten miles or so along the high road, when in the distance I saw a motorcar. And then, very far beyond it, away down the slope, I spotted several men advancing like a row of beaters at a shoot."

"Pursuers," said Bullivant. "Germans or police?

"It didn't matter to me at the time," Hannay replied. "I immediately dropped down out of sight behind my own ridge. The automobile was still a ways away, and so I ran across the road, intending now to head south. Suddenly, ahead, I espied two new figures in the glen beyond, moving toward me. I realised that I was hemmed in on all sides of a relatively barren patch of land."

"Good lord," I said. "What choice did you then have?"

"The only one possible in that situation, Watson," declared Sherlock Holmes. He cast an admiring glance at Hannay. "Stay in the patch, and let your enemies search it and not find you."

"Exactly, Mr. Holmes," replied the South African. "The problem, of course, was how to escape notice. There were no trees. The bog holes were but small puddles, and the stream I encountered merely a trickle. It was all heather, hill grass, and highway. For lack of a better option, I ran farther along the road, where I came to a bend, and there I found my salvation."

---

[68] Named after French philosopher Jean Buridan, this paradox refers to an imaginary situation where a hungry and thirsty ass is placed exactly midway between a pile of hay and a pail of water. Unable to choose between the two, since they are equidistant from it, the animal dies of both hunger and thirst.

Bullivant and I tilted forward in our chairs, while Holmes leaned back contentedly.

"I saw a roadman," said Hannay. "He was tending to his repairs, splitting stones with a hammer. Suddenly, he dropped his tool and, seeing me approach, began to wail about his headaches."

"Migraines, perhaps?" I asked. Holmes covered his mouth and shook his head.

"What?" said Hannay. "No, not migraines. The man had just caroused a bit too much the night before, against his better judgment, and now found himself in an awful state the morning after. And to top off matters, a road surveyor was due presently to inspect his work, which had hardly progressed at all since the day before.

"I immediately suggested that we trade places. Without much need for coaxing, he gave me his spectacles and dirty hat, as well as an old clay pipe. I, in turn, stripped off my jacket, waistcoat and collar, and gave them him to carry to his cottage, which was visible in the far distance. He briefly instructed me in his tasks, and I sent him off to his home to sleep the rest of the day. Then, after roughing myself up a bit to look the part, I assumed the man's identity, in order to fool anyone who might pass by."

"And you made certain that you fooled yourself as well," said Bullivant.

"Oh yes, I did."

"What do you mean by that?" I asked.

"I believe Sir Walter means that Mr. Hannay needed to convince himself that he was the roadman," explained Holmes.

"You see," said Hannay, "it's like an old scout in Rhodesia once told me: the secret to playing a part is to think yourself into it. You can never keep it up unless you can manage to convince yourself that you are it."

"Yes," said Holmes wistfully. "You must shut out your real identity entirely."

"And so I did," Hannay affirmed. "I thought of the little white cottage in the distance as mine. I made up false memories of sleeping there in a box bed[69] beside a bottle of cheap whisky. I made the road the only purpose I had in life."

"And you escaped detection?" I asked.

"Yes," said Hannay. "The motor I had seen stopped at my worksite. Two men got out and spoke to me, and I was certain they were among my German pursuers, but I deceived them completely. Then, toward the late afternoon, another man happened by in a touring car and stopped. I recognised him as a London stockbroker with whom I had once been very slightly acquainted, and on a daft notion, I revealed my true identity. He'd heard the news of the Portland Place murder and believed me the killer. That fear was enough to coerce him into following my instructions.

"I donned his driving coat and buttoned it to the top to hide my own filthy clothes, and then I told him to sit in the passenger seat and be still while I drove the two of us for several miles, through the cordon of pursuers and on into early evening. I left the frightened fellow to his vehicle and then wandered off to spend the night on a hillside.

"The following morning, I woke to a pale blue sky visible through a net of heather. I raised myself on my arms and looked at my empty boots

[69] A box bed is one enclosed in furniture that looks like a cupboard.

sitting beside me, and then down into the valley. That one glance below set me to lacing up the boots as quickly as I could, for there were men approaching, not a quarter mile off. They were again spread apart across the hillside like a fan, and beating the heather.

"Keeping behind the local ridge as best I could, I ran on for perhaps half a mile, where I deliberately showed myself to them. That set the bunch running toward me, but I once more ducked down and then ran back the way I had come. I somehow slipped past them and did not look back after that. I knew, however, that my stratagem had gained me only a head start of a few minutes. I covered a good deal of ground, though, and came upon a deserted cottage, and beyond that a house with a smoking chimney—the same one you have described, Mr. Holmes."

The detective nodded.

Hannay continued. "I wandered onto the grounds of the occupied house and saw, from various details, that it appeared to be an ordinary moorland farm, though with a pretentious white-washed wing added. The wing had a glass veranda, and through the panes, an elderly gentleman was studying me. I walked across a border of coarse hill gravel and entered the veranda, whose door was already open.

"The room where I found myself was pleasant, with a wall of books opposite the glass. Instead of tables and chairs, however, the floor supported a number of cases such as you see in museums, all filled with coins and odd stone implements. There was a desk in the middle, at which the old man was now sitting. His face was round and shiny. Big glasses sat on the end of his nose, and the top of his head was as bright and smooth as a glass bottle. He remained still as I crossed the room, raising his placid brows as if waiting for me to speak first. Yet, though tired, hungry, and feeling at the end of my rope, I hesitated to confess and seek help from him."

"But did you?" asked Sir Walter.

"No," said Hannay. "The gentleman himself spoke for me. He observed that I seemed in a hurry. I, in turn, nodded towards the window. He rose and picked up a pair of field glasses. Through the glass of the veranda, he scrutinised the distant heather.

"'I see men coming this way,' he said. 'Police?'"

"I nodded, and he declared he would not have his privacy be broken by clumsy rural constables. The old man directed me to another room, where I bided my time in a dark chamber which smelt of chemicals and was lit only by a tiny window high up in the wall. Sometime later, the door opened, and I emerged to find the elderly gentleman, who directed me back into his study. I asked if my pursuers had left, and he said they had.

"He reached for a cigar and repeatedly tapped his knee in an odd way before finally lighting his smoke. As he took the first puffs, he said that he had told the men searching for me that I had passed through his property and on over the next hill. I sighed and thanked him, remarking that I was most fortunate.

"'Yes,' he agreed. 'This is a lucky morning for you, Mr. Richard Hannay.'"

Bullivant and I leaned back in our chairs.

"The moment he uttered my name without benefit of introduction, I realised I had walked straight into the enemy's headquarters," said Hannay. "I would have been safer with those who were beating the heather, who I now understood to have been the police.

"My first impulse was to simply throttle the old ruffian and make for the hills again. He seemed to sense my intention, however, and smiled gently before motioning to the doorway behind me. I turned and saw that two menservants were pointing at me with pistols—they were the same two I had encountered in my pose as the roadman. Standing between them was another man, a plump fellow who studied me with a curious expression.

"'And so our quarry has wandered in on his own?' the plump man asked in a disbelieving voice. He then proceeded to estimate the distance I had walked in all, and speculated about the towns I might have passed through."

"'I am not concerned with his past itinerary,' said the elderly gentleman, staring at me with eyes that were hooded, like those of a hawk. 'What matters is that he is now here. Karl,' he said, addressing one of the servants who held guns, 'you will put this fellow in the storeroom till I return.' I translate that final sentence, for the command was issued in German."

"And so you were imprisoned?" I said.

"Yes," Hannay replied. "Under supervision of the plump man, the servants marched me out of the study, a pistol at each ear, and deposited me in a damp chamber that was part of what had been the old farmhouse. The floor was uneven and uncarpeted, and it was black as pitch inside, for the windows were heavily shuttered. By groping about, though, I eventually determined that the walls were lined with boxes and barrels and sacks of some heavy material. The whole place smelt of mould and disuse. My gaolers had closed the only door and turned the key in the lock, and after a while, I could hear someone shifting feet from moment to moment while standing guard outside the door.

"I didn't know their plans for me," said the South African, "and I could see no way out of the mess I was in. The more I thought of it, the angrier I became, and so I moved about the darkened room, trying the shutters to no avail and groping among sacks and boxes, finding nothing but what I took to be old grain and nuts. Then I discovered a handle in the wall and realised I had stumbled upon the door to a press.[70] There was what felt like a flimsy lock on it, and by working the door steadily, I managed to break it open and, fumbling about, found what I took to be a little stock of electric torches on one shelf. They were in working order, and so now I was acting with benefit of light.

"Using one of the torches, I saw that the cupboard contained bottles, oiled silk, fine copper wire, matches, and a stout cardboard box, inside of which was a wooden case. I wrenched the case open and found within a dozen little grey bricks, each a couple of inches square. I took one up in my hand and found that it crumbled easily. Then, after smelling it, I tasted it with my tongue. Now, as a mining engineer, I can recognise lentonite explosive when I encounter it—and this was it. I'd used the stuff in Rhodesia and, knowing its power, was prepared to use it again."

"You don't say?" murmured Bullivant. "To blast open the door? Would not that have been extremely risky?"

Hannay looked at Holmes and smiled. "I certainly *intended* to use it. I had forgotten the proper charge and the right way of preparing it, and I wasn't sure about the timing, but I knew that if I did nothing, I was a dead

---

[70] A press, in this instance, is a wall cupboard.

man in any case. I remembered the sight of Scudder lying in my smoking room, a knife through his heart. That image decided the matter for me.

"I found detonators in the box, and I took one in order to set things up to blow open the door. Then I paused, for I thought I heard a thud outside. After a moment of quiet, I resumed my preparation and was about to light the fuse when I heard a key in the lock of the door, which then burst open, and I saw a figure silhouetted in the frame."

"'Mr. Hannay,' I called discreetly," said Sherlock Holmes, continuing the story. "'Mr. Hannay, come with me!'"

"And so watching the house and its aerodrome paid a dividend at last," I said.

"Indeed, it did," Holmes replied.

"If nothing else," said Hannay, "Mr. Holmes's fortuitous entrance prevented me from blowing myself to pieces."[71]

"There was no guard stationed at the door when you arrived?" Bullivant asked the detective.

"There was no conscious guard *after* I had arrived," said Holmes. "I gained entry to the house without notice and then sneaked up behind the man watching Hannay's door. My application of a quick baritsu stroke rendering the German unconscious was the thud that Hannay heard."

"And you did not harm yourself in the process?" I enquired.

"From the baritsu stroke? No," said Holmes with raised brow. "I have kept in practice during my later years, old fellow. In any event, I rapidly introduced myself to Mr. Hannay and urged him to follow me away, when I noticed that he held a burning match in his hand."

---

[71] According to *The Thirty-Nine Steps*, Hannay did in fact employ the fictional explosive lentonite by himself in order to escape, contradicting this account.

"I called Mr. Holmes's attention to the lentonite I had set to blast open the doorway," Hannay interjected. "But, as he had opened the door and the match was burnt almost to my fingers, I shook it out. It was then that we both arrived at the same thought simultaneously."

"Mr. Hannay fetched another match," Holmes said, "after we had together set a new, longer fuse. Before he ignited it, I asked that he remove his jacket and leave it in the room, perhaps to be found by the Germans after the explosion and taken as a suggestion that he had not survived the blast. We rushed out the open door, each taking an arm of the guard whom I had rendered unconscious. We pulled him from the house and set him against a wall, presumably safe from the impending explosion, the key to Hannay's cell once more in his pocket. Then we ran."

"We had reached a mill lade[72] when the blast occurred," Hannay told us. "I should have been expecting the sound of an explosion but was too intent on fleeing. When the concussion swept over us, I was so taken by surprise that I slipped on the edge of the lade and fell into the water." He glanced down. "Rather embarrassing, I'm afraid. Even more so, in that I caused Mr. Holmes to stagger as well."

"I tried to catch Hannay before he tumbled into the lade," the detective remarked. "I was unsuccessful, and in so doing, further twisted my already injured leg and went down as well, though only my feet broke the surface of the water.

"We were both prostrate now," Holmes said, "and I saw smoke escaping from an upper window of the house. Confused cries could be heard coming from the other side of the structure. Mr. Hannay quickly

[72] A mill lade or millrun is the channel of water going to or from a water wheel.

climbed from the water—feeling then perhaps a bit refreshed?" he said to the South African.

"Yes," Hannay admitted. "Despite the situation, the water was wonderfully bracing. But though I was now free, it was apparent that the enemy would shortly be in pursuit. We had to run for our lives."

"And it was then that I became the sticking point," said Holmes, "for, with my injured leg now made worse, it was obvious to me that I could not run very fast and thus was a dead weight round Hannay's neck. I urged him to go on without me."

"A suggestion I refused to consider," declared the younger man. "I was determined that it should be both of us or neither."

"And then I saw an old stone dovecot[73] on the far side of the mill," Holmes went on. "I immediately perceived that it might serve as a hiding place. With my leg as it was, I knew I had no chance to ascend to the top, but it seemed likely that Hannay could manage it, and so I urged him to try. My strategy was that, if he hid atop the dovecot until night and I remained at large, we might later reunite and flee together."

"But how did you keep yourself free?" asked Bullivant. "You indicated you could not outrun the Germans at that point."

"The solution will be made clear in a moment, Sir Walter," said Holmes.

"Climbing that dovecot was one of the hardest jobs I ever took on," Hannay admitted. "Every joint was aching like hell during the ascent, and more than once I felt on the verge of falling. But by using out-jutting stones

[73] A dovecot is a structure built to house pigeons or doves, which traditionally were an important food source in Europe. Dovecots usually contain holes in which the birds can nest.

and gaps in the masonry, as well as some very tough ivy vines, I got to the top. There I found a little parapet behind which there was space to lie down."

"I, meanwhile, limped off toward the woods as fast as I could and reached the trees before anyone saw me," said Sherlock Holmes. "However, it was obvious that any pursuers would overtake me before long. I stumbled to a point near the bee colony I had previously discovered, which fortunately lay near the small stream that ran through the woods. Hearing approaching voices, I stepped into the water and proceeded to lie down, making certain to assume a position in which my bad leg appeared twisted. Then," the detective said, "I shouted as loudly as possible."

I gave my friend an admiring look.

"Two men came through the trees," Holmes related. "I gestured for them to help me up while complaining about how the explosion's short, sharp shock, as it were, had startled me and caused me to lose my footing and tumble into the stream. Thus did I explain the reason for my feet being wet and my leg injured. At the same time, I thought that by calling to them I might blunt any suspicion I was aiding their fugitive, for the guard I had subdued back at the house had not seen me before I rendered him unconscious."

"And they believed you?" I said.

"Sadly," Holmes replied, "though they said they believed my story that I was but a visiting apiarist, they insisted upon taking me back to the house, which by now was a scene of furious activity. A fire had indeed been started by the explosion we had set, but the flames were contained in a short while, and by the time I was settled into a chair at the centre of that very same study into which Mr. Hannay had first wandered, the grounds had been secured.

"Into the room came the elderly man whom Hannay had encountered," the detective told us. "He was most compassionate toward me, asking about my leg and suggesting that a doctor be called to the house. I demurred, but those objections did not prevent him from insisting that I remain for rest and observation."

"Do you believe he suspected you to be other than what you claimed to be?" asked Bullivant.

"Oh, of course he did," Holmes replied. "However, I think he soon appreciated my expert knowledge of bees, and he had his men go off to seek the husband and wife with whom I had been lodging—for I had mentioned them as people who might corroborate my story. Still, there must have been some nagging uncertainty in his mind even then, for he was determined that I should enjoy the care and hospitality of his household for the remainder of the day.

"He gave his name as Alasdair Moncrief and described himself as an archaeologist who had been associated with the expeditions of Schludermann and Gerhardt. The blast, he said, had been the result of accidental detonation of old explosives from a stock that had been used to excavate some cliffs in Asia Minor, and he offered me the comfort of his home for the night—thinking, I believe, that in so doing he might prevent me from assisting Hannay, should his worst suspicions prove true."

"When did you eventually free yourself of him?" I asked.

"It was not until the following day," Holmes said. "I was given a room in which to sleep, and two servants were detailed to watch over me and bring me meals, and thus I was not able to rendezvous with our precious refugee that night as planned. Instead, I was kept in bed and observed with great concern—none of it medical."

"All that afternoon, I lay baking on the rooftop of the dovecot," Hannay went on, picking up his portion of the story. "Thirst tormented me constantly. My tongue was like a stick, and the worst part of it was that I could hear the cool drip of water from the mill lade below. Watching the course of the stream as it came in from the moor, I thought I would give a thousand pounds for the opportunity to plunge my face into it.

"From that vantage point, though, I also had a fine prospect of the entire surroundings. I saw a car speed away with two occupants, as well as a man riding east on a hill pony and two others go into the woods. I knew they were looking for me at the least, but I also feared for Mr. Holmes.

"I saw them escort him from the stand of firs, and my heart sank. It was then, while casting my eyes about, that I noticed the plateau ringed by trees. The level of the dovecot was such that I could see what lay within: the great oval lawn that served as aerodrome for the monoplane.

"Late that day, when I had convinced myself that I had eluded my pursuers, the aeroplane appeared in the sky—fortunately, not directly overhead. I heard its engine suddenly cut out, and the craft volplaned[74] onto the lawn. There were the twinklings of lights and sounds of much coming and going from the house. Then night fell.

"The moon was past half and had not yet risen, leaving the early night sky dark. Well into evening, overcome by thirst and hoping for the best, I descended from the top of the dovecot. Mr. Holmes was nowhere to be found, but I decided I could not tarry, and so I crawled on my belly

---

[74] When an aircraft volplanes, it makes a steep, controlled drive, probably with the engine off. The word derives from the French *vol plané*, which means "gliding flight."

across the grounds in the lee of a stone dyke, till I reached the fringe of trees surrounding the house. Briefly, I considered rendering the monoplane inoperable—"

"An admirable thought," said Bullivant, "but foolhardy."

"Yes," agreed Hannay. "I thought it more prudent to simply be off, and so I continued into the woods on hands and knees, feeling carefully before me every inch of the way. It was well that I did, for presently I came upon a wire about two feet from the ground."

Sherlock Holmes smiled as he contemplated the South African. "One of the wires I mentioned earlier," he said. "In our rapid flight from the house before the explosion, I had no time to warn you of it, Mr. Hannay. I compliment you on your cautious observation."

"If I had tripped over that wire," Hannay went on, "it would have rung some bell in the house, no doubt, and I would have been caught. There was another such wire a hundred yards farther on, on the edge of that small stream. I avoided it also, and then plunged deep into bracken and heather. Ten minutes later, after quenching my thirst in the stream, I was running at full gallop, putting as many miles as I could between me and that accursed archaeologist with the hooded eyes."

"But you did not head straight here, for Berkshire," commented Bullivant.

"No, sir," replied Hannay. "I couldn't, for I had left Scudder's notebook with Mr. Turnbull, the roadman I had impersonated. It and my original garments were presumably safe with him at his cottage, and I realised I would need the notebook if I were to make a convincing case to you or anyone else concerning what the truth was."

"Yes," said the spymaster, "of course."

"I determined to reach Turnbull's place, aided by a map supplied by your godson, Sir Harry, which I still carried with me. When, at last, I sat down on a hilltop that night and consulted it, however, I realised that by now I was close to twenty miles from the cottage and couldn't reach it by daybreak."

"And so you must have found refuge somewhere," I offered.

"Yes," answered Hannay. "Just after dawn I came upon a herd's cottage. He was away, but his old wife was there, and she turned out to be a decent, plucky sort. She offered me a bowl of milk with a dash of whisky in it, and let me sit for a little by her kitchen fire. I'm sure she often cast a glance at an axe that sat in a corner, for I presented quite a fright: I had no jacket, waistcoat, collar, nor hat. My trousers were badly torn, and though I had washed as best I could in a hill burn, my face was still somewhat soiled.

"Still, she took the money I offered in return for her hospitality, and she gave me food and a new plaid, as well as an old hat belonging to her man. She showed me how to wrap the plaid round my shoulders, and when I left that cottage I think I must have been the spitting image of a traditional Scotsman. I found shelter below an overhanging rock in the crook of a burn and slept there until nightfall, when I set out for Turnbull's cottage. As a second dawn broke, with the mist lying close and thick, I was knocking at his door."

"An admirable hike," murmured Sherlock Holmes.

"But if I am keeping track correctly," Bullivant said, "that still brings us only to a few days ago, not the present."

"Yes," replied Hannay. "You see, during my youth in Africa, I contracted malaria and have suffered recurrent bouts of the disease ever since. By the time I reached Turnbull's cottage, I was feeling a good deal of fever in my bones—perhaps it was my night journey in damp weather, but whatever the reason, the ailment had chosen to reassert itself within me.

"Turnbull recognised at once that I was ill and immediately put me to bed. The roadman nursed me for days, and even after the fever broke, I found it took me some time to get my legs again." He clasped his hands together. "And by that time, Mr. Holmes had found me a second time."

Bullivant and I turned toward the detective.

"Moncrief, the archaeologist, kept me in his house through that first night and then allowed me to depart the next day, once he was convinced I was who I claimed to be. He even said he would have a man convey me to Dumfries in a motor, an offer I readily accepted.

"It was there that I learned, though discreet enquiry, that a government man had recently left the town after surveying the district for the location of a new RFC aerodrome," Holmes wryly noted.

I shrugged, and the detective continued.

"Though my stay with Moncrief had prevented me from rendezvousing with Hannay, it had enabled me to observe the house and draw conclusions about its possible function as a headquarters for German spies. We will discuss that, perhaps, later tonight or tomorrow, Sir Walter," he told Bullivant.

"Of course," said the spymaster. "I believe that, at present, my principal interest is how you latched onto Hannay again."

"Well, it was not that difficult," said Holmes, "though it did take some little effort." The detective took a deep breath and crossed his arms. "I had had but a few brief minutes in Hannay's company between opening the door to his cell and leaving him to climb to the top of the dovecot. However, in that short span, I had taken stock of several features of interest.

"Stripped, as it were, of coat and jacket, and without baggage of any sort, he clearly did not possess Scudder's notebook," declared my friend. "That meant he must have deposited it elsewhere, at a location from which he could later retrieve it. Then too, there was the state of his hands, visible when we set the second fuse.

"I was most unmindful of yours the other week, Watson," he said to me, "as my brother noted with undisguised glee. This time, I made certain I was not so careless. I had seen that the edges of Mr. Hannay's fingernails were cracked and uneven, to such an extent that I could not believe their condition to be due merely to his scrambling about in the wild. Instead, their appearance suggested that he had, on purpose, recently been scraping them against rocks and pebbles. Then there were the accumulations of white dust on his clothing, artefacts I immediately associated with the local macadam roads. Placing the two observations side by side, I concluded he had been engaged in some type of road work."

"Yes," said Hannay. "My stint in place of Mr. Turnbull."

"It was all I had to begin my search, but I determined to find all instances of current road repair in the county," Holmes said. "It took me the better part of a day to track down a road surveyor, to whom I posed as a correspondent for Baedeker[75] seeking information about local turnpikes, and he supplied me with everything I wished to learn about ongoing building and maintenance in the area. Indeed, he was about to make

[75] The German publishing house Verlag Karl Baedeker was a pioneer in the business of worldwide travel guides.

rounds of inspection in a motor and invited me to join him. I suspect he came to regret that gracious offer, for at every stop I made a thorough survey of the immediate surroundings.

"It was during the fifth such episode that I came upon Hannay's Mr. Turnbull, feverishly pounding rock into pebbles. I engaged the man in discreet conversation and, after assuring him of my true identity and purpose, learned that he harboured Hannay in his home. Bidding the road surveyor farewell, I hiked to the cottage and came upon our friend, still in bed but largely recovered from his bout of malaria."

"Yes, Mr. Turnbull said I had been ill for ten days when you arrived," the South African said.

"And you had already done a marvellous job of deciphering a small but crucial portion of the American's text," remarked Holmes. "I spent another day in Turnbull's cottage completing a bit more. It is a trove of data," he told Bullivant. "Still, many more pages still need to be translated."

"Yes," said the spymaster. "But the key piece of information gleaned from it thus far is, no doubt, the plan to assassinate Karolides."

"There are two additional items of immediate interest as well," amended Holmes. "But, to conclude our little tale, Hannay and I left Mr. Turnbull's cottage in the company of a cattle drover the next day. We arrived in Moffat after twelve miles of slow travel, during which we chose to evade a pair of men in a motor, whom I took to be police inspectors. We then discreetly ate in a public house and waited at the rail junction for the southern express, which was due at midnight."

"And from there," said Hannay, "It was third-class cushions all the way to your station here."

"I allowed my companion to walk a distance ahead of me," Holmes explained, "for I was fearful that, while Hannay's appearance was expected, my arrival might create a bit of commotion." A sympathetic glint in his eye, the detective glanced at me. "I thought it best if the full reunion proceeded at low key instead. Thus, I hid while you greeted our friend and then followed him discreetly to this house, where we both entered, though I had to quickly persuade Sir Walter's servant that two guests were expected for dinner rather than one."

"Well, it all worked out well in the end," said Bullivant. "But if you do not mind, I should like to return to the contents of Scudder's notebook. You mentioned there were two items of additional interest in it beyond the Karolides plot."

"Yes," said Holmes. "First, Scudder's book has some sketchy notes about Moncrief's operation up in Scotland."

"Which may be the third head of Cerberus that we have been hoping to find," said Bullivant.

"I'm afraid that is not likely to be the case, Sir Walter."

"Oh?" said the spymaster. "Why is that? This bunch in Scotland are clearly Germans, are they not?"

"Yes," said Holmes. "But they are Germans who knew of Hannay's importance from the very beginning. How would they know of his value so quickly unless they were part of the Black Stone apparatus themselves?"

"Ah," replied Bullivant with a sigh. "I see. But then, the Black Stone is therefore widespread."

"As is Von Bork's operation," observed Holmes. "Remember, I was recruited for his group up in Skibereen."[76]

"And so the presumed third head of Cerberus lies somewhere else, still uncovered," I remarked.

"I fear that is so, Watson," Holmes said. "Parts of Scudder's notebook that I have translated confirm what we initially surmised: there are indeed three distinct German spy rings in our land, each operating independently, with knowledge of each other but communicating among themselves infrequently, if at all."

"That sounds rather inefficient," I noted. "Three German spy rings? Would they not duplicate their efforts?"

"Yes, but that would seem to be the point. Berlin apparently planted three such groups so that these separate cells might gather information independently, thus unknowingly corroborating data gained by any one ring."

At the last comment by Holmes, Sir Walter shifted uncomfortably his chair. "You mean Moncrief and his Black Stone group may have gathered information in the same vein as that which we supplied Von Bork's ring?"

"Yes, I am afraid so," replied Holmes. "And, of course, in matching those different sets of information, Berlin may have begun to notice how often Von Bork's information has failed to agree with that from the other—and, perhaps, that of the presumed third spy ring as well."

[76] Skibereen is a town in Ireland.

I watched as Sir Walter spent a prolonged moment engrossed in silent thought. Then, after sighing, he said, "Might we be, then, have reached the moment when our charade with Von Bork must end?"

"I think so," replied Holmes.

"You mentioned two additional items of interest in Scudder's book," Bullivant said. "What is the second?"

Hannay silently deferred to Holmes, who pulled from the pocket of his jacket a small black pocketbook and leaned over to hand it to Sir Walter.

"The material about the Black Stone in Scudder's notes mentions not only the plan to assassinate Karolides, the Greek premier, when he visits London this month, but also an intention to steal knowledge of the dispositions of our Home Fleet in the event of mobilisation. Apparently, our General Staff regularly meets with a representative of the French government to coordinate possible strategies, and that information is discussed at those gatherings. That is the second item that caught my attention."

"Yes," Bullivant whispered. "The fact of those meetings is not generally known."

"Well, the Black Stone know about them and intend to infiltrate the next such meeting and come away with the dispositions."

Sir Walter gave a slight intake of breath and set the notebook down on a table beside his chair. "Ah," he said. "I see."

"Has such a meeting already occurred?" enquired Holmes.

The spymaster cast a cautious glance among the three of us and then drew himself up in his chair. "No, but one is scheduled to take place in eight days."

Just then, there was a knock at the door to the study. It was Bullivant's servant, who announced that someone was waiting to speak to our host on the telephone.

"Excuse me for a moment, gentlemen," Sir Walter said before leaving us.

Hannay stared at the carpet for a moment and then said in a soft voice, "I must again express my sincere gratitude to both of you, as well as to Sir Walter." He looked me squarely in the eye when adding, "And I am so sorry, Dr. Watson, that you suffered the hardships you did and yet never made contact with me."

"I have made contact now," I said. "And, as I have noted so many times before to myself, in past years," I added, glancing at Sherlock Holmes, "the joy is in the chase itself. Looking back, I realise that, despite the hardships and frustrations, there was much joy in chasing you, Mr. Hannay."

"A great game, yes," said the younger man.

"That is the phrase often employed," murmured Sherlock Holmes in a bemused tone.

Suddenly, the study door opened again. It was Sir Walter, his face now ashen and his expression quite blank. He held his tortoiseshell spectacles in one hand.

"It was Mycroft who rang," he said, his voice hollow. "The Greek premier, Karolides, was murdered earlier today."

CHAPTER NINE: THE THIRTY-NINE STEPS

I came down to breakfast the next morning, after a night of troubled sleep, to find Sir Walter decoding telegrams in the company of Sherlock Holmes. A moment after I reached the table at which they sat, I turned and saw Hannay appear in the doorway behind me.

"Good morning, Doctor," he said sullenly before glancing at Bullivant with an expectant look.

"Holmes and I had a busy hour on the telephone after the two of you retired last night," the spymaster said. "I talked to Mycroft again, and we agreed that the French military attaché—a man named Reyer[77]—should come over to meet with our General Staff much sooner than originally planned. Moreover, the participants will be reduced in number and the gathering held in a different venue than usual."

"I see," Hannay remarked.

"In fact, Reyer will arrive in London today at five and then dine with Mycroft," explained Bullivant. "He is scheduled to come to my London home in Queen Anne's Gate[78] afterward, where four people will see him: representatives of the army chiefs of staff and the admiralty, the war minister, and myself. There will also, of course, be various aides in attendance.

"We need to start for London presently," said Holmes.

---

[77] In *The Thirty-Nine Steps*, this individual's name is given as Royer.

[78] This should not be confused with Queen Anne Street, the location of Watson's residence. Queen Anne's Gate was a housing development between St. James's Park and Westminster.

"Yes," agreed Bullivant, who turned to Hannay and me and directed us to the hot dishes that remained upon the breakfast table. "I suggest you fill up yourselves," he said. "I believe we have a long day ahead of us."

We four drove to London later that morning, with Hannay acting as chauffeur—Bullivant's butler was to come up by train with the luggage. At half past eleven, we arrived at Queen's Anne Gate and entered Sir Walter's residence to find Inspector Magillivray waiting for us.

"I've brought you the Portland Place murderer," Sir Walter proclaimed jovially.

A wry smile swept over the inspector's face. "It would be a welcome present, indeed, sir, were that the case. However, it appears that you have instead brought me Mr. Richard Hannay. Halloa," he said as he extended a hand. "My department and others have been very interested in you these past few days, as I'm sure you've been aware."

"Mr. Hannay will interest you all again," affirmed Bullivant. "He has much to tell, but not at present. For now, I wish only that you ensure that he will suffer no further inconvenience while in town."

"Of course," said Magillivray, turning once more to the South African. "You may take up your life where you left off," he declared. "Your flat is waiting for you, and your man is still there. As you were never publicly accused, I should think there is no need of a public exculpation. Shall I set a guard on you, though?"

"I don't think that will be necessary," replied Hannay.

"In any event," Sherlock Holmes advised the South African, "I strongly suggest you lie low, for if any member of the Black Stone were to see and recognise you, there might be serious consequences."

"I understand," replied Hannay, who shortly thereafter took leave of us, hailing a taxicab to spend time in the north end of London. Meanwhile, Holmes made use of Bullivant's telephone to ring up Jack James, who at length arrived in his taxi.

"All the news is about the murder of that Greek politician," said the young man as we boarded his vehicle. "Everyone seems quite upset about it all. There's a lot of talk about war breaking out."

I merely nodded in agreement, remembering a comment that Holmes and Hannay had gleaned from Scudder's notebook about conflict being inevitable once the assassination had been successfully accomplished.

"Steiner and Hollins gave Von Bork to understand that I was travelling to Scapa Flow?" Holmes asked the American.

"That they did," Jack replied. "And you are to report directly to the German once you are back. *Are* you back?" he asked after a moment.

"No," replied the detective. He pulled from his coat pocket an object I recognised at once: Scudder's battered notebook. "I have again been entrusted with this for the moment," he told me. "And I believe we should employ the next few hours to continue the decipherment of pages that Hannay and I had not the time to translate before, in preparation for what is to come. To Safety House, Jack," he ordered.

"It is a substitution cipher," Holmes explained as we sat at the table in what would have been the dining room, had Safety House served as an actual residence. My friend had spread the notebook open before us and wrote on a stack of blank foolscap positioned to the side.

"Hannay was very attentive and perceptive," the detective declared. "While still alive, Scudder had told him that a woman named Julia

Dobranski[79] would be the key to the entire affair. And so she is, metaphorically—or, rather, her name, as Hannay cleverly speculated."

"How so?" I asked.

"Scudder's notebook text is written entirely in Roman numerals, each of which we may assume represents a letter of the alphabet. As Hannay related to me on the trip down to Berkshire, it suddenly occurred to him that there are five letters in the name *Julia* and five vowels in the English language. Taking those vowels in order, he surmised that the first alphabetically, A, might be represented by the first letter of the woman's name, *J*. Now *J* is the tenth letter of the alphabet, and so in Scudder's cipher text, the numeral *X* would be translated as *A*. Similarly, the next vowel in alphabetic order, *E*, would correspond to the *U* in *Julia*, and thus *XXI* in the cipher might represent *U*. In this manner, all five vowels are accounted for."

"And how does the last name—Dobranski—come into play?"

Hannay's guess was that it gives consonants, except that there are only nine letters in that surname. Hence, he supposed it was related to merely the principal consonants, and that turns out to be the case. If one makes all the previous assumptions stated, the numeral text in Scudder's book yields partial words, phrases, and sentences, allowing the translator to guess the remainder."

"You mean to say that the letters of the last name specify those consonants in the order of their frequency according to common usage, rather than in alphabetical order? How could an innocent bystander know that frequency?"

---

[79] In *The Thirty-Nine Steps*, the surname given is Czechenyi.

Holmes smiled. "One is often amazed by the range of minutiae our minds collect, almost unconsciously," he said. "However he came by it, Hannay did know the order of the most frequent consonants. With all the vowels known, as well as the most common consonants, the words of the original text can be fleshed out nicely. Of course," he went on, "Hannay did not have the time to complete the job. That is what we must do now, without delay."

"Are we not also to attend the meeting with the French attaché at Bullivant's residence?"

"No," said Holmes as he bent over the notebook, carefully transcribing numerals and letters to the sheet on top of his pile. "I cannot see the need. The gathering with the Frenchman is to be small and well-guarded."

I watched as Holmes continued to decipher the notebook's contents. "And what of your German master, Von Bork?" I asked. "When will you contact him?"

"That remains to be seen," remarked my friend. "Please pass that other pile of papers to me, old fellow."

With me assisting him in some of the transcribing, Holmes started ploughing through those portions of Scudder's pocketbook that had not yet been deciphered.

"We have translated some important material, Watson," said my friend after an hour of work. "And we have also decoded notes by Scudder whose meaning escapes me. Listen to this latest line I have parsed: 'Must disturb the sleeping dog.' What can we make of that?"

"An answer escapes me. In what context was the line written?"

"It stands by itself, and there is no further reference. How odd."

"Perhaps it is nothing."

"Then why would Scudder have taken the trouble to encode and write it down? I must file it in the back of my mind, Watson."

At that moment, as the time was getting on toward eleven o'clock, I heard the telephone ring in the sitting room.

Holmes looked up from the notebook, his face suddenly betraying an expression of concern. Without speaking, he rose and quickly strode into the adjoining room, and there lifted the telephone. I followed him part of the way and then stood in the open doorway to watch and listen.

"Halloa?" said the detective. "Yes, Sir Walter...I see. And Hannay is certain? You have confirmed that fact?" Holmes took a deep breath and turned me as he continued speaking. "We shall rush to Queen Anne's Gate immediately."

Holmes rang off.

"A difficulty?" I asked.

"Worse. A disaster," my friend replied.

He walked past me and gathered up the sheets upon which our decipherment had been written.

"The Black Stone infiltrated the meeting, after all—boldly, and with brazen ingenuity," he informed me. "One of their number apparently attended in disguise and then left with the information we sought so desperately to guard: the Home Fleet mobilisation orders in case of war. Moreover," he added, "he made off with some sensitive French military secrets as well."

"Great God!"

"Go to the bedroom and wake Jack. We need to reach Sir Walter's residence at once."

I turned to fetch the young American, who had gone off to nap while we worked on Scudder's notebook.

"And Watson," added Holmes, "make certain to tidy the bed so that it appears unused. Recall that Jack is not supposed to have been here within Safety House."

"It was the man's expression when our eyes met," Hannay told us several minutes later at Bullivant's residence. We stood amid a circle that included the South African and the spymaster, as well as the British Minister of War, representatives of the army and the admiralty, and the French military attaché Reyer.

"He came out of the meeting room and just walked past," Hannay said for my benefit and that of Holmes. "I'd dined at a restaurant in Jermyn Street, but then I kept thinking I should be doing something, and so I decided to come here. I arrived a bit after half past nine and saw all the motorcars drawn up along the street. Ringing the bell, I was confronted by the butler, who graciously admitted me, despite the fact that Sir Walter was still engaged in the meeting. I was ushered into an alcove and waited there for nearly an hour, at which time I heard a door open at the far end of the hall. There were footsteps, and then a man walked briskly by.

"He caught sight of me from the corner on his eye, and we looked at each other as he passed," Hannay related. "And in that moment, I saw something spring into his expression, and that something was recognition. Do you understand what I mean, Mr. Holmes? You can't mistake the look in a person's eyes. It is a flicker, a spark of light. I was aware that he knew who I was, even though I didn't know him."

"I understand," commented Holmes.

"The revelation made me freeze," Hannay went on. "The man rushed out the door, and the sound of it slamming finally set me into motion. I strode down the hall and burst into the room where the meeting was still in progress."

"The interruption took us all aback," said Sir Walter. "However, Hannay's entrance did not shock us so much as did his assertion that a German spy had just left."

"And no one had questioned the presence of that individual?" asked Holmes, in whom I saw disguised exasperation.

"Everyone took him to be an aide to someone else at the table," explained the admiralty representative. "Apparently, he spoke French to one of the war minister's men, making that person believe he was with Reyer. On the other hand, he suggested to those from my entourage that he was with the army general staff."

"The man was completely nondescript and forgettable," said Reyer. "Even now, I cannot describe him, other than to say that he was somewhat plump. I believe he took a position by the wall during our meeting," the Frenchman said. "He stood there with other underlings, and then volunteered to leave in order to fetch coffee when I expressed an interest in having some."

"And that was after the Home Fleet dispositions had been explained openly?" Holmes asked.

"Yes," replied the war minister. "But you see, no one but Reyer's man took any form of notes during the gathering. The man who slipped out—whom Hannay believes to have been a German spy—could not have left with the information."

"Yes, he could have done so," corrected Reyer.

"But where did he mark down the information?" asked the minister.

"In his head," replied the French attaché. "A good agent is trained to have a photographic memory, is he not, Sir Walter?"

"Quite so," replied Bullivant. "Our best men can memorise places and distances in a host of provinces and still have room in their heads for financial accounts and troop rosters."

"Places and distances," whispered Hannay, whose face now took on a new expression. "By God, I know who that man was," the South African declared, turning to Holmes. "He was the assistant to Moncrief, the archaeologist. He was the plump man who supervised my imprisonment up in Scotland."

"What?" said Bullivant.

"Yes," Hannay replied. "Remember? I mentioned him when I related my capture and escape from that damned house. He was the one who guessed what towns I had passed through and how far I'd gone. He spouted all those distances from memory. The fellow appeared different tonight, but in retrospect, I recall the eyes looked the same as they did in Scotland—they were *his* eyes." Hannay looked around at us. "But is it possible for someone to so completely fool others by disguise alone?"

I looked at Holmes with raised brows, and my friend returned the gesture before responding. "My experience, Mr. Hannay, is that it is well within the realm of possibility."

"But what must we do?" I asked. "Will the mobilisation plans for the Fleet be changed?"

"It would be most difficult," said the Admiralty representative. "Geography is geography, and our current plans are the optimal ones."

"Moreover," said Reyer, "if you all recall, I also revealed many of the detailed dispositions my own government intends to make should war break out in the wake of Karolides's murder."

"The man who left with the information in his head must be apprehended," said the War Minister. "But then, will he not just send that information to Berlin at once?"

"I doubt it," replied Bullivant. "That may be the one saving grace of our situation."

"Yes," agreed Reyer. "Information of that import will be delivered in person. Those behind the infiltration will attempt to leave your country to accomplish that. We must intercept them."

"But how?" asked the war minister.

Indeed," chimed in the army representative. "We haven't a rag of a clue."

"Respectfully, I beg to differ," said Sherlock Holmes.

All eyes fell upon the detective, and Hannay cocked his head. "What do you mean?" the South African said. "Do you speak of the notebook?"

"Yes," replied Holmes, who pulled it from his jacket pocket. "I have completed more of the translation, and one item in it comes to mind."

My friend set the small volume onto a table and pulled from his coat pocket the folded sheets on which we had written the deciphered text.

"There is an entry that Scudder made in the section on the Black Stone. Where is it? Here: 'Thirty-nine steps at high tide—I counted them.'"

I saw that the admiralty representative was staring at Holmes wide-eyed, as if he thought the detective were half mad.

"But what would tides have to do with anything?" asked the war minister.

"My question exactly, Minister," said Holmes. "What would tides have to do with anything involving our current predicament save access to the sea, and what relevance is the sea in this affair other than as an avenue of escape to the Continent?" The detective tapped the notebook. "Scudder must have discovered yet another lair of the Black Stone—"

"That is the code name for this group of German spies," Bullivant whispered to the others, who had now gathered round the table where Scudder's notebook sat.

"He had found another of their dens," Holmes repeated. "Most likely, the location from which they entered and exited our island. A location for which the timing of high tide is somehow critical."

"But they may have gone tonight," someone said.

"No," said Holmes. "I think not. When were the high tides today?" he asked.

"Late morning to midday, I believe, and then in the last two or three hours" said the Admiralty representative.

"There would not have been time for them to reach the coast this evening," Holmes said. "And, if the tide is crucial to their departure, then we have until late morning tomorrow at the worst, and almost another twelve hours if we are fortunate. And these are Germans we are speaking of—they have their own well-perfected plans. They will not be rushed and will stay determined to work to a plan."

"Quite so," said Reyer. "You know them as well as we do, Monsieur Holmes. Are you perhaps in reality French, and English only by adoption?" the attaché asked facetiously.

"I am merely one-fourth Gallic,"[80] my friend genially replied, "but that is enough to be confident in my judgment." Then, laying both palms onto the great table, he asked, "Now, where can we get a book of tide tables?"

The war minister, suddenly appearing more hopeful than before, said, "Let us go to the admiralty."

And so we boarded three of the waiting motorcars—all but Sir Walter Bullivant, who commandeered Jack James's taxicab to take him to Scotland Yard in order to alert Inspector Magillivray.

Holmes, Reyer, the three other representatives of the British government and I, meanwhile, sped to the Admiralty Building. There we marched through empty corridors and huge, spare chambers where, at that hour, the King's business was being conducted principally by charwomen. At length, led by the admiralty representative, we reached a little room lined with books and maps. Though it was now the middle of the night, a resident clerk was unearthed and asked to fetch the admiralty tide tables.

Hannay sat at a desk, Holmes standing over him, while the rest of us formed a semicircle before the two men.

"But where do we start?" exclaimed the South African after a moment. "There are hundreds of entries. How do we determine which are the relevant ones? What if we hunted up all the steamer sailings? Might there be one that is scheduled to leave at high tide?"

---

[80] One of Holmes's grandmothers was a sister of the French painter Émile Jean-Horace Vernet. The detective's quantifying remark suggests that her husband was of a different nationality.

“They would not travel on a regular line,” asserted Holmes. “Indeed, I doubt they will be boarding any large-draught ship.”

“But then, why would the tide be of importance, if not to allow the ship to dock?” asked someone.

“I believe its importance lies not in allowing a ship to reach land,” said Holmes, “but rather in permitting those on land to more easily reach the sea. Is not the significance of the phrase *the thirty-nine steps* evident to everyone present?”

“The reference is to dock steps?” said the admiralty representative.

“Were that the case, there would be no need to mention their number,” replied Holmes. “Scudder must refer to some coastal place—a cliff of some sort—where there are several staircases leading down toward the water, necessitating the use of their number to specify which one.”

“And whichever set of steps has the correct number, that one must lead to the den which holds our nest of spies,” I said.

“Precisely, Watson. And there are other considerations,” Holmes said. “The man seeks a swift and secret passage to Germany. What point of departure would he seek? Not a big harbour, and not a site located on the Channel or the West Coast or our recent tramping ground, Scotland. Consider the map, if you will. He will try for Ostend or Antwerp or Rotterdam, and I fancy he will sail from somewhere on the East Coast between Dover and Cromer.”

Just then, Bullivant arrived in the company of Inspector Magillivray.

“I’ve sent out instructions to watch the ports and railway stations for your Mr. Moncrief, based on your description of him,” the inspector told Hannay and the rest of us. “Too bad the other fellow, the one who actually has the information in his head, is so forgettable. Without a description of him other than 'plump,' it's rather hopeless to think we can catch him that way, should he be travelling alone."

"Inspector? Sir Walter?" said Sherlock Holmes. "May I suggest that Moncrief's house in Scotland, as well as its associated aerodrome, be immediately surrounded, and those within taken into custody?"

"That process has already begun," declared his brother Mycroft, who stood at the doorway to the map room. Seeing that I and others had noticed his slightly unkempt hair, the elder Holmes brushed the balding top of his head with one pudgy hand and then stepped into our congregation.

"My man relayed your call, Sir Walter," he informed Bullivant, "and I got here as quickly as I could. What is our situation, Sherlock?" he asked, implicitly selecting his sibling as spokesman for our group.

The detective explained all that we had discussed in the previous moments.

"They will attempt to leave in a trawler, yacht, or launch, yes," agreed Mycroft, "and undoubtedly the point of departure will lie between Dover and the Wash,[81] as you say. I myself would lean closer to Dover and consider seaside towns in Kent before any others. Tell me," he said to the admiralty representative, "is there an inspector of coastguards we can rouse at this hour, someone who knows the East Coast well enough to suggest how we might refine our search?"

"There is one who lives in Clapham."[82]

"Fetch him," said Mycroft, and the admiralty representative left by car.

---

[81] The Wash is a square-shaped bay on the east coast of England, where Norfolk meets Lincolnshire. The town of Cromer, previously mentioned as the northern boundary of the area under consideration, lies near the Wash.

[82] Clapham is a district of South West London.

About one o'clock in the morning, the member of His Majesty's Coastguard arrived. He was a strapping old fellow with the look of naval officer, which he might well have been in his earlier years. The man was deferential to all and listened attentively as Mycroft Holmes questioned him.[83]

"We are seeking locations on the East Coast where there are cliffs with more than one set of steps leading down to the beach," the elder Holmes began.

"Well, sir," the inspector replied, "there are plenty of places with roads cut down through the cliffs, and most have a step or two in them."

"I want one with nothing but steps," explained Mycroft. "A regular staircase—rather, regular staircases, plural."

"Well," said the man after a moment's reflection, "I know of a place beside a golf-course where there are a couple of staircases to let gentlemen get a lost ball. It's in Norfolk."

"I am thinking of Kent," said Mycroft. "And it is likely a place where there are houses, villas, resorts."

"Oh," replied the inspector. "Well then, I suppose the Ruff is the one for you, then."

"The Ruff?" said the Frenchman Reyer.

"Yes," replied the coastguard. "It's a big chalk headland in Kent, right near Broadgate.[84] There are all sorts of villas for you on the top, and

---

[83] In Hannay's account as related in *The Thirty-Nine Steps*, it is the war minister who interrogates the coastguard officer. But then, Watson's narrative diverges significantly from Hannay's in this chapter.

[84] In *The Thirty-Nine Steps*, the name used is Bradgate. In reality, the coastal town referred to was probably Broadstairs, which lies eighty miles east of London.

several of the homes have staircases down to a private beach. Very high-toned place it is. The residents prefer to keep to themselves."

"An ideal environment in which to set up camp if you are a group of spies," said Sherlock Holmes.

"Agreed, brother," murmured Mycroft Holmes. "Let us choose it and pray."

I suddenly noticed that Richard Hannay had begun feverishly flipping through the table of tides. All other eyes swiftly also turned in his direction.

"We are close!" exclaimed Hannay, planting a forefinger in the middle of a page. "This coming evening, high tide at Broadgate will be at ten twenty-seven. How can we find the exact time of the tide at the Ruff?"

"Oh, I can tell you that," said the coastguard man casually, "for I've spent many nights there in June going deep-sea fishing. The tide at the Ruff precedes that at Broadgate by ten minutes."

The two Holmes brothers looked at one another and nodded.

"There is now but one more thing to do," said Mycroft.

"We must go to Kent, observe the different sets of steps running down the Ruff, and enumerate them," answered Sherlock Holmes.

"*You* must go and enumerate them, dear brother. You are as able to count to thirty-nine as I."

Images of Kentish hedgerows tearing past us in the night existed now only in memory as I stood early next morning with Holmes, Hannay, and Magillivray on a rocky outcrop overlooking calm seas. A lightship lay off shore, bathed in pink, and two miles down the coast, a small naval destroyer sat at anchor.

"My man Scaife should be aboard her now, making arrangements," said Magillivray as we stared at the second vessel. "And we have small squads covering all the hotels; Inspectors Hartley and Carter are overseeing them." Together, we surveyed the cliffs in the distance. "Do you think we should be gathered out here together like this, Mr. Holmes?" the inspector asked.

"The place is rather deserted at this hour," replied the detective as a lonely caw sounded from above. "It is only ourselves and that single gull overhead. In any event, we three will now retire to the hotel room while you survey the stairs," he told Magillivray. "You have the key that opens the gates of the staircases on the Ruff?"

The inspector turned toward the chalky precipice in the distance and pulled his fist from a coat pocket. Opening his fingers, he revealed a key on a chain. "I've never let go of it since obtaining it from that house agent," Magillivray said with a spare grin. "He didn't like being awoke at that hour, did he?" The man's lawyerlike face settled into a determined look. "I'll go and count the steps on the staircases, sirs, and join you in the room shortly."

"Very good, Inspector," said Holmes, who led Hannay and me farther along the little outcrop and back toward Broadgate itself. As we saw Magillivray make his way along the beach toward the greater expanse of the Ruff, my friend gave his goatee a gentle tug.

"I have acquired the habit of grasping this thing," he commented jokingly. "I wonder if I will continue to seize the air once it is gone."

"Will that be soon, you think?" I asked.

"It will not surprise, should that be the case," he replied as we came up over a rise and Broadgate hove into view. "I believe Sir Walter will be forced to tear down our Von Bork façade in the near future." Holmes then explained to Hannay the substance of his past two years of work infiltrating the German spy ring.

"And so," said Hannay, as we approached the town, "should we fail to stop the Black Stone in taking the naval information to Berlin, you must stop playing your role as—what was the name?"

"Altamount," said Holmes quietly, hands clasped behind his back. "Yes, we must scuttle the Von Bork escapade in that event. However," he said languidly, "Our work will hardly be over."

"You refer to identifying the third part of Cerberus?" asked Hannay.

"Yes," sighed Holmes as we entered the town of Broadgate. "But we now have the first of those parts by the throat, and we know the second lies with Von Bork. Let us concentrate on the former for the time being."

It was almost two hours later that Magillivray returned to our room at the Griffin Hotel. Holmes, who was sipping coffee at the window, smiled wanly and cradled his cup in both hands as the man from Scotland Yard entered. I regarded the inspector expectantly from a table where I laboured at a game of Patience. Hannay, who had been reading old issues of several periodicals, rose quickly to his feet in anticipation.

"There were six staircases in all," Magillivray declared as he pulled a paper from his coat pocket. Unfolding the sheet, he read from it. "The various counts of steps in each was as follows: twenty-one, thirty-four, thirty-five, forty-two, forty-seven, and...thirty-nine."

Hannay seemed ready to shout, but he remained silent, quietly slapping fist against palm instead. "We have them!" he exclaimed at length.

"We have identified their probable lair," corrected Holmes. The detective turned back to Magillivray. "And you approached the residence associated with those steps?" he asked.

"I did, Mr. Holmes."

"What did you learn?"

"I got as far as the back door of the house," said Magillivray. "I posed as an agent for sewing machines, as you suggested, and was able to get some idea of the place. It's a red-brick villa with a veranda and a tennis lawn in back. The front sports the usual seaside flower garden, replete with marguerites and scraggly geraniums. There is a flagstaff standing before the house from which an enormous Union Jack hangs."

"Did you speak with anyone there?" Holmes asked.

"Yes, though only briefly, as there was no interest in sewing machines," said Magillivray. "There appear to be but three servants: a cook, a parlourmaid, and a housemaid. The cook shut the door on my face rather soon—I suspect she is not the gossiping kind and quickly got tired of my questions. And, of course, it was still somewhat early in the morning for a businessman to be plying his trade. Still, if I had to judge, I'd say that the three of them are just the type of servant you'd find in a respectable middle-class home, and I doubt they know a thing about any spy business."

"Hum," said Holmes. "And you then went back to the house agent for more information?"

"Yes, I did," replied the inspector. "He wasn't too happy to see me again, though he did praise me for coming this time at an almost decent hour. I informed him which villa I was interested in, and he told me it's known as Trafalgar Lodge. It belongs to an old gentleman named

Appleton—supposedly a retired stockbroker. He's said to be a fine fellow who pays his bills on time and is always good for a fiver when the local charities call at the door."

"Have you any idea if this Mr. Appleton is in the house now?" Holmes enquired.

"The house agent indicated he usually spends late summers there, and that he had been in residence at the place for nearly the past week. Oh, and when I was at the back of the villa, conversing with the servants, I had an opportunity to notice two plates with silverware on a work table, both of them used and not yet washed. The plate was of such quality that I doubt the servants eat any meals of theirs from it. I suppose we may assume that this Mr. Appleton has a guest within the house."

Holmes nodded. "An excellent observation, Inspector."

"I have a yen to go see the house from a distance," Richard Hannay suddenly declared. "Do you think that would be unwise, Mr. Holmes?"

"Not necessarily," said the detective. "Indeed, I was going to suggest it myself. One way or the other, we must familiarise ourselves with the grounds. "Have you noticed any new vessels arriving offshore?" he asked Magillivray.

"None, sir. It's still only the lightship and the destroyer."

"That is a good sign," declared Holmes, checking the time. "Every minute that passes without a ship coming into view means a lesser probability that our friends will attempt to flee during the morning tide. Let us wait a while longer here upon the porch. Once the hour of eleven passes, I believe we may rest assured there will be no effort to escape until tonight."

We all left the room and took up stations outside, which gave an excellent panorama of the coast.

"I wish I had had the opportunity to meet Scudder," mused Sherlock Holmes. "He must have been rather accomplished to have ferreted out this lair, as well as all the other elements contained in his notebook. It is a pity he is not here with us to savour the prospect of victory."

We kept watch for close to a half hour, but no vessel appeared on the horizon.

"Well," Holmes said at length, "Shall we all go have a look at Trafalgar Lodge?"

"Or another look, in my case," replied the inspector.

We went for a walk along the Ruff, keeping well behind the rows of villas. Along the cliff top was planted a line of turf, with iron seats placed at intervals upon little square plots railed in and festooned with bushes. It was from that area that some staircases descended to the beach, and from our vantage point, Trafalgar Lodge could be plainly seen.

It was as Magillivray had described it: a red-brick villa with veranda, sporting an ordinary seaside garden in front and tennis lawn in the back. Looming overhead was a huge Union Jack, now fluttering fitfully in the late morning breeze. We passed Magillivray's telescope among ourselves for a better view, and as Hannay took his turn, he gave a start.

"Someone is leaving the house!" he announced, passing the glass to Holmes.

"It is an older man," said the detective, once he had focussed the telescope. "He wears white flannel trousers, a blue serge jacket, and a straw hat. He carries a newspaper and field glasses—we should be prepared to duck behind our tree at once if he raises them to his eye. He is sitting on one of the seats and unfolding his paper."

"Is it Moncreif?" I asked.

Holmes shrugged. "At this distance, and with his hat in the way, I cannot be certain."

Cautiously, we took turns once more with the glass, this time watching as the old man read the newspaper. Then, as I beheld him, he folded up the paper once more. "He has finished with it," I said quickly as I passed the telescope back to Holmes, who immediately pointed it toward the object of our observation.

"He is staring off at the sea," noted my friend. "To his left."

"That is the direction in which the anchored destroyer lies," observed Hannay.

"Yes," said Holmes. "That ship, no doubt, is where his fancy—or anxiety—lies. He is reaching beside him for his field glasses then moving his hand away from them, and...tapping his knee with his finger! Ha! Our sights are aimed true, gentlemen."

"How do you mean, Mr. Holmes?" asked Magillivray.

"He taps his knee repeatedly in a distinctive manner," repeated the detective.

"Yes," I interjected, but how does—"

"Mr. Hannay," said Holmes, "does that gesture not remind you of someone?"

"Tapping of the knee? It does seem that I've noticed that in someone recently, but I cannot—wait! Good God, do you mean that man there on the cliff is Moncrief, after all?"

"Here, he is no doubt known as Appleton," said Holmes, continuing to watch through the telescope. "Recall that I too spent a while with him up in Scotland—more time in his presence than you did," he told Hannay. "I quietly compiled a small catalogue of his habits and gestures, and that hesitant tapping of the knees which you mentioned in your account was put on the list quite early during my own observation of him."

"Yes," said Hannay. "I recall he displayed it when lighting a cigar in my presence."

"Ah," said Holmes, "he is at last grasping his field glasses and looking out to sea."

"At the destroyer? That ship must be a concern for him, as you said," commented Magillivray.

"Yes," agreed Holmes. "However, surveying the naval craft with his field glasses would tell him little more than he could already surmise. He watches and waits for something else, I suspect." The detective put down the telescope and compressed it. "And so must we. Come, let us return to the Griffin. I do not wish to forgo lunch in the interim."

Once more we occupied the porch of our hotel, the four of us this time lined up in chairs as if we were carefree vacationers. Holmes attempted to cast a leg up upon the railing, but found his ligaments not as pliant as in earlier decades and returned to a more dignified posture.

Then Hannay stood up and pointed at the horizon.

"I believe I see a ship. Can that be it?" he said anxiously.

I, who had the telescope, pointed its lens in the direction indicated. After a brief search, I espied what had caught the South African's attention. "It is a yacht," I said.

"What colour is the ensign, Watson?" asked Holmes.

I had to wait a moment more before getting a sure glimpse of the banner.

"White," I said at length.

"A member of the Squadron," muttered Magillivray. "That could not be the one, could it?" he asked in disbelief.[85]

"Nothing precludes our friends from being well connected," said Holmes with raised brows. "But let us first wait and see where the stranger drops anchor, if it does at all."

The yacht continued to sail in from the south and then circled before anchoring immediately opposite the Ruff.

"That must be it, don't you think?" said Hannay.

"I should think so," agreed Holmes. "But halloa, I believe your man also approaches, Magillivray, though from the north instead."

Turning, I observed Sergeant Scaife walking briskly along the path leading to our hotel. Seeing us upon the porch, he waved and then a moment later joined us there.

"You all have a nice shady promenade," he said pleasantly, "and a good view as well. And company, I see," observing the yacht anchored offshore.

Holmes nodded.

"Well," Scaife said, his eyes flitting between my friend and Magillivray as he spoke, "the commander of our destroyer out there, *HMS Anchises*, confirms that he has received the message sent from London

---

[85] Magillivray refers to the Royal Yacht Squadron, founded in 1815 and based at Cowes. Member ships of the Squadron are allowed to fly the White Ensign of the Royal Navy instead of the merchant Red Ensign flown by most ships registered in the United Kingdom.

and will meet you here at the hotel at six o'clock to put finishing touches on the plan, if that will suit."

"I believe it will. Do you agree, Inspector?" asked Holmes.

"I've nothing else on my agenda for that time, certainly. Well done, Scaife," Magillivray said to his man. "Tell the captain we'll receive him here as he proposes. I shall make the rounds of the other hotels to be certain everyone is prepared for this evening."

"Yes, sir."

"And Sergeant?" said the detective.

"Yes, Mr. Holmes?"

"Do you become ill at sea?"

"Me, sir? Hardly. I was raised in these very parts—Margate, specifically—and I'm most comfortable out on the water."

"In that case," said Holmes, "there is a task in which you may assist Mr. Hannay upon your return."

"Glad to be of further service, sir."

Later that afternoon, after Scaife had confirmed our appointment with the captain of the naval destroyer anchored down the coast, he accompanied Richard Hannay in hiring a boatman for some fishing in the waters off Broadgate. The pair returned carrying an admirable catch of pollack and cod, but also with information gleaned from immediate observation of the newly arrived yacht, which was named the *Ariadne*.

"She's built for speed," Scaife testified. "Her construction lends her swiftness, and there's no doubt she possesses heavy engines."

"And you got close enough to speak with members of the crew?" asked Holmes.

"Oh yes," Hannay said. "I made the boatman row us round the yacht and then closer to her. There was a man polishing the brasswork out on deck, and I spoke to him."

"Any idea where he hailed from?"

"There was a touch of Essex in his speech, Mr. Holmes," Scaife replied.

"Another hand came along almost immediately," added Hannay. "He was unmistakably English as well. Our boatman had an argument with him about the weather, and for a few minutes we lay on our anchor close to the starboard bow."

"Then the two started paying us no attention and bent their heads to their work," said Scaife.

"Yes," confirmed Hannay. "They turned from us as an officer came along the deck. This fellow was pleasant enough and clean looking. He noticed us at once and asked about the fishing in very good English, but there couldn't be any doubt about him, Mr. Holmes. His head was too closely cropped, and the cut of his collar and tie never came out of England."

"German, do you think?" asked Magillivray, and Hannay nodded.

"I take it he had no *Renommierschmiss*, but no matter," said Holmes.[86] "I believe we may assume that, though the deck hands are English, the *Ariadne* is commanded by Germans."

"And so we become confidenter and confidenter," I murmured. "With apologies, Holmes, to your late Reverend Dodgson."[87]

---

[86] This is a reference to dueling scars, seen as a badge of honor among upper-class German and Austrian university students of the time.

[87] Charles Lutwidge Dodgson, better known by his pen name of Lewis Carroll, wrote Alice's *Adventures in Wonderland,* in which there appears the oft-quoted phrase,

Holmes smiled. "Our cast continues to assemble," he said. "And the stage is nearly set. I hope tonight's little play is well received by all but a few."

"With the only bad reviews written in German?" asked Hannay.

"*Ja*," Holmes intoned wistfully as he stared out to sea.

Our meeting at six o'clock with the commander of the destroyer *Anchises* proceeded well. Hannay and Scaife conveyed to the captain their impressions of the yacht's deck plan, and the officer made a quick inspection of the craft from afar through Magillivray's telescope. Then, after a spare dinner, the captain returned to his ship while Scaife set off to assemble the many policemen who had followed us to Broadgate and had remained encamped in various hotels about the seaside town.

Holmes and I donned coats and caps, meanwhile, and at half past seven we left for a leisurely stroll, our course set for the top of the Ruff, and the red-brick villa that housed our adversaries.

"There's an east wind coming, Watson," my friend declared as we made our slow ascent.

"You seem to have lost your edge, Holmes," I replied as I took the lead up the path. "Such a breeze has been with us since before we began climbing the Ruff."

"Watson, you are a literal anchor in our new nightmare of an age. I spoke in metaphor," my friend explained as he extended his hand.

"curiouser and curiouser," a line uttered previously in the narrative—in a somewhat different sense—by innkeeper Ewan Clark. Of interest, perhaps, is Watson's reference to "*your* late Reverend Dodgson." This could suggest either that Holmes was an avid reader of Carroll's work or that the detective had been personally acquainted with Dodgson, perhaps as a client or even student, since Dodgson lectured at Oxford, which Holmes may have attended, until 1881.

I gripped his forearm and assisted him briefly up a tall step.

"That yacht below and our friends in the villa above are but harbingers," Holmes said as he once again trod the way on his own. "So is my own adversary of these past two years, Herr Von Bork. They are all precursors of an ominous wind signalling the Armageddon that is to come."

"A wind of war, then?"

"Sadly, yes. Such a wind as never blew on England yet. Still, with the comradeship of men such as Hannay in the struggle, perhaps there is a prospect of victory. But onward and upward, old fellow. Let us reach for the top."[88]

We attained the crest of the Ruff and proceeded toward Trafalgar Lodge, pausing behind a large rhododendron. Then, at the back of the villa, we saw two men having a game of tennis on the lawn.

"Ah," said Holmes. "I recognise the older fellow there as the man who was known as Moncrief the archaeologist in Galloway—and is presumably Appleton the stockbroker here in Broadgate."

The other tennis player was somewhat plump, wearing club colours in a scarf wrapped round his middle. The pair contended with intense spirit, as if they were two gentlemen who sought hard exercise to open their pores. They shouted and laughed in a most innocent manner, and when a maid brought out two tankards on a salver, they paused for drinks.

"Despite all the circumstantial evidence—the thirty-nine steps, the German officer on board the *Ariadne*, your confidence that one of those men is Moncrief—I must confess that I am beginning to question our

---

[88] Sherlockian devotees will, no doubt, recognize portions of this conversation as appearing in "His Final Bow," though in somewhat different form and context.

conclusions," I whispered to my friend. "How can those two be German spies? They seem, rather, to be pure Englishmen, through and through."

"Blame it on atmosphere and its effect upon perception," said my friend quietly. "That is just what they count upon. Recall what was said when Hannay recounted his impersonation of the roadman? To convince others, you must convince yourself, and to convince yourself, you must actually be what you pretend to be."

The detective gazed at the two men as they finished their drinks and resumed volleying. "Here is evidence of that truth," he said. "A fool tries to look different; a clever man looks the same and *is* different."

I stared at the two figures, willing them to become foreign agents in my eyes, without success.

"Yes, they are masters of the art," said Holmes with a wistful smile as he stroked his goatee. "But halloa, I believe we have another poseur joining them."

From the opposite side of the house, a young man approached on a bicycle with a bag of golf clubs slung on his back. He deftly debarked from the vehicle and strolled round to the tennis lawn, where he was enthusiastically welcomed by the other two.

The plump man, mopping his brow, said loudly, "I've got into a proper lather. That will bring down my handicap as well as my weight," he said to the newcomer, who set his golf clubs against a bench. "Bob, I'd take you on tomorrow and give you a stroke a hole were we not leaving tonight."

Both tennis players chaffed the third man in grand fashion, and he in turn gave them both a dismissive gesture, the sight of which brought a distant memory to mind.

I pulled back behind the rhododendron and looked at Holmes.

"That hand gesture," I said softly. "I remember it being made by the loafer in front of Richard Hannay's building. The young fellow there was one of the Germans who was watching at Portland Place."

We heard the old man shout, "You had best bathe quickly then, Percy, if we are to depart on time," and Holmes motioned that we should leave.

We both headed back toward the head of the Ruff, to the plot of turf and its long row of iron seats. A man and wife strolled with their two young daughters at the far end of the line, and we claimed a bench removed from them but still within distant view of Trafalgar Lodge. Holmes turned and nodded to me, and I withdrew from my pocket a kerchief, which I opened up in front of me and waved before folding it neatly and returning the cloth to my jacket.

"I hope they saw it," I said.

"They have—through Magillivray's telescope," Holmes told me. "The hotel room window must be opening and closing, for I see the bright glint of sunshine off the pane—it is flickering, yes. Magillivray will have Scaife alert his fellows at the various other hotels. Shall we walk on for a bit, old fellow?"

"Of course. We are nearing the end of this affair, are we not, Holmes?"

My friend gave me a weary smile.

"Oh Watson, were that it were so," he sighed as we slowly ambled away from the villa and back along the path by which we had come. "There will be war, as Scudder's notes predict, and Britain will be drawn into it. Indeed," he said, looking out over the sea, "I have been engulfed in that east wind for some time—two years, at least—and it will be years more until we find ourselves in the lee."

He paused some distance down from Trafalgar Lodge, hands in the pockets of his coat. "We have not all three heads of Cerberus in sight, but only two, with the last still to be found. And the beast has at least one person planted somewhere in government."

I felt a chill on my spine at this last comment. "What do you mean by that, Holmes?"

"The meeting with Reyer was abruptly changed at the last moment, both with respect to date and venue," the detective noted, "and those alterations were known to but a precious few. And yet, the Black Stone infiltrated it with their man, perhaps one of the three we have just observed—I expect it was the plump one, according to Hannay's description. But whichever man it was, the fact that the Germans knew of the change in plan means that they have at least one of their own somewhere in Whitehall, with timely access to sensitive information such as that."

"I see. And so this will not be the conclusion."

"Far from it," said Holmes. "It is but the end of the first act, and any bows we take tonight will not be our final ones."

Later that evening, Holmes and I returned to the promontory of the Ruff and once more posted ourselves behind the great rhododendron. Lights shone from Trafalgar Lodge through the darkness, and as stars twinkled above, we were greeted by Hannay, Magillivray, and Scaife, who arrived at the head of a contingent of police, which also included Inspectors Hartley and Carter.

"They've not yet left, I hope," Hartley said quietly.

"They remain inside," answered Holmes, "though I expect them to make their move shortly." He looked at Richard Hannay. "Are you certain you wish to take the lead in this?" the detective asked. "The inspectors and Sergeant Scaife can do so instead."

"Yes," said Inspector Carter. "We can handle the chore, Mr. Hannay."

"You know," the South African said, "I feel as if I am the greatest fool on earth, yet it is something I know I must do, after all that has happened—after Scudder, the milkman, Turnbull the roadman, the innkeeper, and Sir Harry. All of them—and all of you."

Inspectors Magillivray, Hartley, and Carter nodded silently.

"I believe it's getting on near ten o'clock," Hannay declared. "When should I go to the door?"

"Once we see several lights dim," Holmes replied.

A quarter hour later, we saw four windows go dark in turn. At a signal from Magillivray, Sergeant Scaife and a portion of the police contingent moved to the rear of the villa and crept slowly and silently onto the tennis lawn, to crouch behind benches and chairs. The three inspectors and their remaining constables, along with Holmes and myself, watched Hannay calmly approach the front of Trafalgar Lodge.

As he reached for the gate, the door to the front of the villa opened, and three silhouettes stepped onto the porch, only to confront our companion.

"Halloa," Hannay said firmly. "I take it one of you is Mr. Appleton?"

"Yes," replied the old man, and I thought I detected a sense of shock and strain in the voice. "I am just leaving with my nephew and a friend of his. I am afraid I cannot meet with you at present, whoever you are. If you have business with me, might you simply leave your card inside, Mister....?"

"Richard Hannay. We have met before, of course, and I guess you know my business."

"Not really," said Appleton. "I haven't a very good memory, you see. I'm afraid you must tell me your errand, sir, for I really don't know it."

"Well then," Hannay said, "I have come to tell you that the game's up. I have in my coat a warrant for your arrest—the arrest of all three of you, in fact."

"Arrest?" said Appleton in a shocked voice. "Good God, for what?"

"For the murder of Franklin Scudder in London."

"I never heard the name before."

The youngest of the three, the one who had arrived on bicycle, spoke up. "That was the man murdered in Portland Place," he said. "I read about it. Good heavens, Mr. Hannay, or whatever your name is, you must be mad. Where do you come from?"

"Scotland Yard."

There was a long pause. Then the third man, the plump one, had his turn. "Don't get flustered, Uncle," he said cautiously. In a most smooth and resonant voice, he declared, "It must all be a ridiculous mistake, but these things happen sometimes, and we can easily set it right. It won't be hard to prove our innocence. I was out of the country when that murder occurred. Bob here was in a nursing home, and you were in London, yes, but you can explain what you were doing."

"Right, Percy," the old man replied, his tone now soothing and confident. "What was the date of that crime? Could it have been the day after Agatha's wedding? I came up in the morning from Woking and lunched at the club with Charlie Symons. Then—oh yes, I dined at Fishmongers' Hall.[89] I remember, for the punch didn't agree with me, and I was seedy next morning. Hang it all, there's a cigar-box I brought back from that dinner."

He stepped back onto the porch of the villa and opened the door.

"Come, Mr. Hannay," coaxed Appleton. "Step inside with me. I can show it you."

I found myself now almost believing the old man and certain our hunt for the German spies had gone astray. Then, as I tried to turn my opinion back the other way, I saw Hannay reach into his pocket. There was a dull gleam as he pulled out an object between his fingers and lifted it to his lips.

The shrill cry of a police whistle pierced the night, and the constables who stood beside us suddenly surged forward. I saw Appleton lurch toward Hannay and knock him to the ground before dashing back into the house.

"*Schnell!*" the old man rasped from the porch. "*Das Boot, das Boot!*"[90]

His two companions leapt for the railed entrance to the beach stairs. Inspector Hartley tripped the younger one, however, and he and two constables collared the fellow with ease. The plump man named Percy, however, made it to the staircase, locked the gate behind him and rushed down the cliffside.

Appleton stumbled inside, just a step ahead of Magillivray and Carter. Holmes and I reached the open doorway an instant later and looked

---

[89] This building is the headquarters of the Worshipful Company of Fishmongers, one of the Livery Companies of the City of London. A trade association derived from one of the city's medieval guilds, the company originally had a monopoly over the sale of fish in London. Today it oversees the quality of seafood imported into the City, as well as acting as an educational charity. See also footnote 41.

[90] "Quick! The boat, the boat!"

into the entry, where we saw the two inspectors on the floor, their arms locked round the legs of Appleton, who remained standing but had reached out to brace himself against a wall.

Scaife and his fellows, who had been stationed behind the villa, came running through from the back of the house, accompanied by screams from the servants. Appleton, still on his feet but held at the ankles, hobbled a short distance, extended his left hand, and gripped a bell pull, which he yanked again and again.

"Ha!" the old man cried as Magillivray and Carter finally pulled him to the floor.

We all heard a low rumble. Turning round in the open doorway, I saw a murky cloud of dust erupt from the shaft of the rocky stairway.

"He is safe," Appleton declared from his prone position, his eyes blazing. "You cannot follow him. He is gone; he has triumphed. *Der schwarze Stein ist in der Siegerskrome!*"[91]

I stared at him, taken aback, for what I saw before me now was nothing like the pleasant old English gent who had been playing tennis or calmly reading his paper on the edge of the Ruff. I saw that, as Hannay had described, his eyes were hooded like a hawk's, and in my perception the man was transformed into a vicious predator suddenly held captive, those raptor eyes holding all of us in contempt.

"There, there," said Scaife, who assisted Magillivray and Carter in hoisting our foe to his feet. The sergeant clamped handcuffs onto Appleton's wrists and declared, "We've got news for you, Fritz."

---

91 "The Black Stone is in the crown of victory!"

"I'm afraid that's true," said Hannay, who stood behind Holmes and me in the doorway. "The *Ariadne* has been in the hands of the British Navy for the past two hours. When your friend rows or swims out to her, it won't be to freedom."

The old man looked up at Hannay and, at the same time, noticed Holmes for the first time.

"You!" he said, staring at my friend. "*Die Biene mann.*"

"Yes," said Holmes, who took two steps toward the elderly German and bowed slightly. "The bee man."

CHAPTER TEN: ANOTHER BOW

I glanced across at Sherlock Holmes from behind the steering wheel of the Fox Type-V that his brother Mycroft had provided me in London. Harwich was now miles behind us as we raced toward my friend's South Downs cottage on the way to our final destination: Von Bork's headquarters on the Essex shore.

"There is no reason to fret," I said yet again, repeating my assurances of the past month, weeks during which the Continent had slid closer to the abyss of war as Britain watched. "You realise that, do you not?"

"The man escaped," Holmes muttered.

"The man drowned," I asserted.

"Have you a body with which to convince me?"

Holmes sat beside me, bundled in a riding coat with arms crossed. His wan expression was of the kind I had witnessed altogether too often during our many years together in Baker Street.

"I should have insisted on having a boat of our own stationed at the base of the Ruff," he said glumly. "It was a sorry case of misjudgement."

"But no one was seen wading ashore in the area that night," I said. "Surely the plump man lies below the ocean—or floats dead atop it—as we speak."

"And why is my brother Mycroft as sceptical as I of that hypothesis?"

I fell silent and gave my full attention to the road once more. While carefully steering round a horse cart and then avoiding an obstinate procession of geese, I said at last, "We should not yet give up hope."

"Our worries have only increased," Holmes said. "In addition to the elusive third head of Cerberus, we now must believe that the plump man has escaped with those naval secrets still in his head, and there is also a mole in our midst."

"I beg pardon?"

"That is Sir Walter's characterisation of the person or persons who let the Black Stone know that the meeting with Reyer was changed," said the detective disconsolately. "'A snivelling German mole with tunnels running the length of Whitehall,' was how Bullivant put it."[92]

"No doubt he or they will be caught as well."

"We will see. The fact remains that our plump man, the Home Fleet mobilisation plans in his head, is roaming somewhere between here and Germany, if he is not already in Berlin."

"And no one is aware of that, other than a very small number of people," I said idly.

"Yes, not even Hannay was told the man slipped through our fingers." Holmes grunted and then slouched in his seat. "Well," he said, "at least you are getting an opportunity to judge the value of this American motorcar that has come to so fascinate you. Do you intend to trade your present vehicle for it?"

"It is entirely possible," I replied. "She runs like a dream, just as Blenkiron predicted."

My friend gave a discontented grunt as he turned away to gaze at the passing scenery, and little more was said until the motorcar had

---

[92] Though employed as early as the Renaissance to denote such a double agent, the term "mole" regained currency in the twentieth century. Bullivant's remark appears to have presaged the word's renewed use in this context.

passed well into Sussex. We drove through the village of Foulworth and on to Holmes's cottage, which was situated upon the southern slope of the Downs, commanding a magnificent view of the Channel. The coastline ran on as chalky cliffs, the Ruff of Broadgate multiplied manyfold.

As we approached Holmes's residence, I saw to one side of the cottage the expanse of his apiary: a rectangular bee yard containing several rows of hives. And there, in the midst of it all, stood Sherlock Holmes.

"What is happening?" I asked as I brought the motor to a stop just short of the house. I slowly opened the door and stepped onto the ground, my eyes still locked upon the figure working patiently among swarming bees.

"Am I losing my mind?" I turned toward my friend, who had also left the vehicle. "Please tell me—"

"Perhaps someday we will learn how to replicate ourselves fully formed," Holmes said with a chuckle. "But the explanation of your current confusion is child's play, Watson. What is the only possible answer?"

"I am seeing an impersonator."

My friend led me toward the apiary as the Holmes doppelgänger closed a hive box and turned toward us.

"The intent is to make others believe you are still here," I said. "To have them think you are in Sussex, tending your bees, rather than flitting about Britain as an agent for Westminster."

"You see?" my friend said. "You grasped it all in an instant. Yes, Mycroft and Bullivant were most insistent that there be no suspicion I had signed on with them, and so they recommended that this young chap attempt to portray me."

"He does not appear all that youthful to me, nor all that different from you," I remarked as we drew nearer the man, who was removing his protective gear. Indeed, as we continued to close on him, I kept seeing the very image of my friend, down to the walking gait and drape of his clothing.

"The fellow was skilled at disguise when he began this assignment," said Holmes, "and with what additional knowledge I have imparted to him in the meanwhile, he has now become among the best at impersonation—and a rather admirable beekeeper as well. Ah, my dear Arbuthnot, how fares the flock?"

"Hale and hearty, Mr. Holmes. Hale and hearty," the man replied.

He was tall, like Holmes, and possessed the same type of lean, high-boned face as the detective. As I studied him at close quarters, however, I noticed that the man's eyes were brown and spritely, almost like those of a girl.[93] That expression dissolved the illusion of Holmes at last, and I now perceived him as a different individual. Mentally casting aside his disguise, I judged him to be perhaps thirty years of age.

"Come then, and meet Dr. John Watson," said Holmes. "Watson, this is Sandy Arbuthnot."

"Actually, Ludovic Gustavus Arbuthnot," corrected the man. "However, 'Sandy' does just fine. I have been waiting forever to meet you, Doctor."[94]

I detected a slight Scottish tinge in his speech, and as we shook hands, I also noticed for the first time how brown was his skin.

"How are you?" I said. "You have been beyond England, I perceive."

---

[93] Holmes's eyes were gray.

[94] Arbuthnot, a major character in John Buchan's novel *Greenmantle*, also appears in many other books by that author. Bullivant's suggestion in chapter 4 that an agent in Sussex be sent north in search of Richard Hannay is no doubt a reference to Sandy.

"Very good, Watson," said Holmes, patting me on the back. "Young Arbuthnot is in fact widely travelled—openly, as an honorary attaché at various embassies, but also clandestinely—and often atop camels, I understand."

"I've done some work in Arabia, the Balkans, and Anatolia for Sir Walter Bullivant," Arbuthnot explained as we ambled toward Holmes's cottage. "Very little that Greats at Oxford[95] prepared me for, but I hope I have fulfilled the expectations of the Secret Service."

"Sir Walter has always spoken highly of you," Holmes assured him. "It was he who recommended you for this assignment, remember—an assignment whose acceptance you may well have come to regret, for I fancy boredom set in long ago."

"I confess that I've often found myself longing for Bokhara and Samarkand, but I put my mind to the bees when such moods strike me, knowing this is all for a vital cause. If I might ask, however, is your crusade anywhere near its culmination?"

"In fact, I was about to suggest that you resume your true identity as the second son of Baron Clanroyden and hie yourself back to London, where Sir Walter will explain in greater detail and perhaps provide you a new assignment more to your liking."

Arbuthnot stopped before the cottage and looked at Holmes with surprise.

"Truly? Are matters vis-à-vis the Germans resolved in our favour, then?" he asked.

---

[95] Greats is the course on Classics: Ancient Rome and Greece, and the languages and philosophy of those cultures. As noted in *Greenmantle*, Arbuthnot attended Eton and New College before going to Oxford.

"Yes, for the most part," Holmes replied without further elaboration. "I will allow Sir Walter to enlighten you in that respect, as I said. Dr. Watson and I must travel on to Essex, however, and I think it best that we continue the journey."

"Of course. You'll be wanting your package, then. It arrived last week."

"Ah, good!" declared Holmes. "Yes, I was rather hoping to present it to Herr Von Bork this evening."

"I will go inside and fetch it," said Arbuthnot.

"A competent sort," I remarked as the young man vanished within Holmes's cottage. "And rather dashing in the bargain."

"Yes. The man's entry into the Secret Service was most fortuitous," said my friend. "His father went to Harrow with Bullivant, and then by chance Sandy became acquainted with Bullivant's son, who often brought Arbuthnot to Sir Walter's place in Berkshire for fishing. The spymaster is ever keen to snare promising recruits for his profession, and he quickly persuaded young Sandy to join the brotherhood of agents."

"Bullivant has a son?" I asked. "He has never mentioned the boy to me."

"Well, of course, he's a young man now and not a boy," replied Holmes. "And I suspect that Sir Walter has failed to refer to him out of a superstitious bent."

"What?"

"Sir Walter's son is a spy as well, old fellow. In this instance, the elder Bullivant was not happy with his offspring's choice of career, but the son was determined to follow in his father's footsteps. Currently, I understand Bullivant *fils* to be in Ottoman territory—on a rather dangerous assignment, no doubt. According to Mycroft, Bullivant never refers to his son because he believes to do so would bring bad luck of a most fatal sort."

"I see."

Just then, Arbuthnot emerged from the cottage carrying a parcel of wrapping paper and string. He handed it to Holmes, who held it in both hands as he thanked the young man.

"Is 'Martha' about?" the detective asked.

"No, sir. The old one left yesterday and the new one is to arrive later today. Shall I tell her the play is over before she assumes the stage?"

"Yes, you might as well do so. The real Martha will be returning within a day or two, I expect."

"I shall stay until then, of course," said Arbuthnot, "and then depart once she's back here on the grounds. I hope she will find the place sufficiently tidy for her tastes."

"We will see," Holmes replied with a sly smile.

The two engaged in short conversation regarding the apiary, and then Holmes and I departed, taking the road back through Foulworth and then off to the northeast, heading for Von Bork's headquarters.

"Your comments regarding Martha confuse me," I admitted as we left the village behind. "Your housekeeper was not in evidence, and you referred to a 'new' one and an 'old' one."

"True," said Holmes. "You see, for the past two years, Martha has been fulfilling her usual duties not for me, but rather for Von Bork."

"What?"

"It was of advantage to have one of our people at Von Bork's residence at all times, and what better person for that purpose than a housekeeper?"

"But to ask Martha—"

"And why not ask Martha?" said Holmes. "She is crafty and calculating in her way, and she has never been in any danger. It was all managed before Von Bork ever met me as Altamount. A position at the German's residence came up, and Mycroft arranged matters so that Martha was the only one who applied to Von Bork."

"That was very deft."

"And very Mycroft," added Holmes. "The Germans have been quite happy with her, by the way. Indeed, I believe she is now the only servant left in the house—Von Bork has slowly been reducing his help in Essex, which suggests that he is preparing to return to Germany."

"That would seem rather ominous," I observed.

"Quite so. In any event, Von Bork views her as quite harmless." He chuckled. "Martha has even overheard another German saying that she personifies Britain, with a complete self-absorption and air of 'comfortable somnolence.' Ha! They shall rue that comment, I tell you."

"But if Martha has been at Von Bork's house these many months, you must have had an impersonator for her at your cottage as well. That was the meaning of your references to 'old' and 'new' Marthas, then?"

"Yes," said Holmes. "Several women have assumed her identity in Sussex over the past two years, each taking turns in the charade. Bullivant's agents are not always limited to our gender, Watson."

"I see."

"There is another small revelation I must make," said Holmes, now in a somewhat lighter disposition than before. "Given our earlier contretemps regarding your embrace of the motorcar, I have been somewhat reluctant to broach the subject."

"I am eager to hear it, then."

"Well, as you know, I have been posing as the Irish-American Altamount, and in that guise passing supposed secrets on to Von Bork."

"You are now sounding rather like me," I said puckishly. "Let me hear the real Sherlock Holmes: direct and to the point."

"Von Bork and I employ an automotive code," revealed the detective. "To outsiders, I pretend to act as a motor expert—I say, is something the matter?" cried Holmes as the vehicle swerved.

"All is well," I replied, turning the car back onto the road. "I was merely taken aback by your words. I believe I am now prepared for the rest. Pray, proceed."

"Well," said Holmes, "my telegrams to Von Bork employ a code related to motors. In the code, everything likely to come up is named after some motorcar part. Thus, a radiator is a battleship, an oil pump a cruiser, and so on. This morning, I wired Von Bork to tell him that I would come to him tonight bringing new spark plugs, which is code for naval signals."

"I see. And so, in a way, you have accommodated the motor age as well."

"My dear Watson, I was never opposed to it."

"As you wish," I replied. "But I was also going to ask if you think that my presence in this automobile will arouse suspicions on the part of the Germans. Jack James has been your chauffeur in the past, and the vehicle was his taxicab rather than this one."

"Ah," interjected Holmes. "Do not worry. I have a compelling explanation for the change."

The sun was near setting as we continued toward Von Bork's seaside headquarters, and after a long period of silence, I idly asked Holmes, "However did you choose to enlist Jack James?"

"I did not choose him, Watson. Rather, he chose me."

"How so?"

"I have already related how I began my pilgrimage as Altamount by travelling to Chicago before I was enlisted into an Irish secret society at Buffalo. I then sailed back across the Atlantic and gave serious trouble to the constabulary at Skibbereen, where I caught the eye of a subordinate agent of Von Bork, who recommended me as a likely man—the rest becoming recent history.

"Gradually, I gained the German's upmost confidence, and from that vantage point have guided his plans into going subtly wrong at every turn. As part of that process, I quietly arranged the capture and imprisonment of his three best agents, whom I persuaded Von Bork to replace, in turn, with Hollins, Steiner, and James.

"All that would have gone undone, however, had it not been for the last man mentioned: Jack James. You see, Watson, shortly after arriving at Chicago over two years ago, I unwittingly ran afoul of a local gang who would have seen fit to make me vanish beneath the waters of Lake Michigan had young James not provided me shelter. I will omit the details and merely relate that, in the course of saving my life, he learnt the details of my mission and eagerly sought to become part of it."

"Out of a sense of adventure?" I suggested.

"Yes, much like your innkeeper, Ewan Clark. The American had me over a barrel, as it were, and I was forced to take him on. And he has earned his place after the fact, I must say."[96]

"What will become of him now, do you think?"

"Oh, Mycroft has arranged for his passage back to America. I shall tell Von Bork that Jack has been arrested and imprisoned at the Isle of Portland, where he actually has been sent for his own safety—that will be my explanation, if necessary, for your presence. The young man is to sail home aboard one of our cruisers."[97]

"Will you tell him similar stories about Hollins and Steiner?" I asked.

"Very prescient, Watson. Yes, I shall be doing just that." Holmes stared up at the sky, which was now dimming. "We should be at Von Bork's house within the hour," he said. "Then twenty-six months of labour come to an end."

It was nearly nine o'clock when we stopped some distance away from the German's residence. The sky was now dark, with but one remnant of sunset: a single blood-red gash lying like an open wound low on the horizon. Stars were already shining brightly, and below the cliffs, ship lights glimmered on the surface of the bay. Even in the deepening gloom, I could discern that the house itself was as Holmes had previously described it: long, low, and heavily gabled.

---

[96] As Holmes admits, his explanation omits several details, but what few are there suggest that the detective may have been guilty of serious lapses in Chicago. Perhaps, someday, that part of the story may come to light. Meanwhile, as mentioned elsewhere in this book, it is the belief of the editor that "Jack James" was actually Sam Spade, some of whose later exploits were eventually chronicled by Dashiell Hammett.

[97] Situated in Dorset, the Isle of Portland—actually tied to the mainland by a strip of land—was a Royal Navy base at the time.

"There is a delightful garden walk with stone parapet just off the study, which is still lit," said Holmes. "But we will wait here until Martha gives us a signal that Von Bork is alone in the house. There," he said, pointing to a bright window on the first floor. "That is Martha's room. Her light will go out once the coast is clear."

"Is Von Bork with someone at present, you think?" I asked.

"Do you not recognise the great motorcar that blocks the lane before the house?" said Holmes. "It is that of Baron Von Herling, Chief Secretary to the German legation in London, whom I have mentioned before as Von Bork's overseer."

"Yes," I said. "That is the vehicle we followed into the City that day we made plans to search for Hannay."

"The very same."

"Did you ever determine the nature of the baron's business on that occasion?"

"No," said Holmes. "Steiner and Hollins made discreet enquiries later, but they discovered nothing."

We waited for near onto a half hour, during which my friend now and then leaned to one side to feel inside a coat pocket.

"You are certain you have not lost your sponge?" I asked with amusement.

Holmes smiled.

"I am. And my bottle is at hand as well. But halloa, look you there! Martha's light has gone out. Start her up, Watson, while I apply the bottle contents to the sponge."

A moment later, the automobile before Von Bork's house sprang into life as ours began to move toward it. Two golden cones from the headlights of the other motor shot through the darkness and then briefly swept over us as the vehicle containing Baron Von Herling sped past.

"I will step out at once," Holmes told me as we approached Von Bork's residence. "Please make as if to settle into a long wait here, but stay only five minutes before you carefully approach the house. Martha will let you in. Follow her, and you will be able to discreetly watch and listen to Von Bork and me. I do not expect anything to go amiss, but I want you in reserve should the unexpected occur."

"I understand."

"And, of course, you will be needed for the denouement," he added as we braked to a halt.

"I will be ready, Holmes."

"As you have always been, old fellow. Ah," said he, putting the moistened sponge into a small sack that he stashed in a coat pocket before taking hold of the wrapped package given him by Sandy Arbuthnot. Holmes then pulled from another pocket a sodden, half-smoked cigar, which he stuck in his mouth. "I believe I see Von Bork coming out now. Wish us luck!"

I observed a silhouette set against the open doorway rush forward eagerly to meet my friend as he left the motorcar.

"Well?" a guttural voice croaked in the darkness.

Holmes waved the parcel above his head, as if in triumph. "You can give me the glad hand tonight, mister," he cried in the voice of Altamount. "I'm bringing home the bacon at last."

"The signals?" I heard the other ask.

"Same as I said in my cable," Holmes declared. "Fresh from Scapa Flow, every last one of them: semaphore, lamp code, Marconi. They're copies, mind you, not the originals, but it's the real goods, and you can lay to that."

He slapped the German upon the shoulder with rough familiarity, and the other stepped quickly away, out of further reach.

"Come," said Von Bork brusquely. "All alone I am in the house, save for my housekeeper. Only for you was I waiting. Come," he repeated as the pair entered the house.

I waited the prescribed five minutes and then left the motorcar, taking care to close the door quietly. I stepped swiftly toward the house, and within three paces of gaining it, saw the door swing open to reveal Martha, Holmes's housekeeper of the past nine years.[98]

"Halloa, Dr. Watson," she whispered. "This way, please, and quietly. The German thinks I've retired for the night."

The old woman guided me along a hallway and then to an alcove, from which vantage point I could see into what I took to be the study.

Masked by great ferns, Martha and I watched as Holmes, in disguise as Altamount, stretched his long limbs while sitting back in an armchair. Von Bork, his back to us, arranged papers upon a table, and then Holmes struck a match and with effort relit his cigar before looking around.

"Making ready for a move?" the detective asked. "Say, mister," he added, as his eyes fell upon a large, brass-bound safe that sat in a corner of the room. "You don't tell me you keep your papers in that?"

---

[98] Many commentators have supposed or wished that Martha was actually Mrs. Hudson, the landlady of 221 Baker Street. However, there is nothing in the accepted Sherlockian canon to seriously support that conjecture, and Watson's treatment of Martha in this narrative argues rather strongly that the two women were entirely different people. Indeed, later portions of the text confirm without doubt that such was the case.

Von Bork turned toward my friend, and for the first time I viewed the German's florid face and aquiline nose, a somewhat a distorted mirror image of Holmes's own visage.

"And why not?" Von Bork said, as if offended.

"Gosh, you put your stuff in a wide-open contraption like that? And you call yourself a spy," exclaimed Holmes with disdain. "Why, a Yankee crook would be into that in a second with a can opener. If I'd known that all those letters of mine were going to lie loose in a thing like that, I'd have been a mug to write you at all."

"It would puzzle any crook to force that safe," answered Von Bork. "You won't cut that metal with any tool."

"What about the lock?"

"It is a double combination lock. Do you know what that is, Altamount?"

"Search me."

"Well," said Von Bork, "you need a word as well as a set of figures before you can get the lock to work."

He walked to the safe and pointed out to Holmes the radiating discs that wrapped round near the opening handle.

"This outer one is for the letters, the inner one for the figures."

"Oh."

"So it's not quite as simple as you thought, eh? Four years ago it was that this was made for me. What did I choose for the word and figures, do you think?"

"It's beyond me," said Holmes.

"Come, take a guess."

"I give up."

"Bah," said Von Bork. "Well, those four years ago I chose *August* for the word and *1914* for the figures. Does that impress you, my American friend?"

"That was smart," said Holmes. "You must have known a lot back then, and had it down to a fine thing."

"Yes, we did."

"'We'?"

The German's eyes seemed to glaze over, and he muttered a single phrase: "*Die Wilden Vögel, ja.*" [99]

A smile broke over his face as he continued. "Yes, a few of us even then could have guessed the date. And here we are, and I am shutting down tomorrow morning, to return to Berlin."

"Then maybe you'll fix me up also. I'm not staying in this gol-darned country all on my lonesome."

"What meaning do you imply?" asked the German.

"Well, John Bull will soon be on his hind legs and fair ramping. The Continent has fallen into war, and Britain's about to join in, ain't she? I'd rather watch from over the water, I tell you."

"Yes, but what do you mean by being alone? You have your friend James, and there are Hollins and Steiner to keep you company as well."

"Not any longer," replied Holmes. "They're all locked up."

"What?" cried Von Bork. "Why did you not already inform me of this? When did it occur?"

"It happened last night. Coppers rounded them all up. For all I know, they might be after me as well. You know of anything that might have

[99] "The Wild Birds, yes."

happened recently to make us vulnerable?" asked the detective, leaning forward in his armchair.

"Nothing," the Germany spy cautiously declared. "My work here has been completed."

Holmes leaned forward. "I've heard that some other spy ring up north has been taken in as well. You know anything about that?"

"If I did, I would not share it with you, Altamount," replied Von Bork curtly. "All you need know is that my own grand plan has reached fulfilment with these naval signals you have supplied. But tell me again: what has happened to those three men of yours?"

"I told you: coppers got them. James is being carted off to Portland, I'm told. Don't know what's planned for the other two."

"What did they do to throw suspicion on themselves?" asked Von Bork, somewhat nervously. "It must have been his own fault in the case of James. You knew how self-willed he was."

"Oh, James was a bonehead—I give you that. But as for Hollins—"

"That man had become mad. I told you we should stop trusting him."

"Oh, he had been going a bit woozy of late, yes," admitted Holmes as Altamount. "But you have to admit that Steiner was a level-headed sort, and they got him as well."

"All three of them," Von Bork said. "All in the same night? This is a serious blow. It must only make my departure more vital."

"But what about me?" said Holmes urgently. "If they've nabbed them three, they can't be far off me, can they?"

"You don't mean that! In any case, you are an American citizen."

"Well, so was James, and it cut no ice with the British coppers who took him. You're the boss. Aren't you going to cover your men?"

"Why—"

"My landlady down Fratton[100] way, where I've got my other place, she had some enquiries about me, and when I heard of it, I guessed it was time for me to never go back there again. How long until they look me up at my London digs, eh? Doesn't it make you ashamed to see this happen to your men?"

Von Bork flushed ever more crimson. "How dare you speak in such a way!"

"If I didn't dare things, mister, I wouldn't be in your service. But I'll tell you straight what is in my mind. I've heard that with you Germans, when an agent has done his work, you are not sorry to see him put away."

Von Bork sprang toward Holmes.

"You are insolent, Altamount! And look," he said, his tone suddenly changing as he gestured toward a salver upon which stood a heavily sealed, dust-covered bottle and two high glasses. "I had brought up a bottle of your favourite Imperial Tokay, and you insult me in this manner? You dare suggest that I have given away my own agents?"

"Well, I figure there's a stool pigeon or a cross somewhere, and I am taking no more chances."

Von Bork paused and narrowed his eyes, as if appraising the other man.

"I have someone who would be able to discover if the British authorities intended to take you into custody," he said knowingly.

"And who might that be?" asked Holmes.

---

[100] Fratton is an area of Portsmouth, on the south coast of England.

"Again, that is no concern of yours. What matters is that from him I have heard nothing concerning the likelihood of you being arrested."

"But you hadn't heard anything from him about James, Steiner, and Hollins, either, had you?"

Von Bork frowned.

"You see what I'm saying? It's me for Holland," said Holmes at last, "and the sooner the better."

Von Bork returned to the table, seemingly once more in control of his temper.

"We have been allies too long to quarrel now, at the very hour of victory," he said diplomatically. "You've performed splendid works and, yes, taken risks, and I cannot forget that. By all means go to Holland, Altamount. In Rotterdam, you can get a boat to New York if you like. No other line will be safe a week from now—keep that in mind. Now," he said, extending his hand, "I will take from you that parcel and pack it with the rest of my things."

Holmes did not offer the package to Von Bork.

The German cocked his head.

"What about the dough?" Holmes asked.

"The what?"

"The boodle. The reward. The five hundred pounds. The gunner up at Scapa Flow what gave all this to me turned damned nasty at the last, and I had to square him with an extra two hundred, or it would have been nitsky for you and me. It's already cost me that from first to last, so it isn't likely I'd give this up without getting my wad. I want to see it with my own eyes."

Von Bork smiled bitterly. “You don’t seem to have a very high opinion of my honour,” said he. “You want the money before you give up the signals in that parcel.”

“Well, mister, this is a business proposition, ain’t it?”

“Very well, have it your way.”

Von Bork sat down at the table and scribbled a check, which he tore from its book. He refrained, however, from handing it to his guest. Instead, he set it upon the table.

“There,” declared Von Bork. “Your payment now is before you, in plain view. You see, since we are to be on such terms as you insist, Mr. Altamount, I do not see why I should trust you any more than you trust me.”

Holmes shrugged. “And what do you mean by that?”

“I mean that I claim the right to examine that parcel before you pick up this check.”

Holmes appeared to think for a moment and then passed the package over without a word. Von Bork undid the winding of string and then removed two wrappers of paper. He sat gazing with surprise at the object he found within, and as he did so, Holmes quietly but swiftly rose from his chair, cigar clenched between his teeth, and gripped the German at the back of the neck.

From the pocket of his long coat, the detective withdrew a chloroformed sponge and pushed it into Von Bork’s face. Fingers gripped still air, and the foreigner’s writhing spine arched backward before consciousness was lost and the spy slumped forward, guided by Holmes, who settled the German with his cheek pressed against the tabletop.

“Bravo!” whispered Martha, who had remained beside me. “Bravo, Mr. Holmes,” she repeated as she stepped out from behind a large fern and into the expanse of the study.

Somewhat hesitantly, I followed.

Holmes turned round to face us and gave a slight, playful bow.

“The comedy is finished,” he said, and tossed the chloroformed sponge aside.

“Is he all right?” the housekeeper asked.

“Oh yes,” said Holmes, also dispensing with his cigar. “He has not been hurt at all.”

“I am glad of that, Mr. Holmes. According to his lights, he has been a kind employer. He even wanted me to go with his wife to Germany yesterday, but that would hardly have suited your plans, would it, sir?”

“No indeed, Martha. So long as you were here, I was easy in my mind. We waited some time for your signal tonight, by the way.”

“It was Von Herling, sir.”

“I know. His motorcar passed ours.”

“I thought he would never go, and I was aware that would not suit your plans, either, to find him here.”

“No, indeed. Well, it only meant we waited a half hour or so. I suppose you have everything ready to leave.”

“Yes, sir. He posted seven letters today. I have the addresses as usual.”

“Very good, Martha. I will look into them tomorrow. For the moment, please fetch some straps, if you will.”

“Yes, sir.”

As the housekeeper left to retrieve material with which to bind the German spy, I stepped to the unconscious man and looked over his shoulder to satisfy my curiosity. There, upon the table, nestled within the unfolded wrapping papers, lay a small blue book whose title was printed in golden letters across the cover: *Practical Handbook of Bee Culture.*

I smiled and reached out to run my forefinger over the gilt words.

"You may take it, Watson," said Holmes as he stepped over to the safe and opened it with the combination that Von Bork had unwittingly supplied him. "That is the first printed copy and is meant for you. That it has passed through the hands of a German spy may give it some additional lustre."

As I picked up the book, Martha returned with straps to secure Von Bork and then retired to her room to continue packing her bags.

Holmes and I bound the unconscious spy and set him upon a sofa in the study, where he remained sleeping. Then Holmes went to the salver and opened its dusty bottle of Tokay, pouring each of us a glass.

I sat at the table, across from Von Bork's emptied chair, and sipped as I watched Holmes alternate between drinking his wine and removing dossier after dossier from the safe. Once the files were all piled high, my friend began packing them neatly into Von Bork's many valises. Finished, he turned round and took notice of my now empty glass.

"More, Watson?" he said, extending the bottle of Tokay in my direction.

"Of course," I agreed. "It is a good wine, Holmes."

"It is a remarkable wine, old fellow. Apparently, it is from Franz Josef's special cellar at the Schoenbrunn Palace. Hum. Might I trouble you to open the window, for chloroform vapour does not help the palate, does it?"

I took one more sip and then rose from my chair.

"We need not hurry ourselves, Watson," said Holmes as he once more rifled through Von Bork's papers. "Ah!" he cried. "We have him!"

"Yes, of course," I said as I opened a window. "He lies there on the sofa, securely bound."

"No," replied Holmes. "That is yes, of course, Von Bork is there. I meant that we also have his underling in Whitehall—Bullivant's mole."

"Oh?"

"Yes," said my friend, holding up a sheet of paper. "It is a certain clerk in the War Ministry, identified here."

"But I thought that the mole was connected with the Black Stone, not Von Bork."

"He is—was Von Bork's man, but on rare occasions the information he obtained was passed on to the Black Stone when it might assist that spy cell, according to these notes. No doubt, this clerk was the one who alerted that group that the meeting with Reyer had been changed."

"And what about the third head of Cerberus?" I asked. "Is it mentioned as well? Has this mole passed information along to that circle also?"

"No other group, including the presumed third head, is mentioned in any of the papers I have seen thus far," mused Holmes. "That is perhaps curious, given the several references to the Black Stone, but it is certainly not conclusive. Still, we have discovered that at least two of the spy groups were not entirely independent. Oh, would you mind touching the bell? I have need of Martha once more."

After a moment, the pleasant old lady again appeared in the doorway and curtseyed with a smile.

"I have told Sandy Arbuthnot about the end of our enterprise, Martha," Holmes said. "He intends to delay his departure from Sussex until you return to the cottage, so you may leave for there tomorrow. The following day, however, I should wish you to report to me in London, at Claridge's Hotel."

"Very good, sir. I'll spend some time finishing with my packing."

The woman left us again, and I strode back to the table, where I pleased myself with more wine. I smacked my lips with glee, and Holmes smiled. He stepped over and briefly took me by the shoulder.

"You are a blithe lad this evening, Watson," he said. "I do not know if I ever saw you in such a humour, even at 221."

"You know, Holmes, after all that has happened these past weeks, I feel twenty years younger." I held up my glass of Tokay in salute. "Time be damned, indeed."

My friend reached for his own glass, which remained half full. "Time be damned," he agreed, and we clinked glasses together before emptying each.

"And so you will have not one magnum opus, but two," I said, pointing to the little blue book I had left upon the table.

"Perhaps, Watson," said Holmes. "If I ever finish my tome on detection. But here, at least, is the fruit of my leisured ease of the past decade, before I set out on my mission to unhorse Von Bork and, for a few days, be preoccupied by the Black Stone."

He picked up the volume and read out its whole title: *Practical Handbook of Bee Culture, with Some Observations upon the Segregation of the Queen.* Holmes smiled. "Alone I did it. Behold the product of pensive nights and laborious days when I watched the little working gangs as once I watched the criminal world of London. Well, sir, I hope that you are none the worse," he abruptly added, now addressing Von Bork, who gasped and blinked as he regained consciousness.

The Prussian's face convulsed with passion, and he broke out into a furious stream of invective in his native tongue.

"Be thankful you are not fluent in the language, Watson," said Holmes primly as he closed up the last of Von Bork's valises and the Teutonic spy continued to curse and swear. "Though unmusical, German is the most expressive of languages," my friend observed when our antagonist had stopped from pure exhaustion.

The prisoner raised himself with some difficulty upon the sofa and evinced a strange mixture of amazement and hatred toward his captor.

"I will get level with you, Altamount," he said deliberately. "If it takes me all my life, I will get level with you."

"The old sweet song," said Holmes. "How often have I heard it in days gone by. It was a favourite ditty of the late, lamented Professor Moriarty. Colonel Sebastian Moran has also been known to warble it from his cell. And yet I live and keep bees upon the South Downs."

Von Bork gave a puzzled look at the man he knew as Altamount and then cried, "Curse you, you double traitor." The man strained against his bonds and glared murder from his furious eyes.

"No, it is not so at all," insisted Holmes. "Have you not listened to my speech, now so different from that which, heretofore, you have heard from me? As it shows you, Mr. Altamount of Chicago had no existence in fact. I used him, and he is gone."

"Then who are you?" asked Von Bork.

"It is really immaterial who I am, but since the matter seems to interest you, sir, I may say that this is not my first acquaintance with members of your family. I have done a good deal of business in Germany in the past, and my name is undoubtedly familiar to you."

"I wish to know it," said the Prussian grimly.

"It was I who brought about the separation between Irene Adler and the late King of Bohemia when your cousin was the Imperial Envoy. It was I also who saved from murder, by the nihilist Klopman, Count Von und Zu Grafenstein, who was your mother's elder brother. It was I—"

Von Bork sat up in amazement.

"There is only one man," he cried.

"Exactly," said Holmes.

Von Bork groaned and sat back on the sofa. "And most of the information that I sent on to Berlin came from you and the men you recruited," he moaned. "What have I done?"

After that, our prisoner spoke no more and, at length, we took to moving him to the motorcar outside. That proved no easy task, for he was a strong and desperate man. Finally, however, by holding either arm, we walked the German very slowly down the garden walk and, after a short final struggle, hoisted him into the spare seat of our motor, where we rebound his feet. The valises were wedged in around him.

"I trust that you are as comfortable as circumstances permit," said Holmes when the man and his case were arranged in the automobile.

All the amenities, however, were wasted upon the angry German.

"I suppose you realise, Mr. Sherlock Holmes," said he, "that if your government bears you out in this treatment, it becomes an act of war."

"What about your government and all this treatment?" said Holmes, tapping each valise in turn.

"You have no warrant for my arrest. The whole proceeding is illegal and outrageous."

"Absolutely," said Holmes.

"Kidnapping a German subject—"

"And stealing his private papers," chimed in my friend.

"Well, you and your accomplice here understand your position, then," said our captive. "If I were to shout for help as we pass through the next village—"

Holmes smiled. "My dear sir, if you did anything so foolish you would enlarge the limited titles of our village inns by giving us The Dangling Prussian as a signpost. The Englishman is a patient creature, but at present his temper is a little inflamed, and it would be as well not to try him too far. No, Herr Von Bork, you will go with us in a quiet, sensible fashion to Scotland Yard, whence you can send for your friend, Baron Von Herling, and see if even now you may not fill that spot on the diplomatic list that he has reserved for you. Perhaps your new status will make you immune from prosecution, and you will simply be returned to your homeland."

The German bristled.

"*Wir werden sehen*," declared Holmes.[101]

Von Bork turned from us, and Holmes took my shoulder to direct me back to the house and into the study, where I retrieved the blue book, depositing it in my coat pocket.

---

101 "We will see."

We finished the small amount of remaining Tokay and then stepped out upon Von Bork's terrace. The lights in the sky were even brighter than before, as were the earthbound stars attached to ships or, in the distance, the town of Harwich. By now the vault of night was graced by the presence of the moon, which cast its own shimmering web of soft brilliance upon the sea, and Holmes pointed to the rough waters limned by its celestial glow.

"Your east wind, Holmes?" I asked as we leaned against the stone parapet.

He nodded. "It is hard to imagine at this moment, but it will be cold and bitter, Watson, and I fear its consequences more than words can convey."

I stared into the warm August night alongside my friend of over three decades and put my hand upon his shoulder.

"A good many of us may wither before its blast," I told him. "But it's God's own wind none the less, and we must believe that a cleaner, better, stronger land will no doubt bask in the sunshine when the storm has cleared. Let us go, Holmes, and I'll start up the motor."

"Yes, Watson," said he, his mood lightening. "It is time that we were on our way, for I now recall that I have a check for five hundred pounds that should be cashed early, since the drawer is quite capable of stopping payment if he can."

INTERLUDE: Biggleswick

CHAPTER ELEVEN: THE OLD GAME AGAIN

Our captive in tow, Holmes and I returned to a London that had been holding its breath as one empire after another ordered mobilisation and then, seeing its actions mirrored in those of its neighbours, proceeded to declare war upon them. We transferred Von Bork into the custody of the British government, which was able to hold him for mere hours before Berlin claimed the spy as one of its official representatives.

At that moment, Britain had not yet joined the conflict, but rather was waiting to see if Germany would respect the neutrality of Belgium. Amid a clamour from some quarters for compromise and reconciliation, Von Bork was released on the grounds of being a foreign diplomat, and he left London hurriedly the next day, though without his huge pile of dossiers, which Westminster refused to surrender.

That night, as the deadline for German withdrawal from Belgium approached, Mycroft Holmes hosted his brother and me in the Stranger's Room of the Diogenes Club. My friend had since resumed his usual appearance: the goatee had been shorn and his hair colour restored, though I perceived it as more grey than I remembered it being in years past.

Holmes was very subdued, while his elder sibling tried to put a good face on the situation and was reiterating that optimism when chimes tolled the hour.

"Eleven o'clock," said Mycroft with sudden disappointment, consulting his own timepiece. "Midnight in Berlin. The ultimatum has expired, I am afraid."

Sherlock Holmes leaned back in his chair as I heard the muffled sound of a great chorus now singing outside in the distance.

Mycroft echoed the faraway voices. "God Save the King," he uttered. "Well, the war telegram must be going out from the admiralty to the fleet at this very moment: 'Commence hostilities against Germany.'"

"The east wind has picked up," said Sherlock Holmes idly, and his brother cast a questioning glance in his direction. I, meanwhile, merely nodded at my friend before staring into the empty glass I held in my hands.

The following two years and more saw me largely separated from the secret band I had joined during the Hannay affair, though my connections to its members were never entirely lost. Mycroft Holmes assumed tight control over all intelligence activities of the British government, while Bullivant maintained the helm of the Secret Service in particular. Inspector Magillivray was promoted to the highest echelon of Scotland Yard and from that vantage point deftly orchestrated police cooperation with Sir Walter's plans as defined by Mycroft. Sherlock Holmes, meanwhile, agreed to return to London to lend his brilliance to our nation's coterie of cryptographers, becoming a near-constant inhabitant of the mysterious Office 54.[102]

I offered to share my residence in Queen Anne Street with the detective turned spy turned codebreaker, an arrangement he readily accepted, though its consummation was not immediately achieved. Holmes's realisation that his bees could not accompany him caused momentary reconsideration, but eventually he surrendered his apiary to

---

[102] This is probably a fictional reference to Room 40, the section of the admiralty identified with British codebreaking during the First World War.

an experienced Sussex couple who pledged to keep good care of his six-legged brood for the duration, and he moved up from Sussex.

By then, however, I had departed London.

Prior to Holmes's return to the metropolis, I had found myself living in spiritual limbo as Britain's part in the war commenced. My account of Holmes's actions in the Birlstone affair began serialisation, but its appearance did little to refresh my mood.[103] I found myself constantly reading newspaper reports of the first troop and naval movements in the war, saving those articles and literary efforts that appealed to me for the purpose of beginning a scrapbook of the conflict. In that vein, I followed avidly the initial hostilities in France and Belgium, which resulted in retreat until Germany was held at the Marne and the front assumed a profile that would remain largely unchanged until nearly the end of the war.

In late September, however, I was jolted from this passive routine during a chance visit to Charing Cross Hospital. Turning the corner into Agar Street, I saw a huge banner hanging over the pavement. "Quiet for the Wounded," it read, and I realised that heavy traffic had been diverted from the avenue in order to minimise noise for the benefit of those convalescing within the hospital's walls.

Standing there, contemplating the suffering that lay behind that fluttering message, it dawned upon me that, in concentrating upon the great single tragedy of war, I had remained oblivious to the countless individual ones attending it. Recalling with force the oath I had taken

---

[103] As noted earlier, *The Valley of Fear* appeared in installments in *The Strand Magazine* beginning with its September 1914 issue.

decades before when becoming a physician, and without any second thought, I turned round to set matters right.

In part through the influences of Sir Walter Bullivant and Mycroft Holmes, I was admitted into the Royal Army Medical Corps despite my age, receiving a major's commission, and by October—shortly before Holmes began his move into Queen Anne Street—I found myself stationed at Aldershot instructing RAMC inductees, one of whom was young Dr. Blanding, for whom I had so often served as replacement.[104]

I considered my efforts there to be productive and satisfying in their way, but as the First Battle of Ypres raged on into the following month, lecturing trainees seemed a paltry contribution to the cause, and I felt compelled to seek duty in France, a request that was promptly refused in no uncertain terms more than once, and so I threw myself back into the responsibility of teaching the principles of hygiene and disease prevention to those who would be ministering to our men on the Continent.

Being far enough removed from my Queen Anne residence, I set up camp at the Aldershot barracks while Sherlock Holmes transferred his residence to my home. Within days, my housekeeper gave notice, unable to reconcile herself with the singular personal habits my friend had accumulated over the course of a lifetime. Without surprise, I received from him a curt letter suggesting that Martha assume the necessary domestic responsibilities in London, a proposal I readily accepted.

From time to time, I was able to journey to the metropolis, staying one or two nights in my home, which I saw gradually transformed by

[104] Aldershot is a town located about forty miles southwest of London. The site of the first permanent training camp for the British Army during the Crimean War, it has had a continuing association with the military. At the time, the Royal Army Medical Corps's principal training facility was located there.

Holmes into an admixture of its original self, his Sussex cottage, and our former digs in Baker Street. Martha brought a steady hand to the household's management, however, and she convinced my cook to remain in service for the time being, though an endless succession of frustrated parlourmaids would see duty in Queen Anne Street during the course of the war.

Through the following two years, Holmes distracted himself with cryptography while constantly pondering the mystery of the supposed third German spy ring, whose presence was never felt. I, meanwhile, continued to lecture at Aldershot, though in three instances I was assigned to groups of RAMC officers that journeyed to France for the purposes of observation.

Those excursions put my own past military illusions to shame.

The Second Afghan War was as child's play compared to the apocalypse whose scourges I now glimpsed at first hand. Relatively clean wounds of four decades past were replaced by bone-shattering damage from modern high-powered bullets and shrapnel, and poison gas added a dimension of horror previously unknown. Artillery maintained a near-constant din for those at the front, the sound and terror in themselves sufficient to destroy the minds of any who were fortunate enough to escape physical injury. Far above, aeroplanes criss-crossed the sky, most often to spy upon our lines, but now and then dropping explosives that rattled even more the nerves of those on the ground.

The constant flux of wounded seemed to me like a never-ending stream of refugees from Dante's hellish circles, and I never became inured to the horror. Indeed, there are even now images trapped in memory which, at the remove of more than a decade, plague my sleep and intrude upon the enjoyment of these, my later days. I can recall rows of bandaged soldiers lying abreast, their vacant eyes oblivious to all going on round them. Casualty clearing stations were often bordered by hedges of amputated limbs, the heaps stacked to waist height. On more than one occasion, I found I could not shake the hand of a bedridden warrior because there was nothing to grasp, and twice I was forced to communicate in writing with young men who could not speak for absence of a lower jaw.

In one instance, as wounded came steaming into a base hospital, I and my fellow RAMC observers volunteered direct aid when regular staff were overwhelmed. For that brief moment, which nonetheless seemed an eternity, I felt myself truly useful to mankind again as I assisted surgeons, intensifying within me the need to do more than simply lecture.

During these missions, we observers were allowed to visit the front line during what were taken as lulls in combat. The desolation was beyond belief: grim landscapes of earth churning with debris, onto which a harsh geometry had been imposed in the form of zig-zag trenches with their walkways, sandbags, and dugouts drenched in unending moisture. I had seen the barren countryside of Afghanistan decades earlier, of course, but the stark panorama now before me had been shaped entirely by the hand of man rather than that of God, and it terrified me to see what manner of hell our race was capable of forging as I witnessed enemy shells spit up brown rainbows of dirt, stone, and I did not doubt, the grist of human remains.

On two of these journeys to France, I was able to meet with Cecil Harper while he was on leave from his RFC squadron. In the second instance, I could not fail to see a nervous quality to his behaviour, reflected in shaky hands and a tic under his right eye.

"Oh, I've the wind-up,[105] that is for certain," he admitted as we sat outside a café near the Quai d'Orsay. "But it's only exhaustion, Major Watson," he claimed. "Only exhaustion."

Harper lifted his glass and smiled as he caught the eye of a passing young woman.

"I'll return to the hut rested and refreshed, I assure you. And then we'll be making the breakthrough and this thing will be over. Don't you think so, sir?" he asked of Sir Harry Christey, whom I had brought with me that day.

Sir Harry was now a major like myself but assigned to the army general staff. When I had crossed paths with him the day before, I had barely recognised the man: his manner was far more abrupt and uncompromising than I had remembered it before the war in Galloway. Moreover, his political views appeared to have changed dramatically.

"Yes, we'll push back the Hun this year, I do not doubt," he said in reply to Cecil Harper. "And we'll be in Berlin by autumn. Then we'll teach them to mind, as we should have done all these years past."

Staring at Major Christey, I could only hope that would be the case.

"Perhaps I'll live to see that," said Captain Harper with a sardonic air. "And maybe not."

I knew that the prevailing attitude among the flyers was one of "no empty chair": as each member of a squadron was lost, another came to take his place, and an ominous sense of fate hung over the men of the

[105] "The wind-up" was slang for a case of nerves.

Flying Corps, paralleling and yet differing in nature from the futile despair I saw in those inhabiting the trenches, the ones Harper and his fellow pilots referred to as the PBI—the poor bloody infantry.

The breakthrough Captain Harper longed for and Major Christey predicted did not materialise in 1915 nor in the following year, and as the months ground on, I continued my dogged instruction to trainees at Aldershot, punctuated by occasional leave to spend time in London with Sherlock Holmes.

During those two years, I was also able to follow, albeit indirectly, the further exploits of Richard Hannay, for in an effort to bolster public morale at the end of the first year of the war, Bullivant had arranged for a member of the War Information Office to pen a fictionalised account of the Black Stone affair, a narrative that altered events somewhat and completely omitted the participation of Holmes and myself in the matter, on the detective's recommendation.[106]

Hannay himself had joined the New Army[107] as a captain. Sent home to recuperate after being wounded at Loos,[108] he was persuaded by Sir Walter Bullivant to undertake an important secret mission in the company of John Blenkiron and Sandy Arbuthnot.[109] The plucky South African then

---

[106] This was *The Thirty-Nine Steps*, serialized in *Blackwood's Magazine* during August and September of 1915 before being published in book form a month later. The author, not identified in Watson's narrative, was John Buchan, then a member of the War Propaganda Bureau.

[107] The New Army was the huge force, initially comprised of volunteers, formed early in the First World War at the instigation of Lord Kitchener, the British Secretary of State for War, who foresaw a long struggle that would overwhelm Britain's small professional army.

[108] The Battle of Loos, fought in September and October of 1915, was the first great action by the New Army and the largest British offensive of that year. The attack was aimed at breaking through German defenses and restoring a war of movement after months of static trench warfare. It stalled, however, while inflicting heavy casualties on both sides.

[109] That affair, which also involved Hannay's good Boer friend Peter Pienaar, is detailed in the fictionalized account also written by John Buchan and published in 1916 as *Greenmantle*.

returned to military service and distinguished himself in France on into 1917, rising eventually to the rank of brigadier-general.

It was in February of that same year that I was suddenly relieved of my teaching duties at Aldershot and ordered to return to London for reassignment. I did not believe my performance as an instructor had been substandard, and I began to hold out hope that I might see duty of a more active nature, perhaps in Millbank.[110] However, I soon learnt otherwise.

I arrived home once more, this time hoping I would not soon be returning to Crookham Camp[111] and feeling encouraged about my immediate prospects. Stepping foot in Queen Anne Street, I was greeted by Sherlock Holmes, Martha at his side.

"She has provided a much-needed stability for the household these past many months," my friend said later, when found ourselves alone in the sitting room. "It was a much appreciated reversal of fortune after your original housekeeper gave notice within two weeks of my arrival," he added primly, repeating a comment he had never failed to voice during each of my previous visits.

"Yes," I said, once more not mentioning the angry letter I had received from my former servant more than two years earlier. "So I have been given to understand. At least the cook has stayed."

"If only the maid's position were as stable," Holmes complained. "It seems as if a different girl comes in each week."

---

[110] Millbank is an area of central London, formally in the City of Westminster. It was the home of the Royal Army Medical College, where instruction was suspended during the First World War so that the facility could be used to prepare vaccines and conduct research into the development of gas masks. Nearby was Queen Alexandra's Hospital, which served as a general army hospital during the war. Watson is not specific in his comments, but one suspects he was referring to possible assignment at the latter facility.
[111] Crookham Camp was the RAMC depot at Aldershot.

"Perhaps one might find some satisfaction in variety," I suggested, noting yet again how Holmes had subtly made the place his own during my absence. "I observe that you still have the painting of a mountain by that Frenchman, whatever his name is," I remarked while surveying the walls.

"We can certainly remove if you like, old fellow. After all, you will be living here now, and this is your house."

"It need not be taken down," I said, lifting a hand. "In truth, I became rather used to the work when it hung in Baker Street during my final stays with you there. I notice, however, that you appear to have banished that horrible painting of the blue beggar that once adorned the other wall. It is not like you to leave such a gaping, blank space, but I thank you for it."

Holmes smiled.

"Your eye remains sharp," said he. "Yes, I knew you found that work especially offensive. It will not please, but I have recently acquired another by that same Spaniard. It is a study of three women that would make you believe the beggar was by Rembrandt. I very much fancy it, however, and so I hung it in my room, where it now resides beside the picture of the beggar, both of them safe from your view."

"I will never see it?" I asked puckishly.

"It would be best if you did not. However, I have also acquired a painting by a fellow named Dégousse, whose technique intrigues me. I doubt you will care much for it, but I do believe it is something you can tolerate, should you permit me to hang it in this room. On the other hand, perhaps you would wish instead to put up your old portrait of General Gordon to fill that empty space upon the wall—I came across the picture up in the lumber room but last week."

“It is no matter,” I replied. “And perhaps my artistic horizons need broadening. Hang your new painting there on the wall by all means, Holmes.”

“Thank you,” said my friend. “But let us change the subject to a more practical one: should Martha prepare a homecoming meal for you, Doctor? Or, rather,” he said, glancing at my uniform, “Major?”

“By whatever title I am addressed, I remain just as famished. Yes, by all means ring Martha, if you will. And I do hope it is to be a meal for two.”

After a small shared repast, my friend informed me of his intention to go out. “I realise I impose, for you may be tired from your journey, Watson, but might you accompany me nonetheless?”

“You have a purpose hidden behind your request?”

“I do.”

“Then please allow me a half hour, and I will be pleased to join you. I am merely waiting to receive reassignment from the medical corps, and in the meanwhile, my time is my own.”

Holmes quietly nodded, and I left to reclaim my old room, which had been kept intact. There I changed into civilian clothes, and within an hour found myself strolling down Haymarket Street beside my friend in much the same manner as we had ambled through London when our monarch had been the grandmother of the present king.

It was hardly the metropolis we had known thirty years before, however. Horses were in even fewer numbers than just before the war, and electric lighting had replaced gas in many quarters. To my eye, however, it was the change in the female populace that was most striking. By this, the third year of conflict, women had supplanted men in the workforce on a grand scale, and both their manner and style of dress were far removed from what had been deemed fashionable during the previous decade.

"I do not believe we have walked this portion together since, perhaps, that unpleasant Amberley business," Holmes remarked.

"Amberley?"

"Do you not recall Joseph Amberley, the art dealer whose wife was murdered, along with her presumed lover?"

"Ah, yes," I said. "The unsold ticket to the Theatre Royal. I had quite forgotten the matter. When the war is over and I have opportunity to write again, perhaps I should train my pen upon that affair."[112]

"No matter where you aim your nib," Holmes taunted, "the ink will no doubt miss the essence of the case."

"But I shall still chuckle all the way to Cox and Co."[113]

"No doubt, you will. Ah, here we are," Holmes said as we approached the next storefront. "I wish to go book hunting," he declared with a sly smile, "and I believe the waters here to be promising."

"Traill's Bookshop," I said. "This is the establishment owned by Blenkiron, the American, is it not?"

"Yes," said Holmes. "Shall we see what crosses our path inside?"

Minutes later, we were in the natural sciences section, where Holmes pulled a green volume from the bins. "Ah, I have found it," he said

---

[112] These comments refer to a case which Watson did eventually detail in "The Adventure of the Retired Colourman," one of the last canonical Holmes stories published. In the doctor's account, the individual referred to is named Josiah Amberley, and he is described as a retired seller of art supplies rather than an art dealer. The unsold theater ticket was a key piece of evidence in Holmes's resolution of the matter.

[113] It was within the vaults of Cox and Co. Bank that Watson had a tin dispatch box in which were stored papers concerning many of Holmes's unsolved or unfinished cases. The doctor's remark suggests that he had funds deposited in that institution as well.

with joy. "The second edition of my work on bees. What?" he added when he saw my look of surprise. "You cannot imagine such a speedy revision?"

"No," replied. "I cannot conceive of your work in any field requiring amendment all at."

"Well," he said, "I made several novel observations of that colony up in Galloway while searching for Richard Hannay, and they got me to thinking about a few aspects I had neglected to include in the first edition. And so, when not cracking German codes, I made additions to the original text. You see, when I realised that—"

An assistant seller interrupted Holmes's explanation. "The manager's compliments, sirs," he said to us quickly. "He wishes me to tell you that he believes there are some valuable works in just this subject upstairs that might interest you."

"Of course," said Holmes, replacing the volume. "Pray, lead us there."

We followed the man to an upper floor lined with every kind of book imaginable, and with tables littered with maps and engravings.

"This way," our guide said as he rapped upon the wall and then opened a door concealed by bogus book-backs. We suddenly found ourselves in a small, windowless study, where John S. Blenkiron sat contentedly in an armchair, a cup within his reach upon a table.

The assistant left, closing the hidden door behind him, and Blenkiron rose quickly, seizing in turn Holmes's hand and then mine. "Mr. Holmes and—now—Major Watson! This is a pleasure after such a long while. I've heard good reports of you, Major," he said to me. "Your Royal Army Medical Corps should be grateful for having you in its ranks. And

Mr. Holmes, you are a sight for sore eyes. And a better sight, if I may say, without those chin whiskers and dyed hair."

"And you seem more hale than before, Mr. Blenkiron," replied Holmes.

And indeed, though it was still the old Blenkiron, he was immensely changed. His once stout frame was now leaner, as was his face, which previously had been somewhat puffy. Moreover, the man's pale complexion of three years before was replaced by a rosy glow of health.

Holmes glanced at the contents of the cup. "And I notice you no longer limit yourself to boiled milk."

"Ah, the dyspepsia is gone, gentlemen," Blenkiron declared in a booming voice. "Thanks to some doctors in Nebraska, I am a new man. And perhaps, Mr. Holmes, you also deserve some credit for my improved state," he added with a sly look. "M informs me that it was you who deciphered that recent, amusing German telegram that he arranged to be forwarded to my government."

Holmes shrugged. "Oh yes, I believe I was the one whose turn it was to read the message on that particular day, the code itself having already been broken," he said. "I suppose it will raise a bit of a fuss, but how was I to know the Kaiser would suggest to Mexico that it invade your country?"[114]

---

[114] This exchange between Holmes and Blenkiron is unquestionably a reference to the Zimmermann Telegram. That message, sent on January 16, 1917, from German Foreign Secretary Arthur Zimmermann to Berlin's ambassador to Mexico, instructed the latter to propose an alliance with Mexico should the United States join Britain and France in their war with the Central Powers. Germany was to offer financial assistance to Mexico and promise to help recover territory that Mexico had lost to the United States during their 1846–48 war. Intercepted by the British and read by their cryptographers—apparently, by Sherlock Holmes himself—the contents were revealed to the Americans in February, and the telegram's text was released publicly by the Wilson Administration by the end of that month.

"In any case, I have told M that the telegram, combined with Germany's submarine declaration, makes it inevitable that we will soon be joining you formally as allies," declared the American. "Personally, I expect that blessed event to occur within three months, if not sooner."[115]

"Pardon me," I said as Blenkiron gestured for us to take seats. "Who is this *M* you speak of?"

"It is my brother, Mycroft," said Holmes wearily as he sat in an armchair beside Blenkiron's. "As his writing of memos increased in frequency during the Hannay incident, he started signing them with his first initial only, and then sometime between Montenegro's declaration of war on the Ottomans and the first Zeppelin raid on London, he began styling himself so in conversation. I find it an annoying affection, but there's no stopping him."

"Well, certainly," said Blenkiron, "there's no stopping M as the effective overall head of British Intelligence, is there? And may we all thank God for it."

"I do not dispute that view," Holmes agreed as I joined the two of them in a third armchair, leaving a fourth empty. "But never mention that admission to my brother, if you would be so kind."

"It will be our own secret transatlantic pact, Mr. Holmes. Now then," he added, nodding toward me. "Has the Major been informed of our plans for him?"

"Not fully," replied Holmes with an awkward air.

---

[115] This comment refers to Germany's decision to renew unrestricted submarine warfare on February 1, 1917. U-boats would then once more sink freighters and tankers without warning, as opposed to surfacing first in order to search those merchant vessels and safely remove crews before attacking the ships. Blenkiron's prediction proved true, for the American declaration of war came on April 6.

“Ah,” I said. “My return to London was engineered, then?” I turned to Holmes. “You said nothing to that effect upon greeting me.”

“M decreed that I be the one to break the news to you, my dear Major Watson,” declared the American. “And my hope—as well as M’s and Bullivant’s—is that you will be willing to return to the old game.”

“Old game?”

“Espionage, dear boy,” said Holmes. “And you will not find yourself alone, for I will be joining you in the field once more.”

“Has Hannay become lost again?” I asked.

“Hardly,” Blenkiron good-naturedly replied. “If anything, he seems to have found himself. I myself saw the man perform magnificently during the Erzurum business,[116] and in the meantime, he’s done quite well in your army, has he not?”

Holmes nodded. “Indeed, he has. The matter at hand, Watson,” he said, “pertains to the remnants of the Black Stone.”

“There are remnants?” I asked. “Other than the plump man who escaped, I thought that spy ring had been completely destroyed, along with Von Bork’s.”

“Von Bork’s group was thoroughly demolished, yes,” said Holmes. “However, I had infiltrated its apparatus and operated within the organisation for more than a year. All its parts were known, and so we were able to dismantle the thing completely, piece by piece, though Von Bork himself escaped to Germany by means of diplomatic pretence.

---

[116] This is another reference to the events related in Buchan’s *Greenmantle*, which culminated in the Battle of Erzurum, fought between the forces of Russia and the Ottoman Empire.

"On the other hand, we learnt of the Black Stone only through Scudder's notebook, and while we did round up many from that group in both Kent and Scotland, we were aware that we did not get them all."

"Oh."

"Scotland still interests us," interjected the American. "We know that there was a line of communication north from Galloway, reaching as far as Glasgow and likely farther, to Ireland. I believe that conduit has reopened, with its key southern endpoint no longer Galloway, but instead smack dab in the Cotswolds.[117]"

"I see. May I ask, Mr. Blenkiron, how you figure into the picture?" I enquired.

The American agent smiled. "As you've been aware since just before the war, Major, the intelligence forces of our two countries have for several years worked in close harmony, quite unbeknownst to the public at large. Indeed, though my nation will only now be joining yours as an avowed ally against the Central Powers, I and my colleagues in 'the business,' as it were, have been clandestinely acting as if that alliance had been a fact all along.

"I, in particular, have been studying the movements and actions of a fellow countryman of mine: an individual named Abel Gresson. I am certain he was a part of the original network associated with the Black Stone, and I believe he plays a role in the new version of that spy ring, the revived remnant that Mr. Holmes spoke of a moment ago. In the course of tracking Gresson's movements, I acquired evidence suggesting that the Cotswolds also figures into the rebuilt Black Stone apparatus. More

---

[117] An area in the south central portion of England, the Cotswolds is characterized by grasslands, stone-built villages, and stately homes and gardens.

specifically, we have identified the town of Biggleswick as the likely new southern terminus of that spy network."

"Biggleswick?" I said. "Never heard of the place."

"It is a garden city," Holmes told me.[118] "And, in its own way, it is also a thriving centre of local culture, in addition to possible German espionage. It is there that—"

We heard a knock upon the wall and all turned as the hidden door swung open to reveal Sir Walter Bullivant. The spymaster nodded to the bookstore assistant behind him and then stepped into the study, the door closing behind him.

Like John S. Blenkiron, Sir Walter had changed since the war had begun. The Secret Service chief had lost a bit of weight, while his face was etched with several new lines since I had last seen him. Behind the familiar tortoiseshell spectacles, his eyes had altered as well, no longer holding a feisty sparkle but instead conveying the calm reflection of sullen acceptance.

I was well aware of the reason for that transformation, for I had happened to be in London when Bullivant received news that his son, a spy like the father, had perished while on a mission in Ottoman territory.[119]

"I apologise for being somewhat late," Sir Walter said as we all stood. "There was some quick business I had to conduct with M."

---

[118] The garden city movement was a method of urban planning started in Britain about the year 1900. It was characterized by advocacy of planned, self-sufficient communities surrounded by greenbelts with a mix of homes, industries, and agriculture.

[119] The younger Bullivant's assignment was related to the events described in *Greenmantle*, where the son's death in 1915 is mentioned.

Sherlock Holmes raised his brows and exhaled deeply before sitting down again, while Blenkiron and I regained our seats as Bullivant claimed the fourth armchair. The spymaster leaned forward toward me and took my hand in both of his.

"Very good to see you again, Watson," he said. "If only we had our fishing poles in hand and the Kennet before us, eh?"

"Perhaps we will find the time," I replied. "After all this is done, if not before."

"Yes, if not before." He squeezed my hand firmly once more before letting go. "And so, where am I entering the conversation?" Bullivant asked in a tired voice as he leaned back in his chair.

"We have informed the major of the Black Stone regrouping," Blenkiron said. "Gresson and Biggleswick were the last items mentioned."

Sir Walter nodded, and the American, by his posture, indicated that Sir Walter should now take charge of the meeting.

"Well, yes," said the spymaster, turning his head to patiently scratch the side of his neck, "we believe the Black Stone has taken root again, Watson, only this time its tendrils reach from Glasgow down to that town of Biggleswick," he summarised. "To learn more, we must send in forward observers."

He smiled at me.

"And I am to be that observer?" I ventured.

Sir Walter cocked his head and glanced toward Holmes.

"Yes, Watson," said the detective cautiously. "You are, however, to be but one of several. I shall be the second."

"Ah," I said. "Another adventure as Altamount? Will your goatee reappear?"

"I fear not," Holmes replied. "I am finished with impersonation, you see. I go forth in the world simply as myself from now on. After all, naked is the best disguise."[120]

"But that sentiment aside, will not your open presence in Biggleswick arouse suspicion on the part of the German spies, if there are any?" I suggested.

"Yes, of course it will," said Bullivant gently. "That is why we need a plausible excuse for Holmes to visit the Cotswolds."

"You will be that reason, Major," added Blenkiron.

"Isham military hospital is but two or three miles from Biggleswick," Sir Walter said. "M has arranged for you become its administrative head."

I sat silent to the world, but within I made an invisible gesture of exultation.

"Of course, you will be promoted to the rank of colonel, appropriate to your new position," the spymaster said.

"The plan is that, within a few weeks after your installation there, you will be visited by your good friend—me," said Holmes. "That I should pay an extended call on my old compatriot ought not to arouse too much suspicion."

"I see," was my somewhat subdued reply.

"Mr. Holmes's arrival will nonetheless likely heighten their guard," noted Blenkiron. "I refer, of course, to the German agents there, whoever they are."

---

[120] Holmes quotes from William Congreve's 1694 play *The Double Dealer*: "No mask like open truth to cover lies, as to go naked is the best disguise." Coincidentally, this same phrase was used by Samuel Rosenberg as the title of his controversial 1974 study of alleged hidden meanings in the Sherlockian canon.

"The hope of my brother, Sir Walter, and Mr. Blenkiron is that, while supposedly on holiday, I will perhaps be able to narrow the list of those who might be enemy spies," said Holmes. "Moreover, we are both likely to take a jaunt north to Glasgow to observe that fellow Gresson as well."

"And you will have other company," Bullivant told me. "Company beyond just Holmes here. Magillivray's Sergeant Scaife has been temporarily inducted into the army to serve as your batman."

"And I am offering Martha as your housekeeper during the stay in Biggleswick," said Holmes.

"I shudder to think what the subsequent effect will be in Queen Anne Street," I replied.

"We will manage," the detective primly insisted.

"In addition," said Bullivant, "there is already an agent in Biggleswick who will make contact with you there."

"I see. Who is he? That fellow Arbuthnot, perhaps?"

"Young Sandy bides his time in a warmer clime these days," Sir Walter replied cryptically. "No, your contact will be someone else, a person who will be revealed to you when the time is appropriate. That agent has been compiling a list of suspected German spies and will identify those people to you. The individual in question will employ an identifying phrase. That phrase is *blueberry tart*. Keep it in mind."

Sherlock Holmes suppressed a chuckle as Blenkiron looked on placidly.

Isham hospital was devoted to the treatment of officers in the throes of shell shock, that ill defined yet unmistakable state that encompassed everything from enhanced anxiety to sudden, inexplicable panic to complete absence of lucidity. No matter the nature of its manifestation, however, the effects upon those inflicted were horribly real, and the grim charge of the hospital I administered was to make its sufferers whole again, all in the ironic cause of facilitating their return to battle.

Within two weeks of the meeting in Traill's Bookshop, I assumed command as chief administrator of the facility. I was accompanied to the Cotswolds by Martha and the former police Sergeant Scaife, who was demoted to corporal during his period of service in the military.

Biggleswick, as Bullivant had informed me, lay but two miles to the west of the hospital, and I took up residence in the village itself, moving into a vacant cottage let by a Mr. Sacker, which I learnt much later was but an alias for Mycroft Holmes, who had purchased the residence for the government under that assumed name.

The house was one of perhaps two hundred that encircled a lovely Midland common. Built of warm, grey-coloured stone from regional quarries and topped by a steeply pitched slate roof, its frame was well set, though there were eccentricities: the windows were difficult to open, while the doors rarely stayed shut. However, I found it well-furnished and as clean as an operating table. There was a half-acre plot overgrown with weeds, as well as a ragged herb garden just beyond the kitchen windows. Scaife and Martha immediately set upon the tasks, respectively, of clearing the ground outside and organising the household within.

In the end, my residence there assumed a perfection equal to that of the town and district in which it sat. All the ordinary things that I was to see there—streets full of shoppers on market day, parties of hikers trudging down a wooded path, bicyclists setting out along a distant crest, old men reposing with jackets off and pipes in mouths, ploughs opening furrows in nut-brown fields—gave together a pulse, as of a living, breathing thing, and I yearned to become a part of it.

In the days that followed my arrival, the village received me in a friendly if measured way. My immediate neighbours to the north, the Jimsons, welcomed me within the first hour of my entering the cottage, offering a wonderful if rather small mince pie topped by creamy mash.

The wife, a large florid-faced woman with weather-bleached hair, promised me a bouquet of sunflowers in late summer, should I still be stationed at Isham then, but there was no mention of blueberry tarts. Meanwhile, the husband—a lanky managing clerk for some shipping company—offered to assist with my half-acre plot if I desired, suggesting that it be added to the slightly larger patch that the couple owned, adjacent to mine.

"We will, of course, share the bounty," Mr. Jimson declared, stroking his skimpy red beard streaked with grey. The man's blue eyes beheld me behind strong glasses as he added, "Ah, and there is nothing like the good smell of earth and having one's hands taken by Nature's own, eh?"

Both of them were good, kindly souls, proud of their village and more than willing to assist me in every way.

"Never take a major road if you can avoid it," Mr. Jimson would counsel me. "The most winding and wayward journeys are the best, particularly here in the Cotswolds," he declared. "There's no disadvantage in going by the back roads, unless you are in a hurry—and if you are in a hurry, perhaps you don't belong here in any case, eh?" he added with a gentle smile.

"I have generally found that the clock conforms to my movements, rather than the other way round," I replied with a warm grin. "Except when duty calls, which it will the day after tomorrow, when I take the reins at Isham."

And so, the very next day, taking me up on my claim to be an avid hiker, the Jimsons led me for a walk round the town and beyond, during which I crossed paths with several other residents, including a prominent London publisher and long-time local inhabitant, Frederick Shaw, who had been entertaining three guests from the north by joining them in a round of golf.

While passing by the side of the road, all of us—including Shaw's three companions—were almost run down by a tall, lean fellow on a bicycle, an incident which caused the publisher to declare that he would never again accept another manuscript on cycling.

Continuing my stroll with the Jimsons, I encountered more than a handful of young men whom I judged ought to have been in France,[121] including a pair who approached us in the company of a somewhat badly dressed young woman with untidy hair left uncovered.[122] One of these men, a youth named Aronson, was introduced to me by the Jimsons as a great budding novelist, while the other—a slightly older, bristling fellow with a fierce moustache—turned out to be one Letchford, a celebrated reviewer for *The Critic,* a prominent newspaper. Neither displayed a war-service badge.[123] The female, identified as a Miss Lester, was a painter of

---

[121] While conscription had been instituted in Britain—excluding Ireland—in 1916, appeals against service were possible on the grounds of important work, business or domestic hardship, medical unfitness, and conscientious objection. By the time of Watson's move to Biggleswick, more than three-quarters of a million men in the nation had been granted such exemptions.

[122] In this time period, both women and men generally wore hats outside the home.

[123] Those employed in civilian work deemed of importance to British national security were issued official badges identifying their activity as vital to the war effort, so that they would not be seen as shirking military duty.

no small promise, I was told, as well as a close friend and suffragist follower of the Brookhurst women.[124]

As we strolled on and the Jimsons described for me life in Biggleswick, it became apparent that the town was inhabited by a number of talented individuals from the worlds of art, literature, and music, as well as the sphere of political activity.

"The area has enjoyed the presence of noted artists for decades," Mr. Jimson declared as we waited for a small herd of cows to pass down the lane. "Perhaps you've heard of Morton and Emily Clifford, the potters? Or Gordon Pritchard, the furniture maker?"

"I don't believe so," I admitted.

"Possibly the activities of the Aesthetic Guild have come to your attention?" he suggested. "Though they have declined in prominence a bit since the days of the late queen, their spirit remains, I think."

"In any event," I said, "they all have made the area so much the better, I gather."

"It is like living in a great laboratory of thought," Mrs. Jimson said as we approached the Haven Stones, an ancient circle of large rocks. "And it is so glorious to feel the vibrancy of the eager, young people who lead all the newest movements," she declared as we stared at the arrangement of megaliths, whose original purpose had been lost in the mists of time.

"Intellectual history is being made in our studies, sitting rooms, and gardens, that is certain," added her husband some time later, as we returned to the village proper and caught sight of the couple's cottage and my new residence, where Scaife was busy clearing the garden plot.

---

[124] This may be a fictionalized reference to Emmeline Pankhurst (1858–1928) and her daughters, all of whom were active in the cause of women's suffrage in Britain at the time.

"The war is a remote thing to many of us here, I must confess," Mr. Jimson added with strain in his voice as he watched my batman work the soil. "I wish it could be forever remote from everyone. After all, some are sacrificing so that people like us can be permitted leisure and peace to think. Many of those whom you have met today—I speak in particular of Aronson and the reviewer Letchford and Miss Lester—very strongly oppose the war, Colonel, and I must be candid with you and admit that I do not disagree with them on the issue. Still, I can never pretend to the same sort of moral superiority that they claim for themselves."

Mr. Jimson kept staring at Scaife, bent over on his knees. "Never," he repeated.

While settling into my new surroundings, I was to make the acquaintance of many more Biggleswick inhabitants beyond my closest neighbours. Perhaps half of those I met were stolid citizens who had moved to the town for the country air and low rates. The younger men tended to be government clerks, or writers and artists like Aronson. There were a few widows with flocks of sensitive daughters sprinkled amongst the populace, and on the outskirts of town I found several larger residences which had been part of the landscape before the garden city itself was built up. Largely constructed for the gentry in those days when the region dominated the wool trade, these older structures were of a different style than the common cottages such as mine.

One such great house, I was informed, was owned by the publisher Frederick Shaw, in whose company I had almost been run over by the speeding bicyclist. Over the course of the next few weeks, I regularly espied Shaw at the local railway station carrying a little black bag full of manuscripts, which I understood he took with him every working day to his London office. He did not recognise me from our brief meeting days before, and I chose not to renew the passing acquaintance, having at once marked him for further observation at a distance.

Another imposing villa, sitting upon a hill amid sprawling wild gardens, was that of a man named Moxon Ivery, who was described by the Jimsons as a former don and very prominent pacifist leader.[125]

I found myself tolerated, though not intimately embraced by some elements of local society. Being part of the war effort, I was held at arm's length by those, but most people's attitudes toward me were softened by the fact that my role in the conflict was one of ministering to the wounded. In that context, I thought myself treated well, though a few, such as Aronson and Letchford, appeared on occasion to view me with smug, condescending amusement.

At Isham itself, I relished my role as chief administrator of the hospital, where I hoped to at last contribute directly to the relief of human suffering. I found that my predecessor had not been well respected or liked, and that his poor administration had led to falling morale among the staff, with an accompanying decline in the effectiveness of the facility in rehabilitating patients.

I vowed to reverse this downward spiral, and began to undertake great effort to win over the staff, which included several competent individuals around whom I hoped to build a core that would lift the hospital above its current unenviable state.

---

125 A don is a university teacher. The term is often associated in particular with either Cambridge or Oxford, but Watson's narrative does not mention any specific institution.

Of great help to me in this endeavour was Major Collins, the chief surgeon and my *de facto* second-in-command. Below him, Captains Hughes and Simmons managed the details of daily medical routine, such as morning inspections, while each ward was assigned an officer from our small bevy of lieutenants. Those junior officers were all a sober, determined lot—though at times I would find myself casting a half-sceptical eye in the direction of Lt. Hooper, who though dedicated was at times more than capable of being distracted from his duties.

It took me a while to become acquainted with all the staff sergeants and corporals in the facility, as well as the nursing corps, though it was within the first quarter hour of stepping into Isham that I became quite familiar with two individuals in particular.

I had not even entered my office for the first time when I encountered a warrant officer in heated argument with a matronly female nurse.

"Isolation and special care are the best we can do for him," insisted the woman. "We can make the space for him, I tell you!"

"Do that, you fool, and you'll break the man for good," countered the sergeant-major with disdain.

"Here," I said at once, stepping from Major Collins to approach the angry pair. "What seems to be the dispute?"

"We are discussing a hospital matter, sir," the nurse said. "Your rank aside, sir, I would appreciate it if you might let the two of us resolve this matter."

"And as I am your new commanding officer—Colonel John Watson—I believe that resolution is of interest to me as well."

"Oh," said the woman, as if suddenly chastened. "My apologies, sir."

"And who are you?" I asked her.

"This is Nurse Williams, sir," said the warrant officer, saluting as he spoke for the woman. "Sergeant-Major Ffolkes, sir."

"I believe Nurse Williams is capable of introducing herself, Sergeant-Major."

"Quite so, sir."

"And what is the matter that you discuss?" I asked as Major Collins approached to stand at my side.

The warrant officer and the nurse cautiously looked at one another, and then the former reluctantly gestured for the other to speak.

"It concerns one of our patients, a Lieutenant Clayton," said the nurse. "He displays extreme social anxiety, and so I propose to isolate him, so as to reduce sources of irritation and discomfort. As I am sure you are aware, it is the course many recommend in such cases."

"And with all respect, sir," interjected Sergeant-Major Ffolkes, showing the marks of a Queen Alexandra's Staff man,[126] "Lieutenant Clayton shows marked paranoia with respect to his condition. I am certain you also recognise the dangers of such a course as the nurse proposes. There are—"

"Why is this an issue that causes argument between you?" I asked. "Do we not have clear recommendations for the disposition of such cases here at Isham? And in any event, is that determination not made a level higher than either of your ranks?"

I turned to Major Collins, who shrugged.

126 This reference means that the sergeant-major had undergone special training in connection with the Imperial Military Nursing Service, the nursing branch of the British Army.

"In truth, sir," he said, "the previous administration was somewhat lax about adopting guidelines issued from RAMC command, and those we have established ourselves are rather incomplete."

"Then we must complete them," I said.

Collins nodded sharply. "Of course, sir."

"In any event, do not put that man put in isolation at present," I said to Nurse Williams, who was taken aback. "You tell me that Lieutenant Clayton is strained in his relations with patients and staff around him, and while I do not argue that isolation might produce some beneficial effects, I believe, as the Sergeant-Major suggests, that there is a grave possibility that such treatment may lead him to believe his case is more serious than it is.

"As a matter of experience, it is often found that many men cannot stand such clinical isolation for long. They feel they must break out. No," I said, "let us carefully review how we may improve Lieutenant Clayton's relations with us and his fellow patients, but do not place him by himself just yet."

"Right, sir," said Ffolkes, cheered by my support for his position.

"And in future, Sergeant-Major," I added sharply, "allow Nurse Williams and others to speak for themselves. Do you quite understand?"

"Why, yes sir!"

"Very well," I said, leading Major Collins on down the hall, suspecting that I had done nothing to endear myself to either of the two subordinates I had just met.

The facility itself housed at any time about fifty officer patients, some suffering physical wounds, but all carrying the burden of broken psyches, and while our doctors and surgeons were kept occupied, the greatest work was done by the nurses, led by the aforementioned Mrs. Williams, whose pronouncements were often considered by some a law higher than my own—at least, when I was not made aware of them.

The staff also included several VADs[127] in their blue dresses and aprons. Prominent amongst these were Mary Lamington and Edith Finch, the former being especially notable. Though she was young enough that some might have termed her a flapper,[128] Miss Lamington's broad brow-framed eyes conveyed a keen intelligence, and she had an uncanny ability to shift her mood from cheery mirth to grave contemplation within an instant.

During my first week at Isham, she entered my office with a small collection of personal files, which she gingerly deposited upon my desk.

"These are the dossiers of the patients who will be arriving next Tuesday," she said in her lilting voice, and I took the top folder in hand, unopened. "Nurse Williams is uncertain whether we have room for them all. Her understanding is that the senior three patients currently in the north ward, for example, may not be discharged until the end of next week."

"I will speak to Captains Hughes and Simmons; perhaps they might work out the details with her," I suggested, for I was now hesitant to personally confront Nurse Williams, who seemed to view me with

---

[127] The Voluntary Aid Detachment was an organization founded in 1909 with the help of the Red Cross. Each volunteer was referred to as a detachment or VAD. The majority were female, and at the start of the First World War, they sought to serve both at home and in France, an offer which initially was met with resistance.

[128] The term "flapper" was used at the time to refer to a young girl who did not yet put her hair up in the style of mature women. There is no uniform consensus about the origin of the word—one common view is that it is a reference to a young bird flapping its wings when learning to fly, while another holds that it describes instead plaited pigtails flapping on a young girl's back. The word was also British slang for a very young prostitute in the 1890s, but by the time of Watson's narrative, that association had become much less common.

pronounced disdain. I put the file back with the others. "Perhaps we could double up rooms for some of those nearing the end of their treatment."

"In past months, sir, there was occasional talk of billeting the more promising ones in surrounding homes."

"Yes, I remember Major Collins mentioning that." I sighed. "I don't wish to consider it, since that policy would amount to handing our problems off on unwitting and untrained civilians, even assuming that some local residents are willing to accept them."

"Of course, sir."

I pushed the pile of dossiers to one side and hesitated before returning to my correspondence, waiting for the VAD to leave my office. When she did not, I looked up at her with an avuncular smile.

"You have something else, Miss Lamington?"

"I simply wished to welcome you to Isham," she said, taking a moment to adjust her white cap, which sat atop hair that looked like spun gold. "I was present when staff received you, of course, but allow me at this moment to express my personal greeting as well, sir."

"Thank you," I said. "It is most appreciated."

"I would have offered you some gift, had I thought beforehand of doing so," she went on as I again glanced down at the letter I was composing. "Indeed, were it the season, I believe I might have baked you a blueberry tart."

I began to chuckle with amusement, but almost at once the smile left my face. I looked up with surprise at this young woman, barely past twenty years of age, and said in a hushed voice, "You are Bullivant's—"

"Perhaps we should talk of those matters elsewhere," she interjected. "Might we gather some of these dossiers, as well as our coats, and pretend to discuss patients while making a circuit of the grounds?" the nurse suggested.

And so, minutes later, each bundled against the brisk air of early spring, we strolled about outside the hospital, seemingly engaged in hospital business, though our conversation was comprised of very different references.

"Have you been in Bullivant's employ for some time?" I asked as we approached the south garden, where three convalescents, wrapped in greatcoats, stood and stared at a bed of primroses in the company of Lt. Hooper.

"A moment, please, before you answer," I quickly added as we greeted the trio of invalids and enquired if they were in need. With careful, deliberate voices, each man in his turn declared himself to be quite satisfied, and with cautious smiles all round as well as a nod to Hooper, Miss Lamington and I continued on our way.

"I was recruited by Sir Walter not quite three years ago," she said. "Though we never did, you and I might have chanced to meet before now, for I was one of the women who posed as Mr. Holmes's housekeeper in Sussex, you see."

"Ah, so you were one of the Marthas."

"That was my first assignment—a quite trivial one, of course."

"And now you hunt German spies in the Cotswolds."

She smiled. "Well, I keep my eyes open for them, as I have been instructed. And I will assist you in communicating with Sir Walter, for as you have been told, he does not wish you to contact him directly."

"Yes, I am to pass anything of note to the agent already stationed here—you, I now realise."

"I shall fulfil that duty," she replied. "And I am also to facilitate your meeting various people in the community, so that Mr. Holmes may in turn observe them at first hand during his coming visit. My understanding from Sir Walter is that he is to arrive sometime before Maundy Thursday."[129]

"He has been delayed," I said, a statement that seemed to give Miss Lamington concern. "He will arrive not long after, however: on the Wednesday following Easter," I quickly added, and the news appeared to put her at ease. "His stay in Biggleswick will last for over a fortnight. Part of that time, however, will be spent travelling to Scotland with me, as if on holiday. However, we instead will be—"

"Attempting to probe the northern reaches of the German spy apparatus," the young woman completed.

"Quite so," I replied. "And trying in particular to discern its connections with Biggleswick."

By this time, we had circled halfway round the facility and were near the road leading past the hospital, where I observed a man approaching on bicycle. As he drew nearer, I saw that it was the same lanky fellow who had almost run down Frederick Shaw, me, and others during my first stroll about the village. The rider slowed to a halt right before us and stuck out a leg to brace himself.

"Halloa, Mary," he said in a cheerful if whining voice to my companion.

The man was about thirty years of age, wearing grey flannels and dingy shoes, and his thin face was framed by rather more hair than the average man's. His chin was long, the mouth drawn into a firm line with

---

[129] Maundy Thursday is a Christian holy day, the Thursday before Easter, and in 1917, it fell on April 5.

peevish depressions at its corners. What struck me most about the newcomer, however, were his eyes, for in their way they gave off a burning expression—not angry or fierce, but relentlessly active, in much the same way as did the eyes of Sherlock Holmes.

"This is Launcelot Wake, my cousin," Miss Lamington said. "Launcelot, please meet Colonel Watson, our new hospital chief."

"Halloa," said the young man, extending a hand. "You seem familiar," he added, "though I cannot say why."

"We were in close proximity some days ago," I told him. "I was in the company of golfers and was not wearing my uniform then, while you were on that bicycle of yours."

The man thought for a moment and then said, "Ah, yes, of course. I recall it now. You all were standing in the middle of the road, weren't you?"

"I suppose so," I replied untruthfully, realising the man's perception of the incident was not identical to mine.

"Yes," said Wake. "I had a devil of a time getting round all of you, for you were blocking the lane rather completely."

I merely nodded and set my stance as if to defer to Miss Lamington, who took my cue immediately.

"The aunts are planning a grand dinner on Easter Friday,"[130] she said, giving me a significant glance before turning toward Wake. "I expect you will be invited, Launcelot."

"And will you be present?" her cousin asked.

"Of course."

"Then I will attend as well," Wake replied smugly, "invitation or no."

---

130 This refers to the Friday that follows Easter, as opposed to Good Friday, which precedes it.

The woman smiled and then once more looked at me.

"And I was about to inform you, Colonel, that you are on the guest list as well."

"Well then," I said, "I will certainly accept."

"That gladdens me."

"I will have a friend staying with me by that time," I added, almost as if her eyes had coaxed me to say those words in front of her cousin. "Might he, perhaps, be included at the table?"

"Our aunts—they are really distant cousins, but we refer to them as aunts—are very accommodating," said Wake in a sullen voice. "I expect they will allow him to join you—that is, join us."

"I will inform Aunt Claire and Aunt Doria," the woman said. "I am certain the answer will be in the affirmative. Ah, and here comes another who is to be present."

I turned and saw, walking in the road, a stout, middle-aged man. His face was pale and rather nondescript, even when he smiled upon approaching us.

"Miss Lamington, Mr. Wake," he said, and the man's voice more than made up for his lack of physical presence, for its sound was resonant and full, and phrases flowed from his mouth with the smoothness of warm butter.

"And you," he added, looking me straight in the eye while glancing over my uniform, "you must be the new head of hospital."

"Colonel John H. Watson," I said before Miss Lamington could introduce me.

"I am Moxon Ivery," he replied, taking my hand in a firm grip.

"Ah, the great house on the hill," I remarked. "I enjoy the look of its gardens very much," I added.

"Thank you, Major," Ivery said. "You must see my delphiniums, cowslips, and pennycress at closer hand someday."

"So," grunted Launcelot Wake to the newcomer. "You're going to be at Fosse Manor for the Easter Friday dinner as well?"

The young man's tone was not hostile but did convey a touch of irritation. Ivery, however, took no exception to Wake's manner of delivery and once more flashed his forgettable smile.

"This is the first I have heard of such," the retired don said. He looked at Miss Lamington enquiringly.

"You should receive an invitation shortly from my aunts," she said. "I suppose Launcelot's revelation will give you slightly more time to consider."

"I need no time at all to weigh the matter," replied Ivery in his compelling voice. "I accept, even in advance of the formal invitation."

"Excellent," said the woman. "The colonel and a friend of his will be present as well."

"Indeed!" exclaimed Ivery. He looked at me with sly, half-lidded eyes. "Could that friend possibly be Sherlock Holmes?"

"Why yes, it is," I said, taken aback.

"I am but a recent discoverer of your stories, Colonel Watson," said Ivery. "However, I have become a most enthusiastic reader of them. When I learnt the name of Isham's new head of hospital, I could not help but wonder if it could be that very same John H. Watson. And it is! Were you aware of who your new hospital head is, Miss Lamington?"

The young woman gave a bit of a start but quickly regained her composure.

"Why, no," she said, looking at me with an expression of convincing surprise. "That is, I am somewhat familiar with the exploits of Mr. Holmes, of course, but I did not think to consider that you might be the author of those stories, Colonel."

"The illustrious author," amended Ivery.

"I fear that the word *illustrious* exaggerates my status," I replied.

"And who is this Sherlock Holmes?" asked Launcelot Wake.

"There," I said good-naturedly. "I told you it was exaggeration."

Ivery and Miss Lamington chuckled, rather to the confusion and irritation of Wake.

"Obviously," Ivery said, tracing the slanting strap of my Sam Browne belt[131] with his forefinger, "you do not ply the streets of London with your detective friend these days."

"No," I cautiously declared. "I lectured recruits in Aldershot for most of the war before coming here to Isham. And, truth to tell, Sherlock Holmes has been retired from the business of detection for over a decade."

"Perhaps, like you, he is now engaged in war work instead?"

"I believe he is so occupied," I carefully replied. "Its exact nature, however, he has not deigned to reveal to me."

Ivery nodded. "Please do not feel offended, Colonel, but I think it odd that the sisters Wymondham have invited to dinner a military man, though of course you are devoted to healing wounds rather than creating them."

---

[131] The Sam Browne belt is a wide belt supported by a narrow strap passing diagonally over the right shoulder. Once a prominent feature of military and police uniforms, it has since become far less common, other than for ceremonial use.

He looked at me as if appraising my soul. "You see, the majority opinion in these parts is decidedly against the war."

"I have had that inkling, Mr. Ivery."

"*I* am against this war."

"So I have been informed."

"I hope that the prevailing sentiment in Biggleswick does not set you against our community," said Ivery.

"We are all entitled to our views," I replied. "Every Englishman should have his say."

"As well as every Englishwoman," Ivery added, indicating Miss Lamington with care.

"Of course," I agreed as Wake frowned yet again.

"In that connection, Colonel Watson," the former don said, "I have an invitation of my own."

Launcelot Wake scowled and then guided his bicycle past Ivery before the man could continue. "Well, I will be going," Miss Lamington's cousin declared abruptly. "I suppose we shall all see one another again at Fosse Manor."

As Wake pedalled away, I saw Ivery's face contort into a smile that made his jaw and cheeks expand like india-rubber.

"A pleasant, if impulsive young man," he observed. "But then, let me return to the matter of my invitation. Is the colonel aware of Moot Hall?" he asked Miss Lamington.

"Why, I do not know," the woman said without hesitation. She looked between the two of us and then blushed most convincingly. "My discussions with him have concerned only the work of the hospital—we were talking of incoming patients when Launcelot rode by," she said, holding up the dossiers she carried.

"I see," replied Ivery. "Well, Colonel, Moot Hall will be found on the south side of our common, near the rail station. It is a prominent red-brick building and was built with money supplied by Mr. Shaw, the publisher who is my neighbour. Several Christian sects use it as a makeshift church of sorts, while I understand the pagans hereabouts employ the Haven Stones for *their* rituals. Some of us, however, find the hall useful as a setting for lectures and debates—I refer to a committee that Mr. Letchford and I take turns chairing. These gatherings provide all our resident intellects an opportunity to air their views."

"Several speakers from many of the New Movements have appeared there," Miss Lamington added, in a voice that made her seem all too credulous.

"Yes," agreed Ivery. "Would you consider attending our gatherings, Colonel? Perhaps you will find the views expressed enlightening, or possibly you will consider them revolting and seditious. But it is all in the spirit of free exchange of thought, is it not?"

"I will certainly consider your kind offer, Mr. Ivery. Provided," I added with a smile, "that you do not call upon me to speak my own mind."

"Oh, I should be very sad if you do not," he declared with mock disappointment. "But I can understand the reluctance. Your presence alone, even if silent, would be welcomed, I assure you."

"I am certain the discussions are stimulating," I said in a neutral voice.

"We find them so," declared Ivery. He bowed to Miss Lamington and me, and then trudged off along the road.

“He is one to keep an eye out for,” the woman declared once Ivery was beyond earshot.

“Oh? You think him a possible German spy?”

“He is on my list of suspects, yes. Sir Walter requested that I mark those I thought required closer attention. Indeed,” she added, “they all will be at the dinner my aunts are giving.” The young woman smiled demurely. “I had a strong hand in suggesting it and arranging the guest list, you see.”

“And who else is on that list?”

“The publisher, Frederick Shaw, for one,” Miss Lamington said. “He travels almost daily to London, always with manuscripts supposedly within his valise, which never leaves him.”

“Yes, I have seen the man more than once, at a distance.”

“There is also Mr. Letchford, whom Mr. Ivery referred to. And a friend of Letchford, a young novelist—”

“Named Aronson.”

“Why, yes,” said Miss Lamington. “You’ve met him?”

“Both him and Letchford, yes.”

“I believe the latter to be of more interest than Aronson,” the young woman replied. “He is very involved in the activities at Moot Hall, as Mr. Ivery just noted. Moreover, speakers from elsewhere often present their views in the hall, and every one of them boards with Letchford while staying in Biggleswick.”

“You believe these speakers might be part of the Black Stone network?”

“Well, it is possible, is it not?” she said. “And Aronson is so much in Letchford’s company that I believe the pair must be taken together as guilty or innocent.”

"Most certainly." Then, with care, I asked, "And what of your cousin, Mr. Wake? You've indicated that he will be present at the dinner."

She smiled nervously. "Yes, he will, though Launcelot is quite harmless and will be at the dinner only because, were he not invited, he would take offence."

"I wager he is a CO, is he not?"[132]

"Well, he does oppose the war, but his exemption is on account of being a civil servant," she said. "He is a clerk in the Home Office."[133]

"You declare him harmless, Miss Lamington, and yet he is often on that bicycle of his, isn't he? Where does it take him?" I asked idly.

"Rather far afield, I must admit. Launcelot is very active—he hikes and mountaineers as well."

"And where does he hike, Miss Lamington? What peaks does he climb?"

"Innocent ones, or so I believe." Then, after a moment, she added, "I had not considered it before, Colonel Watson, but one of the places Launcelot not infrequently visits is Skye."[134]

"I see. And Skye is close to Glasgow, is it not?"

"I understand your point," admitted the young woman. She looked down with a thoughtful expression, "I suppose it is my duty to place him on the list as well, isn't it?"

"Miss Lamington, I did not mean to cause you—"

---

[132] Watson refers to Wake being a conscientious objector. See also footnote 121.
[133] The Home Office is a department of the British government responsible for law enforcement, security, and immigration.
[134] Skye is the largest and most northern of the Inner Hebrides, an archipelago off the western coast of Scotland.

“It is quite all right, Colonel,” she said, lifting her head and forcing a smile onto her lips. “You are correct. It is just as well, then, that I had my aunts invite Launcelot to dinner with the others.” She swallowed and took a deep breath. “For he is now added to the list of suspects for Mr. Holmes’s consideration. That is my duty, to Sir Walter.”

“Duty, yes,” I said, thinking suddenly of Cecil Harper.

“But shall we return to your office, sir? I believe we should actually take a look at these dossiers I’m holding, as well as the ones still on your desk.”

We stood aside as two VADs escorted a patient, whom I recognised as the fragile Lt. Clayton, from the building and out to the south garden to view the primroses with those already there. Then, briskly, Nurse Lamington and I entered and walked straight to my office.

That evening I made a quiet tour of Isham before going out to the road, where I would wait for Scaife to arrive and drive me home, as he did every other day, in a dogcart borrowed from a neighbour—on alternate days, weather permitting, I walked the two miles to Biggleswick.

I looked into each ward and then passed through the surgical room—vacant at this hour—and on to the library, where several patients sat reading beneath warm amber lights. As I neared the main doors, I hear a scratchy gramophone start up from the recreation room and, smiling gently, stepped out into the early night air to find Corporal Scaife already waiting for me.

“Fruitful day, sir?” he asked as I sat down beside him.

"Yes, Scaife," I replied as the horse began pulling our dogcart along the path homeward. "Very fruitful, and perhaps signifying an even greater bounty to come."

CHAPTER TWELVE: MY DINNER WITH HOLMES

In the second week of April, three days after Easter, I greeted Holmes at the Biggleswick rail station, and together we strolled to my cottage as Corporal Scaife conveyed my friend's luggage in the dogcart. Settled into a spare room and briefly reunited with Martha, Holmes then accompanied me on a walk about the village and its surroundings, in much the same way as I had joined the Jimsons on my second day in the area.

"I trust this is not your first hike in these environs?" he asked with a smile.

"Hardly," I replied. "And I believe I have lost no insubstantial portion of a stone in the bargain. I trust you have planned well your modus operandi while in Biggleswick?"

Holmes shrugged. "That must always be tailored to the specific objective, of course, and in this instance, Watson, we cannot be too restrictive. Bullivant and Blenkiron believe that the northern branch of the Black Stone is once more up and running, but they do not know to what purpose. It could be merely the gathering of information, yes, but subversion may also remain in the group's repertoire—recall, after all, that it was this cabal, in an earlier incarnation, that murdered Karolides and thus helped propel civilisation on its present slide toward the abyss."

"Do you believe the war will end before we all descend into that black hole?" I asked plaintively.

"One side or the other must crack at some point," he replied. "We can only do all that is possible to ensure that ours is not the weaker. And for us, old fellow, that means stamping out the Black Stone once and for all, and then exposing and exterminating that third nest of spies we believe our foe has planted amongst us."

"Yet no sign of the last head of Cerberus has been detected?"

"None whatsoever."

"Is that not troubling?"

"Of course it is, but until such time as the first glimmering of a useful clue is uncovered, I bide my time unravelling coded German messages in London. And you help heal the wounded here in Biggleswick," Holmes added, an odd look in his eye.

At that point, just past the ancient circle of Haven Stones, we came upon the three Weekes sisters, who lived with their mother in a house not far from mine—it was from her that Scaife regularly borrowed the dogcart in which he conveyed me to and from Isham.

Holmes doffed his cloth cap as I introduced him to the trio.

"Oh, Mr. Holmes, your profile is such a bold one," said the first Miss Weekes impetuously. "Has John[135] painted you? He should, you know."

"Yes," agreed one of her sisters. "Look at his eyes: so full of *implication.*"

"You are a lover of Dégousse,[136] I suspect," murmured the third Miss Weekes.

"In point of fact," admitted Holmes. "I am."

"I knew it!"

"Indeed," my friend said. "I own a Dégousse."

All three sisters appeared ready to swoon.

---

[135] This is probably a reference to Augustus John (1878–1961), a Welsh painter and etcher, and an important exponent of Post-Impressionism in Britain at the time.
[136] A fictional artist referred to in the previous chapter. Significantly, perhaps, this same imaginary painter is also mentioned in John Buchan's *Mr. Standfast.*

"We must write Austin about it," one said, and at the mention of that name I gently tugged on the elbow of Holmes's ulster but was too late. One Miss Weekes reached out and lightly grasped the cuff of my friend's other sleeve, a forward act that evinced from him a look of mild surprise.

"Austin is our brother," said the young woman.

"He's been in quod[137] for months now," added another sister.

"That can be the penalty if one is a vocal conscientious objector and not afraid to speak out," declared the third sibling with a hint of anger. "He suffers there in Dartmoor," she went on, bristling as she declared fidelity to her brother. "His hardships are unbearable."

"But I am certain he will bear them in support of his beliefs," replied Holmes, now heeding my silent urging to move along.

"Of course he will," the sisters asserted, almost in unison, as the detective and I hastily bade them farewell.

"You did not wish to linger in conversation with those young women?" Holmes remarked as he once more donned his cap. We continued along a path that led past a copse of beech trees, and he added, "Do you not get along with your new neighbours?"

"They are, most of them, quite well-meaning sorts," I replied wearily. "And, truly, those three young women are good at heart, and their mother the kindest of souls. However, I have seen so much sacrifice, Holmes—both in France and here at Isham hospital—that I find I now cannot take lightly the indulgences heaped upon those who shirk their responsibilities."

"If you refer to the brother of those three sisters—"

---

137 "In jail."

"And others like him," I interjected.

"I do not believe that one who accepts incarceration in Dartmoor prison as a consequence of adhering to principle ought to be considered a shirker, old fellow. And putting a man in gaol is hardly indulging him."

"Have you now become a pacifist as well?"

"Certainly not," sniffed Holmes. "You should know me better than that, Doctor—pardon me, Colonel. I believe the two years I spent as Altamount testifies to my devotion to the Crown, as does my presence here in pursuit of German saboteurs."

"It is I who should beg pardon, Holmes," I said meekly. "I did not mean to suggest that—"

"I merely wish to remind you of something, Watson," my friend said as we strode past the copse and gained a small rise, where we beheld a field of young grass with a rocky outcrop in the distance. "I wish to remind you that the sacrifices to which you refer are on behalf of not only the Crown but also what the Crown itself is pledged to defend: our British way of life, which insists that each should be free to express his own mind."

"Or *her* mind," I amended, recalling Moxon Ivery's comment of the week before. "Of course. I avowed that sentiment only the other day. It is a fault of mine that I should let emotion govern my—"

"To react with emotion is never a fault," said Sherlock Holmes. "Though, I agree, it can sometimes become a disadvantage. Perhaps we should turn our attentions to other matters."

"The landscape, perhaps?" I said, taking in the beauty of the countryside on a spring day as we basked under a sky as blue as a thrush's egg.

"Yes," replied Holmes, bending down. "Or the landscape's details. One cannot avoid marvelling at the local limestone, can one?"

"Well," I said as I heard a lark in the distance. "I suppose not, unless one finds other experiences that are more striking."

"It is an oolite," said Holmes, seemingly oblivious to my remark as he held a small portion of soil in his hand before sifting it between his fingers. "That term is used because it is made up of minute spherical particles resembling eggs. Warm and red-grey when quarried, eventually turning a deep blue-grey," he mused, studying the granules with care before brushing his hands together as he rose to join me in walking on.

"You referred a moment ago to German saboteurs," I said. "Yet, you also indicated that the revived Black Stone network might be dedicated to merely gathering information, as it was before, in parallel with Von Bork."

"Yes," said Holmes. "I did mention both possibilities, did I not? Bullivant is torn between the two views," he said, looking about us. "I thought long and hard in the carriage during my trip here to Biggleswick, and my tentative assumption is that we are seeking saboteurs and subversives rather than those attempting merely to obtain military secrets."

"How so?"

"Your three Weekes sisters exemplify my train of thought," said the detective. "By all accounts—and I am certain I will observe more instances that will confirm the view—Biggleswick is a hotbed of pacifist sentiment. Many here are sceptical of the war effort or stand strongly in opposition to it—some to the point of going to gaol to assert that opposition.

"Persons seeking to gain acquaintance with those who have access to secret government documents or military plans are unlikely to adopt such a pose," Holmes said. "They will, instead, assume the guise of the fervent patriot, the jingoistic blusterer. Based on what you have conveyed to me thus far, I suspect few such individuals are likely to be found within several miles of Biggleswick.

"No, if the Black Stone have planted themselves here at a centre of anti-war agitation, Watson, I believe it indicates an inclination toward subversion and sabotage. It parallels the need the Germans have to strike a serious blow at Britain's heart. Mere information cannot satisfy them at this point. Instead, by infiltrating those who, for whatever motive, oppose war with the Central Powers, Berlin is bent upon stirring up trouble among Britons themselves, much as they attempted to set Mexico against the Americans by means of that coded telegram I conveniently deciphered weeks ago. Blenkiron does not completely agree with me, I know, but that is how I see the situation."

"And to come round to my original question, how does that view affect our strategy while you are here on holiday?"

Holmes smiled. "It means that exits and entrances are equally important," he said enigmatically. "Now then, tell me about this dinner I am to attend with you on Friday."

Two days later, as the first hints of twilight crept in from the east, Holmes and I followed a footpath that climbed through great beech trees just beginning to leaf, and there we encountered a short expanse of hill pasture that stretched to the rim of a vale. Leaving the trees, we found ourselves walking along walls built of thin, flat grey stones without mortar, their edges rendered pastel by the weather and colonies of lichen. Strips of burgeoning meadow weed displayed themselves like carefully planted borders, and beyond, in the enclosed fields, sheep stood calm watch on our progress. Below, our goal—Fosse Manor—was visible through distant woods, and farther away, passing over hills to the south, we could discern the old Fosse Way itself.[138]

We had hiked from my cottage in Biggleswick and now viewed a much smaller village nestled in a crook of the hill upon which we stood. A church tower sweetly chimed the hour, competing with no other sounds besides the twitter of birds and a gathering evening breeze that rushed through the topmost branches of the beeches.

We descended to the manor lodge and there stood before its red-brick façade, which was smothered in magnolias just starting to bud. As I raised my hand to grasp the knocker, the door opened to reveal Mary Lamington.

"I sensed you were there, Major Watson," she said demurely and then smiled. "Actually," she said in a plainer tone, "I have been peering through the window for the better part a half hour and just now saw the two of you approach." She glanced behind before whispering, "Good evening, Mr. Holmes."

"Miss Lamington."

"And you will present your friend, then, Colonel?" the young woman abruptly asked in a louder voice as a servant approached from down the hall.

"This is Sherlock Holmes," I said as the man approached to take our coats and hats. "The famed consulting detective, now retired."

---

[138] Fosse Way is a Roman-built road whose remnants still survive. Its name derives from the Latin word *fossa*, which means ditch.

"Retired by my own wish," added my friend. "And if I am famous at all, it is entirely due to the effort of my tireless biographer."

"It is a pleasure to meet you, Mr. Holmes," said Miss Lamington for the benefit of the servant, who withdrew carrying our garments. "Shall we go in?"

She led us through the large entry and then on past a broad staircase and along panelled walls upon which were hung prim family portraits. At the end of the corridor we caught sight of our hostesses, neither of whom I had yet met, but who were unmistakable even before Mary Lamington introduced us.

The Wymondham sisters, Miss Doria and Miss Claire, were each nearing a half century but dressed in styles common to women half their age. Miss Doria was tall and thin, her pale hair bound by a fillet round her head. Miss Claire, by contrast, was shorter and plumper, as well as less skilled than her sister in the application of cosmetics.

"Ah, Mr. Watson," said Miss Claire, "It is a joy to have you here."

"And we appreciate your wearing of civilian clothes," Miss Doria added circumspectly. "We hope you do not object to our preference for leaving military rank—indeed, everything military—outside these walls."

"I have no objection whatsoever," I replied good-naturedly. "My assignment is irrelevant to the enjoyment of good company."

"And we welcome your friend as well," Miss Claire said. "We hope you are enjoying your stay in the district, Mr.—Mr. Holmes, is it?"

"Yes to both enquiries," said the detective, who refrained from continuing when a young man entered the hall.

It was Launcelot Wake.

"Halloa, Colonel Watson," he said to me, a greeting which caused both Wymondham sisters to wince. "And you are Sherlock Holmes, I am told," he remarked to the detective.

"I am, yes."

"I confess I knew nothing of you until several days ago," Wake declared with blundering innocence. "Odd, I suppose, since I work in the Home Office. However, I have recently read two or three of your stories in old magazines borrowed from Letchford—well, I suppose I should say *your* stories, Colonel. They are rather quaint in their way."

As Holmes smiled in amusement, I acknowledged the remark, uncertain whether to take it as compliment or complaint. Still, I was grateful for no mention of Doyle.

"Launcelot is our cousin," said Miss Claire. "Just as Mary is our cousin. Or distant nephew and niece of some sort, respectively. Have we ever understood the family connections?" she asked her sister.

"Come to the table, all of you," said Doria. "Perhaps we may untangle them there."

The dining room was markedly in contrast to the hall. Here the panelling had been stripped from the walls, which were now covered, as was the ceiling, with a dead-black satiny paper. All round us hung imposing paintings of modernist bent, each in gold frames. I gave the lot but little notice, but Holmes immediately took an interest in them.

"The Weekes sisters inform us that you own a DéGousses, Mr. Holmes," said Miss Claire with enthusiasm.

"Yes," replied my friend.

"We are seeking one ourselves," Miss Doria revealed. "Do you not marvel at his use of texture?"

I turned toward the long dining table as Holmes and the Wymondhams discussed art, observing that there were places set for several more than those of us already present. I ran down, in my mind, the list that Miss Lamington had compiled, comparing it with the empty seats and then, as if cued by my thoughts, three figures appeared at the opposite entry.

Two I recognised at once: Aronson, the novelist, and Letchford, the reviewer for *The Critic.* Between them was a slender woman of early middle age whose face resembled nothing less than that of a classic Greek sculpture. Her eyes flashed about the room, and an impish smile curled the edges of her bright red mouth.

"Ah, we are almost all assembled!" the woman declared loudly, even before being introduced, and the two Wymondham sisters turned abruptly from their artistic discussion with Holmes to face the three newcomers.

"So we are, Vespera," replied Miss Claire. "I believe Mr. Ivery is the only one not yet arrived."

"Perhaps we should arrange ourselves nonetheless," said Mary Lamington, taking charge of the gathering. "But we still have introductions to get out of the way, do we not?"

I declared myself already acquainted with Aronson and Letchford, whom I presented to Holmes. That left only the mystery woman.

"Ah, but the celebrated Miss Vespera Cochrane needs no introduction," said Holmes in a most gallant fashion. I stared in amazement at my friend as he approached the woman and took her hand. "I witnessed your London debut years ago and found it an unalloyed pleasure."

Discreetly, I reached for a chair to steady myself.

"You are acquainted, then?" asked Miss Claire as Letchford and Aronson stifled chuckles.

"I fear not," said the woman identified as Vespera Cochrane, eyeing Holmes with amusement, "but it is a situation easily remedied."

"This is Sherlock Holmes," said Mary Lamington, again stepping into the breach. "Perhaps you have heard of him, as he obviously has of you?"

"I fear that I am not familiar with the name," replied Miss Cochrane.

"Not familiar with the name of Sherlock Holmes? Surely you jest, madam," came the full-throated voice of Moxon Ivery from behind. I turned and saw the man, immaculately dressed, standing by Miss Doria Wymondham in the entrance through which Holmes and I had come. After a momentary pause, he strode to the centre of the room.

"Mr. Ivery," said Holmes, a remark which appeared to surprise the newcomer, who raised his left hand to his chest, exposing a slight discolouration about his smallest finger.

"I shan't bite," said the detective puckishly as he extended his right arm in greeting.

"I do not believe we have been previously introduced," declared Ivery, shaking the other's hand. "I wonder how you knew my name. I am hardly as famous as you, sir, and I should think your acquaintances would predominantly be those of the criminal class."

"My friendships extend to more respectable circles as well."

"I suppose, then," said Ivery, regaining his composure, "that it was your deductive facilities which gave you my name?"

"My identifying you without introduction is hardly remarkable and most definitely does not merit being called a deduction," said Holmes. "A moment ago, one of the Miss Wymondhams remarked that we lacked one guest, a Mr. Ivery. When you appeared, I took it that our missing member had arrived. Anyone else in that same situation would have drawn the same conclusion, I think."

"Ah, I see," replied Ivery. "That's simple enough. Well, greetings to all," he said to those in the dining room, a gesture that earned a frown from Launcelot Wake. "I do apologise for my lateness."

"Apology is unnecessary," Sherlock Holmes assured him. "When one is confronted by a sudden emergency that requires immediate correspondence, all else must come second, must it not?"

"Why do you say that?" asked Ivery, again displaying a hint of anxiety, this time more pronounced than before. "And what do you mean by it?"

"I merely uttered a statement of understanding in support of your apology, Mr. Ivery," said Holmes. "You were engaged in feverish letter writing upon a troubling matter which suddenly came to your attention just before leaving for Fosse Manor, one that no doubt still preys upon your mind. I am certain that it is a justifiable reason for your tardiness."

"And how do you come to know of my recent experience?"

"By the testimony of your person," replied Holmes. "Your right jacket sleeve is creased on its inner side, though the remainder of the garment is pristine, suggesting that your arm has recently been resting upon a surface for some time, as it would if the other hand were engaged in writing for several minutes. That would require you to be left-handed, which is a distinct possibility, since a moment ago you instinctively raised your left arm when surprised by my identifying you by name without benefit of introduction.

"One occasional, unfortunate consequence of writing with the left hand is the smearing of ink upon its fingers and edge, and indeed, your left wrist and little finger are so stained. There are, in fact, several such streaks that overlap, suggesting you spent some time in writing. In addition, the tips of your thumb and forefinger also bear marks that are of identical colour but in the form of blotches rather than streaks, artefacts likely due to a slowly leaking pen. Are you aware of that flaw in your writing instrument, Mr. Ivery?"

"Why, no."

"It should be attended to. Meanwhile, there is no inky imprint upon your collar or left cuff, but I espy a small one upon your right cuff, which would have been fastened with the left hand. Thus, you were writing after you had almost completely prepared for dinner, having already donned your shirt and collar but not yet fastened your cuffs.[139]

"Apparently, the need to write came suddenly, just before or in the midst of dressing, and you debated whether or not to compose a letter then and there as you donned your attire, perhaps causing you to neglect to fasten your cuffs before putting on your jacket. The matter of concern is, as I suggested, a subject that likely still preys upon your mind, Mr. Ivery, for preoccupation with it has made you overlook those small ink stains on your cuff, despite the fact that you are clearly very fastidious in your dress and, I believe, would normally have closely scrutinised your appearance before leaving home."

There was a moment of sepulchral silence after Holmes's declamation, and then Ivery smiled broadly. "A bravura performance, Mr.

---

[139] In this time period, collars were not integral parts of men's shirts but rather obtained separately and then attached to them.

Holmes. Quite perceptive, and quite correct, I must admit. I have a former colleague who is experiencing much family distress, you see," he explained. "I felt compelled to write him as I prepared for this dinner, as you so correctly deduced."

Giving my attention to the exchange between Holmes and Ivery, I had not noticed that the woman identified as Miss Cochrane had quietly made her way to my side and was staring intently at me.

"Vespera Cochrane," she whispered demurely while extending a hand. As I took it lightly in my own, she looked about and lightly added, "I am not above introducing myself when others have neglect to fully do so at all."

"Miss Cochrane is a renowned danseuse," said Holmes, turning from Moxon Ivery to address me.

"Dancer, if you please, Mr. Holmes," she said. "Men and women: we are all dancers alike."

"Dancer," my friend declared, correcting himself. "As I mentioned a moment ago, I attended your London premiere at the Royal Albert Hall and found its evocation of classic Hellenic aesthetics simply breathtaking."

In one corner of the room, Doria Wymondham gently sighed.

"I thank you," Miss Cochrane said to my friend. "But no one has yet told me what you are, Mr. Holmes," she added. "Other than an amusing magician of observation."

"He is Mr. Sherlock Holmes," Launcelot Wake reminded her. "Surely you have heard of him: the famous consulting detective?" he added somewhat self-consciously.

"Now retired," added Holmes.

"Truly?" said Ivery. "You do nothing more than tend bees these days, do you?"

Holmes raised a brow. "Now you make *me* ever so curious about your detailed knowledge of *my* recent experience, Mr. Ivery."

"Oh, I am reading your book, sir," explained the man. "I am not an apiarist myself, but I enjoy the study of nature and find your treatise most interesting and illuminating. I hope to finish it within the week."

Holmes bowed his head slightly and smiled.

"The details about the queen are fascinating," Ivery said.

"Thank you."

"And the portion about dormancy is very intriguing."

"*Dormancy* is a most incorrect term," insisted Sherlock Holmes. "Rather, the practice of the honey bee is to—"

"May we not place people above insects?" asked Miss Cochrane boldly, her eyes once more focused upon me. "I introduced myself," she said to me. "Perhaps you might do the same?"

"This is Dr. John H. Watson," said Holmes before I could speak. "He is the author of those famous stories that you have never read. He is also now Colonel John H. Watson."

"Oh," said the dancer, now seemingly disappointed. "A military man? Here at Fosse Manor?" Miss Cochrane declared, looking at the Wymondham sisters.

"He is an officer in the Royal Army Medical Corps," interjected Mary Lamington. "Indeed, Colonel Watson is our new head of Isham Hospital."

"A healer," Miss Cochrane intoned with a suddenly reinvigorated interest. "A modern Galen[140] for a world in flames." She waved an arm as she spoke and then audaciously hooked it round my own.

"To the table," the woman commanded as she gently pulled at my elbow. "We must all hear of your ministrations, Colonel—when we are not being humoured by Mr. Holmes's deductions."

There was a cynical smile on the face of Letchford, while the others retained neutral expressions—other than the Wymondhams, who appeared completely at sea.

Miss Lamington rushed to add herself to my escort, and framed by both women, I joined the rest of the group in sorting ourselves into seats round the great table. I was placed at one end, with Miss Cochrane and Miss Lamington on either side of me. Launcelot Wake swiftly claimed the chair to the right of his cousin, denying that place to Moxon Ivery, who settled for the seat opposite her and beside Miss Cochrane. Aronson and Letchford took the next positions down the line on either side of the table, each followed in turn by a Wymondham sister, leaving Holmes to inhabit the portion farthest from me, Miss Claire and Miss Doria flanking him on either hand.

For the first time, I noticed a sickly sweet scent in the room, which I thought might be the remnant of incense. Very quickly, however, my attention shifted to the food that servants now brought in, and the meal turned out to be, by far, the best I had enjoyed in many months.

"Excellent," said Letchford as he savoured his bowl of spinach soup. "It suffices in itself, I think. Even should we enjoy nothing else this evening,

---

[140] Galen of Pergamon was a prominent Greek physician in the Roman Empire.

I will be sated. However," he added with a sly smile, "I assume there will be one or more additional courses?"

"Certainly," sniffed Miss Doria. "We are, however, attempting to observe the official guidelines—within reason."

"Are you saying there will be no meat tonight?" asked Launcelot Wake with a sour smile.

"Oh dear boy," replied Miss Claire. "Of course there will be...some meat."

"And war bread, I see," remarked Letchford.[141]

"The shortages are far more acute in London," said Aronson.

"I believe sugar will be the first commodity to be rationed," suggested Ivery. "What is your opinion, Mr. Holmes?"

The detective shrugged. "Only time will tell," he said. "I grant, however, that sugar rationing will undoubtedly come first."

"I suppose that, in addition to aiding the war effort, such restrictions might serve to enlighten some with respect to proper nutrition," commented Letchford as he reached for another piece of bread. "There are so many lower-class mothers who believe their children will die if they do not eat sugar every day."

Aronson looked up from his soup. "Do you mean that may not be true?" he asked.

Letchford raised his brows to the others sitting round the table before stuffing a piece of bread into his mouth.

---

[141] Though Britain did not introduce mandatory food rationing until 1918, attempts were made to encourage citizens to ration on their own and to employ substitutes. For example, "war bread" was made with barley, potatoes, and other materials instead of wheat flour, and sugar was replaced with substances like corn syrup.

"I don't expect the men at the front enjoy a bounty such as this," said Ivery as some empty bowls were removed from the table. "Is that not true, Colonel?"

"Yes," I said. "There are shortages of many things."

"Except ammunition, I should think," said Aaronson with a chuckle.

"Do you ever read anything but your own work?" Letchford asked the novelist in a condescending tone. "The newspapers, for example?"

"You refer to the Shell Crisis?" Ivery asked.[142]

"Of course," Letchford replied, again casting a sceptical eye at Aronson.

"When I was there as an observer, it seemed that many things were scarce in France," I reiterated.

"What deficiency did you find most compelling, Mr. Watson?" asked Vespera Cochrane.

"Oh, I do not know," I said humbly. "There were so many. If we consider just the medical realm, I suppose stretchers are a plausible answer."

"Not enough of them, eh?" asked Letchford with mild interest. The Wymondham sisters looked at one another with apprehension.

"Their number hardly matches that of the wounded, certainly," I said.

"What do the men do when all the stretchers are full, then?" asked Ivery. "Take off a greatcoat, say, and use it instead to carry a man?"

---

[142] The Shell Crisis of 1915 was a shortage of artillery shells caused by a rate of combat fire much higher than initially expected. In Britain, this problem led to the creation of the Ministry of Munitions, as well as the formation of a wartime coalition government. By this time in Watson's narrative, H. H. Asquith had been replaced as prime minister by David Lloyd George, whose successful tenure as the first Minister of Munitions contributed to his political ascent.

"Inexperienced bearers will try that at first," I replied. "But it is a mistake to attempt it."

"Why?" asked Launcelot Wake, his eyes suddenly more intense than usual.

"Well," I explained, "a man will roll about if borne upon a coat, perhaps making his injuries worse."

"And so, if there aren't enough stretchers," Wake said, "what do the bearers do?"

Miss Doria made as if to speak but then remained silent.

"They carry the wounded upon their backs," I said.

"Truly?" the young man asked. "How is that possible?"

"It just is, Mr. Wake. For hours—or days on end."

Aronson whistled under his breath.

"Really?" said Letchford, with a hint of interest unleavened by his usual cynicism. "People actually accomplish such things? It seems rather difficult to believe."

"The capacity of the human organism to surprise is rather well documented, Mr. Letchford," declared Sherlock Holmes, who had been quiet for several minutes. "If you simply read accounts in the newspapers, as you recommended to Mr. Aronson a moment ago, I believe your incredulity will rapidly fade. Or perhaps," he amended, "it will intensify."

"Do *you* read the newspapers regularly, Mr. Holmes?" asked Ivery.

"Yes. It is a habit retained from the days when it was vital to my work."

"Ah, of course," said the retired don. "Agony columns and the like. I suppose they would be important to a consulting detective. I ask about the newspapers only because I was wondering if you read the political articles. Do you follow expressions of opinion regarding this war?"

"I browse them on occasion."

"Please," begged Miss Claire. "Remember, all of you, that the principal rule of this table is that discussion of war is out of bounds."

"But we have heard just a little of Colonel Watson's experiences in the medical corps, and I should like to hear more," said Wake.

"Yes," said Vespera Cochrane, leaning toward me. "Let us have some additional recollections."

Letchford and Aronson good-naturedly struck the table with their palms, joining in the demand that I convey the gist of my past two and a half years of service to all round the table. And so, despite the discomfort of my two hosts, I did so on through the next course, which was a delightful if slightly meat-deficient toad in the hole[143] served with asparagus and onion gravy.

I did not mention in detail any specific horrors which I had witnessed or been told of during my more than two years of recent military service, alluding instead to the RAMC's general approach in comforting those afflicted. In time, however, as we were given the main course of rabbit and turnips—with no evidence of bacon, to my disappointment—matters of art, music, and literature returned to the fore, and I gladly let those subjects dominate the conversation thereafter.

"I have reviewed a most fascinating new novel," said Letchford as dessert was about to be served. "Forgive me, Aronson, but it isn't one of

---

[143] A traditional dish, toad in the hole consists of sausages or meats in Yorkshire pudding batter, usually with vegetables and gravy. There is no consensus regarding the origin of the name.

yours, I fear. No, this is a marvellously crafted Russian work, wonderfully translated, entitled *Leprous Souls*. Have you read it?" he asked of all round the table. "It was published by Mr. Shaw's firm. It's a pity the man isn't here to discuss it."

"He was invited to this dinner," sighed Miss Claire Wymondham.

"But he declined," added her sister. "As he always does."

"Mr. Shaw is a very reticent fellow," noted Miss Lamington, her eyes fixed upon Sherlock Holmes.

"And a Colonial," observed Miss Claire primly. "A native of Canada."

"He does not socialise much beyond his rounds of golf with visitors to Biggleswick," Letchford added. "Of course, it wasn't always that way. Moot Hall was built with his money, and at first, he regularly attended the meetings there."

"Truly?" said Moxon Ivery.

"Indeed," said Letchford. "You wouldn't remember—and neither would you, Aronson—because neither of you lived here before the war, but I recall Mr. Shaw being an almost compulsive member of our discussion groups."

"And when did that change?" asked Sherlock Holmes in an abstracted tone.

Letchford thought for a moment and then answered.

"It was during the first month or two of the war—come to think of it, it was late September. I remember now because the Germans had just been stopped at the Marne, and our Moot Hall committee had decided to stage a series of lectures on the consequences of an indefinite stalemate—how was that for prescience, eh?" he said with a bit of self-satisfaction. "Well, Shaw was to deliver one of those lectures, but he rather suddenly declined. And, indeed, his entire involvement with Moot Hall ceased from that moment on."

The man paused and then added, "Soon thereafter, he seemed to withdraw from Biggleswick society altogether."

"His legacy remains, however," said Moxon Ivery. "To Moot Hall," he added, raising his glass. "Built with the money of Frederick Shaw, noble Canadian turned Englishman."

"Here's to that," said Letchford, lifting his glass as well.

Aronson joined them in the impromptu toast, as did we all.

"And here's to the hope that someday Mr. Shaw will deign to accept a work of mine," intoned the young author. No one followed his lead in that sentiment, however, and so he emptied his glass alone.

"Your time will come, my lad," said Letchford with gentle amusement before taking his first bite of dessert, a delicious rhubarb crumble. He spent several minutes expressing pride in his two children, at which point our general discussion broke into several smaller ones that ebbed and flowed round the table.

Not quite two hours later, beneath a starry, moonless sky spotted with windswept clouds, Holmes and I approached Biggleswick on foot.

"The walk has proved good for my stomach," said my friend. "Our dinner was most filling, despite the influence of the war on its content."

"Has the stroll helped your mind as well?" I asked. "Those whom Miss Lamington believes you should principally consider as candidates for the Black Stone were at that table."

"All save Frederick Shaw, the publisher," Holmes said. "But, as mentioned, the man keeps largely to himself these days."

"But he is not alone in being alone."

My friend smiled. "It occurs to me, Watson, that you might be able to approach Mr. Shaw and thus make it possible for me to observe him at close hand."

"Oh? How might that be done?"

"Are you not the accomplished author?" said Holmes in a taunting voice. "Might you not have another fantasy to pawn off upon an unsuspecting publisher—this time, Mr. Shaw?"

"I have had no time to write, Holmes."

"I am aware of that, old fellow, but Shaw is not so informed. Can you not go to him with at least a proposal of some sort? Another collection of stories? A novel, perhaps?"

"A novel would better serve, if I am to bring him merely the suggestion for a book, but I should have to choose a case the public have not yet been informed of. Which should it be? I have always meant to document the Hoxton beggar case but have never found the right moment for it."

"I do not have the fondness for that affair that you have displayed through the years, and why you should have kept the fellow's aluminium crutch as a souvenir is quite beyond my understanding. Moreover, the matter, though singular, is really worth no more than a few pages. No, I believe that it should be the Abernetty matter."

"Must you again bring up that dreadful business? For the past twenty years, it has ruined my enjoyment of parsley."

"Well then, I suggest you come up with something in the next few days. Recall that we leave for Scotland on Wednesday."

"Yes, I will do my best. And did you reach any understanding of our fellow diners this evening? I did not realise that Miss Cochrane, your renowned dancer, was among the suspects."

"She is not," said Holmes. "According to Miss Lamington, she was included among the guests only after Mr. Shaw declined his invitation. But no, Watson—sadly, nothing of immediate relevance to our quest here presented itself during the evening," the detective replied. "There was one comment by Mr. Ivery, however, that has somewhat altered my perspective on another matter."

"Oh?" I said. "And which remark was that?"

"If you do not mind, Watson, like Mr. Shaw, I should like to be alone with that thought for a while longer. It was not a remark that incriminates the man in any way; rather, it has made me see our Cerebus enigma in a slightly different light. And speaking of light, the landscape is starkly beautiful when stars are the only lamps, is it not?"

"Yes," I agreed, recognising my friend's desire to change the subject of conversation.

"One perceives shapes," Holmes went on, "without the distractions of colour. Form, line, geometric relationship—they all are in much plainer sight, as when one grasps a mathematical theorem for the first time or unravels a thorny riddle with a single insight. It is a pity your lark is not about, so that it might add an aural dimension to this nocturnal beauty."

I glanced at my friend.

"I heard it the other day as well, Watson," he said. "I am not so fascinated with the texture of soil that I am deaf to birdsong."

Silently, I nodded.

Biggleswick came into view as we rounded a small hill, and with the crisp night air wafting into our faces, we made our way to my cottage, where Martha and Scaife awaited us. We assured the former we were in no need of further food or drink, and the woman retired for the night. Scaife, meanwhile, brought to my attention a letter that had arrived while Holmes and I had been absent.

"It is addressed to you and sent from a Mr. Sigerson," the man said with upraised brows as he handed me the envelope.

I took it, dismissed Scaife for the evening, and accompanied Holmes into the small sitting room, where I handed him the letter. "Though formally addressed to me, this is no doubt meant for you," I said.

"As always, Watson, you are quick on the uptake." Holmes opened the envelope and unfolded the letter found inside. "Ha," he said after a moment. "All proceeds well."

I waited for a moment, and then my friend enlightened me.

"I believe I told you, back when I was still playing the game against Von Bork, that my preference would have been to enlist Frank Farrar and Shinwell Johnson for that endeavour."

"Yes," I replied. "You feared, however, that they might be recognised in London and thus chose not to have them pose as recruits for Von Bork's apparatus. You employed Hollins and Steiner instead."

"Correct," Holmes noted. "Both Hollins and Steiner have since volunteered for the New Army, however. I assume you applaud such patriotic fervour," he added in a neutral tone.

"It is to be admired," I said evenly.

"I agree. However, as those two are no longer available to assist in doing Bullivant's work—"

"Do you mean M's work?"

Holmes arched his brows and cleared his throat. "Since Hollins and Steiner are no longer available to assist in *our* work for the British government," he said, "I asked Farrar and Johnson to join us, an offer they eagerly accepted. Farrar has been gathering information in London about our Biggleswick suspects while at the same time searching for any activity that might be associated with the elusive third head of Cerberus."

"Has he been successful?"

"With respect to the latter, no. However, there are some interesting items he has uncovered about those we dined with this evening, as well as Mr. Shaw."

"And what of Shinwell Johnson?"

"Oh, he has been busy travelling about and keeping in regular contact with one of Bullivant's agents, a man in Glasgow," Holmes said. "The coded message in this letter confirms that Johnson left for Scotland yesterday. That is a piece of news I was hoping to receive."

"Oh? Will Porky Johnson be assisting us there?"

Holmes smiled. "Yes, in a manner of speaking."

"Is the hour too late for explanations?" I enquired.

"Not at all, old fellow." Holmes leaned back in his chair. "We are to travel north to Glasgow knowing already that it is one focal point of the Black Stone network. In particular, we will arrive in that city when Abel Gresson, the American whom Blenkiron suspects of being a prime agent for the Germans, will be there. He is supposed to speak to a pacifist assembly at that time, and I hope to observe him.

"Now, we suspect Gresson of passing along information, which eventually reaches the person or persons in Biggleswick who act upon it.

I have suggested to Blenkiron and Bullivant that we fabricate a document and arrange matters so that it passes under Gresson's nose."

"I see. And if a person in Biggleswick somehow demonstrates knowledge of what is in that false document—"

"We have then identified at least one person at the end of the network," completed Holmes.

I thought for a moment. "And Shinwell Johnson will be responsible for placing this fabrication before Gresson?"

Holmes nodded. "Though Johnson and Farrar have achieved some minor celebrity in London, I should be very surprised if either were recognised in Glasgow. This letter you just handed me is from Bullivant and was posted after Johnson had left by train for Scotland. He has with him a page supposedly torn from a German newspaper, a page carrying a most interesting article—but a page that is a forgery. He will not give the sheet directly to Gresson, but rather display it to one of the American's henchmen, who, it is expected, will coax it from him in order to pass it along to Gresson."

"And do you believe that plan will succeed?"

Holmes opened his mouth and then paused.

"*Nous verons*?" I said for him.

Holmes smiled broadly. "Indeed."

Holmes had hoped to spend several days walking about the region of Biggleswick before leaving for Glasgow, but the month was proving both cold and damp, and so the time before our Scottish trip was spent largely indoors. Aside from one evening spent sharing with Holmes a dinner hosted by the Jimsons, who were admirers of my friend, I saw to duties at

Isham while seeking inspiration for the insincere proposal of a new novel that I would attempt to present to Shaw, the publisher. Holmes, meanwhile, devoted the hours to thought alone, in my sitting room.

On the day before our departure, however, we did take advantage of a brief break in the weather to stroll about the fringes of Biggleswick. I had spent a busy morning at Isham, preparing Major Collins to take command during my absence. When Scaife drove me back to the cottage and Holmes expressed a desire to walk, I did not attempt to dissuade him.

"Have you prepared an outline of your proposed novel for submission to Shaw?" my friend asked as we tramped west. "I should very much wish it to be ready by the time we return from Glasgow. Your letter of enquiry has already been sent?"

"The letter will be posted tomorrow by Scaife, and I will sketch out an outline in the carriage during our trip north," I answered. "I have fixed upon the *Matilda Briggs* affair," I said.[144] "You said you wanted something sensational, and that case would seem the most promising candidate."

"One can only hope that Shaw, let alone the world, is ready for it, old fellow," said Holmes with a smile.

As we rounded a hill, I espied Letchford in the company of two children, a boy and girl. The lad was swinging a stick tied with several ribbons, which he occasionally used to strike a mossy outcrop as the girl and Letchford watched.

"Not so hard, Joseph!" cautioned Letchford as the boy slashed viciously at the rocks. "We don't want to actually hurt anyone when the time comes, do we?"

---

[144] The *Matilda Briggs* was a ship connected to the legendary tale of the Giant Rat of Sumatra, one of the most famous of Holmes's cases that Watson never chronicled.

As the boy whirled around in preparation for hitting the rock again, he caught sight of us and stopped abruptly, causing Letchford and the girl to turn round.

"Well halloa," shouted the critic amiably. "You have caught my son preparing for his wager of battle."

We approached the three, and Letchford put hands on the heads of both children and tousled their hair in a playful manner. They in turn giggled and grasped their father at the waist.

"These are Joseph and Lucy," he said, and the boy and girl each greeted first me and then Holmes.

"You are preparing for some battle?" I asked Joseph.

"Yes, if I'm brought before Jack-in-the-Green," the lad said defiantly.

"I hope you are," said Lucy, who drew back as her brother attempted to slap her.

"Here, none of that!" admonished Letchford, who made a face at his children. "It is part of the village's May Day celebration," he told us.

"Which is more than a fortnight away, I should think," observed Sherlock Holmes.

"Yes, but the boy suffered a mock imprisonment last year when he was accused of stealing a fruit trifle and lost his trial by combat, and he's determined to prove himself innocent this time, should the same thing happen again," his father informed us. "Not that he really did steal that trifle last year, of course. It was part of the usual May Day blather, but it's blather that these two enjoy, eh?"

Both children nodded with enthusiasm.

I chuckled. "No one has told me of these local traditions," I said.

Letchford smiled.

"Be careful, Colonel, lest you be drawn into it. You see," he explained, "in Biggleswick, just before the Maypole dance, old Jack-in-the-Green holds court and hands out sentences for all manner of mock offenses. These almost always involve children accusing one another of crimes, prompting a handful of trials by combat. Harmless stuff, really. The children don't hit each other, but rather try to topple each other's rock pile. It's all very harmless."[145]

Joseph gave the outcrop a nasty whack with his stick.

"*Harmless*," said his father sternly, and the boy put his weapon behind him.

"I suppose you shall hope for the best," noted Sherlock Holmes.

"I shall indeed," replied Letchford. "I say, are the two of you trying to slip in a hike between rain showers?"

"Yes," I said. "Apparently the same can be said of you and your son's battle practice."

"He insists on practising well in advance of May Day," Letchford informed us, "and his mother will not tolerate our domestic furnishings being placed in peril. Hence, this venue instead."

"Well, good luck to you all," I said as I led Holmes on.

We left Letchford and his brood and continued through a field and on toward a small wood beyond which lay a main road.

"The man was not his usual, cynical self today," I noted.

"No, he was not the same person I observed at our dinner the other evening, other than when he spoke of his children," Holmes agreed.

---

[145] A Jack-in-the-Green is a participant in traditional May Day celebrations. The individual in question wears a foliage-covered framework, often pyramidal or conical, that covers the body from head to foot.

"Letchford appears a different man in the company of those offspring. Perhaps his life is more divided than one might believe."

"You mean he might have a secret life as a German spy?"

"A hallowed practice, trial by combat," said Holmes, obviously not wishing to pursue my point, as we passed through the small stand of trees.

"Hallowed, but fortunately obsolete," I replied with a sigh. "It is disconcerting to think of our Anglo-Saxon ancestors determining innocence and guilt by means of individual battle rather than reason."

"I do not disagree, Watson," said Holmes. "However, the practice came to our island after the Conquest; it was never an Anglo-Saxon method of justice but rather a Germanic one."[146]

"And now, in effect, we employ it with our present-day German adversaries on a mass scale," I observed.

"That is war," said Holmes in a distracted tone. "Not individual combat."

Holmes now appeared to be lost in thought.

"And what is the subject of your current reverie?" I asked.

"Oh, nothing," my friend replied, an odd smile upon his face.

We passed through a stand of trees and found ourselves standing beside the main road that ran past Biggleswick. Gazing down the lane, we saw a familiar figure approach astride a bicycle.

"Ah, Mr. Wake!" called Sherlock Holmes. "You are drenched, sir."

"Yes," replied the young man, who stopped in the middle of the road and thrust out one foot to support himself upon the bicycle.

---

[146] Holmes is referring to the Norman Conquest of England in 1066.

"I've gone all the way up to Bledwell and back," he said haltingly. "I had a fancy for a long pedal, but I should have kept a keener eye on the weather." Wake's manner seemed less sullen than usual, and his expression, for once, came close to approximating an earnest smile.

"We ourselves are only now taking pleasure in the out of doors after a most rainy morning," Holmes said. "Bledwell, however, would seem too great a journey for us at present, certainly by foot. A main road does not lead there, does it?"

"No," replied the young man. "One has to take one of the minor routes. The two of you leave for Scotland tomorrow, do you not?" Wake asked abruptly. "I recall you mentioning such a trip during our dinner at Fosse Manor."

"Yes," replied Holmes. "In truth, the journey was originally planned solely with Dumfries, in Galloway, in mind. Colonel Watson has been there many times in the past and wished to see the region once more. But then, realising I have not been to Glasgow in several years, I imposed upon him to add that city to our itinerary."

Wake nodded. "Perhaps we will see one another along the way," he added hesitantly. "I leave tomorrow on perhaps the same train as yours, for I will be hiking about Skye."

"An ambitious plan," said Holmes, who took a step along the road. I followed his lead, and as we bade Wake farewell, the man gave a push to his bicycle to continue down the path in the opposite direction.

"I wonder if his wandering round Skye could involve the Black Stone," I said once Wake was out of earshot.

"I, meanwhile, wonder if his cycling this morning concerned the same," replied Sherlock Holmes.

"How so?"

"Wake obviously did not bicycle to Bledwell today, Watson."

"How can you be certain?" I said. "The man's clothing was drenched from the rain. You called attention to that yourself."

"Oh to be sure, Wake has been cycling much of the morning. Bledwell, however, was most definitely not his destination, for it does not lie on a main road."

"I fear I do not understand your reasoning."

"Do you recall when, the other day, I paused to briefly expound upon the local oolite limestone?" Holmes asked.

"Your geological précis is burned into memory so deeply that I cannot expunge it," I replied.

"As you may also recall," said Holmes, ignoring my mild sarcasm, "during the latter stages of the search for Richard Hannay, certain clues led me to Mr. Turnbull, a roadman. That experience drew me into a subsequent, deeper study of road construction and maintenance. It is a subject I found most interesting."

"Rivalling that of bees?"

"Hardly, but compelling in its own right," Holmes said. "You see, the minor roads in this region are constructed from the local limestone oolite of which I spoke the other day, and after several hours of rain, the stuff becomes quite sticky and impassable on bicycle. Had Wake pedalled to Bledwell in this morning's weather, he would have had to dismount and walk, and he would not have been able to complete the round trip in time to meet up with us at this hour.

"The major roads, on the other hand, appear to be paved with chips of hard, dark-blue grit—from Leicestershire, no doubt—which a bicycle's tyres will take to even in heavy rain. If Wake were cycling at length this morning—and I agree that he was—then his destination was not Bledwell but rather someplace else, a location accessible by a main road."

"Ah, and so the most important question is: where did he actually go?"

"No," said Sherlock Holmes as we caught sight of the Haven Stones. "The most important question is: why did Wake lie about his destination?"

CHAPTER THIRTEEN: A STUDY IN SUBVERSION

Accompanied to the Biggleswick station by the Jimsons and Corporal Scaife, Holmes and I boarded a northbound train for Glasgow early the following day. Looking out the carriage window as we prepared to leave town, my friend's mouth slowly turned upward in a sly grin.

"Tell me," he said, "have you sent that letter of enquiry to Shaw?"

"The request that he consider publishing my nonexistent novel?" I asked. "The one that is a work of fiction in more ways than one?"

"Yes."

"Scaife posted it today, as promised. I did not use your title, however, believing it far too sensational."

"Ha! Our usual roles are reversed in this instance, are they not?"

"In any case, there is no guarantee that my letter will gain me—"

"Us."

"Will gain us an audience with Mr. Shaw."

"I believe you underestimate the popularity of your stories among the reading public, Watson."

"At times, Holmes, I do doubt my own so-called popularity, for another is often perceived as the author."

My friend shrugged. "That the relationship you have with your literary agent is an admixture of love and hate, I cannot deny, but—"

Holmes broke off suddenly and drew back from the carriage window. "Watson," he said. "Come, glance through the pane."

I leaned forward and turned my head to behold Launcelot Wake striding beside the tracks. He passed by our window without catching sight of us and then boarded the carriage trailing ours.

I assumed my previous position and said, “Well, he will be travelling north also, as he had told us yesterday.”

“Yes, and by the look of his shoes, not to mention the ice axe hanging from his knapsack, he does appear intent on hiking and mountaineering as claimed,” added Holmes with a languid smile. “I wish we knew if the hiking and climbing will serve a purpose beyond mere pleasure.”

“Miss Lamington was most insistent that he could not possibly be in league with the Black Stone,” I said quietly.

Holmes nodded.

“She is an intuitive young woman,” he said, “and intuition is not to be discounted. But we must not ignore more objective forms of judgment.”

“One should, however, give her credit for not insisting that her cousin be omitted from consideration.”

“Oh, to be sure, I laud her for that. However, we must keep Wake well within our sights.”

Some time later, we had left Biggleswick behind, riding tracks that took us northwest—through Lancaster, Carnforth, and Kendal. A bit past Carlisle, we continued along the main line into Scotland that led to Glasgow, rather than take the westerly fork passing through Galloway, which had been the centre of our search for Richard Hannay three years before.

“Holmes,” I said as we neared the border. “You do not mind that we will return by way of Dumfries? Haste is not of concern?”

The detective lifted his cap, opened his eyes and raised his chin from his chest. Stretching his legs, he replied, “A leisurely journey back to Biggleswick would lend itself to the appearance of this being a holiday outing, and Dumfries is supposedly our prime destination, after all. We will show ourselves there, yes. It is perhaps a shame you did not bring along your fishing gear.”

“I have an earnest desire to see the place once more—and the people, if some of them remain in the area,” I said.

Holmes nodded and studied the passing scenery. “We should be arriving in Glasgow by midafternoon.” He took out his watch and opened it to note the time.

Glancing in his direction, I noticed a small purple-and-white disc affixed to the inside of the watch cover.

“What is that wafer attached to your timepiece?” I asked. “The one with the cross of St. Andrew upon it.”[147]

Holmes smiled wanly. “It will identify us to the resident agent in Glasgow,” he said.

“You’ve not provided much in the way of detail about that person, or the strategy we will pursue once there, by the way.”

“I have never met the agent in question, Watson, and so I have little in the way of detail about him, other than Bullivant’s description of the man, whose name is Andrew Amos. We will meet the fellow in due course,” he replied. “And as for the strategy we will pursue, if I do not instruct you in its particulars, what do you suppose that strategy is to be?”

“One of improvisation?”

---

[147] The X-shaped cross of the patron saint of Scotland forms the flag of Scotland and part of the flag of the United Kingdom.

"Just so," murmured Holmes.

"But you spoke of Shinwell Johnson being there and planting some sort of document with Abel Gresson."

"Yes," said the detective. "It is Johnson who has that specific task to accomplish. We will be idle observers."

"When you observe, you are hardly idle."

"And that is when I shall improvise."

"But your improvisations are always well planned."

Holmes smiled as he leaned back and once more covered his eyes with the cloth cap.

"Well put, Watson," he murmured. "A good biographer always captures the essence of his subject."

We entered Glasgow Central Station at half past two o'clock and remained in our carriage for a few moments while Sherlock Holmes discreetly watched for Launcelot Wake to appear.

"There he is," said Holmes at last, pointing to Wake as the young man strode away from our line of carriages, the ice axe swinging from his knapsack.

"We will make no attempt to follow him?" I asked.

"We are hardly prepared to attempt that," Holmes replied. "Particularly if he is headed for Skye. Moreover, we have our own plans for the evening."

"An evening of improvised observation?"

"Yes."

We took rooms in the Grand Central Hotel and spent the rest of the afternoon refreshing ourselves. Then, as instructed by Holmes, I dressed in a less than elegant fashion and descended to the hotel lobby, where I waited for my friend.

I grew anxious as I sat in an armchair, for my somewhat shabby state attracted silent expressions of rebuke from many passersby. Then, just the lobby clock struck the hour, Holmes entered, attired in a similarly rough manner. Billycock hat rather than usual homberg in hand, he motioned for me to rise, and the two of us quickly left the hotel.

"Are you prepared for a quick stroll toward the Dumbarton Road?" he asked.

"You have me dressed as if for a stroll through Whitechapel instead," I replied with more than a little exaggeration.[148] "I believe you said you were finished with disguises."

"This is not disguise," insisted Holmes. "Rather, consider it mere camouflage."

"Lead on," I muttered.

Some minutes later, we found ourselves in a public square. With the weather still brisk and the sky darkening, there were relatively few people about: only a mother and small child, and a grizzled, bespectacled man who stood feeding pigeons from a small sack.

"Shall we take this bench?" suggested Holmes languidly. "The weather has been dry, at least."

"I suppose cold is preferable to cold and damp," I said with bitter amusement.

"For King and Empire," whispered my friend.

---

[148] Whitechapel is a district in East London. For much of its history a poor, working-class neighborhood, the area is perhaps best known as the stomping ground of Jack the Ripper.

"I assume we will meet your resident agent here? Or is it to be Shinwell Johnson?"

"The former," said Holmes, once more taking out his watch as the man who had been feeding birds slowly ambled over.

"Can ye give us a swatch at that?" the fellow asked. "Ah want the time."

He was a bit over five feet and broad-shouldered. Between his heavy brows and whiskers—the latter joining from either side under his jaw while leaving an enormous upper lip clean-shaven—the man reminded me of an old-fashioned minister. His eyes were solemn, and I did not observe one sound tooth when he opened his mouth to speak.

"Yes, I have it," replied Holmes, holding out the watch so that the man could see its dial, as well as the purple-and-white wafer displaying the St. Andrew cross.

"Thank ye," said the man, reaching into a pocket for his own timepiece. He flipped the case open and looked down at it. "Mine is always fast, as ye can see." He turned the watch so that we both might view the dial, an action that exposed a wafer identical to Holmes's pasted onto the inside.

"Fast and slow are relative terms," said Holmes.

"Indeed," replied the man. "Indeed, they are. Andrew Amos and at your service, Mr. Holmes, for Mr. Holmes was whom Ah was told to expect. Along with," he added, looking at me, "a Mr. Watson."

"Yes." My friend nodded and gestured toward me. "My associate, Dr. Watson."

"Aye," said Mr. Amos, stuffing the small sack of bird feed into a coat pocket.

"Sir Walter Bullivant sends his regards," whispered Holmes.

Amos nodded. "And ye can say Ah was asking for him."

"However, there is no news for him, I gather?" Holmes said.

"No a peep," the man replied. "Though, who may ken, after the great rammy happens this night."

"Mr. Amos is a union leader in the shipyards," Holmes informed me.

"Well," said the Glasgow man, "Ah'm no an actual official of the union, and no likely to ever be one. Still, me word carries more weight than most, and Ah fight for the rank and file against office-bearers who have lost the confidence of the working man. Ah'm no socialist, mind ye, Dr. Watson," he said. "More akin to the old Border radicals.[149] Ah'm for individual liberty and equal rights and chances for all. Ah keep me views largely to meself, though, for the younger lads down at the yards are, some of thame, drucken-daft over their wee books about capital and collectivism.

"Keep in mind, Ah'm with them on the matter of wages and dignity. If men like me abandoned that fight, all the rest would be at the mercy of the first balloon[150] that started preaching revolution. Ye see, those of us agitating for a rise in pay are not for a coward's peace. No, sir. We're fighting for the lads overseas as much as for ourselves. What for should the big man double his profits and the small man be ill set to get his ham and egg on Sabbath morning, eh?"

---

[149] Amos may be referring to the Radical War, also known as the Scottish Insurrection of 1820. This was a week of strikes and unrest in Glasgow and central Scotland that climaxed in demands for labor, economic, and electoral reform within the United Kingdom. The insurrection was put down, and almost ninety individuals were arrested and accused of treason. While some of those charged were acquitted, others were executed or transported to penal colonies in New South Wales and Tasmania.

[150] "Empty boaster"

"And what does an old Border radical think specifically about the war?" I asked idly.

Amos looked at me thoughtfully. "When it started, Dr. Watson," he said with deliberation, "Ah considered the subject carefully for three days, and then Ah came to a single conclusion: at the end of this conflict, either Ah or the Kaiser would be left standing, but not the both of us."

"You spoke earlier about someone possibly preaching revolution," said Holmes. "That will happen tonight, will it not?"

"Undoubtedly, it will," said Amos. "Ah presume you refer to the gathering where Mr. Gresson will appear."

"I do."

The Glasgow man nodded.

"They hope to attract more of the general population this evening, beyond just men from the shipyards." He looked at both of us. "You two look the type they seek to pull in, Ah think." He shrugged. "Then, too, don be surprised if some in attendance are there merely to taunt."

"Do you believe the meeting may become violent?" I asked.

Andrew Amos shrugged. "If the past is any guide, sir, Ah would have to say that may happen, yes."

"You will not be present, however?" Holmes asked.

Amos frowned. "Ah dunna jump about with the likes of thame. Ah canna stand to listen to their drivel," he said. "Comrade this and comrade that. Besides, Ah think it best that Ah seem aloof from that bunch. Ah have my ways of watching them for Sir Walter," the man declared, "and if Ah tried too hard to cosy up to thame, Ah think they might become suspicious of my motives, don ye think?"

Holmes nodded and then conveyed some instructions that Bullivant had requested he pass on to Amos. At length, our meeting concluded, and we rose to take leave of this clandestine observer for His Majesty's government. We walked on for several minutes and found a humble establishment where we ate a spare, early dinner and then set off in search of Newmilns Street, where the rally was to take place.

It was nearing seven o'clock as we approached the meeting hall, into which a crowd was already streaming. Ominously, some of those entering were soldiers in uniform.

Inside, the place was dingy and ill lit. I followed Holmes to the middle of the hall, where we stood staring at a gathering of leaders conversing among themselves on the dais. Below them, huddled against the platform, clusters of followers seemed to hang on their every word. Unlike the rally I had attended at Brattleburn, this one was comprised primarily of men.

"Shall we join the admiring masses, then?" Holmes asked.

I gestured for my friend to lead the way, and we strode to the edge of a small group that was listening to the idle talk of those on the dais. Holmes remained attentive, and when another person joined the group on the platform, he watched carefully as that individual was introduced to the others.

"And this," we heard a fierce little rat of a man say, "is our illustrious American comrade, Abel Gresson."

Holmes and I looked at the newcomer. He was a red-haired man in his thirties, rather sprucely dressed—a flower was stuck in one button hole—and whose small, bright eyes showed great animation. Despite his natty appearance, Gresson appeared to be chewing tobacco. Indeed, he reached into his pocket and bit off a small additional piece in the midst of conversation.

"Aye, we're coming to the end of the last dogwatch," I heard him say with a chuckle as he pulled out a timepiece. "And we'll be raising anchor soon." He nodded to the others and then stepped away to survey the growing audience. Clasping hands behind his back, he nodded as he strode in a rolling gait across the dais, passing by us so that his waist was at the level of our eyes.

I glanced at Holmes, whose eyes were fixed intently upon Gresson, and I saw him gently lift his chin before turning to me.

"Shall we find seats, old fellow?" he asked.

We claimed two chairs in the front third of the audience but remained standing, passing the time in idle conversation unrelated to our true purpose. All the while, I noticed that Holmes periodically surveyed the filling hall with a slow, sweeping motion of his eyes.

Then, as those on the dais began to organise themselves, he whispered, "Ha," and sat down.

I remained on my feet for a moment longer, staring in the direction in which Holmes had been looking before taking his chair. I anxiously gazed at the audience and then, with sudden recognition, I espied Shinwell Johnson sitting on the far side of the hall, fanning himself with his hat. Immediately, I sat down beside my friend.

"I presume you finally noticed our associate," Holmes said quietly.

"Yes." I leaned back in my chair. "And I assume that further explanation will come later."

"As always, old fellow, your expectation is on the mark. But halloa," he said, gesturing toward the dais. "It appears we are about to begin."

"Gresson cuts quite a figure," I whispered to Holmes.

"Yes," agreed my friend as the noise in the hall lessened slightly.

The fierce, diminutive man who had made introductions on the dais earlier appeared to be the chairman of the proceedings, for he stepped forward to call the meeting to order.

"My comrades," he declaimed, "we have come here tonight from many different parts of the globe, but all with one purpose—"

"Yes: to bugger John Bull, you red prick!" came a loud voice from the back of the hall. As did the rest of the audience, I turned round and saw one of many British soldiers standing at the rear, holding his hands to his mouth. As the man lowered his arms, he looked among his compatriots, who all laughed.[151]

"I fear the discord is beginning all too early," whispered Holmes.

"It is John Bull what uses *you*, Tommy!" the chairman shouted back.[152]

"Come away!" yelled someone from the seats.

"Bloody lie!" cried another soldier from the far wall. "King and Empire, I say!"

"You're a pawn of the plutocrats, khaki boy!" barked someone sitting near the front of the hall. "Give imperialism the heave!"

I sat and watched what seemed to be the beginning of an inexorable slide into fisticuffs. But at that moment, as invective escalated on both sides, Abel Gresson rose from his seat on the dais and gently nudged the

---

[151] This is another instance where some explicit elements within the text cast doubt on its authenticity, for this is not the type of language one finds in any authenticated narrative by Watson.

[152] Though already in use during the nineteenth century, "Tommy" or "Tommy Atkins" as slang for a British soldier is especially associated with the First World War. "Thomas Atkins" was used as a generic name by the British War Office in an 1815 publication explaining how to complete military forms, and that may be the origin of the term.

chairman aside. As some civilians joined the soldiers in taunting those on the platform and an increasing number of workingmen got to their feet and fired back insults of their own, the American put his hands in the air and gestured as if seeking to place a lid upon the crowd's restiveness.

"Now boys, please!" he shouted with the smoothness of a practiced speaker. "Let's calm down some and spend the evening talking sense, shall we?"

"I'll spend it shoving that flower up your arse, you damp Bolshie Yank!" cried one of the soldiers.[153]

"If that's what it will take to get you to listen to reason, then have a go, my lad," replied Gresson with a hearty smile as he turned halfway round and bent over. "How's this for a big bahookie, eh?"

The gesture took everyone by surprise, and the hall fell momentarily silent. Then all joined in laughing heartily at the invitation. Gresson himself chuckled before rising again to his full height and turning toward the lectern to once more gesture for calm.

"Now the weather's been blowing up dirty here tonight," he said. "We all have our differences, make no doubt about it, and we are pulling right now all this way and that. Hell, boys, we know some of you have bones to pick," he bellowed, and now there were no taunts from the audience. "But we should tonight dwell on what we have in common, and to accomplish that, let us take a long, hard, and honest look at the aims of this current war."

---

[153] "Damp" is a euphemism for "damn," and "Bolshie" is slang, now dated, for communist or socialist. A shortened form of "Bolshevik," its first documented use was in 1918, a year after the events of this chapter.

He paused, taking an opportunity to look over those in the hall—all of whom, even the soldiers, now appeared willing to give him a fair hearing. Gresson bowed his head, a motion that gave emphasis to his drooping nose, and I saw a subtle smile appear on his face, an expression that vanished as he lifted his chin to continue.

There followed not quite twenty minutes of perhaps the most beguiling public oratory I have ever heard. Beginning from simple observations or self-evident truths that no one could easily dismiss, Gresson wove a clever argument that concluded with a call for peace with Germany, opportunity for all, and universal brotherhood.

As the American ended his speech, most of the audience—shipyard and other workers, largely—stood to applaud in wild abandon, while the sceptics—the soldiers, a few merchants and scattered clerks—remained silent, neither clapping nor shouting down the speaker.

Gresson won handshakes from all his companions on the stage and returned to the lectern to accept the majority's continued applause. As Holmes remained still beside me, I followed his lead; however, I had to admit that the American had made a solid *prima facie* case for his side, though I did not agree with it.

"Let us go," said Holmes as several from the audience jumped upon the dais to further congratulate the American orator and the hall fell into a boisterous intermission. "I have observed what I needed to see."

We negotiated our way through a surging throng and exited the hall to regain Newmilns Street. Following a line of street lamps, Holmes led me briskly away from the neighbourhood and back toward the River Clyde, and it was only after several minutes that he spoke.

"Blenkiron is certain that Abel Gresson is one link in the Black Stone network," he said without preface. "Bullivant has charged us to find the final link in the chain to Biggleswick. The first step in that determination was taken tonight, by Shinwell Johnson."

"He passed on the false document to Gresson?" I asked.

"No, not to Gresson directly," Holmes reminded me. "Bullivant and Blenkiron arranged the creation of a false page supposedly torn from the *Weser Zeitung*—it is a newspaper published in Germany. In Bremen, to be more specific. The sheet holds some interesting news—false, of course—regarding the influence of Berlin on the Austrian government's decision to allow some socialists to attend the upcoming Stockholm conference.[154] It also contains an assertion that, during the crisis of 1914, the Kaiser sent a telegram to the Czar agreeing with Russia's suggestion that Austria negotiate for peace with Serbia rather than pursue war. The contents of that apocryphal telegram are even included in the forged article."

"It all sounds rather esoteric and obscure."

"Yes, it is meant to be. No such reports are known to have been made anywhere, so that anyone citing them in future must have learnt of them from a chain that includes Gresson. Shinwell Johnson, playing the part of a vocal socialist from the south of London, was to casually show the page to a man named Toombs, who is a follower of Gresson. Our hope was that Toombs would take the page and show it to his leader. Johnson has succeeded in that endeavour."

"How can you be certain?"

---

[154] The Stockholm Conference of 1917 was the last of three international gatherings of socialists opposed to the First World War.

“For reasons of discretion, Johnson was instructed not to approach either you or me at the rally. However, if he were successful at letting the false page fall into Toombs’s hands, he was to indicate that in the meeting hall tonight by fanning himself with his hat.”

“I saw him do that constantly.”

“Yes. We have accomplished each of the three goals I wished to attain on this trip: convey further instructions from Bullivant to Andrew Amos, confirm that Gresson has seen the false newspaper article, and glean information about Gresson from immediate observation of him.”

“That third wish was granted also?”

“Oh yes. Thus far, Bullivant and Blenkiron have known nothing of Gresson’s movements south of Glasgow. Where he goes and by what means has been a mystery. From what I saw of his person, however, I believe he travels along the coast while serving on one or more merchant ships.”

“How so?”

“No doubt you caught the nautical references in his remarks on the dais before his speech—a dogwatch, for example, is a period of work duty.”

“I am quite aware of that,” I said. “The last dogwatch is from six to eight o’clock.”

“Just so. You may also have noticed the nautical tattoo on the back of Gresson’s left hand, as well as the fact that he was chewing tobacco, an activity not restricted to but certainly associated with both ships and mining. He has neither the hands nor the face of a miner, however—nor the hands of a common sailor, either, though his walk is clearly that of a man who spends much time at sea.”

“You think he may be a ship’s officer, then?”

"Yes," said Holmes. "At least, he serves in such a capacity intermittently, for we know that he spends a good deal of time on shore as well. I suspect he goes to sea now and then, when it suits his needs for travelling on behalf of the Black Stone, and that suggests he is perhaps a temporary purser or steward aboard one or more vessels. There are several that sail south from Glasgow, travelling down the coast and among the Hebrides, both near and far."

"And that region includes Skye, where Launcelot Wake is supposedly hiking at this very moment."

"Yes," admitted Holmes, who added nothing more to my comment.

We walked in silence, retracing our steps backward along the way we had come, past the park where we had met Andrew Amos.

"We shall enter the subway," Holmes said, "at the Kinning Park station, to be precise."[155]

At length, we found the station entrance and descended to the platform, which was relatively deserted.

"Johnson should be arriving shortly," Holmes said. "Our conversation with him will be brief, and then we shall return to the hotel."

As Holmes stood in thought, I buried my hands in my coat pockets and slowly walked round. At length, I heard other footsteps descending, and turned to see a familiar figure shamble toward us.

"Greetings, Mr. Holmes" came the low, raspy voice of Shinwell Johnson. "And I of course recognise you, Doctor," he said to me. Smiling, he added, "I do not believe I'll have to ask you to produce one of Mr. Bullivant's purple-and-white wafers, eh?"

---

[155] Built in 1896, the Glasgow Subway is the third-oldest underground metro system in the world.

I had not seen Johnson in the flesh for over five years. The former criminal, who had become one of Holmes's principal agents during the later portion of the detective's practice, appeared the same bluff, jovial and earnest person I had known in the past.

"You accomplished the transfer of the false newspaper page?" Holmes enquired.

"I did, yes," said Johnson. "I sidled up to that man Toombs in a pub before first closing[156] and began spouting off about the war and socialism. I mentioned that I had access to a trove of publications from Germany and Austria, and then I pulled out that page. Toombs took great interest in it and asked if he could have it in order to show it to a friend, a proposal I readily accepted."

"Good," said Holmes. "We know that Toombs is one of Gresson's leading henchmen. No doubt he has already shown the article to his boss."

"Sir Walter Bullivant told me that, having completed that task, I am to follow any further instructions you might have."

"Yes, there is one other chore for you to complete," said Holmes. "I wish you to make enquiries at various shipping offices. Ask to see crew rosters and passenger lists for as many independent vessels as you can."

"And what is the goal of my search?"

"The name of Abel Gresson on any of those manifests," said Sherlock Holmes. "Note the vessel or vessels and his position aboard each. Once

---

156 Among other actions, the wartime Defense of the Realm Act that was passed in August 1914 allowed pub hours to be restricted, and within a year, most were limited to two sessions: from noon to 2:40 p.m. and from 6:30 to 9:30 p.m. This change was prompted by the belief that workers in vital industries would demonstrate greater sobriety as a result. On the same grounds, it was also made illegal for anyone to buy drinks for others.

you find him, make certain you do not stop your search at that point. He may be serving from time to time on more than one ship."

"As you wish, sir."

"Once you have concluded that task," Holmes went on, "submit your findings to Andrew Amos and then take them on to Bullivant in London. He will forward them to me."

"Of course. Is that all, Mr. Holmes?"

"Yes," said the detective. "And you performed good work in getting that false document into the hands of Toombs, and through him, to Gresson."

"Another humble contribution to the cause," said Johnson with a chuckle. He turned toward me. "Take care of yourself, Doctor. I reckon I will see you both in London in the days ahead," he said as he vanished up the stairs. "Oh, and Farrar sends his regards, sirs," he called to us.

The following day, Holmes and I journeyed south from Glasgow, enjoying the relatively short trip through Kilmarnock and on to Dumfries, which we had not visited in almost three years.

We debarked our carriage and then left the station with baggage in hand, for our intent was to remain a night in the town before returning to Biggleswick. As we made our way toward the centre of Dumfries, I halted in my tracks and exclaimed under my breath.

"Have you seen a ghost?" asked Holmes amiably.

"A demon, more like it. Look there," I said, nodding ahead and to the right, for both my hands held valises.

"Ah," murmured Holmes. "It is our four-legged friend again."

Trotting down the street came the same ill-tempered cur I had encountered at the train station three years before, only this time approaching in the company of a different master: not the old, drunken man who had been the animal's companion on that earlier occasion, but rather a much younger fellow who appeared to be a herd.

"I recall that dog most pleasantly," said my friend, who had enjoyed a much different experience with the creature.

As we both stood to one side of the street—and I prepared for the worst—the dog and its new master passed us, perhaps from a distance of five feet. The man flashed a quick smile in our direction, but the animal ignored both of us.

"My God," I said, watching the pair recede into the distance. "The dog did nothing."

"Indeed," said Sherlock Holmes. "That is most curious, is it not? Well," he said with a smile, "shall we proceed? I believe you expressed a desire to put up at one local inn in particular."

"Yes," I replied as I set off to the northwest, leading Holmes in that direction. "I wish to obtain rooms where I was taken into custody by Charlie Taylor."

"Do you believe your constable may still be here?" asked Holmes. "Or do you suppose he is in France?"

"I confess that learning the answer to that question is a prime reason for coming here," I said. "If we have an opportunity and he has also remained in Galloway, I should wish to visit Ewan Clark as well."

"Ah yes, the innkeeper who lives off to the east," said Holmes. "There was also Sir Walter Bullivant's godson, was there not? But you have told me you saw him in France on more than one occasion, I believe."

"Sir Harry Christey? Yes, he is an officer on the staff of the high command," I said. "Rather changed in some ways," I said. "Do you remember me telling you how he was a Free Trader and leaning a tad pacifist before the war?"

"I do."

"Well, he's quite the convert these days," I said. "All for crushing the Huns and stringing up the Austrian emperor as well as the kaiser. Ah, the place is in sight," I said, nodding toward the inn ahead.

I quickened my step, and Holmes fell in behind me. Within seconds, we entered the establishment where I had stayed the night more than once in decades past, and within whose walls I had been taken prisoner under suspicion of being a murderer three years before.

I almost expected to see the same two grizzled men that had been amused by my apprehension, but the place proved empty, save for one familiar face that sat behind the counter, reading a book.

"Dr. Watson!" said Charlie Taylor, looking up.

The constable, out of uniform, closed the volume and beamed at me. Smiling, he awkwardly leaned over the counter, extending his arm.

I let go my luggage and eagerly took his hand to shake it with enthusiasm.

"Constable!" I exclaimed. "It is so good to see you after such a long time."

Taylor winced slightly at my words, and he squeezed my hand before breaking off our handshake. He glanced at Holmes and made as if to speak, but remained silent.

"This is my friend, Sherlock Holmes," I said.

Holmes smiled and accepted Taylor's hand, once more extended.

"We are visiting Dumfries for a day," I said, "and thought we might stay the night here, if there are rooms available. That is, should I be asking you? I see that you are not—"

"Not in uniform, no," said Taylor. "Neither police nor army," he said. "Not now." He smiled awkwardly at us and then made his way around the counter so as to be on the same side of it as we.

He did not rise, however, to take the journey on foot.

Instead, we watched him emerge from behind the barrier in a narrow wheelchair, his hands deftly rotating its large wheels. From the waist up, Charles Taylor appeared more robust than he had the last time I had seen him. His face was full of colour and his arms even stouter than before. Below the hips, however, his body ended abruptly, with what I assumed were stumps buried in unused inches of trouser legs rolled up to form two neat cylinders of tweed laid end to end.

"It happened during the Somme," Taylor said simply, without elaboration.[157] "But san fairy ann."[158]

I nodded, and Holmes leaned on the counter respectfully, giving the man his full attention.

"I enlisted in the Galloway Pals," Taylor said.[159] "Along with Boyd Watson, the younger Murray brothers and all the rest, including good old Ewan Clark."

---

[157] Taylor is almost certainly referring to the First Battle of the Somme, which took place during the second half of 1916. In the end, although French and British units forced the German army to retreat six miles, the cost of the offensive was over one million dead and wounded on both sides.

[158] British soldiers in the First World War often picked up French expressions and converted them into phrases that sounded English. One of these was *ça ne fait rien*, French for "It does not matter," which became "san fairy ann."

[159] Pals battalions were units of the British Army in the First World War made up of men who had enlisted together from the same locality, with the understanding that they would serve together rather than be arbitrarily assigned to other units. A consequence of this policy was that, when such battalions suffered casualties, individual towns or

I bent down to address Taylor. "Is he—Clark, that is—is he…?"

"At home," the man said. "At that family inn near the foothills. You'll be seeing him as well, Dr. Watson?"

"Of course," I said.

I looked at Holmes, who silently affirmed my statement.

"He's different too, you know," the former constable said. "You'll see."

"How was your treatment?" I asked. "I have been in France on occasion as well, as an observer for the RAMC."

"Yes, I was aware of that, Doctor," said Taylor. "I once crossed paths with Sir Harry Christey in the trenches, a bit before the big offensive started. He's a lieutenant colonel now."

"Yes, I know."

"He recognised me at once and spoke to me just like a regular person, ignoring our differences in rank—as he ignored our class differences when we tried to start that fellow's aeroplane down in the southern field before the war. He told me you were in the medical corps, teaching the ones that took care of us, and that you'd visited the front."

I nodded.

Taylor smiled, and his eyes glistened. "That were a fun morning, eh? With us and the aeroplane, I mean."

"Yes, Charlie. It was great fun."

A door opened on the far side of the room, and Taylor's wife appeared. The young woman's eyes still sparkled, but her face had

---

neighborhoods at home experienced disproportionate losses. After the introduction of conscription in 1916, no more such groups were raised, and those still existing, most of them now greatly reduced in strength, were eventually absorbed into other units.

acquired its first lines of age. She pursed her lips and then showed great surprise as she caught sight of me.

"Averil," declared Charlie, "look who has come to visit us!"

"Dear Dr. Watson," said his wife, "it is wonderful to see you again. And you are...?"

"Sherlock Holmes," I said at once as the detective bowed. "My good friend."

"And consulting deducing man, or whatever it is called," replied the woman, putting a hand to her mouth in slight embarrassment.

"Consulting detective, aye," said Taylor. "We know well of you, sir. And you've come with the doctor here to visit Dumfries—and us, I hope."

"Yes, of course," I said after briefly taking Averil Taylor's hand. "We thought to stay here, in this inn, while looking up the pair of you. I had no idea that you..."

"After the..." Mrs. Taylor halted and then stepped back to allow her husband to reply.

"After I returned to Dumfries," he said with good nature, "I obviously could not resume my post with the local constabulary. Ross, the man who was keeper here—the one who had me fetched to take you into custody all those months ago—had gone up to Edinburgh to find war work, and so the owner of the place, Mr. Morrison, offered me the position here. Averil helps as well," he added quietly, reaching up to put his hand on hers, which had come to rest on his shoulder. "We having no children or such to tend at home."

Mrs. Taylor, a purposeful smile etched upon her face, asked if we wished to register. "There are two wonderful rooms on the first floor that have gone begging for months," she said. "I believe you will like them. How long will you remain in Dumfries?"

"We had been thinking of remaining only the one night," said Holmes, who kicked both my bags in his direction.

I made as if to take my luggage in hand, but he gently waved me off.

"However," Holmes added, "I believe we have talked of extending that by one or two days. Might you show me to our rooms, Mrs. Taylor?" he suggested as he took hold of our combined baggage. "I believe the doctor and your husband may wish to catch up on old times."

The woman took Holmes's suggestion to heart and led the detective toward the back of the inn. Taylor watched them go and then, as we both heard the pair ascend the stair, he reached out with one hand and murmured, "It is so good to see you again, Doctor."

"It was during the morning hate," Taylor related to us over the dinner table that evening.[160] "Toward its end, really, for the boys were already grumbling about how it would be nice to get rum with breakfast that day, before the company commander made his rounds.

"I heard nothing until the shell hit," the former constable said. "Some of us turned and jumped as it landed, but the thing exploded right in the trench itself, a bit down the line from my group. Men, pieces of men, and debris swept across us. Both my legs took vicious shards of duckboard,[161] the right one ending up with a huge splinter sticking

---

[160] "The morning hate" was slang for "Stand-To," which itself is a shortened form of "Stand-to-Arms." The Stand-To occurred at dawn and evening. Each man was to stand on the trench fire step with rifle loaded and bayonet fixed. This was a precaution against enemy raids that might be mounted under cover of darkness. It usually lasted thirty to sixty minutes.

[161] Duckboard—a platform made of wooden slats—was used to line the bottom of trenches, which regularly filled with mud and standing water.

straight through it. We lay there a while," he told us. "Then those of us still alive were carried off to a casualty clearing station. I lost both legs, and the rest of me is history, I suppose," he said with a wan smile.

"You are doing well now, though?" I asked.

"About as well as could be expected," Taylor replied. "I came back better than some."

"You came back," Averil Taylor said, and her husband smiled as they held hands.

The next day, after a hearty breakfast, Holmes and I set out in a dogcart borrowed through the efforts of Mrs. Taylor, riding dos-à-dos in the carriage.[162]

"I hope you do not mind the delay in returning to Biggleswick," I said yet again as we plod eastward, heading for the hills in whose shadow Ewan Clark's inn lay. "I feel I must see him."

"As I keep reminding you, old fellow, it is no great hindrance to take our time returning to the Cotswolds," replied Holmes, looking back in the direction of Dumfries, which was no longer visible. "Particularly given the story that your Mr. Taylor related to us yesterday and this morning, it would be remiss not to take the opportunity to talk to Ewan Clark as well. There was also that pilot, Captain Harper. Have you written him of late?"

"No, it is an instance where I have been greatly remiss, for I have not sent a letter to him since last returning from France."

"Nor heard from him?"

---

[162] "Dos-à-dos" means that the two seats were arranged back to back. From the text, it appears that on the trip out, Watson drove while Holmes sat behind him, facing toward the rear.

"No, but then I hardly expect him to have the time or inclination to write," I said. "The life of a flyer seems glamourous to some, but it is hardly that."

"Hannay's Boer friend is an RFC pilot, you know."

"The one he has mentioned now and then? The scout?"

"Yes," said Holmes. "Peter Pienaar. He was with Hannay, Blenkiron, and Sandy Arbuthnot during the Erzerum business."

"I know. I have read the book."[163]

"I met Pienaar once," said Holmes. "Hannay introduced us during one of his early leaves from duty on the Continent. The Boer is an interesting fellow. He volunteered for the Royal Flying Corps and became one of its best pilots, until he was shot down last year."

"Did he—"

"He went down behind the German lines," Holmes informed me. "The man is currently a prisoner of war, I believe."

"Ah."

"You must write your Captain Harper when we return to Biggleswick," Holmes insisted.

"Yes," I promised myself while gently urging on our horse.

At length, we reached the vicinity of the inn that Ewan Clark had tended in the company of his bedridden grandmother and the servant Margit. Before, I had approached the cottage along a footpath at night during the search for Richard Hannay; now, travelling by dogcart in the light of day, we followed a different route toward the place, along a road

---

163 This would be John Buchan's *Greenmantle*, previously mentioned, which was published in 1916.

which passed the residence, the route I had taken in the sidecar of Clark's motor bicycle to reach Sir Harry Christey's manor.

As we left our carriage and walked toward the dwelling, a man emerged from the shed where Clark's vehicle had been stored. I saw that the structure was now packed instead with boxes and tools.

"Halloa!" called the man, a bluff grey-haired fellow perhaps a decade younger than Holmes and myself. "Just passing through or needing a place for the night, sirs?"

"I am John Watson," I said. "This is my friend, Sherlock Holmes."

"A second greeting to both of you gentlemen. How may we assist you?"

"We have come to pay a call on Ewan Clark, if he is here," I said.

The man stood still for several seconds, his expression changing to one of apprehension.

"You know him from the war?" he asked cautiously. "You both are roughly my age, and so—"

"I am with the Royal Army Medical Corps, in fact, but—"

"My understanding is that your kind have done all you can for him."

"Yes, but what I meant to add is that I knew Mr. Clark briefly from before the war."

"When he still ran the inn? Before he enlisted and his grandmother passed on?"

"That is correct," I said. "He assisted me some three years ago in a matter of great importance by supplying me a ride in his—" I gestured toward the shed— "his motor bicycle."

The man's expression now changed to one of interest. "Might you be the one who had the aeroplane?"

“Well, I was a passenger in the aeroplane.”

“Yes, Ewan often talked about that ‘adventure’ of his. Before the current situation, of course. Do you know of his present condition?”

“One of his fellow soldiers from the Galloway Pals informed me.”

The man nodded thoughtfully and then stepped closer, extending his hand.

“I’m Malcom Paterson,” he said. “My wife Jean is Ewan’s cousin.”

Paterson then shook Holmes’s hand.

“We’ve been in charge of the inn since Ewan went off to France, and then following his return,” he said. “Come along with me, if you please,” Paterson added as he gestured toward the house itself.

“Mr. Clark—Ewan—still lives here, I was given to understand,” I said as we approached the door.

“Aye. He spent a good deal of time in hospital before being discharged to our care. He’s none the bother, of course. His appetite is still good, as odd as that may sound.”

“I am a doctor,” I gently reminded Paterson.

“Oh, then you’d have a very good understanding of it, then.”

“I do not know that any of us have a very good understanding of it,” I replied mournfully. “Other than those who endure it.”

“Aye,” said the man as he opened the door of the inn.

The sitting room was largely as I remembered it, with the great hearth dominating. Many of the furnishings had changed, however, and the wall had fewer adornments than before. Margit, the stern-faced servant, was still present, carrying a bowl from the room without looking in our direction as she disappeared round a corner. To the right of the hearth, a woman of late middle age did cast her eyes at us, and though her face bore a slight more charity than Margit's, it was still the visage of a hard, practical person.

"Here, Jean," said Mr. Paterson. "These are friends of Ewan. A doctor and a—well, this man here," he said, indicating Holmes.

"Ye're here as physician or as friend, sir?" said the woman. "Ye are...?"

"Doctor John Watson," I said. "Well, these days, Colonel John Watson, RAMC. This is my friend, Sherlock Holmes."

The woman cocked her head slightly, giving her attention to my friend. "Ye are *the* Mr. Holmes?" she asked. "The consulting detective?"

"That I am, madam," said my friend with a gentle smile. "Though I am not personally acquainted with your cousin, as the colonel is."

"Yes," she said as if reciting well-known facts. Her eyes looked me over again. "He spoke often about both of ye before he left. Ye'll be wanting to see him, then?"

"If we may," I replied.

"Take them out back," she told her husband before looking me in the eye again. "He's out by the stream. Just beyond the bridge, in the place he always goes."

Holmes and I followed Malcom Paterson from the house, down the path that I recalled traversing in the middle of a night some three years before. Beyond, we saw the small stone bridge that crossed the stream and there, on its other side, I espied a lone figure kneeling, staring down at the ground.

We approached, but though our heels loudly scraped the rough surface of the bridge, the young man ahead did not lift his head. Ewan Clark seemed neither leaner nor stouter than I remembered him, yet a sense of spiritual emaciation hung about his figure, and when at last he did cast eyes in our direction, I saw that the sparkle they had once possessed was entirely absent.

"Ewan, look who has come visiting!" declared Paterson. "Friends!"

Still on his knees, Clark stared at me and Holmes in turn, and then back to me. He studied my face intently and then nodded slowly.

"Doctor Watson," he whispered. "Halloa."

"How has it been out here today, Ewan?" said Paterson with encouragement. "Would you like to tell us? He's a fortunate one," the man said, putting his hand on the young man's shoulder. "A lucky laddie he is. Off to war and comes back with nary a scratch on him. How wonderful is that, eh? You're the lucky laddie, indeed," repeated Paterson.

Clark did not appear to react, but merely returned his attention to the ground, where he resumed pulling grass from the soil in a listless manner.

"Ewan?" said Paterson with mild urgency. "Ewan, have you no bit of news to tell the gentlemen?"

Clark did not respond. Instead, he kept pulling back the clusters of blades, as if trying to roll them over to expose the roots beneath. Paterson stepped back, eyes silently pleading to us for assistance.

"I have brought Sherlock Holmes with me," I said. Bending slightly, I repeated myself by adding, "Mr. Clark—Ewan?—here is Sherlock Holmes. Do you not remember?" I said. "Sherlock Holmes, the detective? The stories you read?"

For a moment, the young man ceased his efforts at overturning sod and looked up at my companion.

"Holmes," he said evenly, as if trying to remember. He frowned and looked me in the eye. "Stories by Doyle."

"Yes," I said gently. "The stories by Doyle. Do you recall them?"

Ewan Clark stared into empty space for a moment and then shook his head ever so faintly before gripping the partially upturned blades again in order to pull on them.

"He has been like this since they discharged him from the army," Paterson said in a whisper. "Actually, he was worse when he first got out. Couldn't dress himself then, but the boy has made progress. I said his appetite is not bad. And he has good colour, eh? There has been progress, has there not?"

"I am certain there has been," I replied. "I have seen many cases like his. Patience is the key."

"Mud," said Ewan Clark as he kept feverishly pulling at the grass. "Mud!"

Paterson shrugged. "That is what the boy says, over and over."

He and I stared at one another as young man uttered the one syllable again and then once more.

"Yes, mud," chimed in Sherlock Holmes suddenly. He knelt beside Clark. "Mud," he repeated. "There is only mud underneath, is there not?"

Ewan Clark stopped digging at the earth with his fingernails and turned toward the detective, his eyes wide. He said nothing, but his mouth opened slightly, and there seemed once more a glimmer of introspection in his expression.

"Yes," the young man said, nodding sharply at Holmes. "Mud."

"Nothing but mud," whispered Holmes. "As deep as it goes."

Clark nodded again. He smiled, but it was a smile that conveyed not an ounce of happiness. "Mud!" he repeated in a high voice as his eyes filled.

"All mud," my friend agreed in a plaintive voice, eliciting a now more vigorous assent from the young man, his eyes closing as his mouth curled once more into a hopeless smile.

"You know, too," Clark stammered as he leaned toward the detective, whose arms enfolded him.

I stood there and watched a gentle spectacle the like of which I had never before witnessed and was never to see again, for while Sherlock Holmes had, on innumerable occasions, counselled and consoled many—including myself—with his rational words, on this occasion my friend gave solace through silent touch alone rather than reasoned speech, and as Ewan Clark quietly wept in Holmes's steady arms, I could not help but sense that this act of comfort was, in some way I would never fully appreciate, mutual.

CHAPTER FOURTEEN: ENLIGHTENING EXCHANGES

Holmes and I left Dumfries three days later than we had originally planned, after spending the time alternatively with Ewan Clark and the Taylors before concluding our stay with a subdued yet warm reunion uniting us with both parties at the inn now managed by the Patersons.

Charlie Taylor, Ewan Clark, and I spent much time together while Holmes regaled the Patersons and Mrs. Taylor with his own versions of many past exploits, and by the time we left the inn, Taylor was in good spirits and Clark had, for one afternoon, found it within himself to almost hold his own in conversation, with less impulse to upend the ground, though his mood remained fragile.

On the morning of our departure, Averil Taylor provided us with yet another of her fine breakfasts as well as some small treats for the train, and at last we bade farewell to Scotland, boarding our carriage to return to the Cotswolds.

My friend remained quiet during the journey south; the customary impromptu discourses on passing local flora, fauna, and geology were absent, for Holmes's mind was obviously preoccupied.

I chose not to intrude upon his thoughts as he silently stared out the carriage window, instead entertaining myself with a book given me by Charlie Taylor. We ate our sweets from his wife, accompanied by almost no conversation. At length, however, as the rails took us past the village of Bledwell, short of Biggleswick, the detective spoke for the first time in several minutes.

"Bledwell is the village Launcelot Wake claimed to have bicycled to on that rainy day past, is it not?"

"I believe so," I replied. "Have you been pondering him, as well as the others considered possible German agents?"

Holmes smiled wistfully. "Yes, though I confess that it was our approach to Bledwell that only now prompted me to pursue that line of thought. My hope is that, during our absence, Frederick Shaw will have responded to the enquiry about your new novel."

"Ah yes," I said. Wishing to lighten Holmes's mood, I added, "The one I have titled *The Crimson Rat of Sumatra.*"

"I look forward to the interview," said he. "I believe I have told you that Frank Farrar has been collecting information on Shaw's activities in London."

"Do his movements have features of interest?"

"They do," replied Holmes. "As we already were well aware, Shaw travels to the metropolis almost every day, save for Sundays, and always in the company of his black valise. However, Farrar has discovered that on Tuesdays and Thursdays, before going to his office, he visits a particular block of flats in Praed Street."

"Indeed."

Holmes smiled. "Whether that is relevant to the matter of the Black Stone remains to be seen, of course."

Our carriage remained quiet for some time thereafter. Then, as we approached the Biggleswick station, I said, "Holmes, I feel I must yet again thank you for—"

"There is no need, old fellow."

"What you did for young Clark was—"

"Something entirely reasonable," he asserted. He smiled at me again, but this time only with his lips and not his eyes. "Let us speak of other things instead—cabbages and kings, for instance."[164]

Upon arriving at the Biggleswick station and leaving our carriage, we were met by Corporal Scaife, who escorted us to my cottage, where, he said, Martha had prepared a selection of cold cuts despite the ravages of wartime shortages, which had become more noticeable as the spring season progressed.

"Even though we have local children tending the gardens at times, maybe we should find some Land Girls[165] to also help Mr. Jimson and me with the vegetables," Scaife suggested with a laugh. "I don't know if they're sending any of them our way. Oh, and you received a special message yesterday, Colonel."

"It was the servant of that Mr. Shaw who delivered this," Martha informed me once we had entered the house. She held an envelope addressed to me. At Holmes's silent urging, I opened it and read the message inside.

"Well," I said to my friend, "you will be pleased to know that Mr. Shaw is very interested in *The Crimson Rat*. He asks if I might be available this Wednesday to discuss the work at his home, for he will not be travelling to London that day."

"Excellent! Please accept, and ask if—"

---

164 Holmes appears to quote from a poem that appears in Lewis Carroll's *Through the Looking-Glass*, "The Walrus and the Carpenter": "'The time has come,' the Walrus said, 'To talk of many things: Of shoes—and ships—and sealing-wax—Of cabbages—and kings—And why the sea is boiling hot—And whether pigs have wings.'" See footnote 87.

165 The Women's Land Army was a civilian organization whose purpose was to use female laborers to replace male agricultural workers who had gone to war. These women were sometimes called Land Girls.

"If my friend Sherlock Holmes, who is the very subject of this specious novel, may be present as well."

"No," said my friend. "You are to make no mention of me whatsoever, old fellow. I was, rather, going to suggest that you propose a specific time for the meeting."

"Your word is my command. In the meanwhile, will you attempt further contact with Aronson, Letchford, or Ivery? And what of Launcelot Wake? Shall we determine if he has yet returned to Biggleswick?"

"Wake will return when he returns," said Holmes casually. "And as for all the others, let us see what transpires. That newspaper fabrication may be what finally uncovers our man."

"Unless, perhaps, it is Shaw," I added.

I returned to my duties at Isham the next day, eager to discover if the hospital had experienced any changes in my absence. It took me but a quarter hour to discover that it had.

"What was I to do?" implored Major Collins as we stood near the back wall of the recreational room watching Vespera Cochrane dance while Nurse Finch waved a pair of Union Jacks and a collection of patients hummed "Land of Hope and Glory" as best they could.

"Her manner was such that I found it impossible to refuse her," Collins said. "Captains Hughs and Simmons avoided giving me any advice, and the Sergeant-Major voiced no objection."

"Rather uncommon for him."

"Quite. In any event, given the absence of any view to the contrary, I thought it best to let her proceed."

"Divine," cooed Lt. Hooper, standing near, as if in a trance.

"And to be quite honest, sir," Collins added, "Miss Cochrane's performances these past days have buoyed the men's spirits immensely, as is perhaps evident."

"I can see that, yes," I was forced to admit while surveying the small sea of sparkling eyes and waving arms. "Well," I said, "as long as she doesn't put on a nurse's uniform and begin ministering to them, I suppose there's little harm and much good to be had from these pantomimes of hers."

"Well, Colonel, in point of fact..."

I turned to my subordinate. "Are you telling me that—?"

"It has all been under the supervision of Miss Lamington," Collins stammered. "According to her, Miss Cochrane has performed in a nursing capacity almost as capably as she has as a dancer," he said, turning his head to once more view the woman's movements.

I sighed. "And what has Nurse Williams had to say about all this?"

"Truth to tell, sir, the old girl's been very quiet about it all."

"No doubt she has been saving her vitriol for my return," I murmured. "Very well. I will consult Miss Lamington and wait in fear upon Nurse Williams," I added with an acerbic edge. "At least I shan't have Sergeant-Major Ffolkes on my back about it; that is something to be thankful for, at least. I say, Hooper?" I said sharply to the murmuring lieutenant on my other side.

"Yes, sir?" replied the young officer in a suddenly high voice.

I was about to suggest that he get back to his ward duties, but the look in his eye was such that I could not bear to disappoint the fellow.

"Oh, nothing," I muttered and turned to leave the room. "And I should wish to observe Miss Cochrane eventually, of course—as nurse rather than as performer," I barked to Collins while leaving through the open doorway.

A while later, Mary Lamington was in my office to offer explanation.

"She said she was inspired by your comments at the dinner given by my aunts," the woman told me. "We have always accepted civilian volunteers on occasion, and Miss Cochrane was, well, very enthusiastic about donating her services to Isham. In just these past few days, sir, she has shown a high degree of competence—both as a source of morale and as nurse."

I leaned back in my chair and slowly nodded.

"Yes, that is what Major Collins indicated. I do not doubt your word, though I wish to see for myself directly. I refer to Miss Cochrane's abilities as a nurse, having already viewed her dancing."

"I quite understand, sir. If you would tell me—"

A knock came upon the door. It was Vespera Cochrane.

"Ah, you have returned from Scotland," she said, after opening the door and stepping into my office before I could respond. "I trust your journey was worthwhile, Colonel?"

"Yes, it was, Miss Cochrane," I replied with patience.

The woman smiled at Miss Lamington. "I have actually come here in search of you, dear," she said. "I believe I have spotted a dressing on one of the patients that requires changing. It's Lt. Percival. I don't consider myself sufficiently practised to perform the action, and according to what Nurse Finch has told me, he's a very temperamental lad—won't allow himself to be approached by anyone on the staff he hasn't gotten to know well already. I understand he takes to you, and I thought that perhaps...?"

"Of course," replied Miss Lamington. "I will go to his ward presently."

“Thank you.” Miss Cochrane nodded to both of us and then turned to leave.

“Pardon me,” I said quickly, as the woman put her hand to the doorknob. “Miss Cochrane, I wish…”

“Yes, Colonel?” she enquired, turning round to face me with an innocent smile. “What do you wish?”

“I want to watch you in the course of your ministrations,” I stammered. “My understanding is that Major Collins and Nurse Lamington have worked to integrate you into our staff on a voluntary basis, but it is my wish to—”

“I quite understand, Colonel. Please observe me at any time. Is that all?”

She paused silently at the open door, awaiting my next words.

“Miss Cochrane, allow me to also express the gratitude of His Majesty’s Government for your service,” I said, glancing at Miss Lamington. “And excellent service I am sure it is. You may expect me later in the day.”

“I eagerly await,” Vespera Cochrane said with mock sweetness before closing the door behind her.

“Well,” I said, after swallowing audibly, “that is a change in the air, is it not?”

Mary Lamington laughed as she pulled back strands of loose golden hair that had escaped from under her white cap. “A handful for you, sir?” she asked puckishly.

“For us all,” I replied, sensing my face had become warm. “If you do not mind, shall we quickly turn to any developments with respect to the

Black Stone that arose in my absence and that of Sherlock Holmes? Before you leave to attend to that dressing, that is."

"I have had no encounters with Mr. Aronson or Mr. Letchford in the past few days," she told me. "Mr. Shaw continues the daily trips to his London office. My cousin Launcelot wrote me from Skye, informing he will be returning to Biggleswick next week," she added. "And I was accosted by Mr. Ivery on two occasions while you were away," she revealed. "Both occurred when I was strolling with acquaintances in the village: one of the Miss Weekes in the first instance, and with Miss Lester in the other."

"I see. Did he convey anything that might be of interest?"

"It depends on what you mean by that," the young woman said in an odd tone.

I looked at her enquiringly.

"You see, in both instances, he paid much more attention to me than either of my companions or his own concerns."

"Truly? And so...?"

"Colonel Watson, I am trying to tell you that I believe Moxon Ivery has more than a passing interest in me."

I paused, contemplating the meaning of her statement.

"You must understand that I have not led him on, nor undertaken to coax such an inclination from him," she said.

"I understand, Miss Lamington. I did not intend to suggest that—"

"He has demonstrated such an interest for some time, actually. You may have noticed how his attentions inflame Launcelot."

"In truth, I had not put great store in your cousin's reaction to him. He is jealous of Ivery's apparent feelings toward you, you say?"

The woman smiled. "Well, I don't believe it is romantic jealousy, if that's what you mean. Launcelot is very protective of me, but he doesn't fancy me as a wife, certainly. I believe he simply loathes Ivery."

"But Ivery does wish to become your lover, you think?"[166]

"That is my opinion. And though I've not tried to cultivate his attraction to me, I've not discouraged it, either." The young woman blushed slightly. "It has seemed to me that having such leverage over him might be useful to Mr. Holmes."

"A cunning strategy," I said with a gentle smile. "I compliment you."

"It is a cold and heartless strategy," she replied. "I know that, and I hope you do not think less of me for having implemented it."

"I have just praised you, Miss Lamington. We all know it is in the cause of duty."

She nodded. "Yes, it is," the woman agreed, her mood suddenly changed. "Colonel, before I go, I should also mention the arrival of a few new patients."

"Of course," I replied, pulling to me a small pile of dossiers that lay upon the desk. "You have examined these files already?"

"Yes."

"Do any represent novel cases?"

"Well, each case is always its own, I think, but no," she said. "There is nothing in any of them that we have not seen already. They are all from the Arras fighting," the young woman explained.[167] "Each is, in its way, a

---

[166] In this era, the word "lover" did not imply sexual intimacy.

[167] Begun on April 9, 1917, the Battle of Arras was yet another attempt to break the stalemate on the Western Front. British, Canadian, South African, New Zealand, Newfoundland, and Australian troops attacked German lines, making significant gains during the first two days before the offensive faltered. Both sides suffered casualties totaling just short of three hundred thousand.

classic shell-shock case, though one—an officer named Blaikie—is undoubtedly the worst."

"Thank you for noting that. I will study his file most carefully," I said.

"Very well, sir."

"I will attend to it after I read this," I said, holding up a battered envelope that had arrived in the post only that morning. "It is from a dear friend," I added. "A flyer currently in France."

"I hope all is well with him," Miss Lamington said.

"We will see. Please tell Nurse Williams I will visit her this afternoon to discuss these dossiers."

"Of course, Colonel," the woman said.

"Oh, and Miss Lamington?"

"Yes?"

"In that connection," I said haltingly, "has Nurse Williams made any comment regarding me in my absence, or concerning Miss Cochrane's appearance here? Were any such comments inclined to be critical in tone?"

The young woman stood for a moment, thinking. "No," she said after a moment. "I cannot remember her expressing any opinion recently concerning either of you."

"Good," I said with relief. "You may go, then, and attend to Lt. Percival's dressing. I apologise for keeping you."

Brushing a few golden strands of hair from her forehead, she turned and left as I slit open the envelope that had arrived from Cecil Harper.

I had been most relieved at seeing the letter upon my desk, for the recent visits with Charlie Taylor and Ewan Clark had put me in a somewhat disconsolate state. My thoughts kept slipping back to the days spent in Scotland in search of Richard Hannay—a time that, though fraught with tension and danger, I viewed now with a spirit of romance. I especially recalled with pleasure the moments before my departure from Dumfries by aeroplane, with Clark, Taylor, and Sir Harry Christie frolicking while Captain Harper and I had looked on in amusement.

I also could not refrain from dwelling, in contrast, upon how we had all changed in the meanwhile: one had turned his back upon the spirit of benevolence and brotherhood that had once defined his character, another had been shorn of his legs, and the third had misplaced a good portion of his soul. Eagerly seeking some good news, I unfolded the sheets of paper within the envelope and read the message.

The letter had taken its time in reaching me, for it was dated seven weeks previous, well before the start of the Battle of Arras, which was still raging and would continue on for another month. Cecil Harper had miraculously survived over two years of aerial combat while most of his compatriots had fallen; indeed, he was now the most senior flyer of his squadron.

His message provided some small insight into his life in France. As with many flyers, he enjoyed the luxury of sharing a wooden hut with his fellows rather than calling a muddy trench home, and, reading between the lines, I gathered that on those occasions when he was granted leave, Captain Harper made use of his opportunities—principally in Paris—with enthusiasm. To my mind, such pleasures of the demimonde were but slight compensation for the dangerous life he led in support of king and country.

I put down the letter, silently wishing my young friend the best of good fortune in the days ahead. Removing my spectacles to wipe them, I found that my eyes required the same treatment.

§ § §

Arriving at Isham the next morning, I saw that my few but sincere words of encouragement to Vespera Cochrane had taken hold with far greater force than I could have anticipated. The main hall was adorned with a greater proportion of flowers than had been our previous custom, and a handful of intricate paper cut-out figures were now scattered across the corridor walls. Nurses and VADs seemed to have a tad more buoyancy in their step, and their demeanour, though already cheery and helpful, now seemed positively overflowing in those qualities.

"Good morning, Colonel," called Nurse Williams as she entered the dispensary, a greeting I was not unaccustomed to receive from her, but never before in such a good-natured tone. Though we had always held one other in cautious regard, our relationship had been one rooted in hospital business and never inclined toward the warmly personal. Indeed, since my intervention in the argument between her and Sergeant-Major Ffolkes on my very first day at Isham, I had all too often sensed her to be hostile toward both me personally and my approach to administering Isham.

I had, accordingly, tried to steer clear of Nurse Williams as much as possible. In this instance, however, my curiosity got the better of me, and I approached her at the dispensary door to enquire about her opinion regarding Miss Cochrane.

"Yes," said Nurse Williams. "She has changed some things a bit, hasn't she, Colonel? Have you objection to them, sir?"

"Why no," I replied, somewhat taken aback by the question. "Not at all. Indeed, I was fearful that you might be opposed to them."

"Not at all, sir," said the senior nurse. "Perhaps at one time, I might have taken a jaundiced view of Miss Cochrane and her approaches. However, I confess that I find myself quite supportive of them."

"I was rather surprised that she might be the, uh..."

"That Miss Cochrane could be the source of such betterment?" Nurse Williams said. She nodded. "I suppose that makes two of us, Colonel Watson. But I must admit, sir, that she may be the second best thing to happen to this hospital."

I apologised for troubling her, and then, as I left for my office, asked, "And what is the other?"

"Why you, sir," she replied, and entered the dispensary.

Later that day, I made one of several visits to the new patients who had arrived during my trip to Scotland with Holmes, including Blaikie, the officer mentioned by Mary Lamington. He was a Rhodesian who had found himself in a Fusilier battalion at the Battle of Arras. Buried in a huge crump[168] during that action, he was subsequently dug out without a scratch on his person but emerged with his mind quite shattered, in much the same manner as Ewan Clark.

I found him on the edge of his bed in a ward shared with other officers, most of whom were out walking with nurses, though one fellow besides Blaikie remained in the room, asleep in his bed, while another three sat at a table playing cribbage.

"Halloa," I said to the Rhodesian, pulling up a chair. Its legs scraped against the floor, making a short high-pitched squeal, alarming Blaikie

[168] "Crump" was war slang for a shell burst.

and causing him to bolt to his feet. Silently cursing my carelessness, I reached out and put a comforting hand on his shoulder.

The man winced and then looked at me cautiously.

"I apologise sincerely for that, Lieutenant Blaikie," I said.

When he did not speak, I continued. "I am Colonel Watson, the head of this hospital. Other than my most discourteous behaviour just now, have you been treated well since your arrival here?"

He stared at me for a moment and then weakly nodded.

I patted him lightly on the shoulder. "That is good. We want you to be as comfortable as—"

There was suddenly a crashing of metal pans in the hall beyond.

Blaikie jumped at the noise and dove into my arms, while the other officer, who had been sleeping, awoke with a scream. The three convalescents playing cards acted as if nothing had happened; indeed, as if the rest of us did not exist.

"It is all right," I said to Blaikie and the man who had awoke. "We are safe, the lot of us," I assured them.

Blaikie huddled against my chest as my arms folded about him, and the officer in the bed started to weep.

"Come, Lieutenant," I said softly. "Let us get you comfortable again."

Two VADs came rushing in and immediately gave comfort to the other man while I settled Blaikie onto the edge of his own bed once more. Nurse Finch, who was one of the pair who had entered, stepped over to my side.

"Go!" shouted one of the officers at the table in a harsh voice, causing the VAD to hesitate.

"It is just their cribbage match, Finch," I assured her. "He is not talking to you."

She nodded and then murmured, "I can handle Lieutenant Blaikie from now on if you like, sir."

From the corner of my eye, I saw another figure at the entrance to the ward: Vespera Cochrane, her eyes full of concern.

"Very well," I said to Nurse Finch, giving Blaikie over to her care.

I approached Miss Cochrane.

"It was my fault," she whispered to me as we watched the VADs calm both officers and set them to rest. "I was attempting to carry too much and dropped—"

"There is no need to apologise, Miss Cochrane," I said, recalling my own recent carelessness with the chair leg. "We are all examples of human frailty."

"I, in particular, am evidence of that."

"Oh? Quite to the contrary, you appear to have become an uplifting source of strength at Isham, by all accounts. And I cannot recall observing any instance of frailty in you whatsoever."

"It is but an appearance," she confessed. "You, on the other hand, have found the strength to endure this and more for the past three years. I doubt that such reserves lie within me."

"Truly?" I said as we left the ward and strolled down the principal hallway. "At Fosse Manor, you impressed me as a woman who could face any challenge," I ventured.

"Your deductive powers are not as reliable as those of your friend," she replied. "In truth, Colonel, before these past few days, I would have agreed with your perception of me. Seeing the full torment of souls like those, however, has set me straight concerning my limitations."

"We all have our limitations," I said.

"And what are yours?" she asked.

It was on the following Wednesday that I was to have my interview with Frederick Shaw, the publisher. The evening before, I had given Holmes a letter addressed to me that had arrived from the fictitious Mr. Sigerson. I noticed, however, that the handwriting differed from the earlier messages presumably sent by the same person.

"Yes," said my friend, putting on spectacles to read the outside of the letter. "This is Frank Farrar's hand." He eagerly tore open the envelope. "Let us see if he has any more information on Mr. Shaw, prior to your anticipated audience with the publisher tomorrow."

I sat down in my armchair and stared out the window of the sitting room at the low sunlight striking a thicket of trees in the distance.

"Aha," said Holmes quietly. "I curse myself."

"A disappointment?" I asked, reaching for my pipe and Arcadia mix.

"No, a piece that fits," said he. "Any disappointment I show is disappointment with myself—and my slowness of wit."

"I assume you will explain yourself someday, if not this evening."

"What?" said Holmes, looking up from the letter. "Oh, I speak of a small but telling detail in Mr. Shaw's habits. I believe I have related them, some of which you knew already."

"Yes," I said, filling my pipe. "The daily trips to his London office, the valise he keeps close to himself, the regular journeys to Praed Street..."

"A good, brisk enumeration."

“His misanthropy,” I said.

“Ah, Watson, you stumble there,” chided Holmes. “Mr. Shaw does not shun the human race.”

“He avoids society, does he not? Has his refusal to join us for dinner at Fosse Manor slipped from your memory?”

Holmes tossed Frank Farrar’s letter upon a table. “His avoidance is selective, Watson, and it has been a function of time. You admit that the first time you observed the man, he was in the company of friends with whom he had been golfing, do you not?”

“Well, yes.”

“And I believe you characterised him as charming and talkative.”

“He was all that, yes,” I admitted. “Of course, I never spoke to him directly. Indeed, I was never introduced to him, for Launcelot Wake almost ran us down with his bicycle, and Shaw marched off in anger with his friends immediately after. I doubt the man even remembers I was there.”

“And that is to the good,” said my friend cryptically.

“What does that mean?”

“He is hardly the withdrawn person you believe him to be,” Holmes declared, ignoring my question. “He avoids contact only with Biggleswick society, and that reluctance took hold rather suddenly, just after the war had begun. That is what Letchford told us, if you recall.”

“I do.”

“It was his money that built Moot Hall, and he attended meetings there regularly at first.”

“Yes, that is all true,” I agreed.

“If a man’s refusal of society depends upon location and time, it suggests his supposed misanthropy is not an aspect of character but rather the result of happenstance and surroundings. The question in Mr. Shaw's case is this: what are the events and conditions that have caused him to cut his ties with Biggleswick since the war began?"

"And do you now have an answer?"

"Oh, I have always had several. The task has been to identify the correct one."

"And something in Frank Farrar's message allows you to at last make that distinction?"

"Well, my suspicion is now supported by a fresh detail—fresh only because I was remiss in not asking about it earlier."

I reached for a vesta. "And will you tell me about that detail and its relation to the problem, or shall you tease me without mercy, as is your usual custom?'

Holmes smiled and reached for a copy of the latest edition of *The Critic.*

"Mr. Shaw wears a poppy," he said, "but he does so only in London."

I lit my pipe and waited for my friend to elaborate. As Holmes turned page after page of the newspaper, however, I gathered that he would not offer more illumination that night. I exhaled audibly and glanced outside, where the sunlight upon the trees had now faded.

"Apparently, some abnormal behaviours *are* rooted in permanent defects of character," I sniffed. "Specific events and external conditions notwithstanding."

"So I am given to understand," replied Holmes, lifting *The Critic* to disappear behind its pages.

§ § §

The following morning, I called at the house of Frederick Shaw in the company of Sherlock Holmes. At the request of my friend, I wore my military uniform, and also at his insistence, we arrived at Shaw's residence more than a half hour in advance of our scheduled appointment time. When a servant greeted us at the door, Holmes spoke before I could introduce myself.

"If Mr. Shaw is at home, would you please inform him that a representative of the army is here to see him?" my friend requested.

The servant waited to receive a card from either of us, but when none was forthcoming, he closed the door, leaving us standing outside. The detective turned to me and smiled.

"I indulge you far too much, Holmes," I said. "Will Shaw not be put off by this premature arrival, not to mention the failure to properly identify ourselves?"

"It is quite possible," he said. "However, I seek to coax a particular response from him."

"But will this not endanger the case for the book?"

"Do you mean to say that you have now become serious about *The Crimson Rat*?"

As I grasped for a reply, the door opened once more.

"Please follow me," requested the servant.

We entered Shaw's home and were led alongside a flight of stairs and down a hallway that ended in a large ground floor study. Amid books, framed pictures, paintings and piles of paper, Frederick Shaw stood beside his desk, hands clasped together before him.

His eyes fell immediately upon me.

"I am prepared to receive the news, sir," he declared. "I had believed all such ill tidings were relayed by telegram instead, but if this is to be the manner in which my own personal tragedy is revealed, I am prepared."

I stood at the door to the study and glanced at Holmes, uncertain how to respond.

Shaw let both arms drop to his side and then nervously lifted one to take hold of his dark beard. With his other hand, he took his spectacles from his face and briefly closed his eyes before once more staring firmly into mine.

"Do not waste the time," he begged. "Please, I am ready."

"Mr. Shaw," said Sherlock Holmes in a casual tone. "We have most terrible news."

"Oh God!" moaned Shaw. "It is what I feared." He turned away from us and leaned upon his desk. "I should have insisted that Freddy find instead some—"

"Mr. Shaw," Holmes said, "I fear you may misunderstand. This man is Colonel John H. Watson, who wrote you the other week regarding a novel based upon one of my cases. I am Sherlock Holmes."

Shaw turned and stood, mouth open, for several seconds, before his face betrayed a sense of relief, which was almost at once replaced by a stern frown.

"How dare you mislead me!" he barked.

"I admit that we have been most impolite by arriving well in advance of our scheduled interview," Holmes went on. "I thought I had identified ourselves to your servant. Perhaps I did neglect to give him our cards, however."

"You should show some remorse for having—"

"I fear it is all my fault, you see." Holmes said. "During breakfast, I realised that I must take a train into London later this morning, and I did not expect to be able to board on time should I attend your meeting with Colonel Watson at its scheduled hour."

"Why do you—"

"And I did wish to be present when the two of you discussed prospects for his book, since I am, of course, a principal in it."

"What insufferable cheek," said Shaw, now gaining confidence from his growing anger. "If you believe that I will now even consider publishing that—"

"Of course," Holmes added, "I apologise most profusely for causing you anxiety. I quite understand how you might think that we were bringing you sad news concerning your son."

Frederick Shaw's demeanour suddenly changed. His anger dissipated at once, and concern again washed over his face, though of a different nature than before.

"Who said anything about a son?" he asked.

"Why, I just did," replied Holmes with an innocent air.

"I have two daughters," Shaw asserted cautiously. "Only the two young daughters in this house."

"You and your wife have two daughters," the detective answered. "You, in company with another, have a son who currently serves our nation in the trenches, do you not?"

Shaw opened his mouth, perhaps intending to refute Holmes's claim, but as the detective's grey eyes bore down on him, the publisher relented.

"How do you come to think—?"

"Know."

Shaw dipped his head and gathered his thoughts. "How do you come to know this, Mr. Holmes? Are you in the employ of one who seeks to blackmail me?"

"I am the servant of no one individual," declared Sherlock Holmes. "And I have always been the avowed enemy of blackmailers, never their ally. I can state only that I am pursuing an investigation of national importance that, nonetheless, is of no concern to your reputation. However, in the course of that endeavour, I chanced upon information which, on the surface, implicated you in this matter. Further study has exonerated you but also yielded the fact that you have, in addition to your two legitimate daughters, a son who resides elsewhere."

Shaw sighed deeply and then silently indicated that we should be seated. Holmes and I took to chairs as the publisher slowly walked behind his great wooden desk and also sat down.

"It is true," Shaw said. "I am the father of a young man whose mother is a woman other than my wife. His birth preceded my marriage, you see. Moreover," Shaw said, "my wife has always been aware of the child. We choose not to speak of the matter, as one might expect."

"You would not have acknowledged the young man as your son, then, had I simply enquired about him?" Holmes asked.

"Without proof on your part, I would have denied him, yes."

Holmes nodded grimly.

"Well," the detective said, in a tone that belied his words, "I again apologise for the errors that led to your admission, Mr. Shaw. Rest assured that both I and Colonel Watson are most discreet."

"I appreciate your assurances, gentlemen."

“We compliment you on your son’s service,” Holmes added with sincerity, “and we pray for his continued good fortune.”

Shaw smiled timidly. “Again, my heartfelt appreciation, sir. Now then,” he said, “as to the proposed book—”

“You have been prescient in rejecting it, as I believe you were about to do a moment ago,” said Sherlock Holmes. “You see, Mr. Shaw, that is the terrible news that we bring. Colonel Watson now understands that the events chronicled in his prospective novel include certain facts that must remain secret, in the interests of our nation’s safety, until the present war is ended. And of course, from a personal point of view, the Defence of the Realm Act makes publishing those facts punishable.”

“Yes,” I added earnestly, seeking to reinforce my friend’s impromptu fiction. “I do apologise most sincerely, Mr. Shaw, for this change of fortune. It was never my intention to lead you on and then withdraw my proposal.”

“I understand,” said the publisher awkwardly, obviously eager to see us leave his house. “Though I do somewhat mourn the loss of the opportunity, I confess I do feel relief for my son’s safety.”

“Miss Lamington had alerted me to the fact—which you had independently noted—that Shaw travelled to London every day with a well-guarded valise,” Holmes recounted as we walked back to my cottage. “That was sufficient to prompt further investigation, and so, shortly before leaving for Biggleswick, I assigned Frank Farrar to follow Shaw once he arrived at Paddington Station each day. The publisher’s movements were intriguing: on Tuesdays and Thursdays, he invariably travelled on foot to a block of flats in Praed Street, near the station.”

“A habit that no doubt heightened suspicion of him,” I noted.

"Of course. Farrar eventually determined that Shaw visits the block in order to meet with a woman who lives in one of its flats. She was then investigated by Inspector Magillivray, but nothing out of the ordinary was discovered about her, other than the fact that she has a son twenty-two years of age who enlisted in the army in September 1914, and a husband who had abandoned her years earlier. Observation of the woman's movements strongly suggested she was unlikely to be a German agent."

"And you surmised Shaw was the boy's father."

"It was merely a possibility, but my intuition leaned that way. It was then that Farrar, in his recent letter, mentioned that Shaw regularly wore poppies purchased in Covent Garden."

"That is odd," I said. "I have never seen his jacket so adorned when espying him in and around the Biggleswick train station."

"That is because he wears the flowers only in London."

"And what did the poppy suggest to you?"

"Why, that at the least, Shaw supports the war effort, and that perhaps he has a relative serving in France—hence, my assumption that the son of the woman in Praed Street was fathered by Shaw."

"Ah, yes," I said. "He is a native Canadian, is he not?"

"He is, though I do not know if his nation of birth had any great influence upon his manner of showing support for his son. To display the poppy in Biggleswick might have caused argument and disruption, however, given the strong anti-war sentiment there. And no doubt, his anguish would have increased had he continued to attend the discussions in Moot Hall or had maintained constant contact with his neighbours, the vast majority of whom oppose the war. Hence his withdrawal from Biggleswick society."[169]

"I see. But was your method with Mr. Shaw not rather callous?" I asked.

Holmes shrugged as we approached my cottage.

"I had no other rapid means at my disposal, and so I decided to employ the stratagem I did. The story I told him was, of course, false in that it reversed cause and effect: I did not discover that he had a son in the course of exonerating him; rather, I asserted he had fathered the boy, knowing that his confirmation would explain those facts which had falsely suggested he might be a spy."

"And fortunately, he believed that news of his son's death was being delivered in person, rather than by telegram," I said, "causing Shaw no small distress, if only for a moment."

Holmes sighed. "Perhaps he should consider publicly acknowledging his son," he remarked with some indignation. "In any event, Watson, I claim the cause of King and Empire as excuse for my blunt approach. We must get to the core of these matters expeditiously, and few methods are too low for us to stoop in employing them. Though not impossible, I think it now unlikely that Shaw is our German agent."

"Leaving Ivery or Wake or Letchford or Aronson as remaining possibilities."

---

[169] In 1915, Canadian Lt. Colonel John McCrae wrote "In Flanders Fields," which became one of the most popular and quoted poems from the First World War. Its first line alludes to the fields of bright red poppies which sprouted on the scarred battlefield after the first winter of conflict. The work became a propaganda tool for those who supported the war effort—especially in Canada, where the government used it during an especially bitter election in late 1917. The wearing of poppies in remembrance of dead soldiers did not begin until 1918, and then at the instigation of American Moina Michael. Shaw's personal practice of wearing a poppy in support of his still-living soldier son appears to have been a variant forerunner of the practice initiated by Michael.

“Or more than one in combination,” Holmes corrected before adding, “I intend to return to London, Watson. To remain any longer in Biggleswick would prompt suspicion, I believe, and in any event, I believe I have made sufficient initial observation of our principal suspects.”

“And what is to happen in the meanwhile?”

“Perhaps we must simply wait and hope that our false newspaper article gives us the identity of our German spy,” answered the detective.

Two days later, Sherlock Holmes departed Biggleswick.

“We may have largely eliminated but one man from consideration thus far,” my friend declared as I stood with him before his carriage. “However, a seed of decision has been planted in Glasgow by Shinwell Johnson, and I have made clear my expectations of you in the coming weeks.”

“Attend the discussions at Moot Hall.” I sighed. “I do not relish the prospect, but I will do my duty.”

“It is possible that a discussion related to the false newspaper article planted with Gresson will arise there,” Holmes said. “Should it, be certain to listen with care to any comments made by anyone who repeats the contents of the article. I have related those contents to you in sufficient detail?”

“The matter of Germany suggesting to Austria that it allow its socialists to go to Stockholm, and the claim that the Kaiser sent a telegram to the Czar agreeing with Russia’s suggestion that Austria negotiate for peace with Serbia in 1914,” I recited from memory.

“Yes.”

“And what if neither subject is ever mentioned?”

"Keep reading *The Critic*, the paper for which Letchford writes," Holmes told me, as if I had not asked my question. "You may find an interesting letter appearing from an old friend in the next few weeks. In addition," he said, "I have received word from Bullivant that by then you may receive another visitor, though one you cannot acknowledge."

I looked enquiringly at Holmes.

"Hannay has been ordered back to England," he said quickly. "He was pulled out of the Arras campaign at Bullivant's request, and the fellow is joining our campaign against the reinvigorated Black Stone."

"That is perhaps no surprise, and also reassuring in its way."

"Yes, I quite agree. My understanding is that he will be settled somewhere in Biggleswick under an alias, perhaps as early as next month."

"And I am not to acknowledge him," I said.

"Correct, old fellow—unless Hannay himself should approach you in either his real persona or the alias. In the meanwhile, keep your eyes open and relay anything of importance through Miss Lamington."

As the calendar slipped from April to May, I heard nothing more from Holmes while I stayed at the helm of Isham hospital. Following the instruction my friend had left me, I began to attend the public lectures at Moot Hall religiously, and it seemed appropriate that I usually heard the distant, incessant call of cuckoos as I walked to the red-brick building, where I suffered twice weekly through presentations on subjects ranging from the benefits of a purely vegetable diet to the healing power of quartz crystals, in addition to the prospects for peace between Germany and Russia.

Letchford and Ivery took turns chairing the sessions, which were visited regularly by Wake and Aronson, as well as, on occasion, Miss Lamington and Vespera Cochrane, whom I now saw every day at Isham as well. At no time, however, did I hear anything relevant to the fictitious story about a German message to the Czar or the Austrian socialists visiting Stockholm. Though Ivery attempted to coax comments from me following the lectures or, in one instance, tried to persuade me to present my own views concerning medical advances spurred on by war, I remained merely a passive observer.

During the village's May Day festivities, I was dragooned into playing the role of Jack-in-the-Green and had the opportunity to pardon Letchford's son Joseph, who was again hauled before a playful court on the charge of stealing sweets. Mary Lamington at last did bake a blueberry tart for me, and Miss Cochrane and I shared a long twilight walk to the Haven Stones and beyond.

It was the beginning of a very satisfying month as hospital head, as I saw the changes I had begun at the facility take root in earnest, and I spent the first week of June looking forward to even more improvements throughout the summer.

It was then, while making my rounds, that I entered the west garden and saw Blaikie lounging with a visitor in civilian clothes. All at once, a bird flew from a bush, causing the Rhodesian to sit up straight and clasp himself. I realised he was exerting great force to refrain from screaming, and so quickly strode toward him.

His friend, meanwhile, put a hand to his shoulder and began to stroke Blaikie as one might try to calm a frightened horse. When the companion turned to face him, I saw that it was Richard Hannay.

“Colonel!” said Hannay with mild surprise upon noticing me. He started to rise, but I gestured for him to remain seated and continue comforting Blaikie. He glanced round to make certain we three were alone in the garden before adding, “I apologise for the awkwardness—and the breach of protocol—but I absolutely had to see good old Blaikie here.”

“Of course,” I replied as I pulled up a chair. “I have, of course, been instructed not to acknowledge you should our paths cross.”

“And I you, but I have no objection to discreetly breaking the rules if you have none. I am Cornelius Brand now, by the way,” Hannay added quietly.

Blaikie seemed to be paying little attention to us, and Hannay continued. “My persona is that of a South African pacifist. I trust I am not risking myself to exposure by coming here—or perhaps endangering your position as well.”

“If we keep our meeting brief, I believe all will be well. I am glad you came here, I must say, for it is a joy to see you again. We last met in France, did we not? Just about the time of the Somme, when I was on the Continent as an observer.”

“Yes,” said Hannay, lifting a hand to his forehead. “I came out of that fracas with a crack in the head, you know.”

“And a DSO,” I was told.[170]

“Yes, I suppose I did,” he replied, turning toward the other man.

“Halloa, Blaikie,” I said to the patient. “Do you recognise your friend here, then?”

---

[170] The Distinguished Service Order is an order of military merit founded in 1886.

"Africa originally," the convalescing officer said deliberately, somewhat in the manner of a drunken man attempting to sound under control.

"We were friends in Rhodesia years ago," Hannay explained. "Then he wound up in a Fusilier battalion that was part of my brigade at Arras. I suppose you know his story from there?"

"Indeed, I do."

"First time I have seen you today, Doctor," said Blaikie with deliberate slowness. "Do you know yet how long the damn thing will last?"

"I just told you, Blaikie boy," Hannay said in a comforting voice, once more grasping the man's shoulder. "The war will be over soon. At any rate, *you* don't have to worry about it anymore. No more fighting for you at all. And, well, I suspect there will be precious little for me as well. The Boche is done in, all right."[171]

"But I want to know how long it will last," Blaikie insisted as Mary Lamington, in her VAD uniform, approached with a tea tray.

Hannay glanced at me with concern, but I discreetly gestured for him to not worry and continue.

"My lad," said Hannay to Blaikie in the gentlest of tones, "all you need to worry about is sleeping fourteen hours out of twenty-four without stop and then spending half the rest catching trout. We'll meet some of the old gang this autumn and set our sights for grouse, eh?"

---

[171] A derisive term used by the French and picked up by the British, "boche" is a shortened form of *alboche*, which is a slang combination of *Allemand* or "German" in French and *caboche*, which means "head" or "cabbage" in that same language.

Just then, Miss Lamington set the tray upon a table. Hannay looked up, and I saw his gaze linger upon her, though she appeared to cast her eyes only in my direction and nodded before turning to leave.

“Who on earth was that?” Hannay asked a moment later.

“One of the sisters,” Blaikie mumbled listlessly. “Squads of them are roaming around. Can’t tell one from another.”

Hannay looked at me.

“That was Miss Lamington,” I said. “One of the VADs, as you could no doubt tell.”

“Lamington,” Hannay repeated as he watched her vanish round the shrubbery. “Well,” he said, breaking free of his contemplation of the young woman. “Look here, Blaikie, she’s brought some tea for you. Would you like some?”

Hannay rose and poured a cup, which Blaikie accepted. Then, intent on sipping the warm beverage, the patient paid no heed as I rose to join Hannay several paces away.

“You are on your way to Biggleswick, then?” I asked. “To stay for a time?”

“Yes,” Hannay told me. “According to Mr. Bullivant, I’m supposed to be met by a contact of some sort. I take it that person is not you. Have you any idea who it will be?”

“No,” I replied. Thinking of Mary Lamington, I said truthfully, “I am not your contact person, and I am in no position to inform you who that might be.”

Hannay nodded. “I hope I have not risked exposure for either of us by coming here to Isham,” he repeated. “I knew Blaikie was here, however, and I had to see the fellow.”

"Of course. You've not spoken with anyone else?"

"No, other than the nurse whom I asked about Blaikie when trying to find him."

"I am quite certain, General, that you need not fear—your identity has not been compromised."

"I am Cornelius Brand," the man reminded me softly.

"Yes. My apologies. Where will you be boarding?"

"I'll be living with a couple named the Jimsons."

"Ah," I interjected, "you are the one they are taking on."

"You know them?"

"They are my neighbours," I replied. "You will be living next door to me. Do you recall Sergeant Scaife?"

"From Broadgate? Of course."

"As Corporal Scaife, he has been my batman these past months. I've already informed him of your imminent arrival in the village. Should he or I cross paths with you, neither of us will acknowledge you, of course, as anyone other Mr. Brand the pacifist."

"Thank you. Well, I'll spend a bit more time with Blaikie here before leaving," Hannay said. "This evening, before moving in with the Jimsons, I will be staying at a placed called Fosse Manor."

"Ah, the Wymondham sisters."

"You know them as well?"

"I do."

"I am hoping that I might meet my contact person there, perhaps."

"Perhaps," I said, once more thinking of Miss Lamington.

"And, with luck, I will cross paths with you again."

"When this is over," I said quietly, so that Blaikie might not hear. "If not before."

"Yes," Hannay replied with resignation. "Then, if not before. And pass along my best wishes to Mr. Holmes."

"I will."

I took the opportunity to gently place my hands upon Blaikie's shoulders as he sipped his tea. After uttering what few additional words of comfort I could muster, I took my leave of the two men and wandered back into the hospital. As I entered my office, Mary Lamington espied me from down the corridor, and we both discreetly motioned to one another. Moments later, she stood before my desk, the door behind her closed.

"That man with Blaikie," she said at once. "Who is he?"

I smiled. "That, Miss Lamington, is General Richard Hannay. He will be staying in Biggleswick," I said as the young woman began to blush slightly, "under the assumed name of Cornelius Brand."

"Ah," she said, as her normal colour returned. "I will be seeing him later this evening, then."

"At Fosse Manor, yes. He told me he would be staying there before moving into Biggleswick proper. I assume you will be his contact, as you have been as mine."

Miss Lamington nodded. "Yes. And in that regard, Colonel, Sir Walter Bullivant tells me that I am to direct you to make certain to read the *Critic* regularly."

"Did he indicate any reason?"

"No," the young woman replied. "He said simply that you should be alert to encountering a familiar name within the next month."

I said nothing in reply and merelysat back in my chair, realising that this was the second time I had received that same advice.

CHAPTER FIFTEEN: TO GAIN AND TO LOSE

On the first Monday of July, I spent the afternoon preparing myself for yet another interminable discussion at Moot Hall. To inform myself of recent events, I opened the latest edition of *The Critic*, skipping over Letchford's tiresome review of a young American expatriate's book of modern poetry to turn directly to letters.

One of those was a tirade against the reinstitution of Summer Time,[172] while another protested the banning of bonfires. A third letter also caught my eye with its strong invective against American involvement in the war. New World republicanism should not pick up the vices of European aristocracy, declared the writer, who prophesied a great awakening in the United States when the public there finally understood in full its government's policies. The end of the letter made me sit up with greater interest, however, for the diatribe was signed "John S. Blenkiron."

This, I now realised, was what Bullivant and Holmes had told me to be on guard for. It was obvious that the American agent was adopting a public pose as a pacifist, but I did not understand the purpose of the ruse. The answer became more than clear that evening at Moot Hall, however, when Moxon Ivery—as chair of the night's proceedings—disclosed that one of the speakers would be Blenkiron, who emerged from a group standing to one side of the platform and took a seat beside the chairman.

"Well," said Letchford, who sat with me in the company of Aronson. "This should be interesting."

---

[172] What Americans today call Daylight Savings Time had been implemented in Britain for the first time in 1916.

Others in the hall seemed to be of similar opinion, for there was a mild commotion at the announcement. I turned round to survey the audience and saw Richard Hannay slip into the room to take a place on the back benches as the evening's agenda got underway.

Turning once more toward the lectern, I briefly wondered if Hannay had been expecting Blenkiron's appearance, but my attention quickly fixed upon the American himself, whom Ivery introduced at great length as a fearless and indefatigable friend from across the Atlantic.

"Let us see how the fellow performs," murmured Letchford, and Aronson chimed in with enthusiasm.

Blenkiron took to the stage in splendid fashion, and I appreciated with greater force how his recent medical treatments had made him leaner and yet more imposing than before. He stood there, much as I imagined Abraham Lincoln must have appeared more than a half century earlier: tall and thin, with prominent cheekbones and jaw. Every movement had the suppleness of an athlete.

Then, as he surveyed the crowd and his eyes found mine without any betrayal of recognition, I grew tense, realising that he and I—as well as Hannay—were all in the same room together, playing the big game.

Blenkiron's presentation was an odd speech, filled with extravagant vehemence but not well argued. Indeed, as he wandered from one half-demonstrated point to another, I found that his oration reminded me of Sir Harry Christey's meandering Brattleburn declamation in its enthusiastic but often empty bluster.

"Germany is in fine democratic fettle," he claimed, "and it is up to us to help foster that spirit, for we ought to remember that she was forced into this war by the violence and plots of her enemies."

“Is that true?” asked Aronson of Letchford, but the critic only sneered at his younger friend.

Blenkiron went on, employing a number of homely, humorous metaphors drawn from American culture, comparisons which drew their share of laughter from an audience already inclined to his point of view. As I listened, it occurred to me that the man was deliberately shaping his pose as that of an honest, well-meaning naif, and inwardly I smiled at the success he seemed to be having.

At length, he reached the end of his argument, closing with great emphasis on a completely unrelated piece of news: the trip to the Stockholm Peace Conference by Austrian socialists, a journey made with the assent of their government. It was a reference that immediately grasped my attention, for this had been one of items buried in the false newspaper report seen by Abel Gresson.

“They call Austria-Hungary an autocracy too,” Blenkiron declared, “and yet that alleged autocracy allows its dissenters to attend the peace conference, while at the same time, the so-called democracies keep their own domestic opposition trapped within their borders. Now I don’t have any watertight proof,” the American said, “but I will bet my bottom dollar that it was Germany herself that convinced the Austrian government to let those socialists go abroad. Germany, the land that the Allied leaders scorn as intolerant and militaristic.”

“That’s a bit of news, isn’t it?” said Aronson.

“Yes, I suppose,” whispered Letchford. “Rather uninteresting news, though, if you ask me.”

Blenkiron then quickly ended and sat down to great applause, though it was evident that many in the hall thought his praise of Berlin a bit too excessive, even from their pacifist perspective. But for most, it apparently was enough to prove Britain wrong, and it was that criticism that earned the American's oratory the strong approval it received. Even Letchford and Aronson rose to their feet to applaud, while I remained seated and outwardly unmoved.

"I believe I express the opinion of virtually everyone in this hall by saying that Mr. Blenkiron's remarks are taken to heart here tonight," said Moxon Ivery as chairman. "I particularly commend his views on the matter of the Stockholm Conference. Indeed," he said, "I am in a position to bear out all that Mr. Blenkiron has said in that regard. I can assure him on the best authority that his surmise is correct, and that Vienna's decision to send delegates was largely dictated by advice from Berlin. This has been admitted in the German press, for I have seen such a report."

As the audience continued to applaud both Ivery and Blenkiron, I sat still in my chair, realising the significance of the former's assertion. I saw the American beam proudly as he shook hands with the chair. Then, holding Ivery's fist aloft with his own, Blenkiron looked out at the audience, eventually catching sight of me, whereupon his smile grew ever broader. And, as his gaze remained upon me, I raised my hands and began to clap—not for his recent remarks, but rather for his success in exposing Ivery as the compatriot of Gresson, and an undisputed member of the Black Stone.

"I say, Colonel," commented Letchford as he remained standing and witnessed my gesture. "Have you suddenly come over to our point of view at last?"

"I applaud the man," I replied. "Not his remarks."

As the meeting disbanded, I glanced back toward the platform before leaving the hall and saw Ivery and Blenkiron conversing with Richard Hannay in his guise of Cornelius Brand. Realising discretion was called for, I did not allow my concentration to linger upon them and left the hall promptly.

As I walked home to my cottage, I considered going to London the following day to inform Sherlock Holmes about Ivery, though I was certain that Blenkiron would be conveying the revelation soon enough. As it was, when I returned home, Scaife immediately gave me a telegram that decided the matter. The message was from Holmes and displayed his typical brevity: "Please arrive Paddington tomorrow, first train without fail."

The following day, as instructed, I arrived early at Paddington Station in London, where I was met by Holmes.

"My latest housekeeper left but yesterday" were his first words to me. "I suppose she failed to give notice only because I informed her I was considering letting her go," he said as he signalled—silently, out of habit—for a taxicab.[173] "In any case, she took the cook with her this time as well, and I've nothing to offer you save the usual—if fewer—cold cuts, which we shall have to fetch ourselves. There will be ample time before we must attend a meeting at Traill's Bookshop, and countless rounds of dining out thereafter."

"Will Blenkiron be in attendance?" I asked as a taxi rushed by without stopping. "He was in Biggleswick of last night. Holmes, do you know—"

---

[173] During the war, Londoners were prohibited from whistling for taxis after 10:00 p.m. for fear that the sound might be mistaken for an air raid alert.

"That Ivery is our man? Yes, I do. Blenkiron himself sent a coded telegram to Bullivant last night, and Inspector Magillivray came round to convey its contents to me. It seems that later, over dinner with Blenkiron and Hannay, Ivery also admitted to being aware of the second report contained in the false article: the allegation that the Kaiser had tried to coax peace among Russia, Austria, and Serbia before the war broke out.

"That our man is Ivery does not greatly surprise. I always viewed Letchford and Aronson as unlikely spies, so that the choice essentially lay between Ivery and Wake, and I was inclined to trust Miss Lamington's intuition with regard to her cousin. Nonetheless, it is premature to let the younger man off the hook just yet. He may still be allied with Ivery."

I nodded as Holmes signalled to the next taxi, which continued down the street.

"But to return to your question, Blenkiron will be in his bookshop—I believe he had arranged to have Ivery himself accompany him to London on a later train from Biggleswick. Hence, my insistence that you take the first."

"I see."

"Bullivant and Mycroft will be present at this meeting as well, as will Inspector Magillivray."

"Not Hannay?"

Holmes shook his head. "He will be coming to London tomorrow to meet separately with Blenkiron. For him to come to town on the same day as you and Blenkiron was thought to appear a bit too suspicious."

"You know," I added as a third taxi also ignored us, "Blenkiron was most convincing at Moot Hall last evening. I believe that is the first time I have witnessed the man in the field, playing the old game."

Holmes smiled as he gestured, this time successfully, to yet another taxicab. "I do wish I could have seen it myself. However, once we arrive in Queen Anne Street, shall we enjoy the pleasure of my remaining cold cuts? Then, perhaps, I can interest you in allowing Martha to return as housekeeper here."

I gave my friend a sardonic look as he opened the taxi door for me. "Ever the industrious plotter," I murmured. "On several fronts."

Two hours later, Holmes and I made our way to Haymarket Street. It was a bright and sunny morning, with a bit of haze in the eastern portion of the sky. An assistant clerk allowed us entry through an alley door into Traill's, which had not yet opened for business, and led us directly to the second floor, where the door camouflaged by false book spines was ajar. Stepping into the small room behind it, we found Blenkiron, Bullivant and Mycroft Holmes.

"Ah," said the elder Holmes brother. "Greetings, Colonel. I trust your stay in Biggleswick has been doing well by you. Certainly," he added, glancing at his two companions, "it has done most splendidly by us. We now know who our Biggleswick man is—or at least, one of them."

"I believe that was the work of Shinwell Johnson, your own sibling, and Mr. Blenkiron here," I humbly suggested.

"Don't sell yourself short," said Blenkiron. "All for one, and one for all."

"Yes, excellent work, Watson," declared Bullivant, the first to stand and take my hand. "And welcome back to London—though a London now under siege, what with these renewed aerial raids. I suppose it's a return to being under fire for you, eh?"[174]

"My visits to France were but brief ones," I said, "and in each instance I was usually far removed from the front itself, other than one or two direct observations during lulls in fighting. I have not yet truly been fired upon, though I suppose if these assaults from above keep up, that will no longer be true. But then, that will simply put me among all the citizens of London in that regard."

There was a knock at the open door, and Inspector Magillivray stuck his head into the gap. "Halloa, sirs," he said. "Am I late?"

"Not at all," said Mycroft Holmes. "Close the door on your way in, Inspector, and let us get down to business."

We five then settled into a circle, and Blenkiron was given the floor.

"Well, as we were just remarking," the American said, "the Biggleswick operation has succeeded in its first step. We narrowed our list of suspects, threw out the bait, and Mr. Moxon Ivery is the one who has been hooked. This Launcelot Wake fellow may be in league with him as well, according to Colonel Watson and Mr. Holmes, but Ivery is no doubt our big fish in the pond.

"Meanwhile, Abel Gresson's probable routes south have been more closely defined as well: Shinwell Johnson and Andrew Amos in Glasgow have determined that Gresson regularly signs on as purser aboard a vessel named the *Tobermory*, a ship that plies the Hebrides. I believe all we need

---

[174] In 1915 and 1916, German airships had bombed London. As British defenses against those lighter-than-air craft improved, however, airplanes subsequently replaced airships as the prime method of attacking Britain directly. The first bombing of London using heavier-than-air craft had occurred on June 13, 1917.

now is to identify the final link between Gresson in Glasgow and Ivery in Biggleswick."

"And for that, we are employing Mr. Hannay," interjected Bullivant.

"Correct," said Mycroft. "Blenkiron will meet with Hannay tomorrow and direct our friend to travel to Glasgow," he explained for the benefit of his brother, Magillivray, and me.

"He will go in his current guise as Cornelius Brand." Blenkiron continued. "Once in Glasgow, Hannay will be assisted by Andrew Amos in getting acquainted with Gresson. Now that we know Gresson's mode of travel, the hope is that Hannay can arrange passage on the *Tobermory* as a passenger and determine at what location my fellow American passes on his information."

"And to whom," added Bullivant. "That person could well turn out to be Launcelot Wake."

Holmes crossed his arms, saying nothing.

"I believe we will soon be in a position to eliminate this revised version of the Black Stone," said Bullivant with an air of satisfaction.

Magillivray cocked his head and glanced at the spymaster. "And what about that old third head of Cerberus that keeps getting mention every now and then?"

"We have nothing definite yet," admitted Bullivant.

"No," agreed Mycroft Holmes. "However, my brother has an interesting theory about that, which—"

Just then I felt a slight shaking, accompanied by a series of dull roars.

"What is that?" asked Magillivray.

Blenkiron rose in his chair. “Guns,” he said. “Guns firing. Do you think—?”

“Another raid from above,” declared Mycroft Holmes as more shots sounded. “Our defensive batteries must be firing.”

Bullivant opened his mouth to speak but paused as Sherlock Holmes left his chair and pushed open the chamber’s hidden door.

“Holmes,” I said warily. “What are you—?”

“Do you wish to come along to obtain a look as well?” the detective said before vanishing through the doorway.

In a heartbeat, I was up and following behind, alongside Bullivant, Mycroft Holmes, and Magillivray.

“It comes from the east,” said Sherlock Holmes, who stood at a window, looking in that direction.

“Perhaps we are hearing the guns at Wanstead,” suggested his brother as we all crowded to the window. Suddenly, booming from another compass point could be heard.

“And that could be the battery at Parliament Hill,” suggested Bullivant.

Suddenly, even louder reports washed over us.

“More still,” said Blenkiron. “And closer.”

“Those latest are the Tower Bridge guns, I’d wager,” declared Mycroft.

“Look!” said Sherlock Holmes, pointing upward, where great puffs of black smoke now burst across the wide expanse of blue sky. Fresh, dark clouds expanded and entwined with one another, creating a translucent blanket of gloom as the firing grew in power and frequency. To me, it was the front in France revisited in spirit, as well as a new front of conflict in fact, descending upon our homeland from above.

"There they are," shouted Mycroft, lifting a pudgy finger toward the pane. "Some of them, at least." He indicated an area near the horizon from which the black tendrils had receded, revealing a flock of dark specks moving steadily across the sky.

"They must be Gothas," Bullivant said.[175]

"Shall we proceed to the basement?" asked Blenkiron.

The American's suggestion was followed by a series of low rumbles, different in nature than the cannon fire we had been hearing. A moment later, smoke began to well up in the distance, a rising counterpoint to the puffs from artillery shells still bursting above.

"They have begun dropping their bombs," said Magillivray.

"There's no shame in displaying prudence," said Mycroft Holmes, who turned to Blenkiron. "Yes, John, let us seek shelter."

Bullivant and Magillivray followed the American toward the stair, and I took steps in the same direction. The elder Holmes stopped and turned toward his brother, who was still peering out the window.

"Are you coming, Sherlock?" he asked. "I'd rather that I not be forced to give you a direct order."

"That has not occurred in over half a century," replied the younger sibling. "It will not recommence now. Lead on, Mr. Blenkiron," he said, leaving the window.

---

[175] Gothas were heavy bombers used by German during the First World War. The raid described by Watson in this instance is undoubtedly the one conducted by twenty-two Gotha G.IV aircraft on July 7, 1917.

We descended to the ground floor of Traill's, where a small group of assistants were covering bins and storing various items inside cabinets.

"Come along," Blenkiron barked to them, and we all followed the man to a door that led to another flight of stairs ending in a rather sturdy, spacious area beneath the building.

"The pilings and joists have been reinforced in the last two years," Blenkiron noted as we settled onto benches that lined the walls. "Even if bombs should strike in extreme proximity, we'll be safe and secure. If they strike the building itself, however, we shall have to take potluck."

"We need to obtain earlier warning of such attacks," declared Mycroft Holmes. "Thus far, the acoustic mirrors have not adequately proved themselves."[176]

"I've not yet told you, M, but I'm considering having our top agent in Belgium take a hand in this," said Bullivant. "He believes he can provide an early alert when the Gothas are about to take to the air."

"By all means, let us see if he can do that," replied the elder Holmes. "I'd rather be able to take my time to find shelter."

The small coterie of bookstore assistants, who were American agents under Blenkiron's direction, huddled by themselves in a far corner, leaving the rest of us in relative privacy on the oppose side.

"Now then," said our host, as we heard more distant rumbling, "where were we?"

---

176 In an attempt to hear German aircraft approaching Britain, parabolic surfaces were fashioned of concrete or etched into coastal cliffs. These were meant to focus sound onto microphones, but until vacuum tube amplification was employed in 1918, these systems were not effective.

"We were about to discuss that third head of Cerberus, which has eluded us for three years now," said Mycroft. "Sherlock has something to say on the matter, I believe," he added, turning to his brother.

"Yes," said the detective. "It is a thought that, oddly enough, was inadvertently inspired by a comment from Mr. Ivery some time ago over dinner. He referred to honeybees becoming dormant, and I corrected him with respect to that claim. The remark made me think of a singular entry in Franklin Scudder's notebook: 'Must disturb the sleeping dog.' Then it occurred to me that perhaps we have not yet detected the activity of the supposed third spy cell because *it* has been lying dormant."

"Inactive, you say?" enquired Magillivray. "Why would it be sleeping?"

"A sleeping cell," mused Mycroft. "That is an interesting way of putting it."

"We know that Von Bork's spy group and the original Black Stone were intended in part to independently gather information so that Berlin could check the veracity of one's findings against the other," said the younger Holmes. "We also know, however, that the Black Stone went beyond simple espionage to plot and execute acts of subversion, such as the assassination of Karolides. Might the supposed third group be intended to be held in reserve for the same purpose, to be activated only when desired or necessary?"

"And when would that be?" asked Magillivray.

"I believe it must be in the near future," said Sherlock Holmes.

"If not the present," added his brother. "John," he said, addressing Blenkiron, "your nation's entry into this conflict has thrown the advantage distinctly to our side. Berlin must act boldly and swiftly to counter it;

otherwise, the addition of American resources and troops will break the stalemate. If the Germans have hidden reserves of their own, they must bring them into play very soon."

There were louder rumblings than before, and I felt the bench under me quiver.

"They are getting closer," Magillivray murmured.

Blenkiron smiled. "Indeed, they are." He leaned against the foundation wall and looked at Sherlock Holmes. "And have you evidence that this possibly sleeping cell has awoke?"

"Not yet," said my friend. "I keep searching for patterns of interest, however, and—with my brother's and Sir Walter's permission—I intend to continue that activity."

"You know that you always have free rein, my lad," said Mycroft.

"Of course," chimed in Bullivant. "I assume that is why you requested that Watson here return to your side."

"Yes, though I had not yet informed him of that fact," admitted Holmes, who smiled awkwardly at me as the latest round of explosions above lifted dust from the basement walls.

"Your assistance here in London, old fellow, would be invaluable," he said. "With Moxon Ivery now identified as the principal German spy in Biggleswick, your work there is done, and I wish to arrange your permanent return to Queen Anne Street."

I sat there as the rumblings above us died down, finding myself strangely disappointed at Holmes's revelation. While I felt gratitude at my friend's expression of need for my service, I nonetheless sensed mild anger rising within me at the prospect of being removed from Isham, where I had found a true purpose during the war.

I held those feelings in check, however, and forced myself to puckishly reply, "Well, I suppose that it is actually just a very devious method of getting Martha back to London."

Our stay in the underground refuge was relatively brief. From the first firing of ground batteries against the approaching aeroplanes to the final rumbling of exploding bombs, perhaps no more than a quarter hour elapsed. We remained in the basement of Traill's for twice that length, however, and then cautiously regained the ground floor.

Looking out the store windows, we could see no damage in our immediate vicinity, though portions of the sky were obscured by what I took to be dust and smoke from distant fires.

Inspector Magillivray excused himself and hurried off to join his fellows from Scotland Yard to assist in dealing with the aftermath of the aerial raid. As he left, we saw others emerging from neighbouring buildings.

"Well," said Bullivant, "at least people now have the sense to huddle inside when the bombs fall."

"Yes," said Mycroft, turning to Blenkiron and me. "When we had the very first bomber raid last month, I understand most of the population simply stood and watched the aeroplanes out of curiosity, despite the danger." He glanced with amusement at his brother. "You would think they would have learnt from the earlier Zeppelin attacks. Well, shall we return to our conference chamber?" he asked. "Sir Walter can convey the rest of our agenda to Inspector Magillivray."

"I should like to survey the damage," said Sherlock Holmes.

"Yes, of course," said Bullivant. "However, I suggest you do it somewhat later, when you will not be in the way of rescuers, and after we have finished our business here. I do hope no children were lost this time," he added as we ascended the stair.

"The lad was there when the bomb hit, we are given to understand," said a constable later in the day.

Holmes and I stood in the Boleyn Road, with the rubble from three houses still piled before us.

"He was a grocer's delivery boy, twelve or thirteen years of age, I understand," the policeman said. "The young fellow was bicycling past, and the explosion killed him outright."

Afternoon sunlight cast stark shadows from the debris, which was still being cleared. The wounded and dead had long been removed, but we observed ample evidence that human lives had ended here.

"And so from this location, the German aircraft proceeded south, toward where we huddled beneath Traill's," noted Holmes as we stepped carefully along the street. "Over Dalston, Hoxton, and Shoreditch and then on to the City itself before turning east."

"And they continued dropping bombs even then?" I asked.

Holmes nodded. "Yes, and at the same time, apparently, a second group of aeroplanes reached the City as well."

"We will visit the destruction there also, I suppose."

"Yes," said Holmes, whose eyes swept the scene as we continued along the Boleyn Road. "I wish to see as much as possible before nightfall."

"Do you truly hope to glean anything from these visits?"

"I do not know, Watson. As I have told you repeatedly in the past, hope—even faint hope—must never be explicit in detection, but neither must it be absent entirely."

"But do you believe that attacks from the air such as these can lead you to the third German spy group? Why should there be any link between them?"

"I have no indisputable case to make," admitted Sherlock Holmes. "However, I believe it worth the effort. Consider, Watson: a prime target of both Von Bork's operation and the earlier incarnation of the Black Stone was information about our navy—codes, deployments, weaponry, and the like.

"But war has taken to the air in this new century," he added while staring at debris lining the street. "We have our own aeroplanes, and our defensive guns here on the ground as well. Why would the Germans not wish to learn more of them, as they did of our sea forces in earlier years? Why should they not wish to enhance the devastation wrought by their own craft? At present, I know not what if any connections may exist between what we see here and what we believe a German spy group may be doing or planning to do, but if those connections exist, I mean to discover them."

"And are you certain, Holmes, that you require my assistance in this pursuit?" I asked.

"Of course I am," he replied. "And I assume you are as enthusiastic in your desire to return to Queen Anne Street and join in the hunt. The game remains afoot, Watson. Or perhaps, now, on the wing."

Holmes had halted during these remarks, but now he resumed walking, carefully picking his way amid the rubble. I watched for a moment and then set off after him. We passed on round a corner, walking through damage inflicted in Cowper and Woodsworth Roads, and it was there that we witnessed the anger of local residents.

"Are you with the government?" a man of middle age with a dirtied faced demanded to know. "If you are, will you ask your owners what they'll do about this? And what they'll do about the Germans?" The man kept following us. "I'm talking about the ones living amongst us, you know," he said again and again. "What's to be done to the bloody Germans who have been living here?"

Holmes merely nodded and walked on. I followed, and at our backs we heard the continued shouting of the man.

"We'll do it ourselves, if we have to!" he cried.

I returned to Biggleswick the next day and gave my attentions immediately to Isham hospital. I now understood my tenure there was coming to an end, and I felt determined to make certain that the changes I had instituted during my short stay would be permanent. As I worked feverishly on a set of recommendations for Major Collins to pass on to my successor, I received a knock upon my door.

"Enter," I called.

The door opened to reveal Launcelot Wake. The young man stood cap in hand, his thick hair appearing even more vigorous than I had remembered it. A cautious smile played across his face.

"Colonel?" he said. "Are you available at present? May I have a word with you, if you are?"

"Of course, Mr. Wake," I said pleasantly. "Sit down, won't you?" I suggested, motioning toward a chair that sat beside a filing cabinet.

Miss Lamington's cousin closed the door behind him and pulled the empty chair forward, so that it sat opposite mine across the desk top. Bowing ever so slightly, Wake sat down and then drew forward on the edge of his seat.

"I've come here because I've reached a decision, and you had a great deal to do with its making," he said.

"Oh?" I said, pushing my paperwork to the side and leaning back. I placed my right hand upon the desk. "What decision have you made?"

"I've arranged to join the Labour Corps."[177]

I sat and stared at the young man, taken aback by his declaration.

"I know it seems most odd, given my position with respect to the war," Wake interjected before I could speak. "And you must understand that I have not changed that position. The conflict is unjust and unnecessary, and that is that. But it is a struggle that will not go away, and I've concluded that, since the fates have made me a government servant, I might as well do my work from a vantage point somewhere less cushioned than a chair in the Home Office."

"I see."

"It's not a matter of principle so much as self-indulgence, for I am certain I make a better clerk than a navvy.[178] I enjoy fresh air and exercise, however, and feel in the need for more. That is all."

"Have you been contemplating this action only recently?" I enquired.

---

[177] The Labour Corps was a distinct body of troops, organized in 1917, whose purpose was logistical: building and maintaining roads, railways, canals, builds, camps, telegraph and telephone systems, as well as moving supplies. In addition to Britons, the Labour Corps also included large numbers of men from India, Egypt, China, and elsewhere. It was a precursor to the Royal Pioneer Corps, created in 1939 and similarly employed during the Second World War before being united with other units to form the Royal Logistic Corps in 1993.

[178] "Navvy" is a now dated term for a laborer employed in the excavation and construction of roads, railways, and canals. It was coined originally in relation to navigation canals.

"No, I have been thinking about it for some time, and I'm informing you of it first, Colonel Watson, because it was you who inspired me to consider it."

"Oh?"

"Yes, it was during that dinner at Fosse Manor just after Easter. You told us about what you saw in France, and I confess I was enthralled. It got me thinking about many things."

"Have you considered joining the medical corps instead?"

"Oh no," said Launcelot Wake with a gesture of dismissal. "While I may turn out to be a mediocre navvy, I am certain I would be a horrible stretcher-bearer. I could never match the qualities of the fellows you saw at the front, sir, but I believe I could be credible as a labourer."

"And OTC is out of the question for you?"[179]

"I am a noncombatant and will remain so," Wake avowed. "When I had decided upon the Labour Corps, I bicycled all the way to Cheltenham to learn more about it. I got drenched that morning, but it helped decide the issue for me."

"Was that in April?" I asked. "The day that you met Sherlock Holmes and me along one of the local roads?"

Wake thought for a moment. "I suppose it could have been. Oh yes, it was," he suddenly admitted. "I recall it now, for I remember that I lied to both of you about where I had gone. I did not wish anyone to know what I was contemplating."

"And you would have cycled to Cheltenham along the main road," I added.

---

[179] Officers' Training Corps.

“Yes, of course. The main road is the most direct route in any case, and given the bad weather that day, the only route by bicycle, really. Well, I will go now, Colonel Watson. It was my wish to tell you about what I am about to do before I inform anyone else. I am certain that my aunts will be at a complete loss for words when they learn my plans.”

“If anything can produce such an effect, I believe it will be that revelation. I congratulate you, Mr. Wake, and I wish you the best.”

“Thank you, sir. I’ll take my leave now.”

“Here,” I said, rising an instant before the young man got to his feet. “Allow me to act as an escort of honour from the building.” I patted my chest while looking down at my papers. “I believe I am due for a bit of fresh air myself, if for only a few minutes.”

“I would appreciate your accompanying me.”

I took my cap and opened the door for Wake, who followed me down the hall and out the main entrance of the hospital. Beside the steps, where he had left his bicycle, I shook the man’s hand and once more wished him well.

“I should be pleased to receive a letter from you now and then from France, when you are able to spare the time,” I said.

“It will be a pleasure to write you, sir,” Wake declared. “You will be remaining here?”

“In truth,” I said, “I have been informed that I am to be transferred yet again. I believe my new assignment will still be on the home front—London, I am given to understand. You may write me at my residence in Queen Anne Street.”

I gave him my address and then sent him on his way. Watching Lake pedal off to the road and then down the lane toward Biggleswick, I felt minor satisfaction at having confirmed his innocence with respect to the Black Stone.

Heeding my own excuse for accompanying Wake out of the hospital, I resolved to take a quick walk round the grounds and strode over to the west garden, where I saw a small group of unfamiliar faces: new patients, who must have arrived the day before while I was in London.

I advanced to introduce myself, when one officer in particular caught my eye. He had a moustache now, and his face had aged significantly in the past three years, but there was no mistaking the man.

"Excuse me," I said, stepping up to him. "Captain Ashley Tate?" I asked. "Forgive me, but I have forgotten your given name."

He glanced up at me, and I could see in his eyes all the signs of shell shock. I gave him whatever time he required in which to form a response, and after a few seconds, he smiled weakly and said, "No, it is Cap-cap-captain, as you just said. Oh, wait a moment. Sorry, it is Edward, yes."

Squinting, he shielded his face with his one free hand, his right arm being restrained by a sling, and studied me for several minutes.

"I know you," he said at last. "I don't recall your name, either, but you were the fellow who was in that aeroplane landed near Birmin-birmin-birmingham. That's you, isn't it?"

"I am that person, yes. Colonel John Watson," I said, extending my hand. "I am head of this hospital."

"Well, fancy that," he said, grasping my right hand weakly with his inverted left. He allowed me to shake for both of us, and I then released his limp fingers.

"Have we a chair?" he asked of no one in particular. "Indeed, fancy this," he repeated. "I remember you. You were in the aero-aero-aeroplane, weren't you? The Midlands? Just after the start of the war?"

"Just before, actually," I said, pulling up an empty chair. Two of the other new patients watched with vacant eyes and then returned to contemplating the garden in its midsummer glory. "I see you are back in Britain for a time, then?" I noted, leaning forward toward Ashley Tate.

"Yes. Oh yes," he replied, gesturing to his bandaged arm. "I got my blighty wound, I did."[180]

"So I see."

"Dear Old Blighty," whispered Ashley Tate. "So you are head of this place, you say? Been here long?"

"A few months," I said. "And you arrived yesterday, I believe."

"Indeed, yesterday. My blighty wound," the officer repeated, cradling the sling in his free hand. "And there was the other thing," he said, his manner suddenly changing. He smiled. "Do you know about it?"

I shook my head. "Not yet. Do you wish to tell me about it? If you would rather not, I can—"

"It was an ordinary raid," Ashley Tate began calmly, an odd look in his eye. "We were to commence the attack at dawn, but it was cloudy, you see, and so all was still dark. We advanced mightily, but the Germans were just letting us walk deeper into a trap. My company was destroyed, and I myself was shot twice.

---

[180] In India, "vilayati" is an Urdu word meaning "foreign" which eventually came to refer primarily to the British. A regional variant, "bilayati," was picked up by British troops stationed on the subcontinent, and they used it—now transformed to "blighty"—as slang for home. During the First World War, use of the term spread. A blighty wound was one that resulted in a soldier being sent back to Britain for recuperation.

"The Germans then started advancing themselves. Came walking right over us, bayonetting and shoo-shoo-shooting those who still moved. I had to lie still," Ashley Tate said. "I could not move. I could not breathe—that is, I know I must have kept breathing, but I could swear I didn't. And my arm had been smashed up rather badly," he added, lifting his sling ever so slightly. "But even if I didn't move, they might have speared me. Spear me if I move; spear me if I don't move."

Ashley Tate's eyes held the recollection of his fear, but he continued to relate his tale in clinical detail.

"I wan-wan-wanted to make time stop, you see. And it did. That's how I stopped breathing. Everything went dark. And the next thing I knew, I was being gently prodded. I was sure it was a Hun with a bayonet, ready to run me through. And then I heard a voice with a touch of Dorset in it. I opened my eyes and saw a shadow holding a screw picket. That's what it was nudging me with: a bloody screw pi-pi-picket.[181]

"It was night, you see, and the shadows were one of our wiring parties. They found us—except all the others were dead. And time really had stopped, Colonel, for it was two days after I'd fallen. I looked up at the man with the picket and told him to take me away," he said with sudden urgency. "I begged them to pull me out of there!"

I reached out and took his good arm by the elbow, to steady him.

Ashley Tate looked me in the eye, anguish washing across his face before it abruptly vanished.

---

[181] A corkscrew picket was a round steel bar whose lower section was bent into a helix, enabling it to be silently screwed into the ground. It had several loops, which were used to support barbed wire.

“That’s a nice little story, isn’t it, sir?” he asked in a suddenly abstracted tone. “Did you appreciate it?”

“I can appreciate you,” I replied. “As to fully appreciating your experience, however, we have other men here who are certainly able to. Indeed, I think there is a fellow whom you should get to know. Blaikie is his name.”

“Will we have a lot to compare—him and me?” Ashley Tate enquired with a chuckle. The chuckle expanded into a high laugh and then abruptly stopped. “So tell me—Colonel Watson, you said it was?” Ashley Tate said, wiping his eyes. “Tell me, did you succeed in that mi-mi-mission of yours three years ago?”

“Yes, in large part,” I replied. “Thanks to you. And Captain Harper.”

“Ah, Harper,” he said. “Good old Ce—”

I watched him struggle to get the name out.

“Good old Ce-ce-cecil. Ran into him more than once over there, you know. His squadron was based near our brigade. Always envied the RFC boys for the huts they slept in. Beats a dugout any day.”

“I met with Captain Harper in France as well,” I noted, “and I have corresponded with him since. A letter from him arrived only the other week.”

Ashley Tate nodded. “I see,” he said. “Yes, yes. I would enjoy reading that, if you would allow me the plea-plea-pleasure.”

“Of course.”

The officer leaned back and sighed. “Too bad the fellow bought it.”

It was as if the entire world went silent. There must have been birdsong and the rustling of dry leaves in the midsummer breeze, but my ears were deaf to them once I heard those last words.

At some point I felt fingers grasp my elbow. Ashley Tate, his good hand clasping my forearm, shook me ever so slightly as he leaned forward.

"Colonel?" he said. "Colonel, are you quite all right?"

"Yes," I said in a flat tone. "I am fine. I—"

"Did time stop for you, too?"

I opened my mouth but had no words to speak.

"You did know, did you not?" he asked. "About Har-Har-Harper. I assumed you knew."

"I do—I did know," I assured him, not wishing him to think he had caused me distress.

"But you said you received a letter from him last week."

"I received a letter *about* him," I said, heaping deceit in a great mound.

"Were you told the details?" Ashley Tate asked. "It happened in our sector, you know. I heard it from one of the stretcher-bearers who saw it happen."

"Tell me," I said, pleading rather than demanding. "Yes, please tell me the story as you received it."

"It was during Arras, of course," the officer said, and I sat up straight at the news, for the last letter I had received from Cecil Harper—the one I had as yet failed to answer—had been written just before that battle. Delayed by the not uncommon errors and inefficiencies, it had arrived into my hands long after the pilot had died, I now realised.

"Yes, Arras," repeated Ashley Tate. "Some wounded had been taken to a burnt out farmhouse, where the doc-doc-doctors were treating them. The Huns started pouring artil-artil-artillery into the little valley where the house was, and I'm sure they would have eventually hit the place and taken out everyone inside.

"Then along comes Harper in the sky. Don't know if he was returning from a mission or just starting out on one, but from his vantage point, he must have sorted out what was happening, and so he swooped down and drew the German fire away from the farm-farm-farmhouse.

"The surgeons were able to finish and then evacuate the wounded. The Boche kept their sights on Harper, though, and one shell tore off parts of his wings, sending the aero-aero-aeroplane into a vicious spin, according to the stretcher-bearer who saw it all. Old Cecil crashed behind the German lines."

"I see."

"The Huns gave him a decent burial, we were told, and one of their planes flew over our lines to drop his possessions in a packet." Ashley Tate leaned back in his chair and sighed. "I suppose they still do that sort of thing for the airmen now and then. Nothing like that for us on the ground, though. Yes, there is still a bit of honour up in the clouds, wouldn't you say? And just hell in a mud field for those of us in the poor old bloody infantry, eh?"

"Yes," I agreed. "Mud."

Two nurses came round then, and I rose from my chair before putting my hand on the officer's shoulder.

"We will talk again, Captain," I assured him, and he gave an anxious smile. I then left Ashley Tate and the other officer patients in the charge of the two nurses and walked back to my office, feeling as though I trod a path made of fragmented bone.

As I approached my door, I saw Miss Lamington in her blue dress and apron with white cap, dossiers in her arms. Her cap was slightly askew, slanting down on her left side, a gesture that had always been a signal that she wished to convey something of substance to me in private.

"You have more profiles for me?" I said, uttering the oft repeated phrase in a wooden voice.

"Why, yes," she said. "If, however, another time would be more convenient—"

"No," I insisted, opening the door and stepping aside to let her pass. "The present time is acceptable. There is also a matter I wish to discuss with you."

The young woman entered. I followed and closed the office door before walking round to my desk chair as she sat down in a chair facing me.

"Something is wrong," Miss Lamington said at once, holding the dossiers in her lap.

"I will be leaving Isham soon," I told her. "Moxon Ivery having been identified as our German spy, Sherlock Holmes now wishes me to return to London to pursue another matter with him."

"So I had been informed earlier today."

I looked at her earnest face and added, "I should tell you as well that I have evidence that removes your cousin, Mr. Wake, from consideration as a possible accomplice to Ivery."

Miss Lamington nodded. "I knew he could not be involved," she said, "but there was no proof. I will not ask you to share more of that information with me, but I thank you for telling me of its existence."

"I am glad that the matter has been resolved in the manner that it has." I considered telling her of Wake's decision to join the Labour Corps, but remembering his desire that it remain secret until he himself revealed it to others, I said nothing.

"Will you then tell me what bothers you so?" Miss Lamington enquired as she rose from her chair.

"Why, I regret having to leave Isham, of course."

"I am sure that is the case, Colonel, but I am also quite certain that there is a greater trouble gnawing your soul at this moment."

After several seconds spent staring at the top of my desk, I glanced up and into her eyes, which silently urged me to free myself.

"An officer with whom I was acquainted—a flyer—was killed in France some time ago. I have only this moment learnt of his death, from an offhand comment by a patient."

"Oh, dear Colonel Watson," she said.

Miss Lamington placed the dossiers on my desk and stepped behind me to boldly place a hand upon my shoulder, a comfort I did not refuse. "That is an awful thing, and all the more that you should learn of it in such a manner," she said. "I do so wish it were otherwise, but the war is taking from everyone, is it not? None of us is immune."

"I suppose not."

"I have an older friend—a fellow VAD from Derbyshire—who has lost her fiancé to the war. Imagine how her life has been turned inside out."

"Her loss is far greater than mine," I freely admitted. "Captain Harper—his name was Cecil Harper—was a momentary acquaintance, but he made a vast impression upon me, Miss Lamington."

“Perhaps,” she said, “perhaps, in these guarded moments when we converse as spies for Sir Walter Bullivant, you might call me Mary instead?”

I opened my mouth and then shook my head and gave a bittersweet smile. “It would seem odd to me to do so, Miss Lamington, for Mary was my late wife’s name.”

“When did you lose her?”

“Years ago, though each morning it seems to me as if it had happened the night before.”

A second hand took my other shoulder. I steeled myself against tears, and after a time Miss Lamington asked, “What was she like?”

“Small,” I said evenly. “Dainty and blonde. Her face might not have been viewed as lovely by some, but her expression was the sweetest one could have imagined, and her blue eyes so large and singularly spiritual.”

“And Captain Harper?”

“Cheerful, upright, devoted to duty. Worldly, to be sure, yet still an innocent boy in his way. And as fine as any son I might ever have wished to have, had I children of my own.”

“But you have lived long after your Mary’s passing, have you not?”

“Yes,” I said calmly. “She has a place in my mind and heart, but the soul does move on, does it not?”

“There,” declared Miss Lamington. “You have said it. Grasped it and stuffed it into a nutshell. Your soul will move on after the loss of Captain Harper as well, as it must.”

“I know that in my mind, Miss Lamington, but my heart has yet to be dragged into agreement.”

"Oh dear Uncle John," she said. "For that is what I will call you in our guarded moments from now on. You will never fear to confide in me? Tell me so. Whatever troubles befall you, never fail to search out my ear. Do you promise?"

I reached up and put a hand on one of hers. "You are ministering to a doctor now, instead of to patients as you should. I will be all right, Miss Lamington. I have become inured to the loss of my wife, as you have said. I have not become a hermit, to be sure. And, certainly, I will come to accept this latest loss in time."

"Yes, in time," she said. I could feel her determined eyes bearing down upon me. "But in the meanwhile, promise me you will talk to me if you feel such a need, Uncle John. Promise me?"

"Very well," I said. "I promise I will seek your counsel, though recall that I will not remain long here at Isham. Sherlock Holmes beckons me to London, you see," I stammered with a bitterness that surprised even me.

"And you do not wish to go?"

"I have found myself—here!" I said sharply. "It is here that I belong. At Isham. With my staff. With our patients. Everything and everyone here—which is my true place, one I do not wish to leave."

"Then do not," the young woman told me, lifting her hands from my shoulders. "Inform Mr. Holmes that—"

"But I cannot fail him," I said. "I cannot, you see, for I also found myself many years ago with him."

I turned round to look up at her.

"I was living in a private hotel on the Strand, having just returned from Afghanistan and leading a comfortless, meaningless existence—spending money and doing little else. And then I chanced to meet Sherlock

Holmes, and all that changed. I discovered friendship, meaning, and a renewed devotion to my profession—indeed, found a second profession as well, though Holmes will never admit to the legitimacy of it," I added, chuckling through my tears. "I cannot disappoint him, you see. He calls, and I must answer."

"I understand," said Miss Lamington. "And I cannot resolve your dilemma, Uncle John. I can only express my wish that you be happy. And as for this place," she said, stepping back to the front of my desk, "Well, I will be departing Isham as well, I suspect. Once Sir Walter decides what to do with Mr. Ivery, he will no doubt assign me elsewhere."

"I find it astounding that one so young as you and—if you do not mind my antiquated perspective—female should carry off so well this game of espionage."

"Thank you," said the young woman. "I take that as a compliment."

"And so it is." Feeling my composure returning, I gestured to her rakishly set cap and asked, "What is the subject you wish to bring to my attention?"

"I am to inform you that General Hannay departed for Glasgow earlier today."

I nodded. "Moxon Ivery is *his* battle now. Actually, for the moment, his and yours," I added, and I thought I detected a slight flush in her face as she stepped away from me.

"Well," I sighed, "I suppose we each should return to our work here, completing our duties before we are both scattered to the winds. Thank you, Miss Lamington—many times over." I put a hand upon the dossiers, still sitting before me. "I shall read these presently."

She gracefully stepped to the door and, with her hand on the knob, said as she left, "Take care of yourself, Uncle John."

Corporal Scaife arrived late that afternoon to take me home in the dogcart, and when we arrived at the cottage, a local boy was tending the burgeoning vegetable garden, framed by two rows of lavender. Though Mr. Jimson and I had discussed autumn crops, I knew now that my part in those plans must now be laid aside.

When I told Scaife on the journey home of our impending return to London, he expressed pleasure at being able to rejoin the service of Scotland Yard. I was also aware that Holmes was preparing to welcome his old housekeeper Martha back with uncharacteristically open arms, and I was certain that she, upon learning the news, would be more than ready to tend to his domestic needs again.

"Dinner will be ready at the usual hour," she said as I stepped into the cottage. "Oh, and Mrs. Jimson visited earlier. That South African fellow staying with them is off on holiday, she informed me. And she brought something for you, Colonel. It's in the sitting room."

She passed me with a smile and scurried off, and I stepped into the next room, where a bright bouquet of freshly cut sunflowers adorned a small table near the window.

Military cap in hand, I sat down in my armchair and stared at the cluster of large blooms, remembering Mrs. Jimson's promise of them when I had first arrived in Biggleswick. Each bronze seed stood out in a round centre, all spiralling outward with their fellows toward radiating petals of brilliant yellow. The etched contours of the vase in which their stems sat caught the tired light of a dying day, distilling it into phantom diamonds.

"He will not grow old," I said in a quiet voice, "as I have been left to grow old. Age will not weary him."

I sought my armchair and sat there as the sky outside faded and my vision filled with blurred patches of gold. And there, in undisturbed quiet, I remembered a beloved, fallen comrade while contemplating another, more than equally dear, who had called me yet again to his side.

Age, I promised myself, would not weary friendship, either.[182]

---

[182] The words uttered by Watson in his sitting room are a paraphrase of lines from "Ode of Remembrance," which itself is a portion of the poem "For the Fallen," written by Laurence Binyon and first published by *The Times* in 1914. It may be recalled that, in chapter 11, Watson relates how he saved newspaper articles and features during the opening campaign of the war. His reference to Binyon's piece suggests that "For the Fallen" may have been one of those items, and that its words had remained with him during the conflict.

BOOK TWO: THE WILD BIRDS

CHAPTER SIXTEEN: CHANGING THE GUARD

In the days following the revelation of Cecil Harper's fate, I found some small purpose in redoubling my efforts to prepare Isham for an imminent change in command, as well as gathering my household for moving back to London from the Cotswolds. I had been responsible for the hospital for less than half a year, but I believed that I had, in the course of those five months, significantly bolstered morale and made meaningful improvements to everyday practices, so as to leave the institution in a state far better than that in which I had found it.

And, indeed, as I participated as guest of honour at a farewell gathering, I felt touched as, in turn, patients and staff expressed appreciation for me. From Major Collins to Captains Simmons and Hughes on down to Sergeant-Major Ffolkes and Nurse Finch, I felt the strength of the ties that we had forged. Even Nurse Williams was moved to tears, and though Lieutenant Hooper nearly dropped the cake, Vespera Cochrane came to the rescue, taking hold of that treasure before its sublime layers tumbled onto the recreation room floor.

Glancing at Mary Lamington as I was given the first ceremonial slice, I savoured once more a sense of fulfilment in the secret knowledge that I had played a minor role in plumbing the depths of the reorganised Black Stone espionage group, as well as helping to unmask Moxon Ivery as its prime agent in Biggleswick. That feeling acquired an ironic twinge later that day, when I received through the post a present from the German spy—an ivory letter opener—along with wishes for a pleasant return to London and apologies for being unable to attend the gathering at Isham.

Still, as I received the congratulations of everyone, including Blaikie and Ashley Tate, who represented the patients, I was fearful that my return to Queen Anne Street would begin a descent into uselessness.

A day before my departure, I made my usual rounds, intending in particular to welcome yet another small group of new convalescents who had shipped in the night before. As I approached the north garden, I saw Ashley Tate and Blaikie sitting with two of those recent additions. The former, as I had noticed at my party, was beginning to exude a new calmness of the soul, though he still retained the nervous mannerisms so evident upon his arrival.

I strode closer, glad to see such swift progress in him, and noticing as well a far more vigorous spark of life in Blaikie's eyes than before. Smiling, I greeted the four men, silently wishing that somehow the war might end before they were all once more thrust into the breach.

"Ah, Colonel Watson!" declared Ashley Tate, raising a somewhat palsied hand in salute as I gestured for him and the others to remain seated. "Blaikie and I have been counselling the new boys here."

"Yes," declared the Rhodesian. "We have, we have been telling them all the wonderful secrets of Isham."

"And what are those?" I asked genially.

"Where Nurse Williams hides the extra sugarelly, for one," said Ashley Tate with a knowing smile. "And, for another, which doctor will let you pil-pil-pilfer his shag without a scolding afterward."

"And how to coax Nurse Cochrane to dance *extempore* in the wards," added the Blaikie with enthusiasm.

I smiled and turned to the pair of new men, who had been listlessly perusing week-old newspapers. They looked at me with the all too familiar mixture of worried hope and animal fear, and introductions were made in a very low key.

"Much happening in the world beyond the trenches," Ashley Tate remarked, motioning to the papers that our newcomers were holding. "What with all the rioting against German-born shopkeepers over here, I'm glad to read that we've finally got ourselves an English king, eh?" he said, playfully poking Blaikie, who laughed while holding up palms in defence, as the two other men looked on questioningly. "It's about bloody time we were ruled by one of our own, if you ask me."[183]

"I know it won't be in the papers, but will Nurse Cochrane be leaving as well?" asked Blaikie.

"What?" I asked.

"Will she be leaving with you, Colonel Watson?"

"Why would she be so inclined to join me in departing this place, Lieutenant?"

"Do you not like her?" Blaikie said.

"Well," I stammered, "I do respect her abilities greatly."

"Come now, Colonel," taunted Ashley Tate in a sly manner. "You can't fool an Old Contemptible like me, you know.[184] You fancy her greatly, just as she does you. Everyone is aware of it."

"But I do not—"

---

[183] Ashley Tate's remark is probably in reference to the British Royal Family's change of surname, which at the beginning of the war was Saxe-Coburg and Gotha, derived from Prince Albert, husband of Queen Victoria. Because of strong anti-German sentiment in Britain during the First World War, however, King George V changed the family name to Windsor by proclamation on July 17, 1917.

[184] The relatively small professional army that Britain fielded in the fall of 1914 was virtually destroyed during the first months of the war while helping blunt early German advances through France and Belgium. Kaiser Wilhelm was alleged to have expressed exasperation with the "contemptible little army" that was delaying the victory of his forces, though there is no proof he ever made such a statement. The British survivors of 1914 thereafter were referred to as The Old Contemptibles, however, a title they bore with pride.

"We talk about it," said Blaikie without a semblance of discretion. He turned to the two new patients. "We all do," he told them. "The nurses speak of it as well."

Ashley Tate suddenly burst into song:

Smile the while you kiss me sad adieu,
When the clouds roll by I'll come to you...

Blaikie joined him in the next lines:

Then the skies will see more blue,
Down in lovers' lane my dearie...

Ashley Tate gestured to the pair of newcomers who, though uncertain of the words, haltingly made it a quartet:

Wedding bells will ring so merrily,
Ev'ry tear will be a memory...

Seeing the sudden joy flowing from the faces of the four men, I could not burst their bubble of passing happiness and so joined them for the final refrain:

So wait and pray each night for me,
Till we meet again.[185]

Blaikie applauded, and the other three followed. The clapping being directed at me, I playfully bowed to them all in turn, patted Blaikie's shoulder, and bade all the officers a good day, wishing to be off before I let slip that I would be dining with Miss Cochrane that very evening.

---

185 These words are the chorus finale of the song "Till We Meet Again," written by the Americans Richard Whiting and Raymond Egan. However, Watson's memory seems faulty here, for the song was not published until 1918, a year after this episode in the narrative occurs. A recording of "Till We Meet Again" by Henry Burr and Albert Campbell was the number one hit of 1919, though, and the recollection of that success may have led the doctor to misremember which piece the men sang. That he knew the words, no matter what the song, suggests a musical aspect of Watson's character that perhaps remains unexplored.

§ § §

The meal, however, was not unchaperoned. In addition to Martha and Scaife, who of course were present in the cottage during my last night there, Mary Lamington and Launcelot Wake, as well as the Jimsons, shared the table at this farewell dinner.

"We will so greatly miss your company," said Mrs. Jimson with regret.

"That we will," agreed her husband. "A better neighbour one could not hope for. Yes, your absence will leave a void, Colonel."

"And you will very much be missed by the patients of Isham," said Vespera Cochrane over soup. "Missed most grievously."

"You will be missed by everyone," corrected Miss Lamington, and Miss Cochrane nodded agreement as she stared into her bowl. "But duty is duty," the younger woman added.

"Indeed it is," I said, and as Miss Cochrane looked up at me while Wake, the Jimsons, and Miss Lamington paid attention to their soup, I added, "But duty does not exclude all else."

"Speaking of duty," said Launcelot Wake abruptly, "I have a confession to make to you all."

The three women and Mr. Jimson put down their spoons and turned toward the young man as he glanced at me before announcing, "I shall be joining the Labour Corps next month."

Miss Lamington gave a start and the Jimsons both gasped, while Miss Cochrane calmly returned to her soup.

"Good for you, young man," the latter intoned before taking a sip.

"Thank you," said Wake. "I've decided it is what I must do," he added, speaking directly to his cousin.

"But why?" asked Miss Lamington in disbelief.

"Is it not something you might do, Mary, were you a man?"

"But all that you have said about the war—"

"Does not contradict the choice I have made," Wake decreed.

"Aye," said Mr. Jimson thoughtfully. "I can see the philosophy in that."

"I believe you do yourself well," Miss Cochrane interjected. "My own opposition to the war does not preclude volunteering at Isham, after all," she explained. Her eye lingered on me for a moment, and then she turned to Wake to complete her thought. "And Mr. Letchford, as pacifist as I, has offered to hold regular literary gatherings at the hospital as well. Is that not correct, Colonel?"

"Oh yes, he has. I believe the first of those meetings, which I will of course not be able to attend, concerns young Mr. Aronson's recent novel."

"A pity," said Vespera Cochrane as she again dipped a spoon into her broth. "I expect discussion of that travesty will set many patients back somewhat. I am certain, however, that you, Mr. Wake, will extract some shred of nobility from this awful conflict through your action. I say more power to you."

"Hear, hear," said Mr. Jimson, patting the table with his hand while his wife smiled tearfully.

"But will you not be amid the fighting?" asked Mary Lamington with concern. "While you do your vital work for the government here, Launcelot, you are at least safe."

"Sometimes, physical security should be the least of our worries," the young man said. "In any event, I am signed up and will not back out, though I am leaving tomorrow for one last trek around Skye. I suppose I will miss that place, but there will be new vistas in France. You can attest to that, can you not, Colonel Watson?"

I paused, uncertain how to answer, for though I could confirm that fresh panoramas would greet the new enlistee across the Channel, I also knew that they would, most of them, be desolate ones beyond the common imagination. And so I merely shrugged and finished my soup, still uncertain of my parting words to Vespera Cochrane later that evening.

The following day, I left Biggleswick knowing that should I ever return in future, it would be as visitor rather than resident. I had, over the course of the previous week, bade farewell to those in the village with whom I had had any degree of real intercourse, including Letchford and Aronson, the three Weekes sisters and their mother, and the two Wymondhams—Miss Claire and Miss Doria. The Jimsons, Mary Lamington, and her cousin, Launcelot Wake, saw me off at the station, where Frederick Shaw and I caught sight of but did not acknowledge one another. At nearly the last moment, Nurse Williams arrived, scurrying onto the platform to present me with a bouquet of flowers from the staff and patients of Isham and, to no little embarrassment on both our parts, hold me in a farewell embrace.

Martha accompanied me in the carriage, with Scaife to follow on a later train with the greater bulk of my luggage, and so I arrived in Queen Anne Street that afternoon burdened by only a single valise, the one that had flown with me in Cecil Harper's aeroplane to Dumfries three years before.

"Ah, you are a welcome sight!" exclaimed Sherlock Holmes as he greeted Martha, who still held Nurse Williams's flowers, leaving me to enter relatively unnoticed with my baggage. "I trust you are ready to reassume command of this abode," he told the returning housekeeper, "assuming that the colonel is still amenable. You have, I trust, no objection, Watson?" he asked, paying attention to me at last.

"Was it not understood from the beginning?" I said wearily as I headed, valise in hand, toward my room. I stopped after but a few paces, immediately noticing the untidiness that had continued to blossom in Martha's absence. Turning round to face Holmes, I said casually, "How long have you been maintaining this residence on your own?"

"A bit too long, I fear."

"And the cook left as well, you said."

"Yes," replied my friend. "That was the housekeeper's fault entirely."

"And what have you done for meals?"

"I have dined out with regularity," the detective replied primly.

"I see. Martha," I declared, "you appear to face a most—"

"It will take no time at all to whip this house into shape, Colonel," the housekeeper declared cheerfully. "And as for meals, I expect I can find a suitable cook in little time, but until then, I will be happy to provide you with meals—for a proper temporary adjustment of wage."

"Done," said Holmes without hesitation, and though formally the decision was mine, I voiced no objection.

"You have no idea what a challenge I faced when I moved into his Sussex cottage years ago," the woman said. She glanced round and sighed. "Granted, I was younger then. Still, as bad as all this looks at present, it will be child's play compared to my earlier experience."

"Why, Martha," said Holmes incredulously, "I had no idea—"

"You never do, sir," interjected the housekeeper. "Now go to your rooms, gentlemen—or take refuge in the sitting room, if you like. I wish to get an immediate start on this task."

We chose the latter course. I spent some time relating to Holmes my experiences at Isham after he had departed Biggleswick.

"Allow me to once more express my condolences regarding Cecil Harper," said my friend, who had written to me following news of the young man's death. "Though I never met him, I am certain he was as fine an individual as you have described."

"It is the finest that this war is consuming," I replied.

"Then join me in stopping it," said my friend.

"That is why I have answered your summons," I replied in an even voice.

"And it is most appreciated, old fellow." The detective leaned back in his armchair. "The third German spy ring has still not made itself evident," he said. "Yet I know in my bones it lies somewhere, dormant, on our island."

"Its hibernation must be very deep. Certainly, it has been very long."

"Indeed, Watson, and it is—"

Just then the house bell rang.

Moments later, Martha ushered Sir Walter Bullivant into the room. After greetings and casual talk, the spymaster discussed a few matters of business with Holmes and then unexpectedly spoke of my new duties for the RAMC.

"Formally, Watson, you have been gazetted to the general staff of the medical corps, serving as a secretary," Bullivant declared. "Your work in setting Isham hospital on a good footing created quite an impression here in London, even more so than your admirable two years as an instructor at Aldershot. Your superiors believe your bureaucratic skills are impeccable and are looking forward to adding you to their administrative cadre. Of course, M and I have arranged matters so that the demands on you will be minimal, allowing you to devote most of your time to assisting Holmes, as he requested."

I nodded, making certain I displayed no disappointment. Though I had hoped that I might be given some kind of duty at one of the many military hospitals in the metropolis, I knew that Holmes was insistent that I remain on call for him.

And so it would be, I silently told myself.

"Sir Walter has assured me that much of your clerical work may be done here in Queen Anne Street," added Holmes cautiously. "That allows me to draw upon your counsel directly while searching for the elusive third branch of Cerberus."

"You referred to that investigation earlier," I said to Holmes. "But what of your work in Office 54? Do you no longer crack codes for them?"

"I do, from time to time," my friend replied in a plaintive voice. He smiled, though his eyes did not sparkle, as he added, "For recreation."

"Holmes now works on the greatest cipher of all, Watson," Bullivant declared. "His energies are directed at the enigma of that German sleeping cell, as we now term it."

"And a great mystery it has become," said Sherlock Holmes. "But Shinwell Johnson and Frank Farrar are due here within the hour, to give me another report of any signs of possible activity they may have come across."

"And do you anticipate any joy from that meeting?" Sir Walter asked.

"*Dum spiro spero,*" was Holmes's succinct reply.[186]

"I suppose I can say the same with respect to Richard Hannay," Bullivant sighed, a comment that prompted Holmes to enquire about Bullivant's once and present agent.

"We have received nothing since Andrew Amos's report that Hannay had taken passage aboard a ship on which Abel Gresson is serving as purser," related the spymaster. "It's a waiting game for us now, as far as the matter is concerned. We can only hope that all goes well, and that Hannay ferrets out Gresson's contact in the Black Stone network."

"And what of Mary Lamington?" I asked, for though I had seen her that very morning, I was anxious concerning Sir Walter's future plans for her.

"She remains in Biggleswick at present," Bullivant said. "Her assignment is the continued watch over Moxon Ivery, as well as determining what contacts he may have in his portion of the German spy network. We know, after all, that Blenkiron's false article reached him from Gresson, but we still do not know through what intermediate chain of agents that was accomplished."

"Do you expect to apprehend Ivery and Gresson soon?" I enquired.

"Once we have something firm with which to form the basis for an arrest, we will take them in," replied Sir Walter. "Thus far, we are confident that we have our men—or at least, some of them—but there is not enough evidence to satisfy a court of law, even in wartime. Until then, we wait on both Mary and Hannay to supply us with the final proof."

§ § §

---

[186] "While I breathe, I hope" is a modern paraphrase of the sentiment expressed by, among others, the Roman statesman Cicero.

It was not quite an hour later, just after Sir Walter had departed Queen Anne Street, that the unlikely pair of Frank Farrar and Shinwell Johnson were escorted into our sitting room by Martha.

"Greetings, sirs," said the bluff Johnson as he shambled into our presence, billycock hat in hand. "And welcome back to your digs here, Doctor," he added. "I hope the place is as cosy as you remember it."

"I agree with that sentiment," said Farrar, another former agent of Holmes who had, with his companion, formed a detection enterprise of their own.

"Do the two of you have any items of interest today?" interjected Sherlock Holmes with a hint of impatience. "The past week brought nothing, if you recall."

"As have all the weeks previous, sadly," agreed Farrar. "However, we can offer three reports this time, sir," he added. The man ran fingers through his auburn hair as he sat down beside his colleague Johnson, who had already accepted Holmes's silent offer of a chair. "Two of them are from individuals who came to us as potential clients," Farrar said.

"The third springs from a very interesting observation that Frank here made only yesterday off Piccadilly Circus," added Johnson.

Sherlock Holmes leaned back in his armchair and tilted his head, supporting it in the palm of one hand. "That all sounds most promising. Pray proceed, then," he said. "Select one item and give me its details."

"Well," replied Shinwell Johnson, leaning forward in his chair, "the first is from a case brought but yesterday by a woman in Ilford. She came begging us to investigate a matter for no monetary fee, offering instead a collection of shawls she had knitted."

“We accepted, for otherwise she would not tell us her story,” interjected Farrar, “and we feared letting the opportunity slip.”

“The matter formally does not involve her,” explained Johnson with a coy expression. “Rather, she claims to be acting on behalf of a friend.”

“I see,” said Holmes with a wan smile. “Pray, proceed.”

“The supposed friend is the wife of a dockworker, as is the woman who spoke to us—so her story goes. The husband—that is, the husband of the woman who is her friend—”

“Presumably,” interjected Farrar.

“Whoever’s husband it is,” said Johnson, “he is not eating his breakfast.”

“Did you make clear you were consulting detectives, not physicians?” said Holmes.

“It does not appear to be a case of loss of appetite, sir,” replied Farrar. “The wife has seen the man slip his morning bread and cheese into a pocket, after which he claims to have hastily eaten the meal. She provides him with a lunch that she understands he consumes at the docks, but of course she does not witness him do so. She can, however, testify that he hungrily devours his evening meal—bread, drippings, jam, and tea, say—right before her. It is the breakfast that he pockets, and perhaps the lunch, but she does not know why.”

“Perhaps it is better that she not know,” said Holmes.

“You think it best we not pursue it?” asked Johnson.

“How the two of you choose to run your agency is, of course, not my concern—other than during the intervals when you assist the government in flushing out German spies and saboteurs.”

“The husband’s behaviour seems out of the ordinary,” said Johnson.

"Oh, I grant that it is hardly commonplace," admitted Holmes, "though, I must say, it is not unheard of, either—do you recall the similar events at Madeira Lodge years ago, Watson? One or more possible solutions come to mind at once, though certainly not the one we fixed upon two decades ago."

Both Johnson and Farrar leaned forward expectantly, and Holmes reached for his cherrywood pipe and shag.

"And what might those solutions be, sir?" Shinwell Johnson enquired.

"I will leave that determination in your capable hands," said Holmes, stuffing his pipe. "I suppose the man could be foregoing his breakfast—and possibly his lunch as well—in order to give the food to someone else, and that individual in turn could be a German spy, though I doubt it," he said, while reaching for a vesta. "Berlin may be...callous at times...toward its agents in many ways, but...it does not leave them to starve," the detective declared, successfully lighting his pipe.

Farrar and Johnson looked at Holmes cautiously.

"On the other hand," said the detective, tossing his spent vesta onto the coals, "if the man is trading his unconsumed meals for goods or a service, one wonders what they might be." Holmes gave a listless shrug as he exhaled a cloud of smoke upward. "Should you find yourselves with little else to do, taking the case might be of interest, particularly if you have a use for the shawls. I doubt that it will help us much with the Cerberus riddle, however."

"I suppose we will consider it," Farrar replied, looking sheepishly at his partner.

"It appears we continue to disappoint, Mr. Holmes," said Shinwell Johnson.

My friend smiled in a kindly way and held his pipe above his lap. "The two of you never disappoint," he said. "I must admit, of course, that the story you have just laid before me seems somewhat unremarkable, and capable of explanation without the use of foreign agents. Nonetheless, I encourage you to pursue it, and we will see what develops. As you mentioned but a moment ago, we should not throw any opportunity out the window. But you have two more reports, you said. Might I know the details of the next?" said Holmes, studying his cherrywood before inserting the stem into his mouth once more.

"There is a matter involving the master of a sailing barge that usually ties up at the old St. Katharine Docks," said Johnson.[187] "The man is named Tatty Evans, and his barge is the *Belisama*."

Holmes listened carefully to the agent.

"The *Belisama* was plying its trade three weeks ago, coming in from the coast with a load of bricks before it was to take on some coke for shipment to Murston[188]. As the barge was passing the pumping station at

---

[187]Sailing barges were flat-bottomed sailing boats, mostly built of wood and perhaps ninety feet long with two masts. They were common commercial vessels on the Thames into the early twentieth century, used to carry cargo such as bricks, sand, coal and other goods. They were manned by small crews that often numbered only two. Meanwhile, the St. Katharine Docks were located on the north side of the Thames, just east of Tower Bridge. Unable to accommodate large ships, these docks were not a great success after opening in 1828 and in the 1860s were incorporated into the neighboring London Docks. The area sustained heavy damage by bombing during the Second World War, and the site is now a housing and leisure complex.

[188] "Coke" refers here to the fuel usually made from coal. Murston is located near the Kentish coast, a few miles southeast of the mouth of the River Thames.

Crossness,[189] a motor launch sped by, crossing dangerously close to the *Belisama*'s bow."

"Rudeness is known to occur upon the waves as well as ashore," Holmes observed.

"And water does not necessarily calm the soul," replied Farrar. "Master Evans on board the *Belisama* shouted angrily at the person steering the launch."

Holmes raised his brows slightly.

"An individual at the stern of the launch then shouted back these words: 'I have the nose full with your complaint.'" Farrar said. "He also called out, 'Our errand is the more important: you can take poison on that.'"

My friend's brows surpassed their previous acme, and his lips curled into a smile as he gripped the cherrywood with his teeth. "Gad," he said before withdrawing the pipe from his mouth. "The simple elegance of the observation it makes your report all the more sweet."

"We thought you would be pleased," said Shinwell Johnson with satisfaction.

"I clearly do not grasp the reason for your shared sense of fulfilment," I noted. "Are rudeness and disdain for the safety of others sufficient to mark a person as being a German spy?"

"No," said Holmes, holding his pipe aloft. "Our own countrymen exhibit those tendencies altogether too often themselves. Rather, Watson, it is the method of expressing such attitudes that is of interest. 'I have the

---

[189] Crossness is on the southern bank of the Thames in the eastern reaches of the metropolis. The sewage pumping station there was constructed in the mid-nineteenth century and decommissioned in the 1950s.

nose full' and 'you can take poison on that' are the direct English translations of distinctly German phrases."

I waited for elaboration.

"A German might say, 'I have the nose full' instead of 'enough is enough,' as we would," explained Farrar.

"And 'you can take poison on that' is roughly akin to saying 'you can bet your life on it,'" added Johnson.

"The hand aboard the motor launch may have lost his temper when Master Evans berated him for recklessness," observed Holmes. "He had sufficient control to speak in English, but he still expressed himself through his native idiom," he added. "That is my conclusion. Did Master Evans note the name of the launch?"

"Yes," said Johnson. "It is called the *Nemesis*."

Holmes smiled as he again studied his pipe. "A perhaps revealing title."

"One you will no doubt take to heart," I said in a droll voice.

"Just so," replied my friend. He turned to Farrar and Johnson. "Have you more?"

"There is a sequel of sorts," said Farrar. "The *Belisama* reached the docks safely and unloaded her cargo of brick. After taking on the coke for Murston, she set sail three days later, heading down the river toward the coast. As the barge passed the Trinity lighthouses,[190] she encountered the *Nemesis* again, also headed downstream, but this time at a safe distance.

---

[190] Located at Trinity Buoy Wharf, which was used for the docking and repair of lightships, the lighthouses were built in the 1850s and 1860s and used to train lighthouse keepers and to conduct experiments in new technologies. One was demolished in the 1920s, and the surviving structure is no longer used as a lighthouse.

"Nonetheless, Tatty Evans recognised the launch and shouted at the crew again, venting his anger at the previous incident. Everyone on board the other craft ignored him, except for two men—one pointed a finger at his own temple, and the other threw an object at the barge. That hit the water nowhere near the *Belisama*, but the mere act outraged Master Evans even more.

"As the launch was the much swifter vessel, it quickly vanished from view, and that was that, but Evans was now bent upon vengeance. Returning to London days later, he tried to discover where the *Nemesis* tied up in order to speak to its captain. His enquireies failed to locate her, however, and so he came to us in hopes that we might track down the launch."

"And what does Mr. Evans wish to do when the other boat is found?" asked Holmes.

"Give the captain and crew a piece of his mind, apparently," replied Johnson. "It has become an obsession with the man, if you ask me."

I stared knowingly at Holmes as the agent characterised Evans's state of mind, but my friend did not look in my direction. Instead, he took two more puffs on his pipe before setting it down.

"There is nothing conclusive contained in those events," he remarked, making a steeple of his fingers. "However, it would appear that at least one crew member of the *Nemesis* is a native German, though that says nothing about his loyalties in the present conflict, let alone the likelihood that he is an agent of Berlin. Still, it is a most intriguing brace of episodes that you have presented."

Farrar and Johnson shifted in their seats as Holmes fell into silent thought.

"And where is the *Belisama* now?" my friend enquired after a moment. "I assume that, since Master Evans has just brought the matter to your attention, his vessel is still here in London, at its usual mooring?"

"It is, sir," replied Johnson. "Until Tuesday."

Holmes turned to me. "Do you fancy a trip to the St. Katharine Docks, Watson?"

"Now that I am returned from Biggleswick, I am at your disposal."

Holmes reached again for his pipe. After making certain its fire had not gone out, he said to the pair of agents, "There was one last matter to which you referred, I believe."

Farrar glanced at Johnson, who nodded.

"Yes, sir," said the former. "It is not a potential case brought by a would-be client, in the manner of the other two, but rather something that I myself observed yesterday—or, rather, some*one* whom I observed."

Sherlock Holmes brought the pipe up to his lips and nodded for Farrar to continue.

"Well," the younger man said, "yesterday I stopped at the Lloyd Corner House in Piccadilly to meet with friends.[191] It was there I chanced to see at a far table a man I knew who frequented the Golden Lamb's Cave before the war.[192] That fellow was a German who went by the name of Dietrich Baumann. I knew him as Dieter then."

---

[191] This is likely a fictionalized reference to the Lyons Corner Houses, which were owned by the Lyons conglomerate that included restaurants, food manufacturing, and hotels. The Corner Houses were generally large buildings which contained food counters, hair salons, telephone booths, differently themed restaurants, and more.

[192] This may an alias for the Cave of the Golden Calf, which was perhaps the first openly gay bar in London, as that term is understood today, though by the time of this episode, that establishment had closed. In passing, it should also be noted that during these years, waitresses at the Lyons Corner House in Piccadilly regularly reserved a section of that establishment for homosexuals; the area became known as the Lily Pond. These references—as well as others—suggest that Frank Farrar was gay, and they may also casts doubt on the authenticity of this narrative, for—based on his earlier writings—it is

Holmes's eyes widened as he puffed.

"On this occasion, I did not accost him, nor did I give him the slightest attention," Farrar said. "I am certain he never noticed me, but I did discreetly observe him, getting close enough at one moment to even hear his voice, and I can swear it was Dieter, sir. He appeared to now be going by the name of Denis, however, and there was no trace of foreign accent in his speech, as there had been five years ago. He was talking like an Englishman, and I heard him claim to hail from Manchester—and certainly he sounded as if he had been born and raised in Canal Street itself."[193]

"Yet you are certain he was the German with whom you were acquainted before the war."

"Without question, Mr. Holmes." Farrar shrugged. "Dieter had two distinctive moles on one cheek, as did this man. And, having become closely acquainted with him, I am quite sure that this fellow was Dieter."

"Did you pursue him further that day?"

"Once I was certain of his identity, I thought it best to steer clear and not attract his attention in turn," Farrar said. "But after he left in the company of an army private, I made some discreet, indirect enquiries, and I gleaned small pieces of additional information."

Holmes looked expectantly at Farrar.

---

unlikely that Watson would have included such direct suggestions of Farrar's presumed sexual orientation.

[193] Canal Street is in Manchester. Ironically, it is now the center of that city's gay village.

"He spoke to more than one person about working in the vicinity of the gasworks," said the young man. "Though in what capacity and for what firm, he did not mention."[194]

"Did you make any observation of his person from which conclusions might be drawn?" asked Holmes.

"Aside from identifying him as Dieter, only one," Farrar replied. "I recalled the fellow having soft, gentle hands," he said, somewhat self-consciously. "Now, more than once in the Corner House, he hoisted a glass while I watched from within my own coterie of friends, and I caught a good look at his hands. They appeared as smooth as I recalled them being years ago. Whatever work he performs, sir, it cannot be heavy manual labour."

Holmes nodded. "What more did you know of this Dieter before, when he lived openly as a German?"

"At the time, he said he was from Berlin and employed at the German embassy as a footman. He waited upon one of the diplomats in particular."

"Do you recall which one?" Holmes asked pointedly.

Farrar thought for a moment. "The fellow he served had a title," he said. "It was a Baron Von Hertung or Herling, I believe. He said that person was—"

"Baron Von Herling," said Holmes. "The Chief Secretary of the legation."

"Yes," said Farrar. "That was his position."

---

[194] From subsequent descriptions, this may have been the Beckton Gasworks, opened in 1870 for the purpose of manufacturing coal gas and coke. It was located in the eastern portion of London, on the north bank of the Thames, and was one of the largest such plants ever constructed.

"Chief Secretary," repeated Sherlock Holmes. "And the overseer of Heinrich Von Bork, we may recall," he added, casting a look in my direction.

Farrar and Johnson looked on expectantly.

"Well, I believe you have given us a very slight but also very firm handhold," Holmes said. "The mountain top is not assured, but we now have something with which to begin our ascent."

Johnson reached over and gave Farrar a friendly slap on the back. "You've done mighty well, lad," he said. "Should we follow upon this opening, Mr. Holmes?"

"Yes, but discreetly," said my friend. Pointing the stem of his pipe at the pair of assistants, he first addressed Farrar.

"Attend the Corner House in Piccadilly with regularity," Holmes said. "And discreetly make the rounds of those clubs you think Dieter might visit."

"Yes, sir," said Farrar, appearing somewhat puzzled. "You mean for me to observe him only, or to follow him as well?"

"You are merely to note his presence. For the moment, do not attempt to observe him at length, should your paths cross. I do not wish him to notice you. I merely desire to learn what premises he frequents; we will not worry at present about whether there is any pattern to his visits to those establishments."

"I understand, Mr. Holmes."

"Dieter will be more closely observed and followed in time, but by someone else," my friend said without further explanation. "Your charge is to lay the groundwork for that task."

"Of course," said Farrar. "I'll be certain to not exceed my boundaries."

"Good. Meanwhile," he said to Shinwell Johnson, "I wish you to reconnoitre the area of the gasworks."

Johnson curled his nose. "I don't fancy having to endure the aroma of that district," he said, "but I will do my best, sir."

Holmes smiled. "Have Farrar describe his German in greater detail to you, if he has not done so already, and of course keep an eye out for the man. However, your prime duty is to discreetly investigate the nature of any businesses—particularly newer ones—in the area surrounding the gasworks, as well as to keep an eye out for any items of interest that present themselves. Our opening is a slim one, and we must try to coax it wider, rather than apply brute force."

"We understand, sir," replied Johnson.

My friend sat silent for a moment and then motioned for Farrar and Johnson to depart. Both rose from their chairs, and Holmes and I got to our feet as well.

"The information about the German was excellent work," declared Holmes, "and I believe that the matter of Tatty Evans and the *Belisama* will also prove most fruitful. Meanwhile," he added in a light tone, "I hope you have good fortune in resolving your female client's case of the uneaten breakfast."

"We will see to them all, sir," said Johnson. He stood and shook hands with Holmes, as did Farrar, and the two bade me farewell also before seeing themselves out of the sitting room.

Holmes leaned against the mantel as we heard Martha escort the pair to our house door. He placed the cherrywood between his teeth and raised his chin. "With these developments, Watson, we have our first glimmerings."

"The beginning of the next act?"

"Yes," he said. "After Galloway and Biggleswick, the third act, which I expect to play out here in London. Let us hope it is the final one in our drama."

The next day, Holmes and I journeyed down East Smithfield Road to the St. Katharine Docks, which a half century earlier had been amalgamated into the London Docks.[195] We passed furious activity while skirting both the East and West Basins, observing ships being unloaded and their goods immediately placed in warehouses that were built right upon the quayside. At length, we came across the barge *Belisama,* anchored in a far reach.

She was a fetching craft, having been recently painted, with a yellow stripe running round her flared sides and ends, and a transom as shapely as any champagne glass. Standing on deck, between the mainmast and one leeboard, was a tall lad in an open, ragged wool coat whom I took to be the mate or perhaps a hand, if the master was able to afford an additional crewmember. Holmes called down to him, and the fellow looked up, shielding his eyes against the sun.[196]

---

[195] Begun a generation before the St. Katharine Docks, which they came to incorporate, the London Docks were finally closed to shipping in 1969, and portions of the land were eventually used for development.

[196] The transom of a vessel is the surface that forms its stern. Those of Thames sailing barges were indeed shaped like champagne glasses, with a large rudder hanging from them. Leeboards, meanwhile, are foils on the side of sailing vessels used to prevent a craft from lifting from the water when it leans under the force of the wind. Thames sailing barges possessed two such devices. That Watson was familiar with naval terminology and this type of craft in particular suggests another unexplored aspect of his personal history, one consistent with his apparent love of nautical fiction: a possible connection with sea or river transport.

“Aye, what ye want?” the young man asked.

“I wish to speak with the master, Tatty Evans,” replied Holmes. “Is he about?”

“No,” said a large bearded man who emerged from the open fore hatch. “He’s below. Well,” he added, looking at his upper body, which was visible above the opening. “Half below, at least. I am Tatty Evans, sir,” he said amiably, stepping onto the deck. “Might I do something for you?”

“May we come aboard first?” asked my friend.

Evans gestured for us to join him on the *Belisama*, and I followed Holmes onto the sailing barge. The young man we had first encountered stepped aside to allow us to pass him and face the vessel’s master directly.

“I am Sherlock Holmes,” said my friend, extending a hand. “I come as an ally of Mr. Johnson and Mr. Farrar, whose agency I believe you recently consulted. This is my associate, Colonel John Watson.”

“Aye,” replied Evans, accepting Holmes’s greeting and then taking my hand in turn. “I read of your adventures when I was younger than Old George here. Go back down below and finish what I started,” he told the boyish mate, who disappeared down the fore hatch.

“He’s a halfway decent one,” the master remarked. “He’ll be better when he truly is old and more practised, eh? Now then,” he said, “you are here in the matter of that accursed motor launch and its blaspheming crew?”

“Yes.”

“Very good, sir,” said Evans, twisting his face up into an expression of indignation. “Incivility riles me,” he confessed. “Some may suggest I forgive and forget, but behaviour such as theirs does not belong anywhere along the length of our sacred river, I tell you. I want nothing more than to dress down that irresponsible captain and crew, as is proper."

"I understand," said Holmes. "And I am prepared to assist you."

"That is much appreciated, sir. Where do you propose to start?"

"First, of course, we must find the craft. It is called the *Nemesis*, I understand."

"That is what was etched upon her stern plate," Evans said. "When she came so close to us that first time, there was no difficulty reading it, by God. Uncivil and reckless, it was."

"I concur."

"And how will you find her?" the man asked. "Old George and I have looked up and down the docks here ourselves when we had the time, but there was nary a sign of her."

"I was going to suggest that you continue to seek her out upon the river, Master Evans, since you are the one with the sailing barge."

"But I have cargo to haul, Mr. Holmes. I cannot take days or perhaps weeks to find the *Nemesis*. Had I that luxury, I should not be here talking with you."

"Do you haul independently?" asked the detective.

"Yes. I own the *Belisama* and hire her out to those who need her services, but I do have regular clients, such as the local Borough Council and the Smythe Brothers. Why?"

"I propose to hire you to prowl the river in search of the *Nemesis*, Master Evans."

The burly captain laughed. "Is that not dressing the wrong man? I came to your associates in hopes that they would find her for me—and I am prepared to pay for the service. Now you wish to reverse the relationship?"

"One may look upon it in that manner," replied Holmes, reaching into a jacket pocket. "And yes," he said, drawing out a leather booklet, "it is I who am now prepared to pay you, Mr. Evans."

The master of the *Belisama* was taken aback.

"May I use that crate as a writing desk?" asked Holmes, who pulled out a kerchief, spread it upon the deck, and then knelt beside the box despite Evans's lack of immediate response.

"Well, of course you may, but—"

"I am only slightly familiar with shipping rates these days," said the detective as he unfolded the booklet, revealing a tablet of cheques. He removed a pen from another pocket and began to fill out the topmost form. "Still, I will multiply by a factor of five to be sure, yielding what I believe you will find to be a more than adequate payment for the amount of time you are likely to spend in your search. There," he said, pulling the completed cheque from the booklet and holding it out to Master Evans. "I assume it is Tatty with a *y*?"

"It is," said the man before accepting the cheque. He held it with the fingers of both hands and read the amount many times over before exclaiming, "Llŷr, Poseidon, and Davey Jones combined![197] This amount is more than I would expect to reap in—"

"And it is yours," said Holmes with a smile. "If you agree to become my agent rather than my client. Of course, accepting the role of the one will serve the needs of the other."

---

[197] Llŷr is a Welsh god of the sea, as Poseidon is the ancient Greek god of waters. Davey Jones is the devil of the sea in sailor and pirate lore.

"I see that point clearly, Mr. Holmes! You've a deal. The *Belisama* is your hire for—"

"For as long as it takes you to locate where the *Nemesis* ties up. Should that require another payment," my friend said, gesturing toward the cheque, "you need only inform me."

"Of course," stammered Evans, carefully putting the slip of paper into a coat pocket. "But understand this, Mr. Holmes: the *Nemesis*, she's fast. She's like a clipper out there on the water, for sure, and the *Belisama* can hardly compete with her speed."

"I supposed that to be the case. However, I believe that by careful, successive positioning of your boat over the course of time, you may narrow your search effectively without need of actual pursuit. I will advise you with respect to such a strategy."

There was the sound of footsteps from below, and then the young man called Old George appeared in the forehatch.

"Ha, Georgie!" said Tatty Evans. "You've come back up just in time to share a life of luxury. Here, lad, and listen to the man," he added, gesturing toward Holmes.

The master of the *Belisama* briefly explained his arrangement with Holmes, and my friend then spent a quarter hour discussing with the two men how their barge was to be employed in searching for the *Nemesis*. Afterward, the detective and I departed in order to make our way, silently at first, across the docks and on back to the East Smithfield Road.

At length, I asked, "Do you believe Evans can possibly find the *Nemesis*? And we have no way of knowing that the motor launch is being used by a German spy ring, do we?"

"There is no absolute assurance, certainly, with respect to your second question, Watson. Yet between the strong suggestion that at least one member of the launch's crew is a native German and Farrar's espying of the enigmatic Dieter, we have little else on which to base any action at all. It is all or nothing, even though we possess little or nothing."

"I do hope you have not mortally damaged your financial standing with that cheque you gave Tatty Evans."

Holmes nodded. "Oh, I am naturally generous," said he. "Especially with the government's money."

I looked at my friend, who smiled back. "Mycroft deposited a rather large sum in my account some time ago, for use as a slush fund."[198]

I shrugged. "Well, Evans is certainly dedicated to finding the *Nemesis*," I said.

"Yes, and that is a principal reason for paying him to conduct the search, rather than the other way round. His familiarity with the river and those who inhabit it are other points in favour of the present arrangement. Even at the price Mycroft has paid, Evans will prove a bargain, I think. But come along, old fellow," he said, rubbing his hands together. "There is a chill in the air, and I fancy a bath at the Imperial. Do you care to join me?"[199]

"Allow me to signal for a taxicab," I said.

"I am certain you will find your staff duties with the medical corps challenging enough to suit you, Watson," said Sherlock Holmes that

---

[198] The phrase "slush fund" dates from the mid-nineteenth century. It was originally a nautical term for money collected from selling slush, the leftover grease from meat cooked aboard ship. That money, in turn, was usually employed to buy luxuries for the vessel.
[199] Holmes is expressing a desire to experience a Turkish bath at the Imperial Hotel.

evening as we occupied the sitting room: I reading in the basket chair and Holmes on the carpet, with papers and books scattered about him. Neither of us had spoken for the past half hour.

"I beg pardon?" I said.

Holmes put aside the magnifying glass with which he had been closely examining photographs of German naval vessels.

"Though you picked up that book of sea stories nearly an hour ago, it has lain open and facedown upon your lap for the better part of that time. Your gaze has instead lingered alternately on four items in the meanwhile: the photograph of the staff at Isham Hospital that you have set upon the mantel, your framed commission in the RAMC that hangs here upon the wall as it did in your Biggleswick cottage, the hearth, and your open palms.

"No doubt, you have been thinking of the duties of your service and rank, Watson, and the great good that you have performed for large numbers of people these past months. In comparison, keeping me company round the hearth must seem a disappointing gruel indeed, as empty as the palms into which you have stared so often these past minutes."

"Holmes, I must confess that I often feel as if—"

"I understand your resentment at returning to London in this manner, even if it is to your own home." He caught sight of my suppressed smile of irony and added, "Though it is a home, I suppose, which I have commandeered—and in your eyes and Martha's, nearly laid ruin to—without your leave."

"Permission was implied from the start," I replied wearily. "For the commandeering, at least."

"Still, after thirty years, I continue to take much for granted from you, do I not?"

"Perhaps," I said after a moment's consideration. "But that liberty has been earned, Holmes. You know I value our friendship, far more than I can say in words."

"Friendship is best expressed in a medium other than words, old fellow, and you have always proved most eloquent in that respect. It is I who have invariably abused the bond, Watson. I know that."

"Nonsense."

He looked at me with a wan smile.

"*Nous verons*," I heard him whisper under his breath.

CHAPTER SEVENTEEN: A DEAD MAN'S FIST

It took less than a week for my new responsibilities as a staff secretary for the RAMC to assume the nature of tedious routine. Though my superiors had informed me that I might work most days from Queen Anne Street, where material would be delivered to me, I insisted that I labour instead at my assigned office in Whitehall, at least for the first few weeks of my assignment.

Each morning, a different motorcar arrived at my door so that one chauffeur followed by another in turn could transport me to an imposing building where I dutifully transferred papers from one side of a desk to the other. In the evening, after countless documents had passed beneath my eye, yet another driver conveyed me home. So intent was I upon doing my work—even in the motor, both coming and going—that it was only on the third day that I realised that all those behind the wheel were women.

Just short of a fortnight into this tedium, I resolved to walk to my office instead. And so, waving off the *chauffeur du jour*, who that morning was the youngest daughter of a Cabinet minister, I bade farewell to Holmes, whose time was now almost exclusively spent in our sitting room, where he continued to puzzle over the enigma of Cerberus's third head while waiting to hear from Tatty Evans concerning the *Nemesis* or from Shinwell Johnson regarding suspicious activity around the gasworks, or learn from Frank Farrar that the mysterious Dieter Baumann had once more been seen.

On my way to Westminster that day, I passed a newsagent's shop in Soho and saw on display a magazine whose cover produced in me a numbing sense of shock, followed by the most profound fit of anger. With shaking hands, I purchased a copy of the issue and carried it to my office, where I read the offending article contained within. I seethed throughout the rest of the morning and on into the afternoon, and I was wise to walk home that evening as well, for the effort drained from me at least a portion of the ire I felt as I threw the periodical down before Holmes, who still sat upon the floor, a map of London to his right and half a dozen copies of the *Daily Telegraph* on his left.

"I shall sue!" I thundered in such a voice that Martha was compelled to poke her head into the sitting room.

"Colonel?" she enquired cautiously. "Are you quite all right?"

"No, I am not!" I replied. "But my cure is beyond your abilities, I fear. Go on, dear lady. Your best course is to let me stew."

Bowing her head sheepishly, our housekeeper withdrew, taking care to gently shut the sitting room door, which was usually left ajar. I turned and saw that Holmes had picked up the magazine I had thrown upon the carpet.

"The audacity!" I said.

"What?" said Holmes. "You believe that war secrets are being revealed in this article on the development of the tank?"

"Do not play coy with me," I replied tensely. "I speak, of course, of that!" I shouted, bending down to point at the banner that ran across the middle of the cover.

"'Sherlock Holmes Outwits a German Spy,'" said he, sniffing.[200]

---

[200] The periodical in question is the September 1917 issue of *The Strand Magazine*, which included the first appearance of the short story "His Last Bow," based on events chronicled in chapter 10 of this narrative.

"It is Doyle! I read the story at my office. I read it six times, by God. How can he have the audacity to write it? How can *The Strand* have the temerity to print it?"

Holmes took a deep breath, paused, and then exhaled. "I am afraid, Watson, that *The Strand* printed the tale because Mycroft asked them to print it."

"And why did your brother make such a request?"

"Because I urged him to do so."

"You?" I said, breathlessly. "You had a role in this back-stabbing cabal?"

"I admit that I have been remiss," said Holmes after a moment. He held the magazine in his hands, contemplating it. "I should have asked your permission beforehand."

"Ask permission?" I asked cynically while stalking across the room. Reaching the far wall, I found myself face to face with the painting by DéGousses. Disgusted, I turned.

"Why should Sherlock Holmes deign to ask my permission for another person to chronicle his exploits? A friendship of over thirty years should never pose an obstacle to anyone seeking a replacement biographer," I declared, approaching him. "Of course, that it should be Doyle—"

"But it is not Doyle."

"It is so printed right here," I said, ripping the magazine from his hands and turning to the story's first page. "'His Last Bow,'" I read with a bitter voice. "'The War Service of Sherlock Holmes.'"

"Watson—"

"'By A. Conan Doyle,'" I concluded before closing the periodical and hurling it across the room. "Your treachery wounds me grievously."

Holmes covered his mouth with a hand and then let it drop down to massage his jaw. Allowing the arm to fall into his lap, he looked up and extended his other hand.

"Please sit down, Watson," said he. "If you are determined to render punishment, having already cast judgment, you might be gracious enough to at least hear my confession."

Brusquely, I took up position in the basket chair.

"It will come as no surprise to you when I say that I have spent the better part of recent months attempting to discern evidence of our fabled sleeping German spy group," Holmes began.

"Ah yes, the third head of Cerberus," I remarked in a jaded tone. "As if I am not quite tired of hearing that phrase by now."

"I apologise for the repetition. You recall, no doubt, my hypothesis that this spy ring may be dormant at present, waiting to become active," said Holmes.

I crossed my arms.

"Understand, Watson, that I must grasp at every straw I can imagine."

Still camped upon the floor, Holmes leaned against the armchair that sat behind him.

"What do you suppose ever happened to Heinrich Von Bork?" he asked abruptly.

"You caught him," I said curtly. Motioning to the copy of *The Strand* that lay askew upon the carpet, I added, "One can read all about it in that accursed story."

"After that," he said. "I am speaking of afterward, Watson."

I shrugged. "The man returned to Germany, as we both know."

"There to remain, unused and inactive?"

"Why not?" I replied. "Such is the state in which *I* find myself these days."

"The staff work you do for the medical corps is important, I am certain."

I gave a voiceless sound of disagreement.

"And your mere presence here in London is most vital to me, old fellow, as I have professed time and again," Holmes added in a quiet but heartfelt voice. "I could not pursue this work," he explained, motioning to the newspapers and map that lay before him, "I could not sustain the effort without your companionship and perspective. Consider me selfish and callous if you like, but I dearly need you in this enterprise, Watson—for my own sake."

I could not easily dismiss the earnest sentiment my friend had expressed, yet my fit of pique remained. More calmly than before, I said, "Then how could you—"

"I do not believe Von Bork will sit in Berlin forever, fated to do nothing more than contemplate his last failure or his next match of tennis," asserted Holmes. "It is possible that he will or has already secretly returned to Britain, and if that is the case, what better role for him to assume than that of chief agent of our supposed third head of Cerberus? And I apologise for employing that phrase yet again."

"You have evidence that Von Bork has returned to our shores?" I asked, taking sudden interest.

“Utterly none,” replied Sherlock Holmes. “My statement is pure speculation. But if you grant the possibility of Von Bork’s return, Watson, can you then grasp the reason why I should wish that story to see print at this time?”

I sat back and uncrossed my arms, pondering my friend’s enquiry. Finding myself less irate than before, I reflected upon my reaction to coming across the hated magazine article that morning. And then, in sudden revelation, I said, “It would enrage him, remind him of your victory over him. Prick his pride. Goad him into making, perhaps, a rash miscalculation.”

“Precisely, Watson!” said Holmes, his eyes sparkling. “Do you recall the loathing he expressed toward me as we removed him from his house on the Essex coast? ‘I will get level with you.’ That is what he said to me. ‘If it takes me all my life, I will get level with you.’”

“The old sweet song,” I declared, recalling Holmes’s characterisation of Von Bork’s tirade. I gestured toward the issue of *The Strand.* “If he is here in London, waiting to activate the spy cell that he may now lead, then this is your way of rubbing his nose in his past failure, reminding him of humiliation at your hands and spurring him to rouse that sleeping cell of agents all the sooner—and perhaps recklessly—in order to prove his superiority to you.”

My friend smiled and nodded. “Presumed superiority,” he amended.

“That still fails to explain why you did not ask me to write the story,” I said, as curiosity supplanted rage in fuelling my protestations.

“I did not wish to distract you,” Holmes replied. “It was not my wish to lure you from your war work with the demands of what may be a useless errand.”

"You said earlier that Doyle did not write the piece. Who did, then? And why is Doyle identified as the author?"

"I proposed the ploy to Mycroft and Bullivant some weeks ago," Holmes replied. "When I told them I did not wish to trouble you with composing the tale, Sir Walter suggested we employ instead the fellow who had already penned those two fictions based on Hannay's adventures.

"That man is well-practised, having been in the intelligence corps and before that the War Communications Office. Of course, it could not appear under his name, for he would then be publicly associated with me as well as Hannay, thus indirectly linking me with Hannay and suggesting I remain in the field as an active espionage agent for the government rather than a sedentary cryptographer. Thus, I asked Mycroft to approach Doyle about lending his name to the enterprise."[201]

"An excellent choice," I said with sarcasm, "since most people seem to think that Doyle writes my stories."

"In that regard, Watson, there is one more delicate point that needs mentioning."

I sat up straight in the basket chair and cast a beady eye at Holmes. "And what might that be?"

"It seems that Doyle has written a play about me," Holmes said cautiously. "It is fiction, of course, and I doubt that you would approve of either the prose or the plot, but he asked—as his price for allowing the Von Bork story to be published under his name—that I give my blessing to the

---

[201] This disclosure answers a question which has long puzzled Sherlockian experts: the authorship of "His Last Bow," which is one of two Holmes stories written in third person, rather than narrated in first person by Watson—two others are supposedly written by the detective himself. From Holmes's explanation, it is apparent that the author of "His Last Bow" was John Buchan, though credit was given to A. C. Doyle.

play's production, and that I permit him to adapt the play into a short story, should he ever care to do so—and that Mycroft promise to convince *The Strand* to publish it."

"The nerve of that man—Doyle, that is."

"For King and Empire," said Holmes wanly. "But in all seriousness, Watson, if you do not approve, I will withdraw my endorsement of Doyle's play and prospective story."[202]

"No," I said wearily. "I will pose no objection. However, I insist on imposing two stipulations."

"Name them."

"First, you shall allow me to finally chronicle the Phillimore and Ferguson affairs. I understand your past resistance to my writing stories based upon those cases, but you will henceforth drop your objections altogether."[203]

"Done."

"Second, you shall, at some time in future, write one—no, two stories of your own," I demanded.

"What?"

"Were you not listening? You will compose two stories based upon cases of your choice."

---

[202] The play in question is *The Crown Diamond*, written by Doyle and produced after the war in 1921. That same year saw first publication of the short story adapted from it, "The Adventure of the Mazarin Stone." The latter is one of two Holmes tales written in third person—the other being "His Last Bow"—and is often considered the weakest of all of the stories in the Sherlockian canon. Some may argue that is because it is pure fiction by Doyle rather than true memoir by Watson.

[203] It cannot be absolutely proved, but one of these names probably refers to the matter of James Phillimore, who vanished after stepping back into his house for an umbrella, a case to which Watson refers in "The Problem of Thor Bridge" but apparently never did chronicle after all. Meanwhile, the other reference may be to Robert Ferguson, Holmes's client in "The Adventure of the Sussex Vampire," published in 1924.

"I heard you the first time, Watson. The difficulty I have is with understanding your motive. Why should you wish me to emulate your efforts in fabricating melodrama?"

"Perhaps you may then gain some appreciation for my efforts these past many years," I said primly. "It is not an easy thing to distil your cases into literature. And do not take issue with the last word of my previous sentence."

"I do not, old fellow," said he, raising his hands in protest. "And I agree to your conditions, though it may take me some time to get around to fulfilling my obligations to you."

"I am willing to be patient."

"As am I, Watson, to wait and see if Von Bork is out there—and if he is spurred by my provocation."[204]

Sherlock Holmes did not have long to wait for stronger evidence of renewed German activity in Britain, whether under the command of Heinrich von Bork or not, for two evenings later, we received a call from Inspector Magillivray.

"A man has been run down by a taxicab in Kings Cross," I heard the man's voice declare from the telephone. "He was holding a very interesting piece of paper that may have a bearing on your current pursuits, Mr. Holmes."

---

[204] Holmes apparently kept his word, though it took almost a decade. In 1926, the October and November issues of *The Strand Magazine* featured, respectively, "The Adventure of the Blanched Soldier" and "The Adventure of the Lion's Mane," both ostensibly penned by the detective.

"We will be there presently," said my friend, looking at me as he spoke. "Just off Eversholt Street, you say? Colonel Watson and I will be there presently."

Even before Holmes's conversation was finished, I had fetched our waterproofs and hats and stood ready to present my companion with his garments.

"Perhaps this is the moment when your dam of frustration breaks," I said.

"We shall see," replied Holmes, accepting his coat and hat. "I do hope I am up to this, Watson, for I have not examined a dead body in more than three years. One loses one's touch."

A taxicab bore us through darkness to the site of the accident. Its victim lay upon a pavement near the kerb, evidently having been carried there following the collision that had claimed his life. The deceased's own greatcoat shrouded the corpse, which was encircled by a group of constables, who separated it from a gathering of onlookers.

"I hope this is not another wild goose chase," said Inspector Magillivray, stepping past the small crowd and into the ring of policemen as Holmes and I followed. "I fear you have suffered too many of those, sir," the inspector added.

My friend's smile was revealed as he turned his face toward a street lamp. "I suffer the chases gladly, knowing I will someday have the goose in hand."

"Fortunately," the man from Scotland Yard said, "the accident was reported rather quickly, and in view of what the fellow was clutching, word was quickly passed on to Sergeant Scaife and through him to me, and so I alerted you."

Holmes knelt over the remains and lightly withdrew its covering garment. “It would be preferred the body had not been moved, but one cannot have everything.”

“He was still alive after the taxicab struck him,” Magillivray explained. “The chauffeur and three other men carried him off the street to this spot. A policeman was on foot at the far end of the lane and immediately ran to the scene. That is another reason I learnt so quickly about the incident.”

Holmes nodded as he studied the dead man. “There has not yet been an examination of his person or garments?”

“Not a thorough examination, no.”

“But the slip of paper was removed before being replaced in his hand, I see,” the detective declared.

“Yes, sir. As I said, the man was still alive at the time. He did not speak, other than to groan most horribly, I am told, and he held the paper tightly in his hand, refusing to surrender it, until he expired.”

“And death came swiftly?”

“Within five minutes of his being struck by the taxi, according to the policeman’s estimate.”

“There is no apparent connection between the chauffeur and our corpse?”

“As I am sure you would tell me, Mr. Holmes, there is always the possibility of such a relationship, but I think it doubtful. According to all witnesses, the man here was in a great hurry and dashed into the street without looking to either side. The taxi came rumbling swiftly round the corner quite by chance and, though the chauffeur made a mighty effort to stop in time, the vehicle ploughed straight into the fellow. He is being held at the nearest station and is beside himself with grief—the chauffeur, that is."

"I understand," said Holmes, who reached for the small piece of folded paper that lay in the corpse's hand.

"It was the constable at the scene who pulled it from him," said Magillivray. "And it was what was written upon it that suggested the incident might be of importance to you. He placed it back into the dead man's fist."

I bent down behind Holmes as he unfolded the paper and brushed several flakes of dark reddish grit from it. Upon the small sheet were scrawled, in ink, but two words: Wolfram Schwefel.

"That's about as German a name as I can think of," said Magillivray. "Do you believe we should attempt to search for such a man?"

Holmes ignored the inspector's question as he slid the paper into the pocket of his jacket and began carefully searching within the victim's clothing. That exploration yielded only five items: a penknife, two unsmoked cigars, a matchbook, and a metal ring bearing several keys, all of which the detective placed in his coat pocket after a cursory examination of each.

Holmes turned back the collar of the man's jacket and also picked up the greatcoat to examine its inner lining. "There is nothing to identify him," my friend said, brushing more bits of grime that adhered to the outer garment down one side and along the corresponding inner arm.

"Do you believe that he himself was Wolfram Schwefel?" asked Magillivray. "Perhaps that note was by another hand, meant to identify him to a third party."

Holmes once more failed to respond to the inspector's comment. Instead, he rose to his full height and said, "From which direction was the man running?"

"From there," answered one of the constables, pointing past the small crowd of onlookers and out across the street. "According to those who saw the accident, he emerged from that alley and rushed into the lane, where he was struck by the taxicab."

"Let us survey that area between the two buildings," said Holmes, who led Magillivray, me, and another of the constables across the street and toward the alley opposite.

"Will we be looking for something in particular?" asked the inspector as we passed the alley entrance.

"Yes," said Holmes in an abstracted voice as he withdrew an electric torch from his coat pocket. My friend took a moment to cast light on both brick walls that lined the corridor and then said, "On this side, I should think," as he pointed to the left. "We will, all of us, reach above shoulder height and search for any loose brick that moves. Here," he directed, "and if you stagger yourselves along the length of the alley, we will complete the task that much sooner. Do not bother at first with areas below shoulder height."

Thus directed, the four of us each took a section of wall and slowly progressed along our respective portions, reaching up and pulling on one brick after another. Holmes completed his segment first and then moved past me to continue searching. A moment later, however, the hunt ended.

"Halloa!" cried Magillivray. "I have found one that moves."

Holmes motioned for me and the constable to remain at our stations as he approached the inspector. Reaching up, my friend grasped the loose brick found by Magillivray and pulled it free of the wall. Then Holmes stuck the fingers of his free hand into the resulting cavity before withdrawing and examining them.

"The slip of paper was contained behind the brick?" I suggested. "Our deceased stranger retrieved it from there?"

"Yes," said Holmes, indicating that I and the policeman might now join him and Magillivray at their end of the alley. "The paper had a dark reddish grime on its surface, as I assume you noticed," he said. "Similar material adhered to the right side of the dead man's greatcoat, as well as along most of the length of the coat's inner right arm. This alley has no outlet, and of the two brick walls, the one on this side has a coloration more closely matching that found on the paper and coat."

"And so the man leaned against the alley wall to reach up, pull out the brick and extract the piece of paper," said Magillivray.

"Yes," Holmes answered. "That appears obvious at this point. There is no ledge here upon which to hide the paper, and such a manner of deposit would risk discovery, in any event."

"And the loose brick was high enough so that a passer-by might not accidentally dislodge it and discover the message within," I added.

Holmes nodded.

"The message must have been most urgent, for it sent him quickly running from the alley," the constable asserted before putting a hand to his mouth, for fear he had been too bold.

"Yes, just so," said Holmes with a kindly smile as he withdrew from his pocket the paper found in the dead man's hand and reached upward to deposit it in the wall cavity.

"You are leaving that note in place?" asked Magillivray.

"I am," replied Holmes as he restored the brick in the alley wall. "I have taken from it all that I can, and failing to replace it would inform our adversaries that the message was seen by others in one manner or the other. Fortunately, the paper has not been badly crumpled and will appear intact when they choose to retrieve it."

"Certainly, they will learn of their man's death soon enough," I said.

"Hopefully, not so soon that they are already here to observe us at present," remarked Holmes. "It is my wish that they believe he died by accident as he approached the alley to retrieve the message. Come," he said, guiding us back toward the street. "You and I must depart this locale at once, Watson."

"Well," said Magillivray, following Holmes toward the alley entrance, "I suppose that all makes sense, though I wish to know when you desire that we begin searching for the individual named on that piece of paper."

"Oh, you should not trouble yourself by seeking a man called Wolfram Schwefel," replied Sherlock Holmes.

"Why?" asked the inspector as we left the alley. "Do you think the body across the street is that of Herr Schwefel?"

"No. The slip of paper does not refer to a person."

"What?" said Magillivray, stopping in his tracks.

"*Wolfram* is the German term for the element tungsten," said Holmes abstractedly as he continued walking, "and *schwefel* is that language's word for sulphur."

"In some sense, are you not more removed from your goal than before?" I asked later that night, as I sat across from Holmes while, for the first time, he more carefully examined the items taken from the dead man.

“There are now additional conundrums blocking your path,” I said. “You have ‘tungsten’ and ‘sulphur’ to contemplate, in addition to Frank Farrar’s elusive Dietrich Baumann and his activities near the gasworks, not to mention the matter of the *Nemesis*. And there is no certainty that any of those items are related to the enigma of Cerebus.”

Holmes smiled. “As a great philosopher has said, the journey of a thousand miles begins with one step. What is sometimes not mentioned in that well-worn adage, however, is that many of the succeeding steps may lead sideways, or even backward. Nonetheless, I am confident we will arrive at our goal in time.”

“In time to foil whatever the Germans have in mind, you mean?”

“Yes.” He held up the collection of keys that had been found on the body of the dead man. “We do know a little more about how this presumed new spy cell functions, whether or not Von Bork is associated with it.”

“Oh?”

Holmes tossed the keys down upon the table beside him. “The business of hiding cryptic notes behind alley bricks is a revealing practice. A rather clumsy method of communication, it tells us nonetheless that some of the underlings are not instructed in person by their superiors.”

“And what is the reason for that arrangement?”

“Perhaps it is meant to prevent the underlings from identifying those superiors or unconsciously leading our agents back to them,” my friend replied as he picked up the penknife that had also been found on the man run over near Eversholt Street. “That may in turn suggest that our deceased friend was an Englishman who had unknowingly hired on with German spies. Or, alternatively, that the Germans do not trust their own people.” He held the knife, contemplating it.

"But as you say," I said, "the note the man had picked up was hardly explanatory. There were but two words in it, yet seemingly he knew what to do. He must have earlier received detailed instructions from someone."

"At a previous time, yes," said Holmes, unfolding the blade. He delicately ran a finger along its length. "Before suddenly being called to action, perhaps."

"Do you believe that everyone in this third branch of Cerberus has received his instructions already and is waiting merely for the passwords or gestures that will set those directives into motion?"

"That is the view toward which I presently lean," admitted Holmes, bringing the knife closer to his eye.

"You glean something from that object?"

"There is tar on the blade. Nothing more."

"And the keys you tossed down a moment ago?"

"They appear associated with padlocks. There is no identification of any sort, however. Still, they are well worn, though of recent make."

"And do you expect the dead man to remain anonymous?"

"Yes, perhaps even after the rest of our puzzle is solved," replied Holmes. "There was nothing by which his nationality could be ascertained and no personal markings of any kind. If this incident represents our first definitive encounter with the supposed sleeping cell, then it suggests that they are not only awake but also very alert and cautious, leaving very little by which we might detect and trace their actions."

"Is the alley where the message was left being watched?"

"No, though Magillivray kept expressing a desire to keep it under constant surveillance. Of course, that effort could result in disaster, for if our German friends realised the area was being guarded, they would suspect we knew of the message. Fortunately, the inspector soon came round to my point of view. Now Von Bork will be none the wiser."

As my friend set down the penknife, I decided not to contest the assumption that his former foe was indeed a participant in this shadowy drama.

"That leaves us with nothing but an unidentified corpse, some keys, and a blade stained with tar," Holmes went on. "And a matchbook and two cigars." He examined both of the latter minutely before setting them aside.

"Are they useful?" I asked.

"The cigars? No, and they are a common variety, not even worth burning for the purpose of cataloguing their ash."

I watched my friend pick up the last item recovered from the dead man: a matchbook. Holmes looked at the cover and then opened it.

"You are spending more time in a study of that final item than all the others combined," I observed after a while. "It is an object of interest?"

"Certainly, it is sparking my curiosity," said he, holding up the matchbook.

"Why? I see that it carries an advertisement."

"Yes, one that heralds the advantages of some device known as Gussiter's Deep-breathing System. Have you heard of the contraption, Doctor?"

"Perhaps," I said with a dismissive gesture. "Along with countless other examples of medical quackery. You think it could possibly have significance?"

"I do wonder that it might," replied Holmes. "You see, the inside of the cover has a printed display that is intended to be employed to determine which version of the deep-breathing system is best suited for oneself."

"I suspect they are all equally effective," I declared glibly.

"I do not disagree with that assertion, but you see, Watson, I can envision circumstances in which this array might also be employed to decipher simple coded messages."

"Oh?" I said, leaning forward in my chair. "Can you be certain?"

"No, I cannot," replied Holmes, tossing the matchbook onto the table. "That is the devilish nature of such tools: they appear innocent while harbouring a secret purpose."

"And you cannot discern the latter?"

"Without another part of the cipher or code system—a message, say—I cannot." He stared at the open matchbook. "We must store this away and wait to determine its value to our effort. It may be a priceless treasure. Or rubbish."

"An uncertain find," I declared.

"Yes," agreed Holmes. "Quite unlike the unquestionable bounty we will be receiving tomorrow."

"Oh?" I said, reaching for my pipe and Arcadia mix.

"Young Sandy Arbuthnot is returning to London, and Bullivant has put him at our disposal."

"Where has he been since the Erzurum business with Hannay and Blenkiron two years ago?" I asked, stuffing my pipe. "After Arbuthnot masqueraded as you in Sussex and then engaged in that mission in support of the Russians, I believe all that Bullivant ever said to me about him was that the fellow had been assigned to 'a warmer clime.'"

“When informing me of Sandy’s return, Sir Walter filled in the details of the agent’s itinerary during the past several months,” said Holmes. “In the wake of Erzurum, Arbuthnot continued roaming the area at the behest of Bullivant. Apparently, the subsequent Russian victories at Bitlis and Erzincan were in no small part due to his efforts, and he played a role in stopping the Ottoman advance at Gevaş as well.

“The revolution in Russia threw the entire Caucusus campaign into turmoil, however, and Sandy was pulled from that assignment to be posted farther south in the Levant, where he performed more than one feat of clandestine magic: I am told that Jerusalem will be ours by winter largely on account of him. The campaign there is now going so well that Sir Walter had no hesitation in bringing our friend back to Britain upon my request, though he had originally intended to send Arbuthnot on to Persia.”[205]

“The young man has been busy,” I observed after lighting my pipe. “No doubt, he soon will be even busier.”

Holmes smiled. “Yes. He is the one I will put on the trail of Frank Farrar’s acquaintance, Dieter Baumann.”

“Has the German been seen again?”

“No. Farrar has discreetly frequented diverse locales where Baumann might be expected to show himself, but to no result. However, assuming the fellow truly is the one who was at the German embassy before the war—and Farrar is most certain he is—there can be no doubt

---

[205] Bitlis, Erzincan, and Gevaş are cities in present-day Turkey, and the sites of battles in 1916 between Russia and the Ottoman Empire. The Russian Revolution, actually a series of revolts, began in early 1917 and disrupted that country’s campaign against the Ottomans, as noted by Holmes. Jerusalem, meanwhile, was captured by British forces under the command of Edmund Allenby in December of that year.

that he is wrapped up in the spy ring we seek to uncover. Arbuthnot will be excellent for the purpose of flushing out and observing the fellow."

"And what of Richard Hannay?" I said. "Has nothing more been heard from him since he boarded that ship for the Hebrides, alongside Abel Gresson?"

"Not a word," admitted my friend. He gazed at the hearth. "One can only hope that Bullivant hears from him soon. I am not inclined to go hunting for the man a second time."

The next day, I found myself once more sitting at a council of war with Holmes and Bullivant at Safety House. However, the other participants were not Mycroft Holmes, John S. Blenkiron, and Inspector Magillivray, but rather Frank Farrar, Shinwell Johnson, and a very brown-faced Sandy Arbuthnot.

"I must confess," said the new returnee, stiffly moving his arms within a tweed jacket, "these togs take some getting used to after spending years in izaar and thawb."[206]

We had spent several minutes listening to Frank Farrar relate his sighting of Dietrich Baumann to Arbuthnot, followed by a detailed recounting of fruitless efforts to subsequently locate the German. Shinwell Johnson also reported on his own failure to come across the man, or espy anything suspicious in the immediate vicinity of the gasworks.

"Well, based upon your description of him," Arbuthnot said to Farrar, "I am certain I can pick out Dieter in a crowd, should I be fortunate

---

206 An izaar is a lower garment akin to a sarong, while a thawb is an ankle-length robe. Both are traditional wear in Arab countries.

enough to cross his path. All I needs do now," he added, "is to follow your lead in frequenting the right crowds."

"We will meet here according to the schedule I have given you," Holmes told Sandy. "I do not wish to have you coming anywhere near Queen Anne Street, however."

"You believe Von Bork is watching the residence?" I asked.

"We must admit it as a possibility, though I do not know that such surveillance would be worth the trouble in the German's eyes," Holmes replied. Smiling, he added, "Were I Von Bork, I would let me come to me, so to speak."

"And so you no longer wish me to pursue Dieter Baumann, Mr. Holmes?" asked Farrar.

"Not intentionally. Rather, you will join Johnson in regularly scouring the area surrounding the gasworks, widening the radius of search."

"That has yielded nothing thus far, sir," Johnson gently reminded the detective. "I've seen nothing but routine comings and goings."

"Of that I am all too aware," admitted Sherlock Holmes. "At present, however, we have few other locales with which to associate Herr Baumann, and Sandy will be responsible for those. I suggest you two continue to discreetly enquire among various building agents whose concerns lie near the gasworks."

"We will do so," Johnson replied wearily.

"And that barge master, Tatty Evans—he has still not espied the presumed German motor launch again?" asked Sir Walter Bullivant.

"No, he has not," admitted Holmes. "He began his search in the eastern reaches of the river and has been gradually moving closer to central London. I do have hopes he will sight the *Nemesis* at some point, and when he does, we will begin to narrow the choices for the endpoints of her travels."

"Do you believe Baumann may serve as part of the crew of the *Nemesis*, at least from time to time?" I asked.

"I think all our items of interest are part of the same animal," Holmes declared. "However, their anatomical relationships to the whole and each other remain to be uncovered."

"Well, until that motor launch comes to light again, I suppose it's the gasworks and vicinity for the pair of us," said Johnson to Farrar.

"And it is the hunt for Dieter Baumann that is for you, Sandy," interjected Bullivant. "But you are an old hand at flushing out a quarry, are you not?"

"It's a familiar assignment," said Arbuthnot. "But my guise in this endeavour will be a new experience for me, I suppose. But it is always good to expand one's repertoire, eh, Mr. Holmes? I must be certain to watch my back."

Frank Farrar appeared slightly uncomfortable and Sir Walter Bullivant showed not a small bit of embarrassment.[207]

"I trust in your abilities," Holmes said quickly. "We can, however, only wait to see what your efforts yield. I thought John Blenkiron would be in attendance," he remarked abruptly to Bullivant, a comment I perceived as an effort to deftly change subject.

---

[207] This is possibly another example of implied content which may cast doubt on the narrative's authenticity, for the nuances of this exchange are perhaps beyond the spectrum found in Watson's authenticated writings.

"The man is spending an increasing amount of time on the Continent," Sir Walter explained. "The first American troops are beginning to arrive here in Britain, and Blenkiron is focussing his energy on strengthening his own network of spies in France and beyond. Indeed, part of his mission is to attempt to coordinate his agents with ours—including our prime man in Belgium, the one we are hoping may provide us with advance warning of future German air raids."

"And I need not ask for news from the Hebrides concerning Hannay?" Holmes said.

Bullivant sighed and shook his head gently. "No, for I would tell you that nothing has yet been heard from him. The man's silence has gone on quite longer than I had anticipated. Something has no doubt happened—we can only hope something in Hannay's favour. And we can only pray that when we eventually learn of events up north, they will gladden us."

"Here's to that," said Arbuthnot. "I know that old Dick Hannay will come through for us, though. He brought down Ulric von Stumm and Hilda von Einem, and he'll help do the same to Abel Gresson and Moxon Ivery."[208]

We all expressed agreement with that sentiment.

"For the moment, however, Sandy," said Holmes after a pause, "we must see to our own obligations."

"I will get on with searching for Dieter this very day," replied Arbuthnot. He smiled at Frank Farrar and offered his hand. "I'll do my best

---

208 Ulric von Stumm and Hilda von Einem were German adversaries of Richard Hannay during the mission that culminated in the Battle of Erzurum, as related in John Buchan's novel *Greenmantle*.

to follow up on your excellent spotting. If this fellow is still about London, I promise I shall find him."

As Farrar and Arbuthnot shook hands, Shinwell Johnson wistfully said, "Hope piled onto hope."

"Yes, and there are so many irons in the fire," remarked Bullivant. "Baumann, the *Nemesis*, tungsten, sulphur. And that matchbook that you have mentioned," he added to Holmes. "Not to speak of Ivery and Gresson—"

And, possibly, Heinrich von Bork, I thought.

"Can they all be related, as you claim, let alone mastered?" Bullivant asked.

"They are but portions of the same elephant, I assure you," replied Holmes. "And when at last we glimpse the full pachyderm, we shall know the answer to your quandary."

After the meeting at Safety House had concluded, Holmes and I returned to Queen Anne Street in a taxicab. Upon paying the chauffeur, I immediately bombarded my friend with a series of questions I had dared not ask in the vehicle.

"Please, Watson," cried the detective in mock protest as we stood upon the steps. "I beg you to wait until we gain the sitting room before unleashing your curiosity upon me."

"My apologies," I said as I opened the house door. "Had it been the old days, with Jack James driving, I should not have hesitated to raise these points in the taxicab. But in the presence of that chauffeur, I could not say a word, of course."

"Your discretion is admirable, Watson," replied Holmes, who was now chuckling.

"You find something amusing?" I asked as I placed my hat and coat in the wardrobe and stepped back to allow Holmes to do the same with his garments.

"It was your characterisation of the time when Jack James was here as the 'old days' which prompted my laughter," he explained before heaving a great sigh.

"What mirth lay hidden in that remark?"

"For most who might consider it, I suppose none. However, you use 'old days' to refer to a period of but three years ago, while to me that phrase describes what you, perhaps, may think of as the 'even older days.'"

"Baker Street, you mean?"

"Yes," he said.

I nodded with understanding and looked at my friend expectantly, waiting for further elaboration. Holmes, however, merely strode down the hallway toward the sitting room. "Yes, indeed," I thought I heard him murmur again, his back to me.

I at once followed Holmes into the sitting room, where he was already taking stock of the great masses of maps, newspapers, and documents that were heaped in piles from one corner to another.

"You seem to have recreated Baker Street here, to no small effect," I observed, attempting to prolong the jest.

He gave a gently bitter smile. "Do pardon the mess I have created," he said without humour. "Rather," he amended, "I should say messes."

I shrugged and then strode to the breakfast table, where Martha had left our mail.

"Here you are," I said to Holmes, holding out two letters that had arrived for him. "I suppose you may pin these to the mantel with your jackknife, should you wish."

Holmes turned toward me with a wan smile and accepted the letters. "You are kind to grant me that permission. And would you complain were I to engage in target practice against that wall?" said he wearily, reluctantly joining in my whimsy as he pointed in the direction of the DéGousses painting.

"I should think that my neighbours would not be pleased, though I might tolerate such disruption," I said. "Especially if you aimed at the painting rather than the wall itself."

Holmes gave a pained expression.

"I cannot predict Martha's reaction, however." I continued. "In any event, I believe that 'GVR' would be more difficult to successfully achieve than a mere 'VR.'"[209]

"Granted," said he, opening one letter. "And I am quite out of practice. Moreover, my revolver is not presently loaded, while the jackknife now rests at the bottom of the Chicago River."

"You dropped it into the water?"

"As it was embedded in the back of my would-be murderer at the time, I had no recourse but to allow it to fall through a layer of ice, along with the body. Time was in short supply, you see."

I stared at Holmes for a moment, my mouth open.

---

209 "VR," for Victoria Regina, was used as postmark on British mail during the queen's reign. While George V was monarch, the corresponding mark was "GVR." In their Baker Street lodgings, Holmes once fired his gun at the sitting room wall so that the bullet holes spelled "VR." Meanwhile, mention of Holmes's jackknife refers to his habit of affixing unopened mail to the Baker Street mantel with the blade.

“And no, Watson,” he said as while reading the letter. “It is an episode about which you shall never write. Now, may I trouble you to ring Martha?”

CHAPTER EIGHTEEN: TERROR AND FLIGHT

As my stay in the Cotswolds receded into the past and the experience of Isham became only memory, I chafed at the paltry duties I bore as a staff secretary of the Royal Army Medical Corps, finding those inconsequential obligations matched by my seemingly superfluous role as assistant to Sherlock Holmes. I understood that I was too old for the Western Front itself, but my new assignment at a London desk—and my own desk in my own home, at that—produced in me a sense of guilt far worse than that which I had suffered that day in 1914 beneath the banner spanning Agar Street, in the shadow of Charing Cross Hospital.

Though I granted that it was of upmost importance that Holmes uncover the organisation, methods, and goals of the presumed third German spy group, my role in that effort hardly seemed that of an active collaborator. What progress that Holmes might achieve would, I thought, owe more to the efforts of Frank Farrar, Shinwell Johnson, and Sandy Arbuthnot, and perhaps Inspector Magillivray and his Sergeant Scaife, rather than mine.

Though the man originally known as Dietrich Baumann was nowhere to be seen in the metropolis, Arbuthnot began a systematic survey of several East End neighbourhoods in hopes of finding evidence of the young German, when he was not inhabiting various focal points of the London demimonde. A the same time, Farrar and Johnson cast their nets across a wider span centred about the gasworks, reaching to the docks and river embankments beyond the facility, even as Magillivray and his colleagues continued to stand alert for more incidents such as that which had drawn us to Eversholt Street. And all the while, Tatty Evans maintained a quiet vigil afloat, plying the river for signs of the *Nemesis*, though also to no avail.

And, in a more distant place, Mary Lamington stood in watch over the comings and goings of Moxon Ivery in Biggleswick, while we all waited in anticipation of Richard Hannay's reappearance from his trip north in pursuit of Abel Gresson's secret network of contacts.

I faithfully kept to my role as mere companion to my friend, allowing him to sharpen his thoughts against a human whetstone. That in itself was valuable service, I admitted, though to me it was one that could have been taken up by anyone. As the days wore on, I wished for some dramatic turning point to occur.

Very soon, it did.

On a Tuesday evening, I found myself in the sitting room, waiting for Holmes to return from Office 54, where he had gone to obtain enemy war communiques for decipherment in Queen Anne Street as an occasional respite from fretting about the riddle of Cerberus's final head. The Third Battle of Ypres was still raging under a new commander, and I read with anxiety reports that, on the Eastern Front, the Germans had captured Riga.[210]

---

[210] The Third Battle of Ypres, also known as the Battle of Passchendaele, ran between July and November of 1917. The Allies sought to take control of ridges to the south and east of the Belgian city of Ypres and, in so doing, disrupt the railroad network supplying the German army, as well as break through to the coast of Belgium, where enemy U-boats were based. Rain turned the battlefield into a sea of mud, however, and progress was stalled. This lack of advancement was blamed on the commander immediately in charge of the offensive, General Hubert Gough, who on August 25 was replaced by General Herbert Plumer. The campaign ended when Canadian forces captured Passchendaele. Meanwhile, on September 1, the Baltic city of Riga was taken by Germany.

It was well past eleven o'clock when Holmes arrived home. Upon hearing the door close, I put down the newspaper, rose from my chair, and crossed the sitting room. Seeing the offending issue of *The Strand* still upon a table, I turned the magazine over as I passed. Then, reaching the doorway, I peered down the hall and saw Holmes hanging up his coat, Martha having retired for the night some time before.

"Have I kept you up waiting, old fellow?" said he, approaching along the corridor.

"No," I replied as Holmes passed me and entered the sitting room. "I have been somewhat deep in thought," I told him, intending that to be prelude to yet another confession of dissatisfaction with my current state of idleness, prior to laying out an argument for asking the RAMC to give me an alternate assignment.

"As have I, Watson." He took his black clay pipe from the mantel. "Deep in thought, indeed."

"Perhaps you are still grappling with our friend, Wolfram Schwefel?"

Holmes smiled as he filled his pipe.

"On my way back here, yes, I thought of him, but to no effect." He reached for a vesta and, glancing across the room, espied the issue of *The Strand* turned facedown. Sighing deeply, Holmes lit his pipe and then extinguished the vesta.

"Watson," said he, tossing the match onto the coals, "I do apologise again for any indignity which you may feel you have suffered on account of the appearance of that Von Bork story."

I returned to my chair. "As always, I assume your intentions are—"

My sentence was interrupted by two sharp bursts.

Holmes and I stared at one another.

"Great God," I exclaimed. "Sound rockets. Are they—?"

"Bombarding us by night, as they did from the Zeppelins?" Holmes uttered, completing my question. "Such appears to be the case, old fellow. I will gather up Martha and join you in the basement before the aeroplanes arrive."[211]

No bombs were yet falling in our vicinity, but we heard many distant explosions as we descended. The three of us maintained a cautious vigil in the basement for at least an hour: Holmes and I read newspapers by candlelight while Martha slept upon a cot she had previously prepared for such an emergency. More than once, her snoring served as reminder that the elderly woman was in no way bothered by the potential danger from above.

At length, after a long interval of quiet, we ascended to the ground floor as the hour approached one.

"Do not bother rising at your usual time," Holmes told our housekeeper. "The colonel and I will manage for ourselves in the morning."

"It is already morning," I noted disconsolately. Then, with concern, I added, "I do wonder how many were killed tonight."

"More than a few, I fear, judging from the number of explosions we heard," Holmes replied. "I expect Bullivant or Mycroft will inform us tomorrow—or, rather, today, for we have a meeting with them at Safety House at ten."

"Well," I said with resignation, "now that you have informed me of that fact, I shall have at least a handful of hours in which to try to gain some sleep. In truth, however," I added as Martha trod off to her room, "it

---

[211] In July 1917, the practice began of firing rockets in quick succession from the tops of all London fire stations as warning of an impending air raid.

occurred to me earlier this evening, Holmes, that I am nothing but baggage in this endeavour of yours. Perhaps I need not attend that meeting at all."

My friend paused and tilted his head, as if prompting me for more.

"I long for a return to action of some form directly relevant to the war," I declared abruptly. "At Isham, I felt I was being of use. In the current instance—"

"In the current instance, Watson, your value to me is beyond words. Please," he said, as I saw a hint of desperation flash in his eyes, "let us have no more such talk."

After daylight had returned, Holmes and I took a taxicab to the vicinity of Safety House and then entered the building through its back door. We passed into the sitting room, where Mycroft Holmes waited with Sir Walter Bullivant.

"Do you already know the facts surrounding last night's raid?" asked the elder Holmes brother. "Or do you wish to learn them?"

"The latter," said Sherlock Holmes as he took a chair.

I claimed a seat beside my friend.

"The German aeroplanes crossed our shores in waves, between half past ten and a bit after midnight," said Sir Walter. "Two of our squadrons put craft into the air, but not a single one of the pilots was able to engage the enemy. However, an Archie battery at Borstal[212] appears to have shot down at least one of the German aircraft. A search is being conducted for wreckage and crew."

---

212 "Archie" was Royal Flying Corps slang for anti-aircraft fire. Borstal, meanwhile, was a village on the coast of southeast England near Rochester, which has since absorbed it.

“I thought you were hoping to receive advance warning of such attacks from that agent of yours in Belgium,” said Sherlock Holmes.

“We did receive warning,” replied his brother. “Unfortunately, the methods of transmitting such alerts along our own spy network are not yet well coordinated. The message from our Belgian agent arrived after the attack was completed.”

“We heard the first bombs about half past eleven,” said the detective.

“Some fell in West Ham and Stratford,” Mycroft informed us. “Another landed near Oxford Circus, and yet another exploded in Agar Street.”

“Was there damage to the hospital?” I asked.

“I am not aware that it suffered structural damage” was Mycroft’s reply. “All I know is that a bomb struck just outside the building’s entrance, and there were casualties.”

“Still others fell in and around the Victoria Embankment,” added Sir Walter. “One of those struck close to Cleopatra’s Needle and killed three people in a passing tram, including its operator.”[213]

“How many any other deaths have been reported?” asked Sherlock Holmes.

“At least three, though I have already alluded to them” said Mycroft grimly. “A woman and two Colonial soldiers, from the bomb that fell near Charing Cross Hospital. There are, as well, perhaps ten or more injuries

---

[213] Completed in 1870, the Victoria Embankment is a road and walkway along the north bank of the Thames, part of a project which reclaimed marshy land next to the river. Within its borders sits Cleopatra’s Needle, an ancient Egyptian obelisk that has nothing to do with the aforementioned queen; it was transported from Africa to London and reerected there during the nineteenth century. From the descriptions, it is apparent that this was the raid of September 4, 1917—the first nighttime London raid by German airplanes, as opposed to airships.

that resulted from that explosion. I have no doubt that additional casualties will be reported as we move into the afternoon."

"Well then, M, shall we proceed to our planned agenda?" asked Sir Walter, as if eager to move to another subject.

"Yes, I believe so," said the elder Holmes. "If we first—"

Mycroft was interrupted by a loud, patterned knock upon the front door of Safety House. He and Bullivant stared at each other.

"Magillivray, perhaps?" said Sherlock Holmes.

"I will go and see," said his brother, much to the detective's surprise.

A moment later, Mycroft Holmes returned to the sitting room with the Scotland Yard inspector and a breathless Richard Hannay, who was dressed in the rumpled uniform of an army private.

"Hannay!" said Bullivant, excitedly rising to his feet. "Where have you been? We have been waiting—"

"I thought they were shot!" were the first words from Hannay's mouth. "I thought the three men we collected on the Ruff years ago were all shot."[214]

Bullivant did not reply, while Mycroft Holmes once more took to the sofa and remained silent, as did Sherlock Holmes and I.

"The plump man escaped, didn't he?" asked Hannay.

"Yes," admitted Bullivant after a moment.

"When?" Hannay asked. "Where? How?"

"We failed to intercept him at the base of the Ruff in 1914," Mycroft Holmes calmly declared from his perch on the sofa. "He was expected to

---

[214] This is the first indication in Watson's narrative of the grim fate planned for the three German spies—and apparently carried out on two of them.

swim for the *Ariadne*, as you recall, where he would have been seized, but he never arrived at the ship."

"What happened? What did he do? Where did he go?"

"Some presumed that he drowned," Mycroft replied, looking at Bullivant. "Many of us were not so certain." He glanced over at Hannay and raised a brow. "I apologise for keeping the information from you. It was deemed most secret. Dare I ask how you came to learn of his escape?"

"I saw him last night," Hannay replied with an edge to his voice. "The third one. The plump man. Good God, he is the one we have known as Moxon Ivery!"

"What?" exclaimed Bullivant as Mycroft Holmes gripped one arm of the sofa.

Sherlock Holmes leaned back and drew a deep breath.

"Where did you last see him, Mr. Hannay?" asked the detective. "Do you know his current whereabouts?"

"I ran across him at the Strand Tube entrance[215] last night. I'd gotten to London after a rather eventful journey up north and back."

"Yes," said Bullivant, glancing at the uniform that Hannay wore. "I cannot wait for that story."

"It must wait, sir," Hannay said urgently. "Moxon Ivery is more important at the moment. I was in Charing Cross when I heard the first bombs explode last night. I took to the Tube entrance, as did almost everyone else in the vicinity, and while I stood amongst the crowd—all of us cheek by jowl—I saw him."

---

[215] This refers to an entrance of the London Underground, the public transit system which incorporates the world's first underground railway, opened in 1863.

"You saw Ivery, whom you now believe is the plump man?" said Sherlock Holmes.

"Yes," replied Hannay. "I saw Ivery—and yet it was not Ivery. At that moment, in my mind, for what reason I do not know, he seemed to change shape. I saw him not as Ivery but as that stout, plump man who had been at Trafalgar Lodge in Broadgate three years ago. I thought that fellow long dead, but there he was. And then he turned his head and saw me."

"And his eyes betrayed understanding that you had recognised him at last?" enquired Holmes.

"Exactly!" said Hannay. "He knew that I knew. I saw him slip farther back into the crowd huddled in the Tube entrance, and I resolved to rush to Blenkiron's bookshop, for it was the closest place I could think of where I might sound the alarm."

"Blenkiron is in France at the moment," said Mycroft Holmes, pulling out his watch. "Or, rather, he was, for by now he now should be in transit back to London. Still, one of the Americans would have opened the door to you. I take it you never arrived there."

"I did not." Hannay motioned to the uniform he wore. "It was tied all in with this."

"On his way to the bookshop, Mr. Hannay was picked up by the military police," explained Magillivray, who apparently had already heard Hannay's full story. "Some pompous fool provost marshal kept him confined and under guard in his office all night, on suspicion, until permission was granted to call me at Scotland Yard. I arrived and freed our friend, and then thought bringing him to Safety House might be the best thing to do, in case any of you gentlemen were here."

"And so we are," said Mycroft Holmes. "Well, Mr. Ivery was obviously playing you from the start, wasn't he, Mr. Hannay? No doubt he recognised you from the confrontation on the Ruff and knew who you were when you first entered Biggleswick under your alias."

"Yes," Hannay said disconsolately. "He flattered me, applauded my remarks—even urged me to go to Glasgow, and no doubt was laughing at me all the time. I met Gresson, by the way, and I'm certain Ivery had already put him on to me. I was almost drowned on board Gresson's ship, you see, and they set the local police against me, and—"

"As you said earlier, Mr. Hannay," interjected Sherlock Holmes, getting to his feet, "we will have time to hear your full saga later. For the moment, we must attempt to capture Ivery before he leaves Britain."

"He has hours of head start," Hannay declared. "I'll bet you a pony he's already across the Channel."

"And I'd give a load of monkeys[216] to have the man taken," said Sir Walter with desperation, "but all we can do is hope for the best. Inspector, shall we go?"

"Yes, sir," replied Magillivray. "I've already put our men on alert."

"And I will contact the military authorities at once," said Mycroft, heaving himself to his feet with a mighty effort. "The RNAS[217] boys can patrol the coast from the air." He turned toward Bullivant and Magillivray. "We have our work cut out for us. Shall the three of us leave together?"

---

[216] "Pony" is slang for £25, while "monkey" means £500. Both terms may have been introduced by British soldiers returning from India in the nineteenth century.

[217] The Royal Naval Air Service was the air arm of the Royal Navy, just as the Royal Flying Corps served the corresponding role for the British Army. Both services were merged in 1918 to form the independent Royal Air Force.

"Of course, M," said Bullivant, who glanced at Hannay. "What should we do with—?"

"Colonel Watson and I will take Mr. Hannay in tow," said Sherlock Holmes. "That is, with *M's* approval," he added sardonically.

"Interview him by all means, Sherlock," answered Mycroft. "Forward the gist of Mr. Hannay's story to me. And if you have suggestions that may assist us in snaring Ivery, do not hesitate to make them. And, of course, let yourselves out the back when you depart. Gentlemen, as much as I hate impromptu journeys, we must be going," he said to Bullivant and Magillivray.

The three departed Safety House, leaving Holmes, Hannay and me in the sitting room. The South African appeared even more dismayed than before.

"He knew me from the outset," he said again. "All the while he was toying with me."

"I believe we have established that beyond doubt, Mr. Hannay," agreed Holmes. "It is not impossible that he saw Colonel Watson and myself as objects of play as well."

"Should we not go out also, to find and seize Ivery?" Hannay asked.

"I think it best that we let my brother work his will unattended by us. He has ample support from Inspector Magillivray and Sir Walter. I suggest instead that you relate to us your activities these past many days."

Hannay exhaled, leaned back in the sofa usually occupied by Mycroft Holmes, and told us of his trip north to Glasgow as the pacifist Cornelius Brand, where he made contact with Andrew Amos, met Abel Gresson at a political rally, and then accompanied the latter aboard a ship to the Hebrides. Along the way, he had been involved in a fight with British soldiers, almost drowned by an unknown assailant, and chased by the police on account of his tussle with the soldiers. Through a string of good luck, which had included an aeroplane ride with a Royal Flying Corps friend met by chance—somewhat akin to my own journey with Cecil Harper—he had reached London safely, disguised as an army private.[218]

"The important thing is, I found Gresson's mailbox, as it were: a peak on the island of Skye, where he transfers his information to a Portuguese fellow, who must carry it on south, perhaps to Ivery himself," said Hannay.

Holmes nodded.

"Oh, and I ran into Launcelot Wake, of all people," Hannay said. "He's a good fellow, after all. Indeed, he provided me invaluable assistance. The man is not a German spy, after all."

"Yes," said Holmes, glancing at me. "We determined that after you had left for Glasgow."

Hannay related all the other details of his journey, to the moment when he recognised Moxon Ivery for who he was and on through his incarceration by military police. At the end of a half hour, it was clear that he was more than ready to leave Safety House.

"I'm going to Westminster," he said. "I've kept rooms there as Cornelius Brand, my alter ego. Then I'll take a taxi to my Park Lane flat, which I keep as Richard Hannay."[219] He laughed cynically. "I believe I'll need some time there in order to return to my real persona."

---

[218] These travails are chronicled in detail in *Mr. Standfast* by John Buchan.

[219] Widened in the 1960s, Park Lane has become one of the busiest and noisiest roads in London. At the time of this narrative, however, it was a fashionable residential address bordering Hyde Park.

"I quite understand," said Sherlock Holmes. "I wish you well, Mr. Hannay. Once again, you have performed a magnificent service."

"Do you believe so, Mr. Holmes? Even though Ivery no doubt recognised me from the start?"

"Yes. If nothing else, you have determined the next link in the Black Stone chain beyond Abel Gresson. And you are certain that neither he nor this Portuguese fellow were aware that you were watching them in that wilderness on Skye?"

"Quite certain."

"Good. No doubt, Ivery's house in Biggleswick will be occupied by the police, if it is not being invaded as we speak."

"We can only hope that is the case," sighed Hannay. "Tell Sir Walter to reach me at Park Lane. I will be chomping at the bit for news, of course."

Hannay's sentiment paralleled my own, and after saying our farewells to him in the alley behind Safety House, Holmes and I returned to Queen Anne Street, where we passed several anxious hours. Holmes poured over numerous fruitless reports already received from Frank Farrar and Shinwell Johnson, and he occasionally decoded more German war communiques brought from Office 54.

I, meanwhile, busied myself with staff paperwork for the medical corps. We ate an early dinner, which did not discommode Martha, and then received a telephone call at seven in the evening.

"It was Sir Walter Bullivant," said Holmes. "He wishes us to be at his residence in Queen Anne's Gate within the hour. I propose to make that within the half hour."

"Shall we try for a quarter hour?"

"There is no harm in attempting the impossible, Watson."

We arrived at Bullivant's house at twenty minutes past seven and were admitted by a stolid, impassive butler who led us down the green-panelled entrance hall, past an alcove, and on to the end of the corridor, where we reached a back room in which Sir Walter Bullivant was pacing back and forth upon a hearthrug, an unlit cigar between his fingers.

"Greetings, gentlemen," came a doleful voice from the side and, turning, I espied John Blenkiron ensconced in a plush armchair. "Bad business this evening, I'm afraid," he remarked. "Not the sort of thing I'd hoped to hear upon returning from France, to be sure."

Holmes glanced expectantly at Bullivant, who sighed and turned toward Blenkiron.

"We're still waiting for word from Inspector Magillivray," the American said. "At the moment, all we have is hope."

"One should never be without it," said my friend with a tired smile. He then repeated to Blenkiron and Sir Walter the full story of Hannay's Scottish journey, which had been told to us earlier.

"Well," said Bullivant. "There is some small shred of good fortune there. Scotland Yard has been directed to organise the seizure of Ivery's house in Biggleswick, and we are assembling forces in Glasgow to await my order to round up those associated with Abel Gresson. Gresson himself may still be out on the water on board that ship, but we will nab him as well."

"May I suggest, Sir Walter, that you not interfere with Gresson and his immediate gang?" said Sherlock Holmes. "If left free, they may lead us to still others of whom we are not yet aware."

“Of course,” agreed Bullivant after a moment’s thought. “That leaves this Portuguese fellow free as well, but with luck, we’ll have them all in the end.”

“Yes, but it’s the big bird that we want now,” noted Blenkiron. “The man we know as Ivery.”

Sir Walter sighed again and put the unlit cigar between his teeth before nodding vigorously. “I wish I had told Hannay to come here,” the spymaster said. “He may have more details about the Portuguese that might be helpful, and in any event, the fellow deserves to be on hand when Inspector Magillivray brings us the news, either good or bad.”

At perhaps half past eight the house bell rang. As if in answer to Bullivant’s desire, it was Hannay, who arrived on his own accord and at once sensed the glum mood that hung over the room.

“Is there any news?” he asked at once. “I am sorry that I failed to—”

“It wasn’t any fault of yours, Dick,” said Blenkiron at once. “You did fine.”

“Yes,” agreed Bullivant. “It was the devil’s own work that our friend Ivery looked your way last night. You are certain you recognised him?” he asked in desperation.

“Absolutely,” replied Hannay. “As certain as I am that he knew I saw him for who he truly was.”

“That little flicker of perception that you can never be wrong about,” said Blenkiron. “Land alive! I wish Mr. Magillivray would arrive soon.”

The bell rang as if on cue, and we turned in anticipation. The person who came through the door, however, was not the Scotland Yard inspector but rather a young woman in a white ball gown, a cluster of blue cornflowers at her breast. At the sight of her, Sir Walter sprang to his feet, almost upsetting a coffee cup that sat upon a table.

“How did you come to be here?” said Bullivant. “I expected you to arrive on a later train.”

“I was in London already,” said Mary Lamington. “With Aunt Doria, but when Sergeant Scaife happened to telephone me to say you wanted me here, I cut her theatre party. Doria believes I’m at a dance, so I needn’t be home till morning.” She glanced round the room and added, “Good evening, General Hannay. I’m pleased to see that you have made it safely back to town.”

“Safely, yes,” he replied, “but not victoriously.”

Bullivant then explained the situation to Miss Lamington, who nodded thoughtfully as the news about Ivery was related to her. There was also, however, an odd look in her eye as Hannay related the incident at the Strand Tube station. She almost interrupted his story once or twice but hesitated. Then, as Hannay concluded, we heard the house bell yet again.

“Are you expecting anyone other than Magillivray?” asked Blenkiron.

“No,” said Sir Walter, and all eyes turned toward the doorway.

One look at the inspector’s face told us all the news.

“So he’s skipped across the Channel,” said Blenkiron as a statement of fact. “Long gone.”

“Gone, for certain,” repeated Magillivray, who removed his hat and silently asked permission to sit. He leaned on the edge of his chair, gripping the hat’s brim. “We have just established how he left the country, and it was cleverly done.”

Sherlock Holmes stepped forward and took hold of an empty chair back. The look in his eyes was enough to cause Magillivray to explain all.

"There was no sign of disturbance at his home in Biggleswick when our men entered it," the inspector began, "or in any of his other lairs—for we now realise that he had more than one, just as he had more than one identity. Moxon Ivery was but one of his many poses. He had scheduled a dinner party for this evening in Biggleswick, in fact, and the guests arrived and the meal served, but the host, Moxon Ivery, was nowhere to be seen.

"Instead, he was flying to France as a passenger of a different name, in one of our own planes. You see, in this second persona, he had gotten close to the people comprising the new Air Board."[220]

"Same man, different face," grumbled Blenkiron.

"The plane bearing him landed in Normandy this afternoon," Magillivray informed us. "By now, I reckon the fellow is in Paris."

"Or beyond," said Sherlock Holmes.

Sir Walter took off his tortoiseshell spectacles and laid them carefully on the table. "This is total defeat," he moaned. "Suddenly, I feel very old."

Magillivray continued to fiddle with his hat while bearing the expression of a man in the throes of bitter disappointment. Blenkiron's face was flushed, and I could see that he was blaspheming under his breath. Mary Lamington quietly strode over to Sir Walter and took his hand.

"What is the extent of the damage?" I asked calmly from across the room.

"We do not yet know," replied Bullivant.

---

[220] The Air Board was one of three successive panels intended to oversee military aviation in Britain prior to the creation of the Air Ministry in 1918. It was partially reorganized in January 1917.

"But there is perhaps no limit to its potential," said Sherlock Holmes, who glanced at Magillivray. "If, as you say, Ivery had several identities, he likely had a few we do not yet know, each one as cleverly conceived as the next."

"Who knows what politicians he may have beguiled?" said Blenkiron. "Perhaps as someone else, he even may have breakfasted at Downing Street with forged letters of introduction."

"Or visited the Grand Fleet as a distinguished neutral," added Bullivant. "We do not know what he may have learnt." The spymaster gingerly withdrew his hand from that of Mary Lamington. "We should have realised that, having escaped from the Ruff three years ago, he would return and wreak even more havoc. And to think that we do not even know his true name."

"We must still try to neutralise him," said Blenkiron.

"We can round up his remaining organisation," said Magillivray. "Would that not be enough?"

"The greatest danger comes from what he may have in his head," Bullivant explained. "That was the threat three years ago, if you recall, when he escaped the shadow of the Ruff, and that is our peril now. He may know enough to make an impact upon the present campaign in the field, or to make the next German offensive truly deadly. Both sides are struggling for an advantage over the other at this crucial juncture of the war; Ivery may now give that edge to Berlin. The awful thing is that we don't know for certain."

"Then we've got to push off and get after him," Hannay said with an odd, boyish enthusiasm.

"But what do you suggest we do?" asked Magillivray. "If it's a question of destroying this one man, how are you going to find him? Need I say more than the phrase *needle and haystack*?"

"All the same, we've got to do it," Hannay countered. "My old friend Peter Pienaar—"

"The Boer?" asked Sir Walter.

"Yes," said Hannay. "Him. Peter gave me more than one lesson on fortitude and—"

"I wish I could be an optimist," interjected Bullivant with impatience, waving off Hannay's remarks with a tired hand. "I do so wish, but it looks as if we must own defeat this time. I have been at my work for some twenty years, and though often been beaten, I've always kept a few cards in the game. Now I'm hanged if I have any. This is a knockout, Hannay. It's no good deluding ourselves. We're men enough to look facts in the face and tell ourselves the truth, and the truth is that I don't see any glint of light in this business. We've missed our shot by a hairsbreath, but that's the same as missing by miles."

Sherlock Holmes opened his mouth to speak, but then, observing as did I the play of expression that passed between Hannay and Mary Lamington, he remained silent. And in that moment, Hannay came to the fore again.

"Sir Walter," the South African said, "three years ago we sat in this room, after that same plump man had made off with vital military secrets. We thought then that we were done to the world, as we think now. We had just a miserable little set of clues, all contained in a few words scribbled in a notebook by a dead man. We had given up hope, and then Mr. Holmes grasped the essence of those words in Frank Scudder's book, and in twenty-four hours we had won out."

He paused, perhaps thinking of that same plump man who had eluded our grasp in 1914. "Largely won out, at any rate," Hannay amended.

Bullivant nodded.

"At that moment, we were very much fighting against time," Hannay said. "Now we can enjoy a degree of leisure in our approach. Moreover, we have a greater body of knowledge concerning our enemy than before, based on observation. The point is, in this round we have something with which to work. Sir Walter, do you mean to tell me that, when the stakes are so very big, you're going to chuck in your hand?"

"We do know a good deal about Ivery," admitted Magillivray, raising his head. "But Ivery's dead. We know nothing of the man who came to life when that plane landed in Normandy."

"I beg to differ," said Sherlock Holmes. "There are many faces to this man, but only one mind, and we know a good deal about that mind."

"Should we not catalogue that knowledge?" I suggested.

"An excellent thought, Watson," Holmes said. "And I strongly endorse Mr. Hannay's sentiment, expressed a moment ago, that we continue the chase without fail."

"You would pursue him, Holmes?" Sir Walter asked.

"To France and perhaps beyond?" replied my friend. He shook his head. "Not I; that is a younger man's task. Moreover, I have my own grail to pursue here in Britain."

"The mythical third head?" asked Bullivant.

Holmes nodded, and Sir Walter silently concurred.

"Unless I miss my guess," said Blenkiron slyly from his chair, "it is Dick Hannay who wants the job of finding Mr. Moxon Ivery."

Hannay smiled. "Of course I want it," he said. "I've got a stack of personal affronts to settle with the fellow, not to speak of the interests of the nation in mind as well. Mind you, I'm going back to my brigade in France first. I want a rest and a change, as strange as that remark might sound. Besides, the first stage of our effort will be office work, and I'm no use for that. But I'll be waiting for your summons, Sir Walter, and I'll come like a shot as soon as you call for me."

"You're certain?" Bullivant asked.

"I've a presentiment about this thing. I know in my bones that there will be a finish and that I will be in at it."

Sherlock Holmes looked down with an abstracted expression.

"And I've no illusions," Hannay added. "It will be a desperate, bloody business."

"I fear you are all too correct in that sentiment, General Hannay," said Mary Lamington. "And, acknowledging that, I can make only one suggestion at present."

"And that is what?" asked Bullivant, looking up.

"That we go upstairs to your drawing room, Sir Walter, and take some tea."

In less than an hour we found ourselves buoyed by a renewed sense of hope. Within the elegant lines and décor of Sir Walter's drawing room, we found solace in tea and Miss Lamington's skill at the piano. Then, at length, we began to assemble what we knew about the man behind the face of Moxon Ivery.

"I observed Abel Gresson pass on instructions to another man on the Isle of Skye—the Portuguese whom I've mentioned," Hannay reminded us at one point. "They didn't know I was hiding a short distance away and watching. Their conversation included some other names, and there were some strange remarks between them about birds."

"Was the phrase *The Wild Birds* employed?" said Sherlock Holmes.

"Why yes, it was," exclaimed Hannay. "How did you know?"

"Watson and I once heard another German speak of wild birds," the detective explained. "At a many-gabled house on the Essex shoreline, three years ago."

"The lines that Ivery and the Portuguese uttered were poetry," said Hannay. "Launcelot Wake said the passages were from Goethe."

"You saw Launcelot in Skye?" asked Miss Lamington with sudden urgency.

"I did," replied Hannay. "And it's a bit of relief to know your cousin is not a spy, after all."

Holmes glanced at me, and I turned toward Hannay. In the corner of my eye, I saw Mary Lamington bow her head.

"In any event," Holmes went on, "the names you overhead being mentioned and the phrase *wild birds* are items with which we may start." He looked at Magillivray. "Surely, Inspector, we may hope they lead us somewhere?"

The man from Scotland Yard looked less despondent. "There might be something in all that," he said, "but still, it's a slim chance."

"Of course it is," said Blenkiron. "And so let's get out our small-tooth combs and get to work on it."

"I wish to heaven there was one habit of mind we could definitely attach to the fellow and no one else," Magillivray said.

"That may not work with this man," asserted Blenkiron. "He possesses multiple facets, multiple strengths."

"What about weaknesses, then?" asked Sherlock Holmes.

"Weaknesses?" Magillivray said.

"Yes, blind spots," said Holmes. "A fault that causes him to ignore or overlook, to become careless."

"Yes," said Hannay. "Places he won't go to, things he can't do—well, things he can't do well, anyway. I reckon such knowledge would be useful."

"Perhaps," said Magillivray, "if we knew what they were. It's not what you'd call a burning and shining light, though, is it?"

"There's one chink in his armour," Hannay said. "There's one person in the world he can never practise his transformative disguises on, and that's me. I will always know him again, even though he should appear as my own commanding officer. That will give us an edge."

"It would give *you* an edge," said Magillivray.

Mary Lamington got up from the piano and stepped to the side of Sir Walter Bullivant, who sat comfortably in an armchair.

"There is one huge blind spot of which none of you are yet aware," she said, her cheeks suddenly flushing.

"Oh?" said Sherlock Holmes. "And what is that, Miss Lamington?"

"Just before I last saw him in Biggleswick yesterday, Mr. Ivery asked me to marry him."

Hannay returned to France a few days later. About the same time, I received a letter from Launcelot Wake, informing me that he had been formally inducted into the Labour Corps and would soon be crossing the Channel to France. Making no mention of his meeting Hannay on Skye, the young man reiterated his view that the war was unjust, once more attributing his decision to serve to a desire for fresh air and exercise. I put down his letter with a smile, though in my heart, there was nothing but trepidation for him.

Leaving the search for Moxon Ivery to Magillivray, Scaife, and other agents of Sir Walter Bullivant, Sherlock Holmes devoted himself once more to a concerted search for oddities, anomalies, and inconsistencies in the daily life of our nation and its inhabitants, hoping that by turning over some small, curious pebble he might uncover a clue leading him to the third German spy ring. I noticed that he also took to thumbing through his commonplace books, some of them decades old, in which he had stored a variety of articles on esoteric topics and little-known individuals.

Farrar, Johnson, and Arbuthnot, meanwhile, kept dredging every street in London for the unusual in general and for Dietrich Baumann in particular, but they found nothing of value during those searches. Similarly, Tatty Evans aboard the *Belisama* observed only regular river traffic, with no sign of the *Nemesis.*

I continued to wrestle with the dual discontents of fulfilling what I saw as trivial office duties for the medical corps on the one hand and, on the other, the near useless responsibilities of being a mere listener to my friend's speculations. I found myself with nothing of value to contribute as Holmes relentlessly poured over newspapers, periodicals, and government reports. More than once each day, I sat and envied Launcelot Wake for his fresh air and exercise, as well as his contribution to our nation's cause.

In the weeks that followed, Abel Gresson remained free and apparently unsuspected, but his every move was closely watched, as Sherlock Holmes had recommended. The man travelled to France as part of an official labour delegation to observe the front, while the individual identified by Hannay as the Portuguese courier was subsequently seen by British agents and later observed discreetly in London by Magillivray's Sergeant Scaife.

As we entered October, I received a letter from Charlie Taylor, who was faring well in Dumfries but informed me that Ewan Clark's soul remained in limbo. Three days later, I also received a note from Captain Edward Ashley Tate, who had been discharged from Isham to rejoin his brigade to France. His second week back at the front, the officer had narrowly escaped a German whiz-bang,[221] but the incident had not fazed him, he wrote, for he told me he now believed he lived on borrowed time in any case.

One person I did not hear from was Mary Lamington. I presumed her still to be at Isham, though her task of discreetly watching Moxon Ivery had ended. However, upon being reminded of the Cotswolds hospital by Ashley Tate's letter, I resolved to write her that very day. As I finished that task, Holmes returned to Queen Anne Street with a loud slamming of the house door. I waited calmly in the sitting room, wondering if his loud report was one of victory or frustration. The buoyant energy of his step upon entering the room answered that question at once.

---

221 "Whiz-bang" was a term for the shell of a small-caliber, high-velocity gun.

"I fret over the jigsaw puzzle here in London," he said with amusement. "Only to learn that Hannay, recuperating in his dugout in France, has confirmed a key piece almost without effort."

He threw his coat and hat upon a chair, covering the stacks of books and clippings already piled there.

"And it is both remarkable and delightful!" he exclaimed. "Though I am humbled by my negligence, I am overjoyed that our quest is suddenly advanced by countless leagues."

I set aside pen and paper and turned to address my friend. "To which quest do you refer?" I asked. "The search for the plump man or the uncovering of your missing head of Cerberus? And what piece do mean?"

"Insofar as quests are concerned, either or both," replied Holmes. "And it is this piece," he said, tossing down a folded newspaper before me.

"What am I supposed to notice?" I asked. I picked up the paper and stared at the page, which contained headlines and text that were overshadowed by a huge advertisement whose subject I immediately recalled from memory.

"Gussiter's Deep-breathing System," I read. "The silly device that was advertised on the matchbook taken from the man hit by that taxicab."

"The very same."

"An apparatus that is 'a cure for every ill, mental, moral, or physical that man can suffer'?" I said, quoting from the advertisement. "What does this add to your plate? And how did Hannay even catch notice of it?"

"Because of these cousins," said Holmes, reaching for his discarded coat to withdraw from a large pocket three more newspapers, all of them German. He laid them out before me, folded in such a manner to display advertisements which, though not in English, were accompanied by an illustration almost identical to that in the first paper.

"My word!"

"The *Frankfurter Zeitung*, *Volkstimmes,* and *Volkszeitungs*," said Holmes, naming each of the publications in turn.[222] "All of them carry the advertisement. Oh, the name of the company in these is Weissmann rather than Gussiter, and there are choice quotations from Schiller that you won't find in the English versions, but they are all clearly from the same source. Bullivant is attempting to ferret out where this Gussiter or Weissmann business originates, and I believe he's put Blenkiron onto the scent as well."

"But what could be the significance to all this?"

"Communication, as suggested earlier by the matchbook alone," replied Holmes. "The advertising text varies from one to the next in the German publications as the weeks progress. The same is true of those English newspapers in which the corresponding displays appear."

I thought for a moment. "And you believe that these advertisements contain coded messages?"

"I think it is certain. You see, British agents have been doing much the same thing in Dutch newspapers, planting advertisements there that contain coded messages in order to get their information to our people here in Britain.[223]

---

[222] The *Frankfurter Zeitung* was apparently a real newspaper, but the other two may be fictional. Tellingly, however, those same two publications are referred to in Buchan's *Mr. Standfast*.

[223] Like Switzerland, The Netherlands remained neutral in the First World War. Consequently, it became a hotbed for espionage activity.

“Insofar as these advertisements are concerned, I will attempt to draw out any such messages as I can. The samples are few and short, but by comparing them to that display on the inside cover of the matchbook, I believe there is a chance of success. For the moment, it is enough to establish that messages are conveyed by this means, even if we cannot yet read them.”

“And you say that Hannay came across all this?” I said, pointing at the foreign newspapers.

“Yes,” said Holmes. “His division has been embroiled in the current campaign,[224] but he came down with another bout of malaria, such as troubled him when he was on the run in Galloway three years ago. While convalescing in a dugout, he began reading a number of old newspapers, including some German ones sent him by our fellows in Intelligence—Hannay is fluent in German, if you recall.

“It was then that he noticed the repeated appearance of these deep-breathing advertisements in our papers ás well as those of the enemy. He got to speculating and communicated those thoughts to Bullivant, who recalled my mention of the matchbook and conveyed Hannay’s discovery.

“There is certainly something to it, Watson, though at this point one cannot say if these advertisements for Gussiter’s Deep-breathing apparatus might be a message system for our Mr. Moxon Ivery or the third head of Cerberus—or perhaps both. But now that we have full appreciation of it, thanks to General Hannay, there will be no letting go.”

§ § §

---

[224] This would be the Third Battle of Ypres, mentioned in footnote 210.

Two days later, I returned home from a general staff meeting, one of the few occasions when my superfluous position with the medical corps required me to absent Queen Anne Street. Entering the sitting room, I saw Holmes studying a large map of London that overflowed the breakfast table.

"The *Nemesis* has been sighted at last," my friend said without prologue, looking up from the chart.

"By Tatty Evans and Old George?"

"Yes. And not once, but twice in the same day. Come here and let me relate their observations."

I put aside my valise of documents and removed my military cap. Stepping to Holmes's side, I saw before me a depiction of the river and bands two miles wide on either side of the waters, stretching from Twickenham all the way to the Estuary.

"It was here," revealed Holmes, pointing on the map toward the Isle of Dogs. "Just opposite the West India Docks, where the *Belisama* caught sight of our *Nemesis*."[225]

"Twice, you say?"

"Yes. Recall that Master Evans had begun his search much farther to the east, without success, but at regular intervals, according to my recommendation, he has been anchoring his barge at points progressively to the west of that starting point. Yesterday, he espied the *Nemesis* heading east. About one hour later, the launch reappeared, this time cruising in

---

[225] Now a part of Greater London, Twickenham is about ten miles southwest of the center of the metropolis, while the Thames Estuary is the area where the river meets the North Sea. The Isle of Dogs, meanwhile, was originally a peninsula in the East End of London and became the site of the West India Docks, first opened in 1802 and closed to commercial traffic in 1980.

the opposite direction." He glanced at the clock. "I am awaiting word from him regarding another possible appearance today."

I looked at the map for a moment and then said, "But not from the same point of observation."

The detective smiled. "Correct, Watson. Having determined that the *Nemesis* does not ply the waters to the extreme east, we can conclude that between that region and Evans's position of yesterday lies either the place where the launch moors or a point of interest for her."

"A headquarters or storage place?"

"I have entertained such possibilities."

Just then, our doorbell rang, and Holmes looked at me with an expectant smile. Moments later, Martha appeared, an envelope in her hand.

"A commissionaire[226] just brought this to the door, sir," she said as Holmes crossed the sitting room to accept the letter from her. Before she left, the woman asked, "Now that you are home, Colonel, may I have cook complete dinner preparations and serve within the hour?"

"The half hour, if you like," I replied as Holmes tore open the envelope. Martha departed down the hallway, and I watched my friend's face for an indication of the nature of the message.

His smile told the tale soon enough.

"Tatty Evans has located the eastern mooring point of the *Nemesis*," Holmes declared, tossing the note down upon the map.

I stepped to the map, and my friend pointed to a spot near its centre.

---

[226] Martha is probably referring to a member of the Corps of Commissionaires, a security firm founded in 1859 by Sir Edward Walter as a means of supplying employment for former servicemen.

"It is here," said Holmes. "Just south of the gasworks."

"The gasworks. The parts of your elephant begin to coalesce," I said before leaving to dress for dinner.

CHAPTER NINETEEN: A SPURNED WATCHMAN

"Yes, Watson," said Sherlock Holmes the next morning as he entered our sitting room in Queen Anne Street. "I will gladly consider venturing out in order to acquire some marmalade, in the improbable hope that any can be found."

I looked up from the breakfast table, moved the leg I had stretched out before me, and gave my friend a jaundiced eye. "Why would you ever think that I should—?"

"Ask such a favour of me?" Holmes said, finishing my thought. "I believe the evidence is all in plain view, old fellow."

Grasping the arm of my chair, I drew in my leg and hoisted myself into a more upright sitting position. "Am I now to receive the most recent deductive enumeration of these past thirty—no, thirty-six years?"

"The decades have groomed your expectations to a tee," said the detective as he strode past and assumed the chair opposite mine at the table. "And the enumeration, as you term it, will be mercifully brief. We both know that marmalade is your first choice of material to spread over toast in the morning. Indeed, for years it has been your only willing choice; yet, there on your table, I see no container of the beloved substance, only an untouched knife beside a piece of toast that lies quite naked and only partially consumed." He glanced round the table. "Evidently, you will deign to put neither butter nor berry preserves upon your bread this morning."

"Or any morning. It is personal preference."

"Of course it is, and your right to that choice I shall defend to the death. I am certain that the bitter memory of dry toast has caused you to resolve that, by tomorrow's breakfast, the situation will not repeat. That will require someone to travel to a grocer's, however. You might have considered requesting Martha do the deed, but she is wandering about burdened with the after-effects of a rather nasty cold, and you would never send her out of doors in that state. And since acquiring your new cook, you have taken care not to impose on her, for fear that she may leave as did the previous one."

That the first cook left because of Holmes's impositions I did not mention.

"This month's maid is so distracted in personality that you would never entrust her with such a task." Holmes continued. "Of course, you would have no compunction about completing the errand yourself, but it appears that venerable jezzail bullet from the late Afghan War is once again making itself felt, for when I entered, you had positioned yourself with an outstretched leg, which is your habit when that old wound acts up. It would make for a painful journey in search of marmalade, Watson, and so your thoughts naturally gravitated toward me as possible errand boy," he declared as he stood up from the table.

"Holmes, you make it sound as if I view you—"

"It is no bother to me, old fellow. I have just told you it is a task I will gladly perform for you, though with wartime shortages becoming rather acute, there is no guarantee that any marmalade is to be found." Holmes smiled while grasping a poker with which he stirred the coals. "If I am successful, however, you may take the purchase price off my rent."

I viewed my friend with mock dismissal. "You do not pay rent!"

"I have offered to, on more than one occasion."

"It is out of the question. However, the marmalade is not—if you do not mind."

"I do not. It will be a pleasure to repay you for your invaluable assistance these past months—indeed, years."

"By my count, it is decades, but no matter. The task will not take too much away from your pondering of Gussiter's Deep-breathing System?"

"Not at all," replied Holmes cheerfully, as he continued to rake the coals, now without necessity. "I am, after all, capable of transporting myself by foot and thinking, both at the same time."

Just then, there was a knock upon the sitting room door, which by custom had been left ajar. Both Holmes and I turned to witness Martha's head appear in the opening.

"It's Mr. Johnson and Mr. Farrar, sirs," our housekeeper said with a nasal voice. She gave a quick sneeze. "They are with another gentleman."

"Send them in," commanded Holmes, setting aside the poker. "That is," he added in a whisper, "if your marmalade can wait, Watson."

"Of course it can."

"Mr. Holmes? Colonel Watson?" came a voice from the doorway.

Frank Farrar, hat in hand, entered and then stepped to one side to allow Shinwell Johnson and another man entry into the sitting room. Farrar's brilliant blue eyes sparkled, and his mouth turned up in its usual coy smile as he announced, "Porky and I have brought you a most intriguing story, we believe."

"Oh?" said Holmes, stepping away from the hearth. "Well, I am eager to hear it."

I stood up from the table to greet the two agents and their companion: a short, clean-shaven man of late middle age, who wore an old-fashioned, multicaped ulster. He held a billycock hat in one hand and shifted his feet back and forth against the carpet.

"Hello, sir," the stranger croaked in a hoarse voice.

"Retired hansom drivers seem to go for a shilling a dozen these days," remarked Sherlock Holmes as he stared at our visitor, "though I suppose that one who has traded driving horses for work in a mews[227] and then yet other employment may still have some few choice experiences to relate."

"Yes," said the beady-eyed stranger in a casual voice. "Driving a hansom cab was my calling in life, I suppose, but I've few stories to tell about it, and it's a chapter that's sadly ended for me now."

Shinwell Johnson, who had been observing the man, gave a slight start when his as yet unnamed companion evinced no surprise at Holmes's comments. "Do the owner's conclusions about you not shock and amaze?" he asked.

"Why should they?" replied the man in his crackling voice. "You two told me he was Sherlock Holmes. Is that not what he is supposed to do? Draw conclusions from little or nothing?"

"I would not call it either little or nothing," said Johnson with a defensive air. "Rather, we usually found, when he was still in the business, that Mr. Holmes's clients were rather astounded by—"

"I am not looking to be set back on my heels," announced the man impatiently. "I do not seek stupefaction but rather satisfaction. Though,"

---

[227] A mews is a group of stables built around a yard or along an alley, often with rooms above.

he added with an air of annoyance, "at the moment, I believe I most earnestly desire a simple introduction."

"Mr. Holmes," said Frank Farrar with deliberate slowness, "this is Mr. William Grace."

Holmes and Grace nodded to one another, and the detective gestured for the newcomer to take the basket chair, positioned between the sofa, which Holmes now claimed, and the table, at which I once more sat down.

"This is my colleague, Colonel Watson," Holmes added, nodding in my direction.

"Yes, I'm a great reader of yours, sir," said Grace with enthusiasm. "I observe, however," he added with great effect, "that you are back in the army—"

"The medical corps," I confirmed, pushing my breakfast plate away and tugging at the Sam Browne belt of my uniform. "For the past three years."

"Of course," replied the man. "That makes sense, with your experience and all. But may I ask you, sir: Is that Doyle fellow now taking over for you? I read the last story just the other month—and it was a long wait for it—the tale about Mr. Holmes here and that spy Bork, and it wasn't like your others. Is Doyle going to be writing them now?"

I sternly looked at Holmes, who glanced away.

"Doyle may take over my responsibilities briefly while I am in service to our nation," I said. "Or so I understand," I added in an icy voice. "Rest assured, however, that once this war ends, I hope to resume full authorship of my friend's adventures."

"Ah, that will be most welcome."

"Now then, Mr. Grace," Holmes said with a pained smile, "Let us get to what prompts your visit."

"We ran into the gentleman at an establishment in Stepney," said Frank Farrar.

"Yes," said Shinwell Johnson, smiling at the stranger. "He was hoisting a glass while bitterly complaining to anyone who might give a listen."

"And we listened very closely," added Farrar. "We think you will find this man's tale most interesting, Mr. Holmes."

"Well, I don't know that it is interesting to me so much as very frustrating," Grace declared as Shinwell Johnson and Frank Farrar took up positions to one side, standing near the sitting room wall.

"Pray unburden yourself," Holmes said to Mr. Grace. "Tell us the facts concerning your anguish."

"Well, as you correctly surmised, Mr. Holmes—I suppose from my coat here and perhaps my voice—I drove a hansom for many years, but we all know the trade is vanishing on account of those motors. Every bus you see these days is a motor—the horse-drawn ones have all gone away. It'll be the same for the hansoms—sooner rather than later—and I quit the trade, having seen the handwriting on the stable walls.

"I have tried my hand at a few other endeavours in the meanwhile—working first in a mews and then seeking employment in fields unrelated to horses, which I'm certain will become extinct within ten years."

Holmes nodded as he smiled.

"Most recently, I thought I had found a sufficient livelihood from working as a watchman. It was in that capacity, however, that I experienced my present misfortune."

"And Mr. Farrar and Mr. Johnson heard you speak of it?" asked Holmes, reaching for his cherrywood pipe.

"Yes, they did," replied Grace. "They suggested I come to you for assistance, though I understood you to be retired."

My friend he stuffed his pipe. "From time to time, I have no objection to being challenged in my old age. I should enjoy having you tell me your story, Mr. Grace."

"Well, two months ago, I was approached by a fellow to keep a regular eye on a building the far side of Poplar, within smelling distance of a gasworks."[228]

Holmes paused in the act of filling his pipe and glanced at Farrar and Johnson. "Pray, continue," said the detective.

"The building is a warehouse of sorts, I suppose," the man said, "though I never saw the insides, nor was I ever told exactly what was happening behind its walls."

"Where is the structure located?" Holmes asked.

"Just off the high street," said Grace. "I can give you precise directions, if you wish."

"I should like that very much. However, for the moment, you said your duties...as a watchman...extended only to the exterior of the warehouse?" enquired Holmes as he lit his pipe. "You never stepped within?"

"Not once, except to enter a small, separate addition that housed personal facilities, which I used when necessary."

---

[228] Poplar is a district in East London.

"Describe the man who hired you," said the detective, shaking his vesta and tossing it onto the grate. "How did he initially contact you? What was his name? Whom did he represent, if someone other than himself?"

"I had placed myself with an employment agency," responded Mr. Grace. "It was through its auspices that the fellow learnt of me. He was a Swede—introduced himself as Mr. Borge, and he was a mite like you in appearance, Mr. Holmes, though a bit younger: prominent nose, if you don't mind me saying so, penetrating eyes. And a florid face. A bit haughty, in my opinion—of course, in that way he was quite unlike you, I mean to say—but he was all business and did not waste his time or mine."

"Go on," urged Holmes languidly.

"Well, he told me he was a representative for something called Gussiter's Deep-breathing System."

At the mention of Gussiter, the detective betrayed interest with his eyes alone. The name also caused me to straighten suddenly in my chair, the pain in my leg becoming quite irrelevant.

"And what were your specific duties?" asked Holmes.

"Well, they were mildly curious. You see, this Mr. Borge wished me to keep an eye on the building, yes, but that and nothing more: just watch it from the outside and not guard it as such, you see. Indeed, he told me that if I ever saw any suspicious or threatening activity, I was to do nothing to stop it, and on no account was I ever to call the police for assistance. He wished only to know if I had noticed something out of the ordinary."

"And did you ever observe suspicious activity outside the warehouse?"

"None whatsoever," replied William Grace. "Oh, there were lorries—drawn by horses, all of them—that regularly pulled up before the warehouse, and crates were unloaded from them and carried into the building, and other crates were removed from within and carted away."

He scratched his head.

"Now that I think of it, during those last few days there were far more removals than deliveries. In any case, Mr. Borge told me to expect such activity—that parcels would arrive every day while others would be shipped out. And there were a few workmen who did go in and out of the building during the night—but though they were dressed the part, they did not have the air of simple labourers, if you know what I mean."

"I believe I do," Holmes assured him. "Did you ever speak to any of those men?"

"Oh no, for you see, that was another instruction given me by Mr. Borge: I was never to approach anyone going into or coming out of that building. I was to speak to someone only if they spoke to me first."

"Did you not consider that unusual?"

"Of course I did, but they way I saw it, I was getting paid to follow directions, wasn't I?"

"True, you were," admitted Holmes. "And beyond those instructions, rather singular in themselves, you say you did not observe any unusual activity outside the building?"

"Besides the somewhat suspicious appearance of those coming and going, I never witnessed anything that was out of the ordinary, no."

"And what were your hours of observation?"

"From nine o'clock in the evening through to the same hour of the morning: twelve hours straight. I had a key which allowed entry into that portion of the warehouse I previously mentioned, where there were private facilities in case I found myself in need during the night."

"I see," said Holmes, now enveloped in a smoky miasma. "Well, your story thus far is of interest, to be sure. You said, however, that you had a particular complaint."

"Yes," said Mr. Grace. "You see, though there was no written contract with Mr. Borge, I did enter into a verbal agreement with him. The man promised me a full year of work. For the first six weeks, I was paid regularly by a man who had been at Mr. Borge's side when I signed on. It was to that individual that I made my daily reports."

"And from what you have told me, I assume he emerged from the building and accosted you each day?"

"Yes, he came out very briefly every morning to ask if I had seen anything unusual, and each time I told him I had not. He was the only such person from the place with whom I ever spoke. And every Friday, he would give me my week's wages."

"Can you describe this individual?" asked Holmes.

Mr. Grace shrugged. "Well, that brings up something a bit odd in itself, for you see, every time I saw him, he appeared just a bit different. Oh, he was tall and a tad on the thin side, but his style of clothes, the cut of his hair, the manner of the man's walk—each time these and other aspects of him changed a bit. Some days, it was only by talking to him that I could be sure it was the same gent. Well, that and the two ugly moles on his face."

Holmes exhaled noticeably, and his eyes made a circuit round the room, catching in turn Farrar, Johnson, and me before returning to Grace.

"Go on," he said. "You said you were given wages every Friday."

"Right, but you see, this past Wednesday, when I came to the warehouse to take my nightly station, I thought it somehow seemed vacant."

Holmes stared at the man as if willing him to continue.

"Well, I stayed for two hours nonetheless," Grace said, "for in the past there had always been deliveries after such an interval, as well as those odd workmen coming and going. This evening, however, there was no activity at all. At length, despite my standing orders, I knocked upon the main entrance door, but to no effect. Then I happened to see, strolling by, two other men employed elsewhere in the area. They worked during the day, and I had often chatted idly with them as they were on their way home while I was about to begin my nightly vigil. I took them aside to ask about the warehouse.

"'Heard it was evacuated earlier today,' one of them says. 'I saw them take many crates out of it this afternoon,' the other one tells me."

Holmes nodded.

"I went to the building door again," Grace said. "This time I pounded on it with force, but there was still no answer. Judging the warehouse was indeed vacant, I trudged home, reckoning there was no point in watching over an empty shell.

"I returned the next day and found the place still quiet, except for a band of small boys who were poking about the back. I thought to chase them away, but then I decided that if Mr. Borge had abandoned me, I'd not lift a finger for his blasted warehouse. I went in search of a pint or two instead. Indeed, that has been my principal activity since."

"It was late yesterday that we saw Mr. Grace, glass in hand, declaiming for all to hear," said Frank Farrar. "We spoke with him then and there, received his full story, and convinced him to tell his tale to you."

Holmes leaned back in his chair and stared at the ceiling for a moment, the arm holding his pipe extended out to the side, and then he brought down his chin and cast a neutral glance at Farrar and Johnson before saying, "It is a story that has more than one element of interest. Great interest, indeed."

"But there is more to tell, Mr. Holmes," said Shinwell Johnson.

"Yes," agreed Grace. "For I've not yet fully stated my great discontent. You see, I was promised work and pay for a full year, and I received money for less than two months. I want my sovereign a week for the rest of those weeks I was guaranteed, I tell you!"

Once more, Holmes's expression became one of rapt interest. Cocking his head, the detective asked, "Did you say a *sovereign* per week?"

"That's right. He wasn't paying in any of those paper Bradburys. Mr. Borge's man gave me sovereigns, what you can depend on."[229]

Holmes looked with sparkling eyes at Johnson and Farrar, who nodded to him in unison. Holmes returned the gesture, and all three men smiled. There followed several more minutes of interrogation by Holmes, then instructions to his pair of agents, after which he promised to William Grace that he would investigate the matter thoroughly and attempt to gain justice for his new client.

---

229 Before the First World War, some sums of money were still paid in gold coins, one of which was the sovereign, worth £1. In order to conserve gold reserves for the war effort, however, the British government in 1914 began issuing £1 paper notes signed by the Permanent Secretary to the Treasury, Sir John Bradbury, and within a year, gold sovereigns had essentially vanished from public circulation. Bradbury's name became a slang term for the paper notes, which subsequently became a permanent fixture of British economic life.

"Thank you for hearing me out," said Grace as Farrar and Johnson prepared to escort him from the house. "However, what will be your fee, Mr. Holmes?"

"I leave it to you, sir," replied the detective, whereupon William Grace let out a hearty laugh.

"Very well said," chuckled the cabman. "Very well said, indeed."[230]

Grace turned to go, but then, glancing at me with a mixture of apology and hope, asked, "Do you think, Dr. Watson, that there is a bit of a chance that someday this might serve as the basis for one of your stories?"

"We will see," I replied in a soothing tone.

As Grace left in the company of Farrar and Johnson, Holmes tended his pipe thoughtfully. I patiently waited for him to utter a comment, and at length, after the house door had closed, my friend said, "We have more than a few strands now, Watson—we have enough to twist into a hefty thread. I should like to see what pulling on the skein will yield."

"And will Farrar and Johnson do the tugging?"

"I believe I will take a hand first," Holmes replied. "Tomorrow, your leg willing, we will together examine that warehouse site."

"For evidence of Gussiter's Deep-breathing System?"

"For that and more. Meanwhile, the matter of Mr. Grace's wage deserves a careful pull as well."

"The use of sovereigns is significant, I gather."

---

230 "I leave it to you, sir," was the frequent answer given by cabmen when their clients asked to know the fare. Drivers gave that response in hopes that they would be paid more than the legal rate.

"Of course it is," replied Holmes, standing up suddenly. He strode to the mantel and knocked out his pipe. "No one pays in sovereigns any more. I cannot remember the last time I saw one in common use."

"Why would anyone employ them?"

"To avoid the risk of utilising a bank," said Holmes. "If Mr. Grace has been unknowingly working for the Germans, their payments would of course be made in currency drawn from funds previously stockpiled for such use. Assuming that accumulation was made prior to the war, it would be composed of sovereigns rather than paper notes."

"Even if this is the tip of some Germany espionage activity, can you be certain that Von Bork is involved?" I asked.

Holmes leaned upon the mantel and smiled. "I cannot be absolutely certain—yet—but to my mind, the name of Mr. Grace's employer, Mr. Borge, is suggestive of 'Von Bork,' is it not?"

"I get your point. And what is your plan?"

"To get on with my own business," Holmes said. "May I?" he asked, gesturing toward the pile of yellow foolscap that I kept at my writing desk in the corner of the sitting room.

"Of course," I replied.

"The examination of bodies, the questioning of clients, it all slowly comes back to me after all these years," said Holmes as he reached for one of my pens as well. "So too with placing notices in the newspapers.

"Ah," he said, putting pen and paper upon the table as if something had suddenly come to mind.

"Only after I have secured your marmalade, Watson."

§ § §

The next morning—a rainy and glooming one, but also one that saw my physical condition much improved and my outlook on life brightened by the presence of marmalade—I accompanied Holmes down toward Poplar, where—using William Grace's description of the warehouse he had watched—we found the aged brick structure in question.

Grace had exaggerated somewhat about the building being near the gasworks, which in reality was perhaps three-quarters of a mile away, though in the distance, we could see smoke rising from its slag heaps, and from some locations the top of a great gasometer.[231]

"It seems Dieter Baumann was somewhat loose in his description of his place of work as well," Holmes noted. "Farrar and Johnson have been combing an area too far to the east. No wonder their searches came up dry."

"Still," I replied, sniffing, "the gasworks seem close enough this morning."

"Yes," my friend agreed. "We may blame that upon the direction of the wind."

In a state of mild discomfort from the noxious tinge wafting in from the facility, I was led by Holmes through a slow circumnavigation of the block upon which the warehouse sat, during which we contemplated every angle of its design.

"I wouldn't go in there" came a sudden, high-pitched voice from behind.

---

[231] Gasometers—inaccurately named by William Murdoch, who developed gas lighting—do not measure anything, but rather are large cylindrical containers that store gas at near atmospheric pressure. For that purpose, they are now obsolete.

Turning, we saw three young boys staring at us. After a moment, one stepped forward and said, "I told you gents you better not go inside."

"And why do you say that?" asked Holmes.

The small fellow looked at his companions and then replied cautiously, "It's haunted," he said, pointing at the warehouse. "It is, you know. Best not to go inside."

"Do you know someone who has taken that chance?" enquired my friend. "What fate did he suffer?"

Again the boy glanced at his two friends before responding. "We got a pal what paid for the trespass," he told us. "He got a nasty hurt."

"What kind of hurt? Did a ghost strike him?"

The boy did not respond.

"Was the building deserted then, as it is now?"

"Yes," said another of the lads. "It was empty, except for the spirits."

"What spirits do you keep speaking of?" asked Holmes. "What should we fear from going inside?"

"Boils," said the third boy. "Like what you get when you touch a ghost."

Holmes looked at me and then asked the first lad, "Is your wounded friend about? May we speak with him?"

"He didn't do anything wrong."

"Of course he didn't. We would merely wish to—"

Before Holmes could finish his statement, the three turned and ran down the street, vanishing round a corner.

"Though my leg is better, I doubt I can follow in pursuit," I said.

"No matter," said Holmes. "We could never overtake those streetwise tykes, even were we both in fine health and a good thirty years younger. And to give chase would only further alarm them."

He turned toward the vacant warehouse.

"Perhaps their curiosity will draw them back within a short time. But come," my friend said, beginning another circuit of the block. "I believe I espied a door in the back alley that will provide us discreet entry."

"You risk the wrath of ghosts and retribution at the hands of the law as well?" I asked humorously.

"The one is nonexistent and the other may be finessed, Watson."

"In which order do those descriptions apply?" I gently taunted as we entered the alley that extended behind the building.

"Thus do you abuse your supplier of marmalade," Holmes sighed as we walked over cobblestones covered with refuse. Approaching a door at the rear of the warehouse, we passed a small window at pavement level that had been broken. Three boards with nails protruding lay a few feet away.

"The place has already been violated," Holmes noted with interest. "Perhaps this is the work of those boys, related to the incident they spoke of. Perhaps someone else is responsible. In any event, we will not be the first to trespass here, Watson."

Bending down, he examined the door carefully before reaching into a coat pocket to extract a set of fine tools with which he easily opened two locks, which sat one above the other.

"I take it that the finessing has begun?"

Holmes looked up with a smile. "Quite so, old fellow." He rose to his full height and dropped the tools into his coat pocket. Slowly pushing open the door, he said, "Let us relive the illegalities of old."

"Shall I use my torch?" I asked.

"In a moment," Holmes replied as he entered the building and then stepped aside to allow me to follow. "Wait until I close the door then aim your light at the floor, if you will."

The latch clicked shut behind us, darkening the interior, and I immediately pointed my torch beam toward the floor of the warehouse. From the light reflected upward, we could discern that we stood in a windowless corridor leading into the bowels of the structure. Holmes took three steps forward and gestured for me to accompany him.

I cast the light ahead of us, and we walked down the hall, past a series of doors, finding that the corridor gave way to a large open space. Its windows had been boarded over from within, and overhead there were the remains of great ducts that reached down from the ceiling to a point perhaps ten feet above the floor, which was dusty and bore innumerable marks and stains. The floor itself was largely barren, though littered here and there with nails, rotten wooden boards, and scraps of newspaper. To one side, I observed two well-used floggers and a valinch.[232]

We stood in the centre of the huge room and slowly spun round, taking in the ghostly panorama.

"I cannot wonder that those boys thought this place haunted," I said.

---

232 A valinch is a tube usually employed to draw liquor from a cask, while a flogger is a mallet used to move the bung, or stopper, of a cask.

"But they spoke of boils, Watson. That is a tangible effect, not a sensation conjured from imagination." He pinched his nose repeatedly, as if sniffing the air. "It has a chemical aura, does it not? Tar of some sort?"

"Perhaps," I said. "Though I confess it smells somewhat like horseradish to me," I added with raised brows.

"Would that be significant?"

"It brings to mind HS."

"You mean the sulphur mustard gas the Germans have recently begun employing?"[233]

"Yes. I have read that it can possess the aroma of horseradish."

Holmes abruptly cocked his head. "That would explain the boils on the boy, would it not?"

"Yes, if we allow three assumptions: mustard gas was produced or stored here, some was left behind, and one of the boys touched a remnant while exploring this place."

"It would not simply waft away?" my friend asked.

"It is called mustard gas, but at room temperature it remains liquid—looks a bit like sherry, or so one army doctor who recently returned from the front told me. Indeed, it is quite viscous, does not dissolve in water, and can remain in place for weeks or months, I understand."

"We must return with Magillivray and his men to investigate this place more thoroughly, Watson. For now, let us see ourselves out."

"You do not wish to examine the building further?"

"When this interior is surveyed, I prefer it to be accomplished quickly and completely by several men. I also wish to return to the outside, on the

[233] Mustard gas was first used by the German army in July 1917, just before the Third Battle of Ypres. British solders called it Hun Stuff, or HS.

chance that those boys may have reappeared. If they were inquisitive enough to gain entry to this place and prowl about, they may be inclined to come back in order to observe our progress—or to see us run from ghosts. It would be most desirable, if possible, to speak to the lad who was injured here."

We left the warehouse and Holmes restored the door to its initial, locked condition. The two of us stood in the alley for a moment and then strolled toward the street. Halfway there, a small head poked around the corner.

"Half a crown!" shouted Sherlock Holmes, stopping to pull a coin from his pocket. "Half a crown for each of you if you stay this time!"

The head appeared to be yanked back around the building corner, and then the boy appeared again. Hands reached for him from behind the bricks, but he evaded them and stepped fully into the alley, toward us.

"I'll take one," he said. "I'll take the ones for the others, too, if you want."

"A half crown per lad," said Holmes, steadily walking toward the alley entrance.

From around the corner, the other two boys appeared. "What do we have to do?" asked one of them.

"Tell us more. Take us to your friend," said the detective, pulling two additional coins from his pocket. "The one who encountered the ghost."

"Well, maybe it wasn't a ghost," admitted the first child, taking one of the crowns. "It didn't scare you, did it? You two gents went inside."

"We did," replied Holmes, handing coins to the other boys as we stepped beside them. "And now we would like to compare what we saw with what you observed."

“We saw nothing much,” said the third lad. “All of us went inside, but there wasn’t anything there, other than a couple hammers. And a little bit of tar. Billy touched it, but none of us did, and by the next day, the blisters were growing on his hand.”

“Can you take us to Billy?” Holmes asked. “Is he at home?”

“Oh yes. They put him to bed,” said the third boy. “Most likely to get him out of sight. The boils are so ugly and awful, with yellow pus and all.”

“And they hurt,” another added.

“Tell us more as we walk,” said Holmes. “My companion here is a doctor and is interested as well, are you not, Watson?”

“Of course,” I said, falling into step with Holmes and the others.

We listened to the boys tell their story as we followed them south and west, entering the heart of the Poplar district, where destruction from the Zeppelin raids of previous years was still in evidence. In the course of walking just over a half mile from the vacant warehouse, we passed through streets lined with shops associated with the marine trades—ropemakers, chandlers, ironmongers, and sailmakers, as well as an old seamen’s mission. Those with whom we shared the pavement included a large number of dockworkers—some with skin like black leather from the tar they scraped from the tanks of oil ships, others with faces as pale as ghosts from unloading potash. Many were lascars, sporting turbans or queues.[234]

---

[234] A lascar was a sailor from any of the countries east of the Cape of Good Hope—quite often India—employed aboard European ships. The East India Company recruited many, most of whom settled in Britain. At the start of the First World War, over fifty thousand lascars lived there.

As we passed a group of children playing Dead Man, we came upon terraces of shabby lets. [235] Eventually, the lads escorted us inside one such building. On its second storey, we paused before a door.

"Look," said one of them. "You see, his mum doesn't know the full story. Thinks he touched something in the fields round the gasworks. She doesn't know he went inside that old building."

Holmes nodded.

"We don't want him to get into more trouble," another boy said.

The detective set a firm expression on his face and merely said, "Knock, please, or I will do so."

Reluctantly, one of our escorts struck the door with a fist and loudly identified himself by name. A woman's voice from within responded with permission to enter.

Opening the door, we saw a small, sparsely furnished room where a woman leaned against an iron bedstead while sitting on a horsehair mattress darning stockings. Her youthful but haggard face signalled alarm at the sight of us, and she stood up suddenly.

"You're not a brand new pair of tallymen, are you?" she asked suspiciously.[236]

"Not at all," replied Holmes. "My companion is a doctor, and we are here merely to see the boy Billy."

"They said he would be all right," she said in a raspy voice. "There is not supposed to be nothing to fear."

---

[235] Dead Man is a variant of Blind Man's Bluff, and terrace lets are what Americans would term townhouses or rowhouses that are rental units.

[236] A tallyman was a debt collector who took payments for goods obtained under hire purchase, somewhat analogous to what Americans call an installment plan.

“We have no reason to believe there is,” I interjected. Glancing at Holmes, I added, “We wish simply to check on the progress of his wounds.”

“At no cost?” she enquired, with eyes narrowed.

“At no cost,” I assured her.

“All right, then,” she said with reluctance, setting her work upon a table fashioned from fruit crates.

She studied Holmes and me and then glanced at the three boys. “There won’t be room for everyone at once. You saw him yesterday,” the woman told the boys. “You can wait. In here, gentlemen.”

Holmes and I followed her across the small room. Passing before a window partially covered by newspaper, I glanced down through the pane at a small concrete backyard where two girls were drawing water from a standing tap. An old man emerged from a privy that stood near the tap, and I turned my attention back to Holmes and the woman.

“The other doctor didn’t know what it was he touched round near the gasworks,” she said. “And those boys,” she added, nodding back toward the boys. “*They* keep saying it was ghosts. As if.”

She opened a door, and we stepped into an even smaller room, in which another horsehair bed was pushed up against a bare wall. One small window sat high up on the opposing side, and light diffused in through another sheet of newspaper to reveal a small figure beneath bed covers, a hand hanging out from the edge of a cot.

“His brother sleeps on the floor now when he’s around, instead of with Billy, him being injured. Billy?” she said sharply. “Billy, wake up.”

The blankets stirred. The hand moved and then winced. A boy’s voice mumbled wordlessly, and the occupant of the cot pulled himself up into a sitting position with one arm, revealing a round, dirty face. The other hand, on which I could see yellow blisters, twisted slightly, back and forth at the wrist.

"These men have come to give you another look," the boy's mother said quietly. "He has gotten better," she told us. "In the beginning, I was so worried. Thought it was plague."

I knelt down beside the boy, who smiled sleepily at me.

"May I look at your hand?" I asked.

"Don't touch it, please," the lad said. "Not if you don't have to."

Handling only his forearm, which was unaffected, I turn the entire limb round and observed more closely the blisters on his fore and middle finger, as well as two on the palm. Their nature was immediately obvious to me at such close range.

"It is as we suspected," I said to Holmes.

"Sulphur mustard?"

"Yes. Do you have any wounds elsewhere?" I asked the boy.

He shook his head.

"The exposure must have been minimal," I said, again addressing Holmes. "If these are the only blisters, he is very fortunate."

I let go the boy's arm, reached forward and gently pulled back both his eyelids in turn. "The eyes are normal. Have you had difficulty breathing?" I asked the boy.

"No," he replied. "Just the boils."

I nodded and then with a little effort rose to my feet.

"Is he doing well?" the woman asked. "And what was that about mustard? Was it spoiled food he touched? The doctor what treated him said it was something chemical."

"The boy will heal in time," I told her. "He seems to be progressing well. And the doctor was correct," I added. "Your son was exposed to a substance akin to some with which our soldiers in France are sometimes attacked."

"You mean he was gassed?" she said, drawing back in fright.

"The chemical was in liquid form, and he appears to have innocently touched it," I told her.

Stepping past me to speak with the lad, Sherlock Holmes asked, "Did you see any stain that was yellow or brown when you were in that warehouse?"

"In what warehouse?" said the woman. "Did he go inside the gasworks?"

Holmes ignored her comment. "It is of vital importance that you tell me the truth, Billy," he said. "The entire truth."

"What warehouse?" repeated the woman, and Holmes raised a hand in her direction as he kept staring at the young boy, who anxiously looked back and forth between his mother and the detective.

"Please," said Holmes, his voice softening as a show of kindness flowed into his eyes. "It will be all right if you just tell the truth."

"Yes," Billy stammered after a moment. "There were stains, but it was dark in there, and I didn't see them until I had put my hand on them."

"And it was the next day that you felt your hand hurt?" asked Holmes.

"That night, in truth," answered the boy. "It began to hurt so badly."

"When did you go exploring in the warehouse?" asked Holmes. Billy's mother continued to mutter under her breath, but my friend ignored her.

“Thursday,” Billy said nervously. “Thursday, just before sunset, when it was still light about.”

Holmes nodded. “After the warehouse had been abandoned. It was dark inside, wasn’t it, Billy?” he asked.

“Yes. We’d been playing Ginger[237] with the men in the building for days. They didn’t like it, of course, and that made it all the more fun. Then, that day, we tried it again, only no one answered. After a time, we realised there wasn’t anyone there anymore. So we decided to go inside.”

The boy paused for a moment and then continued. “We had no matches for light. We had to walk slowly down that hallway—

“You did not enter through a door, did you?” Holmes said.

The boy looked at his mother, who remained in the doorway, and shrugged. “No. There was a little window down near the alley pavement that was boarded over. We had seen the men nailing planks over it.”

Holmes eyes widened slightly, and he nodded but did not interrupt the lad.

“Well, we pried the boards off,” Billy said slowly, looking warily at his mother. “We used one of them to break the window.”

The mother gave a cry of disgust and turned away, leaving the room. The boy bit his lip and began to tremble.

“Go on,” said Holmes dispassionately. “I know that it is difficult, but you see, this is for king and country.”

The boy looked at him with a suddenly puzzled expression and then continued. In the absence of Billy’s mother, the other three lads slowly

---

[237] Also known as Knocky Door Ginger and by other names, Ginger is a children’s prank involving knocking on the door or ringing the doorbell of a building and running away before anyone answers.

crept into the room, gathering round their wounded friend as he continued.

"I was the one who volunteered to go in first," Billy said. "Harry dared me to go inside."

One of the other boys bowed his head.

"I crawled in through the broken window and dropped down into this hallway with a low ceiling," Billy said. "I followed it by keeping my hand against the wall and found a huge room with big metal pipes and such. Then I came back for the others."

Holmes nodded.

"It was dark, like I said," Billy went on. "Windows was boarded over, but some light still got in. We wandered about the place, and I started feeling around on the floor, trying to find what was there, you know? It must have been then that I touched it—in a corner, I think. We never found anything much, though, and left the place..."

The boy stopped, as if uncertain of what more to say.

"Afterward, you told your family that you had touched something in a field near the gasworks," completed Sherlock Holmes. "You did not wish to admit to entering the warehouse."

The boy nodded.

"She'd have beaten him," whispered one of the other boys. "Maybe his da would have, too."

"I know your hand gives you distress," the detective said, "but it will heal eventually. And, in the bargain, you have done our country a great service. Now," Holmes added, leaning forward, "you said a moment ago that the four of you watched that window be boarded over. Did you observe more? Perhaps objects being carried from the warehouse?"

"No," replied Billy, and the other boys nodded.

"We just saw them boarding up some of the windows," said another of the lads. "Then the men left in a lorry."

"How many men were there?" asked Holmes. "What did they look like? Did the lorry have any identification?"

"There was two of them," said one of the boys. "Just a pair of men in work clothes."

"Yes, but they were clean work clothes, weren't they?" said another. "And the two of them didn't act anything like regular blokes. They didn't behave quite right."

"As if they were acting the part of workmen?" asked Holmes.

"Yes, that's it," said the first boy. "They knew how to use their tools, but it seemed like none of it was natural for them."

"There was nothing," said Billy from his cot. "Nothing written on the lorry."

"Yes, that's right," said another of the boys. "What writing there might have been on the side was painted over."

"Thank you, lads," declared Holmes, who spent another few minutes questioning the young witnesses before leading me back into the first room, where Billy's mother sat, furiously darning.

"Your son has performed a great service for our country," he told the woman, who continued her work.

"He will recover fully," I added.

"I don't know that he'll recover from the beating I'm going to give him," she said angrily. "Lying and breaking into a building! I was angry enough when I thought he'd trespassed onto the gasworks, but this...I've not raised him and his brother to be—"

The door suddenly opened and a burly mad with a florid, leathery face entered. He was of early middle age, with the bottom of one ear lobe missing. Tossing a canvas bag of tools onto the floor, he calmly considered Holmes, the boys, and me for a moment.

"So what's this, then?" he asked.

"Bill lied to us, Len," the woman said at once. "The boys all broke into some warehouse down the high road. That's where he got the boils."

"Oh," said the man, as if the revelation were a minor one.

"Your son will be awarded for his daring contribution to the war effort," Holmes quickly declared. "I think it not at all unlikely that he will receive a medal for his efforts."

"A medal?" the woman said, abruptly looking up from her needles. "What do you mean by telling me he'll get a medal?" She snorted and returned to her work. "That's a fantasy and a half."

"Medal's got some value," asserted the man. "But what's all this about? You two still haven't explained yourselves."

"Billy did enter a warehouse, sir," Holmes told the man. "And by telling me what he observed, and by suffering with his wound, he has helped our nation's war effort greatly."

"How can that be?" the man asked. "Hell, if getting hurt now and then is worth a commendation, I'd be scooping up heaps of medals down at the iron works."

"Your son undoubtedly *will* receive a commendation for the information he has provided me today," asserted Holmes. "It would not surprise were it signed by the king himself."

The husband and wife looked at each other, dumbfounded.

"But he lied," said the woman. "He trespassed."

"His indiscretion was on behalf of our country," declared my friend. "And if a penalty must be exacted, has he not paid it already? Surely you have witnessed the agony inflicted upon his hand."

"Well, of course I have," the woman said defensively. "That, however, is beside the point. He has—"

"He has earned his badge of bravery already," the detective said, reaching into a pocket. "And he has given our government invaluable information in the struggle against Germany." He held out a handful of half crowns.

"What's this?" the husband said.

"A small portion of Billy's coming financial reward, quite beside the medal he will receive. The balance will be forthcoming."

"What?" cried the woman, while the man simply snatched the coins from Holmes's palm.

"Are they real, Len?" she asked.

"Real as real," he answered. "There's nearly two quid here. And you say there's to be more?" he asked Holmes. "Much more?"

The detective nodded.

"And a medal and being commended?" the woman asked, her mood now changed. "All for my Billy?"

"Trust to it, madam. I speak the truth."

"Well," said the husband. "Eggs is eggs." Heclenched his hand round the coins he had taken from Holmes and walked past us to peer in at his son, still on the bed and surrounded by his friends.

"Da" came Billy's voice from the other room.

"Just stay there, son," said the man, who turned round to face Holmes and me.

“All right, then,” he muttered. “We’ll take your word for it.”

“The one there is a doctor,” said his wife as she gestured toward me. “Said he’s doing fine.”

“Yes,” I said as the husband gave me an inquring look. “Your son is progressing well and will fully recover from the wounds he received.”

“All right, then,” the man repeated. “All right, I say.”

Later, after we had departed the building, we chanced across a hansom, one of the dwindling examples of its kind. Holmes gave me an expectant look, and I answered with a shrug. We both tumbled into the vehicle and told the driver to take us to Queen Anne Street.

“It seems a wonder we were ever satisfied with such conveyances,” I remarked after we had gone but a few blocks, for I found the interior much smaller than those I remembered from the past.

“Well, you now have your motorcar,” said Holmes, “though I don’t believe you have taken it out of the stable since early spring. With the general shortage of petrol, I doubt you will find opportunity to use it until this war is over. I hope you can afford the upkeep for a luxury you cannot enjoy, old fellow.”

“In truth,” I admitted to my friend, “I sold it shortly before setting out for Isham. Got a pretty penny for it, if you must know.”

“There are no plans for a replacement?”

“Oh, there are plans, to be sure.” I watched the blocks pass as our horse kept up a steady gait. “Once the war ends, I will purchase one of those American vehicles recommended so long ago by Blenkiron.”

I glanced at Holmes, whose gaze was fixed upon the passing store fronts as he fidgeted beside me.

“Perhaps you would enjoy a ride now and then,” I added.

“Perhaps,” he said, still seemingly uncomfortable as we rode along.

“Were you not somewhat free in your pledges to the young boy’s parents?” I asked after a while. “Or will you once again raid your brother’s resources and prey upon his goodwill.”

“Of course I shall,” replied my friend. “The government funds Mycroft has deposited in my account will cover an additional reward for Billy many times over, and if my brother cannot have a special medal struck, we will have him requisition a spare DCM or some such.”[238]

“And can Mycroft produce a commendation signed by the king himself?”

“I believe so,” my friend answered. “Indeed, my brother can do more than merely believe in six impossible things before breakfast, Watson; he can accomplish them.”[239]

“And what of the empty warehouse?” I said. “When will it be searched more completely?”

“Later today,” replied Holmes. “I will ring up Magillivray as soon as we reach Queen Anne Street and have him speak to the building’s owners—he will pose as an aide to you, Watson, and you will purport to be a representative of the government, wishing to use the structure for official business. Then we shall all conduct a careful survey of its interior, as well as learn what we can from the owner about his previous tenant.”

---

[238] The Distinguished Conduct Medal, instituted in 1854, recognized an act of gallantry by a soldier below the rank of officer. It was discontinued in 1993, when it and two other awards were replaced by the Conspicuous Gallantry Cross.

[239] Holmes’s remark would appear to be a play upon a comment by the White Queen in Lewis Carroll’s *Through the Looking-Glass*. See also footnote 87.

At length we passed into Queen Anne Street and were deposited in front of my residence. Holmes paid the driver and then stood to watch the cab disappear into the bustling traffic of our modern metropolis.

"Hum," he said. "I agree with your earlier pronouncement, Watson: I cannot see how we managed with those vehicles when we inhabited Baker Street. Remind me to never ride in one again. Nostalgia has its limits."

CHAPTER TWENTY: THE TRANSPORT LEAGUE

Holmes rang up Inspector Magillivray and instructed him to make arrangements with the warehouse owners to meet with their land agent at the building later that day. In the midst of his conversation with the man from Scotland Yard, however, the house bell rang. With Holmes still engaged on the telephone, Martha approached me.

"It is a gentleman who wishes to discuss the gold sovereign offer," she said, handing me a card from a Mr. James Lewis.

Her comment quite puzzled me. "Well," I replied, turning to watch my friend conclude his discussion with Magillivray, "I suppose you may escort him here to the sitting room. We should be able to receive him in a moment, I believe."

Holmes rang off as our housekeeper left the room, and he gave me an expectant look.

"Did I hear Martha say something about sovereigns?" he asked.

"Yes. There is some fellow at the door who has come concerning an offer of sorts concerning gold coins," I said, handing him the card. "I took the liberty of inviting him in, but I do not understand what—"

"Ah," said Holmes, setting down the card without looking at it. He rubbed his palms together. "Our first enquiry. We can only hope the person has a story of interest."

"I believe *I* can only hope to grasp an understanding of what is about to transpire before it does so. That, however, is contingent upon your rapid explanation."

"You saw me write out a notice for placement in the papers but the other day," the detective reminded me.

"I recall you requisitioning a portion of my foolscap for that purpose, but you never revealed the substance of the posting."

"Did I not? Well then, forgive my oversight, Watson. You see, given William Grace's tale of being paid in gold sovereigns by Von Bork, I thought to give notice that I would pay any holder of such coins many times their actual worth."

I thought for a moment as we heard footsteps approaching along the corridor.

"The expectation being that perhaps some of those who reply to your advertisement will have unknowingly received the gold coin from the Germans, and that their stories will give you more information on our enemy's plans," I hurriedly whispered.

"Just so," said Holmes with a smile as Martha knocked upon the open sitting room door.

"A Mr. James Lewis," the old woman said, ushering into the room a very thin, bespectacled young man who struck me as rather bookish.

"Halloa, gentlemen," he said at once, glancing between the two of us as Martha withdrew. "Which of you has made the offer of payment for sovereigns? Or, perhaps, it is both in association?"

"I am the person who placed the notice," answered Holmes. "Pray, be seated, Mr. Lewis, if you wish. I am Sherlock Holmes."

"The retired detective?" replied Lewis, who remained standing. "I had no idea you had moved back to London. My, what an honour it is to meet you." He turned toward me. "May I then boldly enquire as to whether you are Dr. John Watson?" he asked.

"I am," I answered humbly.

"It is my honour to make your acquaintance as well," the man said. "And a pleasure in your case, Doctor, for you see, one of my distant cousins is Edmund Warburton."

"Ah," I said in an even voice. "It has been some time since I have thought of that name. Well, if you are his distant cousin, I suppose that makes us even more distant relations, at least through marriage."

"Yes. I was but a child when the matter of Edmund's father came to a crisis, and I was told of the affair only much later. However, Mr. Holmes, I congratulate you on your efforts all those years ago on behalf of the colonel. He did not deserve the troubles he had to bear, that is certain."

"In the end, it was but a trifle," declared Holmes with modesty. "Though my journey to the affair's conclusion was rather more than humdrum." He gave me a kindly glance and then turned back to Mr. Lewis. "You say you have come about my offer."[240]

"Yes, sir. It is that current prospect that brings me, not the travails of my family's past. You see, over the years, I have accumulated a rather sizable collection of gold coins, including rather many sovereigns."

Holmes smiled at the man while he searched for a pipe, and as I gestured for Mr. Lewis to sit down, I could tell that my friend realised he had not found one of the individuals he sought by placing his notice in the papers.

---

[240] This brief exchange contains some mildly intriguing implications. It would seem almost certain that the affair referred to is that involving Colonel Warburton's madness, one of Holmes's unchronicled cases that is mentioned in passing in "The Adventure of The Engineer's Thumb." According to Watson, it was one of only two instances in which he referred a client to the detective. The suggestion in the present narrative is that Watson was related by marriage to the Warburtons, but it is not clear if that was through his only known wife, Mary Morstan, or another spouse. On the other hand, it is conceivable that the Warburtons were instead related to Watson's sister's husband—see Appendix A.

"In truth," said Holmes, grasping his cherrywood, "the notice you read in the newspaper was somewhat incomplete. I am seeking not just any gold sovereign, but rather a particular mintage. A moment, if you will," said he, putting down the pipe and taking up pen, with which he dashed off a brief notation upon a piece of scrap paper. Holmes offered the note to Mr. Lewis.

"Thank you," said our guest, who looked at the detective's scrawl. "I am a coin fancier and know my collection well, and I can tell you immediately that I do not have the variety you seek. Indeed, I was not even aware that such a mintage exists."

"I regret that you have been inconvenienced," said Holmes as he once more grasped his pipe.

"Oh, I had but a short distance to travel from my work, which is here in Marylebone," said Mr. Lewis. He smiled at me. "I suppose, Doctor, that someday we might share a dinner together and renew family ties, eh?"

"It is possible, certainly," I replied in an even voice. "To echo my friend, I regret that you have journeyed here to no result."

I rose from my chair, which had the desired effect of eliciting the same action from our visitor.

"Well," Mr. Lewis said somewhat awkwardly. "I suppose I will leave, then. But not empty-handed," he added. "For I have met Mr. Sherlock Holmes and re-established connections among the greater Warburton clan."

I offered to escort Mr. Lewis to the door, forcing myself to play the part of a convivial relation, at least for a short while longer. After several minutes of further conversation as we slowly made our way along the corridor, I sent him on his way without making any commitment with respect to his offer of a meeting at Simpson's.

Returning to the sitting room, I found Holmes now wrapped in blue veils of smoke, glancing about while one of his old commonplace books lay upon his lap.

"Watson," he said, "is my copy of the *Almanach de Gotha* [241] lying about in your vicinity?"

"No," I replied after quickly surveying the piles of books, charts, and papers that lay scattered near my feet.

"Hum. Well, I shall find it eventually. I trust you caught up on family matters on your own?" he said languorously.

"As much as I should wish to," I replied quietly. "And so, will we now be bombarded by supplicants offering gold sovereigns?"

"I fear that may be the case," said Holmes, not looking up from his collection of clippings. "I do apologise for your being discommoded, but it strikes me as the approach that best combines effectiveness with discretion."

"I cannot argue that point."

"I am only interested, of course, in those coins that may have passed from German hands," Holmes remarked. "The hands of one German in particular."

Late that same afternoon, Holmes and I again stood at the centre of the great room within the empty warehouse where young Billy had received his blisters. We were in the company of Inspector Magillivray, Sergeant

[241] The *Almanach de Gotha* is a directory of European royalty and nobility.

Scaife, and a handful of constables—all in civilian clothes. According to Holmes's direction, I wore my military uniform and, for the moment, acted as if I were the leader of our delegation.

"I do hope you will recommend that the government employ this building, Colonel," said the land agent who had opened the structure for our examination. "It was only just vacated, and of course we will arrange for it to be cleaned. If you would—"

"I believe what I and my civilian staff prefer above all else at the moment is to be allowed to thoroughly examine the arrangement of rooms and facilities ourselves," I said abruptly after receiving an anxious look from Holmes. "This is but one of many sites the government are considering, and we must be timely in our assessment. You will then not mind leaving us alone for a time, so that we may complete that task?"

"But of course," replied the agent solicitously.

"And you will provide us a list of previous tenants for the past three years?" I added.

"It is being prepared even as we speak," the man declared.

"Good." I glanced at Holmes before addressing the agent one last time. "We will meet with you outside within an hour, then," I told him. "And I thank you for your cooperation."

"Colonel," said the man hesitantly, "there is one other matter on which my employers do wish reassurance."

"Yes?"

"Their understanding is that this building will not be used for weapons manufacture. Is that correct?"

"It is," I said. "There will be no munitions or volatile materials of any kind on these premises, I assure you. That is, should the government decide to make us of this structure."

"Oh, that is excellent news," replied the land agent. "Particularly with the site being so near the gasworks, there is no desire for another Milvertown[242] to happen here."

"I can assure you that there will be no danger imposed by the government's use of this building," I told him. Then, after a moment of awkward silence, I once more suggested that our party be left alone to survey the site.

"Of course," said the agent. "I do hope that—"

"Allow me to escort you, sir," volunteered Holmes, gently taking the man by the elbow to guide him to the building entrance, where he was to wait. Moments later, the detective returned and assumed his place as true leader of our coterie.

"You all have been given instruction in the manner of examining this interior," he told Sergeant Scaife and the constables before glancing round to Magillivray and me. "Let us begin the process."

For the better part of the next hour, we all gave full attention to a minute inspection and thorough scouring of the warehouse. Very soon after we had begun, Inspector Magillivray came across a small residue I believed to be a deposit of sulphur mustard and that Holmes theorised was the spot where young Billy had become infected with the noxious

---

[242] This is probably a fictionalized reference to the Silvertown explosion of January 1917, in which fifty tons of TNT ignited at a munitions factory. Over seventy people were killed, and substantial damage to the surroundings occurred. It was not the only such accident that occurred in Britain during the war: a similar incident at Faversham resulted in the accidental detonation of two hundred tons of TNT, and another blast at Chilwell killed 137 people.

substance. We marked the area, and Magillivray indicated he would contact Sir Walter Bullivant, who would arrange for the army to dispose of the material, as well as any other such dangerous remnants we might come across.

During the ensuing minutes, Holmes and I oversaw the efforts of the policemen in identifying items of interest. Many of these struck me initially as hardly of importance, but on more than one occasion, Sherlock Holmes disabused me of that notion.

"Notice the dried soil and vegetative remnants here about the entrance and along the principal corridor," the detective declared as we stood together near the building door, while the rest of our party busied themselves elsewhere within the structure.

Holmes got down upon his knees, quite indifferent to the effect his action might have upon his clothing. He took quick, short intakes of breath. "I am again reminded of your sense of smell, Watson, so superior in native ability to mine. However, I do not suggest you share my present mode of indignity."

"To what conclusions does your nose lead you?" I ask.

"These portions of debris likely came from a marshland," said Holmes as I helped him to his feet. "I have no doubt that the area in question is the river's edge."

"The marsh near the gasworks, perhaps?"

"Yes. I suggest that men debarked a vessel moored in that area—"

"The *Nemesis*, perhaps?"

"No doubt."

"Stores of sulphur mustard were unloaded from the launch and conveyed here?"

"Quite possibly," said Holmes. "Perhaps also with 'tungsten.'"

"Whatever might have been brought here has since been removed, however," I declared, "The question is, to where?"

"It appears that several trips were required to load this building with its temporary store of mustard gas," said Sherlock Holmes as we walked back toward the main room of the structure. "Perhaps those who moved it elsewhere left evidence of that other terminus, since more than one journey would presumably have been needed to lodge the gas in another place, and those making that transfer may have brought with them evidence of that second endpoint."

We returned to the great space in the middle of the building, where Inspector Magillivray, Sergeant Scaife, and their group of constables had assembled a collection of items retrieved from all reaches of the warehouse.

"We found no other pools of mustard gas," the sergeant said. "This is everything that we could lift, Mr. Holmes. We marked the original positions. It's just a collection of odd items, really: an assortment of nails, screws, and bolts, as well as some dining utensils and a hammer, and the valinch and floggers you had seen before. And a couple of broken knives, both of them soiled with tar. Oh, and we also found that copper pan, there at the side," he said. "That is the largest item in the lot."

"What of the newspapers?" I asked.

"Newspapers?" Magillivray said. "Oh yes, there were stained scraps of newspaper as well. We simply piled them in that corner."

Holmes walked past the principal set of artefacts and stopped directly in front of the discarded papers. He rummaged among them for but two or three seconds before exclaiming, "Ha!"

"Something of interest, sir?" asked Magillivray, seemingly taken aback by Holmes's search among the discarded sheets.

"I believe so," replied the detective, bringing one piece to the inspector, who looked at it for a moment. "Did you bother to read these newspaper pages?" asked Holmes.

"Why no," said Magillivray. "There's nothing but Chinese writing on them."

"All the more reason for reading them—as evidence," Holmes declared. "And as you say, they are stained." He cautiously sniffed the sheet he held. "Oil associated with cooked food."

"And all that tells us something?" asked Magillivray as Holmes stepped toward the collection of items assembled by the constables.

"It suggests the possibility that those who transferred the mustard gas to another location may have returned with food wrapped in these papers," my friend said. He dropped the newspaper sheet and picked up the copper pan, which he also brought to his nose. I saw a broad smile break out upon his face as he turned and held up the piece of metal.

"Limehouse," Holmes declared. "There is a good chance that the sulphur mustard has been moved to Limehouse."[243]

"The copper pan," said Magillivray, stepping to Holmes's side. "Are you suggesting it has been used for—?"

"Boiling opium," declared Holmes, lifting the pan to Magillivray's nose.

The inspector took a whiff and nodded. "Right you are, sir."

---

[243] Limehouse is an area of east London, on the north bank of the Thames, whose population was at the time largely made up of foreign sailors, including many Chinese. By the late nineteenth century, the district had achieved notoriety as the home of several opium dens.

"It strikes me as odd that Von Bork should allow such lack of discipline," said Holmes.

"Perhaps he is not the leader of this new spy group, after all," I suggested.

"Or he has been absent of late," replied Holmes. "But you are correct, old fellow," he said. "I have no firm evidence of Von Bork's presence, only an intuition of his spirit. Well," he declared, setting down the pan before kneeling to observe the other items assembled upon the floor, "I will give the various rooms my own quick examination, but I suspect that will yield nothing more than your own fine efforts have provided us."

"And so the focus shifts to Limehouse?" I enquired.

"I beg pardon?" said Holmes, who had picked up the two knives which Magillivray and his men had found.

"Limehouse becomes our target now?"

"Yes," said the detective in an abstracted tone. "However, I believe that Sandy Arbuthnot's talents are best suited for that locale. We will put him onto it at once."

"And are those two broken knives of interest?" I asked.

"Perhaps," replied Holmes. "You see, as the inspector noted, they are stained with tar, just like the blade we found on that body in Eversholt Street."

On the following Wednesday, I shared lunch at a restaurant with Vespera Cochrane, who had travelled into town to spend several days with a friend in Kensington. During our meal, I was sorely tempted to reveal to her the details of our discovery of the warehouse where mustard gas had been stored, but the uniform I wore was a silent reminder to me that discretion was upmost, and so we passed the time in idle if enthusiastic conversation concerning topics unrelated to the war, until my lunch companion finally broached that subject.

"I have seen my first American soldier," Miss Cochrane revealed to me. "Or, rather, soldiers. They were walking near Olympia Station: perhaps ten in all, and at least two of them were officers, I believe."

I nodded as I set my cup of coffee down upon the table. "Yes, they are assembling here at last. I do not know that they will go into action by the end of this year, however."

"Oh?" said Miss Cochrane. "They are not going to plug holes in the front?" she asked with a coy smile.

"That is not my understanding," I said awkwardly, concentrating upon my cup before lifting it again. "I believe that Blenkiron—the American fellow I have previously mentioned to you—has said their leaders wish them to fight as units under their own separate command, not mixed with our troops or those of the French. Moreover, I am told they will be undergoing additional training before being sent across the Channel."

"I should not think the Americans would need more training in how to fight," she said. Sighing, she added, "After all, some men do not require additional training in anything, do they, Colonel?"

I gulped the last of my coffee and checked my wristlet watch.[244]

Arriving at my residence in Queen Anne Street later that afternoon, I was greeted at the door by Martha, who in hushed tones advised me that

[244] Although wristwatches had been worn by military men since the late nineteenth century, they were, in general, considered more appropriate for women until the First World War, when the British War Department began issuing them to soldiers, starting in 1917.

Holmes was embroiled in heated discussion with a caller named Gawain Owen. Allowing her to take my coat and cap, I quickly strode down the corridor and approached the sitting room door, which, as usual, had been left ajar.

Cautiously, I tiptoed to the entrance.

"It is not my obligation to tell you anything, sir!" I heard a man's voice declare in gruff tones.

"But this may have a critical effect upon our nation's safety, Mr. Owen," Sherlock Holmes asserted. "I must demand that you give me the details."

"And who are you to tell me what's right for England, eh?" replied Owen. "Who are you? I got my orders from a real military officer. I'll not betray that trust. I'll tell you nothing!"

I thought feverishly for a moment, and though I had no idea of the substance of the discussion I was hearing, I nonetheless grasped the dynamics of the moment and, glancing down at my own RAMC regalia, immediately decided upon a course of action. Reaching toward the open door, I silently pushed against it and stepped into the sitting room.

"You can forget about any accommodation, sir!" the visitor said sharply as he turned away from Holmes, who was sitting in his armchair. "If treason is part of your offer, I will never—"

The man stopped as he caught sight of me standing in the doorway. I, in turn, found myself facing a short, stocky fellow of late middle age sporting a walrus moustache whose grey colour matched a ring of hair surrounding the bald spot upon his head. Holding a billycock hat with both hands, he brought it up to his chest and reared back slightly as he studied me.

The stranger stammered a series of unintelligible syllables and then took a step sideways.

"I congratulate you, Mr.—Mr. Owen, is it?" I said.

"Yes it is, sir—or colonel or major or captain, or whatever your rank is," he said haltingly, motioning at my insignia. "I am Gawain Owen."

"Mr. Owen responded to my newspaper offer to exchange gold sovereigns for paper notes at an advantageous ratio," Holmes said quickly.

"Yes, so I did, sir," growled Owen, his back to my friend. "But this fellow here suddenly changed the subject and tried to get information from me of a most sensitive matter as part of the deal," the man told me. His right eye began to exhibit what I took to be a nervous tic, but after moment I realised he was attempting to wink at me as he spoke in hushed tones.

"This here...Mr. Holmes, he tried...to get me to talk about...certain things. The LTL, for instance," he whispered. "I told him nothing, I swear."

"And again, I congratulate you," I said, thinking feverishly. "You have passed the test, Mr. Owen. Do you not think so?" I said, looking past the man at Holmes, who cocked his head.

"Test? What test?" asked Owen.

"A test of your loyalty and discretion," I said, stepping past him and into the middle of the sitting room. I casually reached for my pipe and Arcadia mix. "Perhaps, after this trail at the hands of my friend, you wish to sit down and calm yourself?"

"What?" said Owen, turning round to follow my actions with a questioning eye. "I've been examined, you mean?"

"Of course you have," I said, smiling as I packed my pipe. "You have been examined for loyalty and discretion. And you passed marvellously, for you revealed nothing about the, uh, LTL." I turned to Holmes, whom I asked nervously, "Perhaps you might explain to our friend here?"

"I should be happy to, Colonel," said my friend with a sly smile, immediately grasping my ploy.

Leaning back in his armchair, Holmes opened his hands to Mr. Owen as a gesture of reconciliation. "I do apologise for any upset I may have caused you, sir. However, my…orders from Colonel Watson here were to put you to as stern a test as I might. I am certain you understand."

"Well," said Owen, hesitantly taking to the basket chair in response to my silent gesture. "I am certain I *will* understand, once you explain it all to me."

He delicately set his hat upon his lap and sheepishly watched as I lit my pipe, tossed the vesta onto the coals, and leaned against the mantel.

"I assume I will have that explanation presently?" the man ventured cautiously.

"You volunteered for special government service?" I asked, glancing at Holmes as I posed the question to Mr. Owen.

"Well, I answered the advertisement, yes," said the man. "Not his, I mean," Owen added, gesturing to Holmes. "That is, I did respond to his notice, but I speak of the earlier one in the papers."

"Which earlier one?" asked Holmes sharply.

"The one calling for the services of men in the moving and delivery trades," Owen replied hesitantly.

"Ah, yes," said Holmes, reaching for pile of newspapers. "Perhaps you can verify your statement by identifying the very posting in one of these—"

"Oh, they don't seem to advertise anymore," said Owen. "I haven't seen any for weeks. They must have collected all the men they need. I told my wife's brother about it soon enough and got him hired, though."

"Of course," remarked Holmes. "Perhaps you should recount your experience in all this, Mr. Owen—I believe Colonel Watson expressed a desire to make certain all was going well with your part of the endeavour."

The man shrugged. "I suppose all is well with myself. The endeavour, however, is a great unknown to me. Since my initial hiring, you see, I haven't heard from anyone about it, until I spoke with you two gentlemen today."

"Nothing at all?" I said as Holmes pondered Owen's remark. "That is somewhat strange. Perhaps, as my colleague just suggested, you should recount for us your complete experience in this matter."

"Well, there isn't much to tell, but I can do that now, I think, seeing as how you are a military officer—and you know of the organisation, obviously."

I gave the man an expectant look.

"The LTL, I mean."

Oh yes," I replied. "Of course. The LTL. Go on, then."

"Well, the advertisement in the newspaper sought men in the moving and delivery trades, with the promise of good money, and that came true, all right."

"Your pay was in gold sovereigns," said Holmes.

"Yes. I didn't expect that, but who was I to argue with such a plan, eh?" Owen looked down at his hat. "I stored mine away, since the coins were gold, but I couldn't resist the appeal of your advertisement, either, sir. And so," he said, the glimmer in his eyes seeming to brighten, "you gentlemen said you have been testing me. Testing, perhaps, to see if I would divulge all those details of the LTL that I had pledged to keep secret?"

"Precisely," said Holmes.

"Ah, I understand it now," muttered Owen with a chuckle. "And I didn't squeal one bit to you," he said. "I never revealed anything to you about the London Transport League, did I?"

"No, you did not," replied Sherlock Holmes. "Not even its name."

"From time to time, we lure our volunteers into situations such as you found yourself, Mr. Owen," I said, still leaning upon the mantel. "We test their loyalties and sense of discretion."

"And I passed," the man said again.

"Superbly," replied Holmes. "Now, might you proceed with your story?"

"It was that uniform what done it," said Owen jovially, pointing to me. "If you hadn't slipped in at the conclusion of my examination here, I never would have revealed a thing to your man here. I'd have walked right out—oh yes, I would have."

"Indeed, you would have," answered Holmes with growing impatience. "I should have gotten nothing from you at all. Now then, again, might you recount your full experience with the League to Colonel Watson?"

"My experience?"

"You were going to tell us about how you were accepted into the London Transport League," I interjected. "And also your instructions and obligations. You see, we need to catalogue your present recollection of the

League and its workings, to compare it with what you should be aware of at this stage."

"And so will you proceed with your story?" Holmes asked earnestly.

"Oh, of course," said Owen. "The tale is short and simple. I happened to see the advertisement in one of the papers, as I said, and always willing to add to my sources of income, I replied to the posting."

"You did so by applying at a residence or building?" asked Holmes.

"It was a flat, yes, in Ilford. There were two gentlemen: a tall man who resembled you somewhat, Mr. Holmes, and a young army officer. The tall one never gave his name, but merely said he was secretary to some Cabinet minister. The officer identified himself as a Captain Beaman."

"Pardon me," said Sherlock Holmes. "I realise this may seem an odd question, but did this Captain Beaman have blond hair and two prominent moles?"

"Yes, he did, as a matter of fact. That is, I cannot be sure about the hair, you see, for it was under his cap, which he never removed." The man chuckled. "However, my eyes couldn't avoid coming back to those moles upon his cheek. One was an ugly brown brute, I must say. So you know him?"

"We are mildly acquainted," said Holmes as he raised his head and glanced at me.

"Well, the two of them explained that transportation of goods was vital to the war effort," Owen said, "and that included transport not only in France but here at home as well. They told me that the government had formed a secret Transport League composed of men expected to haul crates from one part of town to another at a moment's notice. Somewhat like the Ambulance Column, I supposed.[245]

"In any event, they told us that our services might not be employed in any given week or month, but that we were nonetheless to be constantly at the ready. And while we would be waiting in reserve, we would still be paid at the rate of two pounds a week, whether we hauled or not. Two pounds a week! That's what you'd get in a shipyard for skilled work, ain't it? And this for just sitting and waiting to be called."

"And you were paid regularly?" Holmes enquired.

"No, sir. They said they'd pay in advance, and was they true to their word! When I signed on, they gave me six months wages then and there. Fifty pounds, just like that! It were like a rich uncle had died—two rich uncles, for that matter."

"And when was your application made?"

"Oh, let's see...I suppose it's going on four months since I was accepted into the League."

"And your pay was all in gold sovereigns?"

"It was," said Owen. "The sight of those coins was more than enough to convince me then and there. I signed up for it, pledged myself to secrecy, and was given my assignment and pay for a half year, all with the understanding that I was to do the government's bidding when called upon, which I haven't been since."

He pulled a gold coin from a coat pocket and held it up. "Not that I'm complaining, mind you."

---

[245] The London Ambulance Column was a voluntary civilian organization whose members met trains arriving in the metropolis with wounded soldiers, whom they conveyed to various hospitals. Providing this service freed members of the RAMC to serve directly at the front.

"And did you return to the Ilford flat after that?" asked Holmes.

"Twice," replied the man, putting the sovereign back into his pocket. "The day after I signed on, I brought my wife's brother over to Ilford to get him registered with the LTL as well. The two men were still there in the flat with a short line of men waiting to apply, but they gladly signed on my own recruit, who got his assignment and advance pay as well."

"And the second time?"

"Ah, that were a week later. I had told a neighbour that I knew how he could pocket half a year's wage in one afternoon, and so he came with me to the men's flat. By then, however, it had been vacated, and the landlord said he knew nothing of those to whom he had let it for a few days. My neighbour did not believe my claims and still won't speak to me."

"Did you not show him your pile of sovereigns?" asked Holmes.

"Of course not!" avowed Owen. "I had pledged complete secrecy. I was allowed to recruit others, but I could not give them any details or show them any specific proof until they was signed on as well—under threat of a firing squad! I was allowed only to declare that I knew of an offer that paid remarkably well."

"You said you were given an assignment," said Holmes. "What assignment was that?"

Gawain Owen looked sheepishly back and forth between Holmes and me. "Well," he said, "I wasn't supposed to reveal that above all else, but seeing as how you're a captain, sir—"

"Colonel," I corrected.

"Right, a colonel there...Well, I was told that if I were to be called—and they never said how I was to be called, just that I would know it when I was—were I to be called, I was to park my lorry in the middle of Theobald's

Road—what some call King's Way— right where it meets Old Gloucester Street."

"That is in the vicinity of Russell Square," I said.

"Yes, you got that right," answered Mr. Owen.

"And do you know what your wife's brother's assignment is?" asked Holmes.

"Well, that assumes he told me what it was, which he wasn't supposed to do," replied Owen coyly. His expression became one of pleading. "And if he were to have done that—which he knew he weren't supposed to—he wouldn't be reprimanded, would he?"

"Of course not," replied Holmes. "We are testing only you, Mr. Owen, not your brother-in-law."

"Ah well, then," said the man, obviously relieved, "he was told to set up station at the intersection of Great Eastern Street and the Curtain Road."

"That is farther east," I said.

"And still just north of the City," added Holmes.[246]

"Once more, simple geography," drawled Owen.

"And you were not told what to expect when you reached your designated location?" enquired the detective.

"No, I was not," the man replied. "I was instructed to simply wait for further orders once I had arrived at my destination and to let no one dislodge me from my station. Not even the police nor anyone else, except a military officer like Colonel Watson here," he said. "I was to stand by and await my cargo, whatever it might be."

---

[246] See footnote 17.

Holmes remained deep in thought for several minutes as Gawain Owen shifted idly in his chair. At length, my friend looked up and asked, "Were you ever told of any preparations you were to make before setting out on such a call?"

"What do you mean?"

Holmes held up his hands. "Were you directed to bring special containers, tarpaulins, or tools?"

"No," said Owen. "I was to bring just the horses with the lorry."

The detective cocked his head. "Your sister's brother is a hauler as well," he said.

"Of course he is. That's why I recruited him, isn't it?"

Holmes thought for a moment and then asked, "Does he employ horses also?"

"He does. Neither of us has invested in motors yet. Wave of the future they are, though, for certain."

"You said that when you went to the flat to apply to the London Transport League, you saw a line of other men with the same intent. Did you recognise any of them?" enquired Holmes.

"Yes," Owen replied. "There were three or four I was familiar with by name, and a few others I had seen but was not acquainted with."

"Can you supply the names of those you knew?"

"I suppose I could," the man said suspiciously. "Though it seems—"

"It is part of our method of evaluating the recruitment practices we employ," I interjected. Conspicuously, I adjusted my Sam Browne belt before continuing. "I am certain that you understand our reasons for doing so."

"Uh, well, yes, of course," stammered Owen. "Makes perfect sense to me. Give me a paper and pen, and I will gladly give you that list."

"Excellent," said Holmes as he motioned for me to fetch the desired items and then leaned back in the sofa. "We will suggest a commendation for this, Mr. Owen."

"No, I have no complaint against the RAMC itself," I admitted to Sir Walter Bullivant as I sat opposite him in the sitting room at Safety House two days later. "I am allowed to come and go as I choose, and to remain in Queen Anne Street if desired for days on end. However, I do wish—"

"Good," replied the spymaster with a chuckle as he leaned over to smile at me. "Remember: your work for the medical corps is subterfuge, Watson. Your real work is to be found at the side of Holmes."

"We call it a covering activity," remarked John S. Blenkiron from a corner chair. The American had once more returned from France, where he was continuing to forge a more effective combined espionage network comprised of agents from all Allied nations.

"In any event," declared Mycroft Holmes from the sofa, "this London Transport League business is rather intriguing. And you have found several men who have enlisted in it?" he asked his brother, who sat beside me.

"Yes," said Sherlock Holmes, shifting in his chair, his eyes still upon me following my comment to Sir Walter Bullivant. "Watson and I discreetly interviewed three haulers from Gawain Owen's list who were accepted into this questionable brotherhood, and once more, the colonel's uniform was all it took to convince them to relate all they knew, including the various locales where they were to drive their lorries—all of which are horse-drawn, by the way."

"You believe that aspect is significant?" asked Bullivant.

"I do not yet know," replied Holmes. "However, we now have identified five members of this League, including Mr. Owen and his brother-in-law, and none of them employ motorcars in their delivery work. In this day and age, from such a sample, I should expect at least one or two would employ motors."

"You think it more than coincidence, then?" enquired Blenkiron.

"Again, I cannot be certain, but I do find it suspicious."

"Well," said the American. "The pattern of their destinations is certainly intriguing, isn't it?"

"Yes," replied Holmes. "Joining those points appears to draw a line curving round the City, leaving the river itself to close the circle on the south."

"But to what purpose?" asked Bullivant. "To distribute mustard gas to various points in London?"

The two Holmes brothers looked at one another, and then Mycroft leaned back in the sofa.

"I am inclined to think not," said the elder Holmes. "If these haulers were to deliver the sulphur mustard to different locales, I believe they would all have been directed to assemble where the substance is being stored. And that is in Limehouse, you think?" he asked his brother, who nodded.

"On the other hand, if the mustard gas has instead already been placed in different areas for immediate use, why load it onto vehicles again?" concluded Bullivant. "Yes, I see your point."

"Could the LTL be connected to the 'tungsten' written on that paper for the messenger that was killed near Eversholt Street?" I asked. "I assume that the 'sulphur' in that note referred to the sulphur mustard gas."

"But who can say what 'tungsten' even means in this instance?" declared Blenkiron. "I know that I cannot at this moment."

"I agree that the mention of sulphur in that message was likely a reference to the mustard gas," said Mycroft Holmes. "Tungsten, however, appears to have no relevance to that aspect at all. The only use for the element that makes any sense in the context of our situation is its employment in light filaments."

"And that advance is but a relatively recent development," said the American.[247]

"But a light filament is the only thought regarding tungsten that we have at present," Sherlock Holmes reminded him.

"And what does that thought suggest?" asked Blenkiron.

"That something is to be illuminated," said Holmes with a smile. "I wish it were ourselves."

"One thing we do know," interjected Mycroft, "is that the Germans will, without question, stage a massive offensive in France by the coming spring. Whatever they are planning for London would likely to be coordinated with that move on the battlefield."

"Agreed," said Blenkiron.

---

[247] Though tungsten had been viewed as a likely substance for making filaments much earlier, the technology required to draw it into fine wire was not developed until a few years before the events of this narrative. By the start of the First World War, long-lasting tungsten filaments were a practical reality.

"I believe it will come within the next two months, for that span will mark the end of the six months for which the LTL members have been paid," said Sherlock Holmes. "I expect that the Germans have planned that the next time they contact their unwitting accomplices, it will be to actually deploy them."

"For whatever purpose they have in mind," interjected Blenkiron.

"Yes," agreed Holmes. "The question is, what is that purpose?"

There was a momentary pause, and then I asked, as I often did at such meetings, "And what of General Hannay and Miss Lamington?"

Blenkiron leaned back in his chair. "Dick Hannay has left his battle post and is now pursuing a number of clues we have uncovered on the Continent that may lead him to the man we know as Moxon Ivery." He paused, glanced at Bullivant, and then added, "As for Mary Lamington, she is..."

"She is in France as well," Sir Walter informed us.

"Also in search of Ivery?" asked Sherlock Holmes.

Bullivant nodded.

"Independently of Hannay?" I enquired with a hint of anxiety in my voice. "Is that not a rather risky venture for her?"

"This grand enterprise is a risk for us all, Watson," said Sherlock Holmes. "I should judge Miss Lamington more than able to safeguard herself."

"I suppose I should convey to you one more item of interest," Bullivant told Holmes. "We have traced that Gussiter firm to Switzerland. Blenkiron found the final link."

Our eyes all fixed upon the American.

"It was a relatively simple for me, Sir Walter, once your man Macandrew performed all the tedious work," Blenkiron admitted.

Our compatriot's mention of Bullivant's subordinate in Lime Street reminded me of the afternoon spent in the man's office learning basic code and cipher practice three years before.

"Between the addresses given in those advertisements and the information you obtained from the agent for that warehouse you examined over by the gasworks," Blenkiron said, "Macandrew was able to trace the Gussiter firm through several holding companies and finally to the ultimate owning company, which goes by a different name. I eventually took that information and located its headquarters in Geneva."

"And there lies the centre of the German code operation," said Bullivant.

"Indeed," said Mycroft Holmes from the sofa, "it would not surprise if it were the real operational headquarters of the entire Cerberus operation."

"And how close do you believe Sandy Arbuthnot is to finding the sulphur mustard's new home in Limehouse?" asked Blenkiron.

"I do not know," said Sherlock Holmes. "I have asked him to not approach Safety House in reporting on that quest. Instead," he added, "I will send successive emissaries to meet with him."

The detective appeared lost for a moment in thought and then resumed. "Those representatives will rotate, and we shall begin with the colonel here. That is," he added, "if you are willing to accept this most vital role, Watson."

All eyes turned to me as I learned of the obligation for the first time.

"As has been the case since before I can remember," I said with quiet patience, leaning back in my chair, "I remain at your disposal."

CHAPTER TWENTY-ONE: CERBERUS ROUSED

I dined alone the very next evening in Soho and just before seven o'clock walked down Old Compton Street to catch the first eastbound motor omnibus I could find. For several minutes, I shared the ride with a pair of inebriated theatregoers in evening dress, a wary young couple and a bumptious clerk, but I kept to myself as the bus entered a district of small, low shops lining streets where the gentle glow of gas still reigned. As the vehicle made its way toward Limehouse, I saw increasing numbers of men with Oriental features or Hindoo attire, and after passing rows of shadowy houses punctuated by fried-fish bars displaying slogans in several languages, I debarked the bus near a hippodrome[248] whose harshly lit exterior blazed with stark beauty into the night.

I walked through Pennyfields and on to the Causeway,[249] mindful of shabby shopfronts with Chinese signs that I passed in the company of a curious blend of off-duty soldiers, rough-looking dock workers, cautious onlookers, and an underlying bedrock of local denizens whose origins were far removed from Britain's shore.

More than once, I thought myself studied carefully by clusters of Celestials,[250] but I sensed no hostility, only veiled curiosity. My instructions from Holmes were to proceed along the Causeway, where at some point I should expect Sandy Arbuthnot to discreetly accost me. Beyond those instructions, I had received no further advice, and as I

---

[248] A music hall.

[249] Pennyfields is an area of London bordering Limehouse, and the Causeway refers to the Limehouse Causeway, that district's central street.

[250] "Celestial" was a nineteenth century synonym for "Chinese."

progressed slowly in the direction of the East India Docks, I began to feel a degree of unease, for though I had not yet espied Sandy, I had the clear sensation of being followed.

Noting my present location on the main thoroughfare, I decided to take a circuitous path in hopes of evading my presumed stalker. Swiftly turning one corner and then the next before attempting to lose myself in the flow of traffic, I occasionally stopped to glance into dusty shop windows. The reflection of one shadowy figure was always present in successive panes, and I soon realised that, conspicuous outsider that I must be, there was no hope of shaking loose my patient pursuer. And so, wishing time to ponder my situation, I entered a dimly lit restaurant, where I parted bead curtains and found for myself a small table next to a pair of seamen who were shovelling food into their mouths with chopsticks.

Having already finished a full dinner in Soho less than an hour earlier, I asked the attendant to bring me only a small portion of spiced fish, duck, and onions accompanied by lychee fruits. The tea was strong and woody, and as I sipped it amid my rough surroundings, I found myself now feeling strangely at ease, though I knew I had waded into a sea of uncertainty.

At length, I paid for my meal and left the restaurant, noticing across the street that same fellow who had been following me since I had set foot in the Causeway: a tall lascar who, bundled in a cloak, leaned in the shadow of doorway. The man appeared to take no heed of me, but I knew he was the one who had dogged my steps for the past half hour.

I paused at the pavement's edge, pondering my choices of action. I could not throw the man off my trail, and yet I did not desire him to watch me rendezvous with Sandy Arbuthnot. And so, unsure of success, I resolved to confront the foreign sailor, hoping to frighten him off by embarrassment, though I understood I was taking a great risk.

"Do you seek something from me, sir?" I called out across the flow of human traffic.

The man ignored me.

Glancing in both directions along the Causeway, I crossed the street and stood three feet from my stalker.

"I asked if you have business with me, sir."

The lascar huddled in his cloak and turned his face to me, though his eyes were still hidden by darkness.

"Answer me, man," I demanded, stepping within an arm's length. "I will brook no harassment."

"I'm not intending to give any, sir," whispered Sandy Arbuthnot. I gave a start as the young man leaned forward, allowing a street light to illuminate his face, which even then I could not recognise as his; voice was the only clue to his real identity.

"Mr. Holmes said we were to meet on the Causeway, Colonel Watson."

"Yes," I mumbled. "I apologise for the misunderstanding. I foolishly thought to look for you in your normal guise."

The young man smiled. "For the past several days, sir, this *has* been my normal guise."

"I see."

"Ask me which way to the docks."

"What?"

The agent held out his hand in supplication and muttered phrases in a foreign tongue.

"Why, which route do I take to the East India Docks? Can you tell me?" I said for the benefit of those passing within earshot. Down the street, I heard the lilting notes of a wooden flute.

Arbuthnot again thrust his hand toward me, and I awkwardly dug in my pockets for a few coins, which I dropped into his palm.

"This way, sahib," he said loudly in a guttural voice not his own.

I walked behind the disguised man at first, but soon he slowed his pace so that we fell even with one another, and at a moment when we found ourselves removed from the nearest of our fellow pedestrians by a few feet, he whispered to me, "I believe we are being followed."

"Could it be one of our own agents, stalking us as you stalked me?" I asked in a low voice.

"Mr. Holmes did not indicate such would be the case, sir. Here," he suddenly said in the accent he had assumed previously. "This way."

We passed through an alley, past a cluster of five Chinamen and on to the adjacent street. As we rounded the corner, I was struck by a strong aroma that I recognised as the sweet musk of opium. Two horse-drawn wagons rolled by in opposing directions, and Arbuthnot, in his alien attire, steered me round both as they passed in turn, so that we might gain the opposite kerb.

"He's a devilishly persistent sod," whispered my guide as we negotiated yet another corner. "If we cannot lose him, I must remove him."

"How?"

"I'm carrying a truncheon, and with it can perform more than one trick taught me by an old dacoit from the Chilapata Forest."[251]

---

[251] A dacoit is an Indian bandit, and the Chilapata Forest is a densely wooded area of that country.

I followed closely behind without comment. We turned yet another corner to enter an almost deserted, dimly lit street, where Arbuthnot lightly pulled me into an alley.

"We wait here," he whispered, taking the thick baton from his belt and raising it above his head, as if ready to strike.

Suddenly, from the edge of my vision, I saw the nightstick pulled out of Sandy's hand from behind. Arbuthnot whirled round, his hand turning to present its sweeping edge, which the intruder deftly avoided by quickly crouching.

"Wait!" whispered the stranger urgently, holding up his hands. "It's me, lad!"

"You?" said Arbuthnot in a low voice. "Good God," he said, extending a hand to assist Shinwell Johnson to his feet. The two smiled at one another in the dark alley, shaking hands with a single stroke before the older man returned the truncheon to Sandy.

"I should have realised it was you," said Johnson, gesturing to Sandy's clothing and facial disguise. "My actions were perhaps a bit rash."

"Heavens," I said in a hushed voice. "Porky, why are you here?"

"Well," answered the agent, somewhat awkwardly, "I was actually looking out for you, Dr. Watson—I mean, Colonel."

"How you address me hardly matters. What seems far more important is your purpose. What do you mean by saying you were looking out for me. At whose request?"

"That of Mr. Holmes," said Johnson reluctantly.

"I do not understand," I said. "Please elaborate."

Shinwell Johnson looked back and forth between Arbuthnot and me, and then he quietly explained. "Mr. Holmes told me that you were going to rendezvous with Sandy this evening in Limehouse, and he asked that I follow you to make certain you came out safe and sound."

I began to speak, but Johnson quieted me with an upraised hand. "Mind you, Colonel Watson, I told the owner that, despite its reputation, Limehouse wasn't going to be a place where you'd be likely to fall foul of anyone." The man bowed his head. "Mr. Holmes said he understood that but that he was not willing to take any chances with your safety. I was to dog your steps until you had your meeting and had gotten out of Limehouse."

"I see."

"Mr. Holmes said his decision to send you was sudden and did not allow for Sandy to be warned that I would be following you, and I in turn had no knowledge of his disguise. I should have realised but did not comprehend that the fellow you had accosted was actually our compatriot," Johnson said. "I saw only a lascar with a stick in his belt leading you off to parts unknown, and I determined that I must—"

"You cannot be faulted, Porky," I said.

"Sirs," interjected Arbuthnot, "this misunderstanding aside, should I not take you to the site where I believe the mustard gas is stored?"

"What?" I said. "You have found it?"

"Yes. I was in the act of leading you there when our most secretive third showed up," the young agent said, playfully patting Johnson's shoulder. "Shall we proceed, then?"

"Yes," I replied.

"And, if I you will permit it," Johnson said to me, "I'll follow discreetly at a distance."

I looked at him for a moment and then, nodding, expressed agreement with that plan.

Holmes's veteran agent departed through the opposing entrance to the alley—the way in which he had come up upon our backs—and though I did not see him, I knew he was behind us as Sandy guided me for several more blocks to where a three-story brick building stood among others of its same general type.

"I believe that to be the one, sir," whispered Sandy in his lascar disguise.

"Is there a watchman outside, as there was at the building near the gasworks?"

"I have not seen anyone outside guarding the place," said my companion. "Here in Limehouse, shuttered buildings with no obvious activity are not unusual fare. I suspect that a sentinel in evidence would only attract attention. The guards are stationed inside."

"How can you be certain that warehouse holds the mustard gas?"

"As Mr. Holmes would say, I cannot be absolutely certain, for I've not seen any canisters. However, I have observed a handful of men go in and out of that building, all of them Occidental—and one of them none other than Dieter Baumann."

I grasped Arbuthnot's shoulder. "You are certain?"

"This time, Colonel Watson, that word applies without any doubt."

"Have you other evidence?"

"I made discreet enquiries in the area," Arbuthnot said. "I dared not question anyone too closely, but while casting about for work in my lascar guise, I learned that several crates were loaded into the building recently, about the time when the warehouse near the gasworks must have been emptied. It could be coincidence, of course, but I am inclined to think not. I hope Mr. Holmes will be pleased."

"I am certain he will overjoyed when I relate the news to him." I paused for a moment and then added, "I am somewhat surprised that I was required to come here to take your story in person, however. Could you not have related this information via a note?"

"Mr. Holmes specified this procedure, Colonel. He wanted nothing written down, and he told me in no uncertain terms not to approach either Queen Anne Street or Safety House."

"As you say. Well, I suppose you may provide me with whatever additional information you have, and I will carry it back to him."

Arbuthnot related to me a small number of other details and then, in his lascar disguise, led me to the area surrounding the East India Docks, where I found a taxicab to convey me back to Marylebone. As the vehicle sped away, I saw the figure of Shinwell Johnson leaning against a streetlight, watching my departure.

The return trip across town was uneventful, and I entered my house late that evening to find Sherlock Holmes waiting for me in his armchair, dressed to go out. Another of his commonplace books lay open in his lap.

"I trust I have not kept you waiting" were the first words from my mouth.

"Indeed not, Watson," said my friend in good humour, quickly closing the notebook. "I have been passing the time to good effect," he added, holding up the cover. "How went your meeting with Arbuthnot?"

"He believes he has found the store of sulphur mustard."

"Excellent!" the detective exclaimed. "The young man never ceases to amaze. You have all the details?"

"I do."

"Good," said Holmes, rising to his feet to set the commonplace book aside. "It will be a pleasure to report Arbuthnot's success to Mycroft."

"I take it, then, that we are leaving immediately for Safety House?"

"Yes. Mycroft sent me a message after you departed for Limehouse. He and Bullivant wish to see us this very evening," he said, reaching for his coat and hat. "I do not know the substance, only that it is urgent. In any case, I am certain that your recitation of Sandy's find will constitute the high point of our discussion. You do not mind leaving almost before you return?"

"No," I said quietly as I followed my friend out of the sitting room. "However, I am curious as to whether Shinwell Johnson will be joining us, or will your company alone provide sufficient protection for me?"

Holmes paused in the hallway. Turning round, he looked at me with a slightly pained expression and asked, "He disclosed himself to you?"

"Under the circumstances, he had no choice—a luxury that was not denied you, however."

"Old fellow, I—"

"Perhaps you should have trusted this mission to someone you think capable of defending himself. Or herself," I added, "since not once have you expressed any concern for the safety of Mary Lamington as she pursues Moxon Ivery on the Continent."

"Watson, you must—"

"I suggest you consider what I have said. And perhaps you may also take to heart my desire to be assigned elsewhere by the medical corps."

The detective looked at me and then nodded. "I shall. Now then, if you are willing, might you still accompany me to Safety House?"

"You wish me to accompany you?"

"I do."

"Then I shall," I replied curtly.

"Good," Holmes remarked quietly, turning to once more proceed down the corridor. "I shall fetch us a taxicab. I suppose, given the need for discretion, I will wait to hear all your report until it is first revealed to my brother."

"Arbuthnot was most efficient," proclaimed Mycroft Holmes after I had related the news that Sandy had found a building that likely housed the missing mustard gas.

"I had no doubt about his abilities," murmured Sir Walter Bullivant.

"Indeed," agreed Sherlock Holmes. His mood was far less ebullient than I should have expected at hearing the news I had obtained. "The pieces come together, do they not?"

"Yes," said Mycroft cautiously. "However, this piece is a keystone of sorts."

"And what does that mean?" asked his brother.

"I refer to the fact that the premier has been insisting that the mustard gas be seized the moment its hiding place is discovered."

"What?" exclaimed Sherlock Holmes. "I was not made aware of that wish."

"The building in Limehouse will be raided within twenty-four hours," said Mycroft to his brother as Bullivant and I looked on. "The premier informed me only today that, when the location of the mustard gas was uncovered, it would then be taken without delay. That is what I had wished to tell you this evening. That Arbuthnot has discovered the hiding place even sooner than expected merely accelerates the schedule for implementing the premier's wishes."

"But that would be most premature!" declared Sherlock Holmes. "We have not yet assembled all the—"

"I do not disagree with you," interjected Mycroft. He leaned back and interleaved the fingers of both hands. "However, I also understand the premier's position in the matter, and it is he who is, well, the premier. I am obligated to follow his commands. So are you."

"You cannot stop him?"

Mycroft smiled wistfully. "My powers of enforcement in government circles are waning these days, Sherlock," he said. "And even my friendly advice is no longer heeded as closely as it once was. No," he said after a moment's pause. "The prime minister is determined to act; he will not allow the mustard gas to sit in London through another sunset."

"He wished to round up the known members of the London Transport League as well," added Bullivant.

Sherlock Holmes bolted to his feet. "But that is more than premature; it is utterly pointless, not to say most dangerous to our cause of rooting out Von Bork!" he declared. "There is no—"

"Calm yourself, brother," murmured Mycroft. "I did achieve one small victory, and that was to persuade the government to keep its hands off the Transport League for the moment. The premier still wishes to take the haulers into custody, but he has agreed to wait awhile longer in their case. However," the portly Holmes added, "he will not wait forever."

Sherlock Holmes exhaled loudly. "I thank you for that much at least, Mycroft," he said as he began to pace back and forth across the room. "The task before us is to implicitly assure Von Bork—"

"Or whoever commands the third German operation," whispered Mycroft.

"To assure him that, though we know of the mustard gas, we have no knowledge of the Transport League, and therefore no awareness that the gas itself is but part of a larger German plan," declared Sherlock Holmes.

"I have been cognizant of that need," declared his brother. "And, if I may say, an approach has been forged that will assure us that the need is met. If you will please be seated again, Sherlock, I will elaborate."

The detective once more took to his armchair. "Who will lead the assault in Limehouse?" he asked.

"Magillivray, of course," replied Mycroft with a faint smile. "And he has invited both you and the colonel to observe the festivities, but—"

"We will pass on the offer."

"Good," said the elder Holmes.

"But do you not wish to witness at least this one fruit of your labour?" I asked.

Both Holmes brothers and Sir Walter looked at me questioningly.

"Having the two of you near the premises during the raid would hardly be prudent," said Bullivant. "You see, Watson, if it were evident that Holmes were involved—"

"If that were evident," Sherlock Holmes interjected, "then Von Bork—"

Mycroft sighed.

"Von Bork would suspect that I might have also discovered the London Transport League and fathomed its purpose," his brother completed.

“But you have not yet determined that purpose,” I observed.

“A fact that does not deny the validity of my analysis,” said Holmes.

“We should try to make certain that whoever controls this spy ring does not realise we know there is more to its machinations than the sulphur mustard gas,” reiterated Mycroft. “To that end, we shall make it appear that the police have stumbled across the cache in Limehouse quite unintentionally.”

He turned to address his brother. “Magillivray will arrange for a disturbance to occur just outside the building: an assault on a man with a German-sounding name. That will elicit the arrival of many policemen, including Sergeant Scaife. In the course of quelling what will become a minor riot, Magillivray and his men will go inside the warehouse and fortuitously discover the presumed stockpile of mysterious containers. Some of the supposed German agents there will be allowed to escape, taking with them the tale of its accidental discovery.”

Sherlock Holmes nodded. “That should suffice.”

“Mind you,” said Mycroft Holmes, “Magillivray has agreed to place himself in a possibly embarrassing and humiliating situation, for no one besides Sergeant Scaife is to know of the arrangement for some Germans to elude capture.”

“Not even the premier himself?” asked Sherlock Holmes.

Bullivant looked at Mycroft Holmes, who returned the spymaster’s glance before lacing his fingers together and admitting, “No, not even he knows.”

The younger Holmes brother smiled. “I should think it is you who places himself in a potentially embarrassing position instead, Mycroft. I thank you.”

"Well," said his sibling primly, "blood is thicker than mustard gas. Or, so they say."

The following evening, Holmes and I ate an early dinner and then took up familiar positions in the sitting room: The detective leafed through yet another commonplace book while I finished editing documents for the medical corps.

At eight o'clock, the doorbell rang. A moment later, Martha ushered Sir Walter Bullivant into our presence.

"The deed is done," the spymaster declared, setting aside his coat and hat. "It all went rather well, just as planned," he said, taking the basket chair. "The disturbance, the arrival of the police, the supposed chance observation of the interior of the building, leading to the discovery of mustard gas—each step succeeded the next like clockwork."

"And was sulphur mustard within that warehouse?" said Sherlock Holmes.

"Oh yes," replied Bullivant. "I'm told there was enough to contaminate many blocks of London. There is an army detachment surrounding the building at present, and the stores will be evacuated to the Albany Street Barracks by dawn tomorrow. There has been and will continue to be a commotion until all is removed, but we are inventing explanations to satisfy the public as matters proceed, with no mention of gas so as to reduce any chance of panic."

"And were there German agents on the premises?" asked Holmes.

"We believe there were five," replied Bullivant. "Sergeant Scaife and Inspector Magillivray allowed two to slip away, as per your request." He sighed. “It puts them in a rather dim light with respect to the Yard, however.”

“We all knew that might be the result,” the detective remarked. “In the meanwhile, I believe the best you can do in reply is continue to employ Scaife and Magillivray as you are able, and to express your confidence in them to their superiors, as you already have. And to hope, of course, that we quickly and decisively foil the further plans of Von Bork’s new spy ring.”

Bullivant nodded.

“There will be no government action immediately forthcoming with regard to the Transport League?” Holmes asked.

“M has promised there will be none for at least the next fortnight, perhaps longer.”

The detective shrugged. “Well, that gives us at least a few days of grace.”

“Yes,” agreed Bullivant. “And there is another item for which we may give thanks: there is no longer any need to search for that Dieter Baumann fellow.”

Holmes cocked his head. “The fellow has not turned up dead, has he?”

“Quite the contrary,” replied the spymaster. “He is alive, and he is eager to come over to our side.”

“What?”

“A note was handed to Inspector Magillivray this very evening as he supervised the final stages of securing the warehouse with army personnel. It was given him by a street boy who said a stranger had paid him to deliver it to the inspector, whom the man pointed out to the lad.”

Bullivant reached into a pocket, withdrew a folded piece of paper, and leaned forward to hand it to Holmes.

"You will see that the note is not signed," the spymaster said. "The boy, however, described the stranger as having two prominent moles upon his cheek. That is our Herr Baumann, is it not?"

"Yes," said Holmes with an abstracted air as he read the brief letter. "This is a most interesting development," he added as he passed the paper on to me.

I took the sheet and viewed its contents:

> *There is more elsewhere. From those keeping me in slavery to their madness free me, and I will lead you to it. I am German but pray for the Kaiser's fall. Answer in the newspaper. God Save the King.*

"The spy ring appears to be cracking, if not breaking," I observed, handing the note back to Holmes, who turned to Sir Walter.

"If it is acceptable," said the detective to the spymaster, "I should like Inspector Magillivray to immediately turn over to me any such notes that he or Scotland Yard may receive in future."

"Yes, of course," said Bullivant. "I will so inform him."

"And in the meanwhile," Holmes said, "please have the inspector place the following message in the *Times*: 'God Save the King: We are listening.'"

"I will have him do so at once," responded the spymaster. "Well, events are turning our way now, it seems. Oh, and there is one more item—one of a personal nature—that I must tell you," Bullivant said. "The store of mustard gas having been confirmed, found, and seized—and the prospect now ahead of taking hold of the rest with Dietrich Baumann's assistance—the prime minister has directed M to have me convey his—that is, the premier's heartfelt thanks and appreciation for your efforts."

Holmes nodded impatiently. "The task is not finished, however," he said. "We do not yet have Von Bork, let alone a grasp of his remaining plans."

"To complete my message," Bullivant quietly said, "I am to inform you that for this and everything else you have contributed in the past several years, a knighthood would not be out of the question, in the premier's view."

"Tosh!" scoffed Holmes, reaching for a pipe. "I have been through that nonsense more than once. What portion of a negative response is beyond the grasp of our government?"[252]

"I leave that issue for you and M to discuss," Bullivant declared. "Consider your brother to be the government's representative in the matter."

"He is the government's representative in all matters that concern me," replied Holmes, reaching for his shag.

"There is news also from Richard Hannay and Mary Lamington," said Bullivant.

"Oh?" I replied as Holmes stuffed his pipe. "Where are they? What is happening to them?"

---

[252] Holmes had already been offered a knighthood at least once, probably in 1902. That was, by coincidence, the year in which Watson's literary agent, A. C. Doyle, was knighted.

"Formally, Mary serves at present at a base hospital in Normandy," the spymaster told us. "And here is something of great import: she has received a brief letter from the man we know as Moxon Ivery."

"Truly?" said Holmes, suddenly losing interest in his pipe.

"Yes," replied the spymaster. "Though I find it surprising that he should attempt to contact her."

Holmes smiled as he searched for a vesta. "It is a testament to the young woman's ability to lead on our Mr. Ivery while not appearing a member of our secret cabal. What was the content of the letter? Did it concern his proposal of marriage?"

"He asked to meet her, an offer that she has not yet accepted, pending my approval. Oh, and the man signed his name as Bommaerts: another one of his many identities, no doubt."

"And are you going to allow her to see Bommaerts née Ivery?" I asked with concern.

"I do not yet know for certain," replied Bullivant. "I thought to ask your advice on this," he added, speaking not to me but rather to Holmes.

"Good God," I exclaimed. "You are not going to use her as bait with which to snare the man, are you?"

"Ivery is too clever to be captured in that manner, Watson," said Holmes as he lit his pipe. "However, he is also…too clever by half, and it would be…to our advantage to allow Miss Lamington to see him, no matter what he is calling himself these days."

"You cannot be serious!" I declared.

"I can be and am quite serious, old fellow."

"Have you no regard for the safety of a woman?" I asked sharply, immediately regretting the remark, for I saw my Holmes's face struggle to hide the pain my comment had wrought.

Knowing the reason for his agony, I saw my friend turn to address Bullivant. "Miss Lamington is perhaps the only person among us whom Ivery does not suspect of being in your employ, Sir Walter," he said calmly. "You should utilise that advantage as best you can."

I chose not to reply to this sentiment, which I admitted was coldly logical, but at the same time also cold-blooded. "And what of Hannay?" I asked in a hollow voice.

"We have made use of Abel Gresson, whom Holmes here wisely suggested we allow to remain free, so that we might observe him," said Bullivant. "When Gresson was touring the Continent as part of that labour group, one of Blenkiron's operatives noticed that he stayed a strangely long while in a small French village."

I listened intently, noticing that Holmes was staring at the carpet.

"Hannay is preparing to visit the village as we speak here," Bullivant said. "We will see if he turns up anything. Oh," he added, "Hannay also wished me to tell you, Watson, that he ran into Launcelot Wake, Mary's cousin."

"Yes," I said. "He is in the Labour Corps."

"Fine lad, then," Bullivant declared. "He is doing his part, certainly, just as Mary is doing hers."

I did not respond to the comment.

"And perhaps if my reassignment ever occurs, the same may be said about me," I muttered with a facetious air.

"Have you not told him?" Bullivant asked Holmes, who frowned and shook his head.

"What?" I asked. "What do you mean by that, Bullivant?"

"I mean that you are certainly prescient," the spymaster told me. "My understanding was that you were not to be informed for another few days, but yes, Watson, you are being reassigned by the medical corps, though you will remain in London."

"And what is the nature of this new charge?" I asked anxiously.

"You are to be gazetted to the staff of Queen Alexandra's Hospital," Bullivant informed me. "I believe it will be effective the first of the month."[253]

"Queen Alexandra's?" I said in disbelief. "Are you quite certain?"

"As certain as I am now that we shall someday capture Moxon Ivery," replied Sir Walter.

"And what is my position to be? My duties? Am I to—"

"I know none of those details," explained Bullivant as he retrieved his hat and coat. "I fear you must wait for your new orders, Watson. But allow me to congratulate you."

Holmes and I escorted Bullivant along the hallway and bade him farewell into the night. As I closed the door, my friend was already returning to the sitting room.

"Holmes?" I called meekly. "Holmes," I said while catching up to him, "did you have any part in this?"

"In what?"

"In my reassignment, of course."

---

[253] See Footnote 110.

"Whatever might suggest to you that I had?" asked my friend, who, re-entering the sitting room, retrieved his pipe from a table to make certain that its fire was still alive.

"The fact that you give such a reply instead of answering my question directly, for one," I stated. "Then too," I added, stepping to the hearth to revive the coals, "Sir Walter enquired if you had informed me previously of my change in duties."

Holmes raised his brows.

"Why should he ask that of you, unless he believed you already knew of the reassignment?" I said.

Holmes sat down in his armchair and reached for another of his commonplace books.

"And why should you know of it," I said, "unless you yourself instigated it?"

"I believe I have heard someone in the past bemoaning being subjected to 'deductive enumerations,' Watson. Could that have been you? If so, then I assure you that I now know how you must have felt."

"I feel you are continuing to evade me."

"Not very well, I fear," Holmes sighed. "Yes, I admit I had a hand in this recent change of assignment for you."

"But why?"

"Is the answer not obvious to us both?" my friend said. "As I have told you, Watson, I must have you here in London, to steady me," Holmes admitted. "To give me an anchor." His eyes assumed a troubled look, and he added, "You are all that is left of those bygone days, Watson. Baker Street and its trappings are gone," he declared, looking round the room, "other than those few mementos that we have salvaged. Indeed, I was instrumental in destroying much of that, was I not? But you were always the rock upon which I built my agency, and you are no less essential now."

I opened my mouth but found I could not speak.

"Your frustration with the secretarial duties that have been foisted upon you has not been lost on me," Holmes said. "If I have had a hand in arranging matters more to your liking, it has been purely from a desire to see you happy, old fellow."

"Believe me when I say that your desire has been fulfilled, Holmes, and I thank you more than words can convey."

My friend smiled wanly.

"And, Holmes, I must apologise most earnestly for my callous remark earlier about—"

The detective gestured as if to wave me off.

"There is no need, Watson," he sighed. "Your judgement is just, and I deserve every—"

At that moment, the house bell rang.

"Who can that be?" asked Holmes, his mood suddenly changed. "Is it Sir Walter returning, having forgotten to convey one last piece of news?"

Just then, Martha appeared at the open doorway.

"A commissionaire was at the door, sir," she told Holmes. "He was bearing this," the woman said, stepping into the sitting room with an ungainly parcel in her arms.

Very quickly, I strode to her side and relieved her of the burden.

"The commissionaire said he had no real knowledge of the sender, only that it was a man of middle age who declared the package was for you, Mr. Holmes."

I placed the box upon a table, and Sherlock Holmes set down his pipe to approach it.

"Thank you, Martha," said the detective. "We will open it presently."

"As you wish," replied our housekeeper, who departed the room.

Holmes, meanwhile, had already removed most of the string and wrapper from a sturdy but elegant wooden box not quite an arm's length in its greatest dimension.

"Hum," said my friend. "Hand me the poker, please."

I stepped to the hearth and returned with the desired tool. Holmes then carefully used it to pry open one end of the box, which appeared stuffed with shredded paper. I heard a dull clink as the box was gently tilted, and then Holmes reached in to extract from the container a large bottle, its dark surface streaked with dust.

"Ha!" exclaimed the detective, holding it in his hands. "What a gesture, indeed!" he cried, holding aloft a bottle of Imperial Tokay. "It were Altamount's favourite," he added in the voice of his erstwhile alter ego.

"Do you mean to imply that this was sent by—"

"Heinrich Von Bork. Yes, of course it was." He dusted off the bottle and then turned once more toward me. "He is most generous, is he not?"

"But why should Von Bork do such an impetuous and foolhardy thing?" I asked. "By this act, he admits his presence to us all."

"He knows he reveals nothing I do not already know," said Holmes, looking once more at the bottle. "However, he does not know all that has been revealed to me. I have told you repeatedly that he was amongst us, Watson, and here is proof at last, in the form of this congratulation."

"But if he is conceding that you have bested him again, does that not mean he realises you were behind the raid on his mustard gas this evening?"

"Yes," admitted Holmes. "In that sense, the gift is bittersweet. Still," he added, "I believe we may also take heart from it, for it is implicit proof that Von Bork does not suspect we know of the London Transport League. Otherwise, I do not believe he would be so brazen."

"Might he not be goading you in the manner you did him with that magazine story?"

"Perhaps," replied my friend. "But I shall not respond to such taunting, if taunting it be."

"You do not propose to drink a toast to those sentiments, do you?"

"Of course not, Watson," he said with a chuckle. "I shall not drink to such sentiments. I should, however, wish to toast your new assignment at Queen Alexandra's Hospital."

I started to speak in concern.

"But do not worry, old fellow," said Holmes, setting down the bottle. "I will propose a toast, but I do not intend to employ this vintage. It would not be beyond the capacity of our German friend to poison the contents, though the stopper appears undisturbed, and I doubt that, with his breeding, he would stoop to ruin such a fine Tokay. Still, one must be prudent."

Holmes strode to the mantel, his bearing, I noticed, transformed to one of confidence. "I have him now, Watson," he said. "I have goaded Von Bork into making this even more a matter of personal emotion."

As Sherlock Holmes reached for our brandy and glasses, I could not help but remind myself that the matter had been very personal for some time, and that Von Bork's gesture had perhaps not been intended to inspire anger in my friend but rather an excess of pride.

CHAPTER TWENTY-TWO: RETURN & REVELATION

I threw myself into the responsibilities of an RAMC staff secretary with new vigour, knowing that their tedium would soon end. Awaiting service at Queen Alexandra's Hospital, I became reinvigorated, feeling that I would soon regain a sense of purpose that was wholly mine, though I did feel slight pangs of guilt, understanding that my duties would leave far less time to stand at the side of Sherlock Holmes.

A few days after learning of my impending reassignment, I remained at home one morning to edit a set of documents. As I put finishing touches on those papers before gathering my things to travel to the staff office in Westminster, Martha slipped her head through the open doorway of the sitting room.

"Colonel Watson, there is an American soldier here to see you," she said with an odd look in her eye.

I set down my pen and gave our housekeeper an expression of puzzlement.

"I have no idea why the Americans should wish to contact me," I said, rising from my writing desk. "No one has mentioned any sort of coordination with them. And why their messenger should call for me here—well, I can only suppose it is a matter both sudden and urgent," I said. "For why else would they seek me here in Queen Anne Street?"

I gently strode past our housekeeper and on down the hall, saying, "He must be received, then."

"The young man is still outside the door," Martha declared with a chuckle as I passed her at the sitting room door and marched down the hallway. "I thought perhaps you should see to him yourself."

"Yes, I shall deal with the visitor," I replied over my shoulder, smiling. "You may stand down, madam."

I opened the door of my residence and saw before me a boyish fellow in the dress of an American private, hands thrust into the pockets of his open coat, worn over a wool khaki uniform. The man, barely over twenty years of age, wore leggings and trench shoes, with a smart overseas cap set rakishly upon his blond head. His eyes bore a look of familiarity, yet I could not place him until he uttered his first words to me.

"Halloa, Dr. Watson," the soldier said.

"Jack James! Halloa, my boy!" I cried. "I confess that at first I did not grasp that it was you."

"Well," he said, stepping into the house after a vigorous handshake, "I suppose the clothes do make the man—and change him—at least some of the time." He looked briefly around as I took his coat and cap. "This place is a bit like I remember it. But also rather different in some ways. I suppose that's because you're now under different management here?"

"Well, there is a new housekeeper since you last visited," I explained as we walked to the sitting room. "We are now under the wing of Martha, who—"

"Was Mr. Holmes's keeper, as well as his spy lodged with old Von Bork. Yes, I recognised her and reintroduced myself, asking that she not let on to you who I was."

I turned and saw the housekeeper standing some feet away, a look of innocence on her elderly face.

"I did remember the young man," she confessed.

I nodded forgiveness, and the woman bowed slightly before disappearing down the hall.

"I take it that the great one himself lives here now," the young man said as I guided him down the corridor.

"He has been residing in Queen Anne Street since just after the war began."

"Well, he did not mention that in his letter. It's just begun for us over on the other side of the Atlantic, of course—the war, that is," the American said with a wistful smile.

"I received one letter from Mr. Holmes after I'd returned home on one of your country's destroyers back in 1914, but nothing since then," he declared as we entered the sitting room and beheld it in all its chaotic glory. "However, I can sure sense Mr. Holmes's presence in here," he added. "Without a doubt. I take it he's not around at the moment, though?"

"He is out," I replied, "but he should return at any time. You are in the American Army now," I said while ringing for Martha.

"Yes, as you are in the British one—or, at least, the medical corps, it appears," he said, gesturing to my uniform, which I had already donned in anticipation of leaving for the RAMC office.

I nodded and suggested James warm himself before the fire.

"I spent two years as an instructor in Aldershot," I told him, "and then a portion of a year as head of a hospital in the Cotswolds. Most recently, I have fought the war from behind a desk here in London, but I am soon to be transferred to a local military hospital, which I anticipate with satisfaction."

"I congratulate you, Colonel Watson," replied James, rubbing his hands as he stood before the coals.

Martha entered, and I asked her to prepare some small plate of nournishment for us.

"And do you ever join Mr. Holmes again to play cat and mouse with German spies?" the American asked me as the housekeeper vanished beyond the sitting room door.

I opened my mouth and then hesitated, wondering whether I should provide him with details.

"I shouldn't have asked," said the young man, at once sensing my awkwardness. "Don't feel the need to enlighten me, Dr. Watson. I'm no longer part of that game, after all. True, I'm here to fight Germans again, but this time with a larger gun," James added puckishly, and I grimly nodded, wishing that the young man might never realise that ambition.

We sat down beside the hearth and reminisced for several minutes about Holmes as Altamount, as well as recalling Von Bork and the taxicab in which James had chauffeured the detective and me about London and beyond.

"I wonder where the old gal is now. The taxi, I mean," he added. "Do you and Mr. Holmes ever go back to Baker Street, together or alone? I remember how he used to have me drive him there. And you did once, as I recall."

"Yes," I answered simply. "I remember that evening. To be honest, the nostalgic impulse has not welled up in me of late. As for Holmes," I said, "I cannot speak for him in that regard. His comings and goings are often his own."

"I understand."

What was for me an uncertain moment ended abruptly as I heard the house door open and close.

"I believe we will share one of those arrivals now," I said.

The dim voices of Martha and Holmes echoed down the hallway, and then the figure of my friend appeared at the sitting room door.

"James!" the detective exclaimed at once. "What a surprise! It is a pleasure to see you again!"

"I can earnestly say the same," replied the young man, rising to shake the other's hand. "I suppose it's a minor victory to have surprised the likes of you, sir. You know, the Murtaugh brothers in Chicago are still looking for you as Mr. Altamount."

Holmes smiled as he invited Jack James to sit down again. Glancing at me, he added, "I am afraid that all they will ever have of me is my jackknife, if that."

"Yes," James said with a sudden note of embarrassment in his voice. "I sometimes think about—"

"But let us not dwell upon what has gone before," said Holmes, briefly taking our visitor by the shoulder. "Past necessity remains past necessity, and we should turn our gaze toward the future, should we not?"

With raised brows, I sat in the basket chair as Holmes invited James to take to the armchair.

Just then, I noticed that our housekeeper was standing in the doorway.

"This is all I could assemble on such short notice, sirs," the woman said. "I do hope that oxo[254] and biscuits will suffice for the moment."

---

[254] "Oxo" is a brand name and in this instance refers to broth made from what Americans call a bouillon cube.

"That sounds pretty fine to me," James declared with a smile.

I nodded agreement, and Holmes gently took the tray from the elderly woman, who once more disappeared down the hall.

"You look older, especially in uniform," Holmes remarked to our visitor while setting the tray upon the breakfast table.

"Perhaps, but I'm afraid I'm likely none the wiser."

"We have often wondered if you would return to London in this manner," said the detective, reaching for his clay pipe and shag while silently encouraging the American to take something from the tray. "Our speculations have obviously come true."

"Yes, I couldn't very well refuse Uncle Sam," replied James as he rose from the armchair and approached the breakfast table. "It's been nothing but training and travelling so far, but at least the conditions have been getting better."

"Oh?" I said, knowing that, for the young man, that trend would soon reverse.

"Yes, London is nothing like the training camp back home," the American replied before taking a bite of biscuit. "Over there, we slept six to a tent. We were told the food was pork or beef, but I had my doubts, though you could always depend on the bread and potatoes. We had to do our personal duties in a pit, but at least we were able to shower regularly, and the linen was kept clean. Still, it was nothing compared to over here. These biscuits are very good, by the way."

"Have you any idea when you will be going to France?" asked Holmes as he leaned against the mantel.

"No. Word is that we're going to be doing even more training before we're sent over."

Holmes nodded as he finished filling his pipe and reached for a vesta. "Perhaps," he said, "you might...consider the possibility of being...seconded, as it were, to the colonel and myself in the interim."

"What, sir?"

Holmes tossed the vesta onto the coals. "Perhaps we could arrange for you to assist me in my present work, much as you did earlier, Jack."

"It is tempting," young James replied, consuming the rest of the biscuit. "Those were fun days. But I'd feel I was shirking if—"

"I understand," Holmes said. "Perhaps, though, you would consider it? A face unknown to most in London, coupled with a most capable mind practised in the trade, would be of great value to our endeavour."

"Well, I suppose there might be times when I could—"

"Then let us consider it possible," declared Holmes. "Give me the name of your commanding officer. We have an American friend you may recall—a Mr. Blenkiron?—I believe he would be able to arrange matters with ease."

"As long as my pals don't ship out to France without me. I won't let them down."

Holmes smiled grimly. "I promise you will not be left behind," he said.

"Well then," replied our guest, "in that case, you can certainly talk to Mr. Blenkiron, for I'd jump at the chance to gad about again with you two gents."

"Consider it done," murmured Holmes.

Our reunion with Jack James continued for the better part of the next hour, and then the young American departed.

As he closed the house door, Sherlock Holmes said, "It is a fortuitous return, Watson."

"You wish to entangle him in the dangerous sport of hooking Von Bork?" I asked cautiously.

"I should think you would applaud my efforts, old fellow, since it removes him, at least temporarily, from even more dangerous prospects on the Western Front. And I suppose his addition will make up for your impending absence."

"I will still reside here in Queen Anne Street."

"Yes, but you will be less available than before, will you not?"

I opened my mouth but found I had no words with which to reply.

"But that is how it should be," Holmes declared in an abstracted tone. "However, the previous state still obtains, and I wish to haul you to Safety House on short notice—and perhaps for one last time."

"What has arisen?"

Holmes pulled a telegram from his coat pocket and placed it on the breakfast table as we re-entered the sitting room.

"Tatty Evans has observed the *Nemesis* change its mooring point," said the detective. "It is now docked closer to the City, just east of the London Docks proper, in the area of the old Hartwell Fish Market.[255] Master Evans noticed the craft absent from its former anchorage, but then espied the craft at the new location early yesterday. He notified me by

[255] This may be a fictionalized reference to the Shadwell Fish Market, whose location was in the area of the present-day King Edward VII Memorial Park, a site matching the rough description of the mooring point in Watson's narrative. At that time, the area was informally used for sporting matches and as a playground for children. Plans for the park had already been made before the war, but they were not realized until 1922.

means of that telegram and is prepared to take us round for a look. I have suggested tomorrow afternoon. Would you accompany me, if that suits?"

"It does."

"That is not the principal reason for visiting Safety House, however," Holmes said. "Bullivant apparently has something to pass on to me as and is expecting us, along with my brother, in slightly more than an hour."

"I suppose I should fetch our hats and coats, then."

"Inspector Magillivray has received a second message from our friend Dieter Baumann," said Sir Walter Bullivant. "He asked me to pass it on to you."

The spymaster glanced with satisfaction at Mycroft Holmes, who leaned back in the sofa of Safety House and looked thoughtfully at his brother.

Sir Walter pulled a scrap of paper from his pocket and unfolded it before offering it to Sherlock Holmes, who read the note before handing it to me. The words were in much the same vein as those in the first, received the night of the raid on the mustard gas warehouse:

> *Time is short. To free myself and save London from more gas, to someone I must talk. Can it be the retired detective Holmes? He saved a friend once. Answer in the newspaper. God Save the King.*

"Should Magillivray place another reply in the *Times*?" Sir Walter asked. "Perhaps one proposing a meeting?"

“And you say Inspector Magillivray received this note?” asked Sherlock Holmes without responding to the spymaster’s comment.

“Yes,” replied Bullivant. “Addressed to Magillivray, it was given to a constable just outside the Cannon Row Station.”

“And who was the person who delivered it?”

“An ordinary clerk on his way to work, I believe,” replied Sir Walter. “The man said he had been handed both the note, in a sealed envelope, and a gold sovereign by a stranger in return for giving the former to the first policeman he saw.”

“What did the stranger look like?”

“The constable did not ask that question.”

“Did the constable at least obtain the clerk’s name?” sighed Holmes.

“He did neither, I fear.”

The detective nodded glumly.

“At least we have another message from Herr Baumann,” said Bullivant. “And its handwriting is identical to that in the first note. I say,” he asked the detective, “did Baumann have a friend who was a client of yours at one time?”

“I very much doubt it,” replied Holmes.

“Should I still have Magillivray place a reply in the *Times*?” asked Sir Walter, his expression puzzled.

The two Holmes brothers cast wary glances at one another, and then Mycroft said, “Yes, Sir Walter. And you shall use prudence, Sherlock.”

“Of course,” said the detective quickly. “Now, Sir Walter, word the reply as follows: ‘God Save the King, you will be free. Let us meet. SH.’”

Mycroft set an elbow upon the armrest of the sofa and let his chin rest on his open palm as he stared down at the carpet.

"Very well," declared Bullivant. "I will make certain that Magillivray places it today. Meanwhile, you said that your man Evans had discovered the German motor launch is now docked in another place along the river?"

"Yes," said Holmes. "It is now somewhat farther west than before. The colonel and I will go on board the *Belisama* tomorrow to make our own observation of the launch at its new anchorage."

"I see," muttered Sir Walter. "The German craft's previous mooring was close to the building where the first store of mustard gas was initially placed. Perhaps this new location lies in the vicinity of the additional stockpile of gas mentioned by our friend Baumann."

"Perhaps," replied Holmes as his brother looked on in silence.

"Well, I expect you will put your men onto it, including Sandy Arbuthnot," the spymaster said as he rose to leave.

"If possible," the detective interjected, "I wish to add to that complement. The young American who assisted me before the war, Jack James, has returned to Britain as part of his nation's army, and he has agreed to become available to us."

"Do you wish him temporarily relieved of his soldierly obligations?" asked Mycroft. "I can talk to John Blenkiron."

"That would be most appreciated," replied his brother.

"Good," said Bullivant, rising. "And I will go to Magillivray in order to get our reply to Baumann placed in the *Times*."

"Thank you, Sir Walter," declared Mycroft Holmes as he struggled to get to his feet as well. "I wish to further discuss that matter of the *Nemesis* with my brother and the colonel, and will ring you up later in the day. You wish an escort to the door?"

"As always, Mycroft, I am able to see myself out. Until later, gentlemen."

Holmes and I rose as Sir Walter departed. When the house door closed, Mycroft sat down and cast an appraising look at his brother.

"As you chose not to make him reconsider his perspective, I thought not to intervene," said the elder Holmes.

"And I thank you for that, Mycroft," replied his brother. "I appreciate your granting me some initiative from time to time."

"You would take it from under my nose in any event, dear boy."

"I beg pardon?" I interjected.

Both men looked at me with kindly expressions.

"Are there facts that I have missed?" I asked.

Mycroft motioned as if to defer to his brother.

"The entreaties we assume to come from Dietrich Baumann are most likely false ones," declared Sherlock Holmes.

"What? They are not from Baumann?"

"Oh, I am certain that Dieter Baumann is the messenger," said my friend. "The messages themselves, however, are undoubtedly from Heinrich von Bork."

I glanced back and forth between the two brothers.

"The circumstances of the first note were somewhat suspicious," said Sherlock Holmes. "Why should the message be passed directly on to Magillivray at the very location of the warehouse? By doing so, Baumann risked capture by Scotland Yard or observation by his fellow Germans. He could instead have sent a boy from another neighbourhood to a police station."

"And why direct the note to Magillivray in particular?" added Mycroft. "I am inclined to believe it is because the Germans know of the inspector's special connection to Bullivant. And to you," he told his brother.

"That is possible," agreed Sherlock Holmes. "Then too, there is the wording of these notes. They are phrased awkwardly, yet Frank Farrar has testified that Dietrich Baumann now is able to pass as English in his speech. No, I believe that Baumann wrote notes that were dictated to him by Von Bork."

"You will be cautious, brother?"

Holmes smiled at his older sibling.

"And you shall accept my advice and assistance," Mycroft declared. "I utter that not as a question."

"As you wish," sighed the detective, who glanced in my direction. "It is all supposition, Watson, but I agree with my brother that it will pay to be sceptical of this development."

The following day, I took a brisk morning walk round my neighbourhood before Holmes and I were to ply the river in the company of Tatty Evans. Having made a broad circuit on foot, I approached my house and saw a vacant taxicab now resting outside by the kerb. Intrigued, I quickly stepped inside, where I found Holmes sitting in his armchair, dressed to go out, and beside him Jack James, who now sported civilian clothes.

"Ah," I said, stepping to the hearth, the still untouched bottle of Tokay resting on the floor near my feet. "That was unnaturally swift. I assume that the taxicab outside is yours now?" I asked young James.

"Well, it has been loaned to me," said the American. "I think you'll find, however, that I am far more practised with both brake and clutch than I was four years ago." He smiled. "I have to say that the automobiles are a mite more advanced as well."

"Our unholy trio has been reunited sooner than I thought possible," I declared.

"When Mycroft wishes to act quickly, he can find ways to do so," said Holmes. "In this instance, with John Blenkiron's assistance, our wishes were accomplished almost instantaneously. Private James has been seconded to our enterprise for at least a month."

"That is good news," I said. "It is time to leave in order to board the *Belisama*?"

"Yes," Holmes added. "I've told Jack that we are going to observe the new mooring place of the *Nemesis*."

"And you have new boots, I see," I remarked.

"Ah, yes," my friend replied. "They arrived last evening, a gift from my brother, whose sudden displays of concern are touching. Are you ready to depart, Watson?" he said, reaching for his hat, which I noticed to also be a recent acquisition.

"That homburg is new as well," I observed.

"It was time to renew my wardrobe," Holmes answered with a smile.

"A bit of river air may not be the most healthful prescription for any of us," I said as I turned to go to my room. "However, I am happy to comply. Allow me a few minutes to change dress."

Somewhat more than an hour later, we three had set sail from the St. Katharine Docks with Tatty Evans and Old George aboard the

Belisama. The craft turned eastward, rounding the river's bend and heading for that point where the *Nemesis* had last been seen at anchor.

"As when I found her earlier mooring, I was sore tempted to land then and there," Master Evans confessed to us as he handed the boat's helm over to Old George. "I've a store of pent up feelings needing to be unleashed upon that uncouth crew. But I remembered you prescribing caution, Mr. Holmes." The stout man smiled heartily. "And I could not forget that you be the one who pays for all this."

Holmes kindly nodded acknowledgement. "And you have seen no activity about the launch?" he asked as we passed dilapidated watermen's stairs leading down to the river's shore.

"None, sir," replied Evans, his breath visible in the chilly breeze. "I've seen only the launch herself, with none of the infernal crew attending her, as near as I could observe."

"The Ratcliffe Highway is just to the north," said Holmes, pointing beyond the waterfront stairs. "That leads off to Limehouse itself," he said softly to James and me as we all wrapped ourselves more tightly in our coats. "Wherever the crew lodges, it must be near this place, I should think."

"Take her farther out from shore," Tatty Evans called to Old George, who swung our vessel to starboard. "There," the master of the *Belisama* declared, pointing toward the near bank. "As those trees slide away from our line of sight, you can see her anchoring spot. Need you a glass, Mr. Holmes?"

"I am already so equipped," replied the detective, withdrawing a small telescope from his pocket. Steadying himself as he gazed through its lens, my friend nodded. “So that is how she appears—the craft seems rather well looked after.”

“Aye,” agreed Tatty Evans. “For a rude, disrespectful crew, they take reasonable care of their vessel.”

“Or are forced to,” suggested Holmes. “Here, Watson,” he said, handing me the telescope. “Take a look, if you wish.”

I spent several seconds watching the *Nemesis*, moored at the edge of a relatively wild patch of ground, and then gave the instrument to Jack James. As we passed the anchored vessel at a distance of perhaps three cable lengths, Holmes declared he had seen enough of the previously elusive vessel.[256]

“Continued cooling of our limbs is too heavy a price for waiting to see if any of the crew come into view,” the detective remarked. “My principal desire was to learn where she ties up and observe her directly. We have accomplished that now.”

Tatty Evans ordered Old George to come about and sail back to our point of origin. As we glided toward the *Belisama*’s own anchorage, Holmes stood pensively, staring at the passing shore. Jack James strode over to Old George’s side to speak with the mate about steering the craft, while Tatty Evans excused himself to go below.

Now alone with my friend, I interrupted his reverie by asking, “Are you thinking of the next full moon, when the German aeroplanes may come

---

[256] A cable length is equal to one-tenth of a nautical mile. That Watson would employ such terminology is perhaps yet another piece of evidence suggesting he had an intimate connection with the sea.

again? [257] And we have not yet determined the purpose of the London Transport League."

Holmes turned toward me with a sad smile.

"Rather, old fellow, I was thinking of the cold, and how delightful it would be to have a warm Baker Street meal waiting for us."

I stood beside my friend for some time, the low conversation between the two young men abaft us the only counterpoint to the momentary silence we shared.

"Do you never cease to lay blame upon yourself?" I asked at length.

Tatty Evans's footsteps were heard as he regained the deck, and Holmes gave me a brief, mournful glance before looking back in the direction where lay the *Nemesis*, now far astern and out of view.

"And now that the well-named craft is found again, sir," asked Evans as he approached, "what am I to do? My vessel, after all, is still under your hire for another six days."

Holmes looked back along the river for a moment and then turned toward the barge's master. Genially, he replied, "I will present you with another cheque after we arrive at the St. Katharine Docks. Your instructions will be to keep watch on the launch for an indefinite period. I shall also have some additional directives for you as well."

"As you wish, Mr. Holmes. You do promise eventual retribution, however?"

"It is guaranteed," the detective quietly asserted.

---

[257] German aerial attacks by this time were staged at night, which gave greater cover for incoming bombers and reduced their losses, and the raids were conducted at or near the full moon to provide crews with a better opportunity to locate targets.

Tatty Evans nodded and then strode over to Old George's side, taking the helm from the younger man, who joined Jack James in admiring the riverine panorama and describing it to the American.

"I do hope that Richard Hannay brings down Von Schwabing," Holmes said abruptly as he too stared at the river's edge.

"Pardon, Holmes? Who do you mean? Not Von Bork, surely?"

"No," said he, leaning upon the gunwale.[258] "I mean the Graf von Schwabing: the man we know as Moxon Ivery."

"What? You have learned his true name?"

"I have deduced his likely true identity."

"By what means?"

Holmes turned round and pulled his clay pipe from a coat pocket. He toyed with it but made no attempt to fill the bowl. Instead, he said, "You may have noticed me frequently perusing my set of old commonplace books in past weeks."

"Of course," I said. "The activity has been difficult to ignore. I believe your *Almanach de Gotha* has made more than one appearance as well."

"You see, Watson," he said, studying the pipe, "Ivery's sophistication and erudite nature were all too obvious in Biggleswick. He was supposed to be a don, of course, but though genius may spring from any class, the man had a presence that struck me as decidedly aristocratic.

"Yet he was portraying another man, and an Englishman at that. A German nobleman would never willingly stoop to play such a role, even in the cause of spying for his own country."

"But Von Bork was a spy," I argued.

---

[258] The gunwale is the upper edge of the side of a boat.

"Von Bork remained Von Bork in 1914," Holmes maintained. "He did not assume another identity and suffer the indignity of getting his hands soiled as an actor for the purpose of espionage."

"He does so now," I asserted, now determined to refute my friend's claims. "Has Von Bork not disguised himself as a Mr. Borge to lie in hiding there?" I asked, gesturing toward shore.

Holmes smiled. "Yes, but you support my argument," he asserted. "Von Bork now prowls the streets and alleys as you say, Watson, but only after suffering the dishonour of being apprehended by me, the indignity of returning home in failure. Coming back to Britain in disguise was his only hope for redeeming his name."

The detective smiled once more, cocked his head, and raised a brow as he looked at me.

"And you believe that Moxon Ivery is a German of noble birth whose reputation was similarly tarnished in the past, causing him to accept the menial status of undercover agent?" I said.

"I have held to that view ever since we discovered that Ivery was our German spy in Biggleswick," declared Sherlock Holmes. "And, believing he would never have accepted such a role except for the reasons just cited, I have been glancing back through all my commonplace books and checking their contents against the *Almanach* in hopes of finding a likely candidate."

"And the minutiae you have gathered in those volumes proved useful, as they so often did back in Baker Street."

"Yes, Watson. What some might consider minutiae is, to the world's first consulting detective, the staff of life. And I daresay that my many volumes of saved cuttings constitute a Rosetta Stone of enlightenment concerning the peccadillos of more than one imperial dynasty—both in our hemisphere and the other.

"It was in those pages that I refreshed my memory concerning one Graf von Schwabing. He was a court favourite in his early years but became unfairly caught in a rather nasty scandal, and his stock with the aristocratic inner circle plummeted accordingly. He vanished from news accounts, and so far as anything was known of him by the general public, he was seen as a rather lazy and dissolute sort.

"However, as we both know, that was but a pose, for I suppose a man who swims for his life in the Channel at night, impersonates a don while maintaining several other identities, and then manages to get himself flown to France during wartime aboard an enemy aircraft is anything but lazy."

"Have you conveyed your discovery to Bullivant?" I asked.

Holmes shrugged and returned his pipe to a coat pocket.

"It is only a strong supposition at present, and I have shared it with no one but you," he said. "However, I will soon relate it to Sir Walter and Mycroft, who will no doubt pass the suggestion on to John Blenkiron. But the St. Katharine Docks now present themselves," announced the detective as the *Belisama*'s mooring place appeared round the river bend.

Smiling, Holmes walked to the opposite side of the barge to join Jack James and Old George. Tatty Evans nodded to me from the helm, and I returned his gesture. After staring briefly at Holmes in conversation with the two younger men, I turned back to watch the docks slowly approach.

Two nights later, I joined Vespera Cochrane for dinner at her friend's house in Kensington. Though I was grateful for our meeting after a separation of many days, I found myself disconcerted when it was revealed that the meal would be followed by a séance.

"You do not care for spiritualism?" Miss Cochrane asked later, when we found ourselves momentarily alone. "If anything, James, I have found you to be a most spiritual man."

"I believe I have asked you to not call me by that name," I noted gently.

"Ah," she said, genuinely contrite. "I did forget. Please do accept my apologies. I did not mean—"

"It does not signify," I said, discreetly taking her hand.

"But do you mean to say that you do not accept the concept of a spirit world?"

"I do not claim that," I answered. "Certainly, I do not deny its possibility, but I confess that, at the same time, I have failed to observe any evidence in support of its existence."

"Were you not moved by the Mons archer or—?"[259]

"I was not there," I said quietly. "And have you physical proof?"

Vespera Cochrane tipped her head. "I have only my heart. And I know you have a corresponding organ, John."

"I have an acquaintance who has been a spiritualist for years," I told her. "He has dragged me to more than one séance, much to my displeasure. Indeed, I had vowed to never attend another."[260]

---

259 The First World War generated many stories of the paranormal from its very beginning. During the Battle of Mons in August 1914, for instance, many British soldiers claimed they had been guided to safety by the apparition of a medieval archer said to inhabit the area, where the Battle of Agincourt had been fought in 1415. As the conflict wore on and casualties mounted, bereaved relatives found in spiritualism a hope that contact could be reestablished with departed loved ones.

260 It is possible that this reference is to A. C. Doyle, who declared himself to be a spiritualist in 1887, the same year in which he arranged for Watson's first Holmes reminiscence, *A Study in Scarlet*, to be reprinted in *Beeton's Christmas Annual*. In 1918,

"Does that mean you will leave prematurely tonight, John?"

I looked at her as she continued to hold my hand, clenching it more tightly, and I strengthened my own grip in return before letting go.

"I will stay," I avowed. "For you. I did not know that you were a follower of these activities. Rest assured that I will respect that."

"In truth, I am not a follower," she told me. "But I possess a curiosity about them. Will you not indulge me?"

"When have I not?" I asked with a wry smile.

Our host then approached and invited Miss Cochrane and me to join her and the other guests in the next room, which was lit by a single candle sitting in the middle of a large round table. A young woman sat there: a thin, big-eyed cadaverous beauty introduced to us merely as Sister Lilian. She arranged us round the table, placing me between Miss Cochrane's friend and a prominent newspaper publisher.

For the better part of an hour, I participated in the charade, holding hands with my fellow participants, all the time recalling the taste of prewar roast beef or taking clinical note of how my eyes were adjusting to the darkness as many of my companions experienced the rapture of communicating with phantoms.

At the conclusion of the night's escapade into ectoplasm, I bade farewell to Miss Cochrane, who would be staying the night in the house, and obtained a taxicab to take me back to Queen Anne Street, where I arrived just before Martha retired for the night.

"Is Mr. Holmes still about?" I asked as I put coat and hat in the wardrobe.

Doyle's son Kingsley and brother Innes would die in the Spanish Flu pandemic, causing him to more intensely embrace and promote the spiritualist cause.

"When is he not, sir?" our housekeeper replied as she shuffled down the hallway. "When is he not?" Pausing, she turned round and added, "He has not eaten this evening. Might you, Colonel, encourage him to—?"

"Consume something? Yes, I shall."

Entering the sitting room, I found Holmes perched beneath a miasma of blue smoke, a lingering remnant from many pipes now extinguished. He held a knife before his eyes and stared at the blade, which appeared stained. Though he no doubt was aware of my presence, his gaze did not leave the tarnished metal edge.

"Is that one of the pair found at the warehouse near the gasworks?" I asked.

"It is," said Holmes, putting the knife upon the table before him.

"And you still contemplate the tar upon it and its brothers?"

Holmes sighed.

"I take that as an affirmative response," I said, picking my way through the maze of newspapers, books, charts, and other assorted ephemera that lay cluttered in piles upon the floor. At length, having snatched both my own pipe and Arcadia mix along the route, I leaned back into the relative safety of the basket chair.

"I rotate the pieces this way and that—speaking metaphorically, of course," said Holmes. "Yet, no matter how I try, I fail to solve the jigsaw puzzle without one contradiction or another."

He ran fingers over his mouth and chin.

"Perhaps you should sleep upon it," I suggested while dipping into my Arcadia. Staring at the thinning veil of haze that still hung just below the ceiling, I added, "After all, some enigmas may turn out to be three pillow problems rather than three pipe ones."

Holmes gave a wan smile.

"I have not the time, Watson," he said, his voice suggesting no small hint of exasperation. "Von Bork must strike soon for his country, before the war is lost to Berlin and its allies. Mycroft is certain there will be a huge German offensive in the spring. A full moon impends. No doubt, whatever terror is planned for our island—more poison gas or some other vile act—it will be delivered within the next few weeks, if not days. I must somehow fix upon the substance and the method."

"Sleep can be a worthy method for grasping at substance," I again suggested as I lit my pipe. "And are you…not…the most methodical of men, as well as the most patient?"

Holmes hung his head. "Perhaps at some time past I was," he replied. "Tonight, however, I find my patience wearing thin, and method is nowhere to be found."

"Retire for the night," I urged again while reaching for a volume of sea stories. From the corner of my eye, I saw my friend rise from his chair. "Perhaps you should take some food before doing so."

"No," murmured Holmes, carefully picking his way across a carpet strewn with the detritus of his researches. "I shall take your advice to heart and declare my day to be at an end—it is straight to bed for me."

"Should I have Martha awaken you for breakfast, or do you wish to substitute starvation for insomnia?"

"Have her knock upon my door, and I will decide the matter then and there. Perhaps I shall embrace both. Oh, and tend to the coals when you finally retire, old fellow," Holmes requested as he approached the sitting room door.

I looked up from my book and surveyed the expanse of scattered books, papers, and maps that lay between myself and the hearth.

"I will do my best," I sighed. "Though you have, after all, made it almost impossible for me to reach the fire through this field of obstacles."

I returned to my reading, but only for a moment, for I quickly sensed that Holmes had not yet made his exit from the sitting room. I turned and saw that he was, instead, standing in the open doorway, his once fatigued expression now replaced with one of sparkling excitement.

"That is it, Watson!" said he.

"I beg pardon?"

"You have blown away the fog, old fellow, as only you can. Find our coats and hats while I ring up Mycroft," Holmes declared in an electric voice. "We meet with him and Bullivant presently!"

CHAPTER TWENTY-THREE: THE CALCULUS OF HELL

Mycroft Holmes once more occupied the sofa in the sitting room of Safety House, thoughtfully reading a war communique, while his brother sat in an armchair beside mine.

"You do not mind waiting for Sir Walter?" asked the elder Holmes, not looking up from his message. "I am all too familiar with your impatience, Sherlock."

"I believe Watson and I know the principal answers already," replied the detective. "Any desire for haste would stem from an anxious wish to forestall what Berlin appears to have planned for our metropolis."

"I understand," replied the elder Holmes, who pursed his lips as we heard the rear house door open and close quickly. "Time, I agree, is not to be wasted."

Seconds later, Sir Walter Bullivant strode into the sitting room and sat down after tossing hat and coat onto an empty chair.

"And so I understand we may be facing an event in the manner of Peshtigo," Bullivant said urgently to Mycroft, who looked up and nodded quickly with a pained expression.

"Might Watson and I know what that name signifies?" asked Sherlock Holmes with sudden curiosity.

"Of course," Mycroft replied cautiously as he put the war communique aside. "Peshtigo is a town in the United States—"

"In their province of Wisconsin," added Bullivant. "The village itself is near the shores of Lake Michigan, and a fire occurred there years ago. A rather terrible fire."

"Rather more than just a fire," corrected Mycroft Holmes. "It was a great storm of flame, nightmarish in power and terrifying in its consequences."

"Blenkiron related the events to us some time ago," revealed Bullivant, to Mycroft Holmes's obvious displeasure.

"Using fire to clear vast areas of forest land is not uncommon in America," the spymaster said. "One day over forty years ago, just such activity was in progress near the aforementioned town of Peshtigo. Strong winds arrived and fanned the fire, setting it out of control and magnifying its intensity many times over. A wall of flame arose, perhaps a mile high and five across, with temperatures that exceeded fifteen hundred degrees, we understand. It swept across the land at many tens of miles per hour, hot enough to turn sand into glass."[261]

"Over a million acres were burned," Mycroft said quickly. "At least a thousand people died, perhaps more than two thousand."

"You may compare it to the Great Fire of London," Bullivant said. "That event very likely possessed many of the same characteristics of the American conflagration."[262]

"And now it appears that the Germans may be attempting to create another such inferno in the metropolis," Mycroft declared. "One surpassing that of long ago, rivalling in intensity that which occurred in America."

---

[261] The Peshtigo Fire occurred on October 8, 1871—by coincidence, the same day as the more famous Great Chicago Fire. Twelve communities were destroyed, and the area of forest that burned was twice the size of Rhode Island.

[262]The Great Fire of London burned for three days in September 1666, destroying the old medieval core of the city.

"I had no knowledge of the Peshtigo event," said Sherlock Holmes, "but I admit that the fire here of two-hundred-fifty years ago crossed my mind once Watson had uttered the words that allowed me to intuit what our enemies wish to accomplish."

Bullivant nodded, while Mycroft Holmes stared at the ceiling.

"Let us suppose that Von Bork arranges for a very few selected blocks of London to be targeted by German incendiary bombs," Sherlock Holmes suggested.

"But how could the bombers know exactly where to aim? How could those blocks be precisely marked?" Bullivant asked knowingly.

"They would be lit," replied my friend. "Lit by search lights on the tops of buildings, bright lights with filaments made of—"

"Wolfram," interjected Mycroft. "Tungsten."

"Yes," said Holmes. "The German bombers would then know upon which blocks to train their bombs in order to ignite intense fires in those buildings.

"And at the same time, Von Bork would summon forth the London Transport League, not to make emergency transfers of supplies, but rather to unwittingly block the streets, making it impossible for fire-fighting equipment to reach the fires in time to quell them."

"Those haulers arriving would be driving lorries pulled by horses," said Mycroft, "animals that could be—"

"Put down by Von Bork's henchman, who would be waiting with pistols, prepared to run off in the confusion after destroying the horses," completed his brother.

"The streets would be clogged for some time, then," declared Bullivant.

"Preventing the separate fires from being extinguished—allowing them to join to produce a storm of flame such as occurred in that American town," Mycroft concluded. "Or here hundreds of years ago," he added, nodding thoughtfully. "I believe we all can see the pieces fitting together in that manner." He looked at his brother. "Do you believe the mustard gas was intended to be used in conjunction with this?"

"It would not surprise," replied Sherlock Holmes. The detective smiled sardonically. "It is the type of flourish that Herr Von Bork might fancy. Fortunately, he will not be able to add that embellishment, but the plan of creating a great wall of flame—if that is the plan—provides sufficient horror in itself."

"That is all very well," said Mycroft Holmes quietly. "However, achieving the objective in question is not a simple matter. Absent the wind that precipitated the Peshtigo event, one must stoke the fire to sufficient size so that it generates its own upward draft, feeding and expanding itself."

"Is that what John Blenkiron has told you?" asked my friend.

Mycroft Holmes studied his brother for a moment and then continued, oblivious to the questions.

"That, in turn, requires a mass of incendiary bombs beyond the capacity of an aeroplane fleet to carry," he said,"though the Americans tell us the Germans are attempting to develop a fire bomb of very small weight; a feat they have not yet achieved. You see, Sherlock, creating such a storm of fire by bombing alone is not yet possible."[263]

---

263 Germany did perfect such compact incendiary bombs in 1918, and plans were developed to use them in attacking London, Paris, and even New York City—by zeppelin, in the last case—but those designs were never carried out.

"But one could have the hearth prepared in advance, so to speak," answered his brother, "and then torch it from above after making certain no one can put out the flame quickly."

"Yes, but how can Von Bork prime London's hearth?"

"Mycroft raises a crucial a point," said Bullivant. "Are the Germans storing countless reams of foolscap in the buildings of central London? What would create an even greater fire in the first place?"

Holmes smiled. "What if the German bombers did not have to drop all the bombs necessary to create such a conflagration?" he asked. "What if some incendiary bombs were already planted on the ground, ready to be ignited—"

"By a few more bombs dropped from above," said Mycroft, completing the thought. "Gad, that would be a brilliant stroke! Horrifying, of course, but brilliant nonetheless. Simple but direct. How do you suppose they brought the incendiary bombs over here? Smuggled to the coast by means of U-boats, such as you suppose the mustard gas to have been?" he asked. "The effort would have to have been a grand one."

"I believe they have been slowly assembled over the years, perhaps even in the period prior to the war," said Sherlock Holmes. "German incendiary bombs are containers of kerosene and oil, are they not?"

"That is the current design, yes," replied Mycroft Holmes. "The containers are then wrapped in tarred rope."

"We recovered tar-stained knives at the warehouse near the gasworks, along with evidence of kerosene," said his brother. "The man killed in Eversholt Road had a knife that was tarred."

"The Gussiter firm had held a lease on that building for many years prior to the war," interjected Bullivant. "Are you suggesting the Germans were constructing incendiary bombs even then?"

"That is a possibility my brother just raised," Mycroft reminded Sir Walter. "And it is a notion I am quite prepared to accept as plausible." He glanced at his sibling. "If those bombs are being secretly stored in buildings throughout the City, they must be in locations leased by the Germans."

"Shall we begin searching for such properties?" asked Bullivant. "My man Macandrew can be put to that task."

"We may not have the time to complete such a hunt," replied Mycroft. "Recall that we were able to trace the Gussiter firm through many holding companies, but that process still took several weeks. For all we know, the buildings we wish to locate have been leased by the Germans under the names of entirely different enterprises."

"Can we not then simply conduct a massive search of the City?" suggested Bullivant.

"We would alert Von Bork with that action and never have an opportunity to seize him," said Sherlock Holmes.

"Failing to take your German spy bothers me less than the chance of creating hysteria among our general population," asserted his brother. "We must operate with the precision of a surgeon."

The elder Holmes paused to look across the room. "It is an immense project that the Germans have undertaken, one long in the planning," he said. "One can appreciate the vastness of it all."

"And is that in part because you had already contemplated unleashing a similar flaming terror upon the Germans?" asked his brother.

"What?" replied Mycroft, as Bullivant looked on with anxiety. "Why would—"

"Why would John Blenkiron have spoken to you of that episode in America some time ago?" Sherlock Holmes said accusingly. "Why would you and Sir Walter appear so knowledgeable of this insane possibility?"

"Sanity, of course, is by definition not an objective term, Sherlock."

"Then ignore my characterisation," replied the younger Holmes. "Has our government discussed with the Americans the possibility of launching such incendiary attacks against Germany?"

Mycroft and Sir Walter looked at one another cautiously, and then the former replied, "It would not surprise if the topic had failed to arise in the past, I suppose."

"I doubt it would not surprise you, brother, for you were undoubtedly part of the discussion, were you not?"

Mycroft Holmes remained silent.

"And what has prevented implementation of such a satanic plan?" the detective asked.

"Our air forces at present cannot drop a sufficient number of incendiaries, just as the Germans are limited in their ability," admitted the elder Holmes. "In any case, your adjectives are steadily escalating to the benefit of no one, dear brother. This aspect of the discussion is at an end."

"Very well then—have you any knowledge of the next German raid from above?" Sherlock Holmes pointedly asked the two men.

Mycroft turned toward Sir Walter.

"Blenkiron's American agents have not yet able to confirm a precise date for the next raid," Bullivant said. "However, our man in Belgium believes that one is coming during the time of the next full moon—and that is mere days away."

"Let us break out the maps," suggested Mycroft. "We are back to the matter of trying to locate buildings in which incendiaries may be stored."

"What maps do you wish, M?" asked Sir Walter. "Those of the City and immediate surroundings?"

"Yes," said the elder Holmes. "That is the section of town that the Transport League is apparently to cordon off by blocking street intersections. No doubt, it is the heart of London that the Germans aim to incinerate first."

"Hoping the flames then engulf the rest of the metropolis," added his brother.

"I will fetch the charts," said Bullivant, rising.

"And to consider for a moment another matter, is there word of Hannay?" Holmes asked Mycroft as Sir Walter left for the map storage room in Safety House.

"And of Miss Lamington?" I added.

"There is a good deal concerning both, actually," replied the elder Holmes. "I have not had an opportunity to yet relate to you their activities, which have been rather dramatic in their way. First, however, I suppose I should give you the good news, as relayed to me from Blenkiron, that the pair of them—General Hannay and Miss Lamington—are now engaged to be wed."

I gave a pleasant start and silently revelled in Mycroft's joyous revelation.

"It was a troth not won without hardship," the elder Holmes said. "Hannay had traced the plump man we know as Moxon Ivery to a chalet

let under his alias of Bommaerts. Miss Lamington had, independently, linked him to the same location, for at the time neither she nor Hannay was yet aware of the other's proximity or purpose. By chance, they each invaded the chalet on the same night and encountered one another."

Mycroft Holmes paused, and his brother gave him an expectant look.

"Ivery or Bommaerts—or whoever he really is—arrived at the chalet the very same evening. Hannay confronted him, but Ivery was able to flee before he could be captured."[264]

"And is Ivery's present location known?" asked Sherlock Holmes as Sir Walter returned with a handful of maps. The detective made no mention of his belief that the German's true name was Von Schwabing.

"Not with any certainty," replied his brother, leaning back in the sofa as Sir Walter tossed the charts onto the large sitting room table. "However, I fancy that he has gone to Switzerland, seeking refuge."

"The nation that is also home to the Gussiter Company," said Bullivant as he dumped a collection of maps onto the dining table.

"Yes," said Mycroft, who rose slowly from the sofa. "It is there that Hannay will continue the pursuit. Well, I believe we now have maps in abundance. Here, let us spread them out."

The charts were rolled out across the wide surface of the table, with drinking glasses used to keep them flat. Mycroft Holmes bent down, as much as his portly frame would allow, and stared at the central portion of one.

"Here is the arc as defined by those destinations assigned to members of your London Transport League," he said to his brother.

---

[264] These events are related in more detail in *Mr. Standfast.*

“It is the City that will be their target,” I said under my breath, immediately feeling embarrassed at having restated the obvious.

“Actually, Watson, it is several buildings that will serve as targets,” said Holmes. “We must speedily determine which ones those are.”

“I can contact Magillivray,” said Bullivant. “The police can scour the area, search every building for suspicious contents, as I suggested earlier.”

“And by so doing, create such a fuss that the Germans will know we are onto them,” repeated Holmes, still staring at the map. “And instilling panic in the heart of London in the bargain.”

“And I believe you have ruled out contacting land agents to obtain the identities of those leasing spaces in the area, Mycroft,” said the spymaster.

“That process could take far too long,” replied the elder Holmes.

“What does that leave us?”

Mycroft Holmes looked at his brother.

“Perhaps we should use the tools that our new century provides,” said Sherlock Holmes. “Aerial reconnaissance will be our method.”

“Ah,” said Bullivant. “Of course.”

“I believe that the buildings containing incendiary bombs will be marked by bright search lights on the night of the Germans' raid,” declared Holmes. “Those must be placed upon the tops of the buildings in question. That in itself narrows our choices somewhat.

“We cannot be certain the presumed lights have yet been deployed atop the target buildings,” declared the detective, “but it is not inconceivable that they are already in place, though hidden, perhaps in crates. We will have aeroplanes fly over the City to take photographs, and then we will examine those images for signs of such containers, or the search lights themselves. There is no guarantee of success, but I think it our best initial course: it does not tip our hand to the Germans, and it does not alarm the general populace. And it is quick."

"Then it will be the course we follow," asserted Bullivant. "I take it you approve, Mycroft."

"Of course," said the elder Holmes brother, stepping away from the table. He strode to the telephone. "I have no idea how soon we can arrange something with the RFC boys. For all I know, all our aerial cameras may be in France."

"Did Mycroft inform you that Abel Gresson has been taken into custody?" asked Bullivant of the detective.

"No," said Sherlock Holmes as his brother spoke into the telephone. "Enough material evidence was found to justify arresting him?"

"Yes, thanks to Blenkiron and the Americans. We've also identified some of the hiding places used by the Portuguese man that Gresson contacted in the Hebrides. He is still roaming at large, but we expect to have him in our nets shortly."

"That leaves only Moxon Ivery," I said, taking care not to divulge Holmes's hypothesis concerning Ivery and the Graf Von Schwabing.

"As well as Heinrich Von Bork," said the detective, adding nothing as he smiled at me.

"All is in the process of being arranged," declared Mycroft Holmes after ringing off. "It is too late to have a man fly over the City today to take photographs today, but we are guaranteed that it will happen tomorrow. At least one camera is indeed available in our area, and an aeroplane will take it aloft from Burton's Farm in Hornchurch.[265] Would you care to supervise?" he asked Bullivant.

"Of course," replied the spymaster. "What time will the plane go up?"

"About nine o'clock," said Mycroft. "We will want the sun low enough to create sufficient shadows for definition, of course."

"Do you care to join me at the aerodrome tomorrow?" Sir Walter asked Sherlock Holmes and me.

Without hesitation, we both agreed.

Early the next morning, Holmes and I accompanied Bullivant in a government vehicle to Burton's Farm. Our chauffeur was a young woman who had driven me to my RAMC office several times previously.

"You know the route?" Sir Walter enquired of her.

"I believe so, sir. We continue out along the Barking Road for a way, and then proceed on past Dagenham, heading east and just a tad north." She smiled. "You can watch and correct me as we go along, if you like."

"Of course," said Sir Walter awkwardly. "Carry on."

On the horizon, we could see the beginnings of London's defensive balloon apron floating against the dawn sky. A distant row of inflated bags hovered in the crisp air, a large cable hanging down to the ground from each of them. Successive horizontal lines, sagging from gravity, linked each vertical cable, and in the space between the balloons, more lines hung

[265] This is probably a fictionalized reference to Sutton's Farm, an aerodrome in Hornchurch, a town in the eastern reaches of greater London. The field was closed after the war, but the land was repurchased by the government a few years later to become the site of what was eventually called RAF Hornchurch, an air base that finally closed for good in 1962.

from those gently curving sideways lengths—all forming a slotted wall at least one thousand yards high.

"In the initial phase of construction, it will stretch from Tottenham to Lewisham," said Sir Walter. "Aeroplanes approaching from the west will be forced to climb over it, and our anti-aircraft guns will be trained to that height. I hope it proves an effective obstacle to the raiders."

We passed beyond the tenuous cordon of the balloon apron and on to the east. As we neared Hornchurch, I noticed many military transport vehicles.

"Is there a depot in this district?" I asked.

"I am not certain," said Sir Walter. "At the start of the war, there was a depot established just north of here at Grey Towers—a mansion that the Army Council purchased when it went up for sale. Some of our troops were based there for a time, before the ANZACs took it over last year." Bullivant turned toward me. "It's since become a convalescent hospital for New Zealand troops, I think."[266]

I nodded silently, as memories of Isham percolated upward in my thoughts.

At length, we arrived at Burton's Farm, an expanse of perhaps somewhat under a hundred acres that served as a field for many of the aeroplanes that stood ready to defend London from attack. We entered the grounds and immediately saw to our right a pair of large hangars, with other buildings on the opposite side of the lane. Our motorcar pulled up

---

[266] Built in 1876, Grey Towers actually served as the command depot for the New Zealand Army during the first half of 1916 and then became a hospital for New Zealand troops, as Sir Walter correctly notes. However, Bullivant appears to confuse the New Zealand command with that of ANZAC, the Australian and New Zealand Army Corps, which fought in the disastrous Battle of Gallipoli. Grey Towers was demolished in 1931; its driveway is now a suburban road known as Grey Towers Avenue.

before what we took to be the headquarters building and debarked, leaving our chauffeur to tend the vehicle. Entering, we discovered ourselves to be in the officers' mess instead and were quickly directed to the station commander's office.

"Ah, I have been expecting you, Sir Walter," that officer said. "A courier arrived last evening with orders that made my responsibilities more than clear. I have the pleasure to inform you that all is in readiness."

"The photographic survey may proceed this morning, then?" the spymaster enquired.

"Yes," replied the officer. "We had no camera here at the field, but one arrived just after midnight. It is a C-camera—not the newest type, but it will suit your purpose to a tee. Our men worked through the night to secure it to the fuselage of one of our two-seaters, and as I just told you, we are prepared to fulfil the desired mission."

"You have men assigned to fly the aeroplane?" asked Bullivant.

"Oh yes, both pilot and observer. The pair readily volunteered when I announced the mission." The man chuckled as he added, "Indeed, the man who will pilot the craft absolutely insisted on taking part after I remarked that you would be on hand, Sir Walter. He said he did not know you, but did know *of* you. Mentioned that a friend of his named Hannay had dropped your name on more than one occasion."

"Well, speak of coincidence," said Sherlock Holmes. "Is this officer about?"

"Let us go to the field proper," said the officer, reaching for his cap. "He should already be there with his crew mate, preparing to go up."

We left the commander's office and reached the main door to exit the building. As we stepped out into morning light, I saw an officer leaning upon our motorcar, engaging the female chauffeur in very friendly conversation.

"Ah, Roylance!" called out the commander. "The government representatives are here; we were just speaking of you."

The young man turned and saluted his superior before nodding at Bullivant, Holmes, and myself in turn. He was a tall fellow with lean, high-coloured cheeks, a bluff if engaging smile, and a manner that seemed devoid of any self-consciousness.

Our chauffeur, on the other hand, appeared somewhat abashed, and she looked away, her face already blushing.

"Taking the trouble to acquaint yourself with our visitors, Captain?" the commander said coyly, indicating the young woman as we approached.

"I am acquainted with the lady already, sir, having danced with her numerous times," replied Roylance. "She's one of Lord Otterbank's nieces, you know."

"This is Sir Walter Bullivant," said the commander, ignoring the young man's comment. "Sir Walter and gentlemen," he said, "may I present Captain Archibald Roylance, the pilot for your mission."

"'Archie' does fine for you civilians," said the young officer. "Like the rat-tat-tat Archie, you know."[267]

"And I understand you are acquainted with General Hannay," replied Bullivant.

"I am, sir. I was one of his subalterns in the old Lennox Highlanders back at the beginning of the war, but I left the company just before the Somme to join the flying corps. Met up with him again recently," Roylance

[267] See footnote 212.

said, smiling at Bullivant. "In the course of one of his missions for you, sir."

"We heard all about it," Sir Walter said, placing a hand on the young man's shoulder. "Good work, I must say."

"And this is Sherlock Holmes and Colonel John Watson," the commanding officer said.

"The retired detective?" said Roylance, shaking the detective's hand. "And Doctor Watson? But you said he was a colonel, sir. Retired?" he asked as he took my hand in turn.

"I am out of uniform today, by choice," I replied. "But I remain with the medical corps."

"Ah well, what's good for the goose is the better part of valour, I suppose," said the young man as we left the motorcar and headquarters building behind. I glanced at Holmes, but my friend merely shrugged at Roylance's curious remark as we walked past the hangars and toward open field, where several aircraft were visible in the distance.

"Good fellows, the medical corps," the young pilot said. "To a man. Do you know General Hannay as well?" he asked cautiously.

"Somewhat," replied Holmes.

"Actually, they are acquainted very well," revealed Bullivant. "You may speak freely in front of these gentlemen, Captain Roylance."

"Ah, good," said the officer, now smiling broadly. "You see, I was the one who flew Dick down to London while he was on his latest mission—out of the frying pan and into the breach, more or less. The police were after him. The army was after him. The Hun spies were after him. That was an adventure and a half, I tell you." He laughed. "Who knows, perhaps when all this business is over, it will be part of another book about Dick, eh?"

"One can never tell," said Sherlock Holmes. "Especially when there are eager biographers lurking about, hungry to tell the tale," he added, smiling at me as we crossed the open field.

"Do you know where General Hannay is at present?" Roylance asked Bullivant. "Last I heard, he was back with his brigade in France, but there was some gossip that he'd been relieved."

"He is, uh, on a special assignment as we speak," confided Sir Walter.

"Ah, I understand," said the young man. "Hush-hush and all that."

We now approached two aeroplanes with RFC markings standing apart from the others on the field.

"Ours is on the left," said Roylance. "It's one of the newer reconnaissance craft."

"That is what Command gave us, I am afraid," remarked his superior. "I know you men do not care for the aeroplane."[268]

"It's all right, sir," replied the younger officer. "I've flown them before, and I can certainly handle this one for a peaceful jaunt over London. Not likely to run into an HB on this mission, am I?" he jovially asked Sir Walter.

"I rather think not," answered Bullivant.

"Hostile battery," I whispered to Holmes, for his benefit.

Just then another man emerged from one of the hangars. Clad in flying gear and holding a pair of fur gloves, he appeared to be about

---

268 The craft referred to was probably an R.E.8, a two-seater that served as the principal British reconnaissance aircraft from 1917 to the end of the war. It was generally regarded by pilots as somewhat difficult and unsafe to fly.

Roylance's age, and as he drew nearer, he saluted his commanding officer before giving the rest of us a nod.

"Captain Geoffrey Jenkins," said the commander, who then introduced Holmes and myself to the man.

"I won the coin toss," said Roylance as he stepped away, in the direction of the hangar. "I'll be pilot, and Jenkins here gets to play at being observer."

Jenkins playfully slapped Roylance's shoulder with his gloves as the latter passed. "I think everyone is on to Archie's two-headed coin by now," he said to us in a loud voice. "Halloa, gentlemen," the man added, shaking hands with us. "I never thought I'd be spying on my own folk, but we've got a clear day for it, don't we?"

"You have the maps?" the commander asked.

"Yes, sir," said Jenkins, pulling folded charts from his flight suit. Once Archie is properly clothed, I suppose we can look at them to make sure we'll get the photographs you desire."

We engaged in a brief discussion of aeroplanes and the weather while Captain Roylance was in the hangar. He emerged minutes later wearing flying clothes and holding gloves and leather helmet in one hand.

"Where do you wish to discuss our target?" he asked.

"The ground is as good a place as any," suggested the commanding officer, and we all walked to the aeroplane the men would fly.

I observed the worn mahogany box housing the aerial camera, which was attached to the craft's fuselage. Roylance and Jenkins got upon their knees to spread a map of inner London across an expanse of the tarmac before looking up at us expectantly.

“The area of concern lies within this region,” said Sherlock Holmes, tracing an arc across the map with the toe of his new boot. “It is in essence the City, bounded by this curve on the north and the river on the south.”

“What we seek,” added Bullivant, “are photographs of the blocks within that confine, of sufficient quality that we may distinguish details on the tops of buildings.”

Jenkins nodded. “Those are several blocks you speak of, sir.”

“And even more buildings,” added Roylance. He looked at his fellow pilot. “We shall have to make more than a few runs, no doubt on through midday.”

“Winter will soon be upon us,” observed Sherlock Holmes. “I should think the sun will remain low enough to cast the necessary shadows, even at noon. The photographs you take will not be difficult to interpret, I fancy.”

“You’ve analysed aerial reconnaissance before, Mr. Holmes?” asked Roylance.

“Now and then,” the detective answered with a smile.

Roylance nodded and said, “Well, then, I suppose—”

The young officer suddenly broke off speaking and raised one hand as he cast his eyes around the area. Jenkins smiled knowingly as Roylance cocked his head, as if to catch a particular sound.

“Sorry,” said Roylance. “I thought I heard the bittern again.”

“Bittern?” I said.

“Archie is the base’s unofficial ornithologist,” explained Jenkins with a chuckle. “He thinks he’s been hearing that bird for the past week.”

“Well, it would be somewhat of a novelty,” remarked Sherlock Holmes. “Sighting a bittern in this area, that is.”

"Quite right," agreed Roylance, giving the detective an added look of respect. "Are you familiar with their call, Mr. Holmes?"

"The odd, low booming?" replied my friend. "I have heard it on occasion. I fear, however, that this past moment was not one of those."

"Ah," said Roylance with resignation. "You do not believe it was one?"

"Sadly, I do not," Holmes declared.

"Ah well," lamented the young officer. "I am perhaps too eager to believe one is lurking about."

"It has been a few years since that one specimen set down in Oxford Street, is it not?" said Holmes.

"Quite so!" exclaimed Roylance, his appreciation of the detective's avian knowledge heightened even more. "Were you aware that—"

Bullivant cleared his throat, and the RFC pilot abruptly changed subject. "Well then," he said, nodding at Captain Jenkins, "I suppose that we'd best be about our work, then."

Mechanics were called to pull the aircraft into position and make final preparations for flight. In particular, the aerial camera was examined carefully to make certain it was functioning correctly.

"And you believe you will finish the reconnaissance by early this afternoon?" asked Bullivant.

"I reckon we will, sir," replied Archie Roylance. "From then on, I suppose it's a matter of how quickly the plates can be developed for you."

The two RFC pilots took to their craft. Holmes and I, along with Bullivant and the commanding officer, stood at a distance as the engine was started and the aeroplane began to move away. I imagined the slipstream in my face, and I thought I caught a whiff of castor oil, though

I knew that was but fantasy. Narrowing my eyes as the aeroplane drove toward the morning sun and lifted skyward, I thought of him whose spirit was already and forever aloft.

"We will repeat the procedure tomorrow and each day thereafter, of course, should we find nothing in this batch of photographs," said Sherlock Holmes that evening as he set a small leather box upon the dining table at Safety House. Sandy Arbuthnot and Jack James entered the sitting room carrying two more such boxes each. At Holmes's silent direction, they placed them beside the first and stepped away from the table as Bullivant and I looked on.

"Continuing until we see what you are expecting to see?" asked the spymaster.

"Yes," replied the detective. "The Germans will place or uncover the searchlights upon the target buildings in advance of the actual attack but not so early as to risk premature detection," he explained as he opened the first box and pulled out a stack of photographs, each one with a numerical and letter code in the upper right corner.

"Do you wish assistance in laying out the prints?" I asked.

"No, but thank you, old fellow," replied my friend as he completed a large rectangular mosaic with the images. "We will examine them section by section, one group at a time. Now, where was that—?"

Holmes gave a small start as I held a magnifying glass before him. Smiling, he took it from me and bent over the table, slowly surveying each image, which showed the tops of buildings in the heart of London as photographed by Captains Roylance and Jenkins earlier that day. With minute care, he examined each frame thoroughly, eventually completing the initial set of twelve before moving on to the next group.

Bullivant, Arbuthnot, James, and I sat or stood expectantly, waiting to be of assistance or hear of success. Then, in the midst of surveying the fourth collection of photographs, Holmes gave a sudden start.

"Halloa!" he cried as he squinted, face close to the tabletop. "I believe we have something of interest."

James and Arbuthnot looked at one another.

"A search light?" asked Bullivant, drawing near.

"No," replied the detective, drawing himself up to his full height. "Not a search light, but a large crate that could hold such a lamp, I think. Here," he said, handing his lens to the spymaster while pointing to a portion of one photograph. "On the top of that building. Do you see it?"

"Yes," said Sir Walter after a moment. He handed the glass off to me, and after observing the grainy image of what appeared to be a large wooden box sitting atop one building, I passed the instrument in turn to Jack James and then Arbuthnot, who both quickly confirmed Holmes's observation.

"It is most curious," Sandy said.

Holmes had already marked on a street map of London the known rendezvous points assigned some members of the Transport League. He now noted on it the position of the building bearing the suspicious object and then returned to the rectangle of photographs and finished his survey, in the process discovering a second crate, identical to the first, on another building two blocks away from the initial find.

"The more of these we see, the greater will be our confidence," the detective murmured with satisfaction.

And so the evening was spent, until on toward midnight. Just before that hour arrived, Holmes finished examining the last set of photographs. He put down the magnifying glass and stood back, a subtle smile on his face.

"Well," he said with a contented voice, "we have gained success far sooner than I had expected. Seven crates in all. With that early triumph, however, comes realisation that the danger looms even closer than I had anticipated."

"The German attack is imminent, you mean?" I asked.

"I fear so, Watson. I think our enemy would not have set out the crated search lights, should that be what lies within those boxes, if they did not have plans to break them out and deploy them very soon." Holmes turned to Bullivant. "There has still been no response from Dieter Baumann to the last item placed in the *Times* by Inspector Magillivray?"

"None, I am afraid," said the spymaster.

"Still, you must contact Scotland Yard and have several teams of their men assembled."

"Of course," replied Sir Walter, who immediately stepped to the phone. "With Magillivray in command? Should I inform the Yard of our purpose?"

"No," replied Holmes. "Have you someone besides Magillivray who might take charge of these contingents?"

Bullivant shrugged. "I suppose either Inspectors Hartley or Carter would do. Both were with us at the Ruff when we apprehended Moncrief."

"Yes," said Holmes. "They will be excellent choices."

"And what of Magillivray?" asked Sir Walter.

"I have other plans for him," the detective replied. "But let us not worry about those details at present."

Holmes then gave instructions as to the number and size of each contingent that Inspectors Hartley and Carter were to organise. "Direct them to have their teams at the ready by tomorrow afternoon at Scotland Yard. We will inform them of the purpose and instruct them concerning procedure only just prior to employing them."

"So the big show is about to happen?" asked James.

"We may safely place a wager on that, I believe," replied Holmes.

"And when do you play your hand, sir?" enquired Arbuthnot.

"When Von Bork is about to lay down what he thinks is a winning combination," declared the detective. "Only to find that we have trumped him and his little cabal."

"And have you any notion what date that will be?" I asked.

"No. I believe only that it will be during the next German raid from the air, and that will require a full moon with good weather," murmured Holmes.

"The full moon is less than a week away," said Bullivant. "We, as well as the Germans, must wait upon the weather, however."

The next many hours were filled with feverish activity by several people, activities I either observed at second hand or learned of only by chance, for I was not among the host of busy participants. From the swift comings and goings of Frank Farrar and Shinwell Johnson, I gleaned that they had been in communication with Tatty Evans aboard the *Belisama*, and from Jack James, who more than once whisked Holmes off to consult with Inspectors Hartley and Carter, I discovered that hordes of Scotland

Yard constables were being readied to seize the presumed German search lights—and stores of hidden incendiaries—scattered about the City, though the police did not yet know that awould be the goal of their imminent raids. Martha let slip that Holmes had received a telephone message from Sandy Arbuthnot.

More than once I offered myself to Holmes as another member of this coterie of helpers, only to be gently rebuffed.

"I do not wish to interfere with your preparation for new duties at the hospital in Millbank," he declared. "That assignment is approaching, is it not?"

"But you have kept me here all these months to provide support, or so you have claimed," I argued one morning after breakfast in Queen Anne Street. "Now that you have need of as many trusted men as you can find, you turn me away."

"And need I remind you, old fellow, that you have complained mightily about being denied an opportunity to exercise your medical skills during this war?" countered Holmes. "Now that I free you of any obligation to me, you complain."

"Will you at least inform me of developments these past few hours?" I implored. "Have Roylance and Jenkins observed the crates being opened? Has another note been received from Dietrich Baumann? And what of—"

Holmes raised a hand as, with the other, he lifted a piece of toast to his mouth.

"You cannot deny you have kept me at arm's length during the past week," I insisted. "The matter of Von Bork and the third head of Cerberus is about to reach its grand climax, is it not? Am I not to be allowed in on the kill, Holmes?"

My friend gave a pained expression and put down the toast. He rose from the table and turned toward the mantel to approach its collection of mementos, accumulated over a life's work in the field of detection: a bust of Napoleon, an empty bottle of prussic acid, and a farthing painted green, among others.

"Holmes?" I said, rising also. "Have I somehow offended?"

"You have not," said he quietly after a moment, his back still facing me as he took the farthing in hand. "It was, rather, the last phrase you spoke: *in on the kill.* That was what Mrs. Hudson said when she offered to assist me in...that final matter all those years ago."

I said nothing, merely watched as my friend grasped the edge of the mantel to look into the glowing fire. Listlessly, he put down the farthing and reached for the poker to stir the coals before turning round.

"I do have some matters to attend to with Mr. Macandrew, and there are messages to leave at Office 54," he said, briskly walking past and toward the sitting room door. "You may inform Martha that I shall return in time for dinner."

"Of course."

Holmes did not re-enter the sitting room to bid me farewell after changing clothes. I heard the house door open and close, and then I gave my time to a small set of medical corps documents in order turn to my mind from the offense I had accidentally given. Toward midday, a telegram arrived.

"Is something wrong, sir?" asked Martha as she observed me reading the message.

"I do not know how to answer this," I replied. "It is a summons of sorts from the RAMC. Apparently, plans to assign me to Queen Alexandra's

Hospital have not been changed, but for some unstated reason, I am to report to Crookham Camp at Aldershot immediately—today, in fact. There is no reason given, but these orders are without doubt from my superiors, and their urgency is underscored by the wording of the message."

"Should I assist you in preparing, Colonel?" asked our housekeeper. "Or make arrangements for a compartment on a train?"

I thought for a moment.

"Why, yes, I suppose," I stammered.

"Which is it, sir? Or is it both?"

"You may see what trains are available. There is a Bradshaw somewhere over there, upon those shelves," I told her, pointing past the heaps of books, papers, and charts that remained strewn across the sitting room carpet. "I shall take responsibility for packing my bags."

Within two hours, I was ready for the trip to Aldershot, and passage had been arranged on a train leaving Marylebone Station later that afternoon. My only concern was that I might not have the opportunity to bid Holmes a proper farewell, especially after my unintentional faux pas of the morning. Not wishing to leave, even for a day, without communicating fully and honestly to my friend, I sat down at my writing desk to compose a brief letter, to be left upon the mantel.

I sat there, in the chair on which I had chronicled so many of Holmes's past exploits, and toyed with the letter opener given me months earlier by Moxon Ivery—or the Graf Von Schwabing. Uncertain of what to write, I allowed my mind to reminisce, reliving the initial days of lodging with the world's first consulting detective, my fortuitous courtship of Mary Morstan, Holmes's introduction of his brother Mycroft, the earnest pluck of the Baker Street Irregulars, and more. Inevitably, my reverie was drawn at last to the terrible pain of more than twenty years before, when I thought my friend to be dead at the hands of Professor Moriarty.

As I recalled our desperate trip across the Continent to elude Holmes's archenemy, I imagined in my mind's eye the arrival at Reichenbach Falls, where I had received the forged summons that had separated me from my friend, causing him to face Moriarty alone.[269]

The epiphany shot through me in an instant, and I put down the letter opener, suddenly enlightened.

"Martha!" I called loudly, not bothering to ring for her.

A moment later, our housekeeper poked her head past the open sitting room door.

"Colonel?"

"I will not be leaving for Aldershot after all," I told her. "However, when Mr. Holmes rings up this house, as I am certain he will, tell him otherwise."

"You wish me to lie to him, sir?"

"Yes," I said, looking her squarely in the eye. "If you value his safety at all, you shall lie for me."

"As you wish, sir," she said, with a puzzled yet trusting expression.

Only moments later, the telephone did ring, and Martha poked her head into the sitting room.

"Was it Mr. Holmes?" I asked.

"Yes," replied the housekeeper, "but it is Mr. Mycroft Holmes. He wishes to speak with you."

---

[269] When, in 1891, Holmes and Watson fled to Europe to escape Professor Moriarty, their journey led them to Reichenbach Falls, where Moriarty separated Watson from the detective by means of a false note requesting the doctor's assistance with a dying Englishwoman back at their hotel. This left Holmes alone with his foes.

"I am glad to catch you at home, Colonel," said my friend's sibling after I had spoken into the telephone. "Your housekeeper indicated my brother is not in."

"That is correct," I replied.

"Colonel, I do not know if you are aware of my concerns about him. There are—"

"Mr. Holmes—M," I blurted. "M, is there any way in which you are able to confirm orders I may have recently received from the medical corps?"

"From the RAMC?"

"Yes."

There was a pause.

"Well, that is possible, of course," came the eventual answer. "I could have a clerk look into it."

"I mean at this moment."

Again there was a pause, a longer one.

"Well, *in extremis*, I could personally verify such an order within, say, a quarter hour."

I voiced my appreciation and then related to Mycroft Holmes the details of the telegram ordering me to Aldershot that very day. We rang off, and several minutes later, the telephone sounded again. I answered promptly.

"The RAMC have no knowledge of such an order, Colonel. As far as they are aware, you are assigned to Queen Alexandra's Hospital and are to report there on Monday next, with no further obligation until then."

"I see. The telegram, then, is false."

Once more, there was silence for many seconds, and then I heard Mycroft Holmes saying, "I suppose we both know the source of the spurious command."

"You mean Holmes. Your brother, that is."

"Yes," replied Mycroft. "I suppose that was his method of getting you out of the line of fire during this evening's festivities."

"Festivities? This evening?"

"Yes," he said. "Do you not know? Our man across the waters in Belgium has confirmed that the geese will be taking flight tonight. And our RFC friends have photographic proof that the presents in the City have been unwrapped. The other shoe will drop tonight," he declared, continuing to speak in homely metaphor.

"And all is in readiness?" I asked.

"Yes," Mycroft Holmes replied. "The Yard's men are stationed and ready to act, having at last been informed of the purpose. And I believe that Sherlock has had Master Evans anchor his vessel at an appropriate point in the river near where the *Nemesis* is docked, with Inspector Magillivray and Sergeant Scaife tending three police launches on shore near that location, along with Farrar, Johnson, Arbuthnot, and James, all of whom are to join them later."

"And where is your brother in all this?" I asked. "What are his intentions for this night?"

"In truth, Colonel, I was about to ask you those same two questions, for that is why I rang you up in the first place. I know nothing of his plans for himself, nothing other than what he has instructed others to do. We spoke earlier today, at which time I conveyed him our news that the German bombers would arrive tonight, and that the search lights have been uncovered. I saw him make some arrangements with Magillivray by means of my telephone, and then he left, after saying he would inform you. I assumed he was headed for Queen Anne Street, but obviously I was incorrect."

"Has any further communication been received from Dieter Baumann?" I asked.

Again there was a brief silence. Then Mycroft Holmes responded.

"I cannot say," he said. "Magillivray has been the person receiving them, and he had been instructed to pass them on directly to my brother. Certainly, he has not notified either myself or Sir Walter Bullivant of a new message, though neither of us thought to ask, expecting Magillivray to inform us of his own accord.

"You know, Colonel," Mycroft said abruptly, "I believe my brother has managed to remove several matters beyond my immediate knowledge and control."

Again there was silence for many seconds. Then Mycroft Holmes spoke in an earnest, heartfelt tone I had never heard from him.

"I do implore you watch after him—if such a thing is even possible," he said, "though I wish you to not tell him of this plea."

"Of course."

"It is not an easy thing to read his intentions, but I do believe he may be up to something—something perhaps reckless and rash."

"I shall stand guard," I pledge. "Though that depends on me seeing him before the day and night are over."

Our conversation continued for perhaps another minute, and then we rang off. A half hour later, I heard the telephone sound again.

It was Sherlock Holmes this time, and Martha followed my previous instructions to the letter, misinforming my friend that I had already left for Aldershot. Barely a quarter hour after that, the house door opened, and from the sitting room, I heard Holmes ask our housekeeper about the details of my departure.

"It is a relief to have him safe," Holmes's voice declared as he and the woman approached along the corridor. "Now, Martha, it is also important that you remove yourself as well from harm's way. Though he is not yet aware of such plans, I shall be sending you to Mycroft for the night, for I am expecting—"

As he strode through the sitting room doorway, the detective paused in the middle of his statement to calmly study me, sitting in my military uniform, framed by two pieces of luggage.

Holmes approached the breakfast table, his movements stiff yet measured.

"Good afternoon, Watson, though I must admit surprise at finding you here," he said calmly. "Martha had given me to believe—"

"What I wished you to believe."

My friend silently acknowledged the truth of what I had uttered and strode to the mantel, where he found his cherrywood pipe. He turned as our housekeeper stood at the doorway.

"You may go," he told Martha genially. "Please close the door, if you will. And do pack some things for your stay with my brother."

With a contrite expression, our housekeeper stepped out and pulled shut the door.

“It was a most inconsiderate of you to scheme to have me leave London on false pretences,” I said at once. “And even more loathsome to borrow the tactic of Professor Moriarty.”

“I felt I had no other choice, old fellow,” Holmes wistfully declared.

As he began filling his pipe with shag, my friend looked back at me from the mantel with a contemplative eye. “You know, Watson, had I not expected Moriarty to arrange for that note back at the Reichenbach Falls, I was prepared to perform the same ruse myself.”

“What?”

Holmes continued to stuff the bowl of his pipe.

“I had seen Moriarty’s henchman, Colonel Moran, skulking about the village that very morning—he was always a clumsy fellow: all bluster, though of a most dangerous variety.

“Given Moriarty’s desperation and his nature, I had no doubt the professor intended to confront me alone in some isolated place, and so I chose the Reichenbach as prime objective of our hike that day. Having seen Moran, I surmised his superior was near, and the falls seemed an appropriate place for the final meeting with my nemesis.

“I had no intention that you share my possible fate, Watson, and so I thought to take a piece of hotel stationery on which to write a summons of some kind, which would be delivered to you shortly before we reached the falls. However, from across the lobby, I saw a young man pilfer a sheet himself from the desk. When, after stalking the fellow discreetly, I observed him meet Moran outside and give the paper to him, it occurred to me that Moriarty entertained the same plan, though inspired by a somewhat different motivation.”

"I see. And the lad was the same one who delivered that false note about the dying woman?"

"He was." Holmes smiled. "I confess I found myself rather amused at having Moriarty do my deceptive work for me."

"Well," I said, "it allowed you to practise an even greater deception upon me for three subsequent years, and so I hope you felt no great disappointment."

"It was a far more vicious lie, I grant," Holmes admitted. After a moment of silence, he asked quietly, "You have still not forgiven me that lapse, have you?"

I thought for a moment and then, watching him light his pipe, replied.

"Since I take it that these may be the last moments on Earth for both of us, I suppose I should, at last, grant you pardon. Yes, I forgive you. I hope you will do the same for my unconscious allusion to Mrs. Hudson."

Holmes looked up, a tortured look on his face, as he tossed the spent match onto the grate.

"I do, though God knows I deserve every lashing I receive for that fatal error."

"And so the attack will come tonight?" I asked, ignoring my friend's comment.

"Yes, without a doubt," he said wistfully. "All evidence, including the latest report from Bullivant's Belgian spy, points to a German air raid this evening." He reached into a jacket pocket and withdrew a paper, which he tossed onto the table. "This makes it a certainty, I believe. Dietrich Baumann wishes to meet with me tonight as well."

I sat up in my chair.

"A messenger boy delivered the note to Magillivray at Scotland Yard this morning. As per my agreement with the inspector, he turned it over to me at once. I suggest you read it."

I picked up the piece of paper and looked at its scrawled words:

> *Must meet with Holmes. I have the knowledge of where are the additional stores. At the hour of seven tonight opposite Spitalfields Market. I meet with Holmes only! God Save the King.*

"And this arrived today, you say?"

"Yes." Holmes held his pipe and studied it closely. "I received it from Magillivray when I saw him at Scotland Yard."

"But if the air raid is to be tonight, why would Baumann wish to meet with you during the same evening?"

Holmes gave me a long, cold stare.

"Von Bork wishes to take you prisoner," I said at last, after revelation had come. "And you intend to let it happen."

"Yes, I do," said my friend, striding to the armchair, into which he dropped. Holmes drew the footstool to him with one toe of his new boots and set his heels upon it.

"Von Bork aims to incinerate London, but that alone will not provide him the satisfaction he requires. He must get even with me, remember," Holmes added with a wan smile. He placed the stem of the pipe against his high forehead. "He means to be certain I witness his inferno at first hand—as one of its victims."

"And what do Bullivant and your brother think of this latest note?" I asked cautiously, not wishing to reveal the substance of my previous conversation with Mycroft Holmes.

"They know nothing of it," replied the detective. "Mycroft realised Baumann's pleas were a ruse, as you know. I am certain he also thinks their purpose is to lure me into a trap. And so, after the arrival of the second message, I reminded Magillivray in no uncertain terms to inform me—and only me—when the next one showed up. It did so early this morning, as I told you, but my brother and Sir Walter were not informed."

"And you will not tell them of it."

"No."

"And you were prepared to leave me in ignorance as well."

"Because I wish to leave you in safety," insisted Holmes. He looked at me thoughtfully. "What dissuaded you from departing, by the way?" he asked, glancing at my luggage.

"Intuition, I suppose."

Holmes nodded and gave an amused smile.

"It appears, Watson, that Miss Lamington's corresponding facility has rubbed off onto you. Well," he said, "I assume you will not agree to pick up those bags and go."

"A brilliant deduction, Holmes."

He sighed and then once more studied me.

"Baumann's note demanded that only I meet him."

"As with countless other clients in the past, Holmes, he must accept both of us or neither."

"And you understand the possible consequences if you accompany me?"

"I more than understand the accompanying effects upon my conscience if I do not."

"Very well."

My friend moved one booted foot, which still lay upon the footstool. Staring at the toe, he added, "Please change into civilian clothes, Watson, if you will, for I am expecting Jack James to arrive in a while with Sandy Arbuthnot in tow. If it is your wish, then we shall live out this night—or at least a portion of it—together."

CHAPTER TWENTY-FOUR: HADES UNVEILED

Holmes and I rode without speaking in the back of Jack James's taxicab as the vehicle made its way toward the area of Spitalfields Market, with Sandy Arbuthnot seated ahead of us, beside the American.[270]

"You are certain you do not want your package yet?" Arbuthnot asked, holding up a burlap bag whose contents Holmes had not revealed to me.

"Not at present," the detective replied. "Where we shall be going, its items would be confiscated in any event. Hold on to the bag instead, Sandy, and have it on hand when Dr. Watson and I meet you at the police launches."

"You expect us to eventually arrive at the river front?" I asked in a whisper, adding to my query the single word, "Alive?"

Holmes ignored my comment.

"Inspector Magillivray and Sergeant Scaife should be there, tending the two vessels with a set of constables," Holmes said. "Both Frank Farrar and Shinwell Johnson are to be in attendance as well. Simply wait for us. However, should Tatty Evans give the signal, do not allow too much time to elapse before all of you begin the pursuit without us, if necessary."

"You're certain you don't want the two of us to join the pair of you now?" asked Jack James as he negotiated the busy street. "I'd think that would make it a mite safer for you."

---

[270] What is now called Old Spitalfields Market is a covered market in east central London.

"In agreeing to accept the doctor as companion, I have already violated the conditions of the message. I shall not tempt fate any further."

"As if you aren't doing so already—with all respect, sir," replied James.

Holmes did not respond.

James made as if to speak again, but Arbuthnot quieted him with a discreet gesture, and for a while the two younger men did not attempt to engage us in further conversation until we approached Paternoster Row, where I plaintively whispered, "At least Martha is safe with your brother."

"As you may be, old fellow, if you will but give the word. I have always sought only to protect you," he added, repeating his earlier protestations.

"I understand and appreciate the sentiment," was my hushed reply. "But I would rather be allowed to stand beside you, Holmes, than be protected by you."

"Let us say no more of the matter, then," Holmes replied. "Our thoughts should be aimed at this night and the future of London, not the past in Baker Street."

"Even though what you do now will only endanger you, to no benefit?"

"You may debark at any time, Watson, as I have said."

I stared at the profile of my friend.

"If you wish to sacrifice your life, then I may as well cast mine onto the pyre as well."

Arbuthnot turned his head ever so slightly and looked at Jack James.

"I thought that fiery metaphors were what we are at all costs trying to forestall," answered Holmes.

"You are exasperating!"

"And you are most refreshing when angry."

My friend's comment and smile evoked from me a chuckle I could not contain, and when our laughter had subsided, I said with a wistful air, "Let us drop discussion of the matter, then, and simply live it instead."

"Agreed."

"Time be damned," I announced.

"And ourselves as well, if need be."

Meeting Holmes's eyes, I silently nodded.

Glancing ahead, the detective leaned forward and said with sudden sharpness, "We are close, Jack! Pull to the kerb!"

James brought the vehicle to a halt, and Holmes and I debarked the taxicab some few blocks from Spitalfields Market.

"Proceed to the riverbank, as I have previously instructed," the detective commanded. "Both of you."

"One last time, sir: are you sure about that?" Arbuthnot asked. "I know the Colonel is along with you now, but shouldn't you have a third?"

"And a fourth?" added James.

"We all have our place in this grand scheme," Holmes declared quietly. "Yours has been given you. Follow orders, Sandy. And you as well, Private James," my friend said with a gentle smile.

"Yes, sir," replied the American in a cautious voice. "And you still don't want the package?" James added, kicking with his shoe the burlap bag that now lay on the floorboards between him and Arbuthnot. "You are certain?"

"Yes," replied the detective. "Let the items within it prove their value later tonight."

"Very well," declared James. "Watch yourselves, gents."

Holmes closed the taxicab door, and the two of us started down the pavement toward Spitalfields Market as our companions watched us leave.

"And what was in that bag?" I asked as we reached the end of a block.

"Your old service revolver and my Webley," replied Holmes. "Both are loaded, of course, and there is spare ammunition in the sack as well. I hope you do not mind the liberty I took with requisitioning your weapon."

"Of course not. Are you certain Von Bork can take you prisoner here in these surroundings?" I asked as we weaved through a bustling evening crowd. "This is hardly a deserted moor; there are countless people about, and subjugating us cannot be accomplished without public notice."

"The Germans will no doubt have Baumann lure us to a secluded place, and there we will be taken captive, Watson. You are still certain you do not wish to leave this to me alone? I do not believe Arbuthnot and James have started up their motor yet, and even should they have already left, you may still catch a taxicab or bus to safety."

"You mean cut and run?" I replied. "Certainly not."

"Good old Watson!" Holmes said, patting my shoulder as he glanced about. "You are a rock indeed. As you are so determined to accompany me, I promise you we shall both escape this obvious trap."

"But why place yourself, let alone both of us, in such a place at all?" I asked. "If you have launches at the ready to pursue Von Bork when he flees, why not lie in wait with Magillivray, Scaife, and the others?"

"There is, perhaps, more information that can be coaxed from him in the meanwhile."

"What information could that be?" I insisted. "You have discerned the German plans for this night. You have deduced the probable true identity of Moxon Ivery. What else could possibly be gleaned, Holmes?"

We crossed a street, and my friend failed to answer. Again I saw him look about.

"Do you perhaps intend this as your own, personal wager of combat?" I asked.

"I beg pardon?"

"A trial by combat," I said. "Much the same as Letchford's son's ordeal during the May Day festivities back in Biggleswick. This, however, is not play. And from what accusation are you seeking acquittal?"

Holmes remained silent as we walked.

"It is Mrs. Hudson, is it not?"

"Watson, please do not—"

"Do you believe that by putting yourself at Von Bork's mercy and somehow escaping his wrath you will be absolved of any blame for her death?"

Holmes suddenly paused before a pawnbroker's shop. In his eye, I saw an odd glimmer and, on instinct, took hold of his arm.

"If you have thoughts of bolting away, do not try," I said firmly. "I intend to stick to you as glue, old man."

"Please let go."

"No. I believe we both understand what this is about, Holmes."

My friend stared into my eye for a moment, and then I felt him relax.

"Yes," he agreed. "Further discussion is, I suppose, unnecessary. However, I shall say this to you one last time: go and save yourself. For God's sake, Watson, please do so."

"No."

"A friend cannot allow a friend to die needlessly."

"That is why I shall not leave you now."

Again Holmes looked at me intently. At length, he said, "And you shall not die needlessly. I promise that you shall see the morning."

"Promise me that for yourself as well," I replied. "Win your acquittal and absolution, Holmes, and take me with you."

"Very well. Remove your hand from my arm then, old fellow."

"Promise me you will not run from me."

I saw my friend's expression change again, and he nodded. "I promise that, Watson."

I released my grip, and Holmes motioned for us to continue along the pavement. As we approached the next crossing, I began to sense another presence at my back.

"Holmes," I said, "I feel as if we are being—"

"We have been followed for the past three blocks, Watson. Let us cross the street and pause before that bakery. I have a wish to admire the treats in its window."

I followed his lead, and in a moment we were both standing before the baker's shop. In the corner of my eye, I detected a reflection that moved and then stopped.

Beside me, Holmes gently smiled.

"You are God Save the King?" asked the detective suddenly.

"Yes," came a nervous voice from behind. "Please do not turn about. You were to be alone."

"You profess familiarity with me and my methods," replied Holmes, who continued to stare through the bakery window. "Do you not recall I am never without my confidante, Dr. Watson?"

"Watson, yes," said the voice. "I recall him, I believe. There is no one else?"

"No one," Holmes replied.

"You may bring your friend," declared the man after a moment.

"Thank you."

"Go down the pavement and cross the next street. There you will encounter a watchmaker's shop. Both of you will please enter it."

"As you wish. Come along, Watson."

We did as the man requested, crossing the avenue and finding, about midway along the following block, a watchmaker's establishment.

Holmes opened the door, which caused a bell to ring, and I followed, leaving the door open behind me.

The shop was empty save for numerous timepieces arrayed on tables and shelves, as well as in glass cases sitting before a scratched wooden counter, behind which hung a row of maroon brocade curtains.

While we still faced the counter, I heard the door behind us shut, and then the sounds of a bolt being thrown and window shades pulled down. Turning slowly round, we saw for the first time our escort: a young man of perhaps thirty, dressed in respectable attire, blond and blue-eyed, with a brace of moles upon his cheek that, oddly, gave by contrast an enhanced beauty to the remainder of his boyish face.

"God Save the King?" said Holmes again.

Dietrich Baumann remained silent.

"God Save the King?" repeated the detective.

"Rather, *Heil di rim Siegerkranz*," came another voice from behind, guttural and low.

"Hail to thee in victor's crown—" It continued as we turned back toward the counter to see a familiar face emerge from the curtains.

"Ruler of the fatherland," Heinrich von Bork added with a sneer as he set a walking stick upon the wooden counter and removed his hat. "Hail to thee, emperor!"[271]

"I shall not take off my gloves," the German agent said quietly, "for I will be departing even sooner than you."

There was a tapping at a shaded window, and Baumann unbolted the door to let inside five young men of seemingly rough persuasion.

"No one else there was?" asked Von Bork.

"Not a soul," said one of the toughs in an accented voice. "You can take poison on that."

"*Gut*," said their chief as the door was bolted again.

Von Bork stepped from behind the counter and leaned against its edge.

"Ah," murmured the German as he crossed his arms and studied us with care. "Can I believe that since we last met there have elapsed all of three years?"

"Three years and four months," answered Sherlock Holmes. "Almost to the day."

"It seems as if it were but days ago," murmured Von Bork as the five new men took up stations behind and to the side of Holmes and myself.

---

[271] *Heil di rim Siegerkranz* ("Hail to Thee in Victor's Crown") was the national anthem of the German Empire at the time. It had been the royal anthem of Prussia since the eighteenth century, but because its melody derived from the British "God Save the King," the song never became popular throughout Germany as a whole. See also footnote 91.

"And it is not as if we have not communicated in our way, now and then, in the meanwhile."

"Or felt the presence of one another here in the metropolis," Holmes added.

"You did not cease to be an instrument of your government after 1914, did you?" the German spy said to my friend. "You continue to play the game of espionage in your quaint manner, do you not?"

Holmes did not respond.

"You crossed the Reich's path now and then with your code breaking, and it would have been better for our cause had you not, but you first seriously incommoded us when you interfered in that silly hamlet of Biggleswick," declared Von Bork. "The flight of Moxon Ivery was a setback, the apprehension of Abel Gresson an irritating inconvenience, and the recent capture of our Portuguese messenger a sad loss, but you gravely hampered my own plans with the discovery and seizure of that mustard gas in Limehouse. And now, as winter closes in, I find myself in a place where I am in danger of not achieving my principal aim—all because of you. You have made the situation an impossible one, Herr Holmes. What? You find this amusing?"

Holmes let his chuckle fade into a smile.

"Your declaration reminds me of a similar one I heard many years ago," he said. "Its author protested my interference with his plans in anguished tones at least the equal of yours, but he had a very great fall, as I expect you shall also, in time—and a rather short time at that. But allow me to apologise—for the interruption rather than the irritation."

"Actually, my discomfort ended some time ago, Mr. Holmes. It ceased the moment you walked through that doorway and into this shop. Tell me, did you find the Tokay to your liking?"

"I must confess that I have not tasted it," Holmes replied, glancing at me. "There were fears it might be poisoned, you see."

The German emitted a coarse laugh. "Your judgment disappoints me, Mr. Holmes. Of all people, you should have realised that such an act of desecration would be quite beneath me."

"So I thought, but I was counselled otherwise," the detective replied. "Oh well, I shall open it later, when I have full cause to celebrate."

"A pity that opportunity will never arise," Von Bork said. "I shall also regret never opening that bottle of Tokay, but some losses in any campaign one must expect. Am I not correct?"

I cleared my throat, and the act caused the German leader to at last pay mild attention to me.

"You are the secretary," he said to me. "Watson by name?"

Curtly, I nodded.

"You were the chauffeur when I was abducted three years ago," Von Bork said. "I suppose fitting it is that you share the fate of your master."

"Watson is my friend and associate," Holmes corrected in a firm voice.

"And biographer," the German added. "Several of your stories I read while in Berlin and found not a few somewhat enjoyable. Of course, the slanderous one published some weeks ago is another matter. You did not compose it?" he asked me in an offhand manner.

"No," I said, and no more.

Von Bork nodded.

“It did not read like your previous recollections. Did *you* compose it?” he enquired of Holmes, who shook his head.

“Even so,” Von Bork said, “you had a hand in it.”

“As did you,” answered Holmes. “I hope you are not spurning your own shared creation.”

“Bah!” exclaimed the Prussian, taking a step toward Holmes. “It is a second injustice—my brief incarceration being the first—for which you Englishmen shall pay mightily this night.”

The spy leader motioned to the five henchmen, and hands seized us even as Holmes bade me not to resist.

“Now you will never taste that fine Tokay, Herr Holmes. Well, at least you had your fill at my house in Essex. To the vehicle with them,” he barked to his followers. “I shall meet you at the place.”

Von Bork grasped his stick and hat, vanishing once more behind maroon brocade. Dietrich Baumann, meanwhile, guided me by the elbow along with one other henchmen while the others escorted Holmes. We all passed through the curtains into the back of the shop, where Von Bork was nowhere in evidence, and were led to a door opening onto an empty alley. A motorised lorry waited there.

“Years ago, you once bound our leader as a prisoner and abducted him in your vehicle,” Baumann said with a dismissive tone. “Now the tables are reversed, are they not? I was told to remind you, Mr. Holmes, that you once suggested the name of a new inn if Herr Von Bork tried to escape: The Hanging Deutsche Mann, I believe?”

“It was the Dangling Prussian, as I recall,” said Holmes in good humour as we reached the motor.

"Ah yes," declared our captor. "Well, I am to advise you to make no attempt to resist, Herr Holmes, lest our chief open a beer garden in Munich named, he suggested, The Perforated Englishman."

"I believe we both get your point," Holmes replied.

"Good. Bind them and toss them into the back," Baumann told the other men.

Our wrists were tied behind our backs and our ankles similarly joined—in both cases with sturdy cord—and we were rudely lifted into the rear portion of the lorry, where we sat upon the wooden planks that served as a floor. Leaning against similar timbers that formed the walls of the compartment, we bent our backs beneath the canvas top.

"There will be no gags yet," Baumann declared. "If either of you shouts, however, you will receive a very nasty blow to the head."

"We continue to understand," said Holmes quietly.

"Herr Von Bork has remarked that, as Altamount, always you were good at taking instruction," remarked the German. "I am to remind you of that as well. Apply the blindfolds," he said to his companions.

A pair of the company jumped into the rear of the lorry and covered our eyes with kerchiefs tied tightly about our heads.

"Let us go, then," I heard Baumann say to his companions.

Two men lifted themselves into the rear of the lorry to sit beside us and the pair already aboard. Then Baumann and the remaining henchman walked to the cab of the vehicle, and a moment later the engine came to life.

"Do not resist, I beg you," said Holmes quietly in my ear.

"As you desire," I replied calmly. "We will see this through together, then."

My friend's face held the hint of a smile. "As we always have, old fellow."

The lorry rambled off, heading west at first, though I quickly lost my sense of direction after several turns. The sounds of London traffic flowed about us: angry shouts, the horns of motors and braying of an occasional horse, as well as the rumble of wheels and rustle of feet. The steady shaking of our vehicle eventually lulled me into a trance that was finally broken as we abruptly stopped and the engine was cut.

I felt hands grasp my elbows while others undid the cord binding my ankles. Then I was assisted from the vehicle and through an opening into a building. Still blindfolded, I was guided up at least three sets of stairs before the kerchief was pulled from my face.

I found myself standing beside Holmes inside a small, barren, windowless storage room illuminated by a single electric light overhead. Von Bork stood at the doorway, framed by Dietrich Baumann and the five henchmen, two of whom were silently ordered away by their master.

"Do you find this place to your liking?" Von Bork asked. He reached out to run his finger along a portion of the dusty wall, where plaster had cracked to expose the lathe beneath.

"I believe I have known better," said Holmes.

"As it is destined to become your final resting place, it will have to please, I fear."

Holmes smiled.

Von Bork's two assistants returned carrying chairs and more lengths of sturdy cord. Without a struggle, knowing what was intended, Holmes and I allowed ourselves to be bound, each to a chair, our hands still tied securely behind us while our upper torsos were similarly affixed to the seat backs.

"Make certain there is no slack in the rope," Von Bork directed. "We do not wish for freedom of action by either man to be available."

When finished, they left us sitting side by side, facing the enemy leader. I stared at Von Bork intensely, trying to draw my attention away from the tight cords pressing into my wrists.

The German, meanwhile, completely ignored me, devoting himself instead to my companion.

"I vowed three years ago to get level with you," the German said, taking a few steps toward us. "And now get level I shall, that and then some—not only with you, but with your entire race of Englishmen."

Holmes remained silent.

Von Bork cocked his head, glanced at Baumann with an expression of puzzlement, and then stared once more at the detective.

"For all your crowing in victory three years ago, you are now rather quiet in defeat," the German remarked. "Did my man Baumann tell you of the plans for a beer garden?"

Holmes nodded.

"Perhaps I should instead name it The Mute Londoner, Mr. Holmes. You continue to contribute so very little to this evening's dialogue. Is it because it so pains you to face such a staggering defeat?"

"When I have something worth saying, I will speak it," replied my friend.

Von Bork shrugged.

"Moreover," Holmes said, "I think your description of me being silent in defeat to be at least half wrong, for I have, after all, rendered useless your attempt to terrorise our metropolis."

"Oh?"

"We have taken your mustard gas," Holmes asserted.

"And what of the additional store of it?" asked the German.

"We both know that does not exist."

"True," said Von Bork. Then, after a moment, the Prussian asked, "But if you knew I had no more gas up my pocket—"

"Up your sleeve."

"Pardon, Herr Holmes?"

"No more gas up your *sleeve*."

The German smiled. "As you wish. But again, if you knew there was no more gas, then why did you accept the offer to meet this evening?"

"To find out what you do intend," Holmes replied.

"You believe I have another hammer with which to strike against you English?"

"Yes."

Von Bork approached closer and bent down, studying the detective's face most closely by the light of the overhead electric lamp. I saw odd expressions wash over the face of my friend, but remained silent. Then the German smiled broadly.

"You know there is more, but you have no idea what it is, do you?" he said. "You thought the sulphur mustard was the only deck I had up my sleeve."

"Card."

"Pardon me?"

"The only *card* up your sleeve," said Holmes. "And I know it is not."

"Yes, but as I said, you know not what more I have waiting," replied Von Bork. He crossed his arms. "You have no notion of the grand design, do you?"

Holmes smiled. "I have notions of your colleague," he said. "The man I knew as Moxon Ivery, for instance."

Von Bork smiled derisively.

"The man whom I should have named as the Graf von Schwabing."

The German's smile vanished.

"I am acquainted with the name, you see." Holmes went on, taking a deep breath and glancing at the high ceiling before resuming. "And the man. He did not avoid my notice. I know he became unfairly caught in a rather nasty scandal, and that he required some means of restoring his reputation in Berlin. As does someone else I know."

It was now Von Bork's turn to remain silent.

"To such a man as Von Schwabing, joining your group of Wild Birds must have had great appeal," Holmes said, a comment that brought another silent reaction from our captor.

"You see, I know far more than expected," claimed Holmes, who leaned his head forward toward the Prussian. "Yes, Ulric von Stumm, Hilda von Einem, and Heinrich von Bork: such a wicked, unprincipled set."

"Entry to our esteemed small circle was a privilege for the Graf von Schwabing," Von Bork said at last. "For whom would it not be? To be part of a cabal that sends the history of the world along a glorious new path is distinction indeed."

"A new path you had charted for some time."

"Yes," agreed the German. "I told you as much long ago, that night in Essex, when I revealed the combination of my safe."

"*August 1914*," recited Holmes.

Von Bork nodded.

"Von Stumm and Von Einem had doubts that a war could be ignited by that date, but I convinced them. And history proved me correct, Mr. Holmes."

"History will condemn you."

"As I shall help write it, I think not. Rather, it will extol me."

"No person of sound mind extols mass murder," said Holmes. "For that is what you and your Wild Birds cabal have wrought, Herr Von Bork. Nothing but millions of needless deaths."

"They are cleansing deaths, Mr. Holmes. And from the ashes of the departed shall arise a new Europe—a new world, for that matter."

"Your uncle, the Count von und zu Grafenstein, would think otherwise, were he still alive."

"Do not mention my mother's brother to me, Mr. Holmes. Better that you had not saved his life during that ridiculous diplomatic mission of his."

"Your country—and the world—had better prospects during the brief time he served Germany."

"My uncle was a fool," snarled Von Bork. "He did not serve the Fatherland; rather, he was the slavish errand boy of a false, weakling monarch who was so fortunately short-lived himself."[272]

---

[272] By "weakling monarch," Von Bork undoubtedly refers to Kaiser Frederick III, who assumed the throne in 1888. A liberal who professed hatred of war and was often at odds with the policies of his father, Wilhelm I, and Chancellor Otto von Bismarck, Frederick had developed cancer of the larynx by the time of his accession and died after a reign of

"Your uncle was an earnest diplomat and a noble individual."

"Bah!" exclaimed Von Bork. "*Humanitätsdüselei!*"[273]

Von Bork gestured for his men, other than Baumann, to leave the room.

"Von Schwabing has proved a more than able colleague," our captor declared. "His triumphs came to exceed those of another of our group, the man you knew as Alasdair Moncrief. They surpassed the efforts of Von Stumm and Von Einem, for that matter."

"All three that you just named were subdued by Richard Hannay," said the detective with an air of satisfaction. "As Von Schwabing will be, in time."

"Sadly, Mr. Holmes, you will not be able to learn whether that prophecy ever comes to pass. But I congratulate you on discerning Von Schwabing's hand in the Black Stone, and his presence in that village of Biggleswick. He did great damage against your Allied cause before being forced to flee this accursed island."

Holmes shrugged.

"Still, your bragging has distracted us from the more important point I was making: you cannot tell me what I have planned for this night, can you? You cannot tell me because you do not know what it is."

I watched my friend, waiting for him to relate our knowledge of the coming air raid and the German plans to incinerate London.

Holmes, however, stayed mute for several seconds before declaring in an even voice, "No, I fear that, while I know you have plans, I have not

---

only ninety-nine days. He was succeeded by his son, Wilhelm II, whose militaristic attitudes contributed to the origins of the First World War.

[273] "Humanitarian babble"

learned their substance, Herr Von Bork. Perhaps now, in your hour of presumed victory, you might enlighten me."

Von Bork studied Holmes for a moment and then stepped forward, chuckling loudly as he approached us again.

"You wish me to gloat?" he asked. "Do you hold hope that I will offer a trite declamation of purpose and plan, for your edification?"

The German bent down and sharply slapped Holmes across the face.

"No," Von Bork said quietly, hovering within inches of my friend. "I will not. Never."

He backed away, strolled toward the door, and then stopped to turn round.

"I liked you better as Altamount, you know. You were convivial and amiable in that guise," the German said as he contemplated Holmes. "Indeed, in those days I almost considered you a friend, though in the same manner as my dogs back in Berlin.

"But you—the real Mr. Holmes—you are ever the annoying, curious one! Gathering your facts in your so-called commonplace books. Sifting evidence and clues, trying to unlock one mystery after another. Do you find that satisfying?"

"In its way, it has been a stimulating way to pass a life."

Von Bork grunted. "British fool! This time, it will be you left dangling, not I. In your last moments, Herr Holmes, you will live the agony of a curious mind lacking answers, having no knowledge of what you are about to face, torturing yourself for failing to deduce it. Baumann!" he shouted to his assistant.

"Yes, *mein Führer.*"

"Go and make the vehicle ready," Von Bork ordered as he checked his timepiece. "We shall leave. All depends now upon *Die Fliegertruppe*."[274]

"You will not tell me what is planned to happen tonight?" asked Holmes in a suddenly insistent voice.

"I have just told you so," the Prussian replied as Baumann left.

"You mean you refuse to—"

"I will tell you nothing more," affirmed Von Bork, who reached up for the chain connected to the light overhead. With a sharp pull of his hand, the room became dark, lit only by a faint glow from the doorway.

Our adversary stood in the illuminated opening, his body appearing only as a black silhouette.

"You will not tell me?" said Holmes yet again, his voice more urgent than before. "What, do you expect me to beg?"

"No, Mr. Holmes," declared Von Bork's shadow just before the door closed with a metallic clink. "I expect you to burn."

---

[274] *Fliegertruppen des deutschen Kaiserreiches*, or "Imperial Flying Corps," was the name of the air arm of the Germany Army prior to October 1916, when its name was changed to *Deutsche Luftstreitkräfte*, or "German Air Force." Von Bork here employs the outdated term.

CHAPTER TWENTY-FIVE: BOWING TO TIME

"Can you hear me, Watson?" called Sherlock Holmes in the darkness, his voice now suddenly firm and unwavering. "Can you move your chair?"

"I can hear you, of course," I replied. Then, after pushing on the floor had caused my chair to scrape across the planked floor for a few inches, I added, "I can move, but at a snail's pace."

"That must suffice. Advance in my direction, if you will, old fellow."

"And what will come of that?"

"Our freedom, if fortune can smile through darkness."

I paused for a moment, hearing a constant, rhythmic thumping.

"What is that, Holmes? From below us, perhaps? Someone signalling?"

"No. What you hear is...me attempting to...utilise this damned set of boots foisted upon me by Mycroft."

"I do not understand."

"Were I in your place, I should be at a similar loss, but accept the situation. Are you still sliding in my direction?"

I pushed against the floor as best I could, making what I believed to be slow but steady progress.

"Good," said Holmes. "I can hear you scuttling toward me," he said as the constant thumping continued.

"What are you...doing?" I asked as I kept moving the chair slowly.

"I told you, Watson, I am—"

Suddenly, during a pause in my efforts to push myself across the floor in total darkness, I heard what sounded like the sour note of a spring being released.

"Ah, at last," declared Holmes. "How far do you think are you to me?

"Perhaps three feet," I replied, basing my answer upon the sound of my friend's voice. "Is that your estimate as well?"

"More or less. Stay still, for I am going to tip myself over."

"What?"

"Not enough," I heard him say with a groan. "Better...Come along...Ah! Over I go!"

I heard him hit the floor.

"Holmes! Are you hurt?"

"My present condition is of less interest than your future position. Continue to slide this way, please, but do so cautiously."

Years of service asserted themselves, and I did as requested without further enquiry as to reason. I pushed myself backward, and then abruptly felt my chair butt up against that of Holmes.

"Excellent," my friend declared. "Do I seem to be on your right side?"

"Yes."

"Good. Now slowly rotate, if you will. Clockwise."

I executed the turn slowly in darkness and felt, after a moment, contact with what I took to the bottom of a shoe.

"Stop," commanded Holmes.

Again I felt contact against my heels.

"Do not move, old fellow, and if you feel any pain, tell me at once."

I heard another noise now: a rhythmic sliding, accompanied by a back-and-forth tugging at my ankles.

“Are you cutting the ropes with a blade?” I asked, incredulously.

“I am. With a very sharp blade, Watson. Feel free to spread your ankles, if you can.”

I did as asked, but to no great extent for several minutes. Then, abruptly, I felt a sudden loosening of the cords round my legs. “They are coming apart,” I cried.

“I’ve withdrawn the blade,” said Holmes. “Can you free your lower limbs now?”

“Yes,” I replied as I felt the last small strands burst. Eagerly, I waved my legs in the darkness. “I assume you will work at my wrists now?”

“Yes, but I must ask you to now join me in assuming a horizontal position. However, can you perhaps stand with the chair attached to you, bend down, and gently plant yourself upon the floor?”

“You may watch me,” I said confidently.

“In truth, Watson, given our present circumstances, that will not be possible. I do trust your physical instincts, however. And stay clear of me; I should not wish you to slice an artery with my blade.”

I strained to get to my feet, hampered not so much by the weight of the chair as my awkward, constrained posture. I dropped to my knees, feeling pain there in the process, and then slowly tipped over so that I presented my backside—and bound wrists—to Holmes.

“You still have not told me how you came by the blade, or where it was hid,” I muttered as I felt Holmes probe with the tip of one shoe.

“Pull your wrists apart as best you can,” said he, ignoring my remark.

Again I heard the slipping of the blade against rope, this time feeling the back and forth tugging directed against my arms. Without being so directed, I moved my hands to and fro, matching the cutting rhythm of my friend. More rapidly than before, I felt the strands binding me give way.

"I am free!" I said. In the darkness, I frantically reached for the cord binding my torso still to the chair, eventually undid the knots and cautiously slid from the seat before, with a lack of grace, stumbling to my feet.

"Find the light pull," said Holmes from the floor. "It is behind you, recall. Take care to give yourself ample room and stay clear of me, Watson."

"On account of that knife of yours, whatever its source?"

"Quite so. Once we again have light, you will understand."

Slowly, my hands before me, I turned round and, by flailing my arms, found the light pull. I gave a slow tug, and the lamp clicked on.

Turning again, I beheld Sherlock Holmes, still bound in his chair, which was tipped onto its side. My friend's homburg lay upside down a short distance away, and my own chair and the cords which had recently restrained me lay near it. What attracted my attention, however, was the shining piece of steel protruding from the toe of Holmes's left boot, its razor-sharp edge glinting in harsh light as the prone detective idly turned his ankle back and forth.

"Good God, that is a nasty piece of metal," I said. "Is it attached to your boot? It was hid in the anterior of the sole?"

"Yes," replied Holmes. "The damned thing is supposed to detach, but the mechanism will not respond. I suppose we should be thankful that, at least, the spring worked as designed, releasing it from within."

I bent down beside my friend. "Shall I try to pull the blade free?"

"You may try, Watson, but I fear there is no place to grasp it firmly without risking a wicked cut."

Carefully, I attempted to dislodge the knife from the toe of Holmes's boot, but to no avail.

"I must untie you by hand," I said.

"I thought as much." Holmes sighed. "The knife would have been faster."

"Much faster," I said, beginning to work the cords that bound his ankles. "These knots are intricate, tight, and will take much effort to undo."

"Best get at it, then."

"I have already begun, if you have not yet noticed."

"Yes, of course. My apologies, Watson. Time, of course, is of the essence."

"And how much do you believe we have?" I enquired as I released a large bit of rope.

"There is no way of knowing the answer. I suppose it depends on how much of a head start Von Bork arranged for himself."

"To get out of the City before German bombers arrive?"

"Rather, to get onto the river before the fires take hold."

"He will go there?"

"If London is on the verge of being consumed by an inferno, what other venue offers refuge within a short radius?" asked my friend. "Here, I feel the rope loosening."

I reared back as Holmes carefully but firmly kicked his legs apart.

"I believe you were warning me earlier regarding that blade of yours," I delicately remarked.

"Oh, so I was. Pardon my enthusiasm, old fellow."

I cautiously pulled the loose cords free from his legs and crawled behind Holmes to begin working on those that still bound his wrists.

"I suppose I should thank you for insisting that you accompany me," he said as I laboured with the knots. "Had I been alone, Mycroft's little device would have been useless to me, I fear."

"And so M's present of new boots was actually—"

"To serve as a hiding place for the knife, should I find myself in a situation where a blade would be handy, yes."

Holmes struck the floor several times with the heel of his bladed boot, and at last the knife separated from the toe.

"I am glad to be free of that," my friend said. "There are more of Mycroft's devices that we shall employ shortly. At a more convenient time, I will describe to you even more gadgets he attempted to foist upon me. And, Watson, please do not employ that single-letter sobriquet for my brother again in my presence. As dear to me as you are, your continued reference to him in that manner tries our friendship most seriously."

"I will take those words to heart," I said. "There! I believe your wrists are free."

I backed away and allowed Holmes to wrestle his hands free of the ropes and then reach down for the knife and cut himself free from the chair. We both got to our feet simultaneously.

"We are no longer bound, but we are not yet free," I said as Holmes reached for his hat. "What can we do now?"

"Set ourselves free," replied my friend as he held his homberg. Searching its brim, he pinched the fabric and then extracted from it a pair of long, patterned metal pins.

"Your brother gives you hats with lock picking tools inside?" I said.

Without replying, Holmes strode to the door and within seconds had opened the lock accessible from our side the entry. The door itself, however, did not budge.

"There must be a bolt of some sort on the exterior," the detective said, looking at the sturdy door that kept us from escaping. Striding to an overturned chair, which he righted, Holmes added, "We shall take the required next step."

"And what is that?"

In response to my query, Holmes sat down in the chair, lifted one leg across the knee of the other, and grasped the heel of his raised boot. He pulled and then gave it a twist, and the piece came away in his hand, allowing several small items hidden within the hollow heel to drop onto the floor.

"A small mallet head," I said. "And a length of small cord. Are there other—"

"Yes," interjected my friend as he reached into the remainder of the disassembled heel to extract a thin wooden handle, which he screwed into the mallet head. Slapping the back of the boot against the floor, Holmes caused a small chisel to appear as well.

"These pieces are all very charming," I remarked. "But we are locked within a windowless room that boasts a sturdy door, which is bolted on the outside. We can never hope to bore our way out."

"I quite agree," said Holmes as he gathered up the set of small implements. "That is why I propose to simply remove the door. Here, drag that chair over to it, if you will."

"It is not clear that those diminutive tools can defeat such a large door," I said as I complied with my friend's request. Within seconds, I had the chair in its desired place.

"We will divide and conquer, Watson," said Holmes, standing upon the chair with mallet in hand. "As you correctly point out, the bolt is on the outside. The hinges, however, share this side of the room with us. They are the focus of our attack."

Holmes bent down on his knees and positioned the thin chisel beneath the bottom hinge bolt. Pounding upward upon the chisel, he forced the bolt upward with repeated strokes until it could be worked loose by hand. Then he got to his feet and mounted the chair, standing upon it, now within reach of the upper hinge.

"Steady both myself and the chair, old fellow," he said.

With one hand I took hold of the chair back, and with the other I grasped a portion of Holmes's coat. My friend now performed the same operation on the second hinge bolt, eventually freeing it as well.

"We are done with these," he said, reaching down toward me, the mallet and chisel in his hand. "Pocket them, if you will."

I let go Holmes's jacket and took the pair of tools as he wound a portion of cord round the upper hinge portion attached to the door itself, taking care to thread the fine line between it and the hinge portion affixed to the door frame. Letting out the line, he hopped off the chair and reached into a pocket with his free hand.

"Here," said my friend. "Do the same with this and the lower hinge. Double the cord, Watson, as I have done."

I rapidly complied, and now the two of us stood back from the door, each holding seemingly frail lines that looped round the flanges of the door hinges.

"Mycroft has insisted this cord is the strongest devised by humankind, but all the same, we have doubled it," Holmes declared. "Hope with me that my brother is correct and then some, and pull with me on the count of three."

I gripped my line tightly, listened to my friend's count, and together we pulled on his signal. The one side of the door jerked suddenly and then stopped.

"Again," said Holmes. "One, two, three!"

The door slid again, and this time the hinged side broke free of the frame, sliding into the room with us, though the lines remained taut.

"Now step to the left, maintaining your pull," my friend commanded. "There. Now we pull back once more. One, two, three!"

The door slid in a direction parallel to its plane, coasting into the room as I heard a rough metallic thump on the other side. Holmes dropped his line, and I did the same.

"Here," said Holmes, pushing on the hinged edge of the door, rotating it slightly to widen the opening between it and frame. "Around me and out, old fellow."

I slid past my friend and out of the room. Holmes followed immediately, and without another word, we rushed down the stair toward the ground floor. Reaching the building door first, I found it locked.

"Can your tools breach this barrier?"

"Perhaps," said Holmes, looking round in the darkness before finding a small crate, which he carried to a single pane window. "This approach, however, should prove much faster. He threw the wooden box at the glass, which gave way with a shattering crash, leaving a gaping hole through which we each might squeeze our way to escape.

Holmes wound his kerchief round one hand and struck at the portions of glass that still adhered to the window frame. Suddenly, we heard a voice.

"Stand back and offer no resistance!" a man called. "We are armed!"

I instantly recognised the voice.

"We will give you no resistance, Inspector Magillivray," called back Sherlock Holmes. "If you will give us assistance."

As we waited, Magillivray's face appeared in the open window frame. Behind him, Jack James, Sergeant Scaife, and Sandy Arbuthnot pressed in beside him to look inside.

"I fear you are all blocking our exit," said Holmes, stepping toward the opening and beckoning me forward. "If you will grasp Watson's arms on his way out, I will assist from the other end in extracting him from this place."

In brisk fashion, I was removed through the window frame before helping pull out Holmes as well.

"It appears you would have escaped without us," Magillivray remarked as Holmes dusted off himself.

"Yes, but we cannot reach the river in time without you," the detective answered. "I assume you all arrived in motors."

"I apologise for disobeying your orders," said Jack James from behind the wheel of the taxicab. Holmes and I were crowded into the rear, alongside Inspector Magillivray, while Sergeant Scaife occupied the seat beside the chauffeur.

"And I ask forgiveness as well," shouted Sandy Arbuthnot as he clung to the cab while standing upon the right running-board. "Neither Jack nor I thought it best to abandon the two of you to fate."

"Both the colonel and I would have survived," said Holmes calmly. "But again, had you not followed us, we could not make it to the riverbank in time to snare Von Bork!"

"I followed the advice in that monograph of yours, sir," said James as he drove south. "The one about automotive pursuit. The Germans never saw us."

"I am certain they did not," said Holmes with a smile.

"Once Sandy hopped out and approached silently on foot, he saw them take you into the building. We then sped down to where the police launches were and brought the inspector and the sergeant with us."

"There had not been any signal from that barge master, Evans," Magillivray declared. "The constables tending our launches have been ordered to wait upon our return."

Just then, young James swerved to avoid a horse-drawn lorry.

I looked back at the vehicle and then turned to Holmes.

"Do you suppose that was—"

"One of the members of the London Transport League?" interjected the detective. "It would not surprise. Let us hope that if such is the case, their destination is one of the intersections manned by Scotland Yard. And let us hope the parties directed by Inspectors Hartley and Carter are about to begin their raids, if they have not already initiated them."

For another few minutes, we rambled through the evening toward the river, with Sandy Arbuthnot hanging on the outside of the motorcar. More than once, Scaife or Magillivray called out in the congestion, identifying themselves as policemen in order to clear our way. In that fashion, we reached the river's edge, where three police launches waited, tended by four constables, Shinwell Johnson, and Frank Farrar.

"Sir!" cried Farrar. "We've just seen the signal from Tatty Evans!"

"Not more than a minute ago," added Johnson. "Shall we be off?"

"Sandy, you and Jack take that boat with two of the policemen," ordered Holmes. "Johnson and Farrar, join the remaining constables in the second launch. We four shall go in the third vessel," he told Magillivray, Scaife, and me.

"Wait, sir," cried Arbuthnot, who ran back to our taxicab and retrieved the burlap sack he had held earlier. He handed it to Holmes, who took it before turning round to view the river.

We also looked out across the waters, where a close pair of lights sat off to the east.

"The second one was lit just a moment ago," repeated Porky Johnson.

"Let us head for them, then," said Holmes.

As directed, James and Arbuthnot tumbled into one craft in the company of two constables, who started up the motor. The second vessel, with Farrar, Johnson, and the second pair of policemen, also roared into life. As both boats waited, I boarded the third launch in the company of Holmes, Magillivray, and Scaife, who stepped to the stern to take control.

"Follow our craft," Holmes shouted to the others. "On with it!" he barked to Scaife, and our vessel cast off. Within moments, all three motor launches were nearing the dim set of lights floating in the region of midstream.

"The *Belisama* is attached to them?" I asked Holmes.

"Yes," said he. "Tatty Evans and Old George have been anchored there for the better part of the day, acting as watchmen—a task they eagerly accepted after learning that we were approaching the end of our drama. Once Von Bork left shore on the *Nemesis*, which was docked nearby, Tatty was to signal, as he did."

"Are you confident we can catch Von Bork? The *Nemesis* is fast, is she not?"

"The Nemesis can outrun Tatty's barge without effort," replied Holmes. "And it may give these police launches a good run. However," he added, "I doubt that Von Bork will go far tonight."

A moment later the lines of a sailing barge emerged from the night mist, and through cold winter air I then recognised the *Belisama* sitting before us, anchored against the current. Scaife steered our launch beside the barge and then cut the engine. Behind us, the other police boats did the same.

"Ahoy, Evans," called Holmes in a soft voice as we drifted nearer the other vessel. "Did you see it?"

"If you mean the *Nemesis*, Mr. Holmes, the answer is yes," replied Tatty Evans sharply. "She left the shore a short while ago, headed straight out, and turned east."

"She was anchored in the same place, about half a mile down," said Old George. "About where the old fish market was. Say, see them lights?"

The young man pointed to the sky, where I saw erupting flashes.

"Maroons[275] are signalling the alarm," said Inspector Magillivray as the dull, distant thuds from their explosions washed over us. When the sound faded, I heard aeroplanes in the darkness above.

"Aircraft," I said. "Are they—"

"Ours, no doubt," interjected Holmes. "We have been expecting the German raid tonight, after all, and Bullivant and Mycroft have put RFC aeroplanes into the air in advance. Come!" he called to Scaife and the men in the other two launches. "Along the river to the east!"

"Good luck with it, Mr. Holmes," called out Tatty Evans as we started off in pursuit of the *Nemesis*. "May the spirit of the river protect all of you."

"Thank you, Evans," replied my friend. "You will obtain your justice tonight."

"So will we all," muttered Magillivray.

Abreast of one another, the distance between them gradually widening, our three craft sped eastward, rounding the river's bend and moving on through the night. As Sergeant Scaife steered us, Holmes looked about.

"Where did I place that burlap sack?" he asked.

"Here it is, Mr. Holmes," replied Inspector Magillivray, reaching down to retrieve the bag. Holmes took it and carefully loosened the twine sealing the top. Slipping his hand inside, he withdrew a gun, which he held out to me.

"Why, thank you," I stammered, recognising my old service revolver.

---

[275] "Maroons" is another name for the sound rockets launched to warn of impending air attack. See footnote 211.

"It is freshly loaded," my friend reminded me, "and so do be careful. It has also been cleaned, but I do not believe you have practiced for more than a decade, have you not?"

"Some things are never forgotten," I said, taking hold of the pistol. "This is one of them."

"So true," agreed Holmes, who then pulled from the sack his own Webley, which he clutched in one hand while dropping the sack onto the deck of the launch. "There is more ammunition for both guns in the bag. Let us hope that memory serves both of us well this night, Watson."

As the lines of a motor launch appeared ahead of us, dim flashes appeared on the horizon.

"Those are not sound rockets," I said.

"Our guns, most likely," suggested Magillivray.

"I hope your fellows from the Yard have stormed the target buildings and rendered the roof lights inoperative by now," Holmes remarked.

"We will see," answered the inspector.

Holmes smiled grimly, nodding at the darkness ahead. Suddenly, he pointed ahead at a distant set of lights.

"That may be Von Bork in the *Nemesis*!" he said.

"He would anchor in midstream?" I asked.

"I expected him to do so," he said, "Von Bork will not run completely from the fire, but instead stay at a safe distance and savour the fruit of his supposed guile and ingenuity. Ha! Instead, he will be consumed by his own conceit."

I thought to caution my friend against falling victim to overconfidence himself but remained silent, concentrating instead upon the lights ahead, which grew brighter as the lines of the attached vessel expanded with time.

At this moment, the other two launches were nearly a furlong[276] to starboard and port, one on either side of us. Distant echoes of our ground batteries firing into the sky washed over us, and then I heard a sharper report that gave way to a steady rumble. I stared ahead, at the lights that were our target.

"It is the *Nemesis*!" cried Sergeant Scaife from our helm. "It must be!"

"She's getting under way!" shouted Holmes. "They see us! Von Bork is attempting to flee."

He turned round to address Scaife. "We must increase speed!"

Ahead, the *Nemesis* was accelerating rapidly. Making a sharp turn, the vessel began to steam furiously down river. Holmes clambered to the bow of our launch and leaned forward to peer at our quarry.

"We must catch him," he rasped hoarsely.

"But if Magillivray's colleagues have disabled the German searchlights and kept the streets clear, preventing the firestorm, is that not enough?" I said, wishing to counsel prudence.

"We must catch him!" my friend repeated, this time in a sharp voice.

Our launch had been gaining on Von Bork's craft, but now the object of our pursuit opened up a slightly greater lead as we approached that portion of the river south of Limehouse. Passing Canary Wharf, I glanced back and saw that our sister launches bearing the others had begun to lag behind. As we shot along the West India Docks and prepared to round the

---

[276] A furlong is one-eighth of a mile. Watson's perhaps unconscious use of the term may be a reflection of his affection for horse-racing.

Isle of Dogs, I realised that only our craft would have any chance of catching Von Bork and his remaining allies.

"Go back and tell Inspector Jones that we must stoke it on," insisted Holmes.

"Do you not mean—?"

"Please do as I ask, Watson!"

I approached the stern of our launch and impressed upon Magillivray and Scaife of the need for more speed.

"The boat's putting out all she can, Colonel," protested the sergeant. "It can do no more."

As I turned forward, toward Holmes, my mind rushed back some thirty years, recalling a similar nocturnal chase upon these waters, one that had taken us past these same landmarks. Realising that, in his excitement, my friend had momentarily confused that experience with our present situation, I returned to his side.[277]

"You spoke to Magillivray?" he asked.

"Yes. The craft is travelling at maximum speed, Holmes."

He nodded grimly. "That is all that can be expected, I suppose." The detective turned toward me, his face in shadow. "I show impatience, do I not?" he said with a chuckle.

"Do not we all?"

"Quite so," Holmes agreed as our launch veered northward, following the river's meander. So intent had I been upon the quarry that I had

---

[277] Watson no doubt refers to the conclusion of the case related in *The Sign of the Four*. In the pursuit of the criminal Jonathan Small aboard the *Aurora*, Holmes and Watson were accompanied by Inspector Athelney Jones.

forgotten about the firing of our ground batteries upon incoming German aeroplanes. Now I took notice of other explosions to the west.

"They have begun dropping their bombs," said Magillivray as he stepped to our side.

"Let us hope it is in desperation," remarked Holmes. "If your men have disabled the searchlights, the bombers will have nothing to guide them. Ah!" he cried. "I believe we are gaining at last!"

Looking across our bow, I observed that the *Nemesis* now indeed appeared closer than before. Turning back, however, I saw that the other police launches still trailed in our wake.

"What shall we do should we close the gap, Holmes?" I asked.

"Respond as the moment demands."

We were coming athwart the Blackwall Basin now and had gained such a length on our quarry that I discerned what I took to be the figure of Heinrich Von Bork crouching near the stern of his vessel. Beside him stood another, whom I supposed to be Dietrich Baumann.

"Do you see him?" asked Holmes.

"Von Bork? Yes, I have just made him out, as well as another who may be Baumann."

"Yes!" said Holmes. "He is there as well."

Scaife called out from the stern of the launch. "I don't know long we can keep this pace, sirs," the sergeant shouted. "The vessel is—"

There were three sharp snaps in the air, and then a fourth. Almost simultaneously, Scaife cried out, and I turned to see his body give a sudden spasm. The sergeant's face turned skyward, and before he hit the launch's floorboards, another pair of loud cracks washed over us, paired with twin whistles above us. Immediately, I dropped below the gunwale.

Magillivray and Holmes were both kneeling as well, on hands and knees, while Scaife writhed behind us.

"They've shot him!" Magillivray exclaimed. "Scaife! You're hit, man!"

I crawled to the downed sergeant as another bullet flew over our heads. Peeling back the policeman's coat and shirt, I uncovered the wound, which was to his upper arm.

"I got my German bullet," Scaife said with an almost hysterical laugh. "Didn't have to enlist or cross to France. Got it right here at home, didn't I?"

"That you did, Sergeant," I replied, applying pressure after noting that the bullet had apparently exited through the man's arm.

"Here," said Holmes, passing me a kerchief. "It is clean." I applied the cloth to Scaife's wound and then flinched as I heard two loud reports within inches of me. Looking up, I saw my friend, now standing, calmly lower his revolver and fire a third time. "Faster!" he cried to Inspector Magillivray, who had grasped the helm. "Maintain our speed, Inspector! We are almost upon them!"

Scaife was breathing in gasps as I maintained my pressure. And Inspector Magillivray crouched at the stern. As he kept control of the launch with one hand, he pulled a pistol from his pocket but hesitated to aim, for Holmes remained standing at the prow of our vessel. I heard more bullets whistle overhead, but the detective did not flinch.

"Get down!" I cried to my friend. "For God's sake, man, get down!"

"*Wir haben Ihre Lampen gefunden!*" shouted Holmes at the *Nemesis*, unmindful of my pleas. "*Es wird kein Feuersturm sein!*"[278]

[278] "We have found your lamps! There will be no firestorm!"

More bullets were fired from the German craft. I heard one hit the hull of our launch, while the others passed overhead. Still Holmes stood and calmly fired back, while Magillivray kept us in pursuit. I looked down at Scaife, who stared up at me. Again there was gunfire.

"Holmes, get down," I repeated. "For the love of God!"

Looking up, I saw my friend reloading his pistol yet again.

Scaife gave a rasp. I looked down at him and saw the sergeant's eyes glowing at Holmes. His gaze shifted to me, and he nodded his head.

"Inspector Magillivray," I said sternly. "Put down your gun. Use your free hand to apply pressure here to your man."

"I'm sorry, Colonel," he replied. "I must try to—"

"Holmes is in your line of fire! You cannot shoot in any event! Apply pressure to your man!" I ordered. "Now!"

The inspector put down his weapon and reached for Scaife, replacing my pressure with his as he maintained the helm with his other hand. At once, I rose to stand with Sherlock Holmes, pulling my service revolver from a coat pocket.

As if in a trance, I heard and felt the buzz of a bullet not six inches from my face as I took aim, noting calmly that we lay perhaps sixty yards from the stern of the *Nemesis*. Only one person aboard her appeared to be firing, and that was Heinrich Von Bork. I stayed beside my friend, compelled to join him in this gruesome, foolhardy exercise. Again and again we aimed and fired at the German launch.

The *Nemesis* then made a sudden turn to starboard, throwing Von Bork off balance. At that moment, Holmes and I fired together, and the lurching figure on the other craft's deck flung its arms outward and stumbled toward the gunwale, making impact with it and then rotating over the edge to topple into the river.

I saw the Prussian's head vanish beneath the hull of his boat, but never saw it rise to the surface again.

"*Nicht schießen!*" came a frantic, high voice from across the waves. "*Ich gebe auf! Bitte nicht schießen!*" [279]

From the shadows of the ship's bow, a light-haired figure emerged with hands upraised.

I turned toward Holmes, my fingers tense as they gripped the service revolver. Immediately, I let my hand drop to the side, so that the weapon pointed downward. Holmes was now bare headed, his homburg apparently having been blown by the wind—or shot by a bullet—from his scalp.

The *Nemesis* had cut her engines and was now drifting in the current. Moments before we reached it, two figures jumped from the launch and began to swim toward the river's southern bank. We set grapples to our quarry, and Magillivray jumped aboard her, gun in hand once more. Scaife was now leaning against the inner gunwale of our craft, a large kerchief tied round his upper arm while he maintained the helm with his other hand before cutting our own engine.

Magillivray called to us. Baumann was sitting calmly near the bow, hands on his knees. No one else was aboard.

Scaife cheered, his mood buoyant.

"Under fire from the Germans," he repeated at regular intervals. "Shot clean through."

---

[279] "Don't shoot! I surrender! Please don't shoot!"

Holmes and I looked to the west, where the horizon was not yet lit with the beginnings of an inferno. In the quiet, I heard my friend whisper a phrase that was unintelligible to me, save for the final word: *Hudson.*

There was another moment of quiet, and then Scaife hoarsely asked, "Are there any more bombs dropping?"

"No, Sergeant," said my friend in a soothing voice. "All is silent, for now, on our home front. We have won London's reprieve, I believe."

And your own absolution, I thought to myself.

One of our other police launches—the one bearing Frank Farrar, Shinwell Johnson, and two constables—came up alongside us. Holmes instructed them to pursue the pair who had jumped from the *Nemesis*, and our companion vessel set out in that direction.

Looking back, I espied the third launch approaching, with James and Arbuthnot aboard, and bent down to pick up Holmes's hat, which I noticed sitting beside Sergeant Scaife. Pointedly poking my finger through a hole in the crown before handing it to him, I said, "Wisdom does not always come with age, it would appear."

"The two have been known to diverge," admitted Holmes, putting his hand upon my shoulder. "However, Watson, your loyalty to the occasionally unwise has never been known to waver."

"You have saved London," I said after a moment, in a choked voice.

"If I have had a part in such an act, it was only by virtue of having my old associate at my side. It would not have been accomplished without you."

We both turned again to the west, and I imagined St. Paul's sitting stolidly in the darkness. No more bombs were dropping.

"It is the calm of London turning over in the night after being momentarily disturbed by some trifle," Holmes said as the river lapped at our craft. "We have not withered before Von Bork's blast."

I stood on the gently rolling floorboards as the third launch drifted in beside us. The two constables it bore jumped into the *Nemesis* and assisted Magillivray in binding Dietrich Baumann's wrists after anchoring the launch in place. Arbuthnot and James watched, along with Holmes, as I stepped to the stern to see to Scaife, whose spirits remained high.

"Will he recover?" asked Holmes.

"It seems as if he already has."

Scaife motioned for me to rejoin the detective at the bow, and I stepped back to my friend.

"A cleaner, better, stronger land," said Holmes. "That is what you said we would have when the storm cleared, is it not?"

"Yes."

Holmes stared once into the night and sighed, his fingers lighting upon and then pressing my shoulder. "Let us pray you have the power of true prophecy, Watson."

I stood a few feet from the cliff edge, staring out to sea. Circling gulls shrieked across the Channel's open expanse, a field of blue embedded with randomly sparkling diamonds brought forth by a bright summer sun.

"It is reminiscent of that morning on the Ruff," said Sherlock Holmes as he held his cloth cap in both hands.

"Or, in an odd way, that night at Von Bork's house in Essex, when we thought we were done with him," I added.

Now we had been many months finished with the German spy, and I realised that all bodies of water would henceforth recall his face to my mind. I thought also of other faces, and all the triumphs associated with them over the past five years—as well as the great costs those victories had exacted from the survivors.[280]

Holmes took a deep breath as a sudden gust from the Channel hit us in the face. "The salt is refreshing," he murmured. "When, at least, it does not touch old wounds."

I nodded.

"I have heard from Jack James," my friend said after a moment.

"Oh?"

"Yes, his regiment is being sent back home to America within two months."

"Will he be staying in the army?" I asked.

"No, he will be part of his country's demobilisation, but he will be joining a militia of a different sort. The lad intends to become a Pinkerton agent."[281]

"Perhaps he will be asking your advice in the coming years," I suggested.

"I am certain he will do quite well on his own."

There was the sound of laughter behind us, and we both turned to see Mary Lamington and Richard Hannay scampering along the footpath

---

[280] The original manuscript contains at this point a long paragraph summarizing events following those of the preceding section in this chapter. Most of those details involve the exploits of Richard Hannay and his associates against the Graf Von Swabing in Europe, matters which are treated at length in *Mr. Standfast.* The paragraph has been omitted in this edition; those interested in these events may read the John Buchan novel to satisfy their curiosity.

[281] Founded by Allan Pinkerton in 1850, the Pinkerton National Detective Agency was the largest private law enforcement organization in the world at the height of its power.

leading to the crest where Holmes and I stood. The two held hands as they bounded up the slight incline. In the distance, Hannay's motorcar sat where it had remained the past two hours as the four of us had first enjoyed a picnic lunch before pairing off for separate strolls along the Sussex coast.

"Are you practising for your run from the church?" I asked.

"Indeed, we are, Uncle John," declared the young woman, brushing golden hair from her face. I expect we shall have to run a gauntlet of upraised swords held by Dick's former comrades in arms."

"Actually, I'd rather it not be a military wedding," Hannay said softly.

"Well, whatever type of wedding it is to be, we will have rice."

"Of course," insisted the prospective groom. "I promise you tons and tons of rice."[282]

Holmes smiled. "Did you have a pleasurable walk?"

"We did," replied Hannay. "We took that one fork that you suggested, Mr. Holmes, and found the inlet you mentioned."

"It was most beautiful," added Mary. "I think Launcelot would have very much enjoyed the hiking here," she added wisftfully.

"Yes, he would have," agreed the South African, squeezing his fiancée's hand to coax a bittersweet smile from her. "And it is another addition to my collection of sights. I don't believe I had fully appreciated the British coast until today—even after that time at the Ruff." He paused, lowering his chin before lifting it to glance at Holmes and me. "Indeed, I didn't fully appreciate Britain herself until a certain evening in June," he

---

282 As part of the restrictions implemented under the Defense of the Realm Act, throwing rice at weddings was prohibited in Britain during the First World War as a measure to conserve food supplies.

added, looking again at his bride-to-be. "Two years ago. It was when I was on my way to my first dinner at Fosse Manor."

I saw Mary look into Hannay's eyes and fondly recalled the Wymondham sisters.

"Travelling to the Cotswolds in my first-class carriage, I was a bit troubled and mystified at the time over my assignment from Bullivant," Hannay said. "But my mind was cleared by the visit with Blaikie at Isham—and by meeting you again, Colonel Watson—so that, by the time I reached the hillside above Fosse Manor, I found myself calm at last. And then, there in the twilight, I had a kind of revelation.

"It was a vision of what I had been fighting for, what we all were fighting for. The struggle itself was across the waters, in France," he said as Mary Lamington now squeezed his hand. "But what the struggle was about was there before me: in the little fields enclosed by walls of grey stone, fields holding flocks of sheep in fading light. And my realisation extended to the tiny village below, with its church tower sounding the hour with a curiously sweet chime.

"That realisation was peace, and more: for in that moment, I tell you, Britain first took hold of me. Before then, Africa had been my land. When I had thought of home, it was the wide, sun-steeped spaces of the veld or scented glen of the berg.[283] But now I understood I had a new home," he said. "Here, on this island, and I knew that I should claim it and wrap myself in it till the end of my days."

"The end of *our* days," amended Mary Lamington.

---

[283] "Berg" is Afrikaans for mountain.

"I suppose we ought to be setting out for London," said Hannay, who to me at that moment had ceased to be a South African friend and was now a fellow Briton. "Would you care to ride along as far as your cottage, Mr. Holmes?"

"I think not," said the former detective. "I have a need to further stretch my legs, but I thank you for the offer."

"As you wish, sir," replied Hannay, who turned to go, along with Mary. The woman's eyes glanced expectantly at me.

"I will be right behind you two," I said. "Just give me another moment here."

"Of course," assured Hannay, leading his future wife down the small hill and toward the motorcar in the distance.

"You will also stretch your legs all the way to London now and then, will you not?" I asked my friend.

Holmes smiled and placed the cloth cap upon his head. "Of course, Watson. Nothing will interrupt our correspondence henceforth, nor will I allow any presumed obligation to stand in the way of the company which I owe you, old fellow. And you, in turn, will share the sea breeze and the joys of Sussex with me now and then?"

"As long as I am not forced to lodge with bees."

"That may be easily arranged," Holmes said jovially, placing a hand on my shoulder as we turned away from the broad expanse of sea to make our way cautiously down the hillside.

"There is still the matter of your knighthood," I reminded him.

"I have refused such before," Holmes declared. "And I have no intention of accepting the same in future. That I should—"

"Your previous refusal was under a different monarch," I reminded him.[284] "Surely you will not turn down a just reward this time—after all, you are the saviour of London."

"Such distinctions do not appeal," replied Holmes as we helped one another down the slope toward the motorcar, where Richard Hannay and Mary Lamington waited for us. "I prefer to live without them."

"Then I suppose I must refuse the same offer that has been made to me."

"Watson, surely you would not deny yourself the honour of—"

"I will do so, most certainly. It must be knighthoods for both of us or for neither, Holmes."

My friend drew back away from me and put his hands deep into his coat before sighing deeply.

"At times, Watson, you make friendship a most difficult arrangement."

"I have learnt from the master, have I not?"

Holmes looked down and smiled. After a moment, he nodded. "I will consider the knighthood. Is that response sufficient for the time being?"

"It is," I said, now taking him by the elbow to lead us toward the motor. "After all, if M can be knighted—"

"And will you please cease using that ridiculous appellation for my brother?" Holmes asked in mock exasperation. "In any case, I expect Mycroft accepted the honour only as a parting consolation."

---

[284] While he greatly admired Queen Victoria, Holmes is believed to have disliked her son, King Edward VII, who offered the detective a knighthood in 1902, only to have it turned down. By this time, however, the crown had passed to George V, who was more in the mold of his grandmother.

"What do you mean by that?"

"My brother is leaving the government," Holmes revealed, a statement that caused me to halt in my tracks. "Did I not tell you?"

"What? How can that be?"

"Mycroft returned from Versailles early and in a very foul mood," Holmes said. "I am afraid he met his match in the Wizard, whose willingness to appease the French he finds rather not to his taste. Thus, he is resigning his post in September, though apparently he sees fit to make his exit with a knighthood in hand. Well, if that is what the eldest of the Holmes clan wishes, he is welcome to it, I suppose."[285]

"And what do you wish for yourself in this new world of ours?" I asked, as we paused at the base of the hill.

"Peace," he said. "Leisure," he added with a puckish smile. "Leisure which is not a euphemism for ennui."

"Bees, for instance?"

"Yes, bees," he said. "And salt air," he added, as he took a deep breath. "And finishing *The Whole Art of Detection.* And you?" Holmes asked. "Does Vespera Cochrane not beckon you to London or beyond?"

"I will be attending her benefit for the War Memorial, certainly," I replied in a hesitant voice. "And she is accompanying me to Brigg next month. The town is dedicating its own war plaque, and Cecil Harper is one of the names on it."

"He was from Lincolnshire, I take it?"

---

[285] Holmes's first reference is undoubtedly to the Versailles Peace Conference of 1919, which set the terms for the defeated Central Powers following the armistices of the year before. "The Wizard" probably refers to David Lloyd George, who remained as British prime minister through the conference and on into 1922— a nickname often applied to that politician was "The Welsh Wizard." Apparently, Mycroft Holmes strongly disagreed with the punitive terms imposed on Germany and its allies by the victorious Allies, largely at the insistence of the French government.

"Yes. You are welcome to join us in travelling there."

"As with the knighthood, I will consider it."

A quick series of reports from the horn of Hannay's motor echoed across the hollow, and the pair of lovers waved to us.

"For the moment, I believe it is the young ones who beckon you, Watson."

"I am loath to go, Holmes, but I must."

"I quite understand, old fellow."

My friend accompanied me across the field of tall grass, stalks waving in the breeze, to the automobile, beside which Hannay and Mary stood. I climbed aboard and settled into the tonneau, buttoning my coat and placing a blanket over my lap.

"Are you ready, Uncle John?" asked the young woman as she clambered into the passenger's seat in front of mine.

"I believe he is more than ready, Miss Lamington," interjected Sherlock Holmes. "Old soldiers never completely stand down."

Though I had been a civilian for many weeks, I gave my friend a sharp salute, and he gripped his cap as Hannay started the motorcar.

"Good-bye for the moment, Mr. Holmes," said the younger man.

"May you have a safe trip back to London," replied Holmes with a genial smile. "And take good care of my Watson."

"We shall."

Holmes stepped out of the exhaust stirred up by the automobile's engine and waved his cap as Hannay engaged the clutch, setting us out along our path leading from the sea. The dirt lane curved in a roundabout way, and as we made a wide turn before reversing direction, I looked back to catch one last sight of Sherlock Holmes. He had regained the hilltop and was once more facing out to the waters beyond, which were hidden by the ridge upon which he stood alone, almost like statue.

But then, I thought to myself, this man was his own monument.

"Uncle John?" said Mary Lamington, grasping her seat as she turned round, golden hair blowing about her face. "Is the breeze becoming too much for you?"

"No," I replied as Richard Hannay steered us toward the main road ahead. "Not at all. Truth to tell, I rather enjoy the feel of a slipstream in my face. Very much so."

APPENDIX A: A GIFT IN THE MAIL

Previously, I edited and arranged publication of a manuscript eventually titled *The Hapsburg Falcon*, a lost adventure of Sherlock Holmes supposedly penned by Dr. John H. Watson. The book's appearance showered me with neither financial reward nor critical plaudits by Sherlockian scholars, but it did made me vulnerable to approaches by a small host of Holmesian fanatics. Letters, e-mails, and even a few telephone messages—none of the latter returned—plagued me periodically for many months thereafter.

Most of these communications were merely annoying, but a few did prove intriguing, and one of these was a letter received from Canada. I have agreed to not identify the sender by name, but I am permitted to reveal that he is a man claiming to be a collateral descendant of Dr. John H. Watson and the possessor of a manuscript relating Sherlock Holmes's full record of service during the First World War, activities that also involved one Richard Hannay, the protagonist of a small number of supposedly fictional novels by John Buchan, the most famous of which is *The Thirty-Nine Steps*.

That Hannay might have been a real person like Sherlock Holmes excited me as I read the letter, but what also caught my eye was a passing reference to one Jack James. James, a character mentioned in the Holmes story "His Last Bow," was identified by me in *The Hapsburg Falcon* as possibly a fictional alias for Sam Spade, some of whose later exploits were chronicled by author Dashiell Hammett, most notably in *The Maltese Falcon*. The prospect that this Canadian text might corroborate elements of *The Hapsburg Falcon* was too good to pass up, and I accepted the man's offer to send me a copy of the manuscript, which I edited and now present, with the owner's permission.

The sheer length of the document argues that it is a forgery, for it contains almost as many words as the four authenticated Holmes novels combined. Moreover, there is nothing in the text that proves it was written by Dr. Watson, though many of its elements are consistent with certain references found in stories from the accepted Holmes canon and the Hannay novels of John Buchan. As will be explained in a later appendix, however, there are also many serious inconsistencies with those other records, and the presumed veracity of the tale is only as secure as the belief that it comes from John H. Watson by way of one of the doctor's descendants.

In the first published Holmes exploit, *A Study in Scarlet*, Watson reveals that he has neither kith nor kin in England, a declaration that would not rule out relations in Scotland, Wales, or Ireland—or the Americas, for that matter. The only confirmed relatives of the doctor as of this writing were his father and older brother, both deceased by 1888, the year in which the events related in *The Sign of the Four* take place.

According to the person who supplied the present manuscript, however, there was also a sister in the original Watson household, who left home under a cloud of some sort. As related in the family oral history, this woman initially settled in Dorset, where she married. Years later, the couple emigrated to North America, living first in Newfoundland and then moving—by that time with two daughters—to Nova Scotia. The husband subsequently abandoned the family, and his fate is unknown.

The grandson of the elder daughter—and thus the great-grandson of John H. Watson's supposed sister—is the person who supplied me with the manuscript, which by his account is a typed copy made in the 1960s of the original holograph, which was subsequently lost. There is also, however, a surviving handwritten note, a photocopy of which I was also sent, which reads, "A little treats [sic] for those to whom I really am Uncle John. All my love."

The family tradition holds that Dr. Watson held a deep and abiding affection for his sister, maintained a lifelong correspondence with her, and even visited her and her daughters in Nova Scotia at least once, sometime in the early 1890s. The doctor's will, according to this history, bequeathed to his sister and her descendants many of his personal articles, including the narrative presented in this volume. That text, in its original form, is untitled, and in arranging for its publication, I have chosen to give it the perhaps meaningless and illogical title *Thirty-Nine Steps from Baker Street*, by which I have tried to suggest a merger of the worlds of Hannay and Holmes.

I have made very small corrections to the text, primarily to rectify obvious typographical errors or grammatical mistakes. I have divided the narrative into three sections and have invented titles for them, as I have done for the chapters, which are merely numbered in the typescript. As with *The Hapsburg Falcon*, I leave it to real Sherlockian scholars—a group to which I certainly do not belong—to judge both its truth and value.

—J. R. Trtek

APPENDIX B: AN ALTERED CHRONOLOGY

An added entertainment in reading some Sherlock Holmes stories derives from efforts to pin exact dates on particular cases related by John H. Watson, a task often made more challenging by contradictory details embedded in the doctor's narratives. The temporal parsing of *Thirty-Nine Steps from Baker Street* might at first seem a simple business, for Richard Hannay is rather specific in giving May 24, 1914, as the date on which he set out for Scotland at the beginning of *The Thirty-Nine Steps*, and the events of "His Last Bow" are clearly stated to have occurred on August 2 of that same year.

This tidy state of affairs, however, does not carry through to all portions of the present volume, some of whose events are also presented, in somewhat fictionalized form, in John Buchan's *Mr. Standfast*, or alluded to in his novel *Greenmantle*. Moreover, as will now be demonstrated, Buchan's very specific chronology outlined in *The Thirty-Nine Steps* is itself likely false—indeed, a deliberate lie meant to hide an explosive secret.

In *The Thirty-Nine Steps*, Hannay says that he left his flat near Portland Place on the morning of May 24, which in 1914 would have fallen on a Sunday. From there, a chronology of his activity for the week that follows can be constructed in simple fashion. The resulting timeline has

Hannay escape the dovecot on the night of May 29–30 and arrive at the cottage of Mr. Turnbull, the roadman, on May 31.

At that point, Hannay suffers a return bout of malaria, and Turnbull cares for him for "the better part of ten days." Two more days elapse before the fugitive leaves for the Berkshire home of Sir Walter Bullivant—presumably on June 12. Hannay takes one more day to complete that final leg of his trip, thus meeting Bullivant—and, as revealed in the foregoing narrative, Dr. Watson—on June 13. It is during the evening of that day that news arrives of Premier Karolides's shooting—two days before the date planned for the assassination, June 15.

The fact that the murder occurs earlier than expected is not a fatal inconsistency. Since the assassins knew Hannay to be loose and still able to reveal their plot to the British authorities, they may have chosen to make their move earlier than originally intended in order to better guarantee success.

Meanwhile, various seasonal and other references in *The Thirty-Nine Steps* do not necessarily contradict the presumed chronology and sometimes support it. On his rail journey north, for instance, Hannay mentions newspaper articles about the beginning of cricket season and "starters for the Derby," which presumably refers to the Epsom Derby. That horse race took place on May 27 in 1914, and so indeed would have been imminent as Hannay rode toward Scotland. At the same time, first-class cricket matches had begun in England on May 2 of that year, about three weeks prior to the presumed beginning of *The Thirty-Nine Steps*. Later in the novel, Sir Walter Bullivant is said to be at his Berkshire cottage because he spends Whitsuntide there, a remark that places Hannay's eventual rendezvous with the spymaster in early June. (It may be remembered that Watson's narrative contradicts this, stating that Sir Walter retired to the cottage around the time of midsummer, which would have been a bit later.)

On the other hand, in referring to the time of year, Hannay uses both "spring" and "summer" in his narrative to describe the landscape. He also makes mention of nesting curlews, which usually begin that activity in April, though apparently mating may continue for several weeks thereafter. There are, however, two pointed discrepancies in *The Thirty-Nine Steps* that bear thoughtful consideration.

The first concerns the moon. On the night of his escape from the dovecot, Hannay declares that the moon was "well on its last quarter and would not rise till late." Consulting astronomical records for 1914, however, one discovers that the moon would reach first quarter on June 1 and thus would have set early rather than rising late. Either way, the sky would presumably have been moonless when Hannay made good his escape, and this error may have just been due to a misunderstanding on the part of John Buchan, who apparently authored *The Thirty-Nine Steps* based on interviews with Hannay.

There is, however, a far more profound error in Hannay's narrative as presented by Buchan. Indeed, it is an error not of chronology but rather of simple historical fact: the premier of Greece was not slain in the middle of 1914, and his murder did not precipitate war. Instead, the one significant political murder that occurred during that interval was the killing of Austria–Hungary's Archduke Franz Ferdinand, whose assassination on June 28 was the immediate spark that ignited the First World War.

It is clear that John Buchan altered some details in telling Richard Hannay's story in *The Thirty-Nine Steps*—most notably, the omission of involvement by Sherlock Holmes and Dr. Watson in the pursuit and eventual rescue of Hannay. But one must conclude too that Buchan also altered his fictionalized narrative to disguise the fact that it was not the assassination of Karolides that the Black Stone plotters carried out but rather that of Franz Ferdinand.

Suppose that the target was indeed the archduke, and that it was his assassination that Bullivant and company learn of in Berkshire on the evening of Hannay's reappearance. That would set the latter's arrival at the spymaster's home on June 28, the day of Franz Ferdinand's murder. Moreover, it should be noted that in *Thirty-Nine Steps from Baker Street*, Hannay spends an additional day at Turnbull's cottage while Sherlock Holmes works on deciphering more of Scudder's notebook, an extra twenty-four hours not mentioned in *The Thirty-Nine Steps*. Thus, counting back what is now fourteen days to Hannay's arrival at the Turnbull cottage puts us at June 14, which means that he escaped the dovecot on the night of June 12–13, two days before the moon reached third quarter. While not "well past" that point in the lunar cycle, this is still more consistent with Hannay's description of a night where the moon would rise late than the conditions of May 29–30.

Working further backward, these assumptions put Hannay's initial departure from London on June 7—a Sunday, as it should be. However, it also puts Hannay's flight to Scotland after the running of the Epsom Derby and more than a month into the English cricket season. The latter would make newspaper references to the beginning of that season far less likely, and the former would be completely inconsistent with the presumed articles previewing the race. The mention of nesting birds also becomes a bit more strained in the context of a June start to events.

These issues can be resolved if we assume that Buchan deliberately put false seasonal references into *The Thirty-Nine Steps* for a specific purpose: to make it appear that events had occurred earlier than Franz Ferdinand's murder and thus remove any suggestion that the Black Stone was involved in the archduke's death.

It does seem somewhat odd that Sir Walter Bullivant did not have Buchan expose this truth in *The Thirty-Nine Steps*, for implicating German agents in a plot that set off the war would have been a huge propaganda coup for Britain and its allies. The fact that the Karolides ruse was adopted—and employed years later by Watson in his narrative—suggests that there was even more to this story, perhaps elements that would have had a negative image on Britain's image as well, if they had been exposed. In all likelihood, we will never know the answer to this question.

APPENDIX C: TANGLED TALES

In an addendum to *The Hapsburg Falcon*, clues in both the short story "His Last Bow" and the novel *The Maltese Falcon* were used to propose that, just prior to the First World War, a young Sam Spade acted as one of Sherlock Holmes's agents in events leading up to the capture of the Von Bork spy ring.

In the same vein, the preceding narrative titled *Thirty-Nine Steps From Baker Street* reveals that the Holmes story "His Last Bow" and the John Buchan novels *The Thirty-Nine Steps* and *Mr. Standfast* actually comprise a larger tale involving Sherlock Holmes, John H. Watson, and Richard Hannay, heretofore considered an entirely fictional person. The preceding appendix deals with some elements of the chronology of that saga, until recently distorted by omissions and deliberate obfuscation in those previous, separate texts. This closing section considers a number of additional loose, sometimes contradictory threads that run through the combined set of stories, beginning with "His Last Bow."

This short story is notable for several reasons. Though not the last published tale in the accepted Sherlockian canon, it portrays events later in Holmes's life than any of its companion pieces, taking place a full decade after the detective's supposed retirement. Moreover, it was the first authenticated Sherlock Holmes story published that, on first glance, seems to not have been authored by John H. Watson. Related in third person under the byline of Arthur Conan Doyle, who is believed to have acted in many instances as Watson's literary agent, the story is a tale of espionage whose single surprise, if it can be called that, is that one principal turns out to be Sherlock Holmes in disguise, with John Watson also appearing briefly at the end.

A few questions have always attended the story, not the least of which is the true identity of its author. Several different suggestions have been made, from the aforementioned Doyle to either Sherlock or Mycroft Holmes. Watson obliquely claimed authorship himself in a later story, asserting that his absence from most of the action required framing the narrative in third person instead of his usual first-person style.

The text of *Thirty-Nine Steps from Baker Street* makes clear, however, that "His Last Bow" was actually penned by John Buchan, author of the Hannay novels—Holmes himself tells Watson that the person who wrote "His Last Bow" was the same individual who wrote *The Thirty-Nine Steps*, and Sir Walter Bullivant's description of the man he suggested write the short story fits Buchan to a tee: Bullivant's man has been in the intelligence corps and saw time in the War Communications Office; Buchan had served in the intelligence corps and, prior to that, been part of the War Propaganda Bureau. The parallels are self-evident.

Buchan had already written *The Thirty-Nine Steps* and *Greenmantle* under the direction of Sir Walter Bullivant, using information gathered in interviews with Richard Hannay, and so it is not surprising that he was selected to pen a short story about Holmes's cracking of the Von Bork spy ring. That it was published under the name of Arthur Conan Doyle is also understandable, as explained by Holmes in the narrative: it was not desirable that any connection between Hannay and Holmes be hinted at, lest the Germans become aware of Holmes's continuing involvement in wartime espionage, and so Buchan's authorship was kept secret. Instead, Doyle agreed to pose as the actual author—though with a price, and apparently to Watson's decided irritation.

Another aspect of "His Last Bow" that has troubled commentators is the reasoning behind Holmes's action in taking Von Bork into custody and dismantling his spy ring in the first place. After all, prior to August 1914, the British were playing the German espionage cell for all it was worth, feeding Berlin false or misleading information—why cut short a good thing?

The answer, as made clear in the preceding narrative, is that the Germans had been successful in their Cerberus strategy: by employing independent spy rings, they had been able to verify—or discount—information gathered by their different cells. One member of the Black Stone—Von Schwabing—had, by August 1914, escaped with British naval secrets that exposed as false the corresponding alternate information that Holmes and his agents had been feeding Von Bork for some time. This exposure would have rendered Holmes's operation useless in any event, and so there would have been no reason to continue it.

While the story of "His Last Bow" is correct in the essence of Holmes's infiltration and destruction of the Von Bork spy apparatus, there are elements that appear to have been fictionalized, reimagined, or altered in time. For example, some of Holmes's remarks concerning Von Bork, related during the very first cab ride through London in *Thirty-Nine Steps from Baker Street*, are placed toward the end of "His Last Bow," after Von Bork has been subdued. Similarly, other remarks by Holmes in the short story, such as his comment on the "East wind," appear to have been made instead while preparations were being made to apprehend the three German spies waiting to escape from the Ruff. Perhaps the most significant discrepancy is the paean to a better England that will arise after the First World War, sentiments which in "His Last Bow" are expressed by Holmes but which are revealed in the foregoing narrative as being uttered by Watson! One may wonder if that misquotation by Buchan ruffled Watson's feathers as much as, if not more than the credit that Arthur Conan Doyle accepted for the story itself.

Though some of these errors may have been due to misunderstanding on the part of John Buchan, others may have been deliberate, intended to either facilitate the story-telling or avoid disclosure that Holmes and Watson had been collaborating in much greater depth and for a longer period of time than "His Last Bow" implies. Indeed, the tone and some of the information conveyed in the short story appears to have the purpose of creating the public impression that Sherlock Holmes had gone back into retirement after besting Von Bork and was not engaged in subsequent espionage activities, while at the same time implying that Dr. John Watson would be on duty solely with the Royal Army Medical Corps for the remainder of the war. (In 1917, the year of the story's publication, both men were, of course, actually engaged in uncovering more German spy and sabotage activities centered in both the Cotswolds and London itself.)

While *Thirty-Nine Steps from Baker Street* casts some elements of "His Last Bow" in a somewhat new light, the newly discovered manuscript also allows one to view *The Thirty-Nine Steps* and *Mr. Standfast* from a different perspective.

The escape of Von Schwabing is not mentioned in Buchan's *The Thirty-Nine Steps*, though it serves as a key element in the plot of the later novel *Mr. Standfast*. The reason for the omission in the earlier novel is rather easy to understand: the British Secret Service did not wish to publicly acknowledge that a German spy had eluded capture. By the time *Mr. Standfast* was published in 1919, however, the war was over and won, and so Von Schwabing's escape five years earlier could be admitted without as much embarrassment.

Some parts of *The Thirty-Nine Steps* stretch credulity—two in particular. The first is Hannay's use of lentonite, a fictional explosive stored in the room where Hannay is held prisoner by the Germans. In Buchan's novel, he sets it off to blow open the door to his cell, amazingly suffering no harm other than being rendered unconscious for a few seconds. As *Thirty-Nine Steps from Baker Street* reveals, Hannay's escape was less violent if just as dramatic, and actually orchestrated by Sherlock Holmes.

The other part of the story that strains the reader's patience are details of the theft of secrets from the meeting between British and French officials in Sir Walter Bullivant's home. In Buchan's version as related in *The Thirty-Nine Steps*, Von Schwabing attends the conference posing as the First Sea Lord—at that time Prince Louis Alexander of Battenberg, father of the 1st Earl Mountbatten. In that disguise, with no one realizing he is an imposter, Von Schwabing effortlessly leaves the gathering with top secret British naval plans. That the German spy could accomplished such a feat verges on the ridiculous.

As Watson relates in his own description of the event, Von Schwabing actually was present at the meeting in the guise of a nondescript aide, whom every official assumed to be in someone else's entourage. Why Buchan added his own somewhat absurd version of the episode is a bit mystifying, though it may be that he was instructed to do so in order to draw critical attention away from the matter of Hannay's escape from the Germans, mentioned in an earlier paragraph. By having Buchan romanticize one part of *The Thirty-Nine Steps* to the point of exaggerated, improbable melodrama, Sir Walter Bullivant may have hoped perhaps to make Hannay's fictitious use of lentonite seem more believable by comparison, and thus avoid having the public—and perhaps the Germans, if they read the novel—question how Hannay actually managed to escape his cell in the first place.

In any case, publication of *Thirty-Nine Steps from Baker Street* reveals at last the important role played by Sherlock Holmes and John Watson in the recovery of Richard Hannay, aspects of the drama intentionally kept from the public at the time. The narrative also makes clear that Holmes and Watson laid the groundwork in Biggleswick for the struggle between Hannay and Von Schwabing that took place in Britain and later on the Continent, and that was chronicled by John Buchan in *Mr. Standfast.* As already noted, that novel was published in 1919, after hostilities had concluded, and one can only regret that Bullivant chose not to reveal the contributions of Holmes and Watson with the publication of the third Hannay book.

Nonetheless, eventual acknowledgment is better than none at all, and—a century after the fact—full credit may now be given to The Great Detective and his biographer not only for the rescue of Richard Hannay and the uprooting of German spies on British soil, but also the saving of London from fiery devastation. Watson may have viewed Holmes as his own monument, but a London preserved also stands as continuing testament to his friend's enduring majesty.

Made in the USA
Charleston, SC
28 November 2015